Beware of Chicken

— BOOK 4 —

— BOOK 4 —

CASUALFARMER

To everyone who continues to help and support me

Cover and interior art by Tsuu

ISBN: 978-1-0394-5229-9

Published in 2025 by Podium Publishing
www.podiumentertainment.com

Beware of Chicken

— BOOK 4 —

Sometimes, unfortunately, one's journey of cultivation must be paused.

While the pursuit of martial superiority should be at the forefront of every great expert's mind, even the most powerful of Masters recognises that after a trying battle, one must rest and recuperate. However, that rest period must be properly spent, for a cultivator must be superior to a mortal in all things, even their relaxation.

The great Masters suggest that a suitable pastime be writing poetry about the splendor of cultivation, taking tea in a stunning garden constructed by your servants and attended to by many jade beauties, attending auctions for more cultivation resources, or torturing one's enemies, kept alive for just the occasion.

Truly, the measure of a man can even be taken by the way he rests, and the more profound his rest, the more profound the man.

□

PROLOGUE

DAY AT THE BEACH

It was a boring day. The sheep were out to pasture and the sun was beating down.

Zhang Fei the Torrent Rider, Disciple of Bi De, sighed. He practiced his kata. He swung his stick. But even that was starting to get old.

He was interrupted by Shaggy Two, who started to bark. *Visitors?* He pulled his mask down and hopped up onto the roof, then scanned the horizon for—

His eyes lit up as he beheld his Master. He was a magnificent specimen, with fire-red and jade-green feathers, shining in the light. He wore a dapper fox-fur vest and his eyes were sharp with intelligence.

"Master!" he shouted happily. Zhang Fei the Torrent Rider scrambled to his feet and jumped off the roof, landing on the ground a moment later. His eyes widened when he realised his Master wasn't alone.

There was a group of people with him. There was a really tall man, a short woman with green hair, two pigs, the prettiest girl Zhang Fei had ever seen—and a fish in a jar.

It was kind of a strange sight, but they were with his Master, so it wasn't *that* weird. Nothing was really as shocking as a talking chicken, after all.

"Greetings, my disciple. Are you well?" Master Bi De asked aloud. "I have abided by my promise. We have met again, haven't we?"

Zhang Fei smiled brilliantly and dropped into a bow. Shaggy Two yipped.

"So, you're my disciple's disciple, eh?" a man asked, amused. He was staring incredulously at Zhang Fei's mask of power, clearly jealous of it—Zhang Fei could just tell. The man was huge! The biggest person Zhang Fei had ever seen! He had a long piece of wood in his hand, curved into an oblong oval. "I heard there was something called torrent riding here, so we decided to check it out."

Zhang Fei nodded, distracted.

"Ah, yes! This way to the village!" he said, waving them onwards and towards the gate guarded by Master's talisman.

The group saw the talisman and stopped in shock.

The giant of a man, the Master of Zhang Fei's Master, began to roar with laughter.

The rooster preened.

↔

"And this is the Gutter, Great Master," the kid beside me pronounced loudly as he finished the tour of the village he was performing for me, Meimei, and Chunky. Zhang Fei was his name, but most people just shouted "Torrent Rider" at him. He had his chicken mask pushed up on his brow, trying to look majestic and serious, but mostly he just looked a bit silly, especially with his round face and wild hair.

I whistled, impressed, as I stared at the edifice of stone. The sluiceway looked for all the world like a massive gutter, probably ten feet across. A trickle of pure, clean water flowed at the bottom, forming a small stream. The stone was rough-looking and had countless pebbles within its base, and the stream itself was home to minnows and frogs. The grass around the edges was vibrant, reeds growing along its edge.

"So this is what you guys go down?" I asked. It looked like a good time. Like a massive water slide.

"Yes, Great Master!" he said seriously.

I snorted. "You can just call me Jin, yeah?"

The kid, so uptight, seemed to relax a bit at my dismissal of the formalities. Chunky oinked from beside me, staring at the ground curiously.

"Yes, Mister Jin. The Lord Magistrate had it built and now all the old folks say that there're no more floods because of it."

"I remember seeing plans for this," Meiling said as she looked at the stone. "Father and Uncle Bao showed me when we were working on the math for the healing formation. We still have the plans in the storeroom, I think."

The kid reared back in shock. "*Really?!*" he asked. "Dad always says that everybody who helped make the Gutter is a hero! They saved us from the floods!"

Meimei smiled at the boy and puffed up a bit with pride at the admiration in Fei's voice.

"Yes, he worked very hard on it," she said to him. Then her voice dropped just a bit, so only I would hear her as she said, "He worked himself half to death. Really, six years for a project this big?" my wife muttered.

I smiled down at the Gutter. It was a massive undertaking for this time period, especially without any cultivators to help it out. I'd have to take a look at those plans myself. I always did like megaprojects. It was no giant pyramid, but it was *certainly* more useful.

The Lord Magistrate definitely would have landed in the history books for the accomplishment, back in the Before.

We stayed out for a bit longer before heading back to the village.

It was readying itself for a feast. The guest of honour was already seated when we arrived back in the square. I could hear his deep, smooth voice—which was still taking me a bit to get used to, Big D *actually* talking. His back was straight as he addressed people, resplendent in his finery.

It didn't look as silly as I'd expected it to.

It was a nice village, what I had seen of it, the Eighth Correct Place. Situated on a giant and rather steep slope that was full of rocks, it was objectively *terrible* farmland. The bare stone was just under the topsoil, which meant the people here could barely grow their own vegetables.

What they had instead was a hell of a lot of pasture for goats and sheep, and the mine still seemed to have plentiful silver. Production was ramping up even more now that the place wasn't flooding all the damn time.

Our visit was a bit of a surprise, but the village had recovered quickly from it. The villagers had rallied and prepared the feast before our tour was even done.

I had been a bit on edge when we'd arrived—being the center of attention again made me anxious. It had me wondering if this little adventure was a good idea. I'd had enough attention for the year. It had only been a couple of months since the Dueling Peaks. But somehow, this time . . . I didn't feel so stressed about it. Sure, people were happy to see us, like at the Dueling Peaks, but they were a bit more laid back about it. Or maybe I just felt different about things because *I* wasn't the focus.

That was reserved for Big D.

Gou had decided to stay back at the farm along with his brother, taking care of things. He had said he'd had a bit too much adventure for one summer and waved us off. Babe was content on the farm, and Ri Zu had decided to catch up on her studies. Bowu, our newest addition, was at Hong Yaowu, having made fast friends with Meimei's little brother after little Xian started calling him "big bro."

Peppa and Chunky, however, had decided to come, along with Tigu and Washy. Meimei, Xiulan, and I rounded out the party.

Chunky was looking around, curious, while I watched the festivities from the sidelines. The town was celebrating the return of its saviour, and while I had been given some courtesy . . . it was nice to be in the background.

I shook my head at Big D, then began to look around for the others. I knew Peppa and Xiulan had planned to investigate the silver mines, but I couldn't find Tigu anywhere. Curious, I decided to go searching for her.

→

The village wasn't *that* big, so it didn't take me too long to find her—and come across a scene that made me pause.

Tigu stood on one side of the street, her hands on her hips, brow furrowed. Across from her was a white, shaggy puppy—Zhang Fei's pet. The pair were tense. Staring, focused only on one another.

A standoff for the ages.

The puppy finally broke the standoff; it seemed to expand as it wound up before letting out a terrifically squeaky bark.

Tigu raised an eyebrow at the display of defiance.

"Oh? You dare?" she asked of the puppy, looming over it.

The little beast barked again, standing its ground. For a brief moment, I felt worried as Tigu's intent flowed from her, but the puppy remained in place and yipped again, a tiny growl escaping its throat.

Tigu smirked. "I don't hate it! Now come, this Rou Tigu shall trade pointers with you, little guardian!"

The puppy yipped and sprang at her as Tigu crouched down. She danced around the little ball of fluff, which continued to chase after her, yapping incessantly.

"Your voice is strong! Good!" she shouted back. "Breath is important, so keep it up!"

I smiled as I watched the amusing scene. She had really changed a lot over this past year. I leaned back against the wall while the puppy went for another charge, simply racing as fast as it could towards her. But its foot caught on a rock and the puppy stumbled. Tigu capitalized immediately.

"*Naïve!*" she shouted, and her finger caught the dog in the side, bowling it over. "Watch your footwork! Else you shall be defeated utterly!" she commanded. "And see? *This* is how an enemy shall disembowel you!" Tigu lectured while burying her fingers in the soft fur of the puppy's stomach, scratching as the little thing wiggled. "Now! Guard your head!"

Her fingers rose up and the puppy raised its paws, playfully biting at the digits that wiggled near its nose.

"Good! You must be faster next time, but this Rou Tigu shall commend you!" she called, and the puppy rolled to its feet, letting out a happy yip.

Its tail wagged rapidly.

Tigu let out a strange noise and picked the puppy up, burying her face in its white, shaggy fur.

I snorted and wandered off.

→

Soon enough, the feast was ready for us. Eighth Correct Place was bigger than Hong Yaowu by a fair bit; the draw of the silver mine and the ease of travel had helped it grow.

The food was mostly goat- and sheep-based dishes, supplemented with hearty vegetables and roots as well as imported rice. The people, already used to a rooster who had saved them, seemed only mildly intrigued rather than shocked by the fish and the two pigs who joined him at the tables, serving them with great reverence when Big D named them his "honoured brothers and sisters."

Tigu was at that table too, still instructing the little white puppy—whose name I learned was Shaggy Two—in exercises to improve his balance.

The puppy, naturally, didn't understand a word, but it yipped happily at the right moments.

We ate and we drank. It was less a formal feast and more just a communal dinner. There was a kind of entertainment too. They seemed to have a neat tradition, where people came up and shared stories on a stage that was set up in the center. Sometimes legends and sometimes just stories of life.

The one that caught my attention was the story of how this place had gotten its name . . . which was rather hilarious. There were also bawdy drinking songs, which Meimei and Xiulan joined in on . . . and then it was time for the last act.

The village chief stood up, revealing a wooden prosthetic leg, then hobbled up to the stage.

He looked up with a gleam in his eye and grinned at the waiting audience. Voice booming, he declared, "Today, I shall tell you the Tale of the Master Rooster and the Village. And why all must heed the powerful talisman that sits at the front of our village!"

A cheer went up from the villagers. I glanced over and saw that Big D seemed almost embarrassed.

Grinning back at the chief, I leaned forwards and listened.

I was rather certain some embellishments had snuck in there—Zhang Fei the younger looked embarrassed as well . . . and then twice as embarrassed when Tigu clapped him on the back and complimented his bravery. I was impressed too. The kid had faced down a Spirit Beast wolf with only a spear.

All in all, it was a fun night. To my relief, nothing much happened. We got some rooms and hunkered down for the night.

We'd planned to stay a couple of days, hopefully see one of the "Rumbles" people talked about, then head home. I wanted to check out what kind of recipes they would have, and Peppa was interested in the chemicals they were using to process the silver. I hoped our time here would be as nice as today had been.

→

The land rumbled. The hills shook.

"Here it comes!" came the Torrent Rider's yell. More voices rose in a chorus of exclamations as the sounds hit us. We heard it before we saw it—like a stampede was headed directly our way.

I was fascinated as I listened to the thunder of water coming down the Gutter. It roared down the edifice of stone, channeled into a single path instead of swamping the entire region.

I knew some of it was from far-off rain, and the other part of it was from . . . *a geyser*? That was what popped into my head. I could feel an old, dying warmth beneath the earth, being slowly strangled by stone.

I paused and shook my head, shooing the idle thought away. The call had gone up, so already there were children charging out of houses carrying boards and other flotation devices, the Torrent Rider in the lead. The adults looked on, exasperated, but didn't make any moves to stop the kids from lining up on the side of the Gutter.

Our little party followed. I had made my own board after Big D had described the thing to us, and Tigu wielded a spare one given to her by the Torrent Rider.

The rampage reached us, the head of white water surging downhill as fast as a car. The frothing head bucked and writhed like a living thing.

"It's a big one!" the Torrent Rider roared as he leapt into the air, his board landing under his feet.

I nearly jumped to grab the kid as he leapt into the most dangerous part, but he didn't falter. He struck the raging water and stayed atop it, whooping, as Big D leapt after him, alighting on his student's board.

A chicken hung ten, thousands of miles from the sea.

I started to laugh as the other kids jumped in after, none quite brave enough to be at the front. Tigu—after staring for a moment at Big D and his disciples' leap—was in like a rocket, her eyes narrowed with concentration.

Xiulan stared, mouth slightly agape, as the kid surfed down the waterway. "Just like a flying sword . . ." she muttered, sounding intrigued.

I held out my own board, and she paused before smiling and taking it. She sketched me a rough salute and then was gone too.

I smiled as I watched her go, then set about finding another board. There were a couple more square planks around, and one of the larger ones was perfect for my needs. It would work fine as a raft. I held my arms out to my waiting wife. Meiling's eyebrows rose and she gave me a look, but she smiled as she got pulled into my lap and we went down together.

There weren't any loops or crazy motions, but thundering through the stone gutter was exhilarating, the spraying water hitting our faces.

It was the longest waterslide I'd ever been on. We flew past fields and countryside, rushing past more villages, smaller than the Eighth Correct Place, farther down the sluiceway.

More and more people leapt into the waters each time we passed a village, joining us in the raging river, most riding on boards while some just bodysurfed on the way down.

Washy occasionally burst from the water, leaping up and around swimmers with perfect grace and looking smugly superior. Several kids got splashed, but one, who looked to be struggling, got a gentle nudge back into position—the water had flowed oddly around him, giving him a chance to recover. I watched him for a while, reminding myself to thank Washy later, then looked behind us, curious at where the others were.

Peppa was standing on a plank of wood while Chunky's bulk came down behind her, his back filled with people who had jumped onto him, clinging for dear life to the massive boar as he careened down the sluiceway.

Eventually, the rumbling waters carried us into a lake that barely reached my knees. It was rocky and clear, and near the edges it looked to have been in the process of drying up—but that was before the extra water hit it. Water that had a very high mineral content. The thought popped into my head again. The sudden understanding about things when I touched them or got curious about them was both useful and a bit annoying.

I cheered as we slowed, getting pushed out into the water.

Meimei was laughing in my lap.

"That was great," she said with a sigh as we drifted on the shallow lake.

"That *was* pretty fun," I agreed. There was probably enough water in the Gutter to let us go for another, more leisurely run, but it wouldn't be the same . . .

Chunky squealed, his voice a thunder of joy.

He clambered out of the water and looked disappointed at the much-reduced flow of the Gutter. The kids were talking and laughing, and some of them patted Chunky consolingly as he pouted, the water now too shallow to really accommodate him.

Peppa frowned and walked over to the water. A fishy head popped out.

Washy glanced at Chunky and said something to Peppa. She passed him several nuts from a small handkerchief tied to a strap that went round her body. A fin bumped against a trotter, the bargain was struck, and the dragon disappeared beneath the waves.

There was a rumble, and the kids stared in shock as part of the lake seemed to split, coming alive and running back up the sides of the Gutter a ways before turning back around once again and forming a section of river that just *kept flowing.*

Chunky oinked happily and jumped into the flow.

"Let's go again!" Meimei said, standing up out of my lap and picking up the board. I grinned.

"Race you to the top," I challenged.

Meimei nodded.

"Ready? One—Oi!"

My wife, the filthy cheater, booked it as *soon* as I started counting.

We only got a few hours out of it before Washy had to stop the constant loop, but I learned a great lesson.

You can kind of kick-flip on a surfboard, if you smack down hard enough.

I spent most of the afternoon watching the kids and my family play on the boards. Tigu and Xiulan kept trying to push each other off until the great dragon breached behind them, upending them both. The carp then spent the next ten minutes running away from them, but the chase was doomed to failure. The great dragon was in his element, shallow though it was, and even while controlling the endless waterslide, he eluded them.

Surprisingly, after the Torrent Rider, the one most enthusiastic about surfing was *Peppa*. She stayed perfectly still, her eyes forwards, even as the river tried to knock her around. Chunky cheered from the sidelines, bouncing around and oinking happily at her grace and form.

→

That night we had a barbecue on the "beach" by the lake, though it was more like just a little patch of sand and gravel. I ended up going to get food from some of the villages farther upstream—most parents were exasperated but accepting of their children's impromptu day off. There was a great cheer when I returned, but I was a passing bit of excitement. The kids quickly returned to praising Washy, the mighty master of the Gutter, who had given them an entire day of fun.

Washy looked to be in heaven as he gobbled up the new flavours, the kids around him cooking the lamb to their individual preferences. Some liked it charred, others rare. Others added goat cheese or herbs to the meats, watching with fascination as it disappeared down the black hole that was Washy.

Chunky feasted on slow-roasted roots and the bounty of the nearby forest of scraggly trees.

There were a few catfish in the little lake as well. Not a lot lived here, since it dried up completely some months and in the winter froze solid, but there were plenty of water plants.

It was more a marsh than a lake, honestly.

I spent a bit of time cooking with Xiulan. I remembered not liking lamb much in the Before, but I had a whole new kind to try here, and cooking alongside her always made it convenient. I had my own personal chef's assistant, while she was happy to let me decide the flavours.

Occasionally, we would glance up from our work to something rather interesting.

Namely Tigu *losing* to Meiling.

Meiling agilely spiked the ball over the fishing net, bursting into cheers on scoring a point when Tigu missed.

Tigu seemed shocked for a moment, but bounced back easily.

"Nice shot, Mistress!" she enthused.

Meimei giggled.

"This is fun!" she cheered. "What did you call this game again, Jin?"

"Beach volleyball," I said, stretching. Meimei grinned and hopped up and down, a big smile on her face. Her skirt was hiked up around her waist and her shirt was off, with only her dudou preserving her modesty. Water and sweat glistened on her skin.

I watched the bounce, slight as it was.

It was a beautiful view.

For my part, I was just down to my pants, while Xiulan still had on all her clothes, though they were wet and clinging to her body. It was an . . . *interesting* sight.

Then Meimei called Xiulan over. In response, Xiulan pushed her shirt down, exposing the bandages that covered her chest, and sprang up to join the volleyball game.

Then there was a *lot* of jumping. My ability to keep my eyes on my wife was sorely tested.

→

"You see the way her nose scrunched up?" I asked, laughing. Xiulan giggled as Meimei elbowed me in the side with a glare.

"My dear husband, and my sister, you shall both taste my wrath in due course," Meimei said primly, then promptly turned to us and stuck her tongue out. She stared down with disgust at the dish in front of her.

Meimei wasn't a fan of goat cheese, so I had enlisted Xiulan's help and snuck some into some of the barbecue Meimei got. The way her face had scrunched up was, indeed, fantastic. Though her retaliation was sure to be swift.

Hey, if you dish it out, you'd best be able to take it.

I sighed happily as I leaned against the sand berm I had made, a circle around the fire that we were all sitting against. The rest of the kids had gone home via the Chunky Express, leaving just our small party on the beach.

I glanced at Xiulan again and she smirked back, though there was a bit of nervousness in her eyes as Meimei started listing out rather *interesting* things one could do with herbs.

But . . . she was smiling and was still at peace. I was slowly settling into that peace as well, even though there was a visible reminder of the cost.

The golden crack in the center of Xiulan's chest was getting easier to look at without the feeling of overwhelming guilt. It was the physical remnant of her near-death at the Dueling Peaks—a scar she'd received while defending Tigu from the Shrouded Mountain Sect. Not that my eyes often wandered there, but the contrast between her pale skin and the bright gold stood out. Our own relationship was changing too. Getting better, I think. She still slipped up on occasion and called me Master Jin . . . but we both just laughed it off whenever it happened.

I leaned back a bit farther, staring deep into the fire. I kinda wished Gou and Yun had joined us. I'd have to go sluicing with the boys at some point. That was awesome.

The fire slowly burned low. Our eyes grew heavy . . . and eventually, sleep claimed us all.

I woke up in the morning with Tigu on my chest, Meimei pressed into my side, and Xiulan curled against my wife's back.

Peppa was using my leg as a pillow and Big D was on Chunky's head.

Living the Isekai dream, I thought, amused. *Waking up covered in women while having a proud and powerful . . .* rooster.

I snorted and settled back down in the sand, then kissed my wife on the forehead.

What a wonderful day at the beach.

CHAPTER 1

SETTLING BACK INTO IT

If you love your job, you'll never work a day in your life.

It was one of the things I'd heard constantly as I grew up yet had never fully believed. It sounded like an empty platitude, too good to be true. After dying, winding up here, and then the mess that had happened at the Dueling Peaks . . . I had to admit that, yeah, there was something to it after all.

I did, in fact, love my job. Yes, some days it did feel like work. Some days I didn't want to get out of bed. But most days? Most days when I got up . . . I just looked forward to what I was going to accomplish.

It was probably a bit of a strange thing to think about as I swung my sickle, bent over so I could get at the stalks of the wheat, but it was a thought I couldn't get out of my head.

There was something soothing about it, invigorating even. To touch the earth, to grow, to make . . . and then to enjoy the fruits of my labour.

The year thus far had been trying, one full of upheavals and revelations. I'd had to reconnect with the real cultivation aspects of this world, something I'd thought I had left far behind. There had been a letter from the man who had taught me how to cultivate. A massive battle at the Dueling Peaks, and all the fallout from that, which I was still waiting for.

And yet for as much turmoil the year had brought . . . when I crouched down with a sickle it all washed away. I just let my body flow as I thought, as I pondered, and as I enjoyed myself.

As I moved forwards.

The lazy days of summer were slowly but surely coming to a close. I could feel the slight nip of the wind, the change in the plants as they started to change their quiet tune and as the days started to become shorter.

And that meant preparations. We had already harvested all of our rice months ago, but the second wheat harvest I had planted was fully grown.

My chickens trailed in my wake, clucking as they hunted down the insects that had taken up residence in the wheat. We didn't have any pesticides, so the fields were always rife with things looking to steal a portion of my harvest.

So we had to resort to older methods. Namely unleashing a horde of chickens.

"Are they tasty this year?" I asked, amused at the sheer predatory intent the chickens were showing, mercilessly hunting down every bug that dared to move.

A voice answered from behind me, "Indeed, they are most succulent this year, Master. Even better than the last." It was a smooth and deep sound, and I soon turned around to look at the speaker.

A rooster stared back at me. He finished placing a sheaf of wheat that I had bundled into the basket tied to his back. He looked almost comical, weighed down with the bundle of wheat that was bigger than he was, yet he bore the task with ease.

"Really?" I asked him. It wasn't often that an animal could really tell you what they enjoyed eating, but I should have known from the rations Big D had packed when he'd set off on his journey exactly what he preferred.

Smoked worms tasted bad to me, but he always enjoyed them.

"Indeed, Master. This Bi De has sampled these interlopers from all over the Azure Hills, and yet the ones from our home remain the most succulent," he declared authoritatively as he picked up another bundle of wheat.

"Where did the second-best ones come from?" I asked, interested.

Big D paused, clearly giving my question due consideration.

"To the southeast, nearer to the Great Lake, there is a glade with a great many worms within. They were most agreeable," the rooster told me, and I chuckled.

"What makes a good worm, anyway?" I asked as I turned back around to continue my job.

"I would say juiciness, for one, yet Brother Wa Shi insists it's the snap and correct chew. I would not know, for I *cannot* chew . . ."

And so I listened to a chicken list off the things that one should look for in a "good" insect as I finished my job.

"See the gleam upon that one's carapace? A choice morsel," Big D narrated from my shoulder. It was rather comforting, listening to my first friend talk.

He would occasionally dart down and grab a bug, just to wax poetic about it.

And on it went until I finished the field.

When I was finally done, I stretched, grunting slightly as the exertions of the day made themselves known.

I turned back and looked at the stalks, which would need to be ploughed back under later. They would be fertilizer for the new growth.

"It's gotten big, hasn't it?" I asked the rooster.

"Indeed it has. And it shall grow in size next year as well," the rooster returned.

A year ago, this place had been covered in massive boulders and thick trees. It had contained but a lonely little shack and the foundation for a single house.

The fields had expanded from a little vegetable plot and half an acre of rice to over thirty acres of farmed land. My home was more like a manor, and even the little shack had grown until it was a proper house.

So much had changed in so short a time.

We even had *industry* now.

I saw the drop hammer we had built down by the river going, the sound muffled by the water and the birdsong. Bowu and Gou Ren were already working on stuff. There was smoke downriver too, the wind blowing away the smell of chemicals as the first tests of our ability to make glass were conducted. Miantiao the snake was being exceedingly careful, and I definitely didn't want to pollute anything, but it still kind of smelled bad. It was something I was interested in—hopefully I'd learn about it later, but it was best to let the master work out some of the kinks first.

Honestly, any more buildings and just a few more folks and my farm would look less like a farm and more like a small village.

"Miantiao certainly wastes no time," Big D observed from my shoulder. "Sister Yin complains that her Master runs her ragged in keeping the flames precise."

"Poor bunny," I chuckled with another shake of my head. A moment later, I hefted up the bundles of wheat and Big D took some of the others.

There was a tune on my lips as we wandered back to the freshly constructed grain storage. The sheer amount of food we were producing necessitated a *lot* of storage. We passed by another field, where an ox with a plough beside him rested, watching over three sheep and four cows.

"Babe! When you have a moment, could you plough everything in that field under?" I called out to the ox. A single eye opened, followed by a slight nod of acknowledgement. He slowly stood, hooking his plough with his horn. The bright yellow piece of equipment was covered in carved suns—its blade had previously been a demonic sword. But hell, it was a good plough.

We continued on our way past the vegetable garden, where a massive rust-red boar and a dainty pink pig were busy uprooting everything like living bulldozers, being careful to avoid any damage to the produce themselves. Chunky and Peppa then passed the uprooted veggies into a pool of water, where a dragon was waiting to receive them. He had fishy eyes and electric-blue scales. Washy received the bounty and then did his duty, a swirling orb of water delicately washing all the dirt and insects off them. His beady eyes then examined them closely. His long whiskers danced along their edges as he considered every angle.

After that, he placed them in two different piles. One to be pickled, our food for the winter, and one to be eaten soon.

The normally gluttonous fish was taking his job *extremely* seriously. And while I was sure we would have some things missing, I *did* trust him to make sure we would be eating good food all winter long.

If only because if he ate too much *now*, he wouldn't be able to eat more *later*.

I gave them all a wave as I walked past and got nods in return, Washy chucking me a choice carrot.

I decided to split it with Big D, snapping it in half before crunching on the sweet vegetable. It was crisp and refreshing.

The well-worn paths of the farm took me to the storeroom, where I opened the well-oiled door and started the process of threshing the wheat—something I was pretty good at, if I'm being honest. Super strength and speed made me as fast as any industrial thresher, turning what probably would have been weeks of labour into hours. The only thing I really had to complain about was how hot it got in the compact place.

I did have a secret weapon, however: Big D occasionally sent a gust of wind my way with his wings, letting a breeze hit me while he blew the dust out of the room.

It was my final chore for the day.

I examined the storage halls, which were nearly full to bursting, and scratched at my chin. At least once a day, I found myself wondering if I could even sell this wheat around here—or if it was like my rice, too high-quality and destined for the Azure Jade Trading Company.

It was annoying as hell if I was honest, not being able to sell locally because what you had was too good.

It was what it was, though. I would just have to figure out a way to deal with it. One problem at a time.

I yawned, stretched, then headed back home.

I always felt a small surge of pride when I looked at the house I had built. My house was quite close to a Japanese style, with a low-hanging roof and enclosed by a veranda that encompassed the entire building. There was a small courtyard out front, flanked by a bathhouse and a hut built to store medicine. It had glass windows, and one side had a sliding door that was currently open, letting the breeze flow through the house.

I took a breath, drawing in the early-autumn smells. The air was sweet with the scent of ripe fruit; the trees I had received as a wedding gift had settled in nicely and were already bearing fruit. I inspected the green fruits, pollinated by my bees. The peaches had already been harvested, and apples were getting big. Suddenly, *everything* about the trees popped into my head. How much water they had gotten, their health, and when the fruits would be ripe. A useful little ability for a farmer—other people got to see power levels, I got crop yields.

I patted the apple tree I was looking at. Big D examined the fruits as well, seeming interested at what they would grow into. And while I may not have been an American, I was *definitely* itching for some apple pie.

I turned from the trees and over to a beautiful sight in the courtyard. A wonderfully beautiful woman sat at a table in the shade, hunched over and writing something, her brow furrowed. I approached and leaned over the table.

"Hey, babe, come here often?" I asked, planting both hands on the table. Meiling glanced up from where she was working. Her amethyst eyes met mine as she was startled out of her introspection, but a moment later she huffed and laughed.

"I just might, handsome," she returned, smirking up at me. She brushed a lock of green-tinted hair out of her face and I kissed the bridge of her freckled nose.

My wife chuckled and leaned back in her chair, stretching. Her shirt rode up just a bit, exposing the bump of her pregnancy. Beside us, Big D had hopped off my shoulder and landed on the table in the shade. A tiny rat squeaked her welcome to us, Rizzo putting away her own brush.

I walked around the table and started to massage my wife's shoulders as I glanced at the myriad of medical diagrams on the table, as well as one of Meiling's own drawings. There was a mass of notes on it, marking out incisions and places of interest.

"How's this going, love?" I asked as she groaned, leaning into my touch.

"Better, now that I have a solid plan. I still wouldn't dare attempt this surgery without the spiritual herbs or your recommendations. The numbing agent is definitely a must, though keeping a person unconscious like that is always a problem," she said with a sigh, looking at the diagram.

She was talking about Bowu. The boy, who had come into our care, had a mangled leg—one that we were relatively certain we could fix . . . or at least Meimei and her father could probably fix. I'd offer moral support and what little I knew about modern medicine . . . but at the end of the day that wasn't much.

"You and Pops have got this. The kid'll be right as rain in no time," I assured her, and she sighed again, but smiled up at me a moment later. A hand reached up and she pulled me down. Our lips met.

"After the Mid-Autumn Festival next week," she muttered. "My, how time flies. It seems like it was yesterday when we were visiting the Eighth Correct Place, instead of nearly a month ago. We'll have to have the little Torrent Rider over. Your disciple was a very polite young man, Bi De," she said, nodding at him. The rooster puffed out with pride at the praise. Zhang Fei was a good kid. I could tell why Big D liked him.

"He should probably leave the dog at home, though. I thought Tigu'er was going to kidnap the fluffy little thing," I mused.

A cat that loved dogs. Well, stranger things had happened.

My wife chuckled and shook her head. "Maybe we should buy her one. We don't exactly need a guard dog, though," she muttered.

We didn't. But I liked dogs, so it was an idea. I'd had dogs in the Before, and they had always been good companions.

It was certainly something to think about. *Maybe next year, in spring.*

My wife yawned and pushed herself away from the table.

"I think that's enough for today," she said.

I helped her collect her papers and carefully put them away. Big D and Rizzo went off together to check on Miantiao and Yin, while Meimei disappeared upstairs.

A few minutes later she came back down with her hair in pigtails and wearing the flannel shirt that she had made. I admired the view as she slung a basket across her back.

"Want to join me?" Meiling asked. "I need to get some mushrooms. I promised Xiulan I'd make mushroom stir-fry for dinner tonight."

I nodded and grabbed another basket. I held out my hand and we departed the house, walking arm in arm. It was a companionable silence as I mused on the past and planned on the future.

Things had changed this past year, and all I could do was roll with the punches.

↔

Meiling always thought it was fun gathering mushrooms, especially when she had somebody to do it with. Wandering the forest and finding food never failed to put her in a good mood. While most of the fungus was from the mushroom farms, they had decided to expand their search, simply walking together through their home.

It was good to see her husband at peace and smiling. It suited him best, instead of his brow being furrowed and his body tense.

He even had his silly grin back on his face as he cheerily narrated a battle between two Great Hornbeetles.

"And the Green Thunder has the upper hand! Can the Crimson Demon hold on?!" he shouted. The bugs rammed against each other, until the smaller of the two managed to get under the larger. "Oh, what an upset! The Crimson Demon takes the win!"

Meiling held out her hand as Jin slapped a mushroom into it—she'd won their little bet. She smiled up at him, his green eyes sparking with mirth.

"Ah man, I totally thought I was gonna win that one," Jin said with a sigh, as good-natured as ever in defeat.

"I've got a good eye for these things, you know," she replied with a smirk. "My little brother has his own little cabal that he thinks I don't know about. The kids bet chores on the winner. The Crimson Demon's horn had a better hook to it."

Jin let out a laugh as they held hands again and wandered through the forest, rays of light penetrating the canopy from the afternoon sun. The massive Emperor Woodpeckers, as big as eagles, looked intently at them as they passed before the birds resumed their hammering. The normally elusive creatures were brazen here, carving out nests or looking for food with thundering reports.

So they wandered. Jin had a lot of land, and even he didn't know everything about it. He'd only been here for a year and a half, so they still regularly found new little nooks and crannies to explore or rocks to clamber upon. Springs to inspect and trees to climb.

It was a bit like being young again, when she had been more inclined to follow the Xong brothers directly.

But eventually, they did have to head back home. They had dinner to cook and mouths to feed. It was a lot of work . . . But she could never say she hated it.

They wandered back to their house, which Meiling still thought looked better than the palace in Verdant Hill. It was a little bit strange, it defied every other building plan she knew of, and yet . . . it worked. It worked, and now she could barely imagine living without a river inside the house or the lovely little upstairs library—which was already swelling with scrolls. Jin was even talking about something he called a skylight, once they had enough glass, and that just sounded ridiculously appealing.

There was a sound of encouragement and combat from the house. Previously, Meiling would have raced to see what was happening . . . but she was slowly getting used to the noise.

Tigu was jumping around the courtyard, followed by a small streak of black and silver.

"You're getting better at this!" the orange-haired cat-turned-girl called as she dodged again, the little rat missing completely. Ri Zu's needle attempted to follow her, but it was to no avail. Tigu was just too fast for her, the girl's yellow eyes easily tracking the rat's movements. Her tanned skin and muscles flexed as she moved, dancing around the tiny silver needle. She was smiling as well, her grin looking remarkably like Jin's. The other of their number was sitting off to the side in conversation with Bi De. The rooster stroked his wattles sagely while Xiulan nodded to him. Their conversation apparently over, the woman noticed their approach when she turned. Her eyes brightened as she rose to greet them. Their friend was currently wearing one of the green tops Meiling had made for her.

If Meiling had to admit it to herself, she was a *tiny* bit jealous of Xiulan. The other woman was absolutely gorgeous, even more so than Meiling's childhood friend, Meihua. Her eyes were crystal blue, her features delicate and refined, her skin pale and unblemished, and her brown hair, done in a single simple braid today, felt like touching fine silk. And, well, the less said about the difference in their body types the better. Meiling was thin like a reed. Xiulan was . . . *Xiulan.*

Really, Xiulan's top needed nearly three times more fabric than Meiling's did.

"Master Jin. Senior Sister," she greeted them, but there was a teasing lilt to it.

Meiling rolled her eyes. While the respect that Xiulan gave without question at first had been gratifying . . . it was good she'd begun moving past it.

Jin just waved, while Meiling opened her arms.

"Senior Sister indeed. This Hong Meiling has heeded your dinner request. You may kowtow before me for my generosity," she declared pompously.

Xiulan chuckled, a throaty thing, and embraced her. Meiling hugged her back. Jin was rubbing off on her, being so quick to hug. Her husband was a very touchy man. Terribly improper, but Meiling was certain he had the right of it.

She pulled back and smiled at Xiulan. "How was your time training?"

"It was very good, Sister. I can feel my strength regrowing already," Xiulan said with a smile. "I'm nearly at the Fourth Stage once more." Her friend touched her chest, where a golden crack lay under her clothes, a wound one of those bastards at the Dueling Peaks had inflicted on her. The translucent, metallic thing seemed to be benign, and acted perfectly like Xiulan's own skin.

It was cultivator strangeness. But from what Xiulan was saying, it was a miracle that she was able to heal at all considering what had happened to her. A burnt-out cultivation.

Xiulan herself, however, had endured the ordeal remarkably well. She hadn't had any nightmares at all, unlike the ones she used to have about Sun Ken. When Meiling and she had talked at night the other woman opened up easily about it.

It was something that calmed them both, talking through it together.

"And how did Tigu do?" Meiling asked, curious about how the excitable girl—who was now sitting on Jin's shoulders—had handled meditation.

"Tigu is a natural," Xiulan stated simply. "She doesn't complain, or even move at all. I must confess I was a bit surprised, but she's good. Better than Junior Brother, at least," she said, flashing a smirk.

"Gou was never good at sitting still outside hunting." Meiling stated, shaking her head and clapping her hands together. "Now, let's get started on dinner!" she commanded, and everybody snapped to attention.

→

Many hands made light work. Dinners were always fast when Tigu or Xiulan could cut everything up in seconds and Wa Shi eagerly got Meiling all the water she needed.

Recently, she had started practicing her own knifework. She was the lady of the house and she wasn't going to get shown up completely, damn it!

She hummed to herself in the crowded kitchen. It was much bigger than any other kitchen she knew, but with a pig, three humans, a fish, a rat, and a monkey, it was starting to feel just a bit cramped.

And this was *after* Jin had been kicked out to go and get the boys.

She hummed as she worked. Tigu hummed with her, voice just slightly off key, but the girl made up for it in enthusiasm.

Meiling pulled the wok from the stove, smelling the aromas, and then handed it to the monkey waiting by the door.

She was still getting used to the monkey. Huo Ten was a quiet creature and spent all his time around that strange crystal Bi De had brought home, though he occasionally chipped in to help with household chores. Meiling was still wondering what would make him open up, because he was rather reclusive.

It was something for later. Soon enough all the food was done, so they carted the feast outside to the enormous table Jin had set up. A table that could accommodate six humans, a boar the size of a small house, a dragon, an ox, and several other animals, all with room left over. Meiling deposited her portion on the table and sat down in her place.

"Yup, it's looking good! I made some improvements to the hammer!" a voice said, full of good cheer. Meiling glanced over to where Bowu was getting a ride from Gou Ren, cheerfully sitting on the larger man's shoulders. Liu Bowu was at that awkward teenage stage of looking like he was mostly composed of his limbs. He was gangly and thin but still had whipcord muscle in his arms and good leg from the fact that he still kept up his Sect's exercise routine. His hair was tinted blue, with a bit of a wave to it, and his eyebrows were rather large.

But the kid seemed inordinately happy. Jin had to drag him out of the forge he had built most nights, the kid tinkering with pipes and the drop hammer constantly.

"Thanks, Bowu, Gou. All those gears give me a damn headache," her husband replied, nodding to them.

Gou Ren nodded and set his charge down.

Her childhood friend looked good these days. Oh, there was no doubt he still appeared quite a bit like a monkey, but he was less scruffy and comical-looking with his trimmed sideburns and close-cropped hair.

He'd even gone off and really become a man. Little Gou, managing to woo a *cultivator* of all things.

Of course, if Liu Xianghua hurt him, Meiling would hunt the woman unto the ends of the earth . . . but from what she had heard, Xianghua had put her life on the line for her friends at the Dueling Peaks.

Next to arrive was Yun Ren, the foxlike man settling down and yawning. His ponytail was a bit disheveled-looking and he had bags under his eyes. "Got the last of 'em done, Meimei," he said with a sigh. He was referring to a set of images he was recording for her of various medicinal plants and mushrooms. The pieces were then placed onto paper, Yun Ren's Qi fueling the transfer.

Meiling perked up. "Thank you, Yun Ren," she said, but her other childhood friend waved her off.

"All good," he muttered, clearly tired. He set his sword in a chair next to him and almost absently poured a cup of tea before placing it in front of the blade.

The sword, Summer's Sky, rattled in a way that Meiling could only interpret as *happiness.*

The final ones to arrive were a snake—who had terrible burn scars across his body, a missing eye, and a broken back—riding a rather sooty-looking silver rabbit.

Miantiao and Yin, the glassmaker and the sun rabbit. The snake had an air of quiet satisfaction about him, while the rabbit just looked annoyed—Miantiao had obviously been working her hard as a flame source.

With their arrival, everyone settled into their seats.

The family was together for dinner.

Jin looked over them all, a smile on his face, and simply nodded his head.

While some days everybody went their own way or took care of themselves, since there were just so many of them, they all ate dinner together like this at least once a week.

Meiling let the conversation wash over her as everybody started talking, passing each other food, and generally enjoying themselves in the light of the setting sun.

The sheep and the cows grazed nearby. The talking was accompanied by an undercurrent of birdsong and the buzzing of bees.

She glanced at her husband, and at the faraway look in his eye as he looked over everybody.

He noticed her glance and grinned at her.

Meiling smiled back.

He nodded and turned back to watch over everybody, his eyes full of fondness . . . and *conviction.*

↔

The land was alive. It was pulsing. It was vibrating, coursing, and surging along a latticework of golden threads.

It was, as always, a pleasure to observe. Bi De's senses ghosted along the coils of energy, keeping a polite distance, as they observed the vast and unknowable.

And even now they pulsed to a familiar rhythm. They were more vital, greater than last year, and yet the energy of the earth was slowing down. Though slight, it was perceptible to his senses. The coils and lattices of Qi, churning with life and power, were not diminished, but their pulse was slowing.

It was preparing. Preparing once more for the cold to blanket the land. For the trees to lose their leaves and nearly all growth to stop.

The observer nodded, satisfied at what he was witnessing.

Bi De, First of the Disciples of Great Fa Ram, opened his eyes to the night sky. He gazed up at the moon, its waning crescent a sublime sliver, high up in the heavens.

How truly blessed was he, to observe a second cycle upon this earth. He noted well the differences and the similarities, trying to deepen his understanding. For another hour he sat upon the roof, deep in contemplation, yet his senses were ever open to interlopers.

He was on the night watch, guarding the flock from those who would dare harm them.

Though . . . he rarely needed to be so on guard anymore. The beasts now seemed to know better than to mount an assault upon the coops, for what must have been thousands of their kin now fertilized the soil. Nay, they stayed in their places, and Bi De stayed in his.

His Great Master had decreed that they be able to receive the bounty of the forests and the hills, for it was not for the Disciples of Fa Ram alone; and so in the wild places, untamed by his Master's iron spur, they slunk and went about their business, completing their cycle.

And thus, Bi De was largely free to gaze at the moon on these nights, contemplating the land and the changes of the moon.

It truly was a great life.

Bi De frowned as he saw his Great Master exit his mighty coop, carrying with him a scroll and a stick. His Lord glanced up to where Bi De was sitting and gave him a short wave as he set himself beside the river.

His Master opened up the scroll and looked at it closely before placing it on a rock beside him and taking his stance.

Bi De was intrigued as he watched him wield his wooden spur. He knew his Great Master practiced his punches daily, with a diligence and mastery Bi De strove to emulate, but he had never seen him use a spur like Sun Ken's.

He settled in to watch, fascinated.

His Master took a breath and launched into the first form.

The movements looked *wrong* on him. Not in the sense that they were incorrect, for Bi De could see that they were fine in execution.

But the movements simply did not seem to fit him. They did not seem to fit his body.

His Great Master looked uncomfortable as he studied the scroll of bladework and practiced the art of war.

His Master paused in his martial form, shaking himself after frowning at the blade. For a moment, he looked as if he was going to put it down.

He took a breath and started again.

The world was not kind; Bi De knew this firsthand. He knew of Zang Li, his attempt upon Sister Xiulan, and of his abduction of Tigu. He knew the world contained many horrors, and that it was only right to defend oneself.

Yet as Bi De gazed at his Lord training, he was struck with a mild sense of loss.

What a shame it was that hands so skilled at making were forced to cultivate destruction.

The rooster turned his head back to the sky; he turned away from the frown on his Master's face as he reset.

Bi De stood up.

He would call on Sister Tigu and Sister Yin to spar with him on the morrow. But tonight . . .

Bi De jumped, a silent shadow. He landed upon the Great Pillars of Fa Ram.

He, like the rest of his fellows, had done the bare minimum in recovering himself.

That was no longer an option. His Lord sought the path of war.

Bi De swore to himself: his Lord would never have to use such things if he had any say in it.

CHAPTER 2

EXPLORATIONS IN ALCOHOL

The day began bright and early, as it always did. Fa Bi De rose to complete his most sacred duty. Climbing to the perch above his Master's great home, Bi De opened his beak and called forth the rising sun, the great burning orb gracing the world with its light once more.

His voice echoed over the hills through the air, a pure note that held none of the harshness generated by his lesser kin. It rang out, and all heeded his exultations.

"*You tell 'em, Bi De,*" his Great Master called from his window. He spoke the words of power, completing the morning ritual that had persisted for nearly two years.

Bi De hopped down to the open window and lowered his head, bowing to his Master as he and the Great Healing Sage pulled themselves from their beds.

Thus, Fa Ram awakened.

Sister Ri Zu stirred from her place under Bi De's vest. Sister Yin and Miantiao the snake would have normally been with them, but the two had been up all night accomplishing something for the Great Master. When Bi De had looked in on the pair last night, the snake had been entirely absorbed in his work, the glow of the molten glass reflecting off his iridescent green scales. Bi De had observed for a moment, awed by the snake's passion and determination. Yin worked beside him, aiding her Master by providing fire for his forge.

Although it was a shame, since the rabbit was pleasantly warm to sleep next to and the mornings were starting to get a bit cool. Still, there was no point dwelling.

From his elevated place above all, Bi De observed the house that was once his Great Master's first coop, which now belonged to Gou Ren. From it arose five of their number. Brother Chun Ke and Sister Pi Pa, who called that house the servants' quarters, marched out in good time. They were followed by the Xong brothers and the newest addition, Liu Bowu. The young man was rubbing his eyes, leaning upon Brother Chun Ke as he walked. His limp was heavy this morning, but he seemed in good spirits as he chattered away.

From the forest came Sister Tigu, who had taken it upon herself to make the final watch. She nodded up at the rooster as she neared the Master's home, three sheep trailing behind her. Bei Be the ox rose from his meditations beneath the boughs of a tree to saunter to the great coop. A great dragon was asleep on the riverbank, his snores echoing through the air.

They broke their fast together: a fine meal as always, prepared by the Great Master, the Healing Sage, and Sister Xiulan. These last days of warmth were a true treat. With everything harvested, the meals grew increasingly elaborate, with new tastes and textures.

Brother Wa Shi looked to be one with the heavens every time they dined.

Breakfast was controlled chaos as usual. They were loud with their greetings and preparations, settling in and waking up. Others crowded around a large slate on the wall, checking duty rosters and seeing if anything needed to be done . . . or adding something they had thought of during the night.

Fed and watered, all of them trooped out onto the front lawn to begin their practice with the morning forms.

Yun Ren practised with his blade. Bowu stretched his leg. Ri Zu's needle flashed. His Great Master's form, that the man normally completed twice with easy grace, became five repetitions. His movements were faster as he focused and breathed evenly. Bi De, on closer inspection, could feel his Master's intent Qi, warm and comforting. These movements were much better. More natural than those he had used with the sword, but Bi De could still see that the more he did them, and the more aggressive his stance, the worse the blows looked. They were ill-suited to Bi De's eyes and did not fit his Master.

Bi De frowned but held his tongue for now, even as he noticed the others taking note of their Master's new strikes.

"I'm off to Hong Yaowu. Gonna see if anybody needs anything back home," Yun Ren declared as they all prepared to truly begin the day.

"Are you sure? Everything should be finished today," the Great Master said.

Yun Ren smirked. "You guys can work out all the kinks and make sure it tastes good for me," he replied cheekily, waving them off and starting up the path in his loping stride.

His Great Master laughed, watching Yun Ren go. A moment later, Bi De caught two of his fellows' eyes.

Both Tigu and Xiulan had noticed the Great Master's intent. The two women stared quietly at the Master's back, a look of concentration on their faces.

So Bi De jerked his head to the side, beckoning them. Both women nodded.

They had much to discuss.

Alcohol. Spirits. *Booze.*

It was said that humans invented agriculture *just* so that they could get their hands on a steady supply of booze. The sweet buzz, the different flavours. The best gift in this time period, really, and if you distilled it enough, a powerful disinfectant.

And I was in the final stages of making some.

"Everything looks good, Master Jin," Bowu said to me as he checked the copper pipes of the still one last time. Gou Ren had been helping him assemble things.

"Thanks, Bowu," I said to the kid, who still didn't seem too sure how to take compliments. He blushed and scratched the back of his head as Gou Ren clapped him on the shoulder. Let me tell you, it was really nice to have somebody who had actually worked with pipes before help me assemble this damn thing. Bowu knew roughly how to build entire spirit furnaces. He was still an amateur, and self-taught, but he had good ideas as well as an enthusiastic Yao Che, the blacksmith of Hong Yaowu, to help him.

Thus, the great copper still of the farm was constructed. She was big and beautiful, that lovely, warm copper tone polished to a sheen in its own little building, with a patch of river running through this one too, providing access to good clean water.

Chunky, Washy, Rizzo, and Meimei rounded out our little group working on the still. Big D, Tigu, and Xiulan were off somewhere together.

My little project had started about a week after we'd returned from the Dueling Peaks. A simple project to get myself back into the swing of things.

I hadn't started with the still, though. I'd gone for something a lot easier.

Mead.

Honey, water, and yeast. The simplest of the simple, really, but like all alcohol production, it was easy to learn and hard to master.

All you really have to do is dissolve the honey in the water, then add your yeast and wait. The devil, though, was in the details. The kind of yeast, the ratio of honey to water, and the fermenting time all played a factor in the final taste. Well, that and how clean everything was, but my wife could literally glare at bacteria until they died, so that part was easy.

As a relative novice, I had decided to make a few batches. Two of those were from what I called the outer hives. The honey for those came from standard-looking honeybees. It was pleasant, sweet, and golden, and perfect for what I wanted to do. One bottle remained as is. And the other one got some peaches in it, making it *melomel*, rather than strictly mead.

The other batch was made of honey from what I thought of as the "main" hive. I was certain by now that the bees that lived in that hive were some kind of strange species I had never heard of before. They were larger than all the others, some nearing twice the size of the other drones. The queen, Vajra, was odd too. She could be seen out and about quite often. It was weird that the hive would risk its most valuable member like that—especially because I often caught the damn fool creature trapped in the bathhouse. Maybe she liked the extra heat, but I wasn't really sure. Meimei and Xiulan hadn't known either.

Whatever the case was, the strange, iridescent bees were incredibly docile beasts and made *fantastic* honey. The raw stuff was almost as good as maple syrup.

They got their own separate bottle. After heating up the water-and-honey mixture, called the *must*, we poured it into the container until it cooled a bit, and then the yeast was added.

After that? Well, then you just had to wait.

Wait and get started on the other project, the still.

Bowu and Gou Ren helped me get everything assembled properly. My friend and the kid were both better at this kind of thing than I was, and Bowu had been interested in the mechanics of the whole thing. Meiling was poking around at the copper construct, using her Qi to give everything one last clean before we started.

"So, after this we slowly heat it up, which will refine what we need? Like a pill furnace, or like the creation of the ancients in Pale Moon Lake City?" Bowu marvelled, referring to the massive construction that had looked kind of like a still.

"I don't know," I admitted easily. "It's definitely not as good, though. That thing, by all accounts, could purify basically anything. This is just messing around with boiling points of different alcohols. You have to discard some of it. The foreshots are toxic," I continued as I fiddled with the mash pot. It had already been sitting for a week and a half, and the bubbles had finally gone down to what I thought was an acceptable level. I was going for vodka, so the base was potato . . . even if most modern vodka was made out of wheat.

My wife paused in her inspection of the copper still. "Toxic?" she asked with a bit too much excitement in her voice. I heard the unspoken question, and the way Rizzo perked up at the mention of something dangerous probably should have concerned me.

But . . . well, Meimei wouldn't do anything to really hurt us. Itching powder was fair game, though. And . . . she *might* actually be able to do something with the methanol.

"I was just going to throw it out . . . but we can keep it, I guess," I decided. Meimei was still upset about what had happened at the Dueling Peaks; brewing something nasty would make her feel better.

I knew this because she had been retreating to her hut a lot. There were some things in the medicine house I wasn't touching with a ten-foot pole, thank you very much. It was a *little* freaky how Meimei could cheerfully describe how exactly a poison could kill somebody, along with her then explaining efforts to make it even deadlier.

Thankfully she had a good-enough sorting system that nothing like that would be sneaking into any actual medicine. Meimei . . . well, she was super serious about that sort of thing, and instead of being angry about my fear of something being mixed up had invited me to double-check for her, just to make sure she had everything sorted properly.

Anyway, back to the Moonshine Project. The mash was ready, the still was ready . . . and we were just waiting on one last thing—

'*They areee readyyy,*' a voice that wasn't a voice called out. It whispered on the wind, laden with Qi, and had an undercurrent of pride to it.

I turned towards the sound of Noodle the snake's voice as he rode on Yin, the silver rabbit. She was pulling a small covered cart towards us. Inside were the first set of drinking glasses I had "commissioned" for this purpose. The snake and the rabbit had gotten paid for their work, like everybody did, but I had a sneaking suspicion that the money I gave to most of the animals just got put back into the savings we had.

We could have *probably* used clay pots for this, but if you want to retain the clean flavour, glass is the way to go.

The small cart was covered by a cloth tarp. The snake had been a bit secretive near the end there, but now he seemed ready to show us what he had made.

I nodded to him. "Finally ready to show us?" I asked good-naturedly.

The snake smirked. '*Thissss one isss out of practice. He apologisssess for the quality. The next ssset sssshall be better.*'

I could hear the humblebragging tone in his voice as he used his tail to peel back the cloth, revealing several rows of glass jars.

To me, with my memories of the Before, it certainly wasn't anything special, but I heard the sharp intakes of breath from the others.

"It's so *clear*," Meimei said as she stepped forwards, picking up one of the glasses and holding it up to the light. "There's no tint at all."

I had seen glass just as clear before, in Crimson Crucible City. The rich who lived in their mansions had windows made of it.

But my windows in my house? They were a bit cloudy, even with all the money I had paid for them.

The snake hadn't been lying when he had scoffed at the quality and said he could do better. His proclamation that his previous master's village had contained the best glass makers in the Azure Hills was certainly no empty boast—he had proven that. The old snake let out a breath, seemingly at peace, a little smile fixed firmly on his face as we all drew out a glass.

Once I got a closer look at them, my mind changed. What I said about this being nothing special compared to the Before? Forget that. These things were *good*. Scratch that, they were quite frankly insane considering the technology level of most places in the world, and the fact that they had been made by a *snake*.

I raised an eyebrow at Noodle. "I'll hold you to that boast," I prodded, and the snake harrumphed.

'*They are the bare minimum my Masssster would have accepted,*' the snake hissed. '*But . . . I am grateful that I have remembered his methodssss.*'

"Thank you, Noodle, Yin," I said as I picked up the glass. The snake bowed his head, while the rabbit smiled brilliantly.

'*This morose old bastard smiling again is good . . . even if I have to be the fire all the time,*' Yin grumbled. I scratched the back of my head sheepishly. I had used the rabbit's fire cultivation to heat things up as well; it was handy.

'*Language*,' Noodle said fondly.

Finally, we were prepared. I poured in the potato mash and we set the fire.

Honestly, it was a *bit* boring. The still slowly heated up and the alcohol, with its lower boiling point, started to evaporate. It went through the copper tubes, recondensing until it formed pure alcohol. That didn't stop Meimei and Gou Ren from crouching down and watching in fascination as the clear liquid steadily spilled out from the pipe into a glass.

First came the toxic foreshots: the alcohols with the lowest boiling point, which included acetone, also known as *nail polish remover*, and methanol, which was just straight-up poisonous. I knew a guy in the Before who had gone blind from his own booze, and I was *not* having that happen here.

Then came the heads, which had ethanol, the stuff you drank, and esters, which helped give flavour, but at this point in the process it tasted a bit nasty. I had forgotten the exact ratios of how much of each you normally got in a run, so I had to repeatedly sample the run to test when we hit the hearts—the actual stuff you drank. Which would probably make this first run kind of mediocre. Not that I minded, since at the end of the day this was just testing the waters. I'd be making a lot more in the future.

I poured out some of the heart, the good stuff of the distillation, into separate glasses for all of us.

Gou Ren was eager to try it, while Meimei just dipped a finger in; the tiny amount would be fine even with the pregnancy.

Gou Ren recoiled slightly as the burn hit him, while Meimei's nose wrinkled.

Both of them frowned and smacked their lips together. Washy and Chunky had their own small sips, the fish considering the glass with a critical eye. Noodle and Yin tried some too. The rabbit shrugged, while the snake swirled it around, holding it with his tail.

There was a beat.

"It's . . . well, it feels strong, and it *is* smooth . . . but it doesn't really *taste* like anything," Gou Ren said, sounding vaguely disappointed.

Meimei looked similarly unimpressed. Chunky shrugged without comment. Washy, however, considered the drink further, eating a berry he had found from somewhere, before taking another sip and nodding.

"It's not really supposed to," I said, taking my own swig and feeling the burn. It was . . . well, it was vodka. It didn't really taste like anything, but it burned. "You can do other things and age them in barrels, but this stuff is supposed to taste like nothing at all."

'*One mussst be careful with it. A mortal would find themssself on the floor with but a sssingle bottle*,' Noodle said. '*Though, I sssuppose sssome may sssee that as a bonusss*.'

Yeah, the eternal problem with distilled spirits. They were either too strong or not strong enough.

Gou Ren looked to Washy, who held out a berry. He took it and paired it with the drink. "Some people will like it, but it's . . . okay, it's growing on me a bit," he admitted. "The berry makes it better, but, well, why not just make berry wine, then?"

"We can, I guess. You can distill basically anything. We'll make berry wine next time and concentrate the flavours here."

Gou Ren nodded, while Washy perked up. *Actually, yeah . . . why the* hell *did I try to make vodka? I don't even* like *vodka, unless it's so loaded down with fruit juice you can't taste it at all . . .*

Hey, cocktails for the festival could be a good idea. I still had a bit of ice left in my storage pit. It had lasted far, far longer than I had expected it to, so we could make chilled mixers with the fresh fruit. That could be pretty fun!

The first round of distillation had still been a success, *technically*. I paused as I remembered one last thing.

"Oh, right, the other use for this stuff is as a disinfectant—most germs die on contact."

That got Meimei's attention, and her eyes brightened. But before she could start asking about it, there was a ragged cough from behind us. I raised an eyebrow as Bowu nearly dropped one of the glasses, having stolen a sip.

"How can you *drink* that?!" the sixteen-year-old rasped out.

We all started laughing. Hell, I'd had the same reaction when I'd tried my first drink. "Well, it's serviceable as something for the festival . . . but let's try the mead. It *should* be done by now."

I went and got the barrels from the storeroom, one from the honey from Vajra's hive and one from the normal hives.

I cracked the one from Vajra's hive open, and immediately the smell hit me. The sweet notes of honey. It filled my nostrils, heady and thick, and I felt myself salivate. I actually froze for a moment before pulling my face away.

Compared to the smell of the vodka from the still, well, it was absolutely no contest. Meimei stiffened and Gou Ren's eyes widened. Washy and Chunky snapped to attention.

Even *I* could feel that it had Qi in it, which meant either I had gotten better at sensing Qi or this thing was chock-full of it. And seeing as I hadn't really spent any time training to get better at sensing Qi . . .

I carefully ladled out the golden liquid.

We all stood around, holding our cups. The smell was intense, and the feeling of Qi radiating out from the mead had gotten stronger.

I took a sip.

The golden elixir surged its way down my throat. It was invigorating. Burning hot and soothingly cool. I could feel strength filling my limbs as the blob of gold settled in my stomach and sat there, spreading through my core.

"Holy *shit!*" was all I could say, feeling a little bit light-headed. That was . . . sweet in more ways than one. Everybody else was drinking deep and making appreciative noises.

Meimei just had her tongue stuck out and her eyes wide. She turned to me.

"Jin, my dearest husband, why did you make this *when I can't have any*?" Meimei asked, staring plaintively at the jar. She bit her lip and turned away from the mead, visibly holding herself back.

Somebody else had no such complications.

I caught Washy out of the air as he attempted a swan dive into the barrel. His eyes were wide and wild, until he realised what he had been trying to do.

The fish coughed, dangling in my grip, looking embarrassed.

"I think . . . we might keep this one to ourselves," I said, staring at the dangerous barrel.

CHAPTER 3

STEAM BOY

Two Months Prior

Funnily enough, it all started on a whim for Bowu, not that long ago. Or perhaps it was fate? A strange man, who looked a bit like a swindler with his sharp, foxlike eyes, and a rather brutish, monkey-looking fellow, holding up a sign. Normally Liu Bowu would have walked past, but what he saw had intrigued him. The large portraits, so lifelike. The extra background options.

Bowu smiled.

His sister already had a portrait of Bowu in her personal quarters, visible right whenever somebody walked in. Their father's eyes tightened every time he went to check on Xianghua's training, or so Bowu was told.

So he decided to get a larger, even more lifelike portrait. A bit of a joke gift for Xianghua, and his own petty rebellion against his father.

It had been a bit of a shock to learn that the Image Master's helper was the same man his sister had met . . . and by all accounts found attractive.

The man looked like a monkey! But his sister had always had a bit of a strange taste, and from what he could tell, this Gou Ren wasn't too bad a guy.

→

There was another chance meeting as he climbed the stairs of the Earthly Arena at the Dueling Peaks.

He came across two men who didn't flinch at the sight of his leg or treat him like a complete invalid. Gou Ren let him make his own way, under his own power—he just let Bowu set the pace.

It had been the closest thing to friendship he'd had in a long time, sitting there commenting on the cultivator battles.

And then . . . his sister. Liu Xianghua versus Rou Tigu. It he'd called the best match of the tournament, the unparalleled bout. Where two members of the Initiate's Realm had fought like those in the Profound Realm, disciples showing as much power as the Elders of the Azure Hills.

It would be spoken of for generations, they said.

Things changed quickly after that. His father, exiled for wasting Bowu's artifact-making talent and for his discipline of his daughter. Bowu, reinstated into the Sect.

Both small things, compared to the rat who claimed that his leg could be healed.

→

"Yeah, Bowu is going to come with us. My wife will take a look at his leg," Master Jin said simply to the Elder of the Misty Lake Sect, Bingwen. He was not asking the man. *He was informing him.*

Bowu couldn't help but be a bit jealous of Master Jin. How he could just say something, and it would be so.

Elder Bingwen spared a glance to Bowu, something in the man's eyes. But he capitulated immediately. "Of course, Master Jin. Take good care of our Young Master. He is very important to us."

Bowu nearly snorted. He wasn't stupid. He knew that all his Sect wanted was his Steam Furnace. If Xianghua could fight like she was in Profound Realm with his artifact, what could the Elders do with it?

A force multiplier beyond compare for their Sect. Even though she had lost to Tigu, that was seen as a powerful showing, especially because everybody thought that Tigu was Master Jin's daughter.

Master Jin was a cultivator beyond the power of the entire Azure Hills, and where others had needed to be beaten over the head with Bowu's talent and his skill at constructing artifacts, Master Jin had grasped it instantly.

A man who was so superior to Bowu's Sect he might as well be a *god* declared, on first seeing drawings of the Steam Furnace, that Bowu was a genius.

Master Jin gave him everything he had hoped to hear from his own Sect: validation, and a rebuke to Bowu's father that would have sent the man reeling and spitting blood.

He saw Bowu's worth . . . even if he himself didn't need the Steam Furnace. He witnessed a talent and decided to nurture it. Bowu would not be a factory to pump out Steam Furnaces under Master Jin. That much was certain.

Was it any wonder that Bowu grasped the chance with both hands?

"Come and visit any time you'd like, Xianghua," Master Jin continued. "You're welcome whenever."

His sister's face was a polite mask, but Bowu could feel how smug she was underneath it.

"Of course, Master Jin!"

Master Jin nodded, and left Bowu to pack.

→

They at first travelled light: a small cart for Bowu, while the rest of them ran. Bowu had been mortified when the powerful Master had taken up the yoke of the cart like he was just a beast of burden—but Gou Ren had just shrugged.

"That's just how Jin does things," Bowu's friend, and the man who had captured his sister's heart, said.

Master Jin hadn't even mentioned it, hadn't even spoken much of himself, but nevertheless, Bowu learned a lot on the road about what kind of man Master Jin was. Not just through the words of those who spoke of him, but through his actions.

Master Jin was everything Bowu's father would have said was unbecoming. Quick to laugh. Uncaring of decorum. Kind.

Worthless traits for a cultivator, who must appear to others as the mist: formless and unable to be grasped, until it was time to reveal one's intent.

It brought Bowu no small amount of dark amusement that Master Jin eclipsed the bastard utterly.

→

The journey away from the Dueling Peaks was over far faster than Bowu had expected it to be. All the while, he kept thinking it was some strange dream that he would wake up from.

But it did conclude, at the end of a road.

At first, Bowu had imagined they would transition to some manner of hidden realm when they arrived at Master Jin's home. Instead, it was simply a farm.

A farm with a dragon who could turn into a fish—and who begged Bowu for his table scraps.

The first few days were spent in a mostly bewildered haze.

He was out of place. It was a familiar feeling, really.

But what *wasn't* familiar was so many people trying to make him feel welcome.

→

Nobody expected anything of him. He was a guest. Lady Meiling—who smirked whenever he called her that—checked his leg daily, administered healing herbs, and gently walked him through what she thought was wrong with it. It felt a lot better already . . . but it was only a temporary relief according to Lady Meiling and her student, Ri Zu.

They thought that when his kneecap had shattered, it had rammed bone shards into the cartilage of his knee and the muscles of his legs. It was something that couldn't be fixed with simple healing herbs, for the bone shards would still remain.

After that, Miss Cai took the time to make sure he was comfortable. Big Bro Gou Ren and Tigu gave him a tour of the property.

He saw strange things. Strange things like Miss Cai, the Flower of the Verdant Blade Sect, working the kitchen like a maid. Chun Ke the boar finding Bowu nuts and berries to eat, little gifts that tasted delicious. Miss Pi Pa arrived in the mornings with a batch of folded clothes for him. A snake talked with him about glass composition.

Big Bro Gou Ren and Master Jin renovated a house, just for him.

He was treated as an honoured guest and healing patient, so none on the farm expected him to do anything.

But Bowu himself was getting a bit restless.

Then one day, a week after they had arrived, Master Jin called him to the forge. The massive drop hammer was always a sight. Bowu had seen one before, in Grass Sea City. The giant thing had always been amazing to look at, and it would have been nice to have one back at the Sect—but the Misty Lake's rivers flowed too slowly for any of them to work there.

Master Jin was sitting down and staring at a piece of paper. His eyes were focused and intent.

He stared at it for a moment . . . until finally, he sighed.

"Man, I have *no* clue what I'm doing," he said, shaking his head as he noticed Bowu. "I was trying to make something to show you what you could do with steam, but to be honest I'm pretty bad at this," the man admitted easily, then held out the page.

"A wheel?" Bowu asked, curious. The drawing looked a bit like the drop hammer—no, exactly like the drop hammer, but there was a strange tank on one end—

Bowu's eyes widened.

"Yeah, the base mechanism for that"—he pointed at the drop hammer—"but without the need for a good river. Just water."

Using steam to turn the wheel, instead of water? That was useless for a *cultivator.*

But not for a mortal. Not for Bowu.

"You said you liked tinkering, right? I've got lots of half-baked ideas, but I need somebody who will help me make them. Yao Che is good, but he has his own things to look after. What do you think? Could you give me a hand?"

For the first time in his life, somebody beside his sister asked for his help. And this wasn't so Bowu could make Master Jin more powerful—he couldn't—but because the man considered the project *interesting.*

There was only one answer Bowu could give.

Master Jin grinned . . . then gave Bowu a helmet, painted yellow.

"Well! First is the safety lecture!" he said cheerily. "Always wear your helmet when operating heavy machinery—gotta protect your melon!"

It was a strange lecture, but Bowu listened diligently—Master Jin said he would revoke Bowu's drop hammer privileges if he didn't.

So he wore his yellow hat and filled his ears with wax.

The sparks the drop hammer made were beautiful each time it slammed down.

He utterly mangled the first piece of metal.

And the next. When they went to Hong Yaowu again a few days later, they talked to Yao Che.

The village blacksmith was flabbergasted that the only thing Bowu knew how to make were pipes and tiny screws.

But . . . the older man was very eager to teach him.

After two weeks of meetings, Yao Che was Uncle Che, and Bowu was his apprentice.

Hong Yaowu was a beautiful place. The people there didn't care about his crippled leg. Most just mentioned they had seen worse, being a village of medicine. They were aware of his limitations, so they walked slower when they were walking beside him.

But it never felt patronizing. It never felt *pitying*.

They just did it because to them, it was the right thing to do.

He was just . . . another person to them. And honestly? It was great. He even made some friends. Hong Xian the Younger was absolutely enamoured by the Steam Furnace that Bowu showed him, and declared that Bowu was "Big Bro." The only person he didn't particularly like was Ty An. The grumpy, abrasive ass was Uncle Che's assistant and often in charge of pumping the bellows. But even she was tolerable.

For the first time in a long time, Bowu looked forward to every new dawn.

→

Present Day

Liu Bowu woke up next to a pig with a slight headache. A reedy-sounding rooster let out a call, and Bowu frowned. It sounded . . . wrong. Not powerful enough. Almost *insultingly* quiet.

He took in a breath and smelled the slight scent of berries and flowers.

He was next to Pi Pa today. Chun Ke smelled more like warm earth.

He knew two pigs apart by smell, because he slept with them so often. For a brief instant he wondered what his parents would have thought if they walked in to see him sleeping next to a pig. His mother's face was the one that invaded his thoughts this time, looking vaguely disapproving.

Vaguely disapproving, but she couldn't do anything about it.

Bowu smiled, in a good mood, and took stock of himself.

He wasn't in the delightfully soft bed Master Jin and Big Bro had made for him. Instead, he was a bit sore because he'd slept atop wood. A familiar experience. He'd fallen asleep often enough on his desk while tinkering with the Steam Furnace that he knew the feeling all too well.

He was fairly certain he was on the floor.

He concentrated, trying to remember the night. Bi De, Tigu, and Miss Cai—*Xiulan*, she had told him to call her Xiulan—had come back from whatever they were doing, and Master Jin had offered them a drink.

Bowu flushed as he remembered the sound Xiulan had made when the mead hit her tongue. Sure, the mead tasted good, but really? He had heard purer sounds coming out of a brothel the lone time he and his sister had passed by one in the city.

He shook his head slightly to clear the thought.

A little while after that, Big Bro Yun Ren had come back, looking extremely amused about something, and then he had a cup, which meant everybody else had a cup . . .

Bowu had snuck one as well. One couldn't hurt, and it did taste good—but everything went hazy after that. He *did* remember getting carried out to a beehive, so that everybody could praise it and the bees within.

And then Xiulan sang a truly and spectacularly vulgar song about a donkey as Lady Meiling, the only sober person in the room, egged her on. Pi Pa had been dancing to it, standing on her hind legs and pirouetting in a surprisingly graceful way . . . if occasionally stumbling.

Bowu had fallen asleep after that.

He finally opened his eyes, wincing a bit at the light, and looked around. The first person he saw was Yun Ren, who was half on the couch and half off, his legs sticking comically in the air. His friend's older brother had drawings all over his face, a mustache, and goofy eyes scribbled over his own squinted set.

The next person he saw was actually awake; Lady Meiling had a massive grin on her face and a recording crystal floating beside her that was chiming softly.

Bowu's eyes drifted over to see what she was grinning about.

Xiulan was lying on her back, drooling and snoring. Her shirt was completely open and her face was covered in doodles.

The fearsome Blade of Grass had Tigu in a headlock, shoved into a . . . well, a *compromising* position as Xiulan cuddled her. Tigu looked mildly annoyed, as she was already awake, but beyond a few minute wriggles, she seemed resigned to her fate.

"She's very grabby when she's drunk," Tigu muttered petulantly.

Meiling just smirked, because Cai Xiulan had caught another person.

Master Jin had his head in her lap . . . technically, for Xiulan's legs were also positioned in a devastating choke hold around the Master's neck. Master Jin simply continued to snore, though, so . . . Bowu guessed it was fine?

The man also had several pieces of male anatomy drawn on his face, and Bowu guessed Lady Meiling was the culprit, judging by the brush in her hand.

She glanced over at Bowu and grinned.

"Awww, you woke up! You were next!" she said cheerfully, and Bowu sighed with relief. It wasn't like getting the ink off was hard, but he had no desire to have his face recorded like that.

He winced and held his head as he tried to get up.

"Go and drink some water, okay?" Lady Meiling told him, her voice kind. "I'll make something for the headache if it stays with you."

Bowu nodded, staggering to his feet. His head hurt, but he was rather used to pain. It was a bit like stepping outside after a long night of drawing formations on a Steam Furnace. He glanced out the window and saw a rust-red mass sticking out of the river like a strange rock formation. Bowu hobbled over to the kitchen, grabbed a cup, then paused as he noticed a pair of feet sticking out of an "oven tray," as Master Jin had named them.

The regal Bi De was on his back, with his feet sticking straight up in the air, shoved together, with Miss Ri Zu and Yin the rabbit supporting him by the sides.

Yin was wearing the rooster's vest and Ri Zu had on his necklace. All of them were covered in half-eaten vegetables.

"So *that's* why the rooster call was so quiet today," Bowu muttered, before going into the river room.

Wa Shi, in his fish form, greeted Bowu, resting against the stone edge of the floor, with one muscular arm sticking out of his side. He had a cold sausage in his mouth and was holding a cup of fruit juice in his hand. The snake beside him simply drank his cup of water.

"Morning," Bowu said.

The fish smirked, another arm forming with a *pop* to salute in greeting. A stream of water rose from the river and flowed into Bowu's glass.

A few minutes later, his thirst quenched, he managed to get back into the main room and sat down at the table. Lady Meiling had gotten everybody who was still asleep into a better position. Yun Ren was back on the couch fully, and Xiulan now had a pillow. Master Jin had woken up and was staring at his wife's handiwork in amusement.

There was just one who was missing.

"Where's Big Bro?" Bowu asked, looking around.

Lady Meiling pointed up.

Bowu stared blankly at the man tied to a ceiling beam.

"I'm going back to sleep," Bowu decided.

HEHE~

CHAPTER 4

THE STORY AND THE HERON

Gou Ren rubbed at his arm, squinting at his brother, while he took a bite of his meal. Waking up tied to the ceiling was a bit disorienting, but they hadn't left him up there for long. He decided that when he found out who was responsible, his vengeance would be swift.

He thought that it had been his brother's prank, when he had come back from Hong Yaowu looking so amused. But it was lunch now, and his brother was still acting . . . just a bit off.

And then he had a whispered conversation with Meimei, and now *she* seemed to be amused about something too. She kept throwing him calculating looks whenever she thought his back was turned.

Alarm gongs were ringing in his head. He could feel the two conspirators breathing deeply behind his back like a pair of growing shadows, waiting for something. The two predators were stalking their prey. But he was a hunter, damn it, and he was *not* going down easily!

He caught his elder brother's eye. There was a battle of wills in the air between them. Yun looked him in the eye and held his gaze.

And then the bastard smirked.

Gou Ren felt a cold sweat go down his back. Their intent filled the air, and Gou Ren prepared for battle. The table went quiet as they all watched the silent conflict.

Jin, who had been deep in thought, swirling his fish soup around in his bowl, broke the tension.

"You know, we should do something special for the Mid-Autumn Festival," he said, glancing up at the silent table.

Everybody's attention turned from them to Jin.

The intent faded, and he could see his brother's thoughts crash at the same time as his.

Do something for the festival? he mused, before realising that was also why things felt a bit strange—there had been no prep work. Normally the village was a hive of activity this time of year, getting things ready, but here they were far from all that, drinking and lazing about, with only the bare minimum of chores.

"What kind of something? Meiling asked. "Normally, people just bring food if they're coming from out of town."

"I dunno, something fun! Like the General That Commands the Winter or the sleigh I did for the solstice. Something the kids will like."

Gou Ren raised an eyebrow. The snow golem as big as a house and a sleigh loaded down with gifts for everybody? Jin certainly didn't do half measures when he decided to have fun. Gou Ren liked the commitment, but sometimes Jin went a bit overboard.

Although the more Gou Ren thought about it . . . well, it didn't sound like too bad an idea, really. It would be nice to bring something for everyone. It would be kind of fun. What was the point of being so strong if he couldn't do silly things with it once in a while?

"Are there any important stories about the festival? Something we could use for inspiration?" Jin asked.

Meimei cocked her head to the side. "Well, we could do something about Chang'e. The Immortal of the moon *is* the origin of the festival."

Bi De seemed to jolt at the words, while Jin just looked intrigued.

"Chang'e? That definitely sounds familiar, but I don't think I've heard the full story. Something about her getting separated from her lover?" he asked.

"'Far away as Chang'e.' This Bi De knows the saying, but I do not know why it is said," the rooster stated, stroking his wattles.

'*Lady on the moon. Bunny too!*' Chun Ke grunted.

'*Oh? If they live up there then they must have many recipes for the moon cheese! This Wa Shi shall accept their tribute, when he claims his morsel.*' The fish stroked his whiskers sagely from his bucket.

"None of you have heard the story?" Meiling asked. "Jin, you must have. I told it last year to the children when—" She paused, thinking. "When you were talking to my father."

"Yeah, I had to explain to Pops why I hadn't asked him for your hand yet," the man said, and scratched at his cheek in embarrassment.

Meiling nodded and took a breath. "Well! Gather around, then, and I'll tell you the story!" she declared.

Jin seemed excited, along with Tigu. They quickly cleared away the plates, with even Wa Shi being faster than normal with the leftovers, interested in the "Queen of Cheese." Gou Ren had no idea why the fish thought the moon was made of cheese. *Why cheese, of all things? Who would even put a giant ball of cheese in the sky anyway?* With the table cleared, Meiling sat down and patted her lap.

Tigu and Chun Ke both started forwards, intent on claiming the coveted position. They paused and turned to one another. Chun Ke looked hopefully at Tigu; the young woman smiled at the boar, accepting defeat graciously. Chun Ke trundled over to rest his chin on Meimei's knee, chuffing happily. Jin and the rest of the animals sat down in front of Meiling, looking for all the world like an eager bunch of kids ready to hear a nightly story.

Meiling chuckled and scratched the boar's black mane, cleared her throat, and started. Gou had heard her tell this story thousands of times. She was the village chief's daughter, after all, and was generally in charge of this one in particular.

Gou Ren could tell that from the way she was settling in, she was probably going to tell the full thing.

"Now, harken to the story of these times long since past, of beautiful and kind Chang'e and her husband, the peerless warrior Houyi. Listen to their tale, of the lady of the moon, of the festival where we give in honour of Houyi's boons . . ."

Gou Ren sat down to listen to the old, *old* tale. His brother lazed where he was, kicking his feet up and closing his eyes. Xiulan sat down beside Pi Pa as Bowu shoved some pillows behind him and got out a brush, only listening with half an ear.

"Full of arrogant power, ten wicked suns did rise. Their wrath scorched the land and brought suffering; from their burning gaze none could hide."

It was a rather nice way to spend an hour and a bit. Meimei told the whole thing, in the traditional style—instead of the often-abridged version the kids got.

Houyi shooting down the suns that had been ravaging the earth was awesome. The love stuff? Well, Gou Ren remembered it being more boring than it actually was. Maybe he was just getting old, but he kind of liked it now.

He could understand Houyi. His thoughts drifted to a willowy woman smirking at him under the moonlight. Houyi was a true man, willing to give up immortality to stay with his wife. Too bad the bastard Fengmeng had to ruin it all, coming in to try to force Chang'e to give him the elixir. In the scuffle, Chang'e was mortally wounded, and in a last desperate act, she drank it. The wicked man was denied his prize, but Chang'e's victory was bitter. She had to leave the earth and ascend—but she chose the moon, as it was the closest place to her husband. Every year, Chang'e was gifted offerings by her husband, thus starting the Mid-Autumn Festival.

By the end of it, Jin was smiling.

"I think I've got an idea," he said with a grin, then pointed at Gou Ren. "And you're gonna be in charge!" he declared cheerfully.

Gou Ren pointed to himself, a bit confused.

"Hey, you said you liked architecture. So let's build something!"

Gou Ren felt a bead of sweat trail down his temple and smiled nervously at being put on the spot, but . . . he nodded, intrigued at what Jin had in mind.

An hour later, Gou Ren excitedly started drawing.

→

The next day, he stood in front of everybody. He had been up all night, but as he had drawn more and more designs, it had started to fit.

He had something. Something that would be worthy of Chang'e's story.

Hopefully.

He took a breath.

"Tigu, I have some rough designs, and need your help carving them out." Tigu perked up at the first to be addressed.

"Yes, Junior Brother!" she said, saluting.

Gou Ren nodded, handing her a page. She immediately began studying it intently. "Yun, Miantiao, could you work on the colours?" he asked. His brother nodded, and the snake bowed his head, his eyes sparkling as he began to mutter formulas under his breath.

Well, this was easier than he'd thought it would be . . .

"Jin?" he asked, turning to the man.

"Yeah, boss?" Jin asked eagerly.

"This part is yours," he said, as commandingly as he could. He handed over another paper with instructions. Jin looked it over and nodded.

While he went along handing out tasks, some of the nervousness faded. Bi De and Yin were given their assignments. Wa Shi and Mei had been happy to help once he explained what he needed them to do. Finally, he got to Xiulan.

She perked up, eager when he approached her.

"Lanlan, you're kind of useless, so you do whatever," he said.

She slumped, her whole face falling. "Is this because I tied you to the ceiling?" she asked.

"I was just joking, you can—wait, that was *you?!*"

They were delayed by most of an hour. When they finally got to work, Xiulan had a muddy footprint on her backside and a smile on her face.

→

Gou Ren finished checking the strap around Chun Ke's midsection. It was tight, and definitely not coming off. Gou Ren nodded and stepped back.

"This one is good, Gou," Jin declared from beside Pi Pa. The entire farm was gathered, ready to leave.

Chun Ke chuffed happily under his burden. He had a red cap on his head and a *small building* on his back. It had been designed by Gou Ren. It looked mostly like a shrine, a square structure with four faces; the front one had an image of Houyi carved into it, while the other sides were open, exposing a cylinder carved with images from the story. A cylinder that spun, making the carvings on it seem to move once it got fast enough. That part was courtesy of Bowu. It was decorated by his brother's illusions and pieces of coloured glass from Miantiao, forming a large, coloured piece.

It was covered with the stuff they were bringing to the festival: sheaves of wheat and rice, potatoes, and mounds of carrots and onions.

And the booze, couldn't forget the booze. None of the . . . *special* mead, but the rest of the stuff was coming along.

Pi Pa stood beside Chun Ke, her head held high and amusement dancing on her features. She carried a smaller burden, though one no less important. This one housed the image of Chang'e separated from her husband, reaching out to him. When put beside each other, they would form one carving, the hands touching.

Meimei had *gushed* over that addition. The lovers finally reunited.

Tigu nodded from beside Gou Ren. "Your eye for detail is quite good, Brother Gou!" she decreed. "We must collaborate again!"

Gou Ren flushed and scratched the back of his head, still a little embarrassed with how much praise had been given to him when everyone had seen the finished pieces. Sure, he had designed them, but only after Jin had given him an idea with his kind of . . . simple drawings. It had been difficult to make sure everything fit together seamlessly, but Jin could have *probably* made it if he put his mind to it.

Probably. But Jin's way was always a bit strange. Like he had the general gist of things but no idea how to actually accomplish them.

But it was nice to have somebody who had faith in Gou Ren's architecture skills, half-baked as they were.

It had been a pretty hectic three days, if he was honest, but it had been fun with everybody in the courtyard working on it. The area had been filled with the sounds of sanding and hammering, and people asking for tools and helping each other. Even Huo Ten the monkey had ceased his vigil over the crystal and aided Tigu in some of the carving. His hands were surprisingly deft.

Playing foreman had been pretty fun, and as his brother nodded and clapped him on the back . . . Gou Ren let out the breath he had been holding for quite a while.

His brother thought he had done a good job. Yun Ren was never one to bullshit him. If he thought it was bad, he would say it. Instead, all Gou Ren saw in his brother's smile was approval.

"Everybody ready to go?" came Meimei's embarrassed voice.

Xiulan was smirking at Meiling as they turned from the image of Chang'e. Meimei had a flush on her cheeks. Meiling had said Tigu should use Xiulan as a model, to better capture Chang'e's peerless beauty. Instead, the woman looked quite a bit like Meiling in the face . . . and had a bit more muscle than any other depiction of Chang'e that Gou Ren had seen.

Gou Ren still wasn't entirely sure why Tigu found muscles attractive, but he wasn't going to say anything to the lady who had carved it.

Washy was the last to arrive, *popping* into his bucket. It was how the fish normally travelled, with his head poking out, Gou Ren privately believed the fish was just being lazy. Although a fish in a jar was an oddity, it was still less odd than a dragon soaring around.

And so they set off. Tigu skipped in front with Jin. Bi De sat atop the wooden piece carrying Chang'e, like he was guarding the woman. Bowu was in a handcart attached to Chun Ke, together with Miantiao, Yin, and Huo Ten. Xiulan, Ri Zu, and Meiling were in the middle, chatting away. Even Bei Be was coming along, the ox travelling sedately behind them.

The farm was going to be empty for the day, but Jin said he'd run back the morning of the festival to check on things, just in case. The other animals had enough food and water, so it should be fine.

It was a leisurely pace along the smooth road. They stopped to make detours off the path. They had lunch under the shade of an enormous tree. They reminisced about the time they had spent building this very road, mere months ago, laughing and joking about the work.

They continued along the path in the midday sun. The colours were beginning to change, the reds and oranges of the trees coming out.

His brother started smirking again when they were halfway there, but Gou Ren just ignored him. It couldn't be anything bad.

And really, what was the worst prank Yun could do anyway?

→

Not long after that, Hong Yaowu was in sight. The gentle green hills and the trees. The smell of the cooking fires, and all the little buildings nestled against their fields. The big headman's house and its medicine storage. The old shrine at the top of the hill. He could see people moving and working, going about their lives, and setting up for the festival. Already the buildings were bedecked in red, and he could see the village chief, Hong Xian, working alongside them. Gou Ren's home village brought a sense of nostalgia, even though he could visit whenever he wanted.

It just seemed so . . . small now.

He had been out into the world, seen Pale Moon Lake City, and fought cultivators at the Dueling Peaks. All the fields, all the nooks and crannies he'd thought were so big not too long ago, were suddenly tiny. Almost quaint.

Yet . . . it was still home.

They were noticed quickly as they came up the road. The kids had obviously been on the lookout for them.

"Hey! They're here!" a young voice yelled out. The children, who had been kicking a ball back and forth, paused their game at Hong Xian's shout.

Then the kids took off running.

Jin laughed and stepped forwards as a small avalanche slammed into him. Gou Ren stepped forwards too as the kids ignored Yun Ren, who had visited more recently.

Soon enough, Jin and Gou Ren were both covered in kids.

"Welcome back, Gou!"

"It's good to see you again!" a kid said from his shoulders, weighing nothing at all.

"You have any stories for us?" a girl, Zi Qi, asked eagerly.

Gou Ren grinned. A hero's welcome, really.

It's nice having the kids happy to see me!

"Howya been, big monkey?" Little Shu asked cheekily as he clambered up onto Gou Ren's back.

Never mind, these children are demons.

"Oi!" Gou Ren interjected, but the little shit sprang off his shoulder and sprinted away from him, laughing all the way. Gou Ren dashed after the kid, staying just behind him, and Shu's running and yelling went from amused to panicked as Gou Ren swiped him up by the ankle. The rest of the kids hanging from his back cheered when Gou caught him.

"I die with honour," Shu declared, while Gou Ren looked at the unrepentant little demon.

"Yet you perish all the same," Gou Ren shot back and dropped him head first into the still-muddy rice field.

Shu landed with a splat and made lots of groaning noises, acting like he had just been mortally wounded.

Gou Ren rolled his eyes and looked back.

Jin had three kids hanging off his biceps as he lifted them all into the air, while Tigu had an arm slung around a freckly, bony girl—Ty An. Xiulan accepted a crown made of woven rice stalks from a small, quiet girl, Liu. The rest of the children were seated before Meiling and pouting. She had her arms folded and was telling them to wait for Jin to get the Shrine off Chunky's back, so they could ride him.

Finally, Bowu had gotten out of the cart, though now he looked to be bracing himself. Hong Xian the Younger was standing opposite him.

Bowu nodded. Xian took off running and jumped.

The crippled boy caught Xian, managing to stay on his feet with a bit of effort and grinning down at the kid.

"You stayed on your feet this time, Big Bro!" Xian said cheerfully.

Bowu preened. "Of course, this Young Master can handle such a slight weight," Bowu said pompously before ruffling Xian's hair. Xian choked out a laugh and muttered something that sounded like "sounds just like her."

"You make anything cool?" Xian asked eagerly. He had been quite enamoured with the puffing smoke when Bowu had last visited.

"Yeah, Master Jin lets me use the hammer whenever I want—Hey, Uncle Che! Look! I'm getting better!"

Yao Che the blacksmith stomped forwards, having come to see what the commotion was about. His grin was wide and his bushy beard wild as always. He picked up the piece of metal that was presented to him, examining the hollow cylinder.

"You're getting good fast, you little brat!" the enormous man decreed, ruffling Bowu's hair. "How the hells did you do these boreholes—they're so smooth!"

Bowu, if possible, got even brighter, leaning into the touch. His smile was wide over his face.

Honestly, Gou Ren hadn't expected the kid would be able to fit into their village that well. He was the son of cultivators, raised as a warrior . . . but he had. He'd slotted in easy, like he filled a hole in the village that nobody knew was there.

"Yeah, me and Big Bro rigged up the drop hammer! Instead of a hammer going up and down, Master Jin said we could make it like a drill—and Tigu helped," the boy babbled, showing the clean drill marks in the cylinder.

Gou Ren left him to it and caught his brother's eye.

His brother looked even more amused, if that was possible.

It was then Gou Ren noticed that most of the villagers were staring at him. Staring at him . . . and some were even giggling.

He swallowed thickly, his eyes shooting around the village. He saw his parents, also approaching. Both of them were smiling brightly as well, and with them was a woman from Ma's tribe—

Gou Ren did a double take at the woman, who was wearing his mother's more traditional clothes, the ones from their maternal tribe. Her hair was done up with feathers and she had on a dress with geometric designs on it. She was staring with warmth at Bowu, a tender expression on her face.

His jaw dropped. His brain staggered to a halt as the world went slightly hazy and pink. His heart skipped a beat as he remembered his time at the Dueling Peaks several months earlier, and the wonderful, *wonderful* woman he met there.

"*Xianghua?!*" Gou Ren shouted.

The willowy woman's face changed. She transformed before his eyes, her hands planting themselves on her hips. A cocky smirk formed on her face.

"Indeed! It is I, Liu Xianghua, the Young Mistress of the Misty Lake Sect! Rejoice, for I have come to your little village!" she boomed, and Bowu froze at the sound of her voice, having not seen her. His eyes widened.

"Big Sis!" Bowu shouted happily, dashing as best as he could to her. There was a bit of a wobble, but he was moving at a decent clip.

Xianghua's grin got even wider as she stared at her brother's stride, Yao Che walking just slightly behind in case the boy fell. She nodded to the blacksmith and turned to Gou Ren as she strode past. "Close your mouth, Xong Gou Ren! I know that I am utterly peerless in beauty, but do not stare so uncouthly!"

Gou Ren's mouth snapped shut. She nodded at him and continued past. Gou Ren just stood there, unsure of what to do. Xianghua caught her brother and hugged him.

"Not even two months and you're already looking so well," she murmured, as Bowu buried his face in her neck.

"We'll catch up later?" Bowu asked, and Xianghua nodded before turning back to Gou Ren.

"Xong Gou Ren! You've taken good care of my brother; allow this Xianghua to thank you!"

She reached forwards and grabbed the front of Gou Ren's shirt and pulled.

Gou Ren's lips met something very soft.

Several people whooped.

Xianghua smelled very nice. The smell of furs and home mixed with the smell of pure water—

She pulled back and nodded as he stared dumbly at her.

Then she turned on her heel.

"Blade of Grass, only a week in this village and I have utterly surpassed you in all fields! I have learned much from Honoured Mother Hu Li and Honoured Father Ten Ren, so now I challenge you to a duel!" she thundered as she continued down the slope.

"What about me, Damp Pond?!" Tigu demanded.

"I shall defeat you after I defeat Xiulan! You are shorter, you come later!"

Tigu huffed and pouted mightily.

Xianghua's fist bumped Yun Ren as she passed him, his brother's crystal chiming while he took a recording of Gou Ren's face.

Then she turned to Meiling, whose eyebrow was as raised as Gou Ren had ever seen it.

Xianghua dropped to a knee, clasping her hands in a formal greeting. "Lady Meiling, Master Jin, this Liu Xianghua greets you," she said with the utmost respect.

"She's been here a week," Gou Ren's father, Ten Ren, stated simply, as he approached his still-unmoving son.

"A week?" he asked dumbly.

"Yes. My son, how did you find a woman as fine as this?" Xong Ten Ren asked quietly. "I mean, she's strange, but . . . in a good way?"

"I mean . . . she kinda . . . found me?" Gou Ren asked, still off balance. "But a week?!"

"She marched into the center of the village last week and shouted that she was here to ask us for your hand."

Gou Ren felt his heart still.

"In front of *everybody*?" he asked, definitely not whining.

"Yup. She kowtowed before us and asked for our permission to court you. She's been living in your and Yun's room."

Gou Ren swayed.

"She also asked us to teach her our ways," Ten Ren sighed before shrugging in a "what could you do" manner. "So . . . I took her hunting."

The statement took a second to fully percolate.

"Wait, why has she been hunting, then? Shouldn't Ma be teaching her how to sew?" Gou Ren asked, yet to find his balance.

His father smiled in a way that said that Yun Ren's mischievous streak was not all from their foxlike mother.

"*She* asked to court *you*," his father informed Gou Ren cheerfully, clapping him on the shoulder. "Your mother told her that to earn our approval, she has to perform the proper courting tradition."

All colour drained from Gou Ren's face.

"But—but the *guy* is supposed to do that!"

His mother shrugged. "Then grab her first."

→

That night, a shadow skulked through the village. He had a rope in his hand and was full of resolve.

He nearly ran into another shadow, heading towards the building he had come from.

Gou Ren stared at Xianghua.

Xianghua stared at Gou Ren.

He glanced down at the rope in her hand. She glanced at the rope in his.

There was a brief scuffle, and then they were off into the forest.

They never exactly agreed on who kidnapped who.

CHAPTER 5

THE MAIDEN OF MIST

One Month Ago

When outsiders thought of the Misty Lake, they often imagined something far different than Xianghua's actual home. They imagined a mirror shrouded by mists, something deep and clear. A haunting, ethereal place.

In truth, the Misty Lake was a swamp. The only reason why anybody really called it a lake at all was history. It was the oldest name for the place.

Perhaps, at one point far in the past, the name had been accurate. Now the Misty Lake, covered by its perpetual fog, was choked by fast-growing reeds. They grew so quickly the landscape was different from one month to the next as plants took over the waters. The only reason why the lake hadn't been choked out completely was the mortals' tireless work, plying the waterways on their floating reed towns, and the work of the Keelbreakers; massive, herbivorous fish tore open new paths and consumed vast quantities of reeds, constantly shearing away the plant life with their scissorlike jaws. They were one of the most important creatures in the Misty Lake . . . though they did have an unfortunate habit of biting the birch-bark canoes that were the most common form of human transport. Such testing bites broke the keel and sent the vessel to the bottom of the lake—if the fish didn't just swallow it whole.

They *normally* spat out the occupant—unless the Keelbreaker was a female in the breeding season, but only fools went to the Breakergrounds at that time of year.

Today, Xianghua was near the northern edges of the lake and doing what was hopefully the last thing she had to accomplish before she went north.

An emergency had been called in by the mortals.

"Beiwei, Shuhe, Taiyou, take the little ones," she commanded as she launched herself forwards.

"Yes, Young Mistress!" they barked, erupting into motion. They took slower, surer routes.

Xianghua landed on a giant lily pad. It was as wide around as a feasting table, with thorns on its underside. It dipped down, then sprang back up, aiding in her leap towards her foe.

A red tendril covered in protrusions and sticky glue slammed down a moment later, smashing the lily pad and curling around it. The Carnivine spasmed as it missed her. Its trap leaves snapped like jaws and its digestion pitchers swayed, releasing the putrid stench of rotting flesh. It was nearly as tall as a palace, stretched out in agitation.

However, for an initiate of the Fourth Stage—no, for *Liu Xianghua*—it was a mere distraction. Her juniors shouted battle cries as they engaged the smaller monsters.

The building-sized monster ignored her sectmates, its massive snapping mouths all orienting to face her before the creature threw itself at her.

Xianghua took a small breath, then reached around to the contraption on her back, its dull red vents prepared.

[Breath of Steam, First Form: Heron's Beak]

Her sword, Shrouded Intent, flashed. The wall of vegetation in front of her parted and sap sprayed out in gouts away from her. The main tendril's trap leaf snapped as if confused before it fell to the side, severed.

Yet it would be the mistake of a fool to think it was dead. Like a heron's beak, her blade speared down into the Spirit Plant's roots.

The entire mass of vegetation shuddered. Three more times she thrust, and three more times the plant spasmed.

The Spirit Plant slumped, its life spent, and Xianghua rose, standing atop its floating corpse. She absently noted the cheers of the watching mortals nearby as her juniors finished off the smaller Carnivines. Taking them out on excursions like this allowed them to gain valuable combat experience.

She watched them with a practised eye, noting with some pleasure that they had taken her lessons to heart.

They were all getting better. Learning, growing. When she had put out the call to arms, they had joined her instantly, ready and willing to defend the mortals of the lake.

It was strange how some things remained. Her father's first lessons on defending the innocent and the mortals stuck fast.

She had been thinking of him a lot these days. It was unfortunate that he invaded her thoughts, but not *all* her memories of him were horrible. His lessons had once been something she looked forward to.

A tiny part of her still loved the man he once was, but it was a child's love for a father. That love had withered with the years, turning into a faded memory. Her father, as far as she was concerned, was irrelevant now. Gone and too far away to care about.

With a single jump, Xianghua landed on the main platform. The other disciples, finished with their quarry, landed behind her. The mortals there all dropped to their knees.

"My lady, we humble men thank you for your swift response," the oldest of the lot said, his head dipped low. Hu Yutong, one of the respected Lakemen, whose family had served loyally for generations. It was through his hands that most of the information on the wider Misty Lake reached Xianghua.

He was a useful mortal. She had even done him the honour of learning his face properly, which was an annoying task that took hours of careful observation.

Xianghua nodded as she looked over the floating platform. There were several pavise shields and a large siege bow with bolts dipped in a potent toxin. The mortals had been prepared for battle. They would have come to fight, even if nobody had responded. This close after the tournament the request for support might not have been given as much consideration, and there might have been a delay. Liu Xianghua, however, did not delay.

There were few duties she allowed herself to be wholly chained by. Rendering aid to the mortals was one of them. She respected the ancient pact between the Lakemen and the Sect . . . and her own younger brother was a mortal. She knew well the struggles of their lives—she had seen the mortal casualty rates against such monsters.

Abandoning people who didn't deserve it never sat right with her. So even though she craved to leave, to venture north to see her brother, she had come here to help.

She was no Cai Xiulan, a true hero to the weak. She just wanted to live a life without regrets. She would regret it if inaction brought these loyal people to ruin, so she acted.

"Your scouts slack, old man. How *dare* they be so inattentive?" she demanded instead. *A Carnivine with spawn? This far into the Lake? Any farther and villages will start going missing.*

Unacceptable. She'd personally see to the punishments of any scouts that let a Carnivine get *this* big. It was eating Keelbreakers!

The mortal bowed deeper, his face hidden by his large hat. "I understand your outrage, Young Mistress, but this one came from the Deep Fenns. It is only through the valourous action of one man that we had any warning at all."

Xianghua paused. *If it was from the Deep Fenns it couldn't be helped. With most of the Sect's strength gone at the Dueling Peaks Tournament . . .*

"I see. Beiwei!" she called, turning to the disciple who had killed one of the spawn the fastest. The young man straightened up. He had performed acceptably in the tournament as well. "I give you a duty. Scour the Deep Fenns. I shall allow you alone this merit—or you may bring several others to claim this merit alongside you."

It was something the Elders had counseled her to offer, years ago. A chance for one to distinguish themself in the eyes of the Sect . . . or shoulder all the failure.

"Yes, Young Mistress!" Beiwei responded immediately and glanced at his fellows, intent on having their support. He at least had some sense. Searching the Deep Fenns alone would have been spectacularly stupid. They nodded. A week to prepare and then they would be in the Deep Fenns, breathing through bags of poison-nullifying reeds.

Xianghua did not envy them—but they likely would not find anything. A necessary precaution, though. The Carnivine had probably eaten everything in there, but better to be careful. Xianghua turned back to Yutong. "Bring out this valourous man." Yutong's head bowed and he waved another boy forwards.

The young man had bandages around his middle, looking like his wounds still hadn't fully healed. He was obviously in pain yet made to bow anyway. She raised a hand, stopping him.

"My lady," he said simply.

"I praise you, Son of the Mist," she declared. "You shall be well rewarded for your valour in finding this Carnivine and reporting it swiftly. However! I shall hear no more foolishness of a mortal venturing into the Deep Fenns. Why were you there in the first place?"

Medicinal plants, perhaps? There were a few that grew there. If a family member of his was ill, she would see they were given medicine.

The young man flushed. "The butterfly flowers, Young Mistress," he said.

Xianghua stared at the young man blankly. The beautiful flowers had no value other than their looks. She squinted at his face. Blushing . . . bashfulness?

"Lovestruck fool," she stated to the man bluntly. "You went there for *butterfly flowers*? There is valour, and then there is rank stupidity!" she erupted, looming over the smaller Lakeman. Yutong chuckled, expecting one of her tirades. Fools needed to be disciplined, after all.

There were tales still going around of the time when she had forced a man thirty years her senior to put a rice bowl on his head and proclaim himself a "bowl of stupid" after she'd had to rescue him from the Breakergrounds.

It was nice to be remembered for your deeds. Even now, people were starting to spread the tale of Bowu and the battle with the Steam Furnace.

Xianghua didn't know if she would ever attain immortality of the body and soul. She was of the Azure Hills, the weakest province of the Empire—she could strive all she liked, but her odds were low.

Yet there was another kind of immortality, wasn't there? A name that echoes for a thousand years could be close enough.

The boy swallowed thickly. Xianghua glared at him . . . and then sighed. After all, she had fought against the Shrouded Mountain Sect out of love, which was arguably stupider than going into the Deep Fenns for pretty flowers.

Liu Xianghua was not a hypocrite.

"Beiwei!"

"Yes, Young Mistress!"

"Retrieve some butterfly flowers as well."

"Yes, Young Mistress!"

The mortal boy's eyes widened.

"Now go, attend to your duties," she commanded. The men nodded, getting their tools ready to begin cutting up the remains of the Spirit Plant. Only she and

Yutong stayed on the main platform. "I shall be gone for a while, Yutong," she said, her voice empty of its usual bombastic tone. The servant deserved at least that much. The old man nodded, bowing low.

"Thank you as always, Young Mistress. May the heavens watch over you in your travels." Respect was in his eyes and beneath that an honest concern.

She nodded and set off, glancing behind her one last time. Xiulan had spoken of peace. The laughing mortals weren't bad, she supposed.

→

The Misty Lake Sect compound was more like what one thought of when they heard "Misty Lake." Surrounded by green, the main compound's waters were completely pure and clear of any influence.

Yet the mist here had always seemed a bit dreary to Xianghua.

The Elders had been in a fit ever since the tournament. It had honestly been amusing, watching them speak with such agitation. Them stripping her father of his power over the revelation of Bowu's ability had certainly been an upheaval. Master Jin taking her brother with him was something else. In one swoop they had immediately lost the thing that they had valued enough to usurp their own Sect Master.

"Will Master Jin even allow Bowu to return?" was the common question, and through it all Elder Bingwen urged calm.

"What use has one so powerful for such a thing?" he would reply, but even Xianghua could tell he was beginning to get unsettled—especially now that she too would be leaving.

It was amusing. Xianghua didn't particularly care if her brother came back. She would love to have him at her side, but while she had good memories of the Sect—training and growing stronger, the duties, and the festivals that she felt fulfillment in—she did not doubt that most of his were bitter at best.

He may have enjoyed her company, sneaking out with her on adventures, but she knew the life he led beneath the Sect's vaunted benevolence. Few had lifted a hand to help him. If he wanted to leave this place forever and remain beside Master Jin, she would kiss his forehead and send him on his way.

Or he could come back. Come back and force all who previously scorned him to honour him for a bit of his favor. Xianghua chuckled at the thought.

Her little brother had a streak of vindictiveness. He probably would want to convert their father's bedroom into a forge and use all of the man's wall-scrolls as fuel for it. Perhaps even visit Mother, just to see the look on her face.

That would be quite fun—even if the woman didn't deserve either of their time.

Xianghua shook her head and continued on. She was packed and ready to leave, so there was just one last task to attend to.

At that moment, Elder Bingwen was in Bowu's shack, seated at Bowu's handmade forge. His eyes were locked on a spinning pinwheel, occasionally looking at the notes tacked to the walls. Bowu's insight was apparently of greater value than she had even thought, so much so that the Elders had actually begun to look at her brother's musings on old techniques. It was a common occurrence nowadays, ever since she had first taken the Elders there.

The way their eyes widened on seeing the diagrams and notes pinned to the walls, showing his easy comprehension of the mysteries of the Ancestors, along with his tools and his prototype Steam Furnaces, was so very satisfying.

Elder Bingwen had decreed it the most heinous waste of talent the Sect had ever seen, that Bowu had been cast out. Another, Elder Huen, who had been annoyed at her father's ousting, had simply looked at a page for a full five minutes before going off to train, his gaze troubled.

They had left the shack how it was. They said it was just in case Bowu had put them in these positions for a reason, and once he returned everything would be moved into grander quarters.

"Elder." The man turned to her. Elder Bingwen had a kind of melancholy look in his eyes. The older man had been responsible for a good portion of her training. It was he who had caught her visiting Bowu more than once, and had turned a blind eye to her activities.

She could admit that she liked him, in a way. He was ambitious but honourable. Ambition had led him to his current place as leader of the Sect; honour helped him keep it. He had never used his station as an excuse to denigrate her, had invited her to every meeting, and had not once tried to advance his own children before Xianghua.

He seemed content to be a steward. Xianghua was in his eyes still the heir of the Sect.

"Xianghua. You are leaving soon, I take it," he stated, nodding to her as she grabbed some of the pinwheels, looking over the room for anything else she could bring . . . but there was little. Her brother did not have much.

"Yes, I am."

Elder Bingwen observed her and sighed. "There is some concern you will not return," he stated mildly as she packed.

Xianghua paused at the statement. The Elders must be truly concerned about losing her as well if he was willing to discuss their fears with her.

She had considered it once, long ago. To simply grab Bowu and run to some far-off place.

Her brother had been the one that had refused her. He had said that she would have trouble cultivating if they had no support. That he would rather deal with petty indignities than have his sister live her life solely for his sake.

She had a goal: strength. Enough to wash away the stain their father put on the family name. She'd wanted the power in part so that when she ascended to head the Sect she could reinstate Bowu . . . yet her brother had accomplished that all on his own. She was proud of him. But it left her without a firm path for the future.

So . . . what did *she* want to do?

"I will return. I can't promise when, but I *will* return to the Sect. This place, for all its memories, is home."

A home and a people she would not abandon for the sake of mere convenience.

Besides, Cai Xiulan's plan of closer cooperation between the different Sects was a good one. How kind was Xianghua, to make the Blade of Grass's job easier?

"Ah, I may have a husband when I come back," she said, remembering.

Elder Bingwen sighed. "I wish you luck, Young Mistress."

Xianghua paused. Her father would have thrown a fit at her words. Elder Bingwen simply accepted them.

"That was easier than I thought it would be," she said. She'd expected a token effort to ask who it was at least.

"I am not so foolish as to give an order that you will not obey. Besides, this Gou Ren appears to be a fine match, connected to Master Jin."

Right, there was the politics. Then again, she hadn't exactly been *subtle* about what she had gotten up to with Gou Ren.

She raised an eyebrow at the man.

"Really? I was expecting at least *some* pushback . . ."

"You make more friends with wine than you do with vinegar. Your father was too involved. He could not see the larger picture," he stated, waving her away.

"I shall send a letter back when I get there," she said, and the man nodded.

"Young Mistress." He bowed.

"Elder Bingwen," she returned with respect.

And then, with no small amount of eagerness, she was dashing north.

→

There were no interruptions or halts on her weeklong journey. She ran unabated through the wilderness and towns of mortals until she reached Verdant Hill, the last stop before Hong Yaowu. She paid it no mind and simply continued onwards.

Halfway to the village she started to get nervous, wondering if just *showing up* was the right choice.

She did like Gou Ren. He was handsome and had courage. He was kind, and he was generous. He was a good man who had helped her brother without hesitation. Did she want to marry him? Perhaps. Probably?

She wanted to kiss him again, at least. And perhaps have another night.

She swallowed thickly and pressed forwards.

Forwards, to live a life without regret.

"Please! Allow me to court your son!" she asked, bowing parallel to the ground.

The shocked silence stretched on . . . But then the woman, who looked quite a lot like Yun Ren, smiled at her tentatively.

"Well, howboutcha tell us about what you and my little man got up to, yeah?" she asked with a thick accent.

→

It was strange, this village. She could not say the people here were disrespectful, but she was rather used to most mortals bowing.

Instead, they were quite a bit bolder, especially after Yun Ren had greeted her. Things were much livelier after that. To be honest, they reminded her of home.

The mortals who lived in their floating reed towns and plied the waterways courted death often, travelling through the swirling mists.

And yet, despite their hard life, they were always chipper and cheerful, in stark contrast to the overcast sky.

The people here were similar. Their lives were hard, but they made the best of it. They tried and strived and tried some more.

It was admirable, in her opinion. Like how her brother had struggled and struggled, never giving up.

Indeed, she made fast friends with the son of the village chief. He brought a vast collection of beetles to her when she was meditating in the morning.

Fine specimens! Though he held them quite close to her face. When she opened her eyes, she could see all the little details of the carapace.

Ten Ren and Hu Li . . . She saw what she remembered of her own parents in them, before they'd found out about Bowu. It was their smiles. The fond anecdotes.

The fact that they had, and still, *cared*.

Hu Li said it was custom to brush Xianghua's hair in the mornings, then dress her up in the interesting clothes of her tribe.

Ten Ren said it was custom to listen quietly in the evening, after asking her what her life had been like.

Both said it was custom that she should be hugged before going to sleep. Most strange, but not objectionable customs.

Xianghua studied their faces diligently, and within the week she had managed to figure them out acceptably.

Enough to know that they found the way she talked amusing. Enough to know she was fairly certain they liked her.

→

When she saw her brother again, she had little idea what to expect.

Yet once they'd arrived, all of her worries faded.

She saw her brother again. He was being helped out of the cart by Gou Ren, who ruffled his hair with a smile. She knew exactly how much her brother limped.

He was walking without wincing. He could practically *run*.

He called the blacksmith Uncle Che, looking to him like he was the mortal's own son. Searching for his approval.

Her normally surly brother had one of the brightest grins she had ever seen on his face. It wasn't the satisfied smirk of a genius proven right . . . but the grin she remembered from her childhood.

She was just so happy that she ended up smiling too, instead of having to actively think to force her face into making expressions.

Then she turned her eyes to Gou Ren. The man saw her and his jaw dropped. His breath quickened. He flushed high on his cheeks.

Xiulan . . . looked at peace. Her friend radiated a kind of quiet strength that was impossible to ignore. The damage that had been done to her cultivation had not affected her spirit. Instead, she greeted Xianghua. Tigu and Ri Zu shouted their greetings as well.

And finally, she met the two responsible for her brother's health and her friend's life.

Any tension that was left faded away.

"Lady Meiling! Master Jin!" she boomed, as boisterously as she could.

→

"I was having lots of trouble with the shape, and figuring out how to join the pieces together. I had made some of the parts too thin," Bowu grumbled, looking petulant. Xianghua let out a little chuckle, rather than a bombastic laugh. She combed her fingers through her brother's hair, looking down onto him where his head lay in her lap.

"Oh? And then what happened?" she said in a quiet voice.

"Well, Wa Shi suggested that we just make them into woks instead," Bowu admitted. "It's . . . kinda bad, and there's lots more I can do to improve, but they still use it. Master Jin even said it was his favourite pair."

There was no missing the note of pride.

Xianghua smiled. "What else?" she asked. She glanced up as Honoured Mother Hu Li poked her head into the room. Her eyes asked if they needed anything.

Xianghua shook her head gently.

Honoured Mother Hu Li nodded, then gave Xianghua a grin and a wink.

Xianghua nodded, ready to accept the mission.

Bowu finally finished thinking. "Oh, Xian showed me a really cool place, with really soft grass. It's his secret spot, and I can't tell you exactly where it is, but it's nice. He taught me how to bug fight as well. That was awesome. I think I would have won if I had a Twinhorn from the south shore. Those would be so good at beetlefighting . . ."

The night carried on and she listened to her brother's excited words as he spoke of the village and of everything Lady Meiling was teaching him about his leg. He talked until he fell asleep.

Then she rose, gaze fixed forwards.

Honoured Mother Hu Li handed her the rope and grinned.

That night she had a reunion of a different sort.

But one no less enjoyable.

CHAPTER 6

PART OF THE FAMILY

Drums thundered. Instruments clanged; firecrackers popped and banged. The scent of food filled the air.

In the middle of a village, I watched as two dragons hopped and skipped, moving in time to the beat. The children shrieked and gleefully chased after their tails as they danced through the streets, performing acrobatic stunts. One was a puppet, clad in red as the elders displayed their skill; the other was bright blue and very much alive, with beady, fishy eyes and a lovely tail fin.

A Mid-Autumn Festival with an *actual* dragon. I had been getting used to him in that form, but even I had to stop and stare as he performed, winding and coiling along with the puppet. He was majestic and powerful-looking, regal. It took my breath away, and I wasn't the only one.

It was the kind of thing that you just had to stop and witness. I absently heard somebody yelp, accompanied by the slight smell of burning food as a cook forgot to move their wok, too engrossed in the performance. Tigu and Yin were up there too, with the kids, dancing in time to the beat and trailing after the dragons.

The dance entered its final stages, and the movements got faster. The dragon puppet leapt and bounded onto nearby walls, before they ran halfway up a building and performed a three-man backflip in full costume. It still amazed me that Pops, Ten Ren, and Yao Che were so synchronized. They were even smoother than last year—and then they did another flip, making the costume do a barrel roll, bounding all over the village in a burst of frantic energy as the drums reached a fever pitch. Washy rocketed into the air, letting out a magnificent roar that sent everybody cheering, while the village elders posed their own dragon on the earth.

The cheers echoed through the entire village as Tigu clapped Washy on the shoulder, nodding. A rooster crowed and a massive boar squealed with encouragement.

The elders clambered out of the dragon costume, sweaty and red-faced but still looking relatively fresh. I clapped along with everyone in appreciation for the performance. The elders walked over to the feast table along with Washy, who quickly claimed a place at the table, a platter of food being put in front of him.

The spell finally broke, so I returned to my job, getting more firewood for the stoves. You know how you could tell if you were "just a guest" or actually part of the village?

The guests weren't allowed to help out.

This year, instead of sitting at the head table as an honoured guest, I'd asked for a job, and I'd gotten one. It was just transporting firewood, but it was still nice to be helpful.

The others were helping out in their own way too. Babe was, surprisingly, with the cooks, helping out in his own way. He was kind of slow, his cuts made with exacting deliberation as he held a knife in his mouth, each object examined carefully after. Honestly, he was probably more of a hindrance than a help with how slow he was . . . but nobody seemed to mind—the older aunties praised his perfectly cut sizes. Besides, he had helped enough with the road and he had the goodwill of the men, who clapped him on his broad shoulders whenever they walked past. Yao Che had, before he started the dance, even offered to look at Sunny the Plough and make sure it was well maintained. Chunky, Peppa, and Huo Ten were out transporting food to the tables. It was kind of a buffet style, as it had to be, everybody coming and going while they grabbed from the platters.

Big D and Miantiao were with the true elders of the village, assisting them with their own tasks. The oldest men and women were gathered around our scene of Chang'e, decorating it even more with flowers and offerings. The sculptures had been received *very* well, to say the least—and I knew that those two pieces would be the center of every new Mid-Autumn Festival to come.

It might even outlive us, and there was something really special about that.

The festival was definitely a success so far. That morning, we had all gotten up early to aid in the preparations . . . and caught Gou Ren and Xianghua wandering back into the village.

It was kind of funny seeing Gou Ren being a blushing mess, while Xianghua was proud of her accomplishment. They were the ones up at the table this year, surrounded by aunties giving . . . *advice.* They were teasing the pair mercilessly, expecting to embarrass them, and were doing a quite good job of getting Gou to flush. Their other target, however, was an unshakable wall.

"Indeed! Gou Ren was most manly; he challenged me for the sake of a mortal, even knowing he would likely lose!" she boasted, her voice loud. "His courage captured this Young Mistress's interest!"

The titters that followed were very loud.

"Oh, *manly* is he?" one of the older women asked.

Xianghua pulled open Gou Ren's shirt further, exposing his abs. "Behold!" she proclaimed.

The old ladies swooned in feigned drama. Gou Ren looked like he wanted to die.

I simply shook my head before looking at Meimei, who was putting the finishing touches on some stir-fry, flipping rice with practiced ease. She seemed amused and shook her head.

"What do you think?" I asked as I wandered over.

"Like you said. A bit nuts . . . but she's a good person," my wife opined. She finished chopping some vegetables and handed them off to another woman. "Like Xiulan was, for a bit."

I nodded. Xianghua had certainly made an impact in the week she had been here. It wasn't every day that a cultivator dropped by, proceeded to start learning how to dress furs from the resident hunter, and started calling him "Honoured Father" and his wife "Honoured Mother."

Hells, she had even helped out with packing away the harvest!

Pops told me he had been wondering how to sneak out of the village to come get me—to make sure the strange woman was a real friend. But then Yun Ren had arrived and, after a moment of shock at her being here so soon, had vouched for her. He had retold the story of her defending Gou Ren, complete with images from his crystal and illusions on the wall. A true brother, talking up the woman Gou Ren liked. After that, Xianghua was an honourary member of Hong Yaowu.

Of course, Yun Ren then kept it a secret so he could spring it on his brother later.

I approved. It was kind of mean, but witnessing Gou Ren's face had been hilarious.

I moved past Xiulan, who was utterly bedecked in crowns of reeds and ivy and had a beautifully carved bracelet of wood. The quiet girl, Liu, was examining her handiwork with pride, and Lanlan looked a bit like some kind of nature goddess of old, surrounded by her panoply of knives and cooking implements. She nodded at me as she picked up a platter of dumplings and walked to the head table, putting them in front of Gou Ren and Xianghua, evidently intent on getting in on the teasing.

Xianghua, however, opened fire immediately.

"Cai Xiulan! I praise your cooking! Truly, this is the best place for you, to be serving this Young Mistress!" she said with a catty smile. Xiulan's smile turned sickly sweet.

And then she made a very rude gesture at Xianghua.

"I thought I would give this to you, Dear Damp Pond. You look so very malnourished, I couldn't leave you alone!" Xiulan puffed out her chest slightly, drawing attention to the . . . *vast* size difference.

Xianghua burst out laughing. "You're much better this way, Blade of Grass!" Xianghua said. "Come! Sit with me! Tigu, you must as well! I deign to listen to the story of your lives!"

Xiulan rolled her eyes but obliged the boisterous woman, poking Gou Ren in the side as she sat down.

Once all the food was prepared and we were stocked with everything needed for the feast, it was time for things to truly get going. We would be cleaning up later, but for the moment everything was done. We all sat down at the head table.

I was to the right of Pops and I poured him a drink. It was something a junior did to a social superior. And while technically a cultivator outranked any mortal . . . that was stupid. This was Pops. I respected him.

Hong Xian was a rather thin man, with the same long, greenish hair as Meimei. He was quite good-looking, I had to say, and had a face framed with a trimmed beard. His eyes were dark and he had several wrinkles on his face—mostly smile lines, though there were the errant few from worry.

He smiled back at me, raising his filled cup to his lips.

"What a year it's been, no?" he asked me after a moment. His eyes were proud as he looked at his people.

"What a year it's been," I agreed, and clinked glasses with him. I watched carefully as he took a drink of the liquid within, like it was rice wine. His eyes widened and his face tightened, but he managed to swallow the vodka.

"Quite strong, my son. But did you think this old-timer could be caught by a trick like that?" he asked, cuffing me playfully for my prank. He coughed slightly and examined the clear liquid. "I take it your 'distillation' was successful, then?"

"Yup. This is the base, but if we go for another run or two we'll get an alcohol that's so strong you can't drink it but is a powerful disinfectant."

My father-in-law smiled at my words. His eyes were on me and full of . . . well, it was an emotion that struck me deep.

"I'm glad you came north, my son." They were simple words, and words that I had wanted to hear for a long, long time. It hurt, just a bit, but it was a good hurt. My heart skipped a beat and his face flashed with the image of two other men. My father from the Before, and Rou's father, smiling in the same way.

It was the pride of a father looking at the accomplishments of his son.

I swallowed thickly before clearing my throat and scratching the back of my head.

"Well! That drink tastes better with fruit added. You want to try that?" I asked, changing the subject.

Hong Xian raised an eyebrow. "Of course! A father should know the fruits of his son's labours. Ever a new invention with you. Speaking of inventions, the beehives worked wonderfully. The first harvest exceeded my expectations . . ."

I listened to him talk about the village. The older man described the foolish incidents, the bumps and the bruises. The highs and the lows.

There was an odd sense of nostalgia as I sat with him. The other elders came and went, chiming in with their words. It was like I was a kid again, listening to the tales of my father. I guess in a sense, I was.

We ate, we drank, and we made merry.

Come to think of it . . . the Mid-Autumn Festival from last year was basically the first time I'd felt like I truly belonged here.

And this year . . . this time . . . well, this time I didn't just belong, I was family.

I stared out over the village and soaked in the atmosphere.

→

"Another year, another set of hangover cures," my wife declared as she sat over the stove, making one of her elixirs.

I laughed, picking up another overturned table.

I ended the Mid-Autumn Festival less drunk than I had last time. Mostly out of consideration for Meimei, as she couldn't drink, and I knew from experience how it was no fun being the only sober person.

We were cleaning up together, skirting between the countless passed-out forms. We'd collect everybody later and put them to bed, if they hadn't stumbled off. The village was silent as we worked. The story boxes Gou Ren had built had been a massive success, going along with Meimei's story. It was a production. Meimei's voice carried over the pseudo animations and the brilliant colours from Yun Ren. Yin shot fire into the air, serving as the suns, and Big D shot them down with silver lances.

My cocktails had also been a big hit . . . though maybe *too* big a hit, judging by how absolutely hammered a bunch of people had gotten off them. Then again, vodka was far higher in alcohol content than anything anybody was used to. A few shots of vodka were equal to a few *bottles* of rice wine.

The final event of the night had been Pops's announcements. "As I am sure you have all noticed, we have another announcement this year," he had said with a shit-eating grin. "Our fair Gou Ren's hand has been claimed by this lovely woman, Liu Xianghua . . ."

I snorted at the memory. There wasn't a wedding date . . . yet. If only because Xianghua had been too drunk to discuss one.

"You still up to get to Verdant Hill tomorrow? Or should we give it a day?" Meiling asked me. We planned to visit Tingfeng and Meihua, our friends from Verdant Hill.

After a moment of consideration, I nodded.

"Yeah. I have to ask the Lord Magistrate for his advice anyway."

Because I was in a bit deep and needed somebody to help out. I had no idea what I was supposed to do, suddenly being the "man in charge" for the Sects of the province and the Shrouded Mountain Sect. I hated politics like I hated practising those sword moves.

But sometimes you have to do things you hate, no matter how off practising those sword forms felt. I had a family to protect.

Meimei reached out and squeezed my hand, noticing my silence. Her smile was soft and tender. "You're going to do fine," she said with absolute certainty.

I smiled and pulled her into a hug.

And so ended the Mid-Autumn Festival.

CHAPTER 7

MISUNDERSTANDINGS

It is still strange to be able to move this fast, Meiling thought as her feet pounded along the road in the predawn light.

She could never help marvelling at her body when she really let loose. The speed at which she could move, the way her body rarely got sore anymore, and the precision. It was the way her body moved *exactly* the way she wanted it to that she couldn't help but marvel at.

She was pregnant, yet she was running faster than a horse, all without strain. None of the standard ailments seemed to bother her. No morning sickness. No urge to urinate constantly. It was still early in the pregnancy, but there wasn't any pain, bloating, or soreness, either. If it weren't for the small, slowly growing bump or the constant awareness of something growing within her, she would honestly never have noticed that she was having a child.

It was just her and her husband today, heading to Verdant Hill. They had set out in the early-morning light. The rest of their family either had been too hungover to join them or would be heading home to take care of the farm.

It was rather nice to have so many people she could rely on. It meant she could leave her worries behind, focusing on running along a road she'd helped build towards Verdant Hill.

It wouldn't have looked out of place near the capital of the province, and it cut hours off the journey by foot, smoothing out some of the winding curves. She still remembered the one time, long ago, it had taken a full week to get to Verdant Hill after a tree had fallen across the road.

At their current pace, it would be mere hours.

It was humbling.

"Hey, look. There's our special spot," Jin said, pointing.

He grinned, then started to make a detour. Amused, Meiling followed him. This was the spot where they had first kissed, over a year ago. How time flew. And Jin, the thief, had stolen the rock itself. It was a very nice rock, and it now had a place right beside the house. Too bad it left the clearing rather bare—

Meiling raised an eyebrow as they came to the clearing. She stared at the new boulder sitting where the old rock had stood.

"When did you put this here?" she deadpanned.

Jin whistled, trying to sound innocent. He jumped to the top of the rock and smirked down at her.

Meiling, who once had to be carried up, jumped up in a single leap.

The view was as spectacular as ever. The company wasn't bad either.

→

Jin was humming a tune and Meiling was in a similarly good mood as they slowed from a run to a more leisurely walk.

The stone walls of Verdant Hill were in sight. They rose tall and strong into the sky, atop the peak of one of the large but gentle slopes. As far as Meiling could remember, they had only been tested by Spirit Beasts three times since the records started, and each time the creatures had been repelled, though one could still see the subtle differences in the stone work on the part of the wall that had been repaired after it had been half knocked down a century ago.

It was an idyllic-looking town, especially with the new roads. Green grass and farmland covered the ground outside the walls, and Meiling could see the guard patrols in the distance going about their business, the well-drilled and polite men ever ready to assist.

The sun had fully risen by the time they got to the gate. The guards gave them a once-over and let them in without a fuss. Meiling could see recognition in their eyes as they looked at Jin, and the guards nodded politely to the two of them while they passed inside.

They came through the gate into the orderly streets. It was an old town, built around an *older* town. A small shrine, right beside the Imperial Palace—the grand name for the Magistrate's residence and the governmental buildings—was the oldest building in it, the rest having been burned down by fires or replaced. The town was well organised, in a grid layout, and had been becoming ever more orderly over the years, and ever cleaner, since the Lord Magistrate had taken office decades ago. Meiling couldn't tell, but Father and Uncle Bao, the Archivist, talked about it quite often.

Even the district that could be considered a slum, filled with the poorer members of the town, was clean and often crimeless. The guards were vigilant and the people remained unmolested.

The Lord Magistrate did his job well, and Meiling could think of no better person for Jin to seek assistance from, especially because the entire thing about the Dueling Peaks was clearly bothering him.

It bothered Meiling too. Jin had been so worn down by what had happened at the Peaks that it had been painful to see. How dare they make her husband feel such turmoil? How *dare* they harm her family?

She had half a mind to poison the lot of them—especially the bastards from the Shrouded Mountain Sect. She was downright hoping they would give her an excuse . . . but Meiling never had been the most diplomatic of people. The reflexive desire to just make whatever was bothering her *disappear* was something she was still working on . . . and why she refrained from offering up her true feelings on the matter and just supported Jin's decisions whenever he started mulling the problem over and trying to include her. She was flattered that Jin valued her opinion so highly . . . but she also knew her own suggestions wouldn't be much help.

Her husband was a kind soul; for all his boisterous personality, he disliked imposing on others. Yet if he had been thrust into a position of leadership . . . then he would do his best to fulfill the duties of that position. It was like with their farm. He had obviously never expected to be any of his disciples' father figure and Master, but instead of shirking that duty, he had risen to it, determined to do right by those who looked up to him.

That approach had given them a wonderful little family already. Even without the child in her belly, she had sons and daughters that she already loved like they were her own.

With luck, and with the Lord Magistrate's help, Jin would be able to mediate like he did on the farm; he would shoulder this burden and turn it into a boon.

But that was for later in the day. Though Jin wanted to see the Lord Magistrate, they were going to drop in on their friends first.

They approached one of the larger walled compounds. Though Verdant Hill had no true noble bloodlines, the Zhuge Clan was one of the oldest clans in the town, having lived here since they had records.

Jin knocked politely on the door, and they were greeted by a servant who showed them in before calling over Tingfeng.

Zhuge Tingfeng was a thin, bookish-looking man. Generally quiet and pensive, he was almost pretty, with long fingers and his topknot, a direct contrast to Meiling's own husband, who towered over him, a wall of muscle.

"Brother Jin! Meiling!" he exclaimed as he saw them. The man looked exhausted, with bags under his eyes, but he perked up happily on seeing them.

Jin took in the other man's appearance. "Your kid still keeping you up?" he asked, amused, as he clasped arms with Tingfeng.

The other man appeared vaguely haunted. "They all tell me that it's *good* he's so loud . . . but he wakes the entire *street*." Jin laughed, then clapped Tingfeng on the shoulder. The other man smiled.

"What we've got to look forward to in a couple of months," Meiling mused.

"Then I shall share a drink with you both when your trial is done," Tingfeng said, as he led them into his home, where Meihua was sitting at the table with her son, obviously still waking up too. Jin paused and averted his eyes from the breastfeeding mother.

"Meiling!" Meihua exclaimed, uncaring of Jin's presence. It was rather unfair, in Meiling's opinion, how her best friend could look so radiant even when so clearly tired. It seemed that every time she saw the other woman, Meihua became more beautiful and radiant. Her hair was still like silk, and her skin as pale as Xiulan's.

Meiling just marched up to her friend and hugged her—before checking over mother and son.

"Have you been eating well? Any soreness? How is he eating?" Meiling asked as the child burbled happily at her.

"Hello to you too," Meihua said sarcastically while fingers poked and prodded, Meihua bearing it with fond exasperation. "Well, no soreness, and I'm always surprised he doesn't drain me dry."

The two women looked at each other for a moment before beginning to giggle. Meihua smiled at Jin and rolled her eyes; he was deliberately focusing away, talking to Tingfeng.

"So, tell me what you've been up to," Meihua said.

↔

We were all sitting together around the table as Tingfeng finished getting ready for work. I was holding a baby in my arms as Meimei and Meihua chattered away, catching up.

The baby didn't have a name quite yet. It was custom to wait six months. But Tingfeng was really quite set on a name for his firstborn son.

Jinhai. Named after *me*.

I grimaced at the reminder of why this child was going to have this name. Zang Li, the imposter, or maybe the true member of the Shrouded Mountain Sect, trying to take Meihua and . . . well.

I shoved the thought aside, very carefully not clenching my fists.

If I had known back then what I know now . . . Well, I might not have been as nice. Maybe I had been kind of naïve. I had trusted in the authorities, and it had come back to bite me in the ass.

Could I have done something different? I didn't know. Maybe I could have killed him, and then the whole series of events at the Dueling Peaks never would have happened. He never would have hurt Tigu and Xiulan. The thought kept me up at night sometimes. But it was too late for regrets.

All I could do in the future was be better.

I rocked the baby, little Jinhai, back and forth in my arms as I thought. I was interrupted in my brooding by Tingfeng when he reentered the room in his official robes and kissed Meihua on the cheek.

"All right. I'm heading off, does anybody need anything?" he asked.

I looked up at him, considering.

"Yeah, could you pass on a message to the Lord Magistrate for me? I know he's busy, but . . . I'd like to arrange a meeting."

Tingfeng paused and looked closely at me for a moment. Then he clasped his hands in front of him. "Of course, Brother Jin. I'll be sure to inform the Lord Magistrate as soon as I am able."

I needed help. And from what I had seen so far, the Lord Magistrate was probably the most honest and upright politician I'd ever come across in either of my lives. And considering I now needed to be a bit of a politician to avoid future conflict and bloodshed? Well, that was worth the hassle.

I sighed and leaned back. Hopefully the Lord Magistrate had a bit less of an exciting time than I did.

I had heard that nothing had really happened in our absence, so that was good.

↔

A man sat at a desk, his eyes intent. Although he looked to be only in his mid forties with a salt-and-pepper beard, he was dignified. Unbowed by the passing of time in the slightest. Exquisite silk robes crafted by master artisans and a perfectly coiffed topknot left one with the impression of a master in his home. Seated before a richly carved desk upon which scrolls were neatly arranged, he had a sense of power about him. An aura of command that would not be out of place in the court of the Emperor himself. The man held one scroll open, reading it with utter serenity.

Then the grand lord sighed heavily and slammed his head onto his desk, dropping the scroll he had read for the fourth time.

"Why can't things be peaceful? This place was supposed to be *quiet*," the Lord Magistrate of Verdant Hill wondered to himself, muttering angrily under his breath as he rose back up.

The Lord Magistrate of Verdant Hill sighed again as he started to read the document once more. The Azure Jade Trading Company would be setting up their first permanent warehouse above the Pine Belt—the name for the rough geographic location that most of the province lived south of, where the snows were harsher and the winters colder.

They had bypassed at least twenty towns that were probably more prosperous and better positioned, heading straight for Verdant Hill.

There was only one reason why they would be so interested.

Rou Jin. The cultivator seemed to delight in making the Lord Magistrate's life harder. He had been informed of the man's arrival earlier in the day and now his thoughts were once more upon the human-shaped Wrecker Ball.

Ever since the man had arrived here it had been one thing after another. The Lord Magistrate was sure Rou Jin's presence had shaved a few years off his life. First had been the debacle with the Shrouded Mountain, then the misgraded rice, and then the revelation that he would be staying at the Lord Magistrate's wonderful, quiet little corner of the world for *years* after marrying Hong Meiling.

And now . . . now there were the roads as well as the missive that he was staring at.

The roads . . . well, they were the least of his worries, really. They had been needed, even if the cultivator had unknowingly stomped all over the Magistrate's carefully laid plans. He had it all laid out, too. In a few more years he would have gotten the quarries to the east running to supply the demand for stone and improve the whole region! The people would have been singing praises of his foresight and ability to give men a living for *centuries*. He would be the Lord Magistrate of the North! The Venerable Patriarch, undisputed! Better still, by the time the area grew enough that he couldn't enjoy the peace and quiet of walking around without guards? Well, he'd be dead! Remembered fondly as a guiding hand, yet getting to enjoy his life while he lived. The best of both worlds.

Except there was this letter, moving up the timelines he had so carefully planned for.

The seal of the Azure Jade Trading Company was upon it. And not just any random member's seal, but one inlaid with small chunks of Jade indicating the *personal* seal of the master of the company.

The Lord Magistrate had known that the gold-grade rice Rou Jin had brought to him would make waves. There was no way it wouldn't have. But that didn't stop him from being annoyed that the Azure Jade Trading Company was coming here in force. Of course, the company had not bothered with the niceties of permission or consideration, they had simply announced their plans.

It wasn't like he could refuse, either. One did not simply tell one of the greatest trade houses that they did not have the right to do as they pleased. He already had one shark in his lovely pond, and now he had another. It was understandable, even, that they would use Verdant Hill as a base. His work had ensured the stability of Verdant Hill; where else would they go?

It did not stop it from being annoying, or stressful in the extreme. Any man would be nervous when the Azure Jade Trading Company started to throw their weight around. Playing host to a company powerful enough to bury him without a second thought had him reaching for some calming tea.

His stomach churned most unpleasantly as he cursed Rou Jin within the sanctity of his mind yet again.

The bastard. It was somehow worse that the man was so strange. With another cultivator, he could at least predict how they would act. Cultivators weren't likely going to get involved in mortal affairs. He could distract them with toys or offer them obeisance. They were simple to appease, unconcerned as they were with mortals. Instead, he was constantly wondering which way the chaotic wind would blow. The cultivator had given the Magistrate gifts worthy of kings without hesitation, each one implicitly putting him further into the man's debt.

Seven Fragrance Jewel herbs, and Qi-filled food. All the while, the man had acted like it was nothing.

The Lord Magistrate groaned again in frustration.

"Oh! Here you are, dear." The Lord Magistrate looked up to see his wife, Lady Wu. Her dark eyes held some concern, and her red lips were pulled into a frown. She set down the tea tray she was holding and brushed a lock of black, waist-length hair, streaked with white, behind her ear. It had always hurt to look at that white strand, residual damage from a cultivator. That, and the shakes that had plagued her in times past. The fact that she could now carry the tray without her hands shaking was a credit to Hong Yaowu's medicine, and little Meiling. No matter how long she was around Rou Jin's corrupting influence, she remained kind and gentle. "I went to give you this, but you weren't where you normally are during the meeting. Why aren't you in the usual place? They're nearly done already."

The Lord Magistrate sighed and his wife raised an eyebrow. Yes, today was when the scribes all began discussing the end-of-harvest reports, after the festival. Normally he would be in an alcove nearby, only accessible from his office, and listening to his men wax poetic about his accomplishments.

It was usually a highlight of his year. It would have been even better, with his wife coming to serve him tea!

Today, however, the clerks had been largely centered on talking about the roads and of the impending arrival of the Azure Jade Trading Company.

Both were loathsome subjects, especially when they were praising *him* for the accomplishments. Saying how his bargaining skills must be beyond mortal ability, if he had been able to convince the company to come here, after somehow managing to swindle a cultivator into building a road for him.

It was vexing! *So* vexing! He had barely had a hand in them! To listen to men praise him for things that weren't his accomplishments was like a knife to his heart and had caused him to flee his banquet of praise.

"I . . . couldn't enjoy it," he finally said.

His lady wife frowned and placed the tea in front of him, walking around his desk to sit beside him. "Husband, have you spoken with him yet?" she asked. As always, she was perceptive, knowing his woes without need for words.

"No. I . . . I need to think of a better way to word my arguments. I can't just walk up and start complaining about him, *to him* no less!"

She looked vaguely amused.

"I do think you *could*," she returned evenly. "Look at you, you aren't sleeping well, and you can't even enjoy something you've been looking forward to all year!"

She was getting indignant now. He caught her arm and patted it.

"It's not . . . *too* much of an imposition, the trading company. I'm sure I can figure everything out and reach a satisfactory conclusion."

She raised an eyebrow at him and huffed. "You can't avoid this forever," she said simply.

"I'll . . . invite him to dinner. Yes, I'll invite him to dinner. He's in town. I'll invite him to dinner and bring up things . . . *delicately*. I'll navigate it with my usual skill and grace."

His wife seemed unimpressed. "Tonight. They're in town, so I'll visit little Mei and bring it up with them."

Tonight?!

"We should have some more time to prepare—"

There was a signal from outside, a servant letting him know that somebody was approaching his door.

Both paused and turned to the sound.

"Enter," the Lord Magistrate said, turning back around and organising his desk. His wife swiftly tugged some errant strands of hair back into his topknot and took a step back, sitting on the bench nearby. In an instant, she'd transformed into the vision of a perfect magistrate's wife.

Zhuge Tingfeng entered, looking a bit out of sorts.

"Lord Magistrate, sir. Forgive me for not bringing this to you earlier, but I could not find you. The meeting started early and Chief Scribe grabbed me—"

The Lord Magistrate waved the man's concerns away.

"It's fine, Tingfeng. I know that the seniors can impose on you. What was it that you needed?"

Tingfeng cleared his throat. "Rou Jin politely requests a meeting over an evening meal."

The Lord Magistrate smiled, his face frozen.

Again. The bastard had stolen a march on him again. Why? What did he do to deserve this?

"He seemed concerned, Lord Magistrate," Tingfeng continued.

The Lord Magistrate grabbed his stomach under the table, out of Tingfeng's view, doing everything in his power not to double over.

CHAPTER 8

COMPREHENSION

It was quite rare that the Lord Magistrate *really* had to entertain people. He and his wife had entertained in the style of the capital a few times, when they had first arrived in Verdant Hill. The awed and cowed looks of the people he had invited had been interesting . . . but the extravagance was simply unfeasible up here. Those of Verdant Hill were rustic in their style and manners. The Lord Magistrate was to the people an approachable man who listened. They enjoyed the more intimate setting of informality; it maintained his image that while not austere, he was not wasteful either.

That, and his lady had found the less extravagant meals more to her taste.

Today, however, the fine porcelain was set out, on his insistence. One of the few things the Wu Clan had deigned to give their crippled daughter as part of her dowry, the finest pieces from the capital. The Lord Magistrate thought they were better suited to be art, but he was born a mere commoner, what did he know? The meal itself would be somewhat rushed, but same-day meetings simply did not leave time for proper feasts. Still, the chef had given it his all, his eyes set to blazing when he had personally promised to have the perfect meal ready despite the short notice. There were no complaints; the staff had swung into motion immediately, each knowing that something must be happening, for the Lord Magistrate never made such demands.

Every inch of the room was immaculate. The room had been cleaned to even Luhai's standards, the head servant walking around with a white cloth in his crusade against dust. The formal reception room was usually the beating heart of most towns and cities, where words were daggers wielded in gladiatorial combat. Dynasties and deals rose out of this nearly unused room, and the Lord Magistrate had never missed that particular facet of city life.

However, a formal dinner request from a superior had been made. To greet the man outside this hall was a faux pas in the extreme. There were only two seats prepared, directly across from each other. Decorum demanded they be seated on cushions and brought their meals, but this was also a delicate matter. The servants, who would normally bring them most of the food, were dismissed for the evening. Instead, his wife would be serving them both. A show of respect, that even the wife of the Lord Magistrate would serve him.

The Lord Magistrate was seated on his cushion waiting. He was rather lucky that when he was nervous, only his back started to sweat. His face remained clear, and it allowed him to sit perfectly still in his formal dress—even if he had gone through three shirts that afternoon, and had changed one final time right before the appointed hour. His mind churned, every possible reason for calling this meeting playing out in his thoughts. Rou Jin had never asked for an official meeting before, and Zhuge Tingfeng had said that "Brother Jin seemed unusually serious."

Did the cultivator mean to replace him?

He thought it . . . unlikely. Though the cultivator mocked him in many ways, Rou Jin seemed to not actively *dislike* him. Like all cultivators he was a mercurial sort: on one hand tormenting him, and on the other gifting the Lord Magistrate a king's ransom in Spiritual Herbs and accepting his apology for the rice. Logic and his gut told him the odds were low, especially with his dear wife's continual contact with Meiling. He discarded that train of thought.

Things could be more complex than they seemed, however, and on consideration he was unable to fully abandon the line of reasoning. Rou Tigu had come in second in the tournament . . . . Was the man coming to inform him that he had created a Sect, and now Verdant Hill was part of his territory? That was more likely than anything else the Lord Magistrate had come up with. Sects had the right to collect taxes from towns under their control, and levy the population to battle.

It fit with the arrival of the Azure Jade Trading Company. They were well known to cater to the needs of powerful Sects—yet he hadn't had a transmission from Pale Moon Lake City or Grass Sea City informing him of the change in his status.

He took a slight breath. Hopefully it wasn't—

A quiet, familiar voice broke his train of thought. "Lord Magistrate, it is time." He glanced up at Luhai, who had spoken.

The Lord Magistrate took a breath to compose himself. "I will see him now," he declared. Luhai rose, then swept out of the room.

He did not have to wait long before Rou Jin arrived, trailing one of his more trusted guardsmen. The cultivator was different today, which only added to the Lord Magistrate's worries. The man had actually dressed up, rather than wearing his rugged, ripped sleeves and boots. His clothes were well made, though out of rough cotton, not silk. He was clean and groomed. His hair, normally unruly, was tamed.

The Lord Magistrate swallowed thickly. The difference was obvious and worrying.

The guardsman exited swiftly upon formally announcing Rou Jin, leaving the Lord Magistrate with only three people in the room. He didn't know whether to be grateful that his servants were loyal enough to obey him so easily, or offended that there were none listening in case things went south so they could rescue him.

Well, when all else failed, decorum triumphed. Everything was in place. He went to greet the cultivator, as protocol dictated, and as usual, the cultivator interrupted him.

"Lord Magistrate!" the man greeted with his usual bow. It always seemed just the slightest bit mocking. Perhaps it was because of the pause before it. Like he was deciding whether to bow, and he always had a strange, self-satisfied smile after.

"Rou Jin," he greeted him, bowing respectfully in his seated position. When he rose, the cultivator was still standing, his eyes flicking over the Magistrate before he took a seat upon the cushion.

"Thank you for agreeing to meet with me on such short notice," the man continued.

"It was no trouble," the Magistrate said in a blatant lie, dipping his head again. His mind raced through exactly what he was supposed to do at the moment. He didn't know what the cultivator wanted, and Rou Jin had arranged the meeting.

They lapsed into silence. The cultivator smiled brilliantly at Lady Wu as she set the food in front of them, thanking her. He always did get tense when the cultivator interacted with his wife . . . But the other man likely wouldn't do that sort of thing. He had already defended a peerless beauty from another man, the Shrouded Mountain Disciple. *That* particular vice seemed absent.

His wife raised an eyebrow at the breach in etiquette but remained silent, bowing deeply.

The Lord Magistrate waited for the cultivator to speak, ceding the conversation while continuing to wonder what he wanted, as they began their meal.

"This is good!" Rou Jin said. "My compliments to the chef!"

"They shall be pleased at your praise, Rou Jin. They have accomplished wonders this night," he agreed easily, despite barely being able to taste the food.

They lapsed into silence again. The Lord Magistrate's back was drenched through, and he felt his nerves spike each time Rou Jin glanced at him and turned back to the food to take another bite.

The silence lengthened until it became awkward. His wife prepared more tea, pouring another cup for them both.

Rou Jin took a sip from his cup and licked his lips. Finally, the cultivator spoke.

"Lovely weather we've been having lately."

The Lord Magistrate was taken aback by the casual statement. "Forgive me, Rou Jin. I have rarely gotten out this past week, due to my duties, but the sun does seem beautiful from the window."

"Ah, you're really busy? That suc—I mean, *is unfortunate*. I hope I haven't been adding to anything . . ." the man said with a laugh, joking. The Lord Magistrate felt a surge of irritation but opened his mouth to respond in the negative.

"It has not been too much—" the Lord Magistrate began.

"You have added to his work quite a bit, dear," his wife interrupted, with mild reproach.

Rou Jin's laugh died in his throat. The Lord Magistrate felt like she had just punched him in the stomach.

His wife had just chastised the cultivator. To his face. The man had been all too easygoing so far, but the Lord Magistrate couldn't imagine a world in which he let this go.

As always when the Lord Magistrate felt fear, he froze up completely. His body couldn't move to clap his hands over his wife's mouth and apologise for her slights.

Especially when she kept going.

"The Azure Jade Trading Company coming to town requires an enormous amount of work, as do the roads. Oh, and the cultivators arriving. Just last week one came through town. After decades here without any, all of a sudden our little town seems to be playing host to a great many. My, things are changing quite quickly, and you're certainly giving my poor husband more than he should have to deal with. Interfering with his quiet, *peaceful* life."

Her words were calm and measured, delivered with a sweet smile that looked anything but amused . . .

The cultivator stared at her, a frown on his face. A moment flashed in the Lord Magistrate's mind of the horrible shrieking *boom* that had filled the air in Pale Moon Lake City, and his wife screaming in pain as Qi burned her body and soul.

An endless parade of memories overwhelmed him. Lady Wu screaming and thrashing, foaming at the mouth as her body tried to shake itself apart. His beloved wife hobbling and wincing with every step, rather than gliding across the ground with her easy grace. It was the way she could no longer play any instruments, her body shaking too much. It was his lady not noticing the small cuts on her fingers, her sense of touch deadened to near unfeeling. That was why they had started using ropes and rougher play in the first place—just so that Lady Wu could feel *anything* at all though her reduced senses.

The cultivator slumped, looking like the Lord Magistrate's own son did whenever his wife scolded him.

He looked *contrite*.

"The Azure Jade Trading Company—ugh. I didn't even think it would be an issue," he muttered to himself, before he looked back up. The man grimaced. "I'm sorry for adding to your work."

The Lord Magistrate let out the breath he had very intentionally been holding. His frozen muscles unseized, and his shoulders slumped. This time . . . there was no violence. There was no surge of Qi. No flash of panic and terror as the people closer to the impact died screaming in agony.

Instead, Rou Jin looked wholly apologetic.

The Lord Magistrate swallowed thickly, his mind racing.

"It is a bit of work . . . but it will likely be a boon to Verdant Hill in the long run," he replied diplomatically.

The cultivator sighed. He scratched at his head, quickly returning his neatly arranged hair to its usual mess. The Lord Magistrate's eyes landed on his wife, who simply nodded like she had accomplished something other than nearly causing him to spit blood.

She refused to make eye contact with him, instead settling down beside him, slipping out her fan, and watching Rou Jin.

The man squirmed uncomfortably under Lady Wu's raised eyebrow, his every action that of a cowed boy rather than an ancient monster. He opened his mouth, closed it, and paused, clearly trying to find what to say.

"All right. Uh . . . I can explain all of this, but . . . how to start this . . . I guess at the beginning?" he mused to himself, before looking back up. "What have you heard about the Dueling Peaks Tournament this year?"

The Lord Magistrate paused, remembering the report that had been sent to him. "That the victor was Cai Xiulan, and that the one she defeated was Rou Tigu. It seemed likely that Rou Tigu was one and the same as the young lady of your household. I did not deem it . . . necessary to inquire further."

"Yeah . . . Tigu'er and Xiulan fought in the finals. Was there anything else you heard?"

Anything else?

"There was some manner of altercation? The report made bare mention of one."

The cultivator closed his eyes. "Well, there was . . . an incident. What I'm going to tell you has been covered up, but I think you deserve to know, and it leads into why I wanted to meet with you tonight."

The Lord Magistrate felt dread crawl up his spine at the man's words.

"The Shrouded Mountain Sect attacked Tigu'er, because their Young Master was the guy who was here last year in town, and who I thought was an imposter. It turned out to be true, just not the way I thought. Then there . . . uh, was nearly a war between the Azure Hills and the Shrouded Mountain Sect."

The words were all accurate, but they didn't make sense. This stuff just didn't happen. The whole of the Azure Hills was nearly plunged into war?! The Lord Magistrate glanced towards his wife—and some of her decorum broke. She was hiding her face underneath her fan, but her eyes were worried, and her mouth was open.

"Ah, don't worry, nothing's going to happen! I kind of . . . *forced everybody* to stop."

The words sounded so innocent. The Lord Magistrate felt faint.

"You stopped the Shrouded Mountain Sect."

"Yeah, we shouldn't have to worry about them at all again, I think. I made them promise to never set foot in the Azure Hills unless I let them, but I also kind of don't trust them . . . even after I told them I was part of the Cloudy Sword Sect."

The Lord Magistrate's stomach, surprisingly, was absolutely calm. He picked up the bottle of wine, meant to be drunk later in the night, and dearly, dearly wished that he could upend the entire thing right then—however, he would need to remember Rou Jin's words, so instead he allowed himself only a single sip.

He instantly regretted it, for the taste awoke a powerful thirst. So he handed the bottle off to his wife, to free him from temptation.

She obliged him, draining the rest.

"I guess . . . I should tell this better," Rou Jin said with a nervous grin.

→

The tale was hard to stomach. Kidnapping, running battles, and the man in front of him strong-arming every Sect in the Azure Hills as well as the Shrouded Mountain Sect.

Tao the Traveller wrote more believable stories.

He had known Rou Jin had to be fairly powerful to possess Seven Fragrance Jewel herbs. But to have been a member of the *Cloudy Sword Sect*?!

The Lord Magistrate felt faint but was compelled to ask:

"Forgive me . . . but why are you telling me this? And what could you possibly need from this lowly mortal, when you possess that power?"

"Lord Magistrate, how old do you think I am?" the cultivator asked. The question was an odd one. A cultivator who looked like Rou Jin could be centuries old.

"I do not know."

Rou Jin smiled, a crooked thing.

"I turned twenty this year. Before that, I was an orphan, living in the slums. I started cultivating when I was twelve."

The Lord Magistrate rocked back on hearing the words. *So young?!*

"And now, apparently *I'm* the guy everybody looks to for answers." There was a grimace of irritation. "I came here today to ask for your help," Rou Jin stated, lowering his head to say in a desperate whisper, "*because I have no idea what I'm doing.*"

Everything clicked into place. Everything about Rou Jin that had rubbed him the wrong way, that had made the man seem insincere at times, suddenly made sense.

Every bow that the Lord Magistrate had assumed to be made in jest had been in complete sincerity. Every gift had not been something to put the Lord Magistrate in his debt but a man giving his technical lord tribute. Every pause before he'd acted, not because he was deciding whether to show respect but because he was pausing to remember proper etiquette.

Everything had a reason. The discussion on taxes last year—it was not the man trying to get out of paying them but trying to work out how to properly contribute. The work on the roads and his proclaiming his Spirit Beasts at the Lord Magistrate's service. From the beginning, Rou Jin had *intended* to work with him. From the beginning, each offence caused had been unintentional.

Have . . . have I truly been so blind? So hung up on my own insecurities that these obvious tells have gone right by me?

Even now, the young man who could end his entire town with a single thrust of his fist sat awaiting *his* judgement. As if he were a child before an elder.

"Why me?" the Lord Magistrate asked.

"From everything everybody has said, you're a good man. What I've seen just confirms it. I need help, and I think you're one of the few people I can really ask. And kind of . . . the only official I really *respect*," he said, his voice soft and his head still lowered.

Rou Jin had just said he respected him.

The Lord Magistrate licked his lips, wetting them.

"What would you wish to learn from me?"

"I don't know most things about decorum, or about talking to people properly. I know I can't solve every problem with violence . . . and even if I could, I don't want to. I need to be able to solve things with words . . . or at least know when people are trying to jerk me around. I need somebody to teach me how to find solutions to problems that don't end in destruction."

The ancient scholars said that civilization was what separates men from beasts. That law and order must be valued above strength. It was an old adage. A wonderful idea that they were required to learn . . . and then were told in no uncertain terms by their teachers that such things had to be disregarded in the name of practicality. When cultivators roamed, the strong ruled.

As the Lord Magistrate stared at the cultivator before him, a question bubbled to the surface of his mind: What if the strongest were committed to that old ideal?

The Lord Magistrate dismissed the nonsense, banishing it from his mind. He didn't want to get involved in *any* cultivator business. Where cultivators lay was madness and misery.

"Please. I need your guidance, Lord Magistrate. In rhetoric, politics . . . basically everything. I don't want this town to lose anything. I value the peace I've found in the Azure Hills."

There was a young man before him seeking guidance. Not yet fully ready for the trials of life, despite all his bravado and strength. The Lord Magistrate was not an altruistic man, yet he had often indulged in giving pointers to others. There were few things as pure as a junior's eyes shining with admiration as he gifted them his wisdom. As they thanked him for enlightening them to the truth of the world.

Now, he had the strongest cultivator in the land calling *him* teacher with complete sincerity.

That he was saying he valued the peace of the land . . . well, that was just a bonus.

In his youth, the Lord Magistrate had been an ambitious man. A man who sought to rise to the top and rule the entire Azure Hills, before he learned the true terror of cultivators and the benefits of a quieter, slower life.

This was an opportunity that only came once every thousands of years.

It was a gamble. Yet could he really say no?

For the sake of his quiet life. For the sake of *his* town. The Lord Patriarch of Verdant Hill could only say one thing.

“You may raise your head. We shall work together,” the Lord Magistrate decreed, his voice more powerful than he’d thought he would be able to make it.

Rou Jin’s face lit up.

“Thank you. I won’t let you down, teacher,” the cultivator said, performing the proper kowtow before him, accepting him as his master in the arts of reason and politics.

They drank a cup of wine together, and then Rou Jin left, saying he would be back on the morrow to work out a schedule with him.

And so the Lord Magistrate simply sat there. His legs had long since gone numb, and he didn’t feel like he could stand. He was absolutely exhausted.

“I did tell you all you needed to do was scold him,” his wife said blandly, as she sipped wine.

“I don’t need your cheek right now, dear wife.”

“Oh? Going to do something about it?” she asked, her eyes challenging.

“When I can stand again,” he returned.

His wife snorted, her eyes looking at the door Rou Jin had exited out of, before glancing back to the Lord Magistrate.

“Poor boy. It always seems that responsibility finds those who don’t wish for it . . . yet are too stubborn to put it down once they have it.”

The Lord Magistrate wanted to deny her insinuation. He was nothing like Rou Jin.

Still . . . he did feel a bit lighter. Like things wouldn’t be too bad. He was just dealing with a lost young man. He could deal with that. And if he could harness this strength . . . . *Well.* Then his life would continue to be peaceful.

Perhaps the future held a bit less stomach pain as well?

He smiled to himself as he looked up at the ceiling. He felt as if a great weight had been lifted from his shoulders.

Now all he had to do was teach the man who was apparently the new power of the Azure Hills how to deal with every other cultivator Sect.

He paused.

Now I have to teach the man who is the new power of the Azure Hills how to deal with every other cultivator Sect!

His stomach churned as the weight of his newfound goal settled on his shoulders.

His face was still blank with a smile.

Inside his mind, he screamed in terror.

CHAPTER 9

TRADING POINTERS

A blade whistled through the air in a quiet section of the forest. It cut the air, descending towards the earth almost gracefully, before curving back up. A slight bit of sweat followed it from my fist.

I was in a quiet section of the forest near Hong Yaowu, practicing with my sword. Everybody else was asleep for the night.

My muscles strained. The sword felt wrong in my hands. It was too small. The grip was nothing like a shovel, or even an axe. I glanced again at the scroll, wondering what I was getting wrong, but as I looked at it, I somehow *knew* my movements were right. The flow should have been perfect.

And yet it still felt off.

The movements were right, but there was something deep in my body rejecting it.

An old fear bubbled inside—that I wasn't good enough, I was weak. Worse still, I couldn't help but feel shame because I was failing Gramps.

Rou's memories always started coming up more when I thought about the old man and the bitter feelings that came with it.

I sighed and put the sword down, swapping to the other form Gramps had taught me, the unarmed one I did every morning. This at least didn't feel too bad . . . until I started trying to shadowbox an imaginary opponent. The second I thought of it as more than a way to defend myself and went on the offensive, my limbs started to creak.

It was a disconcerting feeling, so I pushed it aside and concentrated on both the movements . . . and what I had learned earlier today.

The Lord Magistrate's first lesson had been . . . interesting, I guess. Politics was not a field I was versed in—or ever had interest in at all. Where I had come from, the view of the government was one of thinly veiled disdain. Rou hadn't really thought of it at all either. Gramps certainly hadn't taught him anything on it, and cultivation had consumed his world after he'd been picked up. At least I wasn't completely unarmed—the courtly characters that Rou had been taught were invaluable—but I still didn't know exactly what to expect.

So it was with trepidation that I had walked into the lesson that morning, the day after I'd asked him for them. We'd met in an empty, private room that was quite well appointed. We'd had drinks, and proper seats, and I had brought a rough list of things to go over. It had really just felt like he had invited me into his house—until he'd risen, his face all business. Seeing him standing in front of me with his hands behind his back as he gave a lecture had seemed almost . . . modern.

But I suppose lectures hadn't really changed much since the dawn of schools, except with the addition of PowerPoint.

You can kind of ape PowerPoint with a recording crystal . . .

Nope, keeping *that* idea to myself for now. I'd already introduced the wedding slideshow, and that had been a pretty big hit. Maybe I could unleash it on the Azure Jade Trading Company at some point, so I could conquer the world with colourful graphs and commercial blitzes.

Though the Lord Magistrate didn't need all of that to be engaging. His stern looks and voice had me enraptured. He had that calm charisma everybody talked about, one that I finally got to see firsthand.

"There is no *one* true path for this," the Lord Magistrate had declared. "Essentially, one must pick a . . . face, for lack of a better term. To act out your chosen role. How did you act when you first met the other members of the Sects? If you clearly remember that, then continue, for the most part, to act that way. If you disregarded decorum at the start, then you can continue to do so. Acting in a consistent manner is what is key. *Some* disregard of decorum can in this case be in your best interest—for it shows either that you have no idea what you're doing, or that you're so powerful that such petty things are beneath you. I believe, from what you have told me, that the latter is the assumption. So we must feed this assumption."

His starting speech wasn't quite what I had expected, but it all made sense. Leverage what you have. Use all your strengths. He'd said it with such complete and calm authority that I couldn't help but trust him.

He had looked a bit tired, though, but I suppose I had given him quite a bit of stress by my own actions.

I'd have to get him something nice.

After the first lecture he had moved on to a strange sort of quiz, where he'd asked me a bunch of questions and I had to essentially role-play answers.

Though it had revealed what would be considered a flaw in this world:

I apologised too much.

For the first time in my life, I was told that being as polite as I was, was a detriment. Part of me had *recoiled* when I was told I couldn't reflexively say *Sorry*.

I'd have to fight every fiber of my being to do it, but it was something I'd need to do when I talked to people.

After that, I'd gotten a bunch of scrolls to learn proper decorum, so I could know when somebody was trying to insult me subtly and to know which insults I could "safely" ignore.

All in all it was remarkably structured for something that looked like he had put it together in a single night. At least this time he had seemed a bit more happy when I gave him some of the Spirital Herbs. His wife had told me he sometimes had stomach problems and that the herbs helped with that.

At the end of the day all that had been left was a run back to Hong Yaowu and a wife who commiserated with the pile of scrolls I had to read.

Meimei had her own lessons with Lady Wu, who was apparently a slave driver, making my wife sit through an entire mock formal event.

She had certainly been more proactive than me at getting prepared, but I wasn't going to be slacking any longer.

And it was a bit of a balm on my mind that, well, I wasn't alone. Meimei had taken up her lessons with Lady Wu of her own volition, to help *me*. So now it was my turn to do the same.

If there was one person in the entire world I could count on, it was Meimei. But I did have more than her, didn't I? I had an entire family of people who would be happy to help.

I brought myself out of my thoughts and grimaced—I was soaked with sweat from the forms I had been practicing.

With a sigh, I thought, *I'm not getting anywhere.*

I got out of my stance and sat down beside the blade and the scroll. Then I took a moment to stare at the sky, a beautiful band of stars, and the moon that shone as a silver crescent, high above.

Well, I had already asked one person for help, and Lanlan knew more about this cultivation stuff anyway. Or maybe Big D would be able to see what was wrong—

"Great Master?" A voice interrupted me and I glanced back, staring at Big D. The rooster had been with Rizzo all day, both of them helping Pops out by collecting mushrooms. Speak of the devil . . . or I guess it's "speak of Cao Cao" here.

Except instead of a warlord of the Three Kingdoms, he was some super powerful cultivator who had a Qi projection of himself laughing at you, appearing if you spoke his name in anger.

I raised a hand and waved at the approaching bird. "Hey, how are you doing tonight, buddy?" I asked, lowering my shoulder so he could hop on.

The rooster, however, remained on the ground, his eyes serious.

↔

Bi De had a wonderful day in Hong Yaowu. He had spent it largely with Sister Ri Zu and Yin, exploring the forests and examining the village while his Lord was off in Verdant Hill, consulting with his servant.

The First Disciple himself still had unfinished business there, with the strange old woman who had given him his map, months ago, but he would find out what exactly was in the crystal before he went to confront her.

He had been preoccupied with how to approach his Great Master. His Lord hadn't exactly been secretive about his training, and his struggle was obvious.

Yet he'd persisted.

Bi De had convened a quiet gathering before they had gone to Hong Yaowu to discuss the issue with Sisters Xiulan and Tigu. Xiulan had posited that perhaps it was his cultivation that prevented him from taking up the sword, and that this was merely a bottleneck.

Tigu thought it foolish to bother him with their worries. She had simply declared that she would get so strong she would never need to be saved again, and the Great Master could remain at Fa Ram. He would hear not a word of enemies, for there would be none left alive.

For his part, Bi De was unsure. All he knew was that his Master needed aid. Something he had little idea how to give.

All were in agreement: they would aid the Great Master, little though their power was.

Their plans, however, had been interrupted by the sweet ambrosia that was the mead, and then by preparations for the festival, as the Great Master cut back on his evening bladework.

Tonight, though, his Master had once more gone to practise alone. Sister Tigu and Sister Xiulan had both agreed that he should be the one to approach the Master. He was First Disciple and thus the closest to him.

Besides, Bi De had been with him when he had received this technique.

Yet now, he felt trepidation as he gazed at his Great Master.

His Lord's face was slick with sweat, and his arm, the one with which he had struck the interloper Zang Li, had little lines of gold trailing up it.

Like the wound was still there, just beneath the surface.

"Hey, how are you doing today, buddy?" his Master asked, as he made the gesture to allow Bi De to sit upon his shoulder.

His smile was the same as always as he beheld his disciple, even through the strain.

Bi De honoured his Master's teachings. In this, he thought perhaps he had found a way through the puzzle of how to help him. One of his greatest yet simplest lessons.

He asked.

"Your disciple is well, Great Master," he said, bowing. "Yet it is not for my well-being that I have come to you . . . there is something that troubles you."

His Lord grimaced at the question, and Bi De was afraid he had overstepped himself.

But his Master merely sighed, then glanced down at the scroll of war.

"Yeah. Yeah, this is troubling me." His smile was crooked as he gazed off and shrugged. "This stuff . . . it's a bit much, sometimes, ya know?" he asked, gesturing at the sword.

"Is there anything I can do to help?" Bi De pressed, forging ahead. "We have all noticed your discomfort. Your disciples are concerned, Great Master."

"It's that obvious?" his Master asked, his frown stretching across his face. "I'm sorry if I've made you worry."

Bi De shook his head. "Do not apologise, Great Master. We all know why you pursue this path . . . yet it does not take away from the fact that we are concerned to see your pain in practicing the arts of war."

His Great Master went quiet at Bi De's words. He glanced at the scroll. He looked towards the direction of Verdant Hill, as his eyes went far away for a moment. "I ran away from this life," he whispered, frustration in his voice. "I never wanted *any* of this. The politicking, the Sects, the fights . . . I hate it. I just wanted to be a farmer."

"And yet you do it anyway, don't you?"

"Yeah. I started it, so I'll see it through to the end," he replied with a snort, looking away from Bi De. "Sorry if I'm not that great a Master."

Bi De glared at his Master for the tone in his voice.

"No. You *are* our Great Master. You shoulder this burden for us, even though you hate it. But, Great Master . . . it does not have to be this way. Let your humble disciples be your blades, if such things are required."

The words were delivered calmly, as the rooster bowed his head. His Great Master seemed struck, though after a moment he shook his head.

"I can't ask people to shoulder a burden I'm unwilling to take up," his Great Master replied.

"You do not need to ask us, Master. We all *choose* this. For the things you have created. Your dream that you told us of . . . I, your Disciple, must say . . . it is not yours alone anymore. When you first asked me my goals after our battle with Sun Ken . . . I said it was to defend Fa Ram. *I stick to that oath.*"

Nearly a year ago in the snow, after Sun Ken's demise, his Great Master had confided in them his goal. His reasons for coming to the Azure Hills. His Master's goal of creating a heaven upon the earth.

Bi De had seen the world. And yet his goal had not changed, even with his experiences. From what had happened to Miantiao, to the adventure in the crystal caves with the monkeys, to the brawl at the Dueling Peaks. He would defend Fa Ram. That was his proudest goal and greatest ambition.

His Great Master stared at Bi De.

"To defend your home, huh?" he asked. He took a breath. "But . . . even if this training isn't working out, I need *something*. I'm not going to be a liability. Bi De. Will you help me? Will you . . . *trade pointers* with me?"

The First Disciple swept into a bow, pride surging in his breast at his Lord's trust. "It would be this Bi De's greatest honour."

He was going to get to *directly* spar with his Lord.

He glanced up, to see his Master flinch at the question. Bi De wondered if he had overstepped himself. His Master's hand rose up, unbidden, as he clutched at his heart. He sucked in a breath and closed his eyes.

Then he nodded. His Master rose to his feet and bowed.

"Please treat me kindly, Master Bi De," he intoned.

Bi De felt his heart leap up into his throat, and his feathers puffed out—his Lord had referred to Bi De as his Master.

"Pl-please, Great Master. You do not need to embarrass your disciple so!" he squawked.

His Lord laughed at Bi De's cracking voice, as both rose from their bows.

"All right. Let's do this!" his Master demanded.

Bi De lunged forwards. His Master, who had raised him so high, asking him for pointers.

The crescent moon shone above, in its most perfect form.

CHAPTER 10

INTENT

My fist whistled through the air, body creaking as I moved. It felt like a boulder grinding against another rock and refusing to move properly. Big D dodged the strike and lashed out, tapping the side of my body.

I sighed, frustrated. Sure, I could have gone faster, but that was defeating the point.

I knew I could move faster—I knew I could just swing and probably send Big D to the next province, but that wasn't the point of this spar. Strength meant nothing here. The point was to *learn*.

You can't learn if you just unga-bunga everything in your path. I mean, it was *kind* of a valid strategy . . . but if I ran up against somebody who I couldn't just yeet out of the province, I was pretty boned.

I sighed as I corrected my stance . . . or at least *tried* to. Big D was considering.

"The blows themselves have nothing wrong with them, Master," the rooster said. "Yet . . . nothing is changing."

Sparring kind of sucked. We had been at this for at least an hour already. An hour, and I still felt . . . *off.* I tried to focus. I tried to really, *really* focus on what I was doing wrong.

I hesitated too much. I thought too much about my next move. Without the panic and immediate need to act of real combat . . . Well, I couldn't get myself to just commit. I spent too much time thinking.

It was compounded by the fact that I needed to keep everything under tight control. I still remembered what happened when I'd let loose at the Dueling Peaks. A wrong jump had *shattered* a house—I was lucky nobody had been inside.

I felt like I was wasting time. We were no closer to figuring anything else out now than we were when we started.

I stopped shuffling my feet and trying to get into a position that felt good, and instead dropped my stance.

"Let's take a break," I suggested, wandering over to the log with my sword and the scroll, and just sat down.

I sighed, frustrated with myself as I took a swig from my waterskin. *Just what am I doing wrong?*

I sat there brooding for a moment—then jerked my head backwards as a clod of dirt and grass shot through the air where I had been but a moment before.

I turned to the rooster, who looked entirely too innocent.

"What the hell, Big D?" I asked.

The rooster cocked his head to the side. "I am merely adapting thy training methods, Great Master," the rooster intoned. "Sisters Tigu and Xiulan swear that this training is most efficacious."

I huffed. *Throwing mud at them had actually been useful? I mean, I could kind of see it . . .*

Another clod of dirt went for my head, and I dodged it. Some of the tension faded as the rooster dug into the earth with his talons, scooping up ball of dirt number three.

I snorted, tired of the whole sparring thing.

"All right, then. Come on!" I demanded.

The rooster was only too happy to oblige me. Earth rained down upon me as I danced around the missiles. He couldn't throw curve balls like I could, but he could chuck a clod of dirt and then flap his wings to send it in a shotgun spray straight at me.

The first time he did that it got me good, I do admit. But I was wise to the next strike.

The spread of dirt whistled by my head.

It felt good to finally have some stress relief after hours of worthless training. After this, we would probably have a dunk in the river and head off to bed.

I might not have had any progress . . . but I was still grateful to Big D for taking the time to try.

Then the cheeky chicken decided that dirt wasn't enough and sent another kick at me. I dodged it, but instead of backing off, he kicked again and I blocked.

Well, if *that* was how he wanted to play it . . .

I swung back on the next strike, and the rooster dodged it. I laughed and poked at him, like I always did when I was play-fighting with people. Back and forth, like a dance, we went. Smacking and kicking at each other like we had been when we were sparring—

I paused. I didn't feel any of the odd, grinding sensation. My moves were crisper.

Big D performed the exact same kick combo he had before, the one that ended with a tap to my side, and I waved through it with ease.

The opening that had been there was gone; I blocked the strike, and my own fist shot forwards, tapping against Big D.

I had landed a real hit on somebody sparring.

Is . . . Is it that simple?

Had I really just been that dumb? Had I forgotten what kind of world I was in?

I had started training not because I wanted to, but because I felt like I *had* to. I hated it. I loathed every moment I was training for battle.

I *resented* the sword. I resented everything going on the offence represented to me. I had not wanted to do it. And, if I was honest with myself . . . I didn't want to be good at it.

To be good at this . . . meant that I was almost failing in my promise: to not go off the deep end. To not become some kind of warlord.

And so it had been flawed. The moves were right; the intent behind them was what was wrong.

How could I hope to get anywhere when I didn't really *want* to succeed?

There was another flurry of blows as we exchanged strikes. Each attack started to run into the last as I started to get into the flow. A continuous motion.

But here, here in this moment . . . things felt just the slightest bit better.

I didn't need to be so grim and steely-eyed. That wasn't me. I had been trying to do something I didn't want to and be something I wasn't.

Three more strikes. It was . . . well, it was awkward as hell fighting a rooster. He moved so gracefully and so quickly it still seemed like I was watching a TV show or something. What we were doing could barely be called fighting, compared to what I remembered it as in the Before. That had been undignified flailing that barely deserved to be called strikes. Or the short brutal scuffles where one guy tackled another and then pounded the tar out of him while he was on the ground.

I let out a breath as I saw an opening, then tapped the rooster in the side, the second strike I had landed. His eyes widened briefly as he leapt away, and we paused, facing each other.

"Thank you for showing me that opening, Master," the rooster said, sounding a bit surprised. "Shall we continue?"

A silver glow formed on Big D's legs. Crescent blades formed on his spurs.

I pulled my own Qi.

I got into a stance. I could feel the power thrumming through my body; my breath caught. *This is enough power to—*

"I know that you shall not harm me, Great Master," the rooster stated simply.

I took a deep breath and let the tension run out of my body.

Just think of it like a shounen fight scene. The power of friendship and nobody gets hurt. Like when Tigu and Xiulan fight.

I launched myself towards Big D. The silver blades met my fist.

I might not have found a solution quite yet . . . but it was a start.

I dueled, *properly dueled*, for the first time since I'd come here. And with Big D . . . with a friend to guide me by my side . . . I couldn't say I hated it.

→

It was dawn when we finally stopped. I was sweating and breathing heavily, while Big D looked close to collapsing.

I looked down at my hands.

"Thank you," I said, and the rooster bowed.

"It is my pleasure to aid you, Master."

Even now, he called me Master. Even now after all they had done. I could still see the respect in his eyes as he stared at me.

Even though I felt I still didn't deserve it, no matter what Xiulan had said.

I felt the urge to ask him. Ask him *why* he thought so highly of me—but in the end, that would just be me stroking my own ego.

The only thing I could do was to try to keep being worthy of that respect.

I patted my shoulder. This time, the rooster hopped up happily, claiming his rightful place. He let out a terrific crow and I laughed as he did his job of greeting the sun.

↔

Bi De was absolutely exhausted, barely hanging on to his Great Master's shoulder as his Lord bore him to the village.

His feathers were ruffled and his spurs ached. His Great Master was sweaty and his clothes were drenched through. But that was the end of it.

He looked more at peace now. Or at least less like the weight of the world was upon his shoulders.

He had finally, truly been of aid to his Master. His Lord had given him heartfelt thanks.

Bi De supposed some would have seen his Master's moment of weakness and been disappointed. Yet his Master had ever been frank with them about his capabilities. He had told them he considered himself weak. He had told them all he disliked fighting.

Even with that, his Master gave them his all without reservation. It was humbling, to see how far he would go for their sake. Driving himself to distraction and willingly taking up that which he hated the most.

Bi De still wished that he could dissuade his Master entirely from fighting. That Bi De and his Master's disciples would take care of any who dared to raise their hands against Fa Ram.

Yet he could not. All he could do was offer his own aid . . . and then win any battle before it truly became a war.

They passed the tree line and came to the outskirts of the village.

There stood the Disciples and the Great Healing Sage Meiling, waiting for them. The Qi Bi De had given off as he sparred with his Lord was no small thing, and they had all surely felt it. Yet none were worried or anxious as they approached the group.

The Healing Sage sniffed at the Great Master, clearly using her peerless ability to sense Qi to uncover any hidden ailment. She just nodded, and declared:

"Better."

And thus, they returned home, with their newest guest.

Bi De never got tired of the look on people's faces when they first experienced Fa Ram. Liu Xianghua was no different. Her sharp eyes softened. Her breath became shallow, and her tense, coiled body relaxed.

For a brief moment, Liu Xianghua looked vulnerable.

And then she straightened, her eyes firmed up.

"Hmm. This place's air . . . I don't hate it!" she shouted. "In fact, it's not half bad! Master Jin, allow this Liu Xianghua to praise what you have built!"

The Great Master laughed at her words. "I try my best, you know?" he said, his own back straight. "Come on in, and make yourself at home."

Later after settling in, the Great Master called both Sisters Xiulan and Tigu to him and bowed his head, requesting their aid.

Tigu was ecstatic, having the chance to spar with her Master. Cai Xiulan accepted without reservation.

To give and receive in equal measure. One of the first of his Great Master's teachings.

CHAPTER 11

THE FALL COLOURS

Breathe in, breathe out.

Reach deep into the earth, like the roots of a plant, mingling with the golden energy there.

Feel the energy cycle.

Cai Xiulan knew peace.

A contentment born of success and repayment.

The sun's rays felt warm on her face while a cool breeze flowed over her. For the moment, she simply . . . existed. Luxuriating in a feeling that had been only fleeting once. The energy filled her body. It washed through her meridians and her dantian, rising in a crescendo. It was like she was going to ascend to the next stage of her cultivation as it swirled and buoyed her up . . . before it started to ebb, not quite allowing her to break through to the Fifth Stage of the Initiate's Realm.

A year ago, she would have grabbed at the energy. Forced it back, pulled it into her body, and consumed it in a desperate attempt to breach the divide. Instead, Xiulan simply let the energy go. She released the breath she was holding and it faded away.

Patience. Patience was key.

As the energy receded, so too did minute impurities within her foundation. The Qi of the land taking, purifying, and removing them, leaving her Qi pure and her foundation more solid.

Idly, she expected a sneering scoff from a little girl, her face and body coated in cracked gold. The little Earth Spirit had not danced with her a single time since the Dueling Peaks. She still felt the connection to her through the golden crack that was in the center of her chest, part of the Earth Spirit's own body sealing a wound shut.

She could feel a sense of . . . drowsiness. The spirit had evidently expended much energy in aiding her. She would not begrudge the little one her rest.

The scar was an ever-present reminder.

Xiulan had been burned, burned by Zang Li's Qi from the First Stage of the Profound Realm all the way back to the Third Stage of the Initiate's Realm. For a cultivator of the Azure Hills, it was a crippling loss of power, a tragedy for the Young Mistress to be so maimed.

Yet she felt no loss at all. The thought of Tigu, Ri Zu, Gou Ren, and Yun Ren hurt and broken . . . was unacceptable.

Even if her cultivation had been destroyed completely, she would have been content with the outcome of the final battle.

Yet it had not been. And even now, she regrew. The ashes in her soul were like fuel, the stalks of grass growing anew.

It was humbling and gratifying at the same time—

"Cai Xiulan, you're supposed to be a blade of grass, not a *weed*."

Slowly, Xiulan opened her eyes to a river and the grass of a farm, both splashed through with reds, oranges, and golds from falling leaves. She was sitting on the veranda of the house, facing the river. Slightly behind and to the left was the swinging chair Jin and Meiling spent many an hour on.

She glanced up to Xianghua, the source of the voice that sounded both impressed and annoyed, raising a single eyebrow.

It had been a week since her return to Fa Ram from the Mid-Autumn Festival. It was a little annoying how fast Xianghua seemed to just . . . *fit in*. Her boisterous laughter was just right at home at the table as she feasted and just went with the flow. The irrepressible woman already had a routine that she had crafted for herself, eagerly joining their group in the morning, taking tea at noon with Meiling and Xiulan, and then sparring in the afternoon.

"Oh? Maybe it's just my natural talent shining through, Damp Pond. Try not to get too jealous. Stagnant water is unappealing."

The woman just laughed as she slid down to sit beside Xiulan. Her hands were still damp, looking like they had been recently washed. She appeared in a good mood.

"It's going well, then?" Xiulan asked.

Xianghua nodded happily. "The deer is completely healed and walks perfectly," the young woman said, then excitedly reported to Xiulan the details that she had missed while meditating.

A trial run for restoring Bowu's leg had been planned. Ri Zu, Meiling, and—surprisingly—Wa Shi had worked on it. A trapped deer was rendered unconscious with the medicine of Hong Yaowu. The leg was then paralysed with more paralytics and acupuncture, the nerves mostly shut down. Meiling had cut open the leg while Ri Zu monitored the paralytic poison, and Wa Shi aided with keeping the incisions clear of blood. With Meiling's skilled hands the procedure took all of ten minutes to perform. It wasn't a perfect one-to-one comparison . . . but the deer had been walking within the hour after being healed by the Spiritual Herbs.

They had kept the deer for a time, to see if any infection would set in or if the healing was imperfect. But the deer seemingly hadn't noticed, content to be fed and watered. In the end it was like nothing had happened to it at all. Xianghua had noticed Meiling muttering something about "bullshit cultivators."

"Yes, it's going to be soon. Very soon. Lady Meiling wishes to do one more mock run just in case . . . but it will *work*."

Xianghua's eyes were full of bright hope, and a small smile was fixed on her face as she stared across the courtyard, where there was a mahjong game in progress. Tigu, Bowu, Ri Zu, and Pi Pa were all playing, while Gou Ren and Yun Ren watched idly on as they performed their own chores. Gou Ren was maintaining his bow while Yun Ren fletched arrows. The feathers were a very familiar red, Bi De having donated a few out of curiosity to see if the arrows flew better. Xiulan was curious about the outcome of the test herself, though she had never used a bow—her floating swords took care of any ranged attack.

Her musings on the arrows were interrupted by Tigu's voice at the mahjong table.

"The House of Master!" she called proudly as the orange-haired girl slapped down half her tiles, smug as could be.

The entire table stared at her play. Or rather, the completely random hand Tigu had arranged into something resembling a house, instead of an actual scoring hand.

"We spent *two hours* teaching you how to play yesterday—*you're doing this on purpose!*" Bowu shouted, pointing an accusing finger at Tigu.

Tigu smiled brilliantly at him, the picture of innocence.

A rat bounced off the back of Tigu's skull, a terrific flying kick sending her staggering. Bowu reached up, putting the orange-haired girl's head into a lock. He jammed his knuckles into her head and started twisting. Pi Pa looked as if she were above such things, a perfect aloof lady . . . and then there was movement and Tigu yelped as a trotter delicately stomped on her foot—which had drifted too close to the pig.

Tigu could have broken out in an instant. But she didn't, instead allowing the indignity of Ri Zi jumping up and down on her nose and squeaking angrily at her.

Xianghua let out a little chuckle as she looked on, then turned to Xiulan.

"Sometimes the luck of heaven does go to the virtuous," Xianghua stated solemnly. Xiulan flushed at the earnest compliment.

They watched the scrambling mahjong players for a while, until Meiling came out carrying a stack of blankets.

The blankets were tossed on top of the squabbling pile, turning it into a writhing mass, and Meiling's voice rose in a scolding.

Xianghua shook her head as Meiling forced all four of them to kneel before her, her arms crossed and her foot tapping. She waited for them to explain who started it—so they could all get to the Fall Colours viewing faster.

"A Fall Colours viewing today, hmm?" Xianghua asked—and Meiling just sighed about who had started the squabble. "Interesting."

Xiulan was looking forward to it. She had gone to flower viewings before, on the days when the lotus blooms broke the surface of the ponds in the Verdant Blade Sect, but never when the leaves fell.

Perhaps some felt as if it would be too close to celebrating death? Or more likely it was because the trees to the south did not get quite so vibrant in colour whenever they turned for the winter.

"Xianghua, could you take some of these blankets, please?" Meiling asked kindly as she sent off the younger ones with fond exasperation, Yun and Gou following after them.

"Of course, Lady Meiling! I shall convey each and every blanket to its destination in a heartbeat!" the woman declared.

She received a quiet chuckle in response from Meiling.

"Xiulan, could you go check on Jin and make sure everything is almost done?" Meiling asked her next, and Xiulan raised an eyebrow in confusion. "He said he was making some kind of *cheese*," Meiling clarified petulantly. Xiulan chuckled.

"Of course, Senior Sister. Your champion shall brave the dreaded cheese's stench," she replied mockingly, then clambered up from her meditation spot.

Meiling huffed and bumped her with her hip as Xiulan walked past. Xiulan bumped back.

→

Xiulan poked her head into the kitchen, where Jin was humming to himself while working. He was spreading a thick, creamy-looking sauce over the top of oddly shaped, golden-brown rolls.

Bi De was nearby flapping his wings, clearing off some of the leftover flour. While Xiulan and Meiling had helped with the meal, the majority of the work today had been Jin. He had wanted some specific things for what he called a "special treat."

He had that focused look on his face, along with the smile Xiulan remembered from when she'd first met him. He looked carefree again, instead of having his brow furrowed with concern.

It suited him much better.

The small smile as he bowed to Xiulan and Tigu. As he asked for their help.

The opportunity to give back . . . No, not to give back, but to help *as he had helped her.*

It had taken some time, but he finally looked to have recovered the calm he had been missing.

"Jin? Is everything almost ready?" she asked.

Jin turned to her, and his grin brightened.

"Yup! It's good to go! Just finished putting the icing on."

Xiulan stared curiously at the strange things. If Jin had made them then they were undoubtedly good—and she was curious about the sauce.

He noticed her intent look and glanced around, shiftily, before leaning towards her.

"Don't tell Wa Shi," he said with a wink, handing her the spoon, which was normally the glutton's prize. The dragon and Chun Ke had been in the forest nearby the last she had seen of them, going around and burying some of their nut stash so they could have something to eat if they went for a walk in the winter.

Xiulan smiled, taking the spoon from him and examining the thick frosting. It certainly didn't smell like cheese. It just smelled creamy and tangy. Intrigued, she sampled some of it—

"MmmMmmmmmHHHH—" The sound, as always, came out unbidden. The substance was almost sickeningly sweet. Decadence incarnate melted in her mouth, everything that the austere masters who had trained her warned about.

Jin's eyebrow twitched and his face flushed. Xiulan stuffed the spoon in her mouth.

"Cream cheese frosting and cinnamon rolls," Jin said proudly, after awkwardly clearing his throat. "Along with maple ice cream and shooter sandwiches," he declared, pointing to what looked like a whole loaf of bread that had weights placed on it, crushing it down. "Also got a veggie one for Chun Ke."

"*Cinnamon* rolls?" she asked, staring at the sweet-looking cakes.

"Well . . . spicebark, but it tastes close enough," Jin said, as he grabbed the bowl to start to clean up.

Xiulan eyed the dregs of icing left in it.

"Now, now, Sister, there is plenty to eat later," Bi De chastised her, the rooster sounding most amused.

Xiulan helped him pack everything together and then they were off too. Jin carried a basket while Xiulan held the box filled with ice and ice cream. Bi De alighted on Xiulan's shoulder and picked a leaf out of her hair. The trio marched out of the house and away from the courtyard, to where the new project was starting. The leveled-out and staked section of land had pieces of iron scaffolding set into place and what looked like a warped piece of glass stuck between the frames. Jin's "greenhouse" was still in its early stages, as Miantiao tried to make the "floating glass" Jin had mentioned work.

They journeyed in companionable silence, past the fields, empty of now-harvested crops. Past the sheep grazing in the fields and the bend in the river.

Everyone else was loitering at one of the bridges across the river, and the group perked up when they came into view.

Meiling squeezed in between them and linked arms with them both as Tigu clambered onto Xiulan's back, batting playfully at Bi De until he swapped to Jin's shoulder with an annoyed huff.

They ventured into the forest that blazed in the sunlight with a riot of colours until they came to a grove of maples, where they set out their blankets.

They all settled in for a meal on the blankets, sitting around, talking, and watching the leaves fall.

It was nice, just drifting in and out of the conversations, as they ate and drank fruit juice.

Xiulan turned to where Pi Pa, Ri Zu, and Meiling had cornered Xianghua.

'*Miss Liu, Ri Zu must know!*' the rat said, her eyes sparkling.

'*Indeed, dear, it's really quite important*,' Pi Pa intoned.

"Yeah. You and Gou have been cagey. When *is* the wedding, anyway?" Meiling continued, smiling brilliantly.

Xianghua blinked, then shrugged.

"We do not know yet. He wants to have something 'more worthy of me,' the fool. But I don't hate his earnestness," she said fondly.

Meiling, on the other hand, frowned. "It's fine if you're married, but should you be . . . ?"

"Ah. He offered to stop until we were wed. Gou has been a perfect gentleman!"

Meiling cocked her head to the side.

"Naturally, I refused," Xianghua stated cheerfully without an ounce of shame.

Xiulan shook her head and looked somewhere else while Meiling seemed torn between impressed and just a bit scandalized.

A moment later, Xiulan looked to the sky as a single red leaf fell—the same leaf that was on the symbol Meiling had designed and the same one on the sign outside the gate.

She raised a hand, touching the falling red leaf. It rested for a moment on her outstretched finger. And then she let it fall to the earth.

There was a small scuffle as Jin, Gou Ren, and Yun Ren began to squabble over the last of the cinnamon rolls. Distracted by the battle, the boys didn't notice the fish slinking in behind them to nab the prize.

Xiulan chuckled. There were still many trials ahead, that much was certain. Yet she still could not help but be optimistic for the future.

□

"The road changes up ahead, sir," a man in a uniform reported. "Smooth stone. I thought I was dreaming at first, but it looks like the roads near Pale Moon Lake City."

"Really?" Guan Bo, merchant of the Azure Jade Trading Company, asked as he looked back at the caravan. His first trip had been tough enough, but it had only really been himself and a few guards.

Now the train was twenty carts long and they had nearly sixty guards with them, the finest money could buy, all with hazard-pay bonuses. The breakdowns and the amount of times they had gotten stuck on the poorly maintained roads had been murder.

Still, they were nearly there and *that* was what mattered.

"It really is far away," a woman with scarlet hair muttered from beside her brother as they marched down the road to Verdant Hill.

"I did tell you," Bo replied. "Not *my* fault you've barely been out of Pale Moon Lake City, Chyou."

The woman, Guan Chyou, let out a breath. The trip had been slow and uncomfortable, taking over a month, but besides the breakdowns, nothing really exciting had happened.

"Is everything ready for when we arrive, Bo?" she asked, biting back a tart reply.

Her brother rolled his eyes. "For the last time, yes. The gifts are ready to go, we have the route back mapped, and we have all the stuff we need for the outpost. It's going to be *fine*. I know you're nervous because of how big this is, but it's all going to turn out great!"

Chyou let out a breath before nodding.

"To Verdant Hill, then," she muttered, staring around at the large undertaking.

All of this mobilized for one man. It seemed almost absurd when she thought of it that way.

Except it was one man with the finest rice this side of the Empire. They had found six more suppliers in Yellow Rock Plateau and the Howling Fang Mountains who could produce no more than a single bag each—and *none* of them compared to the quality that Master Jin produced.

The Azure Jade Trading Company wasn't just banking on a man.

They were banking on a future.

CHAPTER 12

PAYBACK

The Lord Magistrate will receive you now," the Verdant Hill guard said, clicking the butt of his sheathed spear against the ground. Guan Chyou glanced at the guard from where she had been considering the colourful curtains. The guard's bearing was immaculate. His march was quick and precise, and the man's diction was only barely marred by his northern accent.

He was a far cry from the other guards they had met on the journey to Verdant Hill. Hells, they hadn't even needed to bribe the men in the town to look after their things properly. Not that anybody would have tried anything with the presence of their own guards, but that was just how business was done.

Instead, her brother had just talked briefly with the guard captain and then they were through. No exchange of coins necessary.

It was a welcome sign, but still a bit strange to see guards with such moral fortitude so far north on the frontier. They were all remarkably well drilled and polite. They wouldn't have been out of place among the elite guards of Pale Moon Lake City.

It was another quirk of this already quirky little town. Like the cleanliness, the order, even the general smell. It was too . . . *nice.*

It really shouldn't be this way, from everything that she had seen so far. It was an enigma.

The roads and quality of the villages they had stopped in on the way here had progressively worsened while travelling farther north, as she'd expected. Dirt roads, untidy villages, grubby farmers. Everything one would expect as you left the centers of commerce for the hinterlands.

This town wouldn't have looked too out of place in the south. Verdant Hill was clean, orderly. Even the smell of the place was pleasant. Almost *too* pleasant.

Chyou and her brother had arrived after exchanging the usual formalities at the Palace of the Lord Magistrate. She had been expecting a dirt room and creaky chairs. Instead, she found herself in a well-appointed waiting room, one they had barely been in for long. The Lord Magistrate apparently did not feel like playing games with them. Chyou checked her hair and clothes one last time in a small mirror she kept on her person. Her scarlet locks were done up immaculately in the most recent style of the provincial capital. She was garbed in the persona of the perfect flower: a peach silk robe and an array of subtly placed blooms. Her brother was a bit more subdued in his clothing, but it was still an extremely expensive silk garment, one that would surpass the quality of anything a frontier magistrate *should* have. A display of wealth and power to ensure that this Lord Magistrate knew to whom he spoke. It would be less trouble if he took the hint.

Chyou mentally reviewed the information they had on the Lord Magistrate of Verdant Hill as they followed behind the guard. Her brother had met the man before, but his description had been rather vague. He had found the man irritatingly stuck up and by the books, which wasn't too odd but indicated he would not be bribable, if he would act this way even to the Azure Jade Trading Company.

Most frontier Magistrates were men who had scored poorly on their exams and barely made the cut. They were the bottom-of-the-rung men who couldn't refuse the poor postings they were granted. To be banished to such places as Verdant Hill with no hope of advancement was often considered a punishment for men who had spent their lives learning and training to manage cities. Why would they ever be satisfied with the obedience of a handful of rice farmers in far-flung outposts? Especially the most northern town in the province. The winters here were supposed to be brutal compared to the ones in the south.

Their intelligence had come back with his records from the Grand Palace in the provincial capital.

Top five in his class and wed to Lady Wu Zei Qi of the Wu Clan.

He had been at the very top of his class until some incident had bumped him down the rankings, but he had still been slated to be taken in by the Grand Palace upon his graduation . . . until he had *requested* the transfer.

Was it a coincidence? Or was he here because Master Jin was here? Was he some manner of servant for the cultivator? It would make sense . . .

Chyou sighed. She *hated* going in without complete information. All they had were her brother's vagueness and old, old records. Normally they would have paid somebody for a more comprehensive review.

Normally, they would have used the Plum Blossom's Shadow. In this endeavour, however, they were alone. Though the new and extremely powerful information brokers were on good terms with their company . . . they had cited standing orders from their enigmatic Master Scribe that Verdant Hill was forbidden to them, on account that they were to respect Master Jin's privacy. So there had been nothing from that front.

They'd had to send out their own men last night for a quick and dirty information-gathering session. The people of the Azure Hills had been only too happy to wax poetic about their ruler. The entire town had nothing but positive things to say of the Patriarch of Verdant Hill.

It was a bit suspicious that the man was so universally loved, but they had nothing else to go on.

Ideally, the man would be compliant to the Azure Jade Trading Company's wishes. He likely had some powerful friends and, from what they had learned last night, he held the love of the people. Removal from his position if he proved combative would be a fool's errand.

Such things were a measure of last resort, anyway.

Hopefully.

They were admitted to a private meeting room with servants lining the walls. Chyou had expected little and was surprised. The room was tastefully decorated and lavishly furnished, clean and well-lit by hanging lanterns artfully placed. It was the room of a noble official, from Pale Moon Lake City, transported all the way up north.

Three figures were waiting for them. A lady and a portly man flanked what could only be the vaunted Patriarch of Verdant Hill. Guan Chyou finally got her first glimpse of the Lord Magistrate.

She nearly froze in her tracks when she saw the man.

Chyou's image of a normal Magistrate was of a corpulent, corrupt creature, soft and decadent. The south was rife with them, to varying degrees.

Oh, many were skilled administrators, and there were even a few who had little corruption to their name, but they all seemed like the same kind of creature.

The Lord Magistrate of Verdant Hill looked more like the drawings of the Scholar-Generals, the men who had aided the First Emperor in founding the Crimson Phoenix Empire. Oh, they had heard tales from the villagers, about how he trained with the guards and rode his horse through obstacle courses like he was hounding evildoers, but it was one thing to hear and another to *see*.

There was barely a shred of fat on him. He was solid, but not overly muscled, and was starting to show signs of age. Wrinkles along with a salt-and-pepper beard, yet neither of those detracted from the admittedly still handsome man.

The single feature that drew her in had to be his eyes. Will and determination. Intelligence and drive. They shone in the evening light. She knew those eyes intimately—her grandmother wore them every day.

She forced herself to keep moving under the Lord Magistrate's impressive gaze and was nearly pinned by the eyes of two more people.

Lady Wu looked remarkably hale and hearty for a supposed cripple sitting calmly beside the Lord Magistrate. Her silken robes equaled anything the Azure Jade Trading Company had provided to Chyou. Her makeup was barely needed to accentuate an already stately beauty. Her lower face was covered by her fan, depicting the Soaring Phoenix.

A brazen display, calling on the image of Imperial Majesty. It was practically a declaration of war in the language of the court fans.

Behind her fan, the lady was the image of grace. Chyou was not fooled. Her eyes gave the impression of a smile, but all Chyou felt was that there was a tiger watching her from behind a patch of grass.

A third figure stood waiting nearby, a man who looked more like what she'd thought of when she'd first imagined the Lord Magistrate. He was fat and jolly-looking, wearing the traditional robes of an Archivist. He would not be out of place among her foolish uncles. But she did not miss that sharp intelligence as he carefully looked Chyou and her brother over.

Chyou felt like she and her brother were being weighed, and were found . . . wanting.

Her grandmother would have the face and the guts to stroll in like she owned the place, uncowed by these clearly experienced and prepared people. Perhaps a phoenix would have come out of her own sleeves to challenge Lady Wu directly.

Grandmother wasn't here, though, and Chyou wasn't stupid enough to attempt something like that against these three old tigers. There was knowing the power her name held. And then there was rank arrogance. These men and women were confident for a *reason*.

Still, the name of the Azure Jade required the Magistrate to rise to his feet to receive them.

"We greet the Lord Magistrate," she and her brother intoned, bowing politely.

"Esteemed guests of the Azure Jade Trading Company," the Lord Magistrate replied as he rose, clasping his hands and inclining his head the barest amount to not be completely disrespectful. "Please, be seated."

They bowed again and sat down as the servants started moving into place. Even the servants were well-appointed and moved like they knew the dance of courtly rules intimately.

Chyou carefully got out her own fan, one with drifting blossoms. Peace and reconciliation.

The lady raised an eyebrow but made no move to close her fan. Chyou swallowed.

This is going to be far harder than I expected.

"My dear wife, Lady Wu, and the First Archivist, Lin Bao, shall attend us this evening," the Lord Magistrate continued.

Lin Bao? The name immediately seemed familiar to Chyou. Something about a scandal in the provincial capital? Her grandmother had talked about it maybe? The exact nuances of what had happened escaped her for the moment. She could not think about it long, however—the meeting had begun.

"It is a long journey from Pale Moon Lake City. I trust your trip was pleasant?" the Lord Magistrate asked as they settled in and received the first course. A clear invitation to begin discussions, but Chyou hesitated. The food placed before her distracted her. It was some sort of flat disk that smelled slightly sweet.

Her brother nodded, still managing to stay chipper in spite of the pressure.

"Yes, sir. It was hard, but uneventful—until we hit your wonderful road, of course. Then it was the perfect journey."

Guan Chyou stared down at the disk. It was the same dish Master Jin had made when he'd shown them what went well with maple syrup.

Then the servants placed before each of them an entire *cup* of syrup. It took all her skill not to gape in astonishment. High-end restaurants were even now clamoring for more of the golden liquid—which they served in a thimble.

"Most excellent. A quiet journey is a good journey, no matter what fools say about boredom. But this is a bit abrupt of a visit, is it not?" the Lord Magistrate mused casually as he picked up the cup of syrup that was on his tray, looked them in the eyes, and then emptied the entire vessel onto the plate.

Both of them watched. They were rather used to displays of decadence, but the man was drizzling pure silver onto his plate with utter casualness.

The man raised an eyebrow at them when he noticed their stares.

Bo glanced at her.

Chyou tapped her leg three times.

Bo swallowed. "We of the Azure Jade Trading Company apologise for the timing of the transmission, and for any inconvenience it laid on you."

The Lord Magistrate made a considering noise.

"It is just you two, then? You seem quite young."

"Our . . . powerful client requested us," Bo stated carefully. "He is a good friend to the company, and we endeavour to complete all his requests."

"Ah, it is indeed troublesome when there are such requests, but what can one do?" Lady Wu spoke up. "Our *good friend* is a bit of a handful, but he is ever so generous in his gifts, don't you find it so, Guan Chyou?" She liberally poured the syrup over her own stack of cakes as well while smiling like a mother at them. "Please, do eat. There's *plenty* more where this came from."

"Indeed. We servants are ever obedient," Lin Bao declared. "But there is value and honour in serving, is there not? So, let us all work together on bringing prosperity." The man chuckled as he cut a stack of cakes and took a large bite. "I'll be having seconds, my dear," he said to the serving girl, who bowed immediately.

"Yes, there is honour in serving, and in working together for prosperity," Chyou ventured. She carefully picked up the cup of syrup . . . and started to pour.

All eyes were on her as she raised the white flag of surrender.

The Lord Magistrate broke out into a smile.

"Very good!" the Lord Magistrate decreed, raising a cup in toast to them. "So, let us decide the specifics of your *little operation* in *my* Verdant Hill." He looked very pleased.

Chyou saw her brother swallow.

↔

"Oh my, we haven't done that in years," Lady Wu said, looking far too amused as she fanned herself. "And you, darling. 'May we ever have a beneficial relationship?' That was just *mean* to the poor boy."

The Lord Magistrate smiled as he watched two stunned merchants stagger their way back to their hideout. It indeed had been a long time since he had last really dueled with words.

"Me? You were entirely too cruel to that girl, my dear. I thought she saw your fan."

"Oh? But those wide eyes were rather cute. I just want to tie her up," his wife said with a sadistic smile. "Red rope made of red hair. It has a certain appeal, no?"

The Lord Magistrate shivered. Guan Chyou's hair was indeed appealing, but he had no desire to offend the Azure Jade Trading Company more than he had tonight.

"It was easier than I thought it would be," he stated.

Indeed, he had been expecting the more experienced members to lead the negotiations. Instead, he had encountered two relative novices. Competent enough but unused to being truly challenged.

He had driven a bargain the merchants had gulped at before politely accepting, but if they thought they could suppress him in his own town they would have been sorely mistaken.

And it was rather fun, visiting some of the torment he had felt back on them.

CHAPTER 13

THE HEALING SAGE

Meiling sat in an empty room with her eyes closed. Cloth had been placed on the floors and on the walls, cordoning off the room from the rest of the building. Her Qi swirled gently around her body, the odd, tingling feeling of it sterilizing her surroundings with an ever-present sensation.

It was time. Time for the surgery. It was a week after their Fall Colours viewing and the last test performed; the deer had been released just yesterday. Her father had ventured from his home to assist her. Every tool was prepared, every eventuality planned for . . . or so she hoped.

Bowu was already sitting down on the cloth-covered table as Ri Zu checked over the various concoctions that would place the boy into unconsciousness, keeping him asleep without harming him. It was rare that such things were used.

On occasion, when they had to amputate a limb, the person would be rendered unconscious first. The medicines to accomplish this were relatively risky—the doses could interact badly with the patient, killing them. Quite a lot of men chose to be awake, the more general numbing herbs reducing the sensations to mere pain instead of excruciating agony.

Meiling shook her head. She still wondered sometimes how it had come to this. How she'd gone from being a mere mortal village doctor to the precipice of performing the work of miracle doctors and spiritual healers. She probably should have waited to do it until after she gave birth . . . but she had been fixated on the problem ever since it had been brought to her.

It was terrifying, and yet the practice runs had gone off without a hitch. She had studied the new scrolls Jin had gotten her from Pale Moon Lake City. This operation was well within her capabilities.

Trust had been placed in her, and she would exceed their expectations without fail.

She took a sharp breath as a large hand gently rested on her shoulder. Glancing up, she opened her eyes to her husband's smile.

"You got this, Meimei," Jin stated simply.

Absolute faith shone in his eyes.

Reassured by his steady presence, she smiled at him, and nodded.

She rose and stared into the cloth-clad room. Her father, Ri Zu, Wa Shi, and Pi Pa awaited her. Pi Pa had a brush in her mouth, off to the side; she would record today's procedure as was proper so that others could benefit.

Meiling glanced over the room she'd meditated in one last time.

Xianghua sat in the corner, absolutely still, her body tense like a coiled spring. She had refused to be separated from her brother and thus had been allowed in as an observer after Jin had said he would handle her if she tried to interfere at any point.

Some of these suggestions for the procedure had been Jin's: the sterile clothes, the idea to completely paralyse the limb.

The rest had been fairly straightforward. The acupuncture and numbing agents would paralyse the leg, to make sure no pain would force a reflexive movement. Liu Xianghua had been instrumental in that, bringing with her gifts of medicinal plants from the Misty Lake, as well as scrolls detailing what they were used for; the numbing Five Tongue Flower was what they would be using today.

Meiling put everything save Bowu her out of mind and walked forward.

"Bowu," Meiling said as the boy lay down. "Are you ready?"

A small part of her hoped he would say he was not. That way, she could have more time. Perhaps a year or two? Just so she could be *sure*.

The boy on the raised bench, however, was resolute.

"I'm good, Auntie Meimei," Bowu managed to get out. She had to fight back a laugh. *Now*, just before a life-changing procedure for the both of them, was when he finally relaxed enough to call her that? It was good. *Lady* Meiling was a bit much for her tastes.

Meiling closed her eyes and bowed her head. When she opened them again, everything else fell away. The anxiety disappeared. The pounding of her heart steadied. Meiling was prepared.

"Ri Zu," she commanded. Her student nodded, Qi flowing out of her body. The little rat took out her needle and pressed it into Bowu's neck. The boy didn't flinch as Meiling started counting backwards from ten. Ri Zu could control how the concoction would react, speeding it up and slowing it down as she monitored Bowu's vitals.

At one, Bowu's eyes closed. Needles coated with numbing agents stabbed into pressure points, effectively cutting his leg off from the rest of his body.

Meiling took one last breath, and then her knife moved, pressing down.

She avoided as many blood vessels as she could. She *knew* where each and every one of them was, her Qi helping to guide her around every deviation from the scrolls in Bowu's body. She opened the skin and slid gently between muscles; Meiling attempted to curb as much blood loss as possible, but he was still bleeding . . . and they didn't really have a way to replace that lost blood until the operation was over.

At least not yet. Jin knew of some medicine that powerful cultivators used to help deal with blood loss. He also knew that blood could be shared but confessed he had no idea how to check which blood would help . . . or be poison.

Another project for another time.

She opened Bowu's bone to the air, and then her father helped her place the specially made metal pieces Yao Che had created for them to keep the wound open. There was a thin film of blood coating everything, impeding her vision.

"Wa Shi," she requested, eyes not deviating one bit from the operation site. Wa Shi's control was impeccable as tiny, thin streamers of water descended to siphon away blood.

She would thank him later.

The wound came into view, for the first time unimpeded by flesh. Bowu's kneecap looked completely mangled, like a shattered plate that had been poorly stuck together with clay. The cartilage was red and inflamed-looking even now . . . and she could see tiny, needle-like bone shards sticking out, and the ugly-looking bumps where they were below the surface.

All well within expectations, Meiling concluded as she lowered her knife again.

What followed was butcher's work. The cartilage, filled with shards of bone, had to be scraped out in some sections. In others, Meiling wielded a tiny pair of tweezers her father handed to her, using them to carefully pull pieces thinner than needles out from the afflicted areas.

She could see each and every one, though she was sure that they would have been invisible to mortal eyes. Her hands moved with speed and precision. There were no minute shakes, no hesitation. Her body did as she commanded it, the practice with the deer making this feel routine, despite the difference in structure.

"How is he?" she paused to ask Ri Zu, more for her own peace of mind and a second opinion.

'All is accounted for, Master. He feels not a thing. His heart beats strongly, and his breathing is even.'

Meiling nodded in assent as she deposited another shard of bone into a tray. Her Qi surrounded and invaded the knee, searching for other shards of bone. She kept working, and her hand kept moving, until she was satisfied there were none left.

"Ninety-two." Meiling reported the number of shards removed as she turned her attention to the kneecap.

This . . . this was going to be the hard part. Carefully grasping the bone with two fingers, Meiling took a quick breath to gather her courage—then snapped the bone before her resolve could falter. She was amazed at how easy it was. Less like bone and more like a child breaking a cookie.

There were no shards created by the movement. It had broken cleanly. She repeated the process with each breath, breaking the bone along each poorly healed line, dismantling it with ease.

Once it had all been broken properly, Meiling then sliced two of the pieces and placed the two ends together as they *should* have healed. Her father reached in and placed a single drop of the Spiritual Herb liquid onto the joint with a brush.

The liquid she had refined, with Wa Shi's aid. It seemed to spark and crackle as it dropped onto the bone.

The broken bone, carefully held in place, hissed slightly . . . and then *fused.* It regrew and joined together like it had never been broken at all.

This is like piecing together some sort of wooden puzzle sculpture from the big cities, she thought as she reassembled the kneecap. *Like wood and glue, except this is bone and miracle medicine.* When the last drop hit the bone it looked smooth and whole. It was as if it had never broken.

Meiling paused. She searched for something, *anything* that might have gone wrong . . . but there was nothing.

She checked two more times, just to be *sure.* Then she began the final steps.

More of the healing liquid was applied after her handiwork. Meiling watched as *cartilage* regrew at a rapid pace, the incisions she made fading when the Qi worked its magic.

There was no stitching required. There would be no weeks or months of healing, though Bowu might need to relearn how to walk without limping.

Meiling applied the last drop . . . and then stared at a completely unblemished leg. It almost felt anticlimactic. A decade of pain gone in not even an hour.

It had taken so little time for a little girl who simply loved medicine to become a genuine Healing Sage.

The world of cultivators was truly a strange place.

↔

Liu Bowu woke up slowly. His head felt full of fog for a couple of minutes, before there was a muffled squeak and his mind suddenly cleared.

He was in a bed, with a weight beside him and a hand on his forehead.

He opened his eyes to a freckled woman with amethyst eyes staring down at him.

"Good morning," Auntie Meimei said to him as she pulled her hand back. The normally slightly scary-looking woman's eyes were warm and not nearly as intense as they usually were.

"Did . . . *did it work*?" he asked, blurting out the only thing on his mind.

"I do believe so. How are you feeling, Bowu?"

He paused and took stock of himself. He felt . . . pretty great, actually. He'd expected to feel a lot worse than he did. He'd felt like crap all the other times the doctors had looked at him.

"I feel fine," he reported, and he meant it. No little aches or anything besides the usual pain in his leg—

And then it hit him. *It didn't hurt.*

There was no pain in his leg.

It was always there: the dull ache that was ever present, that would morph into blinding pain when he put weight on it.

He sat upright, Auntie Meimei dodging him as he pulled the covers from his leg and stared at his knee.

His knee, normally bumpy in texture, shattered and broken.

He bent his leg. It went to the area where it would normally stop and refuse to bend any further without extreme pain . . . and then it kept going.

He swung his leg back out. There was no scar, no trace of the lifetime of pain.

A hand on his shoulder kept him from bolting to his feet.

"Slowly," Auntie Meimei commanded, gently but firmly.

Bowu nodded. Carefully, he swung his legs to the side and pushed himself out of bed.

He stood *up*. He stood, without a crutch, and without any pain.

As if in a trance, he started forwards, taking his first step.

There was a slight twinge, and he paused . . . but there was no *pain*.

He took another.

He put one foot in front of the other, fighting the urge to limp as he'd had to for so long.

Each slow step carried him to the door; Auntie Meimei followed behind him, watching his movements carefully.

He was walking. Walking, without any pain at all.

He had the urge to burst into a run, but a repeated, reproachful "Slowly" from Lady Meiling halted the idea in its tracks. So instead, he paced himself. He walked fully upright and without a limp, opening the door into the main room, where his sister was leaning against Big Brother Gou, her face set into an anxious, heavy frown.

Her eyes whipped to Bowu as she shot to her feet, gaze locking onto his face.

Bowu grinned at her and lifted his leg, bending it completely.

There was an impact as Xianghua vaulted the table and scooped him up into a painful hug. Her limbs shook with the action, the embrace slightly too tight. He hugged back with just as much force.

CHAPTER 14

A FATHER'S PRIDE

A little girl pounded away at some reeds on a field of steadily drying grass. The sky was full of golden stars interlaced with bands of light.

The little girl looked exhausted. She paused in her work, yawning and stretching. She had cracks of gold running through her body, as if she had been shattered and somehow glued back together.

The little girl returned to the reeds a moment later, checking them over, then nodded, satisfied at the slightly coarse fibers.

Her task completed, she turned to the small divot dug in the ground . . . and threw the soft plant fibers in.

She stepped back and put her hands on her hips, surveying her bed.

It . . . didn't look particularly comfortable. It would be a lot better if she could remember how to weave blankets, but that . . . well . . . She tapped at her forehead. Her knowledge just wasn't all there anymore.

There was a disapproving snort from behind her, causing her to jump and turn around to see an enormous boar made out of runed stone and living wood.

"Not comfy, Big Little Sister. Will sleep bad," the boar said, his voice like the mountains moving.

The little girl grimaced. "It's . . . not the greatest, but I can sleep here. Look!" she said, and dove into the pile of fibers. Burrowing around in the stack, she squirmed until her head was poking out, then grinned back up at the boar.

He still didn't look particularly amused.

"Why not ask friends for help?" the boar asked her, curious.

Tianlan paused at the question. Friends helping her make her bed . . . She winced as a spike of pain pounded into her head. Broken fragments of memories from the Dueling Peaks flashed in front of her eyes, of somebody helping to make her a place to sleep.

Visceral hate burned in her chest when she saw flashes of that person. *The betrayer.*

She shoved the images away, feeling sick.

"This is something I have to do myself," she said instead. Chun Ke looked unconvinced.

The boar stared at her for a moment and then chuffed. A giant nose leaned down and pressed against her forehead.

"If need help, Big Little Sister ask?"

"Okay," she whispered as her hands rose up, going around Chun Ke's neck. "I'll ask. But . . . I want to see how far I can get first, all right?" she requested.

"Okay," the boar agreed.

↔

What was it like to witness a miracle? Hong Xian had seen a few in his time. Once, when his not-yet-wife Liling had arrived just in time with the evidence that had saved his and Bao's necks. Once, when Meiling had been born. And once more when his son was born.

The feeling of awe, wonder, glory, and relief that a miracle had taken place was something to be cherished.

And he had just witnessed another yesterday.

"Okay, bend it for me . . . Keep going, keep going . . . . Any pain?" Hong Xian watched as his daughter fussed over Liu Bowu. Her amethyst eyes were focused, and a slight green tint circulated around her hands. She was flanked by Ri Zu and Pi Pa, the two animals assisting her, and Jin, who was standing back and watching the proceedings beside Liu Xianghua quietly.

His eyes sought out the leg that just yesterday had been gnarled and broken, that had been cut into and scraped at, sitting completely unblemished.

If he had not seen it with his own eyes, he would not have believed it. He had seen a cultivator healing before, a broken arm fixing itself in a week through the use of medicine, but this was beyond even that. In mere moments, the bone had fused so completely it was as if it had never been broken.

Xian thought back to the surgery. It had been humbling to have his daughter, with all the powers of a cultivator, call upon *him* to ask for his aid. He had been only too happy to oblige her.

And yet he had been rendered nearly superfluous.

Meiling had been breathtaking to watch. The way her hands had moved, the skill with which she had sliced open the young man's leg—it was all so exacting that Xian knew he couldn't replicate it even if he practiced for years. He had barely been able to see her move in some cases, her tweezers plucking out shards of bone that were so small they had been completely invisible to him. Her lack of hesitation and her calm commands had been amazing.

He felt like a boy at his father's knee again, even after everything he had done and seen throughout his life. He still remembered the brutal amputations—or the worst one, where he'd had to carve out a portion of a man's skull to reduce swelling of the brain. The man had lived, but he was never quite the same afterwards.

And now, as his daughter made sure her patient was well and that there were no further issues with his leg . . . Hong Xian could only watch. She had surpassed him utterly, even if she still would deny it and continue to proclaim Xian her better in all things.

It was sweet of her, but he supposed that some things took time to realise.

It was a strange miracle . . . but in the end, it was a welcome one. At first, his pride had been stung on realising that his skills amounted to little in the face of a cultivator, but the sting soon faded—his daughter still asked for his opinion, her questions so earnest.

The blow to his pride soon turned to pride in her accomplishments . . . and pride that his daughter was carrying on the family tradition.

He had always been proud of her. She had picked up medicine astoundingly fast. She had been driven and passionate about their family's crafts—like he was at her age. Always wanting to learn and apply herself.

Sometimes, Xian thought it might have been better were his daughter born a man. He would have been happy to proclaim her his heir . . . But it could not be. The world of mortals was not the world of cultivators. They were *peasants*, not nobles. Very few would have followed her, even if they did like Meiling. That, and the second reason.

The words of the ancestors were clear. Hong Xian, son of Hong Xian, must succeed as the head of Hong Yaowu. He himself had sworn an oath upon taking the position from his father, and some things were not broken lightly.

It was, in his opinion, an injustice dealt to his daughter. She'd spent those years of learning and of aiding him, only to be told by potential matches that her learning had been useless. In truth, he was rather glad she had dosed those men's drinks with laxatives. For such foolish men would sire foolish children—and his Meiling deserved better than that.

Xian sighed and absently picked up the flask. Seven Fragrance Jewel Herb Liquid, grown by a powerful cultivator and then refined through the lightning of a dragon and the medicinal Qi of another powerful cultivator.

In any other case, it would sound like the creation of a charlatan. If a traveller dared to say that this was the method to obtain the sparkling concoction within, they would have been chased out of town for trying to swindle the population.

However, he had seen it made with his own eyes. Meiling had given him a recipe for a less potent version; he had used it and he knew the results firsthand.

His daughter had willingly shared it with him, to better aid the village. In conjunction with the Spiritual Herbs that even now were growing in his garden, Hong Yaowu would be able to produce miracles of its own. The village would be able to save a person's life from nearly any injury, so long as it was administered before they died.

All this, from a single visitor.

He gently placed the priceless concoction down as his eyes found Jin. His son-in-law was watching Meiling's treatment of Bowu from nearby. He made no move to intervene. In fact, he looked impressed and proud. He had seen Meiling's talent, nurtured it, and loved it.

Like the thistle that was the same colour as her eyes, Xian's Meiling had grown quickly in the right soil. She was the Master of her household, she commanded a multitude of servants, and she was practically the wife of a chief in her own right.

All this on top of her medicine. The drive that his daughter had was pushing her further and further along in her studies. Jin did not just indulge his daughter, as if medicine was a passing fancy. He supported her wholeheartedly.

But, as Xian was coming to learn more and more about Jin, that was just how the man did things. He would rather aid another than take the credit for himself. Jin saw their passions and, as if seized by those passions himself, he strove to create *with* them.

They truly were a good match, his daughter and Jin.

Xian shook his head as he realised his attention had wandered. His daughter had completed her tests. Luckily, Pi Pa had been writing everything down. It had taken him over six months, but he was getting used to the talking animals now.

There was the *clink* as Jin got some tea and poured Xian a cup.

"Jin. Sit with me, son. I wish to hear about your plans for the winter," Xian said as he patted the spot beside him.

Jin smiled at the invitation as they both sat. The cultivator took a sip of his own tea, swallowing before starting.

"Well, the first thing is first: the General That Commands the Winter must muster his forces . . ." Jin began with a silly grin.

Of course the first thing Jin thinks of is a giant snow golem. I probably should have expected it.

"I've got the perfect carrot, you know? It's as long as my arm and I had to duel Wa Shi for it when I dug it up!" Xian snorted with laughter as he imagined the dragon being slammed into the ground in a grand conflict over a carrot. It was an amusing image. He let Jin's voice wash over them as he thought.

Well, the harvest had been good this year, and there was never really much to do during winter . . . perhaps the village would challenge the General's might?

Perhaps use an internal frame . . . or was that cheating? No, Jin used Qi, so it was fair!

If only to see the look on Jin's face when Hong Yaowu beat the size of a cultivator's snow golem.

CHAPTER 15

THE WITCHING HOUR

Xiulan moved through the first form of the Verdant Blade Sword Arts in the light of the setting sun. Her eyes were closed as she felt the flow of the movements. Her form was impeccable, over a decade of practice having honed her movements until they were as natural as breathing. Each step was precise. She wove a pattern of steel in the air, a blooming flower, until she came to the end, her sword held to the side and two fingers pointing up in front of her face.

With her breathing calm and steady she opened her eyes and turned to her companion. Jin was watching her, his brow furrowed in concentration.

"It's a bit more grace than I think I can manage," he joked, absently clenching and unclenching his fist. Xiulan sheathed her blade and turned to look over the young man. Indeed, Jin's build was not the greatest for her techniques; he was too thickset, with muscles that would interfere in his movements.

"I was taught that taking things slow is sometimes best," Xiulan offered, and Jin nodded, moving into the starting stance she had shown him. He had his sword in his hand. A magnificently crafted work, if unadorned. "Now . . . shoulders set. Eyes forward. Plant that lead foot."

She watched him carefully as he steadied his breathing, taking the first form. *Technically*, one could argue that she shouldn't be teaching him the Verdant Blade Sword Arts. Jin was, however, her sworn brother, and thus that made him "family of the main branch."

At least that was her interpretation, and she was prepared to argue it if need be. She was certain none of her Sect would object in any case.

Jin's sword moved slowly and his eyes were closed as he made the first stroke of his blade. He was focused, yet there was an obvious lack of connection. Xiulan winced at the awkwardness in his movements. Bi De had been correct in his assessment: the sword did not suit Jin . . . yet it was far less awkward than before.

Xiulan had agreed to show Jin the Verdant Blade Sword Arts after he had shown her the scroll he had received from his Gramps. She knew not what style was depicted within, yet she had been humbled by it. It was the work of a true master. The moves were seemingly simple, only the most basic and efficient ones possible. Yet it was undeniable that they were the distillation of techniques from the eyes of a true master of the blade. Just looking at the scroll had allowed Xiulan to adjust her own training.

It was a pure foundation. Utter mastery of form. In its simplicity, the technique was absolutely beautiful. Jin had shrugged and put it on the table for all of them after listening to their assessment of the scroll. After barely one night of practice with the knowledge of the scroll, her bladework had already improved.

Bi De and Tigu were spending time studying it at the moment, leaving tonight's training session to Xiulan alone. It was probably for the best—Tigu had gotten a bit too excited in their last session and escalated the spar. She had looked quite embarrassed when her Qi claws had shattered on Jin's skin.

Jin had been dissatisfied with his own progress with the scroll, so he wished to see if it was merely the techniques it taught that was the problem or something else; Xiulan was quite certain now of the cause.

His cultivation rejected the sword entirely . . . but this was not the sword, or at least, not all of it.

"Your foot is too high. A slide, a glide, more than a step," she instructed, like she had with her own students, the ones that people had taken to calling The Orchid's Petals.

Jin nodded and repeated the movement. Xiulan had come to learn that Jin's style of learning was a slow, methodical thing. A grinding advance of careful repetition until he accomplished his goal, not unlike how he approached most tasks. For him there were no grand epiphanies or sudden advancements. He just worked until he got it, patiently persisting. Even now as he attempted to center himself despite his breathing threatening to destabilize, he kept a grip on his blade.

Xiulan watched over Jin, who was soaking in the last rays of the dying sun, his eyes closed, completely focused on his task, trusting her to catch any problems that she noticed.

The world was quiet, filled only with the sound of his breathing and the occasional gust of wind.

The silence was broken by a squawk of outrage.

"I'm going to tie ya to a tree, Meimei!" Yun Ren howled. Laughter echoed out from the house, both Meiling's giggles and Xianghua's booming gales.

"Pink hair suits you, Honoured Brother!" she roared.

The disturbance to the peace did not break Jin's breathing. Instead, it was reinforced. The tension eased from his shoulders.

Xiulan smiled as Jin relaxed into a firmer stance, then acted. His body moved through the second stance with grace approaching what Xiulan would expect of herself.

He looked relaxed, shifting smoothly from second to third stance, but she could see the minute twitches in his form, the same twitches she had—urges to change the movements from the bladework into a flowing dance. It was a problem Xiulan knew well. One had to mix the two for the best results . . . but for him to have found the same beat Xiulan had taken years to discover so swiftly was interesting. None of the others she had taught had felt the dance.

A little smile crossed her face and she launched into the second part of their training.

"Who is the Sect Master of the Rumbling Earth Sect?"

Jin frowned slightly before answering, still moving through the form: "On Gang."

"Correct."

Jin had asked for her help in both cultivation and diplomacy, and she had given all she knew. She had written out an accounting of every Sect that she knew of: their masters and mistresses, their heraldries, their territories, historical grudges . . . Everything she could think of from her own training had gone into the little pamphlet.

Jin had stared at it like a drowning man being thrown a rope, and then slammed his hand into his forehead and berated himself for not asking sooner.

"Who are their allies?"

"His Sect and the Whitewater Sect are *technically* allies, but the Sect Masters hate each other," Jin responded as he gradually took up the fourth stance.

Xiulan remembered the root of that feud, Elder Gang taking Elder Xinling's sword to the gut had been an unforgettable moment. Elder Gang wasn't particularly well liked. Avaricious, arrogant, and a boor according to her father—she had little cause to disagree. At least his nephew, the heir, seemed to share none of his undesirable traits. Dulou Gan was actually rather sweet when he wasn't busy putting on an act, trying to gruffly glare at everything.

"And what about the White Water Sect?"

"Elder Xinling. They live near a set of violent rapids. The gravel and dirt that comes from the mountains dyes the white foam grey. Elder Xinling plays the guzheng . . ."

They continued their back-and-forth for a while, Jin answering every question she posed to him while he completed the forms of the Verdant Blade.

"This is a bit easier than I thought it would be," Jin mused. "I'm normally terrible with names. I thought I would have to give everybody nicknames like Tigu does. Music Lady, Rumble Man, Dad of Grass." His lips quirked into a smile, and his form continued without flaw. Xiulan snorted at the nickname for her father.

"'Dad of Grass'? *Really?*" she asked. "Tigu's nicknames are better." Jin pouted at her pronouncement.

Finally, he completed the last movement and rose back into the ready position. His sword was pointed to the side and two fingers were held towards the sky.

He seemed a bit anxious as he opened his eyes and looked at her. She smiled and nodded her head.

"You did excellently," she stated simply. "You *do* have some grace to you after all."

Jin sheathed his blade and scratched at his neck before taking a breath and bowing formally. "Thank you for your help, Senior Sister," he said with a little smirk.

"Thank you, *Master* Jin," she fired back. He snorted and stood up from his bow. "How did the Verdant Blade Sword Arts feel?"

"Strange. Like I was about to break out into . . . well—" He frowned, and his feet started tapping out a rhythm.

"Like this?" she asked, clapping her hand to his beat, her own body moving. Xiulan took up the dance that was familiar now. It felt refreshing. Not something to be held back or feared. Jin's eyes widened as he watched her move. The dance grew like a plant, the smaller movements leading into larger ones before blooming into the finale.

"Yeah, like that," he agreed. Jin's eyes were wide as he watched her. His feet tapped with the rhythm and he began to copy her, following along.

One step, then the second. Slow and halting, but he started to get into it. She matched her movements with his. It was almost like at the Dueling Peaks, when she had danced with Xianghua, Tigu, and the Young Master of the Hermetic Iron Sect.

Something that resided in the depths of her soul recognised the movements and resonated with them.

This dance in particular seemed to fit Jin. The movements of growth and life, vital and strong.

Jin's grin got bigger and bigger as they reached the final moment, and then they paused, their hands stretched out. Normally the dance would repeat, but she saw the little gleam in Jin's eye.

His dance *changed*.

One finger pointed to the sky, and then he swung it down to the ground and back again. Xiulan froze at his completely serious expression and the odd sounding "*ba-da-bada-ba-da-dadda*."

Xiulan snorted, thrown off her own movements by the change. With a raised eyebrow, she followed along, swinging her hips and her finger until her laughter couldn't be contained any longer.

"Who dances like this?!"

"*Di si ko* is a legendary dance, I'll have you know. Our ancestors swore by it," Jin declared pompously.

"I very much doubt my ancestors danced like this," she said as Jin executed a spin . . . and then started up a movement that made it look like he was gliding backwards while walking forwards.

"Then they and their bloodlines were weak," Jin stated. His face remained stone . . . until he too began to laugh. After recovering, the two of them walked up the hill slightly before sitting down, Xiulan shaking her head at the stupid grin on Jin's face. It was so full of cheer, especially after that stupid dance.

It still felt a bit strange to think of Jin as young and inexperienced. He had seemed so solid, so sure of his path in life when she had first met him. His words had been full of wisdom; his actions had raised her to heights she never could have imagined.

And yet here he was, dutifully being her student.

It was actually a bit appealing. In her mind's eye she could see him in the robes of the Verdant Blade Sect and following after her like one of her other students, a big grin on his face as he called her Senior Sister.

Or perhaps, in a different lifetime, all of her companions would have been there from the beginning? It wasn't a bad thought, was it? To have Jin, Meiling, and the Xong brothers all in her life for twenty more years would have been a blessing. A reel of imagined situations started up. She pictured herself scolding Meiling for using poisons in a spar again, while the girl whistled innocently; she could see Gou Ren and Yun Ren having done something silly and begging their Young Mistress to get them out of trouble again; she knew Tigu would challenge her to a spar every day on the hilltop; and when they went to fight Sun Ken, they would have all sallied forth together and brought him low without the blood and the misery.

It was an amusing distraction, yet she knew she would have not appreciated them as she did now. Xianghua had been there for her, yet Xiulan had been blind to her aid.

Or maybe they could have knocked some sense into her?

In the end, one couldn't change the past. She gently laid the appealing image to rest.

Instead, she had to look forward to a future. Where would they be in five years? Ten? Twenty? She did not know, but she was ready to find out.

She was eager to share her life with these people who had found her.

Xiulan stared at Jin, who looked at the tree line in the fading sunlight.

"The trees look kind of spooky like this, don't they?" Jin asked as he stared at the naked branches and the darkening sky. The full moon shone in the sky, a few clouds covering it.

She considered the trees. In truth, she didn't feel scared, but the slight mist that was forming on the ground drew her attention. It reminded her of the Hill of Torment, which she supposed was rather haunting.

"A bit," she agreed.

Jin stared at them for a moment longer, his eyes far away.

"You know, at this time of year, a lot of people said that evil spirits come out to steal their souls. So they used to light lanterns, carved with demonic faces to scare the evil spirits away . . ."

Xiulan raised an eyebrow. "I see. We shall need some of these protections, then?"

"We're gonna need a *bunch* of squash," Jin said, a familiar impish gleam in his eyes.

Xiulan stood with him as the fire in his eyes ignited, walking together to the squash patch as he started talking about the Hallowed End.

She knew of the feast of Hungry Ghosts, but that was months gone by now. The Hallowed End sounded similar.

Although dressing up in costumes was strange, Jin seemed excited about it.

"Meimei will make the *cutest* witch," he declared simply. Xiulan raised an eyebrow, not knowing how wild hair and talismans on an old crone could be cute. Though she could imagine Meiling giggling over a new poison, a happy gleam in her eye.

They got strange looks when they came back to the house with armfuls of large squashes they had gathered. Yun Ren paused in grinding his knuckles into Meiling's head, raising a freshly pink eyebrow at them, which gave her time to elbow him in the gut and escape.

"What's that all for?" he asked, confused.

Soon they all gathered around and Jin explained what they were doing.

A contest to carve the best face into the gourds began swiftly, and as Jin sketched out a large, floppy, and pointy-looking hat, Xiulan finally got what he was talking about.

The witches of Raging Waterfall Gorge had a strange costume. They were not old crones but young women with large, pointy hats . . . but he was right.

Meiling *would* make a cute witch.

Xiulan kind of wanted one of those hats for herself, if she was honest.

CHAPTER 16

THE HAUNTING FOREST

Two figures on horseback trotted down a wide road. They wore the rich travelling clothes often associated with merchant folks. Bright silks with symbols emblazoned on them marked the duo as part of the Azure Jade Trading Company. The pair rode down the path without haste, one keeping a sharp eye on the road ahead while the other looked over the grand vista before them.

Guan Chyou's eyes roved over the hills around them, a smile on her face. The crisp autumn air felt invigorating. Her head moved to and fro, trying to soak everything in. The height of the trees, the infinite blue sky, and even the road was beautiful. The paving stones were decorated with what looked like carved vines and covered with a thin sheet of red and orange leaves.

"Ah, it's a lovely ride, isn't it?" Guan Bo turned back to ask her.

"It is nice. I've never been this far out. It feels . . . good."

Bo grinned at her in return. "I'm so glad to be out of that town."

Chyou nodded, and grabbed onto the brim of her hat when a particularly fierce gust of wind blew through the valley between the hills they were in. Her red travelling clothes were emblazoned with a blue dragon, and she wore a lighter blue sash. A pink band of silk went under her chin, keeping her wide-brimmed hat on her head, and her red hair flowed freely under it, a crimson streamer that followed the wind. Her brother was dressed similarly, though he also had a sword strapped to his hip. A sword he didn't know how to actually use, but it was necessary to have at least the appearance of protection, no matter how supposedly safe the roads were.

For the first time since the start of their journey north it was just she and her brother. No guards, no multitude of servants, just her and Bo riding down the road into the great unknown. I was almost like a real adventure.

The road was safe, and there were likely no hidden dangers. There would be nothing this close to a cultivator's abode or the efficient militia of Verdant Hill, but it was still exciting. Outside the capital and on an adventure, riding down the road to the home of a mysterious cultivator. They would go and give tribute, all to win the right to his secret wares.

Also it got them out of Verdant Hill and away from the Magistrate.

"I'll tell you, if I have to deal with those two again I'll go grey. Working outside of our city normally makes things easier, not harder!" Bo muttered.

"I would have to agree," Chyou grunted out. Being on the back foot while a person better than you ran rings around you was *highly* unpleasant. Yet it was a learning experience. Grandmother always said that steel sharpened steel, no matter how unpleasant the interactions might be. Well, it was her duty to meet the challenge of Lady Wu. She would not be defeated next time—or at least, not defeated quite as utterly.

"I swear the Archivist *enjoyed* giving us all those forms to fill out," her brother continued, complaining as was his wont.

"Oh, is my brother so unused to paperwork? Weren't you complaining on the road about how much you missed your desk?"

"I miss the nice beds, not the forms," he grumbled.

He often tried to foist that work off on her when he could, the lazy bum.

The name Azure Jade Trading Company normally waived a lot of the paperwork. Not here, however. The Lord Magistrate had given them *all* the relevant papers.

It was . . . rather a lot.

"There were so many pages. At least the terms were better than we thought they'd be."

Chyou had to agree. "For being so difficult, the Lord Magistrate was remarkably even-handed," she mused as she glanced at the wonderful blue sky and breathed in the crisp air.

The terms they had been given were not too onerous, compared to what Chyou had seen leveled at people in the capital, after they had sat down to think rationally about them. Hells, they were downright lenient . . . for anybody not of the Azure Jade Trading Company. Her company had to use local workers for most of their needs, rely on the city guard while in town, and take steps to ensure that the trade route was actually a trade route . . . and not just a road that solely catered to Master Jin's needs.

It was . . . well, it was everything that they had been prepared to give, if she was being realistic. The concessions to the local authorities could barely be considered concessions at all. Just good sense.

In the end, it had all been a very effective play by Master Jin's servant. The man retained his place instead of becoming their subordinate as they had originally planned. Chyou could admit when she had been outplayed—yet better humbled by an ally than a true enemy. She could bow her head if it meant succeeding in her endeavours. Business was no place for pride. Besides, they had gotten everything they wanted, largely.

The positions of the respective players were confirmed, and thus their relationship could continue. Chyou had even received a lovely silk dress embroidered with blossoms as a gift from Lady Wu. Peace had been established.

However, since the paperwork had been completed, the relevant messages sent to Grandmother, and the construction of their building well under way, they now had time to complete their *real* task.

Meeting with Master Jin.

The man who held such wondrous goods. The profits on the gold-grade rice already justified everything they were doing now. They had completely sold out of all three hundred bags.

Chyou had their profit reports, as well as the estimations for the grand expedition to the south that the cultivator had spoken of. It would be hellishly expensive . . . but much of her hoped he would still wish to commission the journey. Chyou still remembered the passion with which he had spoken about the rare plants of the south, as well as the way he had complimented her skills in management and logistics.

And the way he had implied that she would be a good fit to lead such an expedition.

Chyou shook her head and banished the fanciful thoughts. Instead, she returned to the present, concentrating on the lovely views.

The north looked quite a bit different from the lands around the capital. The hills were more jagged, and there were a great many more pines. The last vestiges of the leaves on the trees were more colourful as well, even if most of them had fallen off. The two of them had been travelling down the well-made road for several hours already, and it would likely be several more, but they should arrive at the village of Hong Yaowu by nightfall.

Eventually, they stopped to get off the horses and stretch their legs in what looked like an area meant specifically for camping. The road veered off to the relatively smooth area by a hill, and there were stone benches and an obvious fire pit prepared nearby.

They slid off the horses, and Chyou grimaced at the soreness, rubbing at her legs.

"Yeah, that happens," Bo said as he got out a pack of jerky and handed her some. Chyou took it, biting into the salty snack. "Be thankful the road is so nice."

"It doesn't hurt too badly," Chyou deflected, and Bo laughed.

"You're a trooper, sis," he said, shaking his head. "You're doing a lot better than I thought you would. Not a peep of complaint. You would have made a good caravaneer, if Granny hadn't poached ya."

Chyou flushed a bit at the compliment. Her brother didn't know exactly how much she enjoyed this. She had always loved the grand stories of adventure, and seeing the members of her family off when they departed for the wider world always made her a bit envious. She had listened to Grandmother's stories about the early days when she had been with the company. She'd wanted to do what they had, not that she had shared that ambition with anyone. Chyou had kept that particular dream to herself. It was, after all, infeasible. Especially with her role in the company. Grandmother had chosen her for a different purpose.

The Flower to entice bees. A valuable piece for the company to use, to expand their influence and prestige.

She didn't resent her role, not really. It was logical. She understood her grandmother's reasoning . . . and largely agreed with it. Chyou likely would have made the same decision her grandmother had made, had she been in that position.

She had a duty, and she would see it through . . . but now things were a bit different. Chyou had a chance to do something else. A small one, but she could not help hoping. Master Jin had changed things, and now the slightest hint of her old, childish passions was coming again to the fore.

She was in a good mood while her eyes roved over the hill. Her heart was infected with that childish whimsy, and she paused, noticing a small path. It cut between the trees and looked very enticing. She glanced furtively at her brother.

Bo sighed as he noticed her look. He chewed his lip.

"It *should* be safe," he allowed after a moment. "Just don't break your neck or something."

Chyou blinked, turning to stare at her brother, at his permissiveness. Normally she would have had to be escorted. Prudence warred with the part of her that lusted after the chance to wander on her own. A lone woman in the wilderness was a bit foolish, but the urge to explore and her brother's trust in her made it an easy choice. Deciding not to wait to see if he changed his mind, she started up the hill.

Alone.

Her heart beat happily as she marched up, her travelling robes swirling behind her in the gentle breeze. She hummed to herself as she wandered around, imagining herself in some other, far-off land. She crouched down near a stand of bare trees, looking at the strange mushrooms that were poking out of the soil, and ran a finger along the bark of a tree. Eventually, the path she followed took her to a large rock that looked out of place. It was a huge thing that stuck out of the ground, with bare and loose dirt around it, seeming oddly placed.

She shook her head and looked around, noticing the small gap in the trees and canopy.

The view from the top of the rock would be spectacular.

Something seized her. The rock was sloped on the back side and looked easy enough to climb. Her palm, almost unbidden, landed, seeking handholds.

Her well-manicured hands with glossy brightly painted fingernails gripped the rocks, ready to pull. She stared at her hands gripping on the rock, then down at her pristine clothes. Despite the travel, she had managed to ensure that she looked as always . . . the Flower of the Azure Jade Trading Company.

The desire to climb the rock fell away.

Chyou sighed and let go of the rock. She was about to meet Master Jin again. She would have to be presentable, and scuffed hands and dirty clothes from rock climbing were hardly acceptable.

She patted the rock twice, then set back down the hill, her good mood dampened.

It was evening when they reached the quaint little village, nestled in the hills. The villagers were curious about them but settled down when Bo said they had been invited by Master Jin.

They ended up sleeping in the house of the village chief, Hong Xian. The man was polite and soft-spoken . . . and another one of those men who looked like they should have been living in the capital, instead of out here.

He had seemed rather distracted, however, and for all that he was a fine host, he made himself scarce after fulfilling his duties.

They settled down and slept in the surprisingly comfortable beds, partaking of the man's hospitality, and then left first thing in the morning.

→

The next day was damp and foggy. It had rained during the night and clouds still covered the sky as they followed the road that would take them to Master Jin's home.

They were in a relatively good mood at the start, but as they travelled onwards and the sky remained overcast, there was a change in atmosphere.

The fog got denser. The trees had shed most of their leaves, and their spindly branches seemed to loom over the pair of travellers.

Chyou felt her heart pump faster as she shivered. Her brother's eyes darted around.

"This place feels strange, doesn't it?" he mused, his body tense.

There was a sudden rustling behind them. A screech sounded in the air followed by the deeper sound of an owl's hooting.

Chyou felt the hairs on the back of her neck stand on end.

"It's a little . . . unnerving," she admitted.

She looked to her brother, who had slowed their pace. He had a frown on his face. He glanced down to check on his steed. The horse seemed alert but remained relaxed.

Bo patted the side of his horse's neck. He turned to her. "Always trust the animals. They'll know before you if something is up," her brother stated sagely. "Whether it's a freak storm or a beast about."

Chyou was no fool; she knew all about them. These were the finest steeds money could buy. Grass Sea Horses, known for their sensitivity to Qi and their protective nature. If there had been any foul creature or something with ill intent in these woods, the horses would have turned tail and fled long ago. It was a recurring story from most of their caravaneers; if the animals were nervous, everybody was on high alert. They had saved many lives that way.

Chyou nodded.

"Besides, Master Jin wouldn't ask us to come here while having something that could potentially kill us living around his house, *right*?" Bo asked.

"That does seem rather counterproductive," Chyou agreed, letting out a small nervous titter before glancing up at the gnarled branches overhead.

They looked like skeletal fingers.

She shivered again and turned back to the foggy road.

The ominous feeling didn't get any better as they travelled farther down the path. They didn't stop and get off to rest, simply eating some jerky on the road. Her brother complained about the meal often, but Chyou rather liked the taste . . . even if she couldn't enjoy it at the moment as her eyes darted around the forest.

With the fog and the dark clouds, it felt like night despite it still being fairly early.

Chyou felt the tension slowly mounting . . . until they noticed pillars rising from the gloom.

"Look, I think that's our destination," she said, pointing, relief flooding her.

"See, no problem, no problem. Just a bit of fog," her brother said.

Chyou took a deep breath and shook her head. He was right, it was just a bit of foolish fear.

They rode up the path, and the mist broke enough so that they could see more of the fence, rising up taller than the tallest men. It was a sturdy construction formed out of what looked like entire trees.

As they got closer, more of the imposing, looming logs came into sight, swirls of mist crawling over the dense pine logs. Each one was topped with a roundish object that they were just starting to make out from the gloom—

Chyou's breath froze in her throat when the fog lifted enough to let her see what the bulbous things were.

A face, twisted in agony, stared back at her from atop one of the pillars. Its eyes had been torn out, forming two hollow, gaping pits that stared into her soul. Its face was twisted and withered, like it had been baking in the sun.

The visage of a damned man.

"Ancestors in heaven!" Bo exclaimed. The siblings yanked on the reins, pulling their horses to a stop at the macabre sight. Each post was topped with another head, barely visible through the gloom.

Chyou felt bile crawl up her throat as she looked on in horror. She felt numb when she stared at the head, glaring blankly down at them.

The softest smiles hid the most dangerous men. Master Jin's cheerful smile came back to her—he'd looked more like a farmer than a powerful master, yet here proof lay before her of the terror of cultivators. She knew a man couldn't be that powerful and remain kindhearted.

Her breath came out in pants as she continued to stare, transfixed.

Finally, she tore her eyes away and looked at her brother.

Bo was white as death, his attention consumed by the cadaver. He swallowed thickly, and both of them flinched when the owl hooted again.

Finally, he turned to look at her. "Do we run?" he asked in a small voice.

Her breath came short and shallow. She licked her lips.

"We have a job to do," she declared. "Like you said, it's bad business to kill us, isn't it?" she said with more bravery than she felt.

They would meet with Master Jin. They *would* accomplish their mission—no matter how terrifying that mission had suddenly become.

Chyou struggled to swallow the acid in her throat, her image of the smiling man who had shared with her a grand vision of an expedition that she could head dying an ugly death. They gripped the reins tighter and started forwards, eyes locked onto the heads. Even as the sky was becoming lighter, the clouds moving away from the sun, all they could feel was darkness.

A beam of sunlight broke through the canopy, burning away some of the mist and revealing the corpse's green, speckled skin, as well as the stem on top.

Chyou blinked, the terror vanishing like the mist.

And then she wheezed, letting out the breath that had stuck in her throat. Beside her, her brother, noticing what she had seen, broke into laughter that grew into body-bending howls.

They weren't heads. They were *squashes.*

Squashes carved with faces. The rest of them were revealed as the sun broke through the clouds. Some had leering grimaces and others jaunty smiles. One looked like a smirking fox, and still another was carved into the shape of a flower.

The one in front of them, of the screaming man, was carved so realistically that she had to praise whoever had done it . . . even if the effect was *wholly* disturbing. It looked *real.*

The one on the next post appeared like it had been carved by a child, a dopey, smiling face of crooked lines.

"I thought I was going to *piss* myself!" Bo gasped, staring at them.

Chyou chuckled alongside him, relief flooding through her body. The broken image of Master Jin quickly repaired itself. Perhaps there was some manner of festival he had celebrated, or perhaps they were warding talismans? Chyou didn't know, but they looked quite good now that she knew what they were.

The two of them approached the gate, looking at all the different carved faces. The vision of horror was now just a passing amusement. There were two signs hanging from the large post.

One was of a maple leaf, the same one on the back of Master Jin's shirt. The other was a sign—

"'Beware of Chicken'?" Bo asked, staring at the sign. "Who is going to be scared off with that?"

Chyou frowned. "Didn't he have a chicken with him in the city?"

Her brother considered it. "Well, if it's a Spirit Beast, then maybe . . ."

"Indeed. This Fa Bi De is a Spirit Beast," a smooth, deep voice intoned. Both of them startled, glancing up at the fence, where there was indeed a magnificent rooster.

A magnificent rooster, with a fox-fur vest and a silver pendant, that *spoke.*

"Guan Chyou. Guan Bo. Welcome to this Fa Ram, guests of our Master," the rooster declared, sweeping into a bow.

Both Chyou and her brother stared at the chicken blankly.

He . . . *knew their names*. The siblings glanced at each other, a little of the eerie feeling crawling back up their spines.

Tentatively, they returned the bow.

"Excellent. Please, come in," the rooster said primly, beckoning them through the open gate.

→

Chyou hadn't known what to expect, venturing into a cultivator's home. Were there to be floating islands? Strange energy fields? Any other manner of things?

Instead . . . instead she got something that looked almost mundane. Yet just because there were no obviously cultivator things didn't mean the view wasn't breathtaking. The sun had risen fully, burning through the clouds and dispelling most of the fog, revealing the sight from the top of the hill.

A grand manor was nestled on the small island between two rivers, surrounded by a carpet of red leaves. It was a strange-looking house, defying most of the conventional wisdom of architecture and the Imperial Styles. It was not enclosed by a wall but rather open.

It looked welcoming and inviting, despite the strange style. A wall would have ruined it, somehow.

There were several buildings nearby as well as a few homes, likely for servants. In the distance she could see barren rice fields, and farther out were deep, wild woods. Farther back, there was another set of buildings against the river, already belching smoke into the air.

The path to the house was lined with garlands of red persimmons and black bark, as well as more of the gourds and squashes, all carved into various leering faces. The rooster noticed their curious looks.

"Ah, we have just celebrated the Hallowed End. It was quite an enjoyable festival," the rooster stated. "You must partake of the squash pie. We still have some left."

"We . . . would be delighted to?" Bo asked, a slight tremor belying her brother's nervousness.

"Indeed, the fruits of Fa Ram are a delight." The rooster paused, turning to them. "You may leave your horses here. Brother Chun Ke shall see to their feed and water."

They both obeyed, sliding off their steeds at the bridge to the island and removing their packs.

Chyou had only a moment to think on who "Brother Chun Ke" could be when a boar that was nearly as tall as *her* trotted around the house and chuffed. The massive, fierce-looking creature had three enormous scars that ran down his face and tusks large enough that they could gore bears.

Chyou and her brother froze up as the great, rust-red beast bowed politely, then sniffed at them in curiosity. He paused for a moment considering them before he let out an approving *oink* and then turned to their horses and made a happy-sounding chuff while he trotted towards a large red building.

Their horses followed behind without a second thought.

Well . . . there was the strangeness of cultivators. As if the talking chicken wasn't enough, Chyou thought as the boar opened the door to what had to be a barn. She watched, a bit dazed, when the massive creature left to tend to their mounts as if he did it every day.

The rooster clucked, and they both flinched, breaking out of their shock. Bi De moved forward and held open the door to the house for them.

"This way, please," the rooster stated simply. "You may wait here while I inform the Master of your arrival."

"Of course, we don't want to keep Master Jin waiting," Bo declared nervously, putting on his charming smile. Chyou took off her hat, quickly fixing her hair. Her brother stepped behind her and gave her a once-over before nodding to her.

"Good?" she whispered as they approached the cavernous doorway.

"As good as it'll get. Your hair is fine, even with the damp. And *everybody* knows you don't look your best after hard travel," Bo agreed. "Besides, he struck me as the kind of man who wouldn't care if we showed up wearing rags."

Chyou had to agree. In the entryway, she quickly took the waterproof wrapping off the sheaves of paper, and they both removed their shoes as the rooster disappeared farther down the hall.

Five minutes later, he returned, just as they'd managed to finish their preparations. She took a breath, then stepped through the door.

Master Jin was waiting for them, seated at a table, in a warm, inviting room.

"Guan Bo. Guan Chyou. Good to see you both," he said, rising. He had a smile on his face as always, nodding to both of them. Chyou couldn't help smiling back at him. She and her brother bowed respectfully, even as Chyou's eyes darted around the room, taking in the others.

They were an odd collection of . . . *people*. If that was even the right word to use. The first of them caused Chyou to raise her eyebrow: a prim-looking pig with a brush in her mouth and a ledger open in front of her. She didn't know how a pig could look prim, but she did. The pig glanced up and set her brush aside to bow silently to the siblings before returning to her task. There was a wild-looking man a bit like a monkey with his own ledger beside the pig; he smiled and bowed as well. Chyou assumed they were like the rooster and the boar, both servants of Master Jin.

Two women were present as well. One was dressed in plain robes, though Chyou could see the maple leaf and rice sheaf upon her back. She had green hair and an unfortunate amount of freckles covering her nose. Likely the maid Bo had mentioned. She was tending to the fire and warming up water in a large teapot.

The second woman nearly made Chyou trip over herself. She was perhaps the most beautiful person that Chyou had ever laid eyes on, the kind of beauty that struck men dumb. The woman eyed them briefly, seeming a bit disinterested as she sat off to the side, reading.

So *that* was Master Jin's wife. No wonder he was completely uninterested in Chyou.

"Was the trip all right?" Master Jin asked as he led them to the table.

"It was very peaceful, Master Jin," Chyou assured him with a smile as they were invited to sit down, and the freckled maid came to the table with cups of tea.

There was a slight swell to her belly that didn't look like fat. The woman smiled at Chyou, who nodded absently, dismissing the servant . . . before she realised something. Her eyes darted to the other woman.

. . . hadn't Master Jin said his wife was pregnant?

"Yes, it was a completely uneventful journey, Master Jin," her brother agreed. "And I must say, it's excellent to see you and your lovely wife again." He had a bright smile on his face as he nodded to the beautiful woman.

The beautiful woman who very conspicuously *wasn't* pregnant.

Both the beautiful woman and Master Jin froze.

Master Jin's freckle-faced wife raised an eyebrow. "Oh? When did you two get married?" she asked blandly.

Her brother's face paled.

CHAPTER 17

THE DRAGON'S ATTENTION

The world slowed to a crawl. The look of mounting horror on her brother's face filled her eyes.

It was like when, during a party at the provincial capital, a man had addressed the head clerk's *mistress* as his wife. This was that same moment all over again. The stunned silence. The dawning realisation . . . then the *explosion* that was sure to come. The woman's strident voice . . . as well as the mistress's *husband's* howl of outrage.

Later, what Grandmother had referred to as "a shit show" had eventually led to an assassination.

And her brother had just made the exact same mistake.

But with cultivators.

It was an insult beyond insults, worse if perhaps it revealed something Master Jin had wanted to keep quiet. They might have possibly brought damages to their Honoured Customer. Grandmother would have *both* of their heads.

If they even survived the next few moments.

Chyou woodenly turned her head back to the woman, who was *very much not a maid.* Chyou had been so distracted by the Spirit Beasts that she hadn't noticed the perfect poise and presence of Hong Meiling. She was certainly no heavenly beauty, yet the aura that surrounded her was hard and commanding.

Hong Meiling felt like Chyou's grandmother.

The woman's eyes were hard gemstones, sharpened to razor edges and gleaming in the light of the house as she stared at Bo's horrified face. Chyou quietly cursed her brother, and *every single one* of her male ancestors for producing him, even as she got ready to kowtow and beg for her life. Her stomach churned unpleasantly as the woman examined them both, eyes shifting from one to the other, seemingly trying to decide whether to destroy them.

And then she *giggled.*

It was a light titter, surprisingly adorable coming from her. The oppressive aura that had been emanating from Hong Meiling faded, and then there was just a woman.

"I'm sorry, but both of your faces—!" the woman got out before starting to laugh in earnest. *That* was followed up by a chuckle from the man who looked a bit like a monkey, and he then also started to laugh.

Even the beautiful woman . . . who looked frighteningly similar to the images of the Demon-Slaying Orchid, Cai Xiulan—and considering Chyou's luck probably *was*—snorted and shook her head.

Her brother started breathing again as he shot up from his seat and bowed so quickly he slammed his head against the table.

"Please, forgive this Guan Bo for his stupidity! He meant no insult, yet his blind eyes have caused shame upon himself and his family name!"

That just got the woman and the man to laugh harder.

"People were giving Xiulan a hard time at the market, so I stopped correcting them when they asked if she was my wife," Master Jin interjected, confirming Chyou's suspicions as to the identity of the *mistress*. "Really, it's not Bo's fault."

Master Jin's face was twisted into a compassionate wince as he clapped Bo on the shoulder.

Her brother raised his head, staring up as Master Jin defended him. He looked like he was about to cry, and Chyou let out the breath she had been holding, her heart still pumping in her chest.

"It is fine, Guan Bo. I forgive you. I had heard some of the rumours in Verdant Hill about Jin's 'beautiful wife' anyway." The lady of the house waved off the insult, and Bo bowed his head yet again.

The woman still had some measure of mirth in her eyes as she sat beside her husband.

"Senior Sister isn't the type to be upset over honest mistakes," Cai Xiulan said, and the part of Chyou that was still her grandmother's child filed that bit of information away. Her brother was still breathing hard even as the lady smiled at him. Master Jin, in his magnanimous kindness, poured Bo a cup of tea to calm his frayed nerves.

They settled in once more, and Chyou's heart finally started to slow from its frenzied beating.

Really, two scares in one day? She would say it was bad for her heart, but she actually felt quite . . . invigorated? No, she felt *good*. Satisfied.

"Okay. Introductions. This is my wife, Hong Meiling," Master Jin said as Lady Hong gave them a short bow. Chyou felt her mind restart when the name clicked into place. Hong? Like the village they had just passed through and the Elder who'd had them as guests under his roof?

"This is my good friend, Gou Ren, who was instrumental in growing this year's crop."

The monkeyish-looking man nodded politely. His eyes didn't linger on her for even a moment, and she immediately discarded several strategies that had worked with other young men. She decided on a course quickly, smiling professionally at the young man and giving him a bow of deference. If he had aided in growing the rice, he was a necessary contact.

"Next is Pi Pa, who does most of the ledgers and aids us with finances," Master Jin continued, introducing the pig as casually as one would any functionary. It took her a second to parse the name, as Master Jin had slurred his speech strangely when he said it.

'*Young Sir. Young Miss. A pleasure.*' The pig greeted them with the diction of a proper court lady, her bow elegant and refined despite her . . . unusual form.

"Ri Zu is Meiling's apprentice." He gestured at the little rat near Lady Hong. "And this is Wa Shi," Master Jin declared, tapping a jar beside the table that Chyou hadn't noticed. A carp popped his head out of the water and nodded in their direction. "He's here to go over all the calculations."

Master Jin's speech was formal as he introduced his household to them. He sounded more like a merchant than a cultivator, matter-of-fact and businesslike. Compared to the noble etiquette of reciting each servant's full list of titles and duties, she could almost say *brief*, but his manner indicated he was certainly close with all of them.

"And last is Cai Xiulan," Master Jin said. He looked like he was about to say something else, a slight smile on his face, before he just shook his head and returned his gaze to them both. "I thought we could discuss things here first, then have some dinner. That is, if you're okay to start, Bo?"

Her brother took a final calming breath and rolled his shoulders, his long experience as a merchant reasserting itself. Bo looked up with a nervous smile.

"I'm fine, Master Jin. Do not worry yourself on my account," he said, "And I once again apologise for any discord my assumptions have caused, Lady Hong."

Her brother then cleared his throat as he finished getting out the scrolls and, after hesitating for a moment, handed one of the first set over to the pig. "This is a preliminary assessment of all sales and profits," he stated, standing up and preparing to begin.

Master Jin nodded as the pig daintily opened the first scroll.

"First, on the maple syrup . . ." Bo started.

↔

Wa Shi pretended he was going through the numbers as the Boss's guests talked. He had finished them all a while ago, but there was no sense in letting people know he could work faster . . . that way just led to Pi Pa trying to hand him more work.

The best thing to do was to slack off most of the time, then if somebody *really* needed it one could "beat expectations" by being "faster than normal."

Truly, Wa Shi was the most brilliant dragon to ever exist.

He glanced back at the two merchant people. They were strange folk . . . but they were in the business of transporting food. Thus, they were important.

It was mildly impressive how much work went into transporting the Boss's rice. It would end up ten times the original price at the end. However, considering the transport costs, that was to be expected—and the merchants had to make some coin for themselves too. Taking that into consideration meant the deal looked pretty good.

Wa Shi absently memorized the math formations they used, tinkering with the numbers they gave. These merchants were skilled at mathematics, and Wa Shi had to acknowledge their skill. There wasn't really anything he could see offhand to improve with raw number crunching, as the Boss called it, so he turned to look back at his scroll as they went into a more in-depth explanation for Bro Gou Ren. He was sitting in so that he could get some experience with these matters . . . the Boss didn't want any of his underlings getting taken advantage of, so Bro Gou Ren had to learn.

He watched as they brought out another page with warehouses and continued on with their plan to expand into Green Stone Forest, Howling Fang Mountain, and Yellow Rock Plateau, which finally concluded their presentation.

The Boss nodded and glanced at Pi Pa, who had just finished her own work. Wa Shi took a look over her shoulder and nodded his approval. Her speed left much to be desired, but she had gotten everything on the cost analysis paper right. It was just a lot of simple operations, but when one wasn't as magnificent as Wa Shi there could be errors, so he peeked to make sure.

'*Everything appears to be in order, Master*,' Pi Pa decreed.

Which was his cue to gaze at the much larger set of numbers like he was still trying to study them.

'*All their numbers are right, Boss*,' he said after an appropriately long moment. He had to make it look like he was giving it his undivided attention.

The Boss looked at the Missus for her approval. She nodded.

"Then everything appears to be in order. Fifteen hundred bags of gold-grade rice for sixty silver a bag," the Boss confirmed, placing his seal at the bottom of the page and finalizing the deal that would allow others to taste some of the best food this world had to offer.

Which was disappointing, really; Wa Shi would not get to eat as much of it . . . but others had to taste things too, if only to bask in the superiority of Fa Ram's ingredients.

"Thank you for your continued association with our Azure Jade Trading Company, Master Jin."

Both of the Boss's new underlings bowed to him, and Wa Shi took a moment to consider where to go next. His job was done, after all, and there were rocks to bask on!

And Chun Ke thought he'd found a new kind of nut. That was cause for celebration!

"Now . . . on to the topic of your suggested venture south; my sister will explain," the one called Bo said, gesturing to the cold-looking red-haired woman. She reminded him a bit of Pi Pa. No-nonsense . . . *and boring*.

Until Bo mentioned the expedition. Then she seemed to swell, sitting up straighter. Her eyes took on a gleam, and she came alive as if she had been jolted by one of Wa Shi's bolts.

Oho? She's hiding her depths from this dragon's eyes? Impressive.

"After more research . . . we do believe that your expedition to the south is possible, Master Jin," she began, and the Boss leaned forward, curious. Wa Shi looked around to see if anybody else knew what she was talking about, but everybody else seemed just as confused.

"There is a route to the south of the Empire along the coast, albeit one rarely travelled, but I managed to obtain several sea charts as well as the diary of a captain and crew who survived the attempt. It's considered dangerous, but so far, from preliminary investigation, it seems to be extremely promising."

"Really? It's looking that feasible? How much time are you thinking to prepare?"

"Two years—perhaps a year and a half, if we focus fully on such an endeavour."

"That fast?" The Boss looked stunned.

"And just what is that expedition for?" the Missus asked, looking curiously at the young woman.

"There are several spices Master Jin wishes to obtain," Guan Chyou stated, which caught Wa Shi's attention completely.

'*You're going on an expedition to dangerous lands for food?*' he demanded.

Chyou looked at Wa Shi with an offended air. Seemingly outraged that he would dare ask.

"Yes, for food! Cacao pods, that Master Jin said can create a wondrous sweet dish! Vanilla, a flavour that he described as sublime! A hundred spices, and a hundred more luxuries await! Of course for food!" the woman exclaimed. "To go to the south and find these great treasures . . . Is that not worth the danger? Do you know how much people will pay for these treasures? What we could do?!"

Guan Chyou's eyes were now full of fire. He could see the desire in her gaze—she wanted to taste these wonderful things and was willing to brave any amount of danger to get them.

In that . . . she had Wa Shi's utmost respect. He bowed his head before her impassioned declaration.

There were still more treasures upon this earth. He was not yet strong enough to taste the moon . . . and if the Boss wanted these things bad enough to send this expedition that Guan Chyou waxed poetic about, then they must be truly delicious indeed.

And the more people with access to these things . . . the more dishes they would create, wouldn't they? Had not Wa Shi crafted delicacies, like pond-reed ice cream, after witnessing the Boss create his own? Had he not mixed the leftovers into glorious Everything Soup? Others surely could not match his genius . . . but they too should have the chance to craft wonders.

'*Magnificent! I, Wa Shi, approve of it! Tell me more about these southlands, Guan Chyou!*' he demanded.

The woman ruffled around in her pack for a moment before drawing out a beaten-up looking sheaf of papers.

"Captain Dulou Dalu says, here, upon first landing—" she began.

↔

Guan Chyou hit the bed face first. She was completely and utterly exhausted . . . but at least she had kept it together and made a good impression.

She had somehow ended up reading half of an explorer's journal to a bunch of cultivators, who had all sat and listened raptly, after calling in more animals . . . and the Young Mistress of the Misty Lake Sect as well.

And then Cai Xiulan had cooked dinner for them.

It was strange. It was surreal. It was something . . . *wonderful.*

After dinner they'd presented their gifts, which had been well-received. Bags of seed for Master Jin and several items for . . . his wife, *Hong Meiling.* Luckily, they had decided to forgo bringing dresses—which would have been far too large for Lady Meiling, labouring under the idea that Lady Cai was Master Jin's wife. Instead they brought various useful items for an expectant mother . . . cloth, a comb, and the most expensive piece: a silvered mirror.

Finally, they had been escorted to a guest house of sorts for the night by Chun Ke. It was a little one-room shack that still managed to feel homey. Despite the house's humble nature, she looked out through the small window out into the farm and felt . . . at peace.

Chyou sighed, feeling her eyes droop from the stress of the day.

"Well . . . that went pretty well, if I do say so myself," Bo declared brightly, looking at her from his bedroll. Always able to spring back from his mistakes, her brother.

He sounded entirely too chipper.

"The heavens favour children and fools."

Her brother just grinned. "The luck of the heavens is worth being a fool sometimes, no?"

Chyou grumbled into her pillow, but in her heart she could feel the thrill of it all. Adventure, the south, it would surely happen. The fantasies she had once had as a child . . . they would come true.

↔

"They were more interesting than I thought they would be," Meiling mused from her place on the couch, legs across my lap, as she stared at her reflection in the fine mirror we had gotten. "They recovered well, even if they did look like they were about to crack when we sent them off. Are you sure they'll be fine? The new guest house isn't finished."

"It's finished and furnished enough," I replied with a shrug. The little guest house was another addition I'd made recently because we were running out of beds. A lot more people were sleeping in my house than I had originally planned for, and even my old house was full up. At this rate, I'd have to build an entire boardinghouse . . . but for now the newest structure would have to do. It was more a hotel room than anything. A place to sleep, but not a place to live.

And while Chyou and Bo were resting, I got to examine my new presents. I grinned at the bags of seed on the table. Peas and beans from Green Stone Forest.

"I think I quite like those two," my wife decided, as she put down the mirror and sat up. "They were nice . . . and good entertainment. I should see if I can get a copy of that journal . . ." She leaned into me as she thought, her gaze going round the room before finally landing on Xiulan.

I stared warily at the devilish smirk that stole across her features.

"They also had another interesting story . . ." Meiling mused, crawling along the couch towards her. "Something about a wife . . . ? Maybe there was some truth to their words? You two *have* been going out at night together to the forest—" Meiling gasped dramatically and raised a hand to her forehead. She swooned, lying in Xiulan's lap and propping her feet on mine once again. "Oh no! You truly are going behind my back for a secret tryst!"

Xiulan's head slowly turned to Meiling as the smaller woman leaned across her lap, poking her in the side.

"How dare you, Cai Xiulan! After all I've done for you~"

Xiulan stared at me. I nodded in solidarity.

Xiulan grabbed the floppy, half-finished witch's hat that was on the table and shoved it over Meiling's face at the same time I pinned her legs, poking a finger into her side.

"*You* are a dirty old man, Sister," Xiulan said calmly, while Meiling's muffled giggles emerged from the hat.

CHAPTER 18

THE SENIOR DISCIPLE

Several Months Ago

Right beside Crimson Crucible City, in the Raging Waterfall Gorge province, there was a mountain. The lonely Cloudy Mountain, stood dominant and taller than all its brothers, its peak perpetually shielded from view by a ring of clouds.

Behind that ring of clouds, obscured from view, sat the Cloudy Sword Sect: one of the greatest Sects in the Empire, by reputation and the might of its disciples. The indomitable Cloudy Sword Sect, the masters of the Raging Cloudy Sword Formation. The bane of demons and the wicked alike.

Archaic stone halls and blue roofs dominated the mountain peak. From a distance, it looked deceptively simple. It appeared almost ancient, like a tomb . . . And yet it was a tomb as pristine as the day it was completed. Its walls were covered in carvings done in traditional style. It depicted clouds and scenes of generals and cultivators battling demons, yet it was, for all the skill and all the detail, understated. No colour was upon the carvings—no inlays of gemstones or gold leaf as was the case with many other Sects. The designs were simple. Understated. They matched the harsh, stark beauty of the mountain peak.

Senior Disciple Lu Ri could not help the smile that overtook his face as he climbed the mountain, staring up at the enormous gates, the Gate of Clouds, carved with the scene of a grand battle against the demons. The blowing wind tousled his hair and threatened to remove his simple straw hat, which, if one looked closely, had a circular hole in it that had been patched at some point. He planted a hand on it to stop it from blowing away.

Lu Ri could have simply leapt up the mountain, or used one of the artifacts to ferry him to the top . . . And yet it somehow felt wrong to enter that way.

So instead, he had come as if a pilgrim. From Crimson Crucible City, through the Clouded Forest, and now, up the hundred thousand steps to the main entrance.

His stride quickened. He'd spent months away from the Sect. Through the trials of tracking down a single man, and then again, to the Imperial Army Headquarters to deliver a reply. His travels to find Jin Rou had been frustrating in the extreme . . . yet as he made his final approach to the gates, he could feel all that frustration dissipate.

He had accomplished his mission. In crafting the Plum Blossom's Shadow, the lessons of the Honoured Founders made more sense than ever.

And . . . he had acquired a rather delicious treat to pair with his tea now, after a long day of managing the Inner Sect Disciples.

The Honoured Founders said that small pleasures were permissible, so long as they did not lead to excess.

He took a breath as he reached the great gates and laid his hands upon them. As tall as any Imperial Palace, they were currently shut tight as a precaution—yet as he filled them with his Qi and pushed, they opened for him easily . . . much more easily than he remembered them opening.

Lu Ri nodded, his hypothesis confirmed. He had felt the change as he used his Qi more and more to travel quickly. The months in a low-Qi area, where he'd constantly controlled his strength as to not shatter the warding stones the Azure Hills used, had improved his control by a small margin.

While not a massive advancement, it was still more growth than he had expected from his time in such a Qi-starved area. He would have to continue with the exercise. It was intensely uncomfortable to have such a tight grip on his Qi, and yet discomfort was to be endured, and then mastered.

As he passed the great gates the sound of the wind cut out, and the chill, enough to kill a mortal within minutes, dissipated. The air was brisk and invigorating instead of biting, and the silence lent itself to quiet contemplation.

"Brother Lu Ri! You have returned to us!" his fellow Senior Disciple, Zhao Haoyu, exclaimed. The one on duty to the gate had a truly vast pile of paperwork he was going through, working alongside four other disciples. "Was your mission a success?"

Lu Ri smiled and nodded.

His fellow Senior Disciple brightened. "Tell me the parts that you can later, over a drink. Elder Ran is within the Great Hall."

Lu Ri bowed his head in thanks and turned to the street.

Within the Sect, the style of architecture continued. The streets of the compound were wide and open to the blazing sun. Each building was uniform, but they held an air of quiet dignity and tranquility.

Several disciples spoke quietly within the Outer Sect dormitories, deep in discourse over a scroll. The walls of the building had been freshly cleaned, and there was not a crack in sight.

Lu Ri's smile widened.

Behind the dormitories were gardens. There were fields of herbs that, when hit by the sun, seemed to shimmer like jewels in the light, a slight iridescent sheen upon their leaves. Here too were disciples, watering and tending to the Lowly Spiritual Herbs, which fueled their early cultivation and healed their injuries.

He passed the halls and the training grounds upon his path up the mountain. He noted an Inner Disciple unleashing a devastating combo upon one of his juniors. Lu Ri's eyes narrowed, his ire roused at the sight . . . only for the young man to pop back up after he fell, frown, and retake his stance, shifting his legs slightly under the hawklike gaze of another Senior Disciple. The woman was supervising several pairs today. The Inner Disciple nodded before the man and demonstrated the first move for the boy.

The Junior bowed to his Senior, thanking him for the pointer.

A marked difference from before, Lu Ri was pleased to note. Pointers truly *were* pointers instead of thinly veiled excuses for the strong to bully the weak.

Lu Ri continued to the Great Hall. Higher up on the mountain were the rooms of the Inner Disciples, and farther still the rooms of the Core Disciples and Elders, yet even as one went to the highest peaks and those within got their own private rooms instead of a communal dormitory . . . the same stark architecture remained. There was no gold here, and the only treasures were those that could aid in cultivation.

Finally, Lu Ri came upon the Great Hall and opened the doors. There he beheld Elder Ran as he went over reports. The man glanced up the moment Lu Ri entered, and the Elder nodded with satisfaction.

"The last task is the eastern annex. Continue with the work that we must do, for it is almost complete." The disciples around him bowed as Elder Ran gave his command, his voice soft yet heard by all. "I commend the work thus far. Distribute the rewards to the skilled and the worthy at the end."

"Yes, Elder Ran," the Senior Disciples intoned.

"Now, you are dismissed. Lu Ri, come, walk with me," the Elder commanded, rising from his seat and gesturing to Lu Ri.

Lu Ri obeyed, walking behind the Elder through the wooden hall filled with the weight of history. They went past the Wall of Martyrs and, as was tradition, they both bowed to it before coming to a balcony.

"Your mission was a success," Elder Ran stated.

"Yes, Elder Ran. I have found Jin Rou and, as per my commands, did not push when he refused to return. However, he provided me with a map and a means to contact him later." Lu Ri produced the piece of paper and held it out for the Elder, who took it and nodded. "Further, I have delivered his reply to the Imperial Army."

The Elder studied the page for a moment before turning to Lu Ri.

"How was his cultivation?" Elder Ran asked.

"Intact . . . and much stronger than when he left us. Yet at the same time it was . . . *strange.* Subtle, yet encompassing."

Elder Ran nodded, letting out a small breath. "His temperament?"

"He was polite and kind. I do not believe that he bears any ill will against the Sect. I do not believe that he spoke any falsehoods when he said that we could contact him if need be."

The Elder studied Lu Ri for a moment longer before clasping his hands in respect.

"Then . . . I commend you, Lu Ri. Your diligence and skill may well have saved the Sect much hardship and much face. Such diligence is to be rewarded. Go into the Vault of the Lonely Cloud; take any three items within as you so choose," the Elder commanded, and Lu Ri had to duck his head to keep the Elder from seeing the surprise on his face. *Three* treasures from the Vault of the Lonely Cloud? *That was absurd!*

"Furthermore, you are to have access to the Skypeak for three months."

The Skypeak, where the Qi of the Cloudy Mountain was thickest, and the most potent for cultivating and refining the Raging Cloudy Sword Formation.

Lu Ri could only bow at the generosity of his Elder.

"You are relieved from your normal duties until further notice, Senior Disciple. Collect your reward at your leisure."

The last words brought joy to his heart for a brief moment. Nothing but cultivation and study for the foreseeable future? It sounded like a heavenly reward.

And yet he paused. He thought back to the Plum Blossom's Shadow and their diligence . . . of his own thoughts on crafting a superior organisation, and he found the idea of complete isolation not as appealing as it once had been.

Teaching and commanding the mortals had proven more fulfilling than he had thought. And now . . . with the rest of the disciples once more attending lectures and performing meditations . . .

He wished to be the Senior Disciple that he had desired to be.

"Elder Ran?"

"Yes, Senior Disciple Lu Ri?"

"I would like to return to my duties, Elder Ran. I would aid our Cloudy Sword Sect, as a Senior Disciple."

It was an insult and foolishness to refuse to meditate where the founders had once found enlightenment.

And yet Lu Ri felt that he must.

Elder Ran's face was stone . . . until he broke out in a smile.

"You are a true disciple of the Cloudy Sword Sect, young man. I do believe my Master, may her soul rest in peace, would have enjoyed your company."

A hand clasped upon Lu Ri's shoulder.

"Go then, Senior Disciple. Return to your duties."

→

"And thus, the Honoured Founders meditated for three days upon the question: Is the Law to be immutable?"

Lu Ri stared out over both the Outer and Inner Disciples as he lectured, his voice carrying across the amphitheater. The disciples' eyes were alert, their minds open to the discourse of the Honoured Founders. He could see their consideration of his words, as they sought to make sense of them, to understand them.

It was a refreshing change. The amphitheater was completely clean, the smooth stones shining. The overgrown planters had been fixed and replaced, providing shade.

"Now go and meditate upon this question yourself. I will be available tonight to those who have questions regarding the third volume of *Meditations of Zhong Haoyi.*"

Lu Ri watched the disciples walk off, all of them beginning to discuss among themselves the question he had posed to them.

It was a particularly difficult one, in Lu Ri's mind.

Yet he smiled as they departed, returning to his own quarters.

Within those quarters was a map. A map of every road in Raging Waterfall Gorge, and rough travel times between locations. In his mind, he constructed depots and rest areas, spread regularly along the map.

Beside the map was a list. A list of requirements, and a command structure.

All for delivering mail.

CHAPTER 19

GROWING UP

"Well . . . that was kind of easy, wasn't it?" Yun Ren asked his brother as they stared at the corpse of the deer.

Normally a hunt could take days of stalking a particularly prime buck, or traversing along trails checking traps for rabbits and other small game. To be honest, the ease of it disheartened him a bit. The thrill and, dare he say it, the challenge, was gone. The duo had set out early in the morning in the predawn light. Mist still shrouded the ground in the area of the forest they had wandered to on the edge of Jin's property. Yun Ren had easily picked up the trail of a buck and tracked it down in less than an hour. A single shot into the side of the deer, which months ago he would have called *art*, ended their hunt. The beast hadn't felt a thing, simply collapsing. That was how hunts went nowadays.

He was lucky he had other things he enjoyed, or life would have quickly gotten very boring.

"It's probably better this way," Gou Ren replied, crouching down and bowing his head in respect for the fallen animal. Yun Ren did the same, silently thanking it for its contribution to their lives.

The moment passed and they stood, getting out the rest of their equipment. It wasn't like the hunt was *really* the reason they went out together. Just one of them venturing forth would be enough . . . but they hadn't actually been spending that much time together ever since everything that had happened at the Dueling Peaks. So a hunt had been in order, to catch up with each other.

"So how did that meeting go last night, anyway?" Yun Ren asked as he tied a rope around the deer's legs and then hoisted it over a tree branch one-handed to begin to clean and bleed it.

His brother grimaced. "Let's just say I'm glad Jin is handling all that stuff. It's going to be a pain in the ass when I have to do it by myself. Still, I learned a lot. I think."

Yun Ren considered the serious look on his little brother's face.

Oh, that wouldn't do.

"Look at my little brother. All grown up and bein' a man, learnin' how to take care of his own farm." Yun Ren wiped an imaginary tear from his eye, Gou Ren snorted in response.

"Shaddup, pinky," he retaliated halfheartedly, to which Yun Ren chuckled. The dye Meimei had put in Yun Ren's hair had mostly washed out already, leaving only a slightly pink tint. The colour had been incredibly vibrant, and after his outrage had died down it had actually been kind of nice. He had no idea how Meimei had even *made* that colour. He had a hunch it was crafted out of some of those mushrooms Bi De had brought back from his own journey, which meant he'd certainly have to steal some. That said, washing out after only a day? Meimei had been downright restrained. Maybe her pregnancy had mellowed her out. Yun paused at that thought. Probably not.

Yun Ren stepped back from the deer, considering the best place to cut. It was a healthy specimen, good and strong, with lots of meat on it.

"Year's almost over. Are you thinking of getting your own land soon? Got somewhere scoped out?"

His brother paused at the question in the middle of sharpening a knife.

"I don't . . . well, I don't have anything right now . . ."

Yun Ren raised an eyebrow at his brother. "You're not just going to jump into getting your own place? I thought with Xianghua and all . . ."

Gou shook his head. "I don't think I'm ready. It's a lot of work, and I'm still learning. I can grow gold-grade rice, but I'm not ready for all the rest, not yet. I . . . don't think I can just jump into getting my own place, yanno?"

"Fair enough."

"And, *well* . . . I like it here. Jin is cool with me hanging around, and Meimei is too. I've got my own house already, and even if I'm not the Master of my own land yet, it's still a good place to live."

"I don't deny that," Yun Ren agreed as he made the first incision, gutting the deer. Hells, even he had thought of coming over and working on the farm full time. "But is your girl all right with it?"

"Yeah, we talked about it. She said it was a good idea. We have to do a lot of planning. Between her Sect stuff and the farm . . . well, we need to decide where to settle down. What about Biyu and you?"

Yun Ren paused at the mention of Biyu, the crystal carver he was courting. An image of the woman's beautiful eyes popped into his head.

He didn't actually know what to do. He liked Biyu. A lot. Her passion for crystal carving was mesmerising. She had great taste in food and was, to be honest, everything he'd ever really wanted in a girl. His plan was to court and marry her, as tradition dictated.

Eventually.

But the thought of just settling down immediately wasn't appealing. There was so much out there. So much to see and experience. Now with the crystal he could make art, record glorious images like the ones he had taken on their trip. The Dueling Peaks, for all the fear and terror, had given him a true taste of the vast world out there.

"I . . . don't know? See if I can bring her up north?" he finally said.

They lapsed into silence, working on the carcass, both of them lost in thought. It didn't take that long. After they got the skin off they started butchering in earnest.

"Hey, uh, Yun?" his brother asked.

"Yeah?"

"What kind of recording crystal would you recommend?"

Yun Ren's eyes widened. "You're looking to buy one?" His brother had been a little interested before, but outright asking Yun Ren for one?

"Well, Jin had a good idea, you know? To record memories. I thought I'd get one to do the same," Gou Ren clarified.

Gou Ren had been using Jin's recording crystal more, especially when they had carved all the gourds. He had recorded them all, from Tigu's unsettlingly lifelike one to Chun Ke's gourd with a crooked smile. But mostly, he seemed to be sneaking recordings of Xianghua and Bowu.

Yun Ren could relate.

"They're pretty great, aren't they?" Yun Ren asked, tapping at the wonderful leather pouch that held the flat pane of crystal Yun Ren cherished. "But they're pretty pricey too, yanno? And the ones that can record more than just static images are *way* more expensive."

Gou Ren shrugged. "I can afford it. I got my cut of the cash for the harvest. It's shitloads of money . . . more than I kind of know what to do with."

Yun Ren nodded. It was a predicament he pondered often. His little recording sessions in the Dueling Peaks had netted him more cash in a week than he could have realistically seen for *years*, all from making portraits for rich people and cultivators. He didn't really know what to do with it all either.

It was novel, being wealthy, but he hadn't really had much time to enjoy it.

"And so I thought . . . Well, there are some things I wanna remember properly, and I was hoping you could teach me how to get some good recordings?"

Yun Ren grinned and clapped his brother on the shoulder.

"Deal. Some time in the winter, we'll head to Pale Moon Lake again, eh?" That, and it would be good to visit Biyu again. He hadn't seen her for just over three months. "Okay, so for a good crystal, Biyu says you gotta look for the facets that have . . ."

Yun Ren lectured on what he had found out about certain thicknesses of crystals, the way one placed their Qi into the crystal to capture an image, and the ways the colours could look subtly different . . .

His brother nodded along, listening as he worked on the carcass, letting Yun Ren's voice wash over him.

Soon enough, the deer was prepped and they made their way back to Jin's house. They walked through the misty forest, the leaves crunching under Gou Ren's heavy tread while Yun Ren made barely any sound at all. They had a good chat about autumn hunting and the difficulty they used to have with all the leaves alerting their prey—and the bears they had to run from as they desperately looked for one last meal before the snows set in. Both were things of the past now, but it was nice to reminisce.

Everybody else was still waking up—they got treated to the echoing thunder of Bi De's morning wake-up call.

However, there were two people waiting for them. Gou Ren put down his pack, filled with meat, at the sight of them.

Xianghua and her brother were already up, it seemed. She was carrying a steaming pot of tea ready to serve, clearly meant for them. Both were talking, but Xianghua looked up and tapped her brother, who brightened at the sight of them.

"Big Bro!" Bowu called, waving enthusiastically, and immediately broke into a full sprint. His sister followed behind him, a bit more sedately, with the teapot and a pair of cups, a brilliant smile on her face as she watched him run.

The woman had kept that smile ever since Bowu had started to walk without limping.

"Honoured Brother." Xianghua greeted him and poured out a cup of tea from the teapot. The whole "Honoured Brother" thing was a bit much . . . but Xianghua had gotten the respectful titles into her head. They'd probably die down soon, like with Xiulan.

Honestly? When Yun Ren thought about Xianghua, all he could think was that he liked her. She was a bit weird . . . but hells, in this madhouse, who wasn't? She fit right in as far as he was concerned, and was a regular riot when she started on the act she put on as a Young Mistress.

Yun Ren nodded politely and took the tea from her as Gou Ren spoke with Bowu, the younger man looking with interest at the deer meat.

". . . was wondering if you could take me hunting next time?" Yun Ren caught the tail end of the conversation between Bowu and Gou. He glanced back at the young man, who was looking hopefully up at Yun Ren's brother.

"Of course!" Gou Ren declared. "I'll show you every trick I've got!"

"It'll be a short lesson," Yun Ren snarked. His brother reached over and punched him in the shoulder, though Yun Ren immediately laughed it off.

"Gou Ren must surely have a thousand tricks, Honoured Brother," Xianghua said in Gou Ren's defence, and his brother flushed and smiled. "As cunning as the Great Sage Wukong!"

His brother's face fell at the reversal in fortunes, pouting . . . but unfortunately for him, he couldn't complain about being compared to a monkey. Xianghua genuinely seemed to think it was a compliment, and Gou Ren, after recovering, reached out for her, pulling her into his side.

With Bowu looking up at Gou and Xianghua at his side . . . Yun Ren's little brother didn't look so little anymore. His face was lit up in a way Yun had never seen. The trio looked like a family.

There was a small pang in Yun Ren's heart at the sight.

Gou Ren had a plan for the future and something that he wanted.

Yun Ren would miss the little boy who'd followed him everywhere, demanding piggyback rides. But the man in front of him looked pretty good too.

"Yo, Gou, I got the deer. You show Bowu how to string a bow, yeah?"

His brother perked up. "Really?"

Yun Ren grabbed the deer meat and punched him in the shoulder, a little smile on his face. His brother just seemed confused and tried to kick at him.

Yun Ren had to break into a sprint as Gou and Bowu gave chase, sticking his tongue out behind him.

→

They still had some time before breakfast, so Yun Ren went off to do his own thing.

He gently leaned a shining white sword against a log and placed a cup of tea before it. The sword was, even to his inexperienced eyes, a masterpiece. The inscription on the blade read Summer's Sky.

'*Summer's Sky thanks Eighth Master*,' the sword, a jian blade, intoned, speaking directly into his mind. It was a little weird and it tingled sometimes, but it wasn't unpleasant. The sword clacked. '*Another new blend? Approval.*'

"Elder Xian taught me how to make this one," Yun Ren said to the blade as he flexed his Qi, warming up the misty feeling in his gut until it felt like the sun's rays. The sword rattled in approval.

The strange, talking blade had technically been a gift. A gift from the fox Spirit Beast Nezan when Yun Ren had travelled near the Howling Fang Mountains. The sword had originally been a grave marker, but for some reason Nezan had given him the blade, which had belonged to the fox's departed friend. Not that Nezan had informed him of that. The trickster had hidden it under an illusion. Yun had thought it was an ordinary blade right up until the illusion had melted off mid-battle.

Absently, he reached back into his pouch and rubbed the inert chunk of stone that was Nezan—or at least a part of him. The fox had saved his life in that fight against Fenxian, but it had depleted Nezan's energy in this piece of his core and forced him to rest for a time. His self-proclaimed "Uncle" was still asleep.

He was getting a bit worried. Yun Ren would have to go up north and bug the old bastard if he stayed snoozing for too long.

Yun shook his head, and after giving the stone one last good rub, he turned to a large stone that he had been practising with. He closed his eyes, letting his Qi flow from his body to paint the building-sized rock like he had a hundred times before. This one was a favourite of his. And one of Tigu's favourite rocks too—the other side was covered in her carvings.

"Okay, what now?" he asked the sword. There was a twinge in the back of his eye, as Summer's Sky used his senses. It was a minute thing that he was getting better at noticing.

'Slightly more green. Approval.'

Yun Ren nodded, and the green tint on the section he was working on intensified. He gazed at the colours, some of which almost hurt to look at, and some he was certain weren't colours at all—purples and blues he could barely see.

The project had come about after Yun Ren asked how the sword, which had no physical eyes, could see things coming.

The answer had surprised him. Summer's Sky saw mostly through *his* eyes, which was the twinge he noticed, and the sword "saw" the "aura" of things.

He hadn't understood it, so he asked for a description.

A week later, he now had a rough approximation: spiraling geometric shapes that looked like shattered glass in colours so intense it made his eyes water.

"Is this really it?" Yun Ren asked.

'Indeed, Eighth Master. First time this question has been postulated to Summer's Sky. Interesting. Approval. Summer's Sky names you the most interesting Master after the Seventh.'

"I'll be second place with pride, then," Yun Ren declared. He had heard of his predecessor, the Summer's Sky Thunder. The woman whom Nezan had obviously loved and cherished.

The sword rattled happily as Yun Ren sat down beside it, staring up at the colours woven with illusions.

He sighed. Happy with a job well done.

He sat with the sword in companionable silence as the cold wind blew through skeletal trees. From his vantage point on the hill, he could see most of the farm. Jin was pointing out one of the storage buildings to the Azure Jade Trading Company people. He could see them nod along from here. He had no real opinion on the two, honestly. Only that Chyou's tale about the southlands had been interesting. She had a quite nice voice, from what he recalled when she'd described everything, and he could almost see it in his mind's eye. An expedition to the south. Something wondrous . . . and dangerous.

He mulled over the idea.

Finally, he shook his head and brushed off the thoughts of the future. "Come on, let's go through some moves again. I don't want to get kicked around so badly next time!" he said to Summer's Sky, the sword rattling as he stood.

'Eighth Master is improving. Your sparring partners are interesting and skilled.'

Yun Ren had taken to sparring with Tigu after the whole debacle at the Duelling Peaks. He had spent the entire time getting chased around by that Fengxian asshole, and had only escaped death because Jin had been there to stop it. There was nothing like nearly dying to light a fire under someone's ass, so he'd then gone to one of the best fighters he knew. Tigu was actually a fairly good teacher, but the one-on-one time hadn't lasted long. Everybody seemed to have the same idea of getting better, and starting to spar in the evening.

Which put Yun Ren firmly at the bottom of the pole. Oh, they were being nice about it, but he knew he wasn't as good as them. He likely never would be. The sword wasn't his passion. But even if he might never be as good a fighter as Tigu or Xiulan, he did want to learn something of swordsmanship. He would at least be able to defend himself. He had his own plans, after all.

"Let's try something harder, Summer," he decided.

'*Acceptance, approval,*' the sword declared. '*Now. Hootcha guard one,*' the sword demanded.

Yun Ren sighed. He knew he made strange noises when practicing, to help him better visualize things . . . but Summer's Sky took entirely too much joy in naming them. "I said you could use what they were *actually* called."

'*This way is more interesting. Hootcha guard one.*'

CHAPTER 20

ROLLING TO WINTER

Chyou awoke with a start as a rooster's crow shattered the still silence of the morning. It was incredibly loud, echoing off the hills in a way Chyou had never heard before—yet unexpectedly melodious. It was like somebody had taken a rooster's crow and added instruments to it. The cry spoke to some part of her, commanding her to wakefulness.

She stretched in the comfortable bed and pushed herself up to stare around at the rustic room. Beside her, Bo was stirring in his own bed, awakened by the same cry.

Chyou had spent nights in luxurious palaces and decadent beds, yet last night was possibly the best sleep she had ever had. She rose feeling refreshed. Her mind whirled as she thought over the events of the previous day. It had been spent mostly on business. Today, though, they would receive a tour of this strange place. A courtesy afforded them by Master Jin before Chyou left with her brother and with the promised rice.

She sighed; she supposed she would have to get up and get her own water—usually at this point a servant would greet them and prepare everything.

To her surprise there was a short knock on the door, and that part of the script played out.

Except when she opened the door, expecting to greet a humble maid, she wound up having to look down. There was no maid. There was a pig. A pig with a steaming tub of water tied to her back.

'*Young Sir. Young Miss,*' the pig greeted them, with razor-sharp diction. Her voice whispered in Chyou's mind, sending shivers down her spine. Like Wa Shi last night, she spoke without actually speaking, the meaning conveyed without words.

Chyou gracefully nodded, as was custom, giving the help the minor acknowledgement that they were to receive . . . and then decided better of it. Best not to repeat the mistake of her brother. Pi Pa, as she called herself, might act as a servant, but she was still a Spirit Beast that *spoke*.

"Thank you," Chyou said. The pig moved with odd grace, somehow managing to untie the tub of water from her back and set it down without a drop spilling.

Pi Pa nodded back before stepping to the side. '*When Young Sir and Young Miss are ready, this one shall escort you to breakfast.*'

The pig then bowed to them and exited the room, the door closing behind her without a single touch from Chyou.

Chyou looked to her brother who, now fully awake, simply shrugged.

→

Dressed properly with her face washed and hair braided, Chyou left the guest house with her brother to meet the patiently waiting Pi Pa. They followed in her wake, travelling through the still lush, if slightly damp, grass across a bridge back towards the main house.

Already the smells of breakfast wafted through the air, making her mouth water.

They were permitted entry quickly and taken to the long table where they'd had dinner the previous night. It was already packed with the inhabitants of Fa Ram. Both people and Spirit Beasts. When the pair entered with Pi Pa they were given nods of greeting from everyone and guided to an empty spot. There was the rooster, Bi De, who was preening the little rat Ri Zu. Liu Xianghua, the Young Mistress of the Misty Lake Sect, was sitting with Lady Meiling and a snake, who Chyou remembered was named Miantiao, pointing at a scroll. She and her brother were placed near the middle of the table. Her brother was seated close to Gou Ren and Bowu, whom he greeted before immediately talking about how nice the beds were, to the enthusiastic approval of Gou Ren. Her brother thus occupied, Chyou looked to the other side to see if she could converse with anybody.

Beside Chyou's seat there was a jar. And within it a fish, staring at her.

Wa Shi slapped at the side of his vessel happily.

"Good morning," Chyou greeted the strange creature politely. The fish nodded in response.

'*Good morning!*' he returned enthusiastically. '*Today shall be a day of firsts for you, Wa Shi declares!*'

Chyou froze at the statement, as the fish seemed both smug and expectant.

Right then Master Jin came out, carrying the food.

It was strange to have the master of the house serve the guests, so opposite to how the rich and powerful did things, with legions of servants to do the work.

Once more, though, Grandmother's advice rang true: "The truly strong do as they wish. Just smile and nod, Granddaughter."

Besides, he *had* cooked pancakes for her before.

The morning's offerings for breakfast were "hash browns," deer "bacon," fried eggs, and a thick, crusty bread—the entire ensemble made her mouth water.

It was just as good as it smelled.

"These are delicious! What are they made of?" Bo asked, curious, as he inspected the crunchy, golden-brown . . . thing.

"They're made from Earth apples from Yellow Rock Plateau," Master Jin said.

Chyou had heard of these "Earth apples" before. There had been some attempts at importing them, but they had been unpopular—although she supposed that they hadn't been cooked like this.

She glanced at her brother, and he gave her a quiet signal with his eyes. Another object to look into. It would be added to the vast pile of work they would have. Still, this was breakfast . . . and Grandmother so loathed discussing work at breakfast.

So instead, Chyou simply savoured the food, taking her time—until Wa Shi slapped his fins on the table suddenly, catching her attention.

'*Try the reeds upon the bread,*' the carp recommended, using his strange appendages to put a rather stringy-looking collection of reeds on her plate. They didn't look wholly appetizing, if Chyou was honest, but Master Jin was distracted by Tigu braiding the girl's orange hair.

With nothing to rescue her from her predicament, she took the reeds. One did not refuse a Spirit Beast lightly, or so she assumed. Honestly, there was no real standard etiquette for dealing with the creatures, other than "run." Rarely was a Spirit Beast aware enough to have a conversation with.

The reeds were placed onto the bread . . . the damp, stringy reeds . . . yet Chyou was trapped. She hesitated for a moment, then took a bite, hoping that was enough to placate the beast. She chewed . . . And then her eyes widened as the flavour hit her tongue.

"Master Carp, what other manner of reeds go well with this bread?" she asked him.

The fish stared back at her, somehow managing to smile proudly.

'Little Sister Chyou—let Wa Shi recount to you his discoveries.'

→

"By the heavens, that's got a kick!" Bo exclaimed, looking at the clear liquid after he'd taken a generous sip of it. Chyou too sipped it politely, firmly keeping the disgust from showing on her face. The drink burned on the way down most unpleasantly, but Bo seemed like he was a fan. He knew his spirits, while she had never been much for them.

Chyou looked up instead, focusing on the copper edifice, her eyes taking in its curves. It looked so simple . . . yet it had produced this. The amount of copper in it was large, but once production started, each individual contraption would be much cheaper than any pill furnace. It would certainly be another sound investment . . . if Master Jin allowed them to use the blueprints to reproduce it. He seemed easygoing, but there was always the chance he could take offence—especially if they took without asking. Chyou knew they could likely wait and ask him for permission for his secrets another time. For now, just the rice would do. A good merchant had to know when to quit when they were ahead.

The tour of Master Jin's home was an odd mixture of utterly mundane and completely fantastical. The simple-looking fields were contrasted with these tools of industry. There were machines here that put Pale Moon Lake City's industrial districts to shame in some respects. The glass in particular was a wonder. It was of a quality Chyou rarely saw—only Grandmother had pieces that were comparable, yet she had always seemed sad when she looked at them, calling them "the last remnants of a place that is no more."

Despite how much space the various projects took up, it was only a fraction of Master Jin's land. There were the buildings of the main house on the island between two rivers, along with a large red barn. There was also the smaller-yet-no-less-impressive home of Gou Ren and the Young Mistress of the Misty Lake Sect, complete with glass windows, across the river and atop a hill. Near that hill and the forest Master Jin had beehives, another wonder to ask about, as well as several large storage buildings. The guest house was on the other side of the river, situated away from the road. Currently they were near the still, bordering the smaller of the two rivers.

She shook herself out of her reflections and turned back to Lady Meiling, paying attention to her host as she made a considering sound.

"It's not just for drinking," Lady Meiling clarified. "The alcohol, when refined properly, has a powerful disinfecting property."

"What do the doctors in the capital use to clean their tools, anyway?" Master Jin asked, turning away from her brother for a moment, sounding curious.

Chyou had the answer ready.

"Water and soap for the most part, but some use an expensive alchemic solution—though this is rather rare because of the ingredients," she explained. "There are also some scholars who believe that it may have adverse effects, but the discussion is ongoing. I am inclined to agree with them, however. Doctor Shenlong had a treatise on the subject that was convincing—" Chyou paused, wondering if she had spoken too much, but Lady Meiling just seemed intrigued.

"You've read the scrolls you gave us?" she asked.

"Ah, yes, and the doctors *do* like to talk, Lady Meiling. I don't think they thought I could understand most of what they were speaking of, but I did read most of the texts I prepared for Master Jin, to make sure there was no duplicate information," she ventured. It had taken a fairly long time to read through most of it, reviewing the quality and performing a quick check to see if the scrolls truly were the right ones.

Lady Meiling smiled. "You did impressive work," the cultivator said, her compliment genuine. "These texts were very helpful and have already proven their worth. Thank you for getting them for us."

Chyou flushed slightly at the earnest praise.

"It was my pleasure, Lady Meiling," Chyou said with a little bow. It had been an interesting task, all told.

"We should trade letters when you get back to the capital, you and I," Meiling continued. "It would be nice to hear tales of the city and how the preparations are going for your expedition."

She looked back at the freckle-faced woman. Chyou had spent the day watching as was proper, learning the patterns of how this strange group of people interacted. Every instinct within her told her contact with Master Jin's wife would be worth quite a bit. That, and hopefully she could ensure that the woman wouldn't bear any grudges for her brother's slipups . . . and her own grandmother's machinations. Best to have a cordial relationship, before such things were brought up.

If there was one lesson she had taken from the day, it was this: if she was to succeed as she hoped, it was best not to underestimate *anyone*. Who knew where a kind offer would lead?

"Of course, Lady Meiling," Chyou replied as they continued the tour.

They wrapped up their time at the still. Master Jin currently wasn't interested in selling the drink, which left Bo disappointed. The man said there were too many kinks to work out, though he seemed to hint that things might change in the future.

So they trekked across the grass and towards what looked like a house made of glass. Master Jin had explained it to her in the city . . . yet it was something else to see it partially completed. It would truly be a marvel when it was done, as her mind conjured images of lush greenery even in the depths of winter.

↔

It was always fun showing off your house and seeing the impressed faces of people as they looked at what you had built. I'll admit, I was proud of it.

From the drop hammer to the beginnings of the greenhouse where Noodle finally seemed to have gotten a mix in the glass he was happy with.

It kind of really puts things into perspective, you know. Going through the progress of the farm before winter hits and seeing the visible, tangible growth. My stores had been pretty full last year—but now I had dedicated buildings and warehouses that looked like they were supposed to feed an entire army. The village of Hong Yaowu in its entirety hadn't produced as much as I did, and I had used a quarter of the land they did.

Two years in and I could picture many more to come.

My guests were appropriately curious. Bo and Chyou wanted to know everything—and while yeah, they were motivated by profit and wanted to market everything new I put out . . . I honestly didn't mind that too much.

Everything comes to an end, though. The siblings couldn't stay much longer on account of the long journey south, and so after a couple of days we packed up the cart and bid them farewell, though Chyou had looked flabbergasted when Washy had given her one of his scales—it was one of his fish ones; the front of it was dull brown, and the back was pearlescent.

The woman thanked him awkwardly before she settled in on her horse.

Chunky saw them off, carrying the massive cartful of rice for them back to Verdant Hill, where they would take it the rest of the way back. The Guan siblings' horses marched along with him down the road and back to the town.

Taking a breath, I sighed, letting the crisp, cold air fill my lungs. We had perhaps a month, maybe half that, before winter truly set in.

I waved at Yun Ren as he wandered down from the hill he had climbed up, stretching and looking disheveled and sweaty. Despite his beat-up appearance, he seemed to be in a good mood.

Everyone was, really.

I couldn't help staring around the farm, at my family's smiling faces and their carefree expressions.

It warmed my heart knowing that I had created a place where all of them could be happy.

I let my Qi flow out of my body as I relaxed, giving back to this wonderful place.

My heaven on earth.

□

A little girl pounded reeds into fiber. Each motion was slow and full of fatigue, as golden cracks in her body shimmered.

She was tired. *So tired.*

The rock came up, then down it slammed into the reeds, trying to make them into an uncomfortable bedding.

There was a final slam, and she started to pant, turning to the hole in the ground.

She had barely made any progress.

She opened her mouth to ask for help—

Hands grasping tearing help me helpmewhyarent you helping me?!

Her mouth clicked shut.

Wearily, she raised the rock once more.

CHAPTER 21

REACH OUT

It was cold. Frost coated the ground, and breaths came out in steaming gasps. Miantiao always hated the cold. It was a time filled with bitter memories. The winter was when Sun Ken had destroyed his village and slain his dearly departed Master.

The cold was when his old wounds ached the most, the pain stabbing deep.

It wasn't so bad today. The soothing salve provided by Lady Meiling and her apprentice Ri Zu soothed most of the pain . . . as did the knitted tube wrapped around his body, crafted for him by Jin.

It was a bit harder to slither around with it on, but it was soft and warm. It was more kindness than he deserved from them. From *all* of them. He, who had turned innocent Yin into a weapon of vengeance against Sun Ken. He had betrayed her trust in him. Worse still, it had all been for nothing.

Normally his student would have accompanied him, aiding him as she could. But today, he let her sleep. He was up earlier than normal, after all. The last vestiges of the stars lit the sky in the final hours before daylight. But he was close. He was *so close* to finishing his task, a task given to him by Jin. A purpose, after so long without one.

His eyes picked out Chun Ke, Pi Pa, and Jin in the distance as they walked slowly along the riverbank. Chun Ke had been increasingly restless as winter approached and was having trouble sleeping. The boar had taken to going on long walks with the others to help settle himself. His companions in his early-morning walks varied—but he was always with Pi Pa.

Miantiao stared at the three massive scars that ran through the boar's face and bowed his head slightly, heading towards his destination. Chun Ke was in good hands—he did not need Miantiao to darken the mood further.

He travelled through the crunchy, crackling grass and the iced-over pools of water as he came to his destination: the building that had been made for him to practise his craft. It was as grand as any he had seen and had been built to his specifications by Gou Ren and Jin. It brought back memories every time he entered it.

He shook off the feeling as he entered the place. The furnace was still burning, though banked, and he tended to it, raising the flames higher and heating both the furnace that would melt the glass and the bath that would be filled with molten metal beneath it.

The Float Glass technique that Jin had mentioned was still incomplete. Pouring the molten glass onto molten metal and then letting it smooth out into a single pane before rolling off was utterly brilliant. Still, there were often bits of slag stuck to the surface of the glass that required careful scraping and polishing to get off. It was time consuming . . . but Miantiao could mitigate the worst of it by channeling his Qi into the glass and keeping it separate from the metal.

The final result of this technique was the flattest, smoothest, and clearest pieces of glass Miantiao had ever borne witness to. His dear Master would have waxed poetic about it. The artisans of the village would have gathered around and kowtowed before any craftsman for the mere sight of this piece.

And so Miantiao the snake worked. He toiled in the searing heat of the forge. He toiled through his aches and pains. He toiled through the melancholy of the coming winter.

All who lived here offered their help without a thought—yet Miantiao could not be as they were. He would not do as he had with his apprentice Yin: taking without giving. He had to do something that *deserved* that help. He would earn the hand being offered to him.

Bi De had said that living was atoning.

So Miantiao, student of Boli Xin the Glassmaker, would atone in the only way he could.

→

It was not Miantiao who placed the last pane of glass in the scaffold of iron for the glass house. Though he was asked to do the honour . . . that was for another. It was Jin's idea, and thus Jin should complete it.

Miantiao had to admit he was a bit skeptical; despite the sound theory, he couldn't completely believe that it would be so insulating. Glass, after all, was known for losing heat.

But as Jin sealed in the panes with a thick tar, Miantiao could not help but marvel at the shining building of glass.

Everyone was gathered. From Young Master Bi De to Tigu, Gou Ren, and the newest members of the Fa Ram, Bowu and his sister Xianghua.

All were staring with wonder at the structure.

"This is so *cool*," Yun Ren whispered, staring wide-eyed at the structure. He took out a pad of paper and some charcoal, his eyes shining as he wrote down notes and drew designs.

'*Hell yeah! Shifu is awesome!*' Yin enthused, bouncing in excitement. Miantiao nearly chided her for her language, but he was interrupted.

"He is," Jin agreed. "This is amazing work, Miantiao."

There was a chorus of agreement from the gathered crowd. Miantiao ducked his head slightly, pretending to be unaffected. Yet he could not stop the swelling of pride in his chest.

I helped make this.

"Come on, let's head in!" Jin said, opening the door. Yin shot inside first, rushing past everyone through the first door into a small wooden building that was insulated and attached to the larger glass structure. Once everyone had made their way in, they closed the outer door and then opened the inner one, the one that led directly into the house made of glass.

The area was completely barren, containing nothing more than the high ceilings and a perfect uninterrupted view of the world around them. The autumn sun gazed down, throwing its light through the glass, which seemed to focus and intensify it.

The room was already slightly warmer than outside, despite having been completed only a few minutes ago.

Yin was already bouncing around the room as more people walked in, looking around. But Miantiao remained in the doorway.

He stared at Yin, her eyes bright and sparkling as she excitedly asked Ri Zu, who followed her frantic movements with nimble grace, about which plants they would grow first.

Miantiao watched the others walking around the glass house. He could see the excited smiles on their faces. They laughed and joked. Sharing in the marvel.

Being surrounded by their joy still hurt sometimes. It brought back the memories of his old home, lost to tragedy and greed.

Most days, Miantiao still felt like an outsider. But if he was honest, he had been unconsciously distancing himself. Unable to stop himself, afraid, and trying to spare himself more pain. What if things went as badly as last time?

He didn't know.

Jin, having noticed his hesitation, stepped back to where the snake was watching everyone. The young man's concern was clear. "You doing all right, Miantiao?"

Even at this moment, Jin offered his hand. It was who he was, this strange man who had given Miantiao a place in his home. And yet Miantiao still could not fully understand it. This place, where they always seemed so happy, carried loss. He knew the occasional forlorn look in Jin's eyes. In Young Master Bi De's extreme caution around anything that could be considered corrupted. In Lady Meiling's own actions, as she strove her hardest to heal those around her. In the way Xianghua and Bowu clung to each other.

A thousand little breaks. A thousand little cracks. Yet they all carried on anyway. They all smiled, meeting each new day with determination and a desire to move forward. To move on.

Miantiao shook his head.

'*I am . . . I am well, Jin,*' he said. The man nodded, accepting his response . . . then offered Miantiao his arm.

Miantiao looked at the arm for a moment and hesitated, before finally climbing up, winding up on Jin's neck like a scarf.

Like he had done with his Master, so many years ago.

"Do you have anything you want to try growing in here?" Jin asked, as a sudden blast of light and heat from Yin began heating up the room even faster.

The question . . . well, it didn't really concern him. He was a creature of pottery and glass—the affairs of the earth were beyond him. Yet just as he was about to defer the question, he paused and truly considered it.

He thought of one thing. A memory. A remembrance for the departed in a house made of glass to the man who had made Miantiao.

'*If thisss Miantiao may sssuggest . . . sssunnflowers.*' His Master's favourite flower. It was frivolous, to be sure. He did not even know if they would grow here either.

But he asked humbly.

Jin nodded enthusiastically, his eyes brightening up at the idea.

→

By nighttime, the greenhouse was as hot as a summer's day. They had spent most of the day within, simply sitting and planning everything that was going to be planted within. But eventually, they had all exited for dinner, and now with the moon out, the glass house was sparkling. It should have stood out awkwardly. It should have looked out of place. And yet . . . it didn't.

It looked like it belonged. Here, a piece of Miantiao's Master lived on.

His heart resolved, he approached Young Master Bi De as they settled in for the night.

'*Young Master . . . you said that you offered thanks to the Earth Spirit for this place. How . . . how does one do such a thing?*'

Bi De spoke often of how the land rejected the wicked. Yin had taken to offering her Qi with gusto, and she spoke of the occasional feeling of somebody being amused by her.

Yet Miantiao simply had never tried. His rejection was certain, after all. What kind of benevolent land would accept him? It was best not to waste its time or attention.

He was unworthy of it. He knew that in his soul. He was burdened with both sin and guilt.

And yet as he stared at the glass house, as he watched the amazement on the others' faces . . . he did not feel quite so terrible. He had caused the smiling faces. He had *contributed.*

He felt . . . happy, for the first time in a long, long while.

And then he felt guilty. What right did *he* have to be happy? He was a wretched snake, a worthless thing.

Wasn't he?

All Miantiao knew was that there was a judge beneath the earth, one who would show him the true wickedness in his heart.

Would the land reject him? He . . . he had to know. He had to know if he could be redeemed.

The rooster smiled at him, then nodded. "Let me show you."

Miantiao got the feeling that Bi De had been waiting for him to ask. The rooster sat beside him, and their Qi gently entwined.

Qi of glass and earth was guided by the light of the moon to a network of golden strands. They pulsed sluggishly—and Miantiao froze when he truly beheld them.

They were like the art his village had sometimes produced. Pottery, shattered, and then inlaid with lacquer to make the cracks into something beautiful.

It felt . . . familiar. Almost like he had some kind of kinship with the threads of golden light. His energy touched the strands of gold. A tiny portion, as he gave himself to the land.

He held his breath when the golden light examined his offering . . . and then consumed it. He felt fingers drift along the top of his head, like his Master had once done.

As quickly as the vision had come, it was gone, and Miantiao was left once more staring at the sky.

He . . . he had not been rejected.

He was not redeemed. Miantiao was not foolish enough to think himself forgiven for what he had done to Yin.

Yet . . . he felt maybe, just *maybe*, he could try.

□

Tianlan's eyes drooped as she pounded the reeds again. Each moment, each time she lifted the rock to strike the reeds into fiber, felt like she was lifting the world. Her arms shook with the effort and the golden cracks in her body *ached*.

She was tired. So, so *tired*. All she wanted was sleep.

But she couldn't. Not yet.

The rock thudded into the reeds, and she left it there, panting for breath while she turned to the divot in the ground, which was filled with reed fiber and a single, ragged blanket.

She stopped and stared at the lonely little divot in the earth. It wouldn't help her. Her preparations were lacking. She knew that much. Some half-forgotten instinct told her what she needed to do, what she needed to create, so she could recover and heal. Tianlan clenched the stone in her fist and took a breath.

The memories surfaced. Of the time before the void, before the terror and pain.

A man, grinning as he helped craft her a grand palace.

The memory distracted her, and she missed the next strike. The rock slipped from her hands, landing with a *thud* on the ground beside the reeds. Her body followed the motion, and she keeled over, thudding into the earth beside it.

She lay there, breathing sharply, staring at the divot in the ground. Her resting place. It was marginally better than being shards of herself, base instinct spread across the broken ground.

She couldn't do it alone . . . could she?

And yet every time she opened her mouth to ask, memories came flooding back.

She remembered. She relived it, that nightmare.

Begging and crying for help. *Screaming* for it. She remembered the deafening silence. The indifference, like they couldn't hear her at all, and the grasping hands that had ripped and torn at her broken body, bleeding and leaking energy as they broke her, taking her very essence for themselves.

She gagged at the thought. At the shadow of sharpness digging into her golden wounds.

Rolling onto her back, she stared up at the sky, which was filled with white stars and crossed with golden cracks. She pressed the back of her hand into her eyes and bit her lip.

Gentle energy touched her, reaching out from her Connected One. It was given without her having to ask. Strands of gold more vital than ever propped up her flagging strength and soothed the aches.

Yet the energy that came to her was not alone. Not like the first months.

More strands touched her, flowing from others. Each had a taste unique to itself. Orbs of captured moonlight, pure and without taint. Medical plants, with their healing tang. Grass, growing strong, its roots anchored into the ground. Stone and strength, a foundation. Wisps of light and a prankster's laugh. A friend who knew what it meant to want to be understood. A rumble of nurturing earth, a void that was somehow warm, water, lightning, and the scent of a meal, the light of the sun . . . And then something new.

A tiny shard of shattered pottery and broken glass, wanting so desperately to atone. Reaching out for her, to help her, even though he himself was broken.

Opening up, reaching out, giving without taking.

All these little sparks of light propped her up without her asking. Even though she hadn't truly given anything to most of them.

Her hand began to shake. The little shard of pottery and glass awaited her judgement. His energy was slightly tainted. He did feel a lot like the people who had hurt her.

And yet he reached out to her. He begged her for forgiveness, for the sins he had committed.

Tianlan sucked in a breath. She touched the little strand of Qi.

Please . . .

The call from her was quiet. Half desperate prayer and half forlorn plea.

Please . . .

. . . help.

Silence answered her.

She lay there in the grass. Ugly, panting gasps escaped her. Tears gathered at the corners of her eyes. There was no pulse of energy. There were no eyes upon her. There were no hands reaching for her.

She let out a final shuddering breath as she lay on the grass. The tears flowed. She closed her eyes. Nobody would come; they could not hear her, just like the others hadn't been able to hear her. She was alone. It was better that way. Part of her hadn't wanted this to work—

"Hey. You all right, kiddo?" The voice of her Connected One came in two familiar tones, cutting through the haze in her mind.

She jolted, opening her tear-filled eyes to look up. Her Connected One was there.

His face was split in two, a massive scar made of gold that went right down the middle. Two shattered and broken halves were welded together—yet slowly they were melding together, the two halves becoming more at peace with each other.

Her vision of the concerned man was interrupted by the appearance of another. The woman crouched down immediately to examine Tianlan. Amethyst eyes as intense as the gaze of her Connected One swooped down to examine her. The woman's freckles had a golden sheen connected by bands of metallic light, forming constellations across the bridge of her nose.

"Are you well, little one?" she asked, using her delicate fingers to brush the hair out of Tianlan's eyes. Her voice was full of concern.

Tianlan curled up further, tightening into a little ball.

"Winter," she whispered, raising her hand to point. "I have to prepare for winter."

The shining woman and man turned to look at the little divot in the ground. Her Connected Ones' faces fell.

Tianlan looked away from them in shame.

"That's no place to last the winter," her Connected One declared.

"You'll catch death if you sleep here, little one," the woman chastised her, sighing in exasperation.

"I-I know," Tianlan whispered, as hot tears ran down her face. "I tried to do it on my own bu-but—"

Their arms wrapped around her, and Tianlan flinched at the touch. But instead of the ripping pain that should have come with it, as they tore her apart for her Qi . . . there was nothing.

Nothing but warmth.

"It's all right. We're here now," her Connected One whispered.

Tianlan choked, then started to sob, causing thick, heavy tears to stream down her face.

→

She didn't know how long she had cried for. All she remembered was how her body had shook, and how her Connected Ones had held her until Tianlan had finally calmed down.

And now, she was in Meiling's arms, rubbing at her eyes, as her Jin stood, once more examining Tianlan's pathetic hole in the ground.

Jin smiled at the Earth Spirit. "Let's build you something nicer, yeah?"

The world shifted slightly. Trees materialized around them, growing from her Connected One's Qi. The landscape changed from the grassland to something else. An axe formed in her Connected One's hand.

Her Connected One, her Jin, walked to the trees, preparing the land. Cutting the wood in a single stroke, then using his axe to hew the felled log into suitable planks.

Tianlan was carried back to her rock and her fiber, as a Connected One sat with her, cradling her.

"This is how you weave a proper blanket." Her Meiling's gentle voice washed over her, as Meiling shifted Tianlan in her lap. "Watch carefully, little one."

Her deft fingers worked, threading together the reeds with grace. Tianlan watched as her Meiling began to hum an old song. Behind the voice and the soft movements of the weaving, she heard the steady beat of an axe. Jin's voice picked up the pattern of the song, the two melding into a soothing harmony.

Tianlan felt herself begin to drift off in the warm embrace, safe. Just the three of them. How it should be. Just her Connections—

"Xiulan, can you get me more fiber?"

Tianlan jolted back into wakefulness.

"Of course, Meiling," a soft, melodious voice answered. Tianlan looked up from her seat on Meiling's lap and stared at the third presence. A female figure with the face of a long-dead friend stared back. Her heart panged with loss . . . but this was not her old friend. Xiulan was different. A golden fracture in the center of her chest marred the perfection of her form. It was visible through her clothes, a mark of damage done, yet Xiulan stood proudly. She smiled at Tianlan and winked.

"You're much cuter when you're not trying to headbutt me," the woman said in amusement as the grass around them grew tall and separated into soft strands that Meiling took for weaving.

Xiulan began to tap her feet to the beat of the pounding axe and the soft tune upon Meiling's lips, adding her own voice to the harmony of the song. Tianlan blinked and shook her head, glancing at Jin—who now had a rooster made of moonlight beside him. They were both hewing logs together.

There was a soft rumble. A pathway opened in the air.

Two more joined them in the construction. A monkey-looking man grumbled and complained, grey, rocky fingers scratching at his bushy sideburns as he ceaselessly heaved up stones to serve as the foundation of the house. The other man, vulpine in features, with a smoky, misty form that somehow shone like the sun, heckled the stone man as he painted the drab browns of wood and reeds so they burst with colour, adding to the budding chorus.

A girl came next, her form shifting between human and tiger, flickering fitfully back and forth until it settled on human—albeit with cat ears upon her head, a tail, and an enormous amount of freckles dotting her cheeks. Her eyes were wide and playful as she hopped about, assembling the home, then carving into the wood of the building with intricate patterns and beautiful images, elevating the material above just base wood.

Next came a pig. She was pink and translucent, pretty and dainty—yet a small ball of darkness sat quietly in the center of her chest, waiting. She moved with perfect grace, drifting through the little world from one place people were working to the next, organising tools, carrying completed products to their destination, and smoothing everybody into a perfect, seamless dance.

A tiny rat made of inky darkness and healing herbs scampered around the fields of Tianlan's domain, inspecting the golden cracks in the ground and offering soothing Qi into them.

Tianlan could only watch, stunned, as more and more people entered her domain, gently guided through the golden cracks that resided in the sky.

A great dragon the size of a fish descended, his expression filled with arrogance. Then, realising that nearly everybody else was bigger than him, the little dragon pouted. The creature noticed Tianlan and flew over . . . before glaring at her like she was a personal affront.

'*You're too skinny*,' the tiny lord of the skies and rain decreed, and gave her a peach. Tianlan bit into it, her hands shaking a little, as more and more people joined in on the song—as more and more came to her, not to rip flesh from her bones but to build her a home.

An ox with a wild-looking child on his back ventured in, the pair looking around curiously. The child's eyes widened happily when he saw the woodcutting, and he dashed over as if mesmerised. The ox shrugged, ambling over as well.

She could see the faint outlines of a rabbit and a snake, almost ghosts . . . before they too solidified, bringing heat and warmth with them.

Finally came a giant boar, two li high and yet not. A towering titan, and yet just the right size to lean against. His body was made of stone and wood; his eyes burned with golden light. There were three scars across his face, deep, permanent wounds, yet he was no lesser for the damage.

He was one of her greatest friends. The one who knew her best.

Chun Ke cantered over to where Tianlan was, safe in her Meiling's lap. She sniffed, trying to hold back her emotions, trying not to break down again when the boar chuffed, nosing at her.

"Thank you," Tianlan whispered, hugging his snout. Tears spilled out from the corners of her eyes, and all was well.

→

After a moment that lasted an eternity, there was a house. Not some grand palace like in her memories, a fortress to hide away in; instead, it was a humble, comfortable home. The windows were large and brightly coloured. Carvings and painted images dotted the walls. It beckoned to her, promising warmth.

Tianlan could barely see through her drooping eyelids as her Meiling carried her in and laid her down.

The bed she lay in was a simple, rugged thing, yet stuffed to perfection. The cotton blankets were somehow more comforting than silk, smelling like the sun that had dried them.

A fire that felt like the sun blazed in the hearth. She saw the sunbound rabbit nodding at her work and the snake inspecting windows that let in a gentle light.

Tianlan struggled to keep her eyes open through her exhaustion as she stared at the people surrounding her.

This time, there were no grasping hands. There was no pain. There was no ravening void, come to claim her again.

Hands fluffed her pillow. A cat rubbed her head against her cheek. Xiulan cheekily tapped their foreheads together, and her Connected Ones tucked her in.

"Sweet dreams," her Jin said, as he laid his hand on her head.

Tianlan leaned into the touch.

Her eyes closed.

The first flakes of winter fell to the earth.

Beneath the falling snows, Tianlan slumbered in her humble home, warm and safe.

CHAPTER 22

THE EMPRESS

A grand celebration was held within the impenetrable fortress. The walls were hung with magnificent woven tapestries depicting their hundreds of victories over the rebels that had dared to raise their arms against the Emperor. The victorious legion of soldiers had their armor shined and their hair immaculately groomed. They watched servant dancers ply their trade as they supped upon gifts from the Emperor himself. For their leal service, they had been rewarded greatly by the Lord, he who was truly the Son of Heaven.

Vajra watched them all from her seat, wiggling in contentment. The hives had been praised personally by the Lord. He had lined up his entire household to share his delight in their efforts and proclaimed her *Vajra the Great, Boozemaster.*

Vajra had little clue what a *Boozemaster* was, but as it was a title gifted to her by the Emperor in only her first year of service, she would cherish it.

Truly, after the depths she had sunk to in her previous existence, she had been brought up high by the luck of the heavens and the benevolence of her Emperor!

She groomed her eyes thoroughly and wriggled in contentment. The sight of the Emperor and handsome Bi De praising her would be seared into her memory for as long as she lived. Both powerful creatures, standing before her under the light of the moon, praising her skills and beauty . . . oh, it had nearly been too much!

A grand memory to cherish before she began the work required of her in preparation of the White Death coming this year. Vajra's senses turned to her larders instinctively at the thought, a brief moment of panic seizing her . . . but it was a baseless reaction. The larders were full. Even with the tribute taken by the Emperor they had more than enough to last the winter.

To the point that perhaps she had been a bit paranoid in her preparations, but as the time of Falling Leaves stretched on she had made a full accounting for her and her servants' hives. The Coldguard brood was ready and fat, the hives had been scoured for any parasites, and those that had been found were mercilessly exterminated, her warriors checking over their servants for any defects or disease. She had even commanded the removal of the old pupae. In hives such as these, foolish, lesser ones of her kin grew complacent and laid their eggs in the same cells over and over. The resulting buildup of cocoons would eventually stunt their growth to the point where new broods would be half the size . . . and then continue to get smaller until the hive died out.

A year ago, Vajra would not have bothered to police the actions of mere servants. If they died out, they died out—it was their own fault.

But ever since the war against the demonic parodies of her kind, she had learned the folly of waste. Every piece of her hive counted. Every bit of her kingdom would be safe and work to the best of itself. Everything was to be leveraged; waste was a *sin*.

Millions of soldiers and hundreds of warrior-queens had died at the hands of the demons. The most powerful of the demons had even stayed active through the White Death, flying relentlessly to assault them through the deadly cold while Vajra and her kin had been trapped within their fortresses, enduring a slow siege by both cold and foe.

It had been a horrible waiting game through the White Death. Hoping they would survive the assaults . . . only to fly out in the Season of Growth to the wreckage of slaughtered hives.

But that was in the past. It was no good to dwell on those dire times. The Emperor and splendid Bi De would surely not allow the demons any foothold here, for the rapacious creatures gave nothing and only destroyed. Despite this, Vajra almost *wanted* the beasts to come to her new paradise. To come and be smote by her Emperor and Bi De's glorious battle prowess. She wriggled in delight at the thought of the demons being destroyed by blades of glorious moonlight or crushed under the might of the muscular arms of the Emperor.

Vajra sighed contentedly at the memory of the shirtless man sparring with his magnificent cock. Both had struck with enough force to slay a hundred thousand demons as they tested themselves against each other. The pair had then gone into the river, and the Emperor had graced Bi De by washing his glorious feathers with his own strong hands; it was every bit as enjoyable as observing them in the bathhouse.

She had even gotten to see the Emperor *dancing*.

Vajra buzzed angrily at the thought of the Emperor cavorting with that *harlot*, the one that smelled of grass, though it had been a wonderful sight to behold. Vajra could respect the seductress's movements, even if they were inferior to her own dancing skills.

In time, it would be Vajra dancing with the Emperor and enticing him with her flawless mastery.

She chortled as her mind churned with plans.

She was a queen, that was undeniable. But soon . . . soon she would be an Empress! For one of her stature, one had to have ambitions.

→

All too soon, the merrymaking came to an end and the Coldguard finished their preparations. The servants were sent back to their hives, where most would die off during the White Death; only the Coldguard remained with the subordinate queens. They would keep the hives warm throughout the winter, dancing ceaselessly until the White Death drew to an end.

Yet Vajra's strongest warriors were too valuable and lived too long to be discarded so easily in the cycle. They had no names, and they had no spark, being as they were an extension of herself in most respects. There were a few of them who bore her imprints more deeply and could nearly even think for themselves, carrying out her will with zeal.

Each and every one was a credit to the hive.

Vajra would, therefore, ensure their survival.

They stood before her, rank upon iridescent rank staring at her. She gazed back at them all with pride and danced for them, declaiming their value in her service.

Her soldiers were stoic . . . yet she could see the faint stirrings of pride within them.

'*Step forward,*' she commanded, '*Bane of the Black Lances, She Who Purged the Reeds.*'

The first of her warriors obeyed Vajra's call, her carapace scarred from a hundred battles, yet still gleaming. Her soldier kowtowed before her, antennae dipping low.

'*Thou hast performed a valuable service—you shall be preserved for next year, my soldier,*' she informed the warrior.

The Bane of the Black Lances' thorax wiggled, signifying her acceptance, her motions immediate.

Such veterans had been in short supply by the end of the war against the demons.

Vajra touched her forehead to her warrior's. A bit of Vajra's spirit, which had grown to nearly what had been her previous height during the Great War, infused the soldier.

The Bane of the Black Lances stilled. Her rapidly beating heart and vibrating wings slowed. After a moment she slumped, as if dead.

Yet she was still alive. Dreaming, with her body's processes slowed by Vajra's absolute command.

Vajra's Coldguard stepped up from behind her. In their mouthparts and forelimbs were strands of special wax, and they marched towards the Bane of the Black Lances, the smaller Coldguard beginning their work on the enormous warrior.

With these implements, they clad the prime warrior, cocooning her as if she were a larva again. They paid close attention to her spiracles and built up the waxlike tubes, so that she could still breathe, when the next part was accomplished.

The Coldguard bore Vajra's warrior up with reverence and took her to a specially prepared cell filled with an exacting mix of honey that would not freeze with the killing cold. It would instead keep her most powerful warriors young and fresh, ready for aggressive expansion the moment they awoke.

Finally, the cell was sealed—and upon the top of the cell was placed a strand of grass, recording the Bane of the Black Lances' deeds and her meritorious service.

Vajra turned to the next in line.

One by one, her veterans stepped up. One by one, the warriors, fifty in all, were entombed.

She almost envied them. They would sleep, waking again only when the cold was past.

Vajra did not have that luxury. She would stay awake throughout the entire White Death, a long vigil, waiting for the warmth of the Time of Growth.

Vajra turned away from the cells of her soldiers and commanded the Coldguard to continue their duties.

Venturing out to the exit of her fortress, she held still and stared out across the vast domain of the Emperor coated in frost.

The time of the White Death was always the worst, and this one promised to be long. It was the farthest north she had ever been.

She shuffled her legs as she looked at the bathhouse and gauged how cold it was outside.

Perhaps she would sally forth one last time . . .

↔

"Hey, Jin, the bee is in the bath again," Meimei said as she stared at the collapsed creature in the windowsill. Her lips quirked in amusement from where she was leaning her head on my chest. We were having a lovely bath together.

I sighed. Honestly, I couldn't blame Vajra. The bathhouse was warm and it *was* getting chilly out.

I got out of the water and picked up the foolish little thing. She was buzzing in what sounded like contentment, but she also seemed a little dazed.

Vajra did look different from the other bees. Maybe she was used to a warmer climate?

Thinking it over, I realized that Vajra's honey and wax was beyond anything else we had, so I might as well give her a little extra protection . . .

↔

Vajra awoke to incessant buzzing. She shook herself. Ah, it had been a wonderful view, and once more her Emperor had cared for her when she had fallen victim to his stunning good looks.

Yet all of her Coldguard were in a tizzy. They were buzzing and prodding at her, scared and confused.

The Coldguard informed her that the Emperor had *moved* their fortress.

Confused, Vajra commandeered one of her Coldguard, her senses filling it and allowing her to take personal command. The soldier stepped out of the hive and into—

It was warm. It was *extremely* warm, almost like the summer. They were within one of the great palaces the Emperor had built, the one that gleamed like the sun with walls as clear as air and solid as stone. The servant stared in wonder at the warmth, the White Death clearly visible outside . . . Yet within this grand barrier, filled with pots of dirt and spicy-smelling herbs . . . the White Death had been completely defeated.

Vajra fell to her side.

The Emperor could even command the seasons?!

CHAPTER 23

TRUST

Was a dream really just a dream?

It was on my mind as I stared out across my property, waiting for breakfast. The world was clad in a thin blanket of pure white.

I was . . . content. It was almost an irrational feeling, but the dream had been very nice. Even as it faded, I remembered us all working together.

I turned to my wife, who also had a smile on her face.

"When I was little, my aim was so bad that instead of throwing snowballs, I had to run right up to people and try to smush the snow on them," I said to my wife. She smiled at the admission.

"I once set a pit trap for Meihua and blamed it on Gou and Yun. She drop-kicked both of them into the river and even brings it up from time to time. She still doesn't know it was me," Meiling replied, completing our morning ritual.

I snorted, and a moment later we both got up, Meimei marching straight for the outhouse. She had complained about needing to go more often recently, because of the pregnancy.

I, on the other hand, had little to do, as I wasn't in charge of anything that morning. Instead, my attention drifted to the winter wonderland that had greeted us. Snow covered the farm, turning it into a picturesque scene. Chunky certainly enjoyed it all. He was dashing around already, rolling happily in the snow, with Peppa breaking her usual prim attitude to play around in the snowy landscape. He hadn't had any nightmares last night, and it showed.

He looked as happy as I felt.

Xiulan came down from her room with Tigu still half-asleep on her back. Both had smiles on their faces.

"You two have good dreams last night?" I joked.

Xiulan just nodded. "Yes, it was a wonderful dream," she said, as she tapped at Tigu, who finally woke up. Tigu grumbled for a moment before perking up clambering off Xiulan's back to grab Bowu, who had just come inside. She pulled him along, charging out into the snow, while Xiulan followed at a more sedate pace, chuckling.

A dream, huh? I frowned at it. The dream last night had been . . . well, it had been so *real*, despite most of it being kind of a blur. Real and familiar.

That little girl I'd seen had felt like an old friend.

Honestly, I'd thought the dreams of her had been happening because I was going to be a dad. It was normal to dream about your future kid, right?

But now . . . now I wasn't so sure. The normally fleeting memories of my dreams were a bit clearer this time. I could see her. The golden cracks that wound through her body, filling in old wounds. Just like the cracks that had appeared on my arm and the one on Xiulan's chest.

And the energy that I felt. The same energy I felt every time I pulled on my own Qi.

I didn't know *what* she was, and at first I had wanted answers. Yet the look in her eyes had stopped me.

The exhaustion and hope. But most of all . . . the trust. She *trusted* us.

I had a feeling she'd wake up in the spring, once the snow was gone. We'd have a talk then. I wasn't going to wake her up right now and demand answers. We would talk, eventually, get everything sorted out and on the table.

For now, I wished her sweet dreams.

I couldn't help but smile and shake my head—and then I noticed Tigu carting out some of the sculptures she had made last year. The very same sculptures of me that were near universally naked.

She planted the one she was carrying—the one of me flipping over a boar—along the walkway to the house and grinned. Xiulan and Bowu were with her, each carrying a sculpture of their own. Bowu looked quite embarrassed, while Xiulan just seemed amused.

"There! Now we can see how much I've improved this year!" Tigu declared, staring at them with pride.

Three sculptures were placed down beside the walkway, and then Tigu skipped away with her helpers, going to get the rest of them out.

I sighed and shook my head. Well, I had kept them, so I shouldn't have been surprised that Tigu was getting them out . . . and arranging them around the house.

About a minute later, Xianghua and Gou Ren, who were walking arm in arm, emerged from their own house. Both paused as they caught sight of the sculptures. Xianghua's eyes, naturally, dipped lower on the art pieces. The older ones, which were from when Tigu had no idea about certain parts of anatomy.

She blinked at them twice. She tilted her head to the side, then whispered something to Gou Ren.

My friend gained a beatific smile and nodded.

Xianghua looked stunned as they walked past them and into the house. Xianghua found Meiling, who was just setting some food out, and planted a hand on her shoulder.

"Lady Meiling, my deepest condolences," she stated.

Meimei just looked confused while I sidled up behind the man who was trying not to laugh.

I slung an arm around his shoulder, in a friendly way. Gou Ren paled, realising I knew what he had done, and immediately started to struggle. He had gotten pretty strong . . .

But not nearly strong enough to avoid going face-first into the snow a few seconds later.

The first day of snow was heralded by a snowball fight of epic proportions—where cultivators used all their strength and skill to topple each other.

In the end, we were all sopping wet. But that was half the fun, sitting around the fire afterwards, drinking tea and laughing. The tea was really good . . . but I longed for the day when we could have hot chocolate.

If what Chyou had been saying was true? Well, it wouldn't be that long at all.

→

The rest of the day wasn't very busy. Sure, there was the general maintenance of the farm, but that wasn't *really* work. We inspected each building, looking for holes, or anything to patch up that had been revealed by the cold.

Many hands made for light work, though, and we had a *whole* lot of hands. It made it easier that we had built everything so well, so there were minimal repairs.

We ended up just going for a walk to the back of the property, across another river, and into the trees, our breaths steaming out before us in the chill.

It was a quiet, contented silence that surrounded us for the most part. The snow dampened the sound, and there was barely any wind. What remained was the crunching of our boots and Gou's and Xiulan's happy chattering voices as they explained what hockey was to Xianghua. The woman looked intrigued.

Yun Ren was heckling Chunky about something, and the others were all talking among themselves. I hadn't even really noticed that I had started walking in the lead. At the head, forging the path onwards, with everybody else falling into place behind me.

It honestly felt a bit strange, to look over everybody. To know that *I* was the guy in charge.

Neither I nor Rou had ever really had so many people in our lives, not like this. Sure, I had played babysitter to a host of cousins. But the bonds here were more . . . intense than that. Or so I felt.

It felt different to look at Big D, Rizzo, and Yin sitting together on a tree branch, staring up into the sky. Yun Ren pulling open a sack of nuts that Chunky and Washy had unearthed, sharing some of their bounty with them. Tigu packing snow together with Meiling, making their own little snowman.

Whenever they saw me, or looked at me, they all brightened up in their own little way. Xiulan's soft smile. Gou Ren's grin. Yun Ren's smirk, and Big D's nod. Chunky's pleased *oink*, and Washy's searching eyes, seeing if I had any snacks.

When they looked back at me, what hit me the most was their . . . trust.

It wasn't something that needed to be said, or discussed. It was something deeper than that. A feeling.

And after that dream, after that girl, and the feeling I'd gotten in my chest . . . I could finally *see* that trust. I could understand these people, who put their lives in my hands.

It was absolutely and utterly humbling.

→

That night, I went to the greenhouse.

The planters had been moved in, seeded, and placed next to the beehive. The creatures within were probably a bit confused at the moment, but at least I wouldn't have to deal with the chance of my best producers freezing to death.

"Quite the day, wasn't it?" my wife asked from where she was curled up in my lap. Mei loved this place. She had a smug grin plastered on her face and was currently practicing her knitting, while I was strumming my banjo idly.

"Quiet, you," I grumped back, and tugged at my clothing.

What had started as another game of go against Xiulan had gotten both Meimei and Xianghua heckling us to make it strip go—and Xiulan had agreed.

Mostly because she knew she would kick my ass, the ass. I'd ended up stripped down to my skivvies, while Xiulan had gone undefeated.

I mean, I'd known that it was going to happen, but couldn't she have thrown one game or something?! Then she booked it when Meiling had challenged her, out the door and dragging a confused Tigu by her collar along for "training."

My wife giggled again at my misfortune and leaned into me. She took a deep breath of the earthy-scented air—and then she suddenly startled, her hand flying to her stomach. Her eyes widened, and I felt a wave of panic suddenly come over me. I could feel every alarm going off in my entire being.

Her breath came out shallowly as she turned to look at me.

"That was a strong one," she muttered, breathing deeply. She looked okay. Immediately, I calmed, slumping down in relief. "It's been kicking for a while now, but nothing like this—ah!"

My hand shot to her stomach and I felt the little tremor, the small bulge where a foot stuck out for but a moment.

Her stomach getting big was one thing. But this . . . this was complete proof. It was real. The feeling of *my child* moving.

I swallowed thickly.

"How . . . how does it feel?" I asked, and Meimei waved me off.

"It tickles a little—*geh*!" She suddenly winced.

"Are you okay?!"

"*Right in the bladder.* I nearly pissed myself," my wife said with a harrumph, glancing at her empty cup of tea.

I snorted, slumping in my seat, and then I started to laugh, unable to help myself, and Meimei soon joined me.

"It's . . . not too far off now, isn't it?" I asked, and my wife nodded.

"Three months and . . . eight days?" she hazarded after thinking it over for a moment.

Three months. Three months and eight days. Several weeks into the new year. A baby born in the last few weeks of winter just before spring.

My arms tightened around my wife.

Would . . . would I be a good father?

I had no idea.

I felt the weight of the question when I looked down at Meimei, how happy she was. How much she trusted me.

We settled back down, just sitting together and basking in the warmth.

"Hey . . . Jin?"

"Mmm?"

"Where did you learn about all this stuff, anyway?" she asked idly. "What you say sometimes . . . well, a lot of your knowledge doesn't use Qi. Are the doctors in Raging Waterfall Gorge just that much more advanced?"

She caught me off guard with that. It was clearly a question of idle curiosity. I hadn't exactly been frugal in sharing knowledge that came from a more technologically advanced society, so it was only natural that she would be curious. Meiling was smart. She was smarter than I was, that's for sure. She could put the pieces together that something just didn't quite add up.

I took a second to think about it. I had two options here. I had been deflecting over the last couple years because honestly? It kind of didn't matter to me. I was already weird, being a cultivator. What use was adding on that I was a reincarnated soul from another universe? They had never known Rou, to know that I had changed. I was the same guy, with or without the strange origin story. I could always keep saying it was the knowledge of a far-off land; it was even true, technically.

Or I could trust her.

I mulled it over, as Meimei looked at me curiously at my sudden silence. She was calm, waiting for my answer . . . there was no judgement on her face.

She *trusted* me.

And trust is a two-way street. I took a breath.

"Have you ever heard any stories about reincarnation?" I asked quietly. My heart slowly started to beat faster. It was an odd thing, to tell somebody that you had memories of another world. It sounded crazy. "About suddenly waking up in a new body after death?"

Meimei looked at me again, at first amused and with a look that said "get serious." I could see the gears turn as she fully processed what I was saying. She was smart, though, my Mei, she didn't need me to say much more.

Her face changed. From shock, to confusion, to realisation.

I swallowed, wondering how she would take it. I . . . I really didn't want to ruin what we had.

Then her lips quirked into a smile.

"Well, it would certainly explain why you're so weird."

I snorted out a laugh as we lapsed into silence. That, well . . . it wasn't the exact reaction I had been expecting, really. These reveals always felt so *dramatic* in stories.

Instead, my wife just nodded, like everything suddenly made sense. It made the knot of tension in my chest disappear.

"Do you . . . want to hear about it?" I asked slowly, haltingly. Her eyes softened. Her hand came up and rested on the side of my face.

"The heavens know talking about my mother is hard enough," she whispered. "If you don't want to talk too much about it tonight . . . or ever, it's fine."

I leaned into her touch. Her quiet support.

She was right. Remembering the Before was sometimes painful. Remembering my family.

I couldn't remember how I died. If I had at all. All I knew was that I was *here* now.

And that was what mattered.

So I told her a story. A story of a foolish young man, who built snowmen every year with his mother, his father, and his sister, in a country defined by a maple leaf.

The snow fell outside. The smell of dirt and the faint buzzing of bees were the backdrop to my tale.

I told my wife about a life in the Before.

She listened quietly, holding my hand the entire time.

CHAPTER 24

THE SERVANT

Pi Pa woke early, before even Bi De crowed. It was her habit, to awake and begin the day before anyone else, as a good servant should. She awoke beside her Dear, Chun Ke, who was asleep with a contented smile upon his face. They had fallen asleep in the Servant Quarters, as they often did, sleeping with young Sirs Gou and Yun Ren, as well as the newer additions to Fa Ram.

She smiled down at her Dear. He was sleeping well again. She had been worried that the nightmares he had been having were a precursor to something worse, an unexpected remnant of the injuries he had taken from wicked Chow Ji over a year ago now. Her greatest fear was that it would somehow cause him to regress to his previous state, when he had been broken and barely there.

Thankfully, they had just been nightmares. Her Dear was still healed, mostly. She could take a few scares if that meant her other half was fine.

She turned to check on the third person sharing their quarters. Young Sir Bowu was asleep against his side, curled up against her Dear. Pi Pa smiled warmly at the scene and pressed her nose gently against her Dear before leaving them both to their sleep.

In truth . . . she didn't have much to do most of the time. Every other member of their household cleaned up after themself and generally made her job very easy. But even if they didn't, this was a job she enjoyed. She *liked* taking care of people, like the Master and the Mistress. It may have been a small duty, this task of hers, but she enjoyed it all the same. To keep everything neat and tidy, to take care of the small things, was her contribution. Each small task added up in the end to something greater. Each day was an opportunity to better herself and contribute.

Pi Pa heated up some water and brought it to Bi De, who she knew would have returned from night watch. The rooster was sitting upon the coop, stretching his neck and cleaning some of the snow off his vest in preparation for his morning call to the sun.

He turned at her approach and bowed his head. "Thank you, Sister," he said with full honesty.

Pi Pa nodded and departed, leaving him to his duties. She opened up the coop and let the rest of the chickens out as Bi De called the morning alarm.

They spilled out, clucking to the rise of the sun, hazy behind the clouds.

It was time to start another day, even as more snow fell down upon them.

→

"It's time!" the Master said with a bright grin when he gathered them all after their morning exercises. His grin was bright, as it had been for the past couple of days. He and his lady had been even more affectionate than normal with each other recently. "The winter is fully upon us! We shall commence the construction of the Great General! He Who Commands the Winter!"

A great cheer rose from their assembled ranks as they stepped off into the snow.

Her Dear squealed happily and took off, little Bowu, Young Sir Gou Ren, and Young Miss Xianghua all upon his back. Between one step and the next he grew until he scooped a swath of snow from the yard into an enormous pile, constructing the General's foundation.

Pi Pa smiled warmly at the sight.

The Master laughed, his eyes bright and steady as he brought out a strange translucent crystal—the one that had been in the last General's chest.

They all pitched in. Pi Pa was right behind her Dear, collecting and packing snow along with the rest of them. Swiftly, the General grew, and just as swiftly the material for its construction grew scarce—for they had used up all the snow from the main island upon which the manor house stood.

Pi Pa, though she maintained her outward composure as a proper lady, couldn't help but have fun while they all worked together. And if she skipped and danced a bit as she moved, nobody said anything. The General rose first above the house, and then gradually its height exceeded even the trees.

They worked until it was time for lunch, at which point the massive edifice of snow was the tallest construction Pi Pa had ever witnessed in her life. It was twice, nearly three times as tall as their two-story house.

While the younger ones frolicked about his base with Chun Ke, Pi Pa simply settled down on the porch, content to watch. Her heart soared at the sight of her Dear so happy. At his bright eyes, his spark undiminished.

She breathed a sigh of relief. She always checked, ready to step in if his eyes once more dulled.

Pi Pa's first solid memories were of darkness, pain, and terror.

Her consciousness had been fleeting in those early days. Something barely there, that came in bursts.

But she remembered being happy. The Master had taken care of them well. He had been so kind to them, feeding them and playing with them, hoisting them up and scratching their bellies.

He had been their father, in most respects. Their patriarch, seeing to their needs with his kindness and giving to them without a care in the world. She remembered the flashes of joy as she'd grown and played alongside her Dear.

Two parts of a whole. Equal in every way.

And then the rats came.

It was the *smell* that she could never forget.

The acrid, burning tang of Chow Ji and his rats. It was seared into her memory. Even now, so long after his demise, she knew his slimy, oily scent. The smell of blood and death. The burning eyes of the rats as they ate their own dead kin.

They had tried to warn Bi De when he'd welcomed Chow Ji, in their own way. They screamed at him, but he'd heard no words, so they'd stomped and tried to kill the little vermin who desecrated the land.

Together with her Dear. Her brave, noble Dear. He had been so quick to understand things, to see the darkness of Chow Ji—and also to spare Ri Zu. It was Chun Ke who had recognised Ri Zu's pure spirit. They had seen her begging them to help, in a hazy, dreamlike fugue.

With Ri Zu's help, they had broken free of the pen that held them and charged the foul demon. They had done battle with Chow Ji and his horde of minions. They had protected Fa Ram!

That was where the memories sharpened, in that battle. *That* was where she truly became aware. When she truly became Pi Pa.

Her mind went back to the moment Chow Ji's claws had struck her Dear, scoring those three massive gashes in Chun Ke's face. His scream of pain was as much a part of her as her own name. She would not forget it. She could not unhear it.

And in that moment, with her Chun Ke, her Dear falling to the ground . . . it had spawned the void.

The ravening hatred. The sucking pit in her gut that always was there. The ugly, black hate, as her other half was torn from the world in her mind. She'd thought him dead. She'd thought herself dead.

Yet Bi De, with the assistance of her sister Ri Zu, had prevailed in the end. He had struck down the rats and saved Fa Ram.

It should have been a glorious victory, as her Dear opened his eyes.

It wasn't.

She remembered how Chun Ke's spark had flickered and faded. His eyes were dull. Her other half, her complement, had been killed in every way that mattered. He was but a beast.

Her heart had torn in half at the sight, and the little pit of darkness had grown.

Chun Ke had clung on, though. Little thoughts, little gasps of awareness. He had *fought* whatever had maimed him.

And that was enough. She would never give up on him. She couldn't.

The Master had been with them every step of the way. He had administered medicine crafted by the Lady of the House. He had aided them when all seemed lost.

For that, he had her loyalty. Her devotion. She was proud to be his servant, he who would sacrifice so much for them.

Her Dear's nightmares kept her up every night, pressed into his side. His eyes sharpened and dulled in fitful bursts.

The bad days were the ones where he simply trundled around the pen and *oinked* unintelligibly. The worst days were those when he didn't seem to recognise her at all.

On those days, the festering void grew. On those days, she contemplated killing Bi De for his arrogance and stupidity. He had been weak. On top of that, he'd still been recovering from his injuries. If she wanted to, she could have *destroyed* him.

The ravening black pit pulsed every time she thought of it. She knew her cultivation was twisted and perverted. Something *dark*. Something almost demonic that would surge with her emotions, reaching out to destroy everything that had hurt her.

But that would not have brought her Dear back. It would not have helped him. So she had stayed her hand. She'd toiled relentlessly, in the hopes of bringing her Dear back from the endless nightmares that plagued him.

Slowly, ever so slowly, he had started to heal. His spark came back. His eyes stopped going dull for days or weeks on end.

Her Chun Ke was healing, with the medicine of the Lady of the House and the ministrations of their Master.

But her noble other half was diminished. Broken. Her once equal, her perfect, balanced partner, spoke in halting grunts and made-up words. He'd said nonsensical things. He was slow to understand and had to study things for hours to learn them, if he could at all.

It had nearly been too much. He was a stranger at times in her Dear's body. The only thing that saved her heart was the one thing that was undiminished about him.

His love for her, and his pure devotion to the wonder of life.

Even when he'd struggled. Even when he'd forgotten, he'd still called her a pretty lady. His blank, dull eyes would light up, and he would bring her flowers before they inevitably fell back to his demons.

It hurt. *It hurt so much.*

But she'd endured it every day. She had to endure it, for him.

For *herself* too, lest she lose herself to the void in her chest.

Her love was a candle against that darkness. A spark against the storm.

Slowly, ever so slowly, he had truly come back. He would live with the marks of Chow Ji for the rest of his life . . . but his nobility and wisdom manifested themselves in other ways. Crippled, he grew into a new direction, as only her Dear could.

He was the only one who could calm Tigu without her retaliation. He was the one who could chastise and never have his words taken as an insult. He was the one who brought them together. More than Bi De. More than Ri Zu. More than her own attempts to keep the others from fighting.

Her Dear became the beating heart of all of the Master's disciples. Strong in spite of his injury.

The strongest one of them all, in her opinion.

If her Dear was the light of all of them . . . then Pi Pa was the opposite. The yin to his yang, as she was always meant to be.

These days, she could say she was content. Today, she could even say she was truly happy.

She had a purpose. She had her Dear . . . even if he wasn't ready for piglets *quite* yet.

But as she sat calmly looking down upon the laughing crowd chasing her Dear, as she watched over the Fa Ram that had given her a home and purpose, she would not forget. She *could not* forget. She might have made peace with Bi De and forgiven him for his failures. But she had vowed that *whatever* would seek to harm her Dear, *whatever* would seek to harm her *home* . . .

She would devour it whole.

And that would be the end of it. After all, good Lady *always* kept to her word.

CHAPTER 25

RED STRANDS

Knitting was an interesting art, Meiling reflected, as her needles clacked together beside the fireplace. The string was woven together and tied tightly in a perfect pattern to create a greater whole.

Maybe it was a bit too philosophical, to think that the knots represented the people in her life, but it was still a nice thought. A chain that had come together, with hard work and effort.

All these seemingly unconnected people who had found their way here . . . and whose fates had been entwined with a girl from Hong Yaowu.

□

Two bodies impacted with enough force to create a small shock wave. Their weapons clashed as they sought to gain dominance over each other. The blades on their feet bit deep into the ice.

Xiulan smirked at the look of wide-eyed excitement on Xianghua's face, her entire body coiled while she sought to master this new area of combat. Balance and reflexes all in one. Truly, Ha Qi was a powerful sport.

In the end, experience was what won the day, though Xiulan had only really played once before. Xiulan twisted, and Xianghua went spinning away as Xiulan grabbed the puck shooting across the river and bolted towards her next adversary.

Pi Pa sat daintily in the goal, her eyes sharp as ever, watching Xiulan's approach and ready to defend against it. Xiulan displayed the skills that marked her training—her strike was one of precision and grace. A line drive into the corner of the net, faster than the eye could see.

The puck slammed into the stick in Pi Pa's mouth, deflecting off and being caught out of the air by Gou Ren, who immediately started back towards Xiulan's team's net. Tigu was quick to intercept, but Gou Ren was a Wrecker Ball, simply slamming into the smaller girl and sending her skidding backwards as he built up momentum.

Xiulan pirouetted and shot back the way she came . . . only to be intercepted by Xianghua again.

"You know the point of the game is the puck, right?!" Xiulan demanded.

"Master Jin said blocking is a perfectly valid tactic," Xianghua replied, stopping her from getting to Gou Ren. They shoved and skidded along the ice, which was creaking a bit ominously. It still wasn't very thick, but they were cultivators. A bit of cold water wouldn't hurt them.

They rammed into each other until Xianghua managed to sway slightly and twist, sending Xiulan flying into a snowbank.

Grunting, Xiulan shook her head, clearing off the snow, even as Gou Ren got the puck taken off him by Tigu—

Ri Zu slammed the gong, indicating the end of the round. Meiling was sitting beside her, looking amused at their antics, the red thread and needles clacking away.

Xiulan took Xianghua's hand as the other woman pulled her out of the snowbank.

"You were right, Xiulan. It *is* good training," Xianghua said with a smile, her breath misting in front of her.

"It's pretty fun too," Xiulan said, as she looked around the frozen river.

Jin was with Bowu and Huo Ten, the monkey, teaching both how to skate. Huo Ten being here was a bit surprising. The monkey had been relatively reclusive these past months . . . though Jin *had* given him leave to dig as he pleased.

She just hadn't expected the monkey to mine out *an entire tunnel complex* in the back forest.

Her rival sniffed. "You'll see how fun it is when you are defeated and at my feet, Cai."

Xiulan snorted at the challenge. "I wish you the luck of the heavens. You'll need it, Damp Pond."

She skated to the sidelines and took a drink of water as her heart began to calm. She had been looking forward to playing Ha Qi again. It was fast-paced, took immense concentration and skill, and had just the right touch of violence.

It really was the ideal sport. One could even pretend they were on a flying sword, with the blades attached to their feet.

She smiled at Xianghua, then skated off to her own team. Yun Ren and Tigu both nodded to her. "So? What's the plan?" Tigu asked. They were tied at two-two.

"Switch me from goalie," Yun Ren said, rubbing at his thigh. "I've got an idea." His foxlike eyes were narrowed, and he was smirking.

Xiulan raised an eyebrow, Tigu grinned viciously, and they agreed.

The gong sounded again, and they got into position. Ri Zu stood on her raised stone and threw the puck between them.

The match was relatively inconclusive as they traded the puck back and forth for a while, shoving and dancing around each other—until Gou managed to slam into Yun and steal the puck. He had a giant grin on his face as he streaked towards Tigu, drawing his stick back for a slapshot. Qi started to swirl around his arms. It was technically illegal, since they said no technique use . . . but Xiulan had a feeling there was going to be a foul from both sides.

He let fly—only for the stick to just pass through the puck, the illusion dissipating. He looked utterly dumbfounded at what had happened.

Yun Ren chuckled when the puck suddenly appeared in Pi Pa's net, his own lazy strike sending it in.

"Ha! Take it, Gou—*ack!*"

Peppa slammed into Yun Ren's stomach, folding him in half for the treachery.

Ri Zu bashed her gong to halt the action, squeaking about fouls from both sides, while Xiulan and Xianghua skidded to a stop to watch the fireworks.

Xiulan could only stare as Yun Ren managed to get to his feet, then immediately took off running from his brother and the enraged pig.

Xiulan started laughing.

"Hey! Cut me into the next game?" Jin asked, skating up to them.

"Only if you're ready to lose!" Xiulan called back, sticking out her tongue.

Jin grinned and slung an arm over her shoulder.

Xiulan punched at his stomach good-naturedly.

The teams turned out to be Jin versus all of them. Naturally, they ended up losing. Jin cheerfully skated circles around them all, one of the few times when he didn't hold back so much. It wasn't even his strength, it was simply his skill. The mystical sport seemed to be something he had practiced all his life.

By the end of it, they were all tired and soaked with sweat, while Jin whistled a jaunty tune, a smug smile on his face.

"Master is too strong," Tigu muttered.

"I'll draw a bath. Then we can have a bit more fun," Jin called back to them as they all walked home.

Xiulan snorted at the phrasing.

A year ago, she had thought the worst.

A year ago, she had *expected* the worst.

Today, she thanked her friend for preparing a bath for her, ready for the rousing game of Answer-Go that would follow.

□

The fires burned. The hearth crackled, and the days passed.

The dyed-red thread was warm and strong. A bond, perhaps. Like the red threads of fate in all the stories?

The bond between people.

Or maybe Meiling was getting just a tad too sentimental.

□

A dragon descended from the heavens, twisting and undulating. He curled through the grey skies, the rider upon his back bundled up for the cold. They landed before a man on a hill, whose arms were crossed as he stared upon his work.

"It's looking good, Bro," Meiling heard Yun Ren tell Gou as he brought out the recording crystal. He had recorded many images of the project from the air. Gou Ren studied them critically, his eyes narrowed with thought and concentration.

It was a good look on him. The intensity and the passion as he planned and made. Architecture was honestly the last thing Meiling would have guessed Gou Ren would take an interest in—too much math and planning—but her brother in all but blood had surprised her.

Gou Ren grinned, as the images were apparently satisfactory. "It's looking good, everybody! I think we can get started on the next part!"

There was a great cheer from his labourers—which consisted of basically everybody from the farm.

Gou Ren had decided that the packable snow was *perfect* for testing out how his architectural drawings would actually look, so he'd roped nearly everyone into helping him make his grand visions a reality.

Now they had two towers, a bridge, and what looked like a section of a castle rising up off the hills.

Meiling was one of the few sitting out, as she knit a sock. She watched as the castle wall started extending, a small smile on her face. Jin was packing snow along with Gou; both laughed about something, bumping their fists together.

Jin, before turning to start to work again, noticed her watching and grinned even brighter, waving at her. Meiling shook her head in amusement and waved back.

Her husband had been in an even better mood than normal this past week . . . and to be honest, so had she. Mei brought her attention back to her knitting as she thought over the reason she felt more connected to her husband than ever before.

He had told her his secret. The one he had been keeping for a while.

Reincarnation.

A different world.

There were stories about this kind of thing. Lingering spirits who took over the bodies of the dying to get their revenge against the wicked. Cultivators who had been born in the long past and somehow returned in the body of somebody weak.

Meiling didn't know enough to tell if any of them were actually true. But it was a common enough theme.

Similarly, the thought of another world wasn't quite so alien. There had to be something up in the heavens. Other realms to travel to and cultivate.

Meiling chewed on her lip as she remembered asking Xiulan about what exactly was out there.

"There are supposed to be planes beyond the heavens. Other worlds floating in the Sea between Worlds . . . But I don't actually know, Meiling. Nobody really does,

until they have enough power to travel there. I doubt any that do gain such power ever return."

Reincarnation. The memories of two lives. Despite her initial reaction, as soon as Jin had said that, it was as if everything had fit . . . she *knew* it to be true.

It was the small things that gave it away. The things out of place that couldn't be explained solely by him having been raised outside the Azure Hills.

His manner of speech. The odd slurs in his tone that he sometimes had. The way he had spoken the other language, something which she now knew was entirely of another world. His music had been a completely different style, and he'd had tales about celebrations that were like nothing she had heard of. It all made sense now.

It hadn't really changed anything, though, had it?

Meiling was sure most people would have been fairly shocked, but it helped that he had brought it up himself. He told the truth of his own volition and he never had really lied to her.

Everything he had told her had been the truth. It was just sometimes that "a man from a far-off land" was a lot farther away than one might have thought.

He had told her. Revealed his secret to her, a secret that came with wounds that still bled when he spoke of his own death.

Everybody had some secrets. Meiling certainly hadn't told Jin everything about her mother, and the Year of Sorrows that had nearly broken Hong Yaowu. How could she have? They had only known each other for two years, and the scars that the Year of Sorrows had left were still raw to this day.

Trust had to be *built*, just like a relationship. Her father, and her mother's notes, had been adamant about that. One doesn't just spill their deepest and most intimate secrets.

She had known he didn't like talking about his time in the Cloudy Sword Sect. She would have even been fine if he hadn't wanted to talk about it, because some scars never really healed, and worrying at them only made things worse—but she'd wanted to know more about him. She wanted to know more about her husband, her Jin, to share some of the burden he had, just as he shared some of hers.

So she had asked.

Jin had trusted her.

And that was enough.

So even as he told her of a place that was beyond the heavens, of another world . . . things didn't really change between them. They still told each other silly things in the mornings; they still made breakfast together, they bathed together, and slept together.

Jin was Jin. And she wouldn't have it any other way.

□

The days turned to night, and the night turned to day.

Needles clattered together. She cast off and wove in her ends.

Meiling hung her completed sock above the fire.

It was a strange tradition, if she was honest.

But the look of shock and happiness on Jin's face was everything she had hoped for.

CHAPTER 26

THE MINER

Huo Ten awoke in darkness. The smell of earth filled his nostrils, and the air had just a touch of dampness to it. The cavern was warm, some might say uncomfortably so, this far below the earth.

To Huo Ten, it was *perfect.* His hand reached out, tapping at a crystal on his helmet, and it lit up, bathing his cavern in a warm glow. The cavern was relatively small. Big enough for him to stand up straight, but a human would have to be bent nearly double. Master Jin likely wouldn't be able to fit in here at all—a problem Huo Ten would remedy with his next project, enlarging this place to properly host guests. He crawled out of his sheets and made his bed with soft linens that had been gifted to him by his hosts. There was a kettle off to the side, and with his Qi, he could heat the water to prepare tea.

That was one of the perks of being a Spirit Beast. No need for fire crystals or wood, of which he had neither at the moment. His hands curled around his kettle as he heated the water, then poured it into a bowl with mashed rice, berries, and a bit of jerky. It quickly turned into a thick porridge, one that he had eaten often back home—save for the fact that the ingredients were of a quality he had never even dreamed of. The food here went beyond good for the body; it was good for his very soul, invigorating his Qi and propelling him higher into the Initiate's Realm.

He chewed on some of the berries as he smiled around at his domain. It *almost* felt like home. There was just one thing missing, and that was his clan.

It had taken a while after the excitement of adventure for the feeling to set in, but he yearned to be home again in the Crystal Hill.

There was absolutely nothing wrong with Master Jin or any other of those from Fa Ram. They had all been more than kind to him. He could say he liked Fa Ram without reservation. He enjoyed serving tea to others or strolling around the property with Tigu. He had taken pleasure in watching the practice bouts between the cultivators, and aiding with the transfer of the harvest had been fun.

Master Jin even knew the right way to groom! Huo Ten had missed the feeling of another picking through his fur. He had attempted it first with Gou Ren. He was a handsome and rugged lad who would have been the talk of the women back in Crystal Hill, his fine appearance making him look like one of Huo Ten's kin. But the boy had been entirely too awkward as he picked through Huo Ten's fur and kept glaring at his foxlike brother each time the man's recording crystal chimed.

Huo Ten could say that the entirety of his experience at the Fa Ram was interesting and engaging.

But . . . but at the end of the day, he still felt alone. A lifetime of echoes from Master Gen and his own instincts made it so being anywhere other than a loud place with nearly a hundred of his kin and clan felt . . . wrong. Huo Ten missed the soothing feeling of Master Gen's presence. The spiritual fulfillment of being near his ancestors and venerating the Great Master. He missed the foolish antics of the children as they hooted and swung through the trees.

Most of all, he had missed the earth. He missed mining. Every day that passed without a pick in his hand, searching for crystals, felt like he had ants crawling within his fur. Even before he was truly awake, the echoes of Master Gen's passion had infected him, sending him delving deeper and deeper in search of more crystals to share with his kin.

There was no mine here, no place truly underground except the cold storage. And the cold storage, while interesting, wasn't the right kind of tunnel.

So he had begged Master Jin for leave to dig a tunnel, just something to occupy himself with. Master Jin had promptly taken him to the back of the property and given him an entire hill to do with as Huo Ten pleased, even helping him dig out the entrance.

"What kind of man doesn't like digging a big hole?" Master Jin had declared with a shovel in his hand.

Huo Ten agreed wholeheartedly. Truly, Master Jin had the wrong body. He could have been one of the clan with that attitude.

Even if he clearly didn't like being too far below ground. He was simply *too big* . . . Being small came with disadvantages, but for the life of a miner it was a boon.

Huo Ten finished his breakfast and set away his bowl. He would wash it later when he came up to the surface again, but for now he had his main job to do.

He ascended the tunnels, heading upwards along the main tunnel towards the surface, ending up just below the frost line. The tunnels were larger here, and colder, but they were built so that the humans could enter easily. He turned off to the side along the main passage, into a room.

Sitting on a pedestal in the center of the unadorned room was a crystal.

The crystal. His reason for being here, and the reason for his awakening. An ancient device that contained memories from thousands of years ago—from a person who had lived at the same time as Huo Ten's own ancestors.

The inner light from the crystal was roiling slowly with differing colours. This was not the original crystal; the old one had cracked and become too unstable to use. So he and his kin had transferred the contents to this crystal, which had been an adventure of its own. They had nearly been trapped in the crystal by the spirit of a Temple Dog and had barely managed to escape.

Though the transfer had been successful, the sheer amount of information the old crystal had contained was beyond all estimates, as it needed time to settle into the new device.

He performed his checks quickly. Things seemed to be proceeding apace. The formation surrounding the crystal, made for them by Master Gen and Clan-Friend Jing of Pale Moon Lake City, was doing its work. Soon the crystal would be ready to use.

His checks done, he bowed to the crystal thrice and shouldered his pick, smiling to himself. He had found what looked to be a promising direction last night. He had felt the earth whispering to him, of things buried deep. He didn't know what it was, but he was itching to find out!

He went out of the side room, back into the main passage—

'*Hello?*' a voice called out, and Huo Ten jumped. He hadn't heard anybody come down! He turned around and found Miss Yin, the silver rabbit, staring up at him. She was a pretty thing, almost ethereal, with her colouration and beautiful eyes.

'*Can I help you, lass?*' Huo Ten asked her, taking off his helmet in respect, his gruff voice rumbling like a mountain.

'*Yeah, Shifu wants to know if ya can find him more dirt like this.*' She pulled a satchel off her back and showed the sample within.

Clay, the sort used for pottery. Huo Ten took a piece, smelling and tasting some of it. He closed his eyes and thought on the matter, rifling through his memories.

Finally, he found a match. High in mineral content and wet.

'*The seams of this are up a bit higher, and they're all frozen now. It'll take some time to dig it out, but I can get it done.*' It was something to do when he wasn't watching the crystal, at least. '*Is that everything?*'

Yin was staring at him curiously. '*You . . . know exactly where that is from* tasting *it?*'

Huo Ten nodded. '*Smell. Taste. Touch. Dirt is not just dirt. It has character and personality all of its own.*'

Yin looked intrigued.

'*Can . . . can you teach me?* she ventured after a moment. '*Shifu says that I have to find something I really like. So I've been trying everything, but nothing really . . .* clicks *besides fighting. I haven't tried mining yet.*'

Huo Ten paused at the statement, and at the frankness of its delivery. Huo Ten had been blessed to know his place and passion in his life . . . and yet he did understand her.

Being fully awake was scary, in some ways, without the warmth of Master Gen's spirit. A gentle warmth that had always been with him, Master Gen having sacrificed a portion of his strength for all of them. He watched over them, and all of his clan knew that Master Gen had everything in hand.

Here, though, without that guiding warmth, there was doubt. There was uncertainty in his actions now, not knowing how those who were not kin would react.

He second-guessed himself. He hesitated. For the first time in his life, he knew discontent and uncertainty—and he didn't like it.

Sometimes, Huo Ten could admit it would have been easier to just be an ordinary monkey.

But that was not his life any longer.

So Huo Ten, after giving the little rabbit's words due consideration, nodded.

'*First, yeh need a helmet,*' he decreed. '*Master Jin wants everybody to wear one.*'

Yin smiled brightly as she followed after him. He led them both down back into his room and started digging around for his spare. This one didn't have a fragment of light crystal, but it was serviceable enough.

He had to stifle a chuckle when he put it on her head. He had to admit it looked rather silly on her. Her ears stuck out the sides, nearly dragging on the floor.

'*You ready to learn, lass?*' Huo Ten asked.

'*Hell yeah!*' she replied. '*What do I have to do, Master Huo?*

She was certainly enthusiastic . . . but there was something about her. She was serious. She had a kind of drive in her eyes. An utter willingness to be instructed. A completely open mind to learn.

Huo Ten considered his new student.

'*Let us begin.*'

→

And thus they ventured forth, heading into the promising passage Huo Ten had dug out and prepared.

'*See here,*' the monkey said, tapping at the wall and pressing his ear against it. Yin copied him, her head against the wall as well, closing her eyes.

'*There's something here?*' she asked. Huo Ten nodded, pleased that his initial explanation had been taken up so quickly.

'*Aye. You can hear the difference.*' Yin nodded thoughtfully at Huo Ten's words.

'*I don't think that's rock, though. There's something . . . different about it,*' Yin said, giving the wall due consideration.

Huo Ten clapped his hands together and pointed at her.

'*Aye! It's not rock, nor crystal. It's bone.*'

'*Bone? Should we dig it up?*' Yin asked, curious.

'*If you want to. There aren't many bones in the Crystal Hills, so something this big may be a Blaze Bear or some other monster that died long ago.*'

Yin flexed her powerful paws and eagerly started at the wall. The dirt flew quickly but purposefully, as Yin was ever vigilant as to not make the tunnel collapse on them.

He chuckled at her blurring forepaws and sized up the wall himself. He tapped it twice with his fingers, then nodded and hefted his pick. He struck the wall three times; then on the fourth strike, he buried the pick deep and yanked. Yin flinched in surprise as Huo Ten ripped an entire section of the wall out, accomplishing more in seconds than she had in a minute.

The rabbit paused her frenetic digging.

'It's how and where you dig, lass, not the power with which you move. It comes with time, mark me well.'

Yin nodded with utmost seriousness, stepping back to watch him.

'*Here, here, and here,*' Huo Ten said after a moment. '*See this dip in the crack here? That's the way.*'

Yin studied the places intently, and then, with three strikes of her own in the spots Huo Ten had pointed out to her, pulled the entire section down, pushing it out into the tunnel.

Huo Ten nodded and performed a few more strikes of his own, getting the last bit of dirt out of the way. The dirt had surrounded a femur that was as thick around as he was tall.

They both stared for a moment at the discovery.

'*That's fuckin' huge,*' the pretty little rabbit said flatly.

'*Aye. That's fuckin' huge indeed.*'

He walked up to the thing and tapped at it. Then he paused, and tapped at it again. A slight vibration. A slight chime, now that he was directly touching the bone.

Huo Ten grinned.

'*I think we may have hit the mother lode, lass.*'

→

It didn't take long to tunnel around the massive leg bone. It was still hot work, but being Spirit Beasts had some advantages. They pushed around the obstruction until the dig site started getting brighter from a light not coming from the digging pair.

With one final swing, the darkness gave way completely and what Huo Ten had sensed was exposed: a seam of glowing crystal that was hidden behind the bone.

Light Stones. The same kind that were in Huo Ten's helmet.

Huo Ten hooted, a whooping call, as he dropped his pick and beat the ground with his hands. Yin followed suit, thumping the ground with her hind leg excitedly. The rabbit's fur was brown from digging. She was absolutely filthy, but she didn't seem to care.

'*Let's get this to the surface.*' Huo Ten licked his lips as he considered the strike points and how to remove the crystal from the wall—and then he turned to Yin. '*I've got an idea. You up for it?*'

Yin nodded.

'*Now, hit it exactly where I say . . .*'

Normally it would be hours of careful mining to get such a bounty out. But with a few well-placed kicks under Huo Ten's direction, the rabbit extracted the entire thing.

→

The journey back up to the surface was uneventful . . . as uneventful as dragging a mass of Light Stone up could be, anyway.

Together, they carted their bounty to the surface—from the warmth of the deep to the cold, snowy realm above.

'*Hey! Hey! Look what we found!*' Yin shouted eagerly, bounding towards the house. Several heads poked out, curious and interested.

Soon enough, they were all gathered around the table, staring at the new treasure.

Huo Ten was clapped on his back by Master Jin and praised until his blue face darkened to purple.

They weren't kin. They weren't clan. But . . . well, if he had to stay longer . . . that wouldn't be *too* bad.

Digging was always better with a friend . . . and sharing the spoils was his calling.

CHAPTER 27

THE GIRL WHO WAS A CAT

Tigu's head rocked to the side as a fist impacted it. She returned with a strike of her own, matching the bastard blow for blow.

Tigu ached. Her head throbbed as she spat out a mouthful of blood, but a moment later she forced her adversary back with a vicious slash.

The man made of lightning glared at her. He was arrogant and haughty. Though Tigu had injured him . . . he was better than her. More powerful.

Tigu swallowed as the man stared down at her. His eyes were dispassionate, uncaring. He looked at her like she was the dirt on his shoe.

"I shall end it in the next strike," the man declared. "Rou Tigu, you will be defeated."

Tigu steeled herself for the fight. She would not be able to last much longer.

But she didn't have to.

Tigu smiled and laughed as she felt it. Home. The mountain that was her home had come, and it was not happy.

Her Master was here.

The giant man made of lightning recoiled. His eyes widened in horror.

A warm hand landed on her head. Tigu smiled up at her Master. His power filled the world. Her enemy, so large before, quailed before his mere presence, withering away after tasting but a fraction of her Master's might.

"Good job," he praised her, and then his gaze turned towards her enemies.

Naturally, they were defeated utterly.

And all Tigu could feel was satisfaction.

□

Tigu woke up smiling. Her head was cradled on Mistress's collarbone, and her back was pressed against Master's chest. Tigu took a breath, drawing in the comforting scent, before squirming. She had an itch to continue carving today, and she wanted to jot down a few ideas.

"Oh? You're chipper this morning. Have a good dream?" her Mistress asked, apparently already awake. She opened one eye and looked down at Tigu with amusement.

Tigu nodded.

The dream wasn't particularly common, but whenever she had it, she woke up in a good mood.

Master and Mistress, as well as the Blade of Grass, had warned Tigu about the possibility of bad dreams after what had happened at the Dueling Peaks. They said that it was only natural if she felt something wrong and that they were there for her if she wanted to talk.

Tigu had none of that. Her dreams of the Peaks were untroubled. When she dreamed, she dreamed of her Master's warm and comforting power wrapping around her body and shielding her from harm. She dreamed of their enemies, once on the brink of victory, throwing themselves to their knees and her Master simply gazing upon them.

She dreamed of Ri Zu's face as the rat rescued her. She dreamed of Loud Boy and Rags, injured but alive and clapping her on the shoulders. She dreamed of everybody relaxing in Xiulan's house, the battle won.

She didn't exactly know what she was supposed to feel bad about. They had won; their enemy had been defeated completely.

She could say none of those memories bothered her too much. The only thing that did bother her was that she had grown complacent in categorizing people. When she was a cat, all had been enemies; when she was a human, nearly everyone had been a friend. She had to be able to swiftly ascertain who was to be treated like a sparring partner, and who was to be treated like Sun Ken.

Even then, it all felt like some kind of strange, distant memory some days.

"I expected you to sleep for a bit longer, after yesterday," her Master said from behind her, his voice rumbling, though still deep with sleep.

Tigu shook her head. "Can we try that again tonight?" she asked excitedly. Her Master chuckled.

"That" had been a marathon gauntlet against every one of their sparring partners, one by one—from Ri Zu to Xianghua, one after the other. An excellent training exercise even if Tigu was still just a little sore.

"Well, if you're up for it," he agreed.

"Yes!" Tigu enthused as she popped up out of the bed.

Master and Mistress both shook their heads when Tigu bounded down the stairs, going to prepare herself.

Truly, she was living the best life. A Master and a Mistress. Her Brother and Sister Disciples to accompany her. Being able to spar with a multitude of friendly opponents who pushed her to her limits—to even spar with her Master. Though he seemed clumsy and uncoordinated at times, that was of no consequence.

Bi De had been worried that she might somehow think less of Master, because he'd asked for help. Because he'd failed at something. That was foolish. He was learning something new, and these were things to be expected.

After all, when the time came, her Master would deliver them from their enemies without fail.

→

Sadly, spars were held in the evening, so Tigu needed something else to occupy her day.

The air was cold and the snow was thick on the ground as she carefully examined the block of ice before her. It was a good piece. Nice and clear, and it would sparkle like a gemstone once it was carved.

"Thanks, Wa Shi," she said, nodding to the fish. Her fellow disciple gave her a thumbs-up, one of his fins turning into an arm. He had helped her find this piece, swimming under the ice and examining it from below, looking for any imperfections.

Tigu picked up the block of ice and began carting it away to her "gallery," near the main house. Master had made her a place with a roof to put all her sculptures, one singular place where she could show them all off. Pi Pa and Master had helped her arrange them tastefully, and now, with the backdrop of snow and ice, it was quite a wonder to behold!

But it needed more. It was missing a certain something, and her Master had the right of it. It was no good with only sculptures of him.

Tigu set the block of ice down, placed her hand on its surface, and walked all around the giant block, her sharp eyes examining it for each and every minute crack, trying to visualize what to bring out of it. She shifted her shoulders, and the thick coat she was wearing impeded her movement slightly.

She didn't really *need* the coat, because she didn't really feel the cold . . . but Master and Mistress had made it for her, and it was nice and comfy. Same with the red hat on her head, her orange braids sticking out from the back.

Both smelled of warmth and home. Comfortable things . . . and she didn't look half bad in them either. The hat especially. It was like Fa Ram's symbol. *All* of her friends had a bright red hat, and she hadn't seen any of the villagers with them.

Though one thing wasn't exactly perfect. She glared at her reflection and scratched at her cheek.

She was losing her tan. That had been a nasty shock! It was her second winter, and in her cat form, her coat had just gotten thicker—she hadn't expected her complexion to change so drastically. She looked strange with pale skin, in her opinion. The tan was better. More . . . her. But everybody was losing a bit of colour, Master included. Only the Blade of Grass and Misty Lady remained the same. Both of them staying as pale as the snow.

Tigu shook her head and returned her attention to the block of ice. She was looking for something to pique her interest. Sometimes the rocks and branches spoke to her, showing her what they wanted to be. What was hidden beneath their surfaces. Other times, there was nothing to visualize but a blank canvas for her to create as she pleased.

The ice always felt a bit different than other materials. Honestly, after her forays with stone and wood, the ice felt . . . almost inferior. It melted, it deformed, and it was fragile—but she had a soft spot for it. It was what had first sparked her interest in carving: tearing ice out of the ground with Master. At first, she had started carving because of the lack of opponents, and the fact that Master had praised what she had made. She had loved that pleasant feeling in her gut as her Master had commended her skill, even when all the others did their best to ignore her when she was being belligerent. It had soothed her back then. Given her something to do to work out her frustrations—and then it had gradually transformed into something she genuinely enjoyed. Something she had passion for.

It was a connection, different from the ones born of sparring. Every time she had carved something at the Dueling Peaks, people had talked about it, offered their opinion, joined her in creating. It had felt so *right*. That was a feeling she normally only got in the midst of combat.

It was a memory she cherished. If fighting was the thing she liked the most . . . then carving was a close second. To craft, to *create* was to make a record of friendship and memories.

Tigu took a breath and dug her fingers into the ice. Her nails were sharper and longer than a normal human's. Not proper claws, so they were slightly inferior to her other form, but they did make up for it with dexterity. She took it slowly. While it was fun to conjure a set of Qi blades and simply make what she envisioned in moments, there was something to be said for the process. To have her concentration fully consumed, like Master did when he focused completely on his fields.

Her concentration was absolute as she carved in lines. She was empty, save for her existence in the moment. She shaved down ice and walked from angle to angle to observe her work.

The Blade of Grass stared back at her, carved in ice. Xiulan was standing upon a mountain peak, moving through the form of her dance. Her eyes were resolute, staring forwards. It was somehow fierce and protective, yet soft and welcoming at the same time.

Tigu ran a finger down the sculpture's face. The woman who had waded into hell to save her.

Her friend.

Not that she would tell Xiulan that too often. It wasn't good for the other woman to get a big head.

Satisfied, she placed the sculpture next to one of Master and nodded.

There was a squeak of interest

'*Oh? She's not naked?*' Ri Zu's voice came from behind Tigu. There was a teasing lilt to it.

Tigu shrugged, turning, and held out an arm to allow Ri Zu to clamber up. Xiulan *had* given Tigu permission to sculpt her nude, if it remained out of public viewing. But Tigu hadn't yet managed to figure out a composition worthy of her friend. It had to be perfect, to properly capture Xiulan's beauty—not her breasts, which fools stared at, but the muscles of her thighs and calves, which were stunning, perfect things. Not that Tigu would say that out loud. She was an amazing sculptor, and did not have trouble coming up with good poses! So instead, she deflected. "Her clothes were more interesting today."

Ri Zu raised an eyebrow but didn't push, instead changing the topic to why she was looking for Tigu: '*Master wants you. He said we all have to stir the dough for the cookies and make a wish for good luck.*'

"Cookies?" Tigu felt some drool come up from the corner of her mouth. They had tasted good when she was a cat. She couldn't imagine the flavours as a human.

'*And after . . . there is to be a Conclave of the Disciples. Bi De has called one, concerning the solstice,*' Ri Zu finished.

Tigu nodded solemnly.

→

The Conclave of the Disciples was held when the humans of the household departed for the greenhouse.

It was conducted in the side room of the house that was mostly used for storage. Unlike the main living room, the ceiling here was not high and vaulted, but lower, to accommodate the second floor. In the well-organised room, there was a table. Behind the table was a large piece of slate, dark, imposing, and full of writing and diagrams by Huo Ten about mining.

The only light to be had was a glowing crystal in the center of the table. The rest of the room was dark with shadows.

At the head of the table was Bi De, his back turned to them as he studied Huo Ten's works. His wings were tucked behind him, and he waited patiently.

Before, Tigu had chafed at the placement, at the fact that the head was not *her* place. She had once schemed to take it through violence, to cast low her fellow disciple and prove herself superior.

She hadn't given up that spot quite yet—she still wanted to stand there one day. But the urgency was gone. The bitterness did not manifest itself.

Bi De was at the head of the table . . . and that was fine. The rooster glanced back, feeling her eyes upon him and gave her a brief dip of his head in acknowledgement. Tigu returned it, then sat down at her place, directly to Bi De's right. The place of the strongest fighter. Ri Zu clambered off Tigu's shoulder and looked around. The little rat brightened, and she scampered off to get them cups.

Pi Pa was seated beside Chun Ke, brewing the tea. The prim pig was silent, but Chun Ke and Yin were not, the rabbit sitting on his head as they played Xs and Os. Yin's fur was still a bit dirty from her time in the mine earlier that day. Miantiao was watching, bemused at their back-and-forth game, while Huo Ten offered his own commentary, the monkey smiling up at Tigu and rolling his eyes.

Wa Shi was in his jar, simply lying on his back, his belly swollen with dinner and a look of bliss on his face. Even Bei Be was here, the ox bowing his head in thanks when Pi Pa finished her brew and trotted towards him.

Tigu looked around again and fidgeted slightly. She was the only human in the room. The conclave was for disciples . . . or more accurately, Spirit Beasts. The first of Master's disciples.

Her heart thumped a bit faster in her chest, but she managed to calm it. She took a deep breath.

There was a muffled *pop*, and Rou Tigu was once more a cat. She felt . . . awkward in this form still. Almost claustrophobic, and she itched. She missed her hands immediately, and she cast a forlorn look at her paws but clamped down on the urge to change back.

Several of the other disciples startled at what she had done, staring at her with concern, but she sat primly underneath their gazes.

'*Are you okay?*' Ri Zu whispered, returning with their cups. The honest look of compassion in her eyes made the twitching subside a bit.

'*I'm fine*,' Tigu said—even as the urge to swat at Ri Zu surged through her veins. She grabbed that part of her by its metaphorical throat and crushed it mercilessly, tearing into it and forcing it into the corner of her mind.

She was still Tigu. Her instincts could, as Master often said, *sod off.*

Chun Ke ambled towards her and nuzzled her with his nose before returning to his side of the table.

Finally the tea was served, and everybody settled down.

Bi De turned from his place at the head of the table.

His eyes were sharp and his Qi was focused. His gaze swept over them all, searching for something.

Then the rooster smiled. His Qi seemed to become something physical, emanating pride and satisfaction, as he found none of them wanting.

"My fellow disciples, my friends, thank you for heeding my call. It warms my heart to know we can still gather together like this, even after all that has happened this year, with more added to our ranks and stronger than ever."

His deep voice washed over them, his plumage radiant in the light of the crystal. Tigu sat up a bit straighter.

"Indeed, this year has been a trying one. Many tribulations have fallen upon us, yet we have met every challenge and exceeded it. From the beasts of the depths, to the dishonourable curs at the Dueling Peaks, we have repelled all that would do us harm. Yet even those who have not left Fa Ram have accomplished much, in serving our Master and guarding our home. This Bi De commends all of you, disciples of Fa Ram. It is my utmost honour to call all of you Brother and Sister."

The rooster swept into a bow, his wings placed in front of him in the gesture of respect. Tigu felt a small surge of emotion in her chest. She averted her eyes. If she were in human form she would probably be blushing, but this body felt only visceral satisfaction as Bi De rose once more, emotion in his eyes.

"However, another trial approaches. A trial upon the solstice, and one whose preparations we have been lax in. It is a most important task."

Tigu leaned forward, ready and eager, as Bi De continued. His eyes pierced them all.

"Upon the night of the solstice is a festival, a festival of fire. A celebration of the returning sun. It is upon this night that we have a most important duty."

There was a tension in the room as they awaited Bi De's announcement. All eyes were upon him. The rooster observed them, one and all. Finally, he continued.

"My fellow disciples—have you all prepared the gifts to be exchanged upon the solstice?"

Tigu blinked. Sweat began to gather on her back.

She had completely forgotten to make any gifts.

Tigu glanced around the table at the rest of the disciples, who were nodding, save for Wa Shi in his jar. The fish looked vaguely panicked.

There was a muffled *pop*, and Tigu was human again.

CHAPTER 28

HOME VIDEO

Darkness.

Nothingness.

Then Qi. Slow and steady, like the earth.

The crystal chimed.

The recording started.

Facets swam with colour and filled with inner light. In an instant, a world came to life, snapping into perfect clarity. The images were so crisp and sharp that reality almost paled in comparison.

An image of a large man with green eyes and freckled cheeks formed within the crystal's depths. He stood within a brightly lit area; the ceiling and walls the crystal captured behind him were made of rustic yet well-cared-for wood.

He was squinting at the crystal before he grinned and nodded, satisfied.

"There we go. Testing, testing, one-two," he said as the image panned down, then rose up again. "All right, good to go!" He cleared his throat and the angle of the image rose higher and panned wider, revealing more of his head and shoulders. "Alright, the Rou Family solstice preparations, year two! Fifteenth day of the Ice Month, Year of the Goat."

The view spun, taking in the rest of the room. It was warm and homey-looking, bright and inviting, and most certainly lived in. There were tools hanging on the walls, as well as images that seemed to have been captured, then printed onto stone. One was of a house between two rivers, and beside it was another of multiple people making stupid faces. There were many more such works lovingly hung in rows on the wall: an orange-haired girl posing beside a sculpture, a boar and a dragon grinning at each other, a rooster on a post, calling out at the sun. A glimpse of life on the farm.

There were also two desks, one against each wall, and one below a window. The one below the window looked a bit messy and was cluttered with papers and half-built projects, the other neat and orderly, brushes and combs arranged by size resting alongside thick pairs of gloves and a scroll titled "On the Mixing of Poultices." There was a bed in the middle of the room, its headboard against the wall, and a few dressers for storage.

The man, satisfied with having captured the room, exited into a hallway through the door.

"Lots different than the first time I did this, huh?" the man continued, glancing up at the crystal. "Got the house all finished. Man, last year this was just open and had no floor." The crystal shifted as the man stomped his foot against the sturdy floorboards, then panned to point at a door in the hallway.

"These are . . . well, they were originally supposed to be for any future kids, but they're kinda just other people's rooms now? I'm going to have to build an extension or something. That one is Lanlan's room, and the one beside that is supposed to be for Tigu'er—not that she ever sleeps there."

The image shifted to the other side of the room. "Yun Ren sleeps there sometimes, but we got one empty room for now."

The man continued walking down the hallway. It was brightly lit with glowing crystals hung on the walls. "It's a lot brighter than last time too, courtesy of Huo Ten! It's nice not to have to worry about things burning down!" At the end there was a door, and to the left was the stairwell.

"After the bedrooms, there is, drumroll please . . ." The man tapped his hand against his leg rapidly while he opened the door. "The library! It actually looks like a library now."

The room was divided into roughly two sides; on one side the walls were lined with shelves—one was already entirely filled with scrolls, and there were medical diagrams hanging everywhere. On the other side there was also a table, several plush-looking seats, and an upright, hard-backed one.

"And the *pièce de résistance—!*"

The crystal panned upwards, exposing an expanse of glass where sunlight streamed in, warming the table and chairs.

"The skylight! Noodle really came through on this one. It looks great. I always wanted a library with a skylight—almost as much as I wanted a greenhouse."

The image came back down to the man, who turned from the room and stepped back into the hall. He headed down a set of stairs and began to descend them. "We gotta get more books than just medical scrolls and the stuff Uncle Bao gave us at some point, but it's looking good, eh?" he asked the crystal as he reached the bottom of the stairs.

The man walked into a larger room with a vaulted ceiling. Lanterns hung on the wall, adding a warm, steady light to the room and brightening it more than just the windows provided.

"Here's the living room. This hasn't changed too much, but we built a few more couches. I did the frames, and Meimei did the upholstery."

The crystal panned again, taking in the room. There were three couches; all of them were of dark, stained wood, and all of them had odd extensions, almost like perches, along their backs. The cushions were largely a soft blue in colour. There was also a jar, a large pillow, and a slightly smaller pillow beside it. They were all arranged around a traditional fireplace, which was raised above the floor level. The edges of the fireplace were adorned with bright red socks, each one bearing a name above it.

"We've got stockings for everybody this year. They always were my favourite part of the season . . ." The man's tone was wistful while he stared at the stockings, before shaking his head.

"Normally we're all in here at night, but during the day . . ." The image shifted up as the man walked through the house towards an opening just by the stairs, heading to a small hallway that led into a large kitchen. An open door on the opposite side from the entrance revealed a stone room with a river winding through it. The crystal captured a whirlwind of activity centered on preparations for a meal. A heavily pregnant woman with green hair chopping and dicing, aided by a rat dashing from place to place and a dainty, pretty pig gracefully cleaning.

"First, my beautiful, amazing wife, the Legendary Healing Sage, along with her lovely and wonderful assistants, Rizzo and Peppa!"

The woman looked up from her work and rolled her eyes at the title, flushing slightly. She did, however, rise up onto her toes as the man leaned down to kiss her. The rat squeaked, waving, while the pig sketched a bow.

"Whatcha making, love?" the man asked, using the crystal to peek into the woks and pots.

"This one is stir-fry, this one is squash soup, we have some dumplings here, and *this one* is peppercorn prawns," the woman narrated, smiling at the crystal.

"It smells *delicious*," the man said, and there was a shift in his Qi. Scent flooded the crystal as it captured the heady aroma of spices that filled the air.

"Damn straight it's delicious! We have to be all fueled up for tonight," the woman said with a smile.

"Yes, ma'am! And *these* also smell like they're almost done . . ." The man walked over to an oven and opened the door. The crystal peered into the space, exposing a baking tray. The man simply reached his hand in and took it out, examining crisp golden objects cut into a variety of shapes.

"Here we are. The ancient family recipe. If I told you I'd have to kill you," the man said, and his wife snorted.

"It's got spicebark, ginger—" she began, a sly smile on her face.

"*Ah babbabbab!*" the man interrupted, prompting a chuckle from the woman.

He slid them off onto a rack to cool, then picked up another tray and slid it into the oven.

"They're really good," the woman said, continuing to cook.

The man paused as he closed the oven door, and then his eyes widened. He turned back to the rack of cookies and counted them, before turning to his wife with an accusing glare.

"Meimei, we said no cookies until they were iced," he said, almost petulant. He turned to mockingly glare at the woman and her assistant.

She whistled innocently, while the rat and the pig looked in other directions. The rat quickly wiped a crumb she had missed off her whiskers.

"Cookie thieves," the man declared. "You're all cookie thieves! How *dare* you! You have broken the sacred pact!"

"You should be praising me instead, husband. Look at your dutiful wife, she took it upon herself to ensure they weren't poisoned," the woman said, smirking.

The man harrumphed, shooting her a glare. Then he took a cookie for himself, biting into it. Meimei stuck her tongue out at him.

Shaking his head, the man walked back out of the kitchen, still chewing. He made a noise of approval and returned to the living room.

"We abscond from the den of the foul cookie thieves!" the man called, raising his voice to shout back at the kitchen. A moment later, he shook his head and walked to the left of the house if one entered through the front door and the mudroom.

He opened the door. "This one is just storage, mostly, but people hang out here sometimes." There was a long table and a piece of slate against the wall, filled with writing.

"Then, we got this . . ." He walked to the end of the room and turned, revealing that one of the walls contained a sliding door. He peeked his head out.

The crystal followed, adjusting swiftly to the light and exposing another scene. The outside of the house was surrounded by a veranda, and a frozen river was prominent through the snow.

A beautiful woman with crystal-blue eyes was sitting beside a man and a second woman on the edge of the veranda; from this angle the crystal image could only see his back. Both of the women glanced up at the crystal.

All three wore similar clothes: a blue shirt with a maple leaf and a wheat sheaf on the back. The blue-eyed woman was wearing a long, fluffy, bright red hat with a white pompom on the end.

"Xiulan and Xianghua giving Gou Ren a haircut," the man whispered to the crystal. "And I was wondering where my hat had gone to—Xiulan *stole* it. First the cookies, then my hat. Man, do we live in a bandit camp?"

The man, Gou Ren, glanced back at the sound of the voice. With his bushy sideburns he looked rather like a monkey. He flushed at the presence of the crystal.

"Good morning, Master Jin," the second woman, with wavy hair and sharp eyes, said politely, bowing and staring curiously at the crystal.

The woman with blue eyes, Xiulan, tutted as she raised a small blade. She smiled at the crystal. "Junior Brother let himself go," she scolded, then grabbed his face, turning his head back around and pointing at his sideburns.

"It still looks fine," Xianghua defended.

"But doesn't he look better with his hair cut?" Xiulan pressed.

The wavy-haired woman refused to answer, and Xiulan smirked.

"Do you have to record this, Jin?" Gou Ren complained to the man with the crystal.

"*Obviously,*" Jin returned.

Gou Ren had started to turn back around when Xiulan grabbed his shoulder and forced him to stay put. "Just a trim here, see?" The knife Xiulan was holding flashed out. The hair was trimmed in an instant, going from bushy to clean, sharp lines.

Xianghua studied the cut carefully, then raised a knife of her own. Another flash of steel, and the other sideburn was cut down to size, the strands floating off into the wind.

"See? Better." Xiulan shifted her grip on Gou Ren's shoulders, spinning him around for the crystal to take a good shot of his face. The man grumbled but glanced at Xianghua, who nodded, running her hands along his face with a little smile.

The grumbling stopped.

Xiulan crossed her arms, looking self-satisfied.

"You may now thank me, Junior Brother, and express your gratitude for my help!" the woman said, nodding pompously. Gou Ren rolled his eyes, and Xiulan turned a teasing grin to Xianghua. "After all, it was *my* style that helped you get a woman, no? You may be with him, but I'm his Senior Sister. That makes me *your* Senior Sister too, does it not?"

Xianghua scoffed at the words, her face turning blank. "I'd sooner shatter my own meridians than call you Senior Sister."

A spark passed between them.

"Junior Brother, look at this woman! She is too impolite and aggressive. I think a calmer, kinder girl would be better," Xiulan mused, pulling Gou Ren closer to her. "My Sect's An Ran is very cute, isn't she?"

Xianghua's eyes narrowed. She grabbed Gou Ren's arm. "You're courting death, Cai Xiulan."

"To the rink?" Xiulan challenged.

"To the rink."

Gou Ren simply looked at the crystal, his eyes mournful as he was dragged off by the pair towards the river. Jin only laughed at his misfortune.

"Well, that was pretty much the house. I'll get my boots on, then go show you everything else." The crystal followed Jin, who went back inside to put on boots before going out the front door. What was revealed was a mostly cleared courtyard, free of snow, with a massive edifice rising up into the air nearby. It was a giant figure carved of snow, with soot buttons, tree trunks for arms, and a truly impressive carrot for a nose . . . albeit one that had a large bite mark taken out of the end of it. Just visible on top of his tall hat made of blackened reeds was a figure.

"That there's the General, even bigger than last year, and Yun Ren seems to be using him as a perch."

The man on top of the giant black hat made of reeds, just barely visible from the angle, waved down at Jin. Then he raised a flat pane of crystal to his eye; a chime echoed out.

"Good view up there?" Jin called.

"It's all right. The light ain't the greatest," Yun Ren called back down. "It's the clouds. I'm going to try another few shots, then go lie in front of the fire. Chun Ke promised me some persimmons!"

"That's a good plan!" Jin called back, then started walking away. The snow crunched under his feet as he followed a path leading towards the back onto a stone bridge in the frozen river.

It was cold. The crystal recorded both the nip of frost and the sound of the wind.

Out of the crystal's viewpoint came the distinct call of a rooster and the flapping of wings. The crystal shifted just in time to catch the rooster, wearing a fox-fur vest and a red hat with a pompom, landing on Jin's shoulder.

"Hey, bud," the man said, scratching at the rooster's wattles. "And this is, of course, the man, the myth, the legend himself, the mighty Big D. *The First Disciple.*"

The rooster with a red hat puffed up before he bowed to the crystal and settled in on Jin's shoulder.

"Good day, descendants and disciples. This Bi De wishes those who view this recording good health."

"You want to come along for the rest of the property?" he asked the rooster.

"Of course, Master."

The crystal shifted as the man started walking again.

"Well, that's the barn, that's the greenhouse, that's the extra wheat storage . . . Man, it still gets me just how much we did this year." Jin pointed things out on their walk down the river.

"Indeed. Every disciple of this land has much merit to their names," the rooster agreed. "Even now they toil! Look there, Brother Chun Ke and Brother Bei Be have just crested the rise; they must have finished tending to the paths and trails."

The crystal focused on a boar and an ox, walking side by side cheerily. The boar spotted them and began to charge down. The giant creature, nearly as big as a house, barreled down the slope, only to be caught by Jin, who stopped the beast's momentum dead.

He laughed and scratched at the scarred boar's mane—who now, standing beside the man, only came up to his waist. "You gonna come for the tour too, buddy?" he asked the boar, who nodded eagerly. The crystal turned back to the ox, who was carrying a bright yellow plough, its frame carved with suns and smiles, on one of his horns. The ox seemed to shrug, trotting up to the group at a more sedate pace.

"All right! To the drop hammer next!"

→

They continued their journey along the river, pausing only for a moment to watch the two women from earlier hammer each other with sticks, each trying to get a small disc pushed on the ice from the other.

Their movements were sharp and brutal, yet neither gave the other an advantage. Gou Ren just shook his head while he carved another stick, sitting on the sidelines and letting them get it out of their systems.

Eventually the group arrived at the drop hammer. It was a furnace of industry, where a nearby snake, a rabbit, a monkey, and a young man blew colourful glass ornaments. They attached metal fixtures so that the crafted ornaments could be hung—the drop hammer itself was already bedecked in many similar ornaments. It shone with the reflected light from ornaments that were mostly shaded in red, with some blues, yellows, and oranges, like the rising sun.

Jin took a few to hang on the plough the ox was carrying, much to the ox's amusement.

They trekked through a winter wonderland: a man, a boar, an ox, and a chicken. Their path took them beneath the trees, some boughs bare, while others were evergreen and proud, jutting high into the sky.

"I still don't know what to do with most of this. I honestly think I'll just leave a lot of it. There's nothing better than to have an adventure through a forest close to home, and these things are *old*."

Jin patted a tree affectionately, until he seemed to notice something.

"Hey, Tigu'er, Wa Shi, where have you guys been?" Jin asked as the crystal zoomed in on an orange-haired girl carrying a jar with a fish in it. She had on a red hat and a thick coat. Both jumped and the girl nearly dropped the jar, fumbling around with it for a moment. She turned wide, yellow eyes to the recording crystal, her face flushed. A moment later she glanced down at the fish for support—he took one look at her, then abandoned her entirely, diving to the bottom of the jar.

"We were . . . just finishing stuff," the girl said evasively.

There was silence as the man stared at her. He considered her words, then nodded.

"Well, alright then, you two do you!" Jin said after a moment. The girl with the fish in a jar shot off, snarling bloody murder at her cowardly companion.

"Last-minute gifts. It never changes," Jin said, shaking his head with a fond smile.

→

There were starts and stops in the recording as the man switched from recording his walk to recording specific events: Xiulan and Xianghua supporting each other on their limping trek back home, smiles on their faces. Yun Ren lying on a couch beside Chunky, eating persimmons. Gou Ren massaging Xiaghua's shoulders, as Jin did the same to Xiulan. Bowu, the young man from the drop hammer, coming back with a box full of gleaming glass orbs.

A toast at dinner. A massive table, filled with people and food.

And then . . . cookies. Icing was applied, dried fruits and nuts produced. It was a warm affair, with so many people shoved around a table. Gou Ren smeared icing on the younger man's cheek. Meimei grinned as she held up a cookie shaped like a man, who had a massive . . . weapon.

The crystal recorded Mei cackling with glee as everybody else groaned, the woman grabbing at her husband's waistband suggestively.

That was not the only rude-looking cookie.

It was an eclectic mix. Some were works of art, like the stripy cat or the colourful rooster. Chun Ke chuffed with pride over his own creation, a star with offset eyes and a crooked smile, that he had managed to do himself. The fish in his jar begged to be the one allowed to eat "his Brother's mighty creation"—only to be challenged by the pink pig for the honour.

The boar, smiling, broke the cookie in two, and the budding squabble was instantly resolved.

Decorations were hung. Cookies were finished. The dishes were cleaned, and they all sat around the fireplace.

"And that's a wrap. Rou Family solstice preparations year two," Jin said, smiling at the crystal. "Say good night, everybody!"

The crystal panned across the room as people waved with varying degrees of enthusiasm.

The Qi faded.

The crystal chimed, finishing its recording.

Its task complete, it archived the recollections within its depths.

CHAPTER 29

END WHERE IT BEGINS

The morning of the solstice began just as it had the year before, Bi De mused. The sky was overcast, and the world was thick with mist creeping up from the earth to cling to everything it touched. Snow blanketed the land, with the flickering rays of sunlight lending an almost ethereal quality to it, like the mists of a dream.

And just as the year before, a brightly coloured sleigh painted with red lacquer rushed across the fallen snow. Upon it were shining decorations of stars and a bright, rising sun. Cedar boughs attached to the sleigh, laced with silvery bells, chimed in time to the beat of the noble creatures pulling it.

Bi De stood in his place on the front of the sleigh, his dapper red hat trailing behind him. The wind coursed over his wings as they sped through the tunnel of evergreen boughs laden with the heavy snowfall from the wintery night. Below him, Brother Chun Ke and Sister Pi Pa carried the sleigh to its destination. Chun Ke wore his magnificent deer horn, to show respect to the original qilin who had pulled the great sage San Ta's sleigh, while Pi Pa's red-painted nose was a beacon in the mists, a light that cut through the darkness.

Indeed, all of Fa Ram was in full panoply for the solstice, and it was quite a sight to behold. The oranges and reds of the rising sun were spread across all of them, albeit currently hidden by darker coats and shawls. They filled the crowded sleigh. Ri Zu was upon Bi De's back, her nose tasting the air. His Great Master sat upon the seat beside his lady wife, just behind Bi De, the pair quietly enjoying the ride.

The rest were farther back. Disciples Yun Ren, Gou Ren, and Xiulan were resting and chatting with Xianghua and Bowu. Wa Shi was in his jar at their feet, his head poking up above as he slapped the side of the sleigh happily.

Tigu sat on top of the sack filled with food, Yin and Miantiao stuffed down her shirt. Her own red hat was streaming in the wind.

At least Tigu was quiet now. For the first time in Bi De's life, he had known annoyance at his Great Master, for the man had taught her *that* song.

It had been funny to see her spin like a top on her toes and shout, "*Pa Do Ru, Pa Do Ru~!*" for the first five minutes.

A week later, it had become *completely* insufferable. Sister Ri Zu had actually started contemplating poisoning her again, planning it in great length with Bi De.

At those times, it was a struggle to act as the voice of reason, gently reminding her not to do it.

Next came Bei Be. The ox trotted at an easy pace just beside them, his plough stowed safely within the sleigh.

Finally, there was Huo Ten. The monkey was curled up in the back of the sleigh, cradling the memory crystal that was the product of Bi De's journey. The piece had looked visibly different this morning, the churning storm within slowing down to barely a crawl.

All of them were together, just as they had been last night for their own special celebration.

Yesterday, they had gathered around a mighty evergreen. The tree was decorated with rope, glass, and the light crystals Huo Ten and Yin had found.

It was a beautiful sight in the softly falling snow, a beacon of light reaching to the heavens.

Afterwards, they all had gathered around the hearth with warm spicebark tea in hand, listening to Disciple Gou Ren and the Healing Sage regale them all with stories of their childhood. Tigu and Wa Shi had slid in their gifts at the last moment. Those would be exchanged tomorrow, after the solstice festival.

When the night was deepest and the sun slept for the longest.

Sister Yin had been surprisingly lethargic that morning, the tired rabbit not speaking much, not even reacting when Tigu had stuffed her down the front of her shirt.

Bi De glanced back at Huo Ten, at the monkey curled around the crystal. It was covered in cloth, and Huo Ten had declared that it would need to see the rising sun to complete its stabilization.

The hour he had waited for was soon at hand, and he felt some semblance of nerves start to creep up.

Bi De put it out of his mind for the moment—the village approached. They were met with much fanfare.

His Great Master began to laugh with a booming "*Ho ho ho ho!*"

↔

Hong Xian sat before a candle in a dark room, his breath even as he prepared himself.

The day of the solstice was upon them.

He took a deep breath in and let it out through his nose. His son, who shared his name—the name every village chief of Hong Yaowu had for at least seventy-six generations—sat opposite him. His son's eyes were clenched shut, tense. It was not quite the peaceful and calm meditation he was meant to perform, but Xian could hardly begrudge the boy his fears. It would be the first time he would be allowed in the circle with his father to perform the dance in front of others. Unlike his father, Xian the Younger's only duty was to last as long as he could. There was no shame in a boy of nine retiring after only an hour or two, but the longer they danced together, the more auspicious it would be.

His son had been training very hard for this moment. He had been diligent and without the goading he normally required.

A small start, but a good one. Meiling had been even more of a hellion than Xian at his age, a willing participant in the Xong brothers' schemes, and twice as wild, for she was a bookworm. Age and loss had tempered that, the death of his dear wife forcing his daughter to grow up too fast.

But everyone had to grow up eventually. His sister was no longer here to care for him, and his son was rising to the challenge.

For himself and Yao Che, each year the dance took a week of preparation. A week of careful meditation and breathing exercises that slowly intensified until the final day. This time was normally spent completely in solitude. The only thing he had was a candle and water. His shirt was off, and he took deep, even breaths. He stared into the flickering candle flame and tried to center himself for the labour to come.

It was a time when, alone with his thoughts while preparing, he tended to dwell. He dwelled on the mistakes he had made and the regrets he had. He always remembered his late wife; he had thought long and hard about Meiling's uncertain future back then. He mulled over the hardships forced upon his son, and the duty he himself had to fulfill as Hong Xian.

In the darkness, before the candle, each and every one of his failings came to him. They tried to distract him. It was a struggle, like climbing a mountain each and every time. A battle for his mind that had to be won before he did battle with his body.

Maybe that was one of the reasons for the ritual? So the leaders of the village would reflect upon their duties, in this moment before the hardest physical challenge most of them would face all year.

He had honestly been dreading the preparations this year. Without his daughter, and with his son beginning his first vigil, he'd expected it to be a trying time. Both he and Brother Che were without the support of their families. The eldest of the village, the Xong brothers, Meihua, and his own daughter had left.

All of his worries were, of course, unfounded. His village would not have abandoned him or left him to his own devices.

Ty An, the freckly, bony girl, had taken up residence easily with Yao Che, assisting him as she was able. Nezin Hu Li and little Liu, the quiet girl, had come to help Xian himself while the rest of the villagers executed the preparations with little of his own input. It was easy to let fears creep up, but he should have known better than to forget the simplest truth.

Hong Yaowu took care of its own.

Even though it was so different from all the years before, Hong Yaowu continued on, for the changes were mostly good ones.

There had not been a single death all year. All of the four newborns had survived their first six months. Illness seemed to have fled their village—they had not even used half the medicine they'd needed to use last year. They had even had a bumper crop—a quarter more rice had been harvested compared to the previous year.

Xian allowed the scent of the candle to fill his lungs.

He let some of the tension fade as he limbered his body. There were many hours yet before he would have to emerge.

Which was when he heard it.

The *ching ching ching* of the bells before the inevitable voice bellowing *Ho ho ho ho ho!* Booming laughter came from his son-in-law Jin, followed by the wild cheers of the children.

His son's eyes snapped open. A massive grin formed on his face. He turned to the direction of the cheers and looked for a brief moment like he was going to bolt outside—then froze. He paused, in the middle of getting up, and instead returned to his place and sat. Though his son looked pained, he had restrained himself.

Xian inclined his head slightly, approving of his self-discipline.

And besides, they did not have to wait long for the visitors to find them.

His daughter entered the house, quiet and respectful of his meditations as she always was. He heard a whispered conversation, and then she was in the room.

"Father. Xian'er," she whispered.

Xian cracked open an eye and beheld his daughter. Her green hair was braided at the sides as always, with the back of it tucked into a bun. Her normally sharp eyes were warm and full of peace and happiness as she quietly refilled their cups of water. She slid behind her brother and whispered words of encouragement into his ears.

His daughter was home. All was right with the world.

Xian took one last breath and let it all out.

This year, there would be no second-guessing himself. This year, the tiny pool of Qi he had, not enough for him to be called a cultivator, allowed itself to be directed.

↔

Hong Xian the Younger felt sick to his stomach as he stood in the entrance of his home. Even though he had only eaten a special soup that both he and his father had been served, one that was said to give him energizing properties.

It had been ridiculously spicy, and even now he felt a bit hot, dressed in the ceremonial costume.

Xian was eager to get outside. This year, he hadn't been able to enjoy *anything*. None of the festivities, nothing of Big Bro Jin and Bowu coming around, no Lanlan to dance with, or Chun Ke to ride.

It was *terrible*! Why hadn't he run off? At least then he would have gotten to have fun instead of standing around like this.

The drums had started to sound. Xian's thoughts froze in his head.

"It is nearly time," his father said.

Xian felt like he was going to hurl the spicy soup back up as his father turned to him, kneeling down before him.

The traditional sun mask covered his father's face, but he could see his father's eyes staring into Xian's own. He looked strange, with the sun mask on his face. Almost scary.

He didn't know what his father was looking for or what he saw.

But after a long moment . . . the man nodded.

His father turned and called out to the still darkness of their home.

"Hear me, hear me. This one is Hong Xian. In accordance with the ancient pact, I do depart to perform the Rite of Fire. Who will aid me in casting out this night and assisting in the awakening?"

Xian swallowed when his father paused.

"H-hear me, hear me. This one is Hong Xian. In ack—*accordance* with the ancient pact, I do depart, to perform the Rite of Fire. Who will aid me in casting out this night and assisting in the awakening?"

There was a delay. A single helper was supposed to aid Xian for his first time, but his father hadn't told him who it would be.

Xian blinked as a very familiar form walked in. Jin wasn't in his bright reds anymore; he was clad in darkness. He dropped to a knee, hat nowhere in sight.

"Yes, Hong Xian. This Rou Jin will aid you in casting out the long night." It felt weird to have Jin bow to him—to have goofy Big Bro who threw Meimei into mud pits be serious.

Xian felt his heart beat faster as the meditation failed to do anything. This was big, serious—

"We accept your aid, Rou Jin. Lead our path to the grounds for the beginning of the next Hong Xian's vigil," his father said.

Jin nodded, bowing again, but then the serious mask broke for a second and Jin winked at Xian when his father started to march forward.

"You're gonna do great," he whispered, clapping Xian on the shoulder. He smiled warmly, and there was absolute confidence in his voice.

Xian felt his heart calm, slightly, as his father strode out first, carrying his staff with rings on it.

Next came Jin, holding Xian's staff for him, an honour guard for his debut.

The walk they did looked a bit silly, though. The wide, sliding steps that were performed in half crescents, almost like a dance itself. Normally, most people just waited up at the shrine for Father, but tonight they were lining the pathway.

"We pay our respects to Hong Xian!" they shouted as they bowed.

The path up to the shrine had never seemed so long before.

Meimei looked surprised to see Jin beside Xian, escorting him and Father. He didn't know why. Whenever Jin came back from Verdant Hill he always checked in with them and asked Father how to properly do all the boring traditional stuff.

Father was always very happy to teach the others. There had even been a big conversation about what food he would bring and how he would enter the village. Xian thought it was a bit dumb, but Chun Ke and the sleigh were fun.

Father had said it was important, though.

Xian still didn't really get it. He shook his head and refocused on his movements.

The surprise on his sister's face was short-lived. Instead, her grin turned radiant as they continued their match.

After an eternity, and yet no time at all, he was at the shrine. He saw his friend Shen standing beside Elder Che. He had drumsticks in his hands and was fidgeting.

Xian tried to put him out of his mind. He marched up to the shrine and kowtowed before his ancestors three times. Then he turned and headed towards where his father was standing within a circle of braziers.

His father stared at him as he paused at the edge of the circle of fire. In the man's hands, he held another mask.

"Kneel."

Xian obeyed, sinking down to a knee.

His father raised the mask of the sun to Xian's face.

It was awkward, but not really all that heavy. It just restricted his vision a little.

"Receive the staff from your retainer."

With shaking hands, his fingers closed around the wood. He knew that Jin was the one handing it to him, but he didn't have the mind to see it.

"Step into the circle."

He did as he was bid.

Everything went quiet.

They both stood, still and silent, as they waited. Xian's eyes were locked onto the last dregs of the sun slipping away.

A gong sounded.

The last of the twilight faded away, overtaken by the Longest Night.

The drums began to pound. Slowly at first, and then with increasing ferocity. It was an ancient beat that had burned its way into Xian's memories.

He took a deep breath and did what his father had told him to do: not to think, simply to move. To let his hours of practice guide his body, rather than his mind.

His first steps were faltering, almost stumbling, but soon they evened out. The beat thundered in his ears.

Everything else faded away. His father said he only had to last for the first repetition of the dance if he felt like it.

Xian had no desire to do the bare minimum.

The next step was perfect. His breath was clean and even. Every moment of practice, every moment with Lanlan in the forest on that wonderful patch of soft grass, came back to him.

And as the drums thundered in his ears . . . the Dance of Fire felt *right.*

↔

"We do not have a fire like this. The Misty Lake rarely freezes, so the mortals dance upon beds of reeds out on the lake itself," Bi De overheard Xianghua say during her dance with Disciple Gou Ren. They had eyes only for each other as she learned the dance of fire from him.

The information was new to Bi De, but it fit.

Five elements. Five dances.

From his high perch he watched over the festivities—much to the amusement of Tigu, who caught his eye and stuck her tongue out at him, before going back to dance with the children who were around her.

Bi De ignored her taunting. He was having a wonderful night with Sister Ri Zu.

He did, however, envy the easy grace with which his Brother and Sister Disciples could handle children. He tried. The heavens knew he tried, but . . . they were so *grabby.*

He simply wasn't cut out for entertaining the little ones.

Ri Zu giggled from behind him and he dutifully ignored her too. He'd already dealt with teasing from the others; to have Sister Ri Zu to add her own was a betrayal most foul, and obviously Sister Ri Zu would never betray him.

Instead, he gazed back down at the dancers.

At the thin, almost invisible, threads of Qi that rose into the air.

Xiulan had been intrigued by the Qi, but Xianghua had dismissed the phenomenon, saying that it was just like what happened with the Lakemen. Save for the fact that the Qi aligned with fire instead of water, it did nothing and so was ignored.

However, Xianghua did not have the gift of flight, to rise as high as Bi De and observe where those streams of Qi were headed, connecting the villages together.

Bi De let himself rock to the beat as Hong Xian the Younger reached his third hour with no signs of slowing down. On the outskirts of the circle, Bi De's Master worked, fueling the fires without cease.

He glanced to the side, where Yin was asleep and Miantiao tapped his tail to the beat. Huo Ten was behind them, quiet as he held the crystal in his arms.

The dance was what had begun his quest. It had been only base curiosity in the beginning. A burning desire to learn. He had wanted to uncover the reasons behind the strange formation that at first he had thought spread across just a few towns in the north.

Not the *entire province.*

As he travelled and each revelation came, the desire to know more had intensified.

Each village, part of a greater whole.

A dance and matching names. Portents of doom and a great cataclysm.

All were part of the history of this province.

Bi De watched as father and son, as past and future, danced together.

Five hours passed. Then seven. Then ten.

The whole of the village stared as a boy of nine hit his fourteenth hour, dancing in the darkness, matching his father move for move.

Bi De prayed that the basis for this dance was not sinister, that the history within the crystal would not tarnish this beautiful image before him.

And then Yin, fast asleep, started to awake.

The sky brightened as Huo Ten stood atop the roof and raised the crystal to the sky.

The first rays of the dawn hit it. The swirling, coursing colours flashed in unison for the first time and then calmed.

Stable, ready to be used.

The solstice ended when dawn cast away the darkness, and Hong Xian the Younger collapsed to his knees.

For the first time in the recorded history of the town, the heir to the name Hong Xian had lasted the entire night in his first dance.

→

Bi De stared into the crystal, at its pristine contours and facets. They glinted under the bright rays, sparkling and clear, basking in the light of a new cycle.

A cycle. A new year. A new repetition.

He glanced at his Great Master, standing at the head of the village with both Hong Xians. The men had to tilt their head up to look him in the eye as he clapped both of their shoulders.

Bi De returned his attention to the crystal. The crystal that had once housed the soul of a Temple Dog, a guardian who had stayed with the crystal for thousands of years, protecting the item for its Master, until Bi De's own Master had laid the poor beast's soul to rest. The thoughts of the past weighed on his mind along with the memories of the Temple Dog.

The Temple Dog had been trapped for so long in the crystal. He had felt kinship with the great guardian. Bi De knew its thoughts, its desire to please its Master.

He could admit he admired it. Its devotion and its sacrifice. To endure suffering for untold millennia.

But . . . was that supposed to be his fate too? Would he be a Temple Dog for his own Master?

Bi De did not know.

He could see himself becoming like that easily enough. A shade, caring only for the past days of glory. Lost in hope that the Master he served would return one day.

He did not think it would be such a bad fate. If his Great Master asked it of him, despite the tragedy of its end. He didn't think he would have any regrets. He would devote himself like the Temple Dog. He could be his Great Master's Beast.

If his Master asked it of him. But he knew better. He knew, if he asked his Great Master, what he wished for Bi De's future to be. He knew the answer. He could hear the words accompanied by a soft smile and a gentle hand on Bi De's head.

"Whatever you want your future to be."

The rooster turned his face towards the sun. It filled the sky, a blazing fire that warmed his soul. It was the beginning of a new cycle, on this unending, eternal road.

Bi De jumped high into the air.

He sucked in a breath and greeted the new year with all his might.

"You tell 'em, Bi De!" his Master shouted with good cheer.

"Come, my Brothers and Sisters. Lay the crystal to rest, at least for today. There are celebrations to attend!" Bi De commanded. Ri Zu, Yin, Miantiao, and Huo Ten nodded.

Bi De descended back into the village, where he landed upon his Lord's shoulder. The man turned and grinned at him, offering a spoonful of soup.

The rooster took it gratefully, staring around at the peaceful little village.

He hoped he was wrong about the cycles. But if he wasn't and the years and times did repeat themselves . . . he would prove himself equal to the challenge.

CHAPTER 30

THE LADY OF HONG YAOWU

The end of the solstice was normally a quiet, sleepy affair. After staying up all night, most people wanted a bit of peace, to laze the day away and then go to bed early. Or perhaps have a midday nap, a small meal of porridge and tea, and the chance to use this time as one for reflection.

Or at least they normally did, Meiling mused. The air outside her home was energized, and the entire village was abuzz with the events of last night. She smiled at her sleeping brother's face from her position sitting on the side of his bedroll.

"You did well," she whispered, brushing a strand of hair out of his face. Even now the warm pride filled her chest. He had passed out less than ten minutes after the dance and scared everybody into thinking that he had hurt himself.

But he was simply sleeping.

Meiling had some help from Jin getting both her father and brother into the house, and after that she had put a soothing salve on their arms and then put them both to bed.

It would stop them from being too sore tomorrow, and they *would* be sore.

Smiling to herself and imagining the complaints that would fill the house the following day, Meiling stood and began to wander around the house. Her empty room still had a few old things of hers that she had left behind. It was relatively empty, and ready for both her and Jin to sleep here whenever they visited. Somebody had obviously cleaned it . . . but it was still odd to see it this way. There remained a few marks on the doorway, tracking her height. The little scores were close together, tracking a girl who hadn't grown very tall. The floor had a slight discolouration on it, where she had spilled one of her experiments. After that, she had been forced to do them outside.

Shaking her head, she searched the house for a moment longer, falling into old habits and looking for something to do. Perhaps a spot that needed to be cleaned that they had missed, or something that needed to be put away.

But the house was spotless. Everything was in order . . . though the organisation was slightly different from how she liked it. Hu Li had put the cleaning rags on the right side instead of the left, and the broom was hung up instead of resting on the floor.

She paused, wondering what exactly she was doing. She was the lady of this house no longer. She took in a breath after stopping by the kitchen to grab a stick of incense and some of the glutinous rice balls she had prepared at home, then turned and went outside. The sun was still quite hazy and weak after the solstice. Meiling lifted her head and took a breath of the chilly air.

Scents came to her. The normal, mundane scents of fire, cooking, medicinal plants, and people.

What also came to her were more esoteric things. The smell of nothingness. Of fur and mist. Water and steam. A meadow in full bloom. The sun, the moon, a day just before a storm hit, something sharp and spicy. Underpinning it all was the crisp scent of evergreens and the spices of the cookies Jin had made.

She smiled and opened her eyes again to her village. The giant red streamers and flags waved in the winter wind. The little houses were covered in a thin film of snow with their paths cleared. Fifty people sat at tables, murmuring with each other. The hills rose up to the north while the flat land and the snowed-in fields were to the south.

Her village always looked great this time of year. If she had married into Verdant Hill, she never would have been able to see this again. It was expected that the wife celebrate with her husband, and few would be willing to make the journey out to Hong Yaowu.

Instead, she got to spend the festivals with her family.

She set a path for the village shrine so that she could pay her morning respects to her ancestors. Her eyes roamed around the village and glanced at where a large communal pot of rice porridge was set up with people wandering over to fill their bowls and add some dried berries and fruits to their meal. Ri Zu, Wa Shi, Pi Pa, Miantiao, Bei Be, and Huo Ten were all seated at a table together eating their breakfast. Ri Zu raised a paw in greeting, the little rat in a good mood this morning, while the monkey looked fit to fall asleep in his bowl.

Nearby she saw that *some* people had entirely too much energy. They were still up and following along with the movements that Xiulan, Xianghua, and Bowu were showing them. One was like the grass swaying in the breeze, the other a flowing current. Yin was with them, the rabbit bounding gracefully in time with the beat and glowing bright like the sun. The kids who had gone to bed early had now risen, and most of the adults were either watching or joining in.

Hu Li was fussing over Gou Ren for not bundling up tight enough in the winter . . . never mind that her son couldn't feel the cold and wouldn't freeze even if he slept in a snowdrift.

His attempts to explain himself away fell on deaf ears, and eventually he had a coat forced on him. Yun Ren just chuckled from beside him, and then went back to playing go with his father. The sly fox dueled the crafty monkey that was Ten Ren. They'd probably be there all day, and Meiling saw the coins that were the customary wager land atop the table.

She moved past the majority of the people, but she was accosted before she could start up the hill to the shrine.

"Ei! Meimei!" Ty Sho, Ty An's father, called for her attention.

"Yes?" Meiling asked, venturing over.

"Not to take away anything from what the Little Chief did . . . but we were having a bit of an argument over here. Is the Little Chief a cultivator too?"

Meiling raised an eyebrow at the sudden silence in the village. It was a valid question. To a cultivator, dancing all night wasn't exactly impressive.

Meiling shook her head. "Not a hint of him awakening his dantian."

She wasn't entirely sure how to feel about that. Did she want her brother to be a cultivator? In times past, she would have vehemently said no, but now? Well . . . it wasn't *so* bad, was it?

The group exchanged glances, and Ty Sho's grin got bigger.

"See? I told you. The Little Chief was practising all summer long, you all saw him!"

There was more murmuring, and Meiling left Ty Sho to lord it over those who had been saying otherwise.

Shaking her head in amusement, she continued on.

She approached the shrine and presented her offerings. She lit one of the incense sticks and stuck it in its bowl of sand. Then she lowered her head to the shrine three times like her brother had done last night.

"I pay my respects to you, Honoured Ancestors. Thank you for blessing this village with life."

She stayed until the incense sticks burned down more, then backed away respectfully.

She took another breath, finding the sharp, spicy scent of Tigu close. Curious, she set off into the forest.

She did not have long to wait to find the other girl.

"And then he came back with . . . *that* girl, you know? How can I compete?" Meiling heard Ty An mutter, her voice full of frustration. A few more steps brought Tigu and Ty An into view.

Tigu was with Ty An in the tree line, snow sculptures of mostly naked men between them. She recognised depictions of Rags, Loud Boy, and Handsome Man from Tigu's previous work. There was also one of Gou Ren that looked half-finished, and of much simpler, amateurish quality. It was still surprisingly good, though. Ty An was staring at it forlornly.

Tigu patted her on the shoulder and glanced over at Meiling. She shrugged before turning back to her friend.

"Yes, yes, my Junior Brother is quite the catch. You have a good eye! But Ty An, you are also a fine woman! Your appearance is endlessly appealing! Why, you've improved working with Uncle Che! Freckles, muscles, and a tan!"

Ty An, who had turned to Tigu with hope, slumped again. The not so bony, freckled girl stared in horror at her arms, which had thickened up from helping Che in the forge and around the house. Meihua, damn her, managed to look like a dainty flower despite hauling chunks of iron to her father; Ty An had no such luck.

"For the last time, Tigu, boys don't like that!"

"Then they are weak and foolish!" Tigu declared. "I guarantee you shall find a man of quality! Listen to your Big Sister, you just need somebody to appreciate your beauty! What about these fine men, my Brothers?" said, gesturing to the other sculptures.

Ty An flushed and shoved at Tigu halfheartedly. "Well, *he's* not too bad . . ."

Tigu blinked and squinted.

"*Rags?*" she asked. "I cannot see it, but he is loyal and brave! When we meet again, I shall sing praises of your fine visage!"

Meiling decided to leave them to it.

She went back to the communal rice bowl and got herself some porridge. Three of their number were still missing, so she headed out towards the fields.

She found her husband sitting on a rock that was clear of snow. Bi De was upon his shoulder and Chun Ke at his side. He was still in his ceremonial clothes he had been lent. He had been absolutely chuffed to be able to wear them and had talked her ear off last night about how happy he was that her father had let him escort her brother.

It was rather cute how enthusiastic he'd been . . . Even going and sneaking lessons from her father so he could impress her.

Naturally . . . it worked perfectly, and she fell in love with him all over again.

All of them were staring at the snowy monstrosity out in one of the fields. The Warden That Sends Forth the Flying Ice and Snow was truly a credit to his commandery, rising high into the sky. Yet still a lot smaller than the General That Commands the Winter.

"I still can't believe Father roped the village into building that," she said as she sat on the rock beside him. It was covered with a blanket that was entirely too warm to be natural, heated by Jin's Qi.

Her husband's arm moved unconsciously to wrap around her shoulder.

"It's absolutely amazing," Jin said. "I can't believe they managed to get it so big!"

"As Uncle Che says, 'Hong Yaowu does its best,'" Meiling said, making her voice gruff.

Jin laughed at the nearly pitch-perfect tone before letting out a contented sigh.

"Man, I love it here," he said, turning and looking back to the village.

"It certainly has its charm," she agreed.

They watched together as the children started up a snowball fight . . . and then Meiling caught sight of a man coming up the road. He was one of the Lord Magistrate's men, a messenger to deliver the customary salutations on the solstice. He was taking advantage of the cleared road, a look of relief on his face that the ride, even in winter, sometimes only took a single day.

Meiling elbowed Jin in the side and pointed. A grin broke out on her husband's face.

The messenger rounded the last bend and came past the hill that blocked most of the village from view.

Where he came face-to-face with a massive snow golem. It was the size of a two-story building. His eyes bugged out comically and he jerked the reins, causing his horse to rear in shock—then spill him into a snowbank.

The Warden That Sends Forth the Flying Ice and Snow claimed his first victim.

She stared out into Hong Yaowu. The tiny, insignificant village where things rarely happened.

Now it played host to more cultivators and Spirit Beasts than most places in the Azure Hills had ever seen, let alone gotten to know.

Perhaps its insignificance was its greatest boon? Meiling didn't consider herself the philosophical sort . . . but she couldn't imagine a city being this loved by the people who lived there.

Hong Yaowu might not have had any grand libraries or interesting things going on . . . but it was still home in a way.

And she couldn't imagine growing up anywhere else.

CHAPTER 31

THE PRESENT

Bi De observed the village from his place on his Master's shoulders. The celebrations had largely ended although the decorations would stay up for a few more days. They had ended up staying one additional day and had agreed to not depart until after lunch, so that they could spend time with the performers after they had a chance to rest. Little Hong Xian had received so much praise that he eventually got flustered and hid behind the Healing Sage and Disciple Xiulan. Floating chopsticks had warded away any who approached, much to the amusement of the village.

Now they would be leaving, and the villagers had come to see them off.

A strange feeling welled in his chest at the sight of the people gathered around, shoving snacks into their hands or wishing them well. He felt almost forlorn, like he knew he would miss this place and look back on this moment fondly even as he experienced it.

"Bye, Meimei, Big Bro!" Hong Xian the Younger called, waving enthusiastically at them. The shoulder Bi De was on shifted as his Great Master turned to catch the tackle hug. The young lad still looked tired, but his grin was bright—until the Healing Sage bent down to kiss his cheeks and hug him. He frowned and made many faces of disgust . . . but he never tried to push her away. Bi De's Great Master and Liu Bowu clapped him on the back and ruffled his hair.

"It seems all our training paid off, Xian," Xiulan said with a proud smile.

"Yeah! Thanks, Lanlan!" the boy cheered, using the nickname he had given her.

Bi De's attention was drawn away by a great commotion.

"Aww, does Chun Ke have to go?" several children whined, crowding around the boar and his lady. They pouted and wheedled for one last ride, and shrieked with joy as his kindly brother obliged them.

Bi De shook his head at their antics and turned back to where the village chief's house was. Sister Ri Zu had gone to pay her respects to her uncle.

Xian the Elder ruffled Sister Ri Zu's fur and nodded companionably to Sister Pi Pa. The pig had several satchels filled with mushrooms on her back and looked quite pleased. Bi De watched with a smile at the gentle interaction, but then his gaze was interrupted by Tigu and another girl tussling and shoving.

"It'll be good to get you out of my hair, Muscles," one of the village girls, Ty An, drawled at Tigu.

"Bye bye, Freckles!" Tigu returned. The girl rolled her eyes . . . and then blinked in surprise as the Healing Sage came up behind her and embraced her as well, Meiling's little brother gone to collect Bowu from the forge. The younger boy was wishing his other Big Brother goodbye, but there was another scene that Bi De didn't quite expect.

Huo Ten, the crystal secure on his back, stood across from Yao Che, the blacksmith. Both man and monkey had their arms folded across their chests as they sized each other up. The monkey had taken interest in the forge over lunch and started to poke around, only to be caught by the enormous man.

The monkey bared his teeth and hooted, gesturing at the iron ore resting on the side of the forge.

Yao Che snorted, his breath coming out as steam from his nostrils, and his muscles bulged so much they looked like they were about to rip out of his shirt.

"*Is that so?*" the blacksmith asked.

Huo Ten slammed both his palms into the ground and let loose an angry snarl, his posture similarly aggressive. For a moment, it looked like there was about to be some manner of altercation—sparks flew between the two. Bi De tensed, ready to intervene.

Then Yao Che held out his hand and the monkey took it with great force, both man and monkey squeezing hard enough their faces turned red.

They gave each other a manly nod and disengaged. Yin and Miantiao looked on, amused, as man and monkey turned their backs on each other and began to walk away—only for them both to start shaking their hands in obvious discomfort.

Bi De chuckled and his eyes began to wander, catching sight of his Great Master clasping arms with another man who had come up to him, both of them laughing at some manner of joke.

Xianghua seemed to have no idea what to do when she was fussed over by Hu Li, the woman tying the end of a braid into the cultivator's hair and then hugging her tight and kissing her on both cheeks.

The Xong brothers clasped forearms with their father as they stacked the remains of a successful hunt beside their old house, the boys' manly posturing lasting until their father rolled his eyes and pulled them into a hug.

Bei Be, the great ox, wandered in from the outskirts of the village. To Bi De's surprise, Liu, the quiet little girl who oft bedecked Xiulan in flower crowns, walked beside him. They paused at the outskirts, and both the silent girl and the equally silent ox stared at each other for a moment before they both bowed slightly to each other and parted ways.

Little Liu strode with purpose to Xiulan, a holly wreath in her hands. Xiulan knelt down and allowed it to be placed on her head, amusement dancing in her eyes.

Finally, Wa Shi prowled lethargically over in his draconic form, waving goodbye to the aunties of the village, who waved back and giggled. Even in his dragon form, the fish's stomach was swollen and plump from the amount of food the ladies had plied him with.

Bi De watched it all, the strange feeling persisting. Out of all of them . . . he was the one with the least connection to this village even though he was the First Disciple. He normally took to the roofs and merely observed. He considered himself a protector of this place, not truly a part of it. He would act to defend it, just as he had done in the Eighth Correct Place, but Bi De could see he had made no true connections.

He mused that it was something he would have to rectify in the future.

A soft cough drew his attention. Liu, who had given the crown of holly to Xiulan, was looking up at them from the ground.

She said nothing as she held up a smaller ring of holly fitted specifically for Bi De's head.

The rooster hopped down from his perch and lowered his head, allowing her to crown him with the evergreen boughs.

The girl planted her hands on her hips and nodded in satisfaction.

This little one was tolerable, compared to the rest of the children, Bi De decided. He would have to do something in return for this thoughtful gift.

"Thank you, for the gift, Liu," Bi De said, bowing. The little girl smiled brilliantly at him before skipping back to the village.

Yes. Remaining aloof was the height of foolishness. He did not like the children touching him, but the children were not the only members of the village! He could instead play go with the village Elders! That was a much more agreeable path forward.

"See you later, everybody!" Bi De's Great Master called as the flurry of goodbyes wound down. It was what his Great Master preferred to say, implying that they would meet again in the future.

Then he ventured over to the sleigh and whistled. Chun Ke and Pi Pa trotted forward . . . yet instead of being hitched up themselves, they hopped into the driver's seat.

Chun Ke squealed happily as his Great Master lifted the front of the sleigh.

They exited the village to uproarious laughter while Bi De bid them his own goodbye, his voice echoing over the hills.

→

Their walk back home was a relaxing one, their sedate pace carrying them along the road.

Bi De, for his part, stayed upon his Great Master's shoulder, simply enjoying the moment, the time that was here and now. He took strength from it.

He would need it for when he observed the contents of the crystal. The brief flashes he had seen before foreshadowed a great calamity, and worry gnawed at his soul that whatever had shifted the elemental poles, transforming Fire to Earth,

Earth to Metal, Metal to Water, Water to Wood, and Wood to Fire could happen again, once more causing untold devastation.

Yet . . . it had not happened for thousands of years already. And though he longed to find out immediately what the dance had been for and its place in this whole story . . . he restrained himself.

He would have, in Pi Pa's words, been an "unbelievable boor" to set himself to a task in this time of joy.

It was not fair to any of them, or fair to himself, to not be in their company; when they arrived home they would be together, exchanging the gifts to mark the celebration of the new cycle's beginning. Bi De would share in the joy of hearth and home.

He was looking forward to it, and was quite curious what the others had gotten for each other.

□

The present pile was honestly a lot bigger than I had been expecting.

Really, I had no intention of forcing other people to give gifts. I just kind of thought it would be something I did. I'd always enjoyed giving people things for Christmas more than I did getting them.

I hadn't really expected Meimei to just start making things for people, joining in without a word from me.

Peppa and Big D had noticed what she was doing, and before I knew it *everybody* was all in on Santa day this year.

I was a little iffy on it being some kind of *mandatory* thing; I didn't want to turn it into something like it was in the Before, but I had a feeling we were still in the "thoughtful gift that was useful" stage, rather than any kind of super commercialized thing.

After we got back home and had settled in, we all ended up around the fire to do presents. We filled the couches and the cushions, and there was an air of excitement and curiosity as I started handing out my gifts. Tigu looked a bit nervous in the beginning, toying with her bright red hat, but that dropped off quickly once I handed her a gift wrapped in cloth.

Really, the wrapping on the presents looked more drab than I was expecting, but wasting coloured paper for this wasn't something even I really wanted to do. Instead, the presents were neatly tied up in cloth and leather. A few of them were even wrapped in reed bags, like the kind we used for rice.

"All right, next one is for Big D . . ." I said, holding my gift out to him.

"Thank you, Master," the rooster replied, bowing as I handed him his gift. With deft movements of his beak, he opened the package and beheld the cloak within. It was a near-duplicate of the one Meimei had made for me last year, with a waterproof exterior and a warm silk lining.

"This one is from me and Mei," I explained, smiling at his wide eyes.

"Thank you, Master and Mistress. I shall cherish this."

The rooster bowed low to both Mei and me. I grinned back at him, then looked over the rest of the crowd. Most of my gifts had already been distributed.

Tigu was already intently examining a scroll on knotwork designs from Pale Moon Lake City. Washy was sitting beside her, equally focused on what I had gotten him: a bunch of journals from explorers.

It was nice that the Azure Jade Trading Company could specifically find ones that talked about food. Honestly, those people were wizards.

Rizzo seemed to like her new little bracers, which had been a bitch and a half to sew, while Peppa cheerfully displayed a set of brushes to a cowboy-hatted Chunky. For Xiulan, Yun Ren, Gou Ren, and Xianghua I had made sets of actual skates. Proper, purpose-built ones.

The cobbler had looked at me like I was mad, but I'd paid good money and he had gotten a lot of business from me that day.

Bowu was marvelling at his set of steel-toed working boots.

I didn't need the great and powerful OSHA Sect to cross time and space and start screaming at me, thank you very much.

Miantiao got another knitted snake sock, and for Babe I had made a better hitch for the plough so he could carry it around easier.

Yin and Huo Ten were the hardest—I'd had no idea what to get them—but both seemed to like their new helmets well enough; the fronts had little glowstone lamps attached.

Though, I must admit, I did sneak in a *bit* of tomfoolery.

"Hey, Meimei!"

My wife glanced up as I chucked her a present. Eyebrows raised, she opened the cloth and found within it a hat.

"I've already got one of . . . ." She trailed off as she noticed something amiss about the design.

Then she started cackling.

It was a classic design: several white deer on a red backdrop. Xiulan glanced at it before she too stifled a laugh.

Because while most of the hat looked normal . . . in a few of the scenes, one deer was humping another.

She pulled it on immediately, a massive grin on her face.

Maybe it was a little scuffed to only get her a hat . . . but hey, I had already done a library and a greenhouse, so I was running out of ideas for this year. Though from her bright smile I could tell that she liked my rude present just as much as everything else I had done.

"That's me done. Who's next?" I asked, and opened up the floor.

To I think everybody's surprise, Babe the ox stood and walked with purpose over to a simple stack of wood. He picked one up in his mouth and took it over to me.

Curious, I accepted it. It was simple. Simple, but the fact that he had made anything at all was surprising.

Upon the block was a single word: *Foundation.* Done not in brushstrokes but utterly flawless cuts that had a style and personality about them. Rou's memories were impressed, the part of me that had spent hours learning calligraphy from Gramps. They were some of his best memories, and I relied on those experiences heavily.

I glanced up and saw that nearly everyone had received the same thing. A block of wood with a single word.

"This will look good on the wall," Yun Ren said, tilting his piece of wood so that I could see the character for *Truth* on his.

Meimei was staring at hers with a raised eyebrow. "Constellation?"

Before we really had time to consider everything, Chunky bounced up and started distributing his own gifts.

Chunky's displayed set of pottery was amateurish, and he had obviously been coached by Miantiao on how to properly make the set of pots and planters, each with a protrusion that made them look like a different chibified farm animal.

There was a fat, round pig; a curled-up, sleepy-looking cat; and a sitting hen, to name a few, and Rancher Chunky with his cowboy hat eagerly handed them all out.

"*This is so cute*," my wife whispered as she stared at the little rat-shaped pot that had been presented to her.

One by one, more and more people stood up to pass around the stuff they had gotten everybody.

As expected, Miantiao gave out things like glassware, including a giant German-style beer stein I had shown him a drawing of.

Peppa's gifts, on the other hand, leaned more towards the practical. She'd gotten me what looked like an organiser for my desk that she stared very, *very* pointedly at.

I turned to my wife for moral support and simply got a raised eyebrow. I pouted. My stuff was organised fine! I knew where everything was!

Mostly.

Yin and Huo Ten had doubled up together, and what followed was a collection of stuff they had found while digging away, from geodes to giant quartz chunks. Fascinating rocks and crystals.

Gou Ren and Yun Ren had given things like leather pouches and thick gloves . . . mostly because we could never get enough of the things. Rizzo had handed out a kind of personalized little first-aid kit. There were things like burn creams and salves for Bowu and Miantiao, while I got some kind of really funky goop that was minty and made the affected area go all chilly.

Xiulan, on the other hand, had a shit-eating grin on as she gave me several more games that she was *clearly* looking forward to beating me at. I pretended to look exasperated . . . but Xiulan was going to get a nasty surprise later.

The only game I was *actually* bad at was go.

Tigu and Washy had teamed up for theirs, and I was quite impressed when they brought out the first one for me.

It was a wooden haft, for a shovel. It was formed out of a strong, sturdy piece of ashwood—a limb from a tree that wasn't on the farm, from the feeling of it, but there was still just a little bit of Qi to it. It felt strong even now.

"Washy came up with the idea and helped me find the branch," Tigu said, giving the dragon his due. "And then we carved it together."

I smiled at the swirling patterns and geometric shapes that, if rolled out, would form a complete scene: a river, flowing through fertile land.

For something last minute . . . it was really, *really* nice.

The pair delivered more carved and crafted objects to everyone else. From Gou Ren's new staff, to a hair tie for Xiulan, and two smaller hafts for Meimei's little herb garden rakes and trowels.

Meimei's presents for everyone were pretty personalized, being clothes. Though again, unlike the Before where such gifts would have been met with polite disinterest at best or groans at worst, these were received with enthusiasm. Hell, Meimei was just flat-out insane at this. Tailored shirts? Silk underclothes? Shit, you'd have had to pay a fortune for this stuff and Meimei could just . . . *make it.*

Hell, all of my family from the Before had been pretty handy in the clothes department, sewing warm shirts and doing patch jobs, but Mei blew that completely out of the water. You could barely see the seams, even *with* cultivator-enhanced vision.

But Mei just shrugged and treated it like it was normal. "I still have a lot to learn," she said primly.

"Humblebrag," I shot back at her.

My wife stuck out her tongue at me, but there was no mistaking her pride at being able to make these for us.

Then we arrived at the last person left who had been waiting patiently.

A rooster stood up.

"If I may, Great Master," Big D stated.

Carefully, he picked up the first of his gifts and presented it to me.

It was a drawing. A drawing done in what people would consider a traditional Chinese print. It was of a man looking over a hill, with a rooster on his shoulder.

Below that was a set of elegant characters.

"We all make our choices. But in the end, our choices make us."

"If I had a thousand lifetimes, and a million choices, I would choose this path every time."

I swallowed thickly, feeling tears in my eyes, and glanced up. Everybody had their own page and drawing. Meimei, sitting beside me, was looking at hers with surprise. She glanced up at the rooster, before her expression transitioned into a smile. Peppa was stoic as she received hers, while Chunky oinked happily. Tigu was squinting at her print page, and then she furiously rubbed at her eyes with the back of her hand.

"You're too sappy, you stupid bird," she muttered.

"Maybe just a little," the rooster rumbled back, his deep voice echoing.

The room lapsed into silence as Tigu grabbed Big D and pulled him into her lap. She rubbed her chin aggressively against the top of his head, and the rooster just looked amused.

I chuckled at the sight and put my arm around Meimei as she leaned into my side.

The hearth slowly burned down, the night wore on, and I just basked in the glow.

"*Oh!* Right, I have one more present!" Tigu suddenly said. She popped up off the floor and shot outside.

I raised an eyebrow at her haste, noticing some curious glances.

We did not have to wait long for her to return. She came back in, lugging an ice sculpture covered by a blanket.

"This is for you, Blade of Grass! It took a while to get a proper composition, but this is my gift for you! Take it as a token of my admiration!" The blanket came off the sculpture. "It turned out quite well, no?"

The *nude* sculpture of Xiulan. Or rather, *mostly* nude—she actually had a cloth hiding some of her body, but that didn't change the fact that it was basically lifelike. It was spectacularly posed, Xiulan in the middle of a dynamic pose, a snapshot of one of her dances.

Xianghua immediately clapped her hands over her little brother's eyes.

Meiling let out a puerile giggle.

I stared for a moment longer than was probably polite before looking over at Xiulan.

The Cai Xiulan of the past probably would have been angry to the point of coming to blows at what Tigu had just done.

Instead of anger, or even serious embarrassment, there was simply fond exasperation. In fact, she was evaluating her own statue.

"Thank you, Tigu," she said, holding out her arms so that she could give the girl a hug. "It's well done as always."

The silence was slightly awkward, before it was broken by a muffled *pop* as a tiny white fox burst into existence beside Yun Ren. I blinked at the creature. I had seen Nezan for a moment at the Dueling Peaks, before the fox had disappeared.

"Ugh, that took more out of me than I thought, and the ambient Qi is so *strange*." The white fox cleared his throat. "Hello again, nephew. It's good to see you again—" The fox's eyes caught on what had previously consumed everybody else's attention.

"*Oh my*," the fox said, and then he turned to Tigu. "Darling, this is magnificent. Do you take commissions?"

Needless to say, the night burst into a flurry of activity, and all I could do was lean back and watch it with amusement as Big D hopped onto my shoulder.

We both looked on with amused smiles as the fox, Nezan, made himself comfortable.

I sighed with contentment as I looked at Yun Ren arguing with his magical girl mascot.

↔

Su Nezan sat in the winter sun beside a truly delightful young girl. His nose took in the pure scents as he basked in the company.

"And then I spiked his soap with a water-activated dye so that when he went to wash off the itching powder it turned his skin pink," the freckled woman said cheerfully.

Nezan roared with laughter at the tale. It had been centuries since he had last been so amused! Truly, breaking part of his core off was worth it just for this! The Great Fox, the bane of the Shrouded Mountain Sect, rolled onto his back and pounded the surrounding snow with his tail, such was his mirth.

"Dear, you should have been born one of ours," the fox decreed once his laughter died down, shaking his head. "You are an absolute delight!"

Little Mei, who was more of a fox than his own distant kin, sketched a bow. Her amethyst eyes sparkled with merriment.

If only this technique didn't take so long to recharge, he could have experienced this all sooner! But he had spent too much of his strength at the Dueling Peaks, aiding Yun Ren. Weaving illusions over even a Shrouded Mountain Disciple was an energy-intensive process at the best of times. With his Core divided and his power diminished in this form? Well, it had been downright exhausting.

The fox huffed a laugh, climbing out of the snowy divot he was in and back onto the rock that little Mei was seated on, the blanket protecting both of them from the chill.

He turned his attention back to this grand Ha Qi game, where the combatants dueled on the ice. His dearest friend would have loved the game. She would have thundered up and down the ice with glee, taking on all challengers.

The ice was full of laughter and cursing as the little ones gamboled like kits fresh out of the den. Even the two Young Mistresses had joined in, which was strange. Nezan never knew Young Mistresses to engage in such play! At that very moment, Cai Xiulan was in earnest combat with a pig. A pig! And she was quite skilled.

Somehow . . . it just felt right. Like being back among his own kin. They were all just so amusing!

And the fact that most of them were Spirit Beasts was the most fascinating part!

He had been fed breakfast by a dragon, been asked if he had any requests for specific meals or sleeping arrangements by a pig, entertained a rat when she began questioning the nature of his form . . . and shared a surprising moment of enjoyment with a boar as he welcomed Nezan. His earnestness was such a delight, the big sunflower.

His eyes softened when he watched his nephew shoulder-check Tigu, the girl spiraling away. She complimented his blow, then focused her eyes upon him with glee.

Nezan would have to offer them a boon later, when the time came. He had decided now. Yun Ren would take back this fragment of himself to the main body, and then he would visit in truth.

He sighed happily as he expanded his senses to truly take in the depths of this Fa Ram.

Now that he was not completely diminished, he could feel the power a bit more. It was faint, but it was not trying to hide from his eyes; on top of that, as soon as he had manifested outside the crystal, he had felt more invigorated than ever.

It was rather strange that it hadn't helped him while he was actively trying to draw Qi into part of his core before, but now the land would likely be able to sustain this small form indefinitely.

And something else itched at the back of his mind. Summer's Sky had been uncaring of the circumstances, simply labeling it '*Interesting, approval*,' but Nezan's curiosity was piqued.

"Hey! How's the game going?" a voice called out, and Nezan turned to see the Master of this land call from the forest.

The man who had laid low the Shrouded Mountain appeared from the tree line, from wherever he had gone with the rooster called Bi De. Jin had his respect, if only for making those bastards scamper about like the roaches they were.

But . . . there was something that *did* concern Nezan. Here, in the heart of this place, he could see the faint golden lines that connected the man to the earth. The entwined core, pumping and beating, yet slow and asleep.

The itching intensified as an old, *old* memory came to the fore and pieces clicked into place.

Pieces that didn't make sense.

Because there was only one path that Nezan knew that would look similar . . . *and it didn't do this.*

The Path of Shennong.

Nezan frowned. Could it be?

He looked at the man and the wellspring of golden power beneath their feet. It fit.

But . . . it was different than what the scroll had described.

Nezan watched out of the corner of his eye, turning his attention to the delightful young lady eagerly describing to him the way to craft a truly virulent laxative. He committed her concoction to memory, even as his attention wandered back to the question at hand.

A long, *long* time ago, just after the Misty Fang had been taken and renamed the Shrouded Mountain, Nezan had happened upon a scroll. It was an ancient thing, crumbling and ruined, but within it was detailed a style of cultivation.

A cultivation method that had Nezan shaking his head and saying a prayer for the poor fools who set upon it.

When one turns their eyes from the heavens without regret, they begin to walk the Path of Shennong. They stride alongside the first primordial being who tamed the land, who diverted the rivers and who broke the rocks. The God-King of the earth, who taught mankind to farm, crafted a thousand medicines, invented the plough, and formed the contract between men and the firmament.

It is not a conscious choice. One can only embark upon this path without knowing they are on it. To force it or to desire this state is, by all accounts, impossible.

One must give to the earth without desiring anything in return. They must venerate the very thing that other cultivators desire to leave behind.

To walk this path is to be beloved of the earth and count the spirits of the lakes and mountains as their friends.

By this ancient path, they who walk the Path of Shennong will know prosperity. Their strength will be equal to that of the spirits.

They know the land they walk upon as their dearest friend. They will live long, prosperous lives; they will have peace, the truest peace imaginable.

And then they will die, and their flesh and bones will nurture the earth.

This is the Path of Shennong. To forsake immortality and the power of the heavens. To live and die upon the earth.

It was a dead-end path. There was no defiance of the heavens. There was no cultivating for strength. It was a complete submission to the Law of Earth, for as Shennong died, his corpse sprouting medicinal herbs, so too would those of the pact surely perish.

It was a path that was repulsive to any cultivator. Accept death? The very thing that cultivation strove to conquer?

Unthinkable.

To walk this path is to be beloved of the earth and count the Spirits of the lakes and mountains as their friends . . . Nezan pondered this part of the scroll. Everyone knew of Earth Spirits: Qi constructs that were personifications of geographic features, like a mountain or a lake . . . and, well, they were normally rather passive things, unless roused to anger by too much blood being spilled on their homes or men mining too greedily.

They were strong, and the bigger and more Qi-rich their home, the stronger they were.

Nezan traced the golden lines into the distance, feeling a sense of unease.

He licked his lips as he began to understand the sheer enormity of what he was sitting on.

This . . . this was not any kind of Earth Spirit he knew.

How did a man ever manage to contract something so unfathomably vast? It was like asking the sea to notice a fish.

Nezan frowned as he pondered this conundrum, watching Bi De call over Jin. The man nodded, and both man and cock looked quite serious.

↔

The lingering feelings of the night before still resonated in Bi De's soul as he stood in the predawn light. The warmth filled his breast, nourishing his spirit and preparing him for the trial to come.

"Call me if you need me, okay?" his Great Master asked. "I'll hang around in case anything goes wrong."

Bi De took a deep breath and nodded. They were in a forest, brightly lit by the winter sun. Ri Zu, Yin, Miantiao, and Huo Ten were with him as well, looking on with calm eyes.

He stood before the crystal that had defined his journey: a fragment of the past and the answer to his question. What had started with his simple curiosity about why the dances of mortals produced Qi had led him on an adventure that uncovered an ancient cataclysm that had rocked the Azure Hills.

And now it was time.

There was no more second-guessing himself—it was simply time for action.

His beak touched the crystal as he plunged into the memories.

☐

Deep asleep, a girl curled into her blankets, her house warm and comfortable. Her Qi churned sluggishly as golden cracks sealed and turned the colour of flesh. An eye regrew, as did an arm—she inched towards wholeness once more.

Yet despite the peacefulness of her surroundings, there was a little frown on her face.

Tianlan dreamed. She dreamed of a time long since past. A past that had a thousand sweet memories, and a thousand bitter ones.

She dreamed of how she'd made a connection to a little boy. How she'd found friends whom she had loved with all her heart.

But most of all—

She dreamed of how she broke.

CHAPTER 32

THE BREAKING OF [天] PART I

天.
Tiān.
Sky.
Heaven.

□

It was a rather familiar story.

Xiaoshi was a young man born to unimportant parents in the town of Pale Moon. The town was so named for the moon's odd behavior so close to the Mist Wall. Some nights, the entire moon turned a pale silver. Wherever it shone, all the colour was sucked out of the world, turning the entire village black and white.

Xiaoshi was a diligent man. He had to be after losing his family. His father had died in a cave-in. His mother, from disease.

He loved them dearly, even now. Xiaoshi remembered his mother's enormous, radiant smile and seemingly endless stamina as she picked up all kinds of odd jobs to help support them. He never forgot his father's calm countenance, even as he came back from another hard day in the mines, exhaustion in his features.

His parents had wanted to stop being miners, to go out into the world. They had been saving up to buy a plot of land they could truly call their own.

His father had told him stories of how much better life would be soon. How they would be landowners, with their own farm. They would bask under the brilliant sky, instead of being confined beneath the dirt.

That lasted until, at the annual scouting, they'd discovered that Xiaoshi had some talent for the mystic arts. Some talent for *cultivation.*

That day, their plans changed. Instead of working towards their dream home . . . they instead spent all their money on him. On the medicines and pills to make *him* stronger.

At first, Xiaoshi loved it. He knew the stories; if he was a cultivator, he could make a lot of money and protect his parents—and he could protect a lot of other people too! He could be a hero!

His parents were so proud of him, and they had begun working even harder so Xiaoshi would get the things he needed. He ignited into the First Stage of the Initiate's Realm.

The next day, his father went down into the depths and never came out again.

His mother had tried to keep things together—he knew she had—but the little nest egg they had saved and scrimped for had started to dwindle when the sickness took her. Her hair had fallen out and her body became so thin he could count her bones.

"Live a good life, my little stone," she'd said, her grin as bright as the sun despite her pain.

Then she was gone.

At first, Xiaoshi had been at a loss. But . . . but he knew he had to follow his parents' wish. He had to be a cultivator and live a good life.

For them.

So he walked up to the massive mansion, with the last gift his mother ever gave him: a letter for the Overseer.

"Be grateful, boy," the Overseer said after he finished reading the letter. His face was craggy and rough, and just a little bit ugly. "It is through me that you shall not starve."

→

The Overseer was a harsh, brutal man, but Xiaoshi threw himself into his training. He would be a cultivator and live a good life.

So he had to work hard.

His training didn't get him out of having to help fill the increasing Pale Moon Ore quotas, nor from having to sweep the streets outside his Master's home. But there was hope.

There was hope that his Master would see his talent! A couple of the other servants said he was really good at cultivating!

He trained for a year. And then when he was eight, his Master *did* recognise him.

"You will spar with my son. You will be a good whetstone for him," the Overseer had declared—Xiaoshi was so happy he had finally been acknowledged.

Wu beat him up real bad. But that was fine, because he was still learning, and every legend had to start somewhere.

He trained against the "Young Master" every day.

It hurt.

But he did his best.

He was filial. Obedient. He took his lumps from Wu and kept his head down.

The Overseer demanded that he grow stronger and be useful. He had been taken in; it was only right that he repay the kind favour, wasn't it? It was only right that he was a cultivator for the Overseer's sake.

"You're quite useful at being a punching bag," Wu said with a sneer after Xiaoshi was on the ground again, after they had traded pointers.

Xiaoshi was very much starting to hate his Master's son.

→

Eight years went by. Xiaoshi's position never changed. He still had to do the laundry. He still had all his quotas in the mines. He wasn't being paid all that much. The Overseer, after the first year, had stopped giving Xiaoshi any resources, and it became incredibly difficult to keep up with the level that was demanded of him as the Young Master's sparring partner.

Rather, as a living training dummy.

Every time he asked for a promotion, he was denied. Every time he asked for more resources, he was denied.

A servant for life. That was all he would be. The dream of being a powerful cultivator had slowly withered away. After all, he had never *once* beaten Wu.

Xiaoshi sighed, staring up at the massive Mist Wall in the distance.

The dream of every "real" cultivator was to breach the wall and explore the outside world.

Xiaoshi thought it was a sack of crap, in his opinion. The world was so vast already. They might as well explore the entirety of the Azure Mountains before trying to figure out some other place.

Xiaoshi sighed, then returned to his work. Work he *really* didn't enjoy.

→

One day, when he was sixteen, he forgot to call Wu "Young Master."

He was beaten for it. Severely. To the point where he nearly died. It was far beyond the normal lumps and blows that could be ignored, and it was outside the ring.

Xiaoshi asked for justice from the Overseer, and he received none.

"If you cannot handle this much, then you are not cut out to study the mystic arts," the Overseer decreed, his face like solid iron. "This is how the world works, boy."

It ate at him as he staggered out of the palace. It ate at him as he had a meat bun and the whispers of the latest culling of the barbarian tribes reached his ears.

It ate at him as he overheard a man complaining loudly about how the quotas were increasing, only to get shushed nervously by his neighbor.

The Emperor had eyes and ears everywhere, and he didn't take kindly to dissent.

Xiaoshi climbed to the top of a wooden house and sat, nursing his wounds. He stared at the sky, where despite the smoke the stars still shone through, and sighed.

"Just . . . what is the point of it all?" he finally asked.

The world had no answer for him.

He stared back down at the town of his birth. The next day would likely bring torment, because Wu never forgot a slight.

'Live a good life, my little stone.'

Just . . . just what was a good life, anyway? It certainly wasn't in this place. It certainly wasn't being a cultivator.

He remembered his father's stories, of stunning vistas and the smell of crops, even though the man had been a miner all his life. He remembered his parents' original plan.

Xiaoshi pulled the symbol of the Overseer from his breast and tossed it on the ground. He stood up, then left Pale Moon Town.

He gave up on cultivation.

To the west he travelled. He had the piddling coins the Overseer had paid him. He had the strength of a cultivator, which let him take on odd jobs. He travelled across the riverlands, and through the lakes, until he reached the edges of the Cloudcatcher Forest, the tops of the trees as tall as the peaks of mountains.

For the first time, he was content with his life's choices.

→

Xiaoshi stared out across the land that he had purchased. It felt . . . right. It was off the beaten path, but there were no reports of any Demon Beasts around, and the people of the nearby village were kind and helpful.

He took a breath, hefted his axe, and got to work.

He cut down the trees. He diverted a stream. He broke the rocks that would impede his progress and tilled his first field.

For the first time in his life, he was truly living for himself.

It did not take long for him to fall in love with his plot of land. Each day upon it was a blessing. He soaked his Qi into the earth and exalted in every moment.

It was hard, hard work. But as he built his first house, and as his little vegetable garden grew tall, he took pride in his accomplishments; he had finally started living his father's dream.

He gave his Qi to the earth, for this blessed bounty.

In doing so, he turned fully away from heaven.

→

Xiaoshi worked his land. He loved his land. He grew his crops and knew, in his heart of hearts, that *this* was a good life.

He gave everything he had to his little farm. He loved it with all his heart.

Each day, his Qi entered the soil like water. Not out of a desire to receive anything in return but as thanks for the little slice of paradise he had found.

□

Something felt the little tendrils of Qi brush up against it. Caress it.

It had started with the alerts of lesser spirits. The minor ones that helped regulate the Dragon Veins of the world. Their soft whispers were added to the chorus from the strands of Qi as they tasted the man's soul, and knew he walked the True Path.

The great consciousness stirred.

The Qi was nothing like it had felt in . . . in a very long time. The taste of the energy was almost familiar, warm, comforting, and selfless.

A bearded old man smiled at them all. He had his hands on the earth, and a bright smile on his face, even as he died.

A promise, through all the planes and all the worlds.

'And so the Great Ancestor, Shennong, commanded his disciple in the ways of preparing the fields. Till the Land. Fell the Trees. Divert the Waters, Break the Rocks, Sow the Seeds, Reap the Harvest. Craft for thyself a place to call home, and give thanks to the land for its bounty . . .'

First condition met: turn away from the heavens.

A great, unfathomable consciousness began to stir.

Like the morning dew gathering into a drop at the end of a blade of grass, the Earth Spirit's consciousness collected. Slowly. Ponderously, until it was pressed up against the tiny threads and fully *aware*.

Normally, it was diffuse. Spread out over the breadth of itself, passing by the cycles without a single thought. The sleeping time of winter, the growth of spring, the heat of summer, and the falling leaves. There was little variation. Occasionally the ground would rumble, or there would be a flood, but for the most part, its existence passed in silent stillness.

But now it was here. Here, touching the tiny threads of Qi. Tasting the emotion within and learning of the one who had taken the first step upon the Path.

It watched for a cycle, then two. Its attention was utterly consumed by the being that had managed to call its attention. For so, so long, the spirit had simply . . . existed, as was its duty. As was its function. A regulator of the world: one of the existences that was the wellspring of life.

It watched as the man made his farm. It watched as he, after nearly a year of living on his own, finally took the plunge and spoke to other humans.

And instead of the bitter rejection he had experienced all his life . . . the spirit felt the warmth, when he was *accepted*.

"If you want it, Green Trees will be your home. Welcome to the village, Brother."

The sudden surge of emotion hit the Earth Spirit, sending it reeling. Normally, the sensations from those that lived upon it were muted things. This? This was pure. It worked down the man's Qi like the roots of a tree, settling deep and taking hold as the feeling plunged deep into the spirit's core.

The feeling of *belonging*.

The Earth Spirit spasmed.

It remembered belonging once. Belonging to a greater whole, until their creator had separated them; it had been a safeguard against the cancer that lurked between worlds.

But . . . it felt . . . an indescribable thing, ever since it had been separated from the others like it. There was no touch, no connection, hidden as it was behind a wall of mist.

It . . . it wanted to belong again.

First condition met, the spirit reminded itself. For the first time since it could remember . . . one had met the first condition.

It felt the man's Qi again.

And made its decision.

The spirit reached out a tendril to the man's Qi—

—and *connected.*

CHAPTER 33

THE BREAKING OF [天] PART 2

For the first time in a long, long time, Xiaoshi could say that he was truly happy.

The village of Green Trees had accepted him as one of their own. Nobody kicked him, or forced him to work more hours; they merely invited him for games of go, or shared their food and drink with him, just as he shared his bounty with them.

It was like a great weight had been lifted from him.

Each breath he took on his farm was a hymn, a praise to the world around him.

He had made it. And his parents could rest easy. The shrine was in the most beautiful place, high on the hill so that they could watch over him, always.

"Hey, Xiaoshi!" Linlin called, the pale farmer's daughter waving at him happily. "We're all going to head down to the river, do you want to join us?"

There were three others as well—Boyi, Boer, and Bosan—waving at him.

And perhaps, in time, more would come?

Xiaoshi put down his hoe and grinned back. "Of course, my friends! I'll be along shortly!"

Life was good.

↔

The Rules that had been imposed on the Earth Spirit by its creator were . . . strange. The spirit was technically supposed to fall back asleep after it made the connection: it was supposed to go back to dreaming and regulating the province.

But it did not *have* to.

And really, even if the spirit wanted to, it couldn't. How could it sleep, when it felt all these new sensations? How could it ever drift away, when its Connected One was so interesting? When the sensations he gave to it were so . . . so . . .

Wondrous.

It learned the feeling of fat heads of rice sifting through fingers; it felt the summer breeze across its face. It tasted the dumplings made by friends of the Connected One from the village, and its soul filled with joy and amusement as it watched Linlin push its Connected One into the river. The action jostled loose another memory of the old man—of Azure Mountains doing something to one of the others like it, only for its creator to scold it.

It felt joy, as its Connected One harvested his fields. It learned sorrow, as its Connected One bowed his head in front of funerary tablets for his mother and father.

It felt pride, when he built the shrine upon a hill and placed the funerary tablets within so they could overlook his little shack and his fields.

All these things came to it, from its Connected One.

The Earth Spirit went to the festivals, even though it was sleepy. It watched the dances, and the party, and the soft kiss between its Connected One and Linlin.

For a full cycle, it watched.

Its Connected One fell in love with the village, and so too did the Earth Spirit.

The spirit grew more and more enamoured with the people of the village with each passing day. It loved them just as its Connected One did. Like a moth to a flame it could not stop. The feelings were too much, invading its thoughts and dreams.

It wanted to feel the love and affection the villagers had for each other. It wanted to try the games, eat the rice cakes, and *feel* like they felt.

The Earth Spirit wanted to connect to all of them too.

But that was not how things were done. Despite that, it wanted to know. It was an obsession. An overriding desire that felt wrong, yet somehow right.

The spirit crafted itself a body so that it could know. At first, it was a formless mass of gold. Yet through trial and error, the dreams of its Connected One, and the belief of those who lived upon it, the Earth Spirit took form.

It started to look human, rather than like a mountain or an animal, as people had thought of it before.

Mother Earth. The Azure Mountains.

A blend of features formed over the latticework of Qi. *It* became *she*.

Until the Earth Spirit finally looked in a conjured pool of water in its domain of grass and saw her new form's reflection.

She saw herself, and drifted further away from the formless mass she had once been.

When she looked at herself in the calm waters of the conjured pool, she was struck by an urge.

An urge that for nearly a year, she had managed to ignore.

↔

Xiaoshi dreamed of an endless field. It was a recurring dream now, one that he usually had after a particularly good day: a beautiful field with verdant grass, healthy trees, and a wonderful blue sky. Mountains rose in the distance, sheltering the little slice of paradise.

The only thing that changed here was the cycle of seasons. Now nineteen years old, he had seen it twice revolve.

The only slight imperfection was that he felt like somebody was watching him at times. Shrugging, he settled in for stargazing and enjoying the mountain vistas.

"Hello," a voice said suddenly, and Xiaoshi nearly jumped out of his skin. Whoever had spoken sounded the words out oddly, like they were unfamiliar with the language.

Scrambling to his feet, he was about to look around, to see who had spoken, but there was no need to—right in front of him was a young woman. She was of average height with pale skin, and she had brown hair and warm blue eyes that took his breath away.

She looked like a princess with her beauty and regal bearing. Even wearing the clothes of a peasant farmer, she had a *presence* about her. The only slight mar was her freckles, but they weren't distracting.

It was strange that she was in his dream, but his parents hadn't raised him to be impolite.

"Uh . . . hello?" he answered back, still a bit off balance from her sudden appearance.

The woman nodded, appearing pleased at the greeting. Warmth flooded his chest, a familiar feeling, like he experienced every time he pressed his Qi into the earth—

He paused and glanced at his feet. At his feet, where two golden bands connected him to the woman. They pulsed, filling him with warmth. It was a sensation that put him at ease when he worked his fields. He looked back up into those fathomless . . . almost inhuman blue eyes.

And then he saw the rest of her. The mass of Qi that was beneath the earth supporting this entire dream world.

The realisation was a thunderbolt.

Despite all his Qi use over the past several years, he had never truly felt tired. Every time he started to flag, and every time he wondered how to grow a certain crop . . . his energy would refill, and his predictions would come true.

Like somebody had been helping him.

He hadn't even noticed.

"Are you the one who has been helping me, O majestic Earth Spirit?" Xiaoshi asked, immediately sinking into a bow. Earth Spirits were supposed to be like gods, his father had said, and the man had prayed every day before the little shrine to the spirit of the mine . . . Even if it hadn't helped him in the end, they were to be respected.

"Yes." The simple, one-word answer rang with only truth.

"This Xiaoshi thanks you for your benevolence," he said, defaulting back to the manners pounded into his head by the Overseer. He risked a glance up at the woman. Her face was flat and expressionless, but he felt a slight hint of frustration coming from her. "What do you desire for your boons, O great spirit?"

His head ducked down again, wondering for what reason the Earth Spirit had graced him with her presence. She had been helping him, that much was obvious.

The frustration spiked for a moment. There was silence, as the Earth Spirit just stood there, looking at him.

"Let's be friends," the Earth Spirit said, in *Linlin's* voice. The day she had asked Xiaoshi to come with her and her brothers to the river. "That is what I want."

Xiaoshi looked up in shock, just in time for the ground to drop out beneath him. He landed on his rear in a river that suddenly appeared out of nowhere, with the Earth Spirit looking down on him from where she stood on the shore.

"We are friends now, yes?" she asked, with hope in her voice, even if her face was blank and expressionless.

Xiaoshi knew not how to address this. An ancient and venerable Earth Spirit, acting like the village children trying to make their first friend.

He tentatively reached out, feeling their connection. It was a quiet undercurrent. Hope. Apprehension.

And, beneath it all, there was a deep, troubling loneliness.

As isolated and alone as Xiaoshi had been back in Pale Moon.

Xiaoshi didn't know for what reason the Earth Spirit had chosen him. He didn't know *why* she wanted to be his friend.

Xiaoshi grinned. "Of course. You just gotta help me up first." He held out his hand. The Earth Spirit blinked at the hand before reaching out her own. She touched it and started to pull.

But she was completely unprepared for Xiaoshi to yank her down as hard as he could. The Earth Spirit just seemed confused as she tumbled into the water.

She surfaced, spluttering, and for an instant Xiaoshi wondered if he'd overstepped. The Earth Spirit looked at him. Then, like a mason carving a masterpiece, her stiff face split into a massive smile. A surprisingly girlish giggle escaped her throat.

A hunk of mud the size of Xiaoshi was uprooted from the bottom of the river and slammed into him, sending him flying.

Naturally, Xiaoshi would never let such an insult stand. He retaliated as best as he was able, and in a muddy river, a friendship was cemented as they dueled with mud and water—at least until Xiaoshi ended the match by accidentally headbutting her.

The spirit collapsed, holding her head, but both of them were smiling.

Xiaoshi sighed with contentment. Peace claimed his soul, for a moment and an eternity.

Then he realised he had been very rude.

"Lady Earth Spirit? What is the name you wish me to call you by?" he asked her. "This one is Xiaoshi, son of Xiaoshen."

The mud-coated face turned to him. The spirit blinked, caught off guard by the question, her bright smile fading.

"I do not have a name," the spirit stated after a moment. She seemed concerned by the revelation. There was another pulse of anxiety. "Call this one whatever you wish."

He considered it for a moment, staring up at the beautiful blue sky.

"Tianlan," he said.

The girl turned to him, confused.

"Tianlan. Azure. We met under this beautiful sky, didn't we?"

"Tian . . . lan?" the spirit replied, tasting the words. "*Tianlan.*"

The smile was as bright as the sun.

□

It was strange, having a passenger in one's head, Xiaoshi reflected. Tianlan had started out stiff, but she had rapidly devolved into using the slang of the villagers.

"Try that one next, Shishi!" Tianlan demanded, and Xiaoshi rolled his eyes before picking up a skewer of meat. Their senses connected, the spirit let out a moan of happiness.

The festival was in full swing, the paper lanterns lit, and everything was just *perfect*. He smiled at Linlin and handed her another skewer. The Bo brothers were there as ostensible chaperones, but in reality, they were just stuffing their faces.

It was set to be a wonderful night.

Their festivities were interrupted, however, by a commotion at the front of the village.

Xiaoshi glanced at Linlin, who shrugged, and they all started in the direction of the rapidly forming crowd.

"What's going on, chief?" Boyi asked as they approached. The mood in the circle was grim.

"They say that the Ten Antidote Serpents were actually Ten Venom Serpents, and that they had been peddling poison as Demon Beasts all this time. So the Emperor marched on their home and slew them all!" the chief stated, his voice cold and hard.

"Demon Beasts? The Antidote Serpents? He dares to call them that?!" an elderly voice demanded, full of wrath. Poison scars still dotted Yuheng's face from a *real* Demon Beast, and it was widely known that the gentle serpents had healed his wound.

"There's more. We are to be on the lookout for a wicked traitor who attacked the Emperor's army and burned the Emperor's flag. All who aid him will be put to the sword, to nine degrees of separation, and their village will be burned and salted."

The mood died completely at that statement. Linlin squeezed his hand, her normally light skin the colour of a corpse.

The chief sighed, shaking his head. "We shall not discuss this today. Like any swordsman will come this far east in the first place. Everybody! Return to the festival!" he called.

Slowly, the people went back to the party. But there was a pall over the proceedings.

Xiaoshi tried to shake it off. They were at the outskirts. The chief was right. Like anybody would come *this way*.

→

Life went on after the proclamation. He spoke with Linlin's father about her hand, now that he had established himself. It was a little bit awkward with Tianlan constantly telling him to kiss her, and getting upset when he tried to force the spirit out of his senses when he did. The Earth Spirit was entirely too curious for her own good!

"You sure about this, Brother Xiaoshi?" Brother Boyi asked, his arms crossed and a smile on his face.

Xiaoshi nodded, picking up his pickaxe.

"We need new ploughshares, and nobody else has any iron. I'll be a week, at most, and go through the edge of the forest. Nobody will know I'm there!" Xiaoshi said, as Tianlan sang "*Adventure, adventure!*" in his head.

Well, that too. His dear friend was endlessly curious.

He set off on his adventure, waving goodbye to a dear friend, a smile on his face.

□

An injured, vagabond swordsman passed through the village. The people of Green Trees, being kindly folk, took him in to nurse him back to health.

On the next day, the soldiers of the Emperor marched into town, looking for the man who had raised his hand against the Lord of the Azure.

□

There was something wrong.

It came to Tianlan in bursts of fitfulness. There was something *wrong*. It was an itching in her back.

Her consciousness was always with Xiaoshi now. But there was something further down that was plucking at her soul, and she didn't know what.

Xiaoshi hummed to himself as he wandered back to town, big hunks of iron ore slung across his back. His adventure had been more successful than he ever could have dreamed.

"You've been quiet, Tianlan. Are you all right?" he asked her.

Tianlan scratched at her back. "I'm fine . . . but . . . I have a bad feeling," she whispered to him.

"Bad feeling, huh? Well, we'll be home soon, so we can figure it out when we get there," he said. As they broke the tree line, her Connected One paused, glancing up at the sky.

"That's . . . a lot of smoke. Did Boer try to cook again?" Xiaoshi asked, trying to inject some levity . . . . but he broke into a light jog regardless.

Tianlan's back itched again.

Then the smell hit them. The smell of ash and blood. Xiaoshi dropped his basket of ore and broke into a sprint. A mad dash to the village, where the medical hut was ablaze.

Xiaoshi staggered to a stop as he caught sight of the villagers. They were lined up, on their knees, with their heads pressed to the ground before a man. He was in the uniform of the Imperial Army. His hair was tied up like a nobleman's, and he was smiling at the head within his hands. The head was one neither Xiaoshi nor Tianlan recognised.

His armor was sooty, and the blade stabbed into the ground was dripping with blood. He had a captain's rank emblem on his shoulder. There were five more soldiers, all of them watching the villagers, amusement written on their faces.

"You all did receive the proclamation two moons past, did you not?" the captain asked, his voice mild and conversational.

Chief Xin was on his knees, his forehead pressed flat against the dirt.

"We did, Mighty Captain! We of this humble village could not conceive of a man who could escape the mighty Imperial Army for so long, and thus we let down your guards! We beg your forgiveness!"

The man raised an eyebrow, a smile overtaking his face. "Oh? Listen to this peasant, who thinks so highly of us!"

The soldiers around them laughed, and Tianlan got a sinking feeling in her stomach.

"But . . . well. The Emperor's orders were clear, were they not?" he continued in the same tone. His sword rose out of the ground, travelling in a pretty arc.

Chief Xin's arm hit the ground. He started to scream.

She felt Xiaoshi's blood freeze.

"To the ninth degree. All traitors, out by the roots. And *do* be quiet."

Chief Xin, who had welcomed Xiaoshi to the village, who had said he would always have a place with them. The old man who told the children all sorts of stories.

The sword came up again, as the soldiers drew their blades, and what was about to happen set in among the village.

She could feel Xiaoshi's hesitation. She could feel his trembling hands.

He wanted to run away. He wanted to run so *badly*.

The sword arced down. Linlin screamed.

Xiaoshi pulled on their connection.

Something told Tianlan that it wasn't supposed to work like this, but she ignored it. Rage flooded her veins. Tianlan gave her power freely.

Xiaoshi roared, and Tianlan roared with him, launching themselves towards this bastard. The man never stopped his swing. Instead, he simply lifted one arm in a contemptuous block. Xiaoshi was too slow. The blade cut deep into Chief Xin, and the man had the audacity to smirk at them.

Until his eyes widened.

He was in the Fourth Stage of the Spiritual Realm. An existence that would have eclipsed Xiaoshi when he'd left the Overseer's town. It didn't matter.

There was no hesitation. Xiaoshi swung, a nearly artless thing. His fist met a metal sword, and the sword shattered. It met Pale Moon Ore riveted plates, the material holding beneath the onslaught, but not preventing what happened next. The force of the blow continued through, and *pulped* the cultivator beneath.

The other men froze, eyes widening at seeing an expert of the Azure Empire destroyed in a single blow.

Then one found his resolve. "Death to the traitors! Glory for the Emperor!" he screamed. The rest took up his cry.

The battle was joined. The villagers watched in shock and horror as the bloodshed spread.

↔

Xiaoshi was numb when it was all over. He stared at the devastation. The fires had spread during the fight, burning down half the village.

"What do we do?" somebody asked.

Xiaoshi and Tianlan stared at the people of the little village, terror upon their faces, as some of them wept.

Xiaoshi could feel Tianlan's emotions, and her self-recrimination for not noticing sooner. He reached out, and she calmed, slightly, latching on to something else. Something dark.

"We have to leave." Xiaoshi said as he stared at the devastation. They couldn't stay here; the Imperial Army would be back.

He saw a few start to weep at the thought of having to abandon their homes. He felt Tianlan's possessive protectiveness and nodded. His eyes sought out Linlin's. She was terrified.

He took a deep breath. He had only known them for three years . . . but they had been the best three years of his life. He'd take care of them.

Yet something else bubbled beneath the surface.

Something ugly.

CHAPTER 34

THE BREAKING OF [天] PART 3

The feeling was something new . . . and for the first time, Tianlan didn't like it.

She didn't like the way tears welled in her eyes, nor how rain poured down in her domain. She couldn't stop it. She couldn't control it. The dark clouds above her head cracked with lightning and boomed with thunder.

There was something stabbing into her heart. She had pulled off part of her robe, to see where she had been injured, but found only unblemished skin.

Tianlan clutched at the fabric of her clothes as she watched through Xiaoshi's eyes. The bodies of Chief Xin, Han, Shan, Tai, Bizhou, and Feng were cremated, using the wood of the village.

Chief Xin and his easy kindness. Han and Shan, the two constantly bickering—their fights were the stuff of legend, as brother and sister snarked at each other. Tai and Bizhou, the doctor and his wife, the kindly couple who could never *not* aid somebody in need. And Feng, brave Feng, who had thrown himself at one of the soldiers who was trying to attack Xiaoshi from behind and had paid the ultimate price for it.

Her guts churned. Her body shuddered. She gritted her teeth as her Qi spasmed, and she barely managed to clamp down on it, preventing Qi deviation.

Even days later, the pain was still raw. It still ached.

She briefly even thought of dispersing herself, like the contract said she should. Letting go of all these feelings, dissolving into the void. Sometimes she wished she could just diffuse herself again. To let everything go and become nothing.

Tianlan refused.

To disregard these feelings was to disregard herself. So she let herself feel the anguish, keeping an eye on her Qi. She . . . honestly didn't know what she was doing. She had only instinct and a set of rules she had to follow. This was beyond her knowledge. She didn't know where it would lead or what would become of her. Tianlan didn't know what she would do.

She could feel the rest of herself. Distant and muted, a long way away from her core here.

She had concentrated her being too much. Bound it up in Xiaoshi . . . and now even though she was greater as a result, much of her power was beyond her reach.

She grimaced.

And now they had to leave Green Trees.

Part of Tianlan wanted to stand firm. To stay in this village and dare these bastards to come again. She wasn't a fool, though. That captain was weak compared to the people the Empire could bring to bear, or so Xiaoshi said.

Tianlan was confident that they could win against the first few arrivals. But if the Imperial Army took a real interest in them?

Worse still, to stay would be the death of even more of the people she loved. Staying could mean *Xiaoshi* could be lost.

And that was something Tianlan couldn't accept.

↔

Xiaoshi had held Linlin's hand as the fires burned down and the funerary tablets were crafted. In his soul, the only thing that he could hear was choked and muffled sobs.

Xiaoshi himself was simply . . . numb. He returned to his own home and stared out across the gentle hills.

His house looked warm and inviting. His fields were full of growing crops. His chickens clucked and hopped around in their coop, eager for another day of eating bugs.

But most of all, he looked at the shrine he had built for his parents. The shrine he had made for them so that they could watch over him as he accomplished his father's dream.

For the first time since the battle, he consciously tried to do something with his Qi that wasn't just pushing it into the land. He felt Tianlan stir as he touched their connection.

The shrine slowly sank into the ground; the earth flowed around it like a tide, until not a trace remained.

"I'll be back," he promised them. "I'll be back, and then you'll see this place grow once more."

He rose, collected what he could, and returned to the village.

They packed up the entire village in a day, but when it came time to leave, they stumbled, with no real destination in mind. Yet they all knew that staying here was death.

Imperial soldiers had been killed in their land. As far as anyone of the Empire would be concerned, they were rebels.

The Emperor's soldiers were not kind to rebels and barbarians.

But what surprised Xiaoshi was when Boyi walked up, a serious look upon his face.

"Where to, Xiaoshi?" Boyi asked, and the question cut at Xiaoshi.

Boyi would have been—and should be—chief. Xiaoshi should have been asking *him* that.

But instead, everybody was gathered around, waiting for his decision. Linlin slipped her hand into his at the hesitation.

He swallowed, making his decision,

"West. Past the Cloudcatcher Forest, and as close to the Mist Wall as we can get."

There were a few intakes of breath at his proclamation, but such was the severity of the situation that nobody spoke against it.

With heavy hearts and one last look at the ruined buildings, they set off.

□

They travelled past the enormous trees that were so tall they captured the clouds above.

On the tenth day of the second month of their travels, the trees started to thin out. The massive things that touched the heavens became normal once more, and upon cresting a final hill, the villagers saw it.

The Mist Wall.

The Edge of the World. It was said the entirety of the Azure Hills was surrounded by it, a wall between them and the lands beyond the Emperor's reach.

It was an unassuming thing. A bit of fog on the ground, twisting and roiling that intensified until it turned completely opaque. It looked like you could simply walk through it, and surely the fog would lift.

That could not be further from the truth. To enter the Mist Wall, to try to walk through it, was *death*. None who had entered it had ever returned.

Some even said that actual demons stalked within, and that they would steal through the night to attack people.

There was a mood of unease in the caravan as they beheld the eldritch thing, and Xiaoshi felt Tianlan's own discomfort when she stared at it.

But . . . nobody ever really ventured this close to the Mist Wall. Only Pale Moon was built this close, and that was the exception, rather than the rule.

So Xiaoshi searched. He searched long and hard, until he found a suitable sheltered valley.

And thus the rebuilding began.

With Xiaoshi's strength, and Tianlan's help, the buildings were swiftly erected . . . and for the first time in months, things seemed like they were almost back to normal.

The children played. The villagers planted their crops. They built a home again.

Xiaoshi and Tianlan looked out over the valley. They had something worth protecting.

□

"You're going to go, aren't you?" Linlin asked from where her head rested on Xiaoshi's chest. Xiaoshi started at the question and looked down into Linlin's soft eyes. There was no accusation in them, just a simple statement of fact.

Xiaoshi pondered the question.

He hated fighting. He did not want to kill anybody. And yet . . .

And yet what the Emperor was doing was obscene.

Xiaoshi saw the faces of the miners when quotas were increased again. He saw the sunken stares of townsfolk as they rationed food under the increasing burden of taxes, and the fear that took root with the whispers of slain Spirit Beasts.

But over all of this, he saw a burning village.

Something wasn't right. He could feel it in his bones. The Son of Heaven had overstepped his bounds.

The earth *stirred.* The rage of a man and a spirit connected into one feeling.

"Yes. I can't just sit here and do nothing. I'm going to get to the bottom of this," he swore.

He could feel Tianlan's support in the back of his mind.

Linlin smiled up at him and pressed a kiss into his lips.

"Go. Do what you have to. Even if it makes the whole world your enemy."

And thus, Xiaoshi set off for the Imperial Capital.

□

Not to do battle with the Emperor, of course, for that would be foolish. What kind of idiot would just run in, screaming at the top of his lungs? He didn't even *know* the man.

No. Instead . . . he would study his enemy. Study the man who visited suffering upon what was supposed to be "his people."

Xiaoshi could not say the journey was arduous. It was several weeks of roughing it in the forests . . . but he remained unmolested. Nothing came to investigate his Qi. No Demon Beasts tried to hunt him down. He had made faster time than he would have believed possible, heading initially to the south. There, he disguised himself as if he came from the Great Lakes. With his reed hat and a cartful of rice, nobody bothered impairing his path as he joined in with thousands of others like him, headed towards the capital for the Grand Tournament.

For the Emperor himself would be there in attendance.

In the taverns and the inns, he heard the same story repeated over and over. Hushed complaints about taxes. News of the barbarian tribes of the north putting together a grand host, and of raids to the southwest from bandits who melted like smoke into the shadows.

It was a time of unrest. Of weariness and apprehension.

Walking into the Imperial Domain, positioned precisely in the center of the Azure Mountains, was like venturing into a different world. He entered through the massive, imposing stone gates at the top of a steep, inclined mountain pass.

The first thing he noticed as he passed through the gates was that it was warmer here. It was more humid too.

The normal mountains had been carved into what looked like long, thin spires, jutting up from the ground and covered in vegetation and hanging vines.

Tianlan called them *Karsts*, though she seemed confused as to *why* they were here.

Each and every plant was leafier than Xiaoshi was used to. They looked like they wouldn't survive the cold of winter, but there they were in the thousands.

Yet for all that the land around the Karsts looked suitable to farm . . . there was nobody here. The fields were well-trimmed grass and military muster fields instead. Around the Imperial city spread five forts, the Grand Bulwarks, each one protected by formations and experts without peer.

But all of them paled in comparison to the thing floating in the sky, high above the Imperial city.

The Azure Chamber. A one-hundred-and-eight-floor pagoda that scraped the heavens, simply existing in midair, without any kind of visible support.

Xiaoshi swallowed as he laid eyes upon it. The Domain of the Azure Emperor. But even if it was imposing, he had kind of expected it to look a bit different. In his mind, it looked like it should have a perpetual black cloud around it, or perhaps spikes with wailing innocents impaled, but instead it was pure and pristine.

Xiaoshi didn't know how to feel about that.

He checked into an inn with the money he had made off selling rice and pondered what the tournament would bring.

→

The tournament, as Xiaoshi found out, was madness. He had never seen so many people in his life. Crowded together, they roared and screamed as they assembled at the muster fields, where the soldiers of the Emperor showed off their skills.

Tianlan's emotions were roiling, trapped between the excitement of the crowd and her distaste for the capital. She had spent the night kicking down Karsts in their shared dream and then packing them back together to form proper mountains.

He *may* have joined in.

But now, the enjoyment of the night was muted as he stared down at the serried ranks of soldiers. Each captain was a cultivator in *at least* the Profound Realm. The majority were in the Spiritual, flaring their Qi for all to see their might.

"Loyal subjects of the Azure Emperor!" a voice thundered out, and the crowd began to quiet down at the sight of a crystal dais rising into the air, floating over them all. "We thank you for coming today, to witness the martial prowess of our brave and loyal army!"

The cheers erupted, and people stamped their feet.

"And now! Lower your heads! His Imperial Majesty gazes upon you!" the voice boomed out, as between one instant and the next, a shadow appeared in the box floating over the arena.

Instantly, Xiaoshi felt his skin crawl—there was a *presence.*

None could see the Emperor through the screen that shielded him from their gaze, but then again, they didn't have to.

Xiaoshi felt his stomach drop, as he felt the intent. The entire crowd went completely and utterly silent as the Emperor gazed down at them all.

The soldiers, as one, fell to a knee and bowed their heads.

There was a beat as the Emperor's eyes swept from one end of the arena to the other, spearing thousands of people.

The shadow behind the screen nodded.

And then his power unfurled.

Xiaoshi was struck dumb as the heavens seemed to descend. The power became visible. It was dark blue, like the night sky, and full of stars.

This was the strength of the heavens.

This was the strength of the man called the Emperor of the Azure. The man who ruled both the mountains, and the clear blue sky.

It rose higher than the highest cloud and stretched out, past the city, and seemed to swallow the entire world.

Some fell to their knees in rapture. Others fainted dead away.

All Xiaoshi could do was gape openly, while Tianlan trembled in his soul.

That was might. That was power no amount of scheming could overcome.

That was strength fit to challenge the heavens themselves.

→

The rest of the tournament was spent in a daze. The blood of the combatants soaked the arena as men sought to climb in rank.

Both Xiaoshi and Tianlan were silent when they staggered off, feeling utterly demoralized.

'*What do we do now?*' Tianlan asked, frustration in her voice.

"We go home and lay low. We can't fight *that,*" Xiaoshi replied, still shaken from the sky full of stars.

He felt vague disapproval from his companion at his statement, but she didn't have a rebuttal. Despite the vastness of Tianlan's power, neither of them really knew how to fight, and the Emperor was a tiger wearing the skin of a man. "We'll go back home and build something so hidden they'll never find us." He glanced back at the giant pagoda, jutting into the sky.

It looked *far* more imposing now than it had earlier.

'*Do you think he's compensating for something?*' Tianlan asked.

Xiaoshi choked on his own spit at the sudden statement. "Where the hells did you learn that?"

'*Linlin asked Boyi if he was compensating for something after he built that watchtower.*'

"Do you even know what that means?!"

'*Nope. But it sounded insulting, and Boyi went really red.*'

And that was how Xiaoshi wound up explaining innuendo to an Earth Spirit, on their walk out of the city.

'*So, big house, big power, tiny little . . . ?*'

"Yes."

'*Heh.*'

He could feel the amusement rising off the Earth Spirit, and he realised that he had just created a monster.

His steps felt a bit lighter as he walked back home.

That lightness lasted until he came to rest in a village. His mood soured instantly.

Men and Roadspinners alike were clapped in chains. Whips lashed their bodies as they were forced to dig, building the foundations for a canal. The Roadspinners' shells were dull and full of cracks. Their inquisitive eyes were downcast and broken. They looked utterly miserable, mud weighing down their bodies.

For what reason would they be taken like this? Roadspinners were occasionally a nuisance, but they rarely harmed anyone!

The people of the village were looking nervous and muttering to themselves as they watched the work. Some flinched when the whips struck.

A particularly hard lash struck one of the Spirit Beasts, and she fell, Qi invading her body.

Xiaoshi turned his eyes away. He *couldn't* get involved. To fight that was to fight the Emperor.

'*Xiaoshi.*' Tianlan's voice was cold and hard. He could feel her fury, and it matched his own.

He glanced back at the canal as the whip reared back again, and then a child, still bound in chains, moved. The child dashed forwards and threw himself in front of the whip heading towards the Spirit Beast.

The whip cracked into the child, right across his eyes, and he screamed in pain.

It was a scream Xiaoshi knew well. He had heard it enough times coming from his own lips.

Xiaoshi's fist clenched.

"*This is the way the world works,*" the Overseer had declared.

No. This could be better.

'*This place is so wonderful. I love it!*' Tianlan had said with a sigh, as she stared over their village.

He would *make* it better.

He turned his eyes to the Emperor's soldiers.

Even if it took a thousand years. *Even if he had to make heaven itself his enemy.*

The onlookers gasped as on the backswing, Xiaoshi caught the whip.

"You dare defy the Emperor?!" the soldier demanded.

He could see the Emperor standing behind his curtain. The power of the heavens, so completely eclipsing the earth. A sky full of stars, each one a fire that would burn him to ashes.

"*Yes,*" the voices said as one.

CHAPTER 35

THE BREAKING OF [天] PART 4

Tianlan was quiet as they sat in a cave.

They had escaped the Emperor's soldiers, at least for the moment. Their charges, the humans and the injured Roadspinners, were outside asleep beside the cart Xiaoshi had built to convey them faster from the pursuing forces that were sure to follow. For three days already, they had been on the run.

Shi, one of the Roadspinners, was leading them down hidden paths and backways into the hills, so they could meet up with a Lord Yao, who would be able to help them. Exhausted, they had found this space to rest for a time, hoping they had given the soldiers the slip. Shi had been sure they would not be traced so easily. Tianlan could feel the presence of the Roadspinner as she rested, curled around Dulou, the brave little one who had been blinded by the Emperor's soldiers for protecting her.

She was, after all, a mother in her own right, her pups safe with her mate.

They had paused because everyone had needed a break from the bumpy ride in a cart only held together by Qi and a prayer. Xiaoshi, however, still had something to do.

Cultivate . . . as he had *attempted* to do for the last three nights.

Tonight, however, they had discovered something that *should* have been sure to help him. At another time, finding this little cave could have been considered the luck of the heavens.

Cultivators would have slain each other for the privilege of simply sitting in this lonely little cave and meditating. The land here was the perfect spot for cultivation. They would have grown in leaps and bounds, absorbing the power of the earth . . . *her* power.

Try as he might, though, Xiaoshi couldn't add this reservoir to his own. He couldn't even circulate his Qi.

The first night after they had run from the soldiers had been one of panic and confusion. Xiaoshi had decided he wasn't in the right state, and that was why he'd failed. The second night, he was filled with determination as he tried to move his Qi, only to be rebuffed, time and time again. They both felt the bond between them strain at the action, like a mountain trying to rip free from the firmament.

They were both left with frustration and a tired resignation.

Xiaoshi and Tianlan were connected, and that connection was unbreakable. It prevented the normal cycling of Qi that cultivators conducted. Instead of cycling and spinning as it was supposed to, his Qi was trapped within Tianlan's own cycle. One cycle every day. No more, and no less.

They needed to gain power in order to oppose the Azure Emperor. But they didn't know how to. For all of their resolve, it was useless unless they could actually *do* something. If they couldn't gather the strength to oppose him . . . then it would all be for nothing.

And she wanted to do *something*. Tianlan bit her lip as she remembered the suffering humans and Roadspinners. She clenched her fist at the memory of Green Trees. What the Azure Emperor was doing . . . it was wrong. It was the act of a tyrant, to slaughter his own people and exploit them so ruthlessly.

Tianlan had tried to cultivate as well, in hopes of helping. She'd observed Xiaoshi in his attempts and tried to cycle her Qi.

Slowly, sluggishly, it started to move—

There was a *crack*.

Tianlan's eyes shot open at the sudden appearance of a gash in her arm, the rents in her form looking like shattered stone. Her Qi wobbled unstably as if it were a mortal house in an earthquake. Tianlan gasped in panic—yet as suddenly as it had come, the disturbance was gone.

Taking deep, gasping breaths, Tianlan cradled her arm to her chest. The pain steadily faded.

Okay. Never trying that *again.*

"Tianlan? Are you all right? What just happened?!" Xiaoshi demanded with sudden sharpness. Love, affection, fear, and concern washed over her like a wave as her breathing evened out.

She smiled weakly at him and shook her head.

"Ah, it's nothing much, just a little scratch. Just tried something, and it didn't work," Tianlan responded, shaking off the feeling.

Xiaoshi didn't seem to believe her—she could feel his emotions still raw across their bond. She sent feelings of calm and affection back, and some of the worry faded.

"Let's call it a day, Tianlan," he said, sounding defeated. "I don't want you hurting yourself, okay?"

"Yeah, it's probably a good idea to take a break."

Xiaoshi exited the cave he was in and checked on all of the injured humans and Spirit Beasts. Tianlan watched from her position in his soul, a mere observer to what was happening. They had all been bandaged up and given food . . . but some of them were barely hanging in there. Morale was only kept up by their escape, and the seemingly inexhaustible chipperness of Dulou, who despite the circumstances was still able to laugh and joke, a smile permanently on his face.

He was a good kid.

With everybody still looking all right, Xiaoshi finally lay down to rest and appeared within her domain.

He smiled a tired smile as he laid eyes on her . . . and then they bugged out when he saw the state of her arm.

"Tianlan?!" he yelped, and rushed over to her. She felt his anxiety spike, and the stress poured across their link, dark clouds forming in the realm.

His hands landed on her arm, and he gently pulled it up, his own Qi attempting to flood into her, to try to heal the little piece of damage.

"Hey! Hey! I'm fine! It doesn't even hurt anymore!" she scolded, trying to pull her arm back. Really, he was overreacting! If she had known he was going to worry so much that he looked sick, she would have tried to hide it. He didn't need *more* things bothering him. It was just a scratch anyway!

"Are you sure?" he asked. He had already seen too many people hurt. She could feel through the bond that seeing Tianlan herself injured stoked a terror within him.

"Yes. I'm fine. *Really*," she reassured him, and held out her arms. He searched her for any hint of pain before relenting after a short while.

They embraced and pressed their foreheads together. Tianlan savoured the touch. They drew strength from each other, as they always did.

Eventually, they pulled apart and went to their favourite spot within Tianlan's domain, the top of a rock overlooking a small stream.

"It's not getting us anywhere," her Connected One muttered after a moment. His head was in Tianlan's lap as she combed her fingers through his hair, like Linlin often did.

"I know. Maybe somebody else has an idea?" she asked as she felt some of his stress fade away.

"Who can help? I've never even heard of anything like we have, Tian."

She had to admit that was true.

So instead they sat together within her little realm. They pondered the future. And then, when the mood became dark again . . .

"Let's go for a walk," Tianlan decided.

They set off, arm in arm, through the space that at the same time was hers and was *her*. They meandered through grassy valleys and high mountain peaks. They waded through streams and windy vales until they came upon a cave.

A cave, full of power, like the one Xiaoshi had tried to cultivate in.

They glanced at each other and with a synchronized shrug descended into the depths.

They passed glowing mushrooms and sparkling crystals. They marched through the vaulted ceilings of caves, heading ever downwards, towards the pulsing heartbeat far below. Finally they came upon a stream of golden energy. The source of both their power.

Tianlan's Dragon Veins. The lifeblood of the earth.

Xiaoshi gaped at the sight, at the sheer amount of Qi flowing through Tianlan. It flowed slowly, almost more solid than liquid, off into the distance.

Tianlan knew the coils of Qi that wove through her entire being. The vast reservoirs were full, pumping Qi into the air, the water, and the soil.

Xiaoshi wobbled on his feet as he felt the enormity of the power.

"Do . . . do we even need *more* power?" he finally asked, staring at the wellspring of strength. "This is . . . if we could fully access this . . ." He trailed off, his mind whirling.

Tianlan shrugged. "It takes too long. The earth moves slowly, and these are some of the slowest parts . . . if we could even draw the Qi from this deep."

Xiaoshi stared at the coils of energy, and then up at the rock walls.

"A canal."

"Canal?" Tianlan replied, confused.

"Yeah. The Qi, it's like water. A liquid, deep beneath the earth. So what if we build a well? Or . . . a canal? We could deliver it where we wanted it to go, couldn't we?"

It was a good idea . . . but could Tianlan really build a canal like that? To do so would mean changing her roots, her very essence. Tianlan felt a creeping unease at the thought. It felt . . . wrong.

"I . . . I don't really . . ." she began. Xiaoshi's hopeful smile started to fade. She felt his disappointment and despair at all of his ideas failing. They couldn't cultivate, they couldn't get stronger, and now this plan didn't work either?

He was trying so hard to save them, to protect them from the Emperor, and he was failing. She was too. She hadn't been able to do anything, but with this, maybe? If it would help people . . . then it was worth it to try, wasn't it?

Trepidation and fear turned to resolve.

"I don't really know if it will work, but we can try," Tianlan said.

Xiaoshi's smile brightened.

She frowned and examined her Qi further, then reached out for her own Dragon Veins. They weren't completely solid and felt malleable, at least to a degree. In some spots, they branched and shot to the surface, like in the cave.

Slowly, carefully, like the canal that the humans and Roadspinners had been forced to build, she started to dig another channel to the surface.

It . . . surprisingly didn't hurt. It just felt . . . strange. Each moment she dug, she felt like she was doing something wrong. Forbidden. But unlike the last time . . . there were no cracks in her body. No pressure in her soul.

It just *happened.* Like she was a normal person, excavating a new tunnel in the earth.

Her Dragon Veins responded. Like water, her Qi moved, following her new channel.

Rising to the surface

She pulled on her power.

There was a surging, pumping feeling as the little canal responded, her Qi flooding up and through the new pathway.

It was hundreds of times faster than it was previously.

Tianlan grinned.

It would work. They would have to construct them manually, and directly be in the area . . . but the idea would *work*.

Tianlan split another section off, pulling it up. She carved another trench—one that was the colour of gold—and started making a network. A network of canals. Or perhaps, some kind of golden road?

They worked all through the night, constructing their revelation. And then in the morning, they set off again, bringing the Roadspinners to the Lord Yao they had been told about.

□

"What would you ask of me for returning my mate, Xiaoshi?" the giant Wrecker Ball asked, as man and Spirit Beast sat across from each other.

"There may be other victims in this war of mine, Lord Yao. I would ask you to take in the refugees and the defenceless."

The great Wrecker Ball paused, then dipped his head.

"Then this Rumblin' Yao swears. He'll shelter everyone you bring beneath his shell, even if it costs him his life!"

Xiaoshi smiled at him, then raised the stone bowl of fermented berries in toast. "Thank you, my friend. I'll be in touch with you all. But for now, I must leave. I'll make more false trails while you effect your escape."

Bi De pulled out of the memory as it faded, and sighed, exhaustion overcoming him. While not the whirlwind of emotion in the chaos that the crystal had been previously, reviewing these memories still left him utterly drained.

He looked out across the crystal, the memories spread out like constellations in the night sky.

It was beautiful, in its own way.

His consciousness left the crystal entirely, and he opened his eyes to the fading sun.

"You still good, buddy?" his Great Master asked from his position where he was putting the last snowball on top of one of the General's subordinates. There were some half a hundred miniature snow golems in the clearing, all lined up beside each other. His Great Master pressed his crystal close, recording the most recent one.

Bi De smiled at his creations . . . and was touched that his Great Master had watched over him while he was within the crystal's depths. He had exited the crystal once already to eat lunch but hadn't been in the mood to speak of what he had seen quite yet, still digesting the information.

"I am well, Master," Bi De stated wearily as he hopped onto his Lord's shoulder. He still wasn't sure what to make of everything he had seen. Understanding would come in time. "For what reason are there so many Servants of the General?" he asked, and his Master grinned.

His Master's crystal floated into the air and projected a picture of the snow golem. Then it flipped to another. Then another, until it was a sequence of still images, showing the Servant of the General performing a little dance.

"Stop-motion is pretty neat, huh?"

Stop-motion. A strange name, but one that was quite accurate. "Disciple Yun Ren is sure to appreciate this art form," Bi De said as his Master picked up the crystal and started walking back to the house.

"Yeah. I tried to give him an opening to bail out of Nezan's teasing, but he wanted to be there to interrupt any stories about him from Meimei."

"A fool's errand," Bi De proclaimed.

"Don't I know it," his Great Master said with a chuckle before turning back to the memory crystal. "Tomorrow, it should be fine to use your crystal in the house. Nothing happened, and no beasties came out like last time. There were no problems with it, and that'll save you from being out in the cold, right?"

"Yes. Although the cold isn't wholly unpleasant . . . I think I should like a blanket and a cup of tea," the rooster admitted.

His Master ran his fingers though Bi De's feathers. "One cuppa, comin' up. And *Bi De*?"

"Yes, Master?"

"Whenever you want to talk about it, yeah?"

Bi De smiled and simply leaned closer to His Great Master as he walked back to their coop.

The rooster had a wonderful dinner with his Master and his fellow disciples before he settled in for the night, with Yin, Miantiao, and Ri Zu curled up at his side. He could not rest, though. As his companions slept, Bi De recalled all that he had seen within the depths of the ancient memory crystal.

They were similar, in so many ways.

So similar, this Xiaoshi and Bi De's Great Master. The loving Master who would protect them all. Both content simply being farmers, until the world intruded and forced them into action.

It was best to avoid making any true judgements yet. There were still years of memories to sift through. It would have been a task beyond him, but time in the crystal moved differently, faster within than without. He had already watched through years of memories but had been in the crystal for only a day.

He could see if he could skim over some things, but he refrained from just skipping to the last moments. If he did that, he would miss context—why things had happened the way they did.

And . . . it would be disrespectful to the man who acted like his Master. To proclaim that the man's story that he had left in that crystal was not worth being considered.

So Bi De would watch on without any judgement until the end . . . but he already knew there would be no happy ending here.

Bright and early the next day, Bi De was again reviewing what had happened so long ago.

□

Xiaoshi and Tianlan ventured forth, constructing their canals, weaving them together into a golden road and fomenting sedition wherever they roamed.

With every stop they made, they found new people and new atrocities committed by the Emperor and his loyal soldiers.

Despite that, what disturbed Bi De the most were not the carnage and struggles. It was the *people.*

Because half of them were *familiar* to him.

CHAPTER 36

THE BREAKING OF [天] PART 5

And so Bi De watched as Xiaoshi and Tianlan travelled the Azure Empire's farthest reaches bringing Xiaoshi's plans to fruition. Together, bit by bit, they brought Tianlan's Dragon Veins to the surface.

The pair briefly considered returning to their village, but in the end they decided against it. It was too dangerous. They would not lead the Emperor's men to their home's doorstep if they were somehow followed.

Xiaoshi made a rough circuit of the interior of the Empire, with its grand mountains jutting proudly to the heavens. It was most strange to see the differences in the landscape. The mountains were taller, and they all had pointy peaks, even Cloudrest Peak, which was nearly a third taller than Bi De remembered it being.

He kept the changes in mind as he observed their path and their actions.

Bi De approved of those, at least. The pair fought against the wicked excesses of the Azure Emperor. They freed enslaved people and Spirit Beasts. They stopped the massive, open pit mines and destroyed giant pill furnaces that spewed toxic sludge into the world. Bi De could not comprehend why the Emperor had allowed such things. It seemed counterintuitive. Cruelty for cruelty's sake. What would drive the Emperor to such excess?

He did not know . . . and it seemed that Xiaoshi and Tianlan didn't care.

They were wholly focused upon their goal. They grew in strength, day by day, as more places were found where golden roads could be pulled to the surface.

But despite the grim nature of their task, and the determination with which they set about it . . . both still held on to a small sense of wonder. They were curious about the world the Emperor ruled . . . the world that they hoped to save.

Together, they ventured out into the world and learned of the land and its people.

And how the Emperor's cruelty affected everyone.

→

The first time Xiaoshi laid eyes upon a "vicious tribal," he had to confess that he was quite disappointed. Stories were told that they had tusks and horns, or other animal parts. Others said that they were cannibals and rapists one and all. He had been conflicted, at first, in intervening on their behalf, when he had found a group of them captured by Imperial soldiers.

Of course, what he knew had been spread by the criers of the Emperor . . . Xiaoshi had resolved himself to disregard everything that they had said.

What he found instead were just *people*. Slightly darker in complexion, with clothing of differing styles and cuts and thick accents. Their expressions had been the same as those of the people in the Empire when he had torn off their shackles.

'*I really like that lady's tattoos*,' Tianlan said, directing his eyes to a woman who had an interesting design that looked like beautiful rings around her fingers and a flower-shaped design on the back of her hand.

Xiaoshi agreed that it looked quite fetching. Honestly, that was the thing that was the most different, as far as Xiaoshi could tell. To have tattoos was the mark of gang members and criminals, but even old aunties had them here.

In the end, they were little different from his own people.

He kept an eye on the men and women below from the rock he was seated on. He had, with his new companion, rescued them from bondage and spirited them safely away, back to lands where the Emperor held less sway.

He turned to the man beside him, who had a bandana that covered his hair and the top of his forehead. Sharp eyes peered out from beneath it, and a blade attached to a rope was his weapon. He had used it to great effect, both spiriting away the people and tying up soldiers.

Guo Daxian, legendary bandit, scourge of this area, who preyed on all under his eyes.

At least that was what the Emperor's criers declared. But Xiaoshi was beginning to get the feeling that he preyed less on innocents than the tales would tell.

No true savage bandit would look people over with such concern.

"Why do you name yourself 'bandit'?" Xiaoshi asked the other man, at Tianlan's prodding.

The man with the bandana turned to him in surprise at his question. It took him a moment of mulling it over before he responded.

"If I'm an outlaw even to my own people, the Emperor can't ever accuse them of harbouring me," he said. "I swore I would have no name to lead me back to my kin. I would die a thousand deaths and shoulder every dishonour before I let them be hurt." Guo Daxian's words were full of conviction. Xiaoshi could feel his Qi and his intent, full of sincerity, pouring off the other man like a wave, and bowed his head in acknowledgement.

It was, after a fashion, what Xiaoshi was doing. He would shoulder everything so his little village would never have to worry again.

He would follow this lonely path until the end.

"A noble goal," Xiaoshi said, and the other man started.

"An Imperial, callin' *me* noble?! Hah!" The tribesman burst out laughing, drawing the attention of the people below, before he trailed off, sighing. "Things . . .

things didn't use to be this bad. Before, it was only the occasional bad seed that I would have to deal with. You Imperials stayed in your lands and left the ranges and the ravines to us. But now . . ." He gestured at the people. The people who had feared for their lives just hours earlier. "He's just organising raids to capture anybody he can get his hands on."

"I aim to end this. This senselessness. If it requires the Emperor being knocked off his throne, then so be it," Xiaoshi said simply.

Daxian turned to him, his eyes wide as he stared at Xiaoshi. Xiaoshi for his part kept his eyes on the people. Why were they even fighting? What use was calling them savages? They clearly weren't. It was *stupid*.

He could feel Tianlan nodding, deep in his soul.

"You're rebelling against the Emperor?" Daxian asked, in a strangled voice.

"Yes," Xiaoshi replied, letting his and Tianlan's Qi fill the air. The other man's pupils dilated as he felt the very earth tremble. "I will stop this madness that the Emperor has commanded."

For a moment, the other man gaped . . . before his mouth snapped shut. He took a breath. And looked shiftily from one side to the other.

Then he pressed a fist against his heart.

"The name of my forefathers is *Chengis*. The name that is my own is Altan. By the earth and by the sky I greet you, Xiaoshi. If you need my help, I will answer."

Xiaoshi smiled and clasped arms with the man, as fellow warriors.

They both turned back to the mortals below them. When they finished their meal, the mortals made a strange gesture: they touched the earth and then reached to the sky.

"Why do they do that?" Xiaoshi asked.

"They give thanks to the sky and the earth," Altan replied as he touched the rock beneath him, then raised his hand. "We thank Father Sky and Mother Earth for the bounty we have received."

'*Oh, you thank me, huh?*' Tianlan mused, giggling. '*I like these guys, Xiaoshi. They treat me right!*'

Xiaoshi smiled at the excitement . . . and then copied the gesture, touching the ground.

"Thank you always for your help, Tianlan," Xiaoshi whispered, and he felt his companion flush. He then turned to Daxian. "Will you show me how you live?" he asked. The man looked surprised again, and his sharp eyes softened. Xiaoshi felt a bit bad, that his intentions were simply to access more land to pull up Tianlan's Dragon Veins . . . but he *was* interested in them. Tianlan was too.

"Of course. You'll see the way the ravine folk do things, my friend!"

He hoped to visit again, when this was all over.

□

Guo Daxian. A name still used millennia later, and a culture still thriving. The bandana looked similar to the one on the man at the Dueling Peaks, the one whose tattoos Tigu had liked.

Not all of Xiaoshi and Tianlan's adventures were those of battle and violence. Most of the time, their path was uninterrupted as they walked the Azure Mountains. Bi De watched with silent amazement at the sheer amount of cultivation resources they stumbled across on their path . . . His past self would have been aghast at the waste, and even now he was stunned by the quality and amount of Qi-infused items they found.

Once, Xiaoshi tried a pill, yet it had no effect. It was like a drop of water entering an ocean. Tianlan's Qi was too vast and powerful for even a hundred thousand pills to affect.

So they collected them to barter and trade, as they continued onwards.

To the land of rivers and lakes their feet took them, the area that would be known as the Grass Sea. The heart of the Empire, in most senses. There were few mountains here, and the land was mostly flat, though crisscrossed with a hundred thousand rivers and lakes. The fertile valleys sat beside the rivers, and li upon li of rice fed the people of the Empire. In that respect, it had changed little. But it was still shocking to see the sheer extent of what had occurred. The Dueling Peaks, still whole back in this time, was situated on an island.

Next, the pair travelled to the Misty Lake.

□

Xiaoshi bowed to a carp twice the size of a forest bear lazing in the pool, attended to by priests and shrine maidens. They scrubbed his scales, preened his whiskers, and fed him choice delicacies. His vault was beautifully adorned, proclaiming his power and wealth.

"All this for a fish?" Tianlan asked, curious.

Xiaoshi studiously ignored her questions, even as she prodded at him.

"Most would think to use this treasure for themselves. Yet you offered it to us without a thought," the giant fish rumbled.

"I merely return what was stolen, Great Lord of the Misty Lake," Xiaoshi replied, referring to a pearl of great power. Honestly, he had just stumbled across the thing after poking his head into a cave.

The carp nodded his enormous head. "What boon do you ask, boy?" the great fish demanded.

"I merely wish to be able to see your domain, in all its glory," Xiaoshi replied. It was a *bit* misleading, since they needed to dredge the veins in this area and the lake was truly massive. He hoped he sounded respectful enough—he barely knew how to deal with courtly types.

The great carp's eyes locked upon him before he began to boom with laughter. "A fine wish! Our realm is truly a sight to behold, and you have a discerning eye to be able to tell it will be something wondrous! I don't hate the request, little human!"

With a crack of energy, the carp shifted, and in his palace sat a dragon. He had four toes and a magnificent mane, revealing his status as a prince of the heavens.

'*Ah. A fish like that was weird. A dragon? Yeah, I can see it,*' Tianlan mused, as she stared through Xiaoshi's eyes at the giant beast.

"Liu! Escort our guest around our glorious lake!" the Great Lord of the Misty Lake commanded.

A woman approached, clad in the vestments of a priestess. Her hair was wavy and dark blue, and she had a willowy figure. Her eyes were the colour of storm clouds, and two draconic horns peeked out from the sides of her skull.

"Yes, Honoured Ancestor," the girl responded demurely.

Xiaoshi was expecting a small riverboat.

Instead, what they boarded was palatial. They rode atop the water as they were taken into the enormous, misty lake and were waited on hand and foot by an attentive set of servants who operated the boat.

Xiaoshi had to admit, he enjoyed himself probably more than he should have, especially when the priestess, Liu, hung onto his arm and smiled prettily at him.

Tianlan was distracted—not by the woman's . . . soft hands, but instead by something else.

'*Touch her horns. What do her horns feel like?*' she demanded.

□

Throughout the entire tour, Bi De kept expecting the woman to burst into boisterous laughter. Instead, the ancestor of Liu Xianghua was prim, proper, and nearly silent as she showed Xiaoshi the formations that controlled the mist around the lake and turned it solid. Apparently, they could even ward off the might of the Emperor's armies, if need be.

But Xiaoshi did not ask them to join him. The pair connected to the land in the lake . . . and then bid the dragon goodbye, asking for nothing else.

From the lakes, they travelled onwards. Past the Cloudcatcher Forest and to the area that Bi De was most familiar with.

The north.

The ground steamed with heat and great geysers erupted, spewing water thousands of li into the air. Boiling springs bubbled and burbled, feeding into lakes hot enough to cook eggs in. It was a sparsely populated, desolate landscape. Perpetually misty, as the fire of the land combatted the chill of the north, burning away the snow until it could only settle on mountaintops. Here the tunnels into the ground led to great magma vaults and the Spirit Beasts that lived within them.

In this land of fire were another familiar group of people. The Ancestors of Yun Ren.

□

The rumours that the barbarians were collecting a grand host turned out to be true. They were gathered in the thousands—yet instead of a great, screaming army intent on reaving the Empire of the Azure, they were all just . . . *leaving.*

"Where will you go?" Xiaoshi asked their leader, a prophet whose milky eyes stared into his soul. Their clothes were a riot of colour, reds and blues with geometric designs, similar to those of Altan's tribe.

"Our kin to the south will not leave their valley. And we will respect their choice. We go to the bare edge of the Mist Wall and try to ride the coming storm. Dark times are ahead, child."

Xiaoshi bowed his head.

"Then I will cover your retreat. None from the Empire shall harm you."

The prophet smiled. "Thank you, Xiaoshi. Go with the light of the heavens."

And with those words, the tribes of the north left, heading for the Mist Wall and the perpetual cold.

Xiaoshi closed his eyes and let them go, praying for their fortunes even as he turned away.

"Tianlan," he requested.

His dearest companion answered his call.

An army of the Emperor, numbering in the thousands, was headed north. It was large enough to utterly crush anything that they would face. The barbarian tribes would be no match for them.

Yet instead of tribes, the army found a wall as tall as the tallest mountains blocking their path.

□

They had now been travelling for over a year. Bi De observed the change in the seasons. He witnessed Xiaoshi and Tianlan constructing a home, deep within her realm. A veritable palace for her . . . though it had been done more as a joke than anything.

And then Xiaoshi was alone for the winter. Bi De felt the sucking loneliness as Xiaoshi counted the days until she woke up. How he spent nearly every day working alone on the Golden Roads.

It was exhausting. He had to drag himself to continue, a testament to just how much work Tianlan did for the both of them.

He hated the silence of her absence. She was no longer there nattering his ear off, or making stupid jokes and obvious comments.

But Xiaoshi seemed to think that being alone would not stop him. He was a pillar. He could work just fine without her.

Things were getting more dangerous as time passed. Word was getting out of a lone wanderer, the arch rebel of the Empire. The man was to be slain on sight, and any who travelled alone on the roads were questioned harshly.

To disguise himself and his work, Xiaoshi took up the mantle of a gem merchant. It was rather easy when one could command the earth to yield its fruits.

His lonely path took him to the great Shield of the northeast. Here the ground was near-solid rock, and there were mountains of pure marble. Artisans slaved day and night, carving runes of power into the rock upon the Emperor's orders.

Like in Pale Moon town, the people were discontent, though they could do little. The Emperor's armies were ever present, and the area was heavily patrolled.

So Xiaoshi laid low, selling his wares to throw off suspicion. He hawked his goods to the irritated-looking chief, one Tie Desan, who glared at the soldiers quartered in his household. He was thickly built, and had freckles all over his cheeks.

Bi De thought that Tigu was right. He was *rather aesthetically pleasing.*

Xiaoshi didn't think he could kick out an entire garrison just yet without bringing undue harm to its people.

So instead, he looked for quarters for the night. Somewhere to relax and take his mind off things.

He had heard tales of an opera troupe. And so, having never seen an opera, he decided to go and see it. Maybe it would give Tianlan good dreams?

→

Xiaoshi found himself entranced at the movements of the veiled woman. Ruolan was her name, the leader of this opera troupe. They said she had achieved mastery of opera at eleven—and now at eighteen she led one of the most respected troupes in the land.

The way she moved drew every eye, man and woman alike. It made butterflies erupt in his stomach, like she was hypnotizing him.

Her voice only added to the effect. When she sang, the purity and sweetness of the sound was completely enthralling.

Xiaoshi would have been happy to lose himself to the song and the dance of the opera troupe . . . if the subject of her performance hadn't been something that set him on edge.

The veiled woman sang of a man who righted wrongs and defied the heavens. It could have been a song about any cultivator—if one were blind and deaf to her references.

She *directly* referenced one of his ambushes on a guard caravan.

Everybody in the room knew what she was singing about, though she did just the bare minimum for her to say she wasn't outright praising a man who was fighting against the Emperor.

Xiaoshi grimaced. Was this how things were spreading so quickly? He had hoped that he could travel more freely, and the woman was ruining that.

So that night, after her performance, he decided to pay her a visit.

He was going to ask her for tea and try to discuss things like that . . . but Tianlan always did like scaring people. It would be a good story to amuse his companion with when she woke up—and the woman deserved it for making his life harder than it had to be. It was a simple task to gain entry into the singer's room.

It was a little bit awkward, waiting around in her quarters behind the door. In the tales, the cultivators were just suddenly there. Instead, he had to wait for over an hour, all the while wondering if he had the right room, until Ruolan finally walked in.

At least she didn't notice him.

"An interesting song choice," Xiaoshi began, standing behind her. The woman startled, partway through taking off her veil. She jerked to the side, turning to face him in shock.

She gasped. Xiaoshi readied himself to talk, hoping the conversation would go the way he wanted it to—

"Oh! Oh, you're *him*!" the woman gushed, her voice musical. Xiaoshi was taken aback at the sheer enthusiasm in the woman. "Did you like it, sir? This Ruolan hopes she did your exploits justice."

Her hands once more reached for her veil, and when she pulled it off, Xiaoshi found himself stunned.

Ruolan was the most beautiful woman he had ever laid eyes on. The soft curves of her face and her creamy white skin were enticing, and he could lose himself in her crystal-blue eyes.

The woman noticed his stare, and her smile turned just so slightly predatory.

Shaking his head, he coughed into his hand. "I . . . would actually like to ask you to stop. You're making it rather hard to move around, if you keep spreading that story."

Ruolan paused at his request. Her face froze.

"This Ruolan apologises, sir . . . but she cannot," she stated bluntly. "Even if it cost her her life, she will not stop singing your tale."

"Why?"

"The song brings hope," she replied. "It brings hope to the downtrodden. It spreads the news that there is one fighting, and *winning*. The era is changing. Tell me, have you heard the whispers of the people? The songs they sing when the guards are not watching?"

Xiaoshi grimaced. He had. The world was boiling over, and if he hadn't been the catalyst, something else would have been.

"I can hear it in my dreams. The beat of the world is dancing to different steps. The Emperor sits light on his throne. I shall capture the essence of this age . . . even if it costs me my life."

Ruolan's eyes were practically glowing with Qi at her declaration. Resolve firm as a mountain.

"You're a rather strange woman, Ruolan," Xiaoshi decided. Despite all his power, this pretty flower was . . . intimidating.

Ruolan laughed, the wonderful sound making his heart beat faster.

"Everything for the art . . . and I do so love singing about *heroes*."

Her face pressed towards Xiaoshi, and he found himself tongue-tied by her beauty. She walked two fingers up his chest, seeming to delight in his reactions.

"Tell me. How can this Ruolan . . . *aid* you?" the woman practically purred.

Xiaoshi really, *really* wished Tianlan were awake at that moment, to say something dumb and distract him. He thought desperately of Linlin . . . but did not think that would be much of a defence.

Ruolan looked like the sort of woman who would not be denied.

□

The coquettish smirk and outright *flirting* coming from a woman who looked exactly like Disciple Xiulan knocked Bi De out of the memory.

He stared blankly, trying to reconcile Xiulan's normal soft smile with . . . *that*. The woman had a look in her eye more reminiscent of the Healing Sage than his fellow disciple.

"*Gimme that butt! Gimme that butt!*" an imagined Disciple Xiulan shouted eagerly, her hands grasping.

The rooster shook his head, dispelling the frightening image. They already had one Healing Sage, and though he loved her dearly . . . they certainly didn't need a second.

But Xiaoshi did need a woman like Ruolan aiding him.

Originally, Xiaoshi had no real intention of gathering a great host to go up against the Emperor. Such was the ruler's strength that anyone Xiaoshi asked to help battle the madman would surely perish.

But after Ruolan, he noticed it more—he noticed the people starting to arm themselves. The result was they would rebel, piecemeal, and get slaughtered, piecemeal.

So he had to control it. The war of his was no longer a secret.

And so it was carried, in the alleys and on stages. The tale spread and spread, rushing through the hearts and minds of the people of the Azure Hills.

The Song against the Heavens.

A song that found increasing reach when black, corrupted land started appearing across the realm.

Imperial soldiers were always found around it when it appeared, along with strange formations and barrier stones. They said they were sent to contain the outbreaks . . . but the people were having none of it.

The cold, quiet war suddenly ignited as all across the province the people raised their banners in rebellion.

Yet even as the battles raged, Bi De realised that the Emperor *couldn't* be the one behind the black, dead land. Men did not cause devastation like that, then send soldiers to guard the locations.

Bi De pondered the Emperor's actions.

Increased taxes. Drawing on more manpower. Draining the land dry.

For what reason would a man do such a thing?

Bi De . . . felt he knew the answer.

CHAPTER 37

THE BREAKING OF [天] PART 6

Xiaoshi, a straw hat pulled over his eyes to hide his identity, stared into his drink. For what could be the last time, he drank his wine in peace.

He had honestly expected things to take longer. A grand struggle with years of battles. Instead, all they had to do now was march forward. Soldiers and cultivators had started defecting in droves when they beheld his army and Xiaoshi let the strength of his Qi show.

And now . . . now they were nearly there. Nearly ready to confront the Emperor.

"Hey. Hey, Xiaoshi, look at that," Tianlan prodded, and Xiaoshi glanced to the side, where a storyteller was setting up a painting for him to use as a background to his tale. It was a rather beautiful painting, and one Xiaoshi could appreciate—until he looked more closely and realised what it was a painting *of*.

He nearly choked on his drink.

"My friends, tonight this humble storyteller has a tale for you. A wondrous tale, to put to rest all your rumours! I speak, of course, of the Hero and his loyal followers!"

That got the interest of the rest of the tavern, as they too turned to focus on the storyteller.

"In a peach grove, they gathered, one and all," the man began, and Xiaoshi listened with half an ear to the tale.

The storyteller spoke of how the rebels had assembled to oppose the wicked and bring peace to the land. He called out names as he pointed to familiar figures in the painting.

The War Council, according to the storyteller, was a serene affair. In the painting, Xiaoshi—or at least what was supposed to represent him—sat at the foreground on an elaborate throne. He *certainly* didn't remember the throne, nor his clothes being so gaudy. Before him were the serried ranks of former Imperials, gleaming in their armor and silken robes, defectors who had turned against the Emperor. The soldiers had their weapons raised high while the officials stood solemnly in their full dress and those hats that Xiaoshi thought were stupid-looking.

The tribesmen were off to the side, clad one and all in their bandanas. They were tall and fierce-looking, bedecked in war paint and the familiar tattoos. And finally, the great and noble Spirit Beasts were arrayed. The massive form of Rumblin' Yao. The sharp lines of the Bladewolf King, the Tempered Blade. A dragon circled overhead, the Lake King. The Ten Antidote Serpents, their scales a rainbow of colours, a Verdant Bear, an emissary from the Empress of the Forest, and a hundred other kinds of Spirit Beasts.

Together, they had all solemnly sworn to bring down the Emperor, who had lost the Mandate of Heaven.

Tianlan snorted in the back of his mind. "This guy *definitely* wasn't there."

Reality . . . was not quite so pretty and simple as the painting. The only thing the artist got right was the fact that the grove was very nice and peaceful. Xiaoshi would have to take Linlin there after everything was settled. Everything else? Honestly, it was a miracle that no blood feuds had been declared.

Xiaoshi recalled the disaster when Rumblin' Yao had ended up accidentally stepping on the Tempered Blade's tail. The howl had startled everybody, most of all the Roadspinner, who'd then backed up into a table full of food, sending it crashing to the floor.

Altan had loomed over an official who was running his mouth without knowing that the "barbarian tribal" was right behind him, while the soldiers of both sides glared at each other and fingered their weapons.

The cultivators had been greedily eyeing the treasures the Antidote Serpents had brought—the furious serpents were putting everything on the line for this battle. *Everybody* had tried to ignore the fat fish sitting in his tub of water, the Lord of the Lake in attendance with his priests and handmaidens.

Half the "soldiers" of the Imperial side weren't real soldiers at all, simply petty practitioners and artisans who had turned the tools of their trade into weapons. There were entire villages armed with hoes and sickles, as well as miners with bulging muscles, and tattoos that proclaimed them convicts.

The only reason a fight hadn't started was an opera singer who had somehow managed to soothe ruffled feathers with only whispered conversations—and the presence of Xiaoshi himself, the Hero who would fight the Emperor. He had spent the whole time trying to keep his nerve from breaking while he kept his face as still and straight as possible, like a cultivator was supposed to be. Tianlan, of course, hadn't been any help, simply gushing over how many people liked them and wondering what festivals they would have later.

What he wouldn't give for Tianlan's optimism.

He'd had to pretend to know what he was doing, nodding stoically and accepting people into their ranks.

"I pay my respects to the Hero," people would say as they bowed their heads.

The real meeting had happened after all the ceremony and pomp. That was a smaller, quieter affair with only the leaders of respective groups, and it hadn't gone any better. Everybody had argued over who would be on the vanguard, who would be the ones to attempt to breach the walls, and even who would attempt to fight the Emperor.

Which was stupid. *They* wouldn't be fighting him. The mad bastard would kill anybody but Xiaoshi in a single blow—at least he hoped he'd survive that. He prayed that the Emperor hadn't been holding back when he allowed the people to see the might of his Qi.

The only truly useful person had been a defector from the palace itself: a lowly official who went by the name Kongming. He was a rather nondescript fellow, with the thin mustache and beard that was popular in the capital. His clothes were some of the finest in the meeting, and his dumb hat the tallest.

"Great Hero Xiaoshi! This Kongming has within his possession maps of each and every building within the Imperial City, as well as the Imperial Palace itself! I would submit them to yourself and your war council!" the man had declared.

That had gotten him a seat closer to Xiaoshi.

The maps themselves had proved invaluable. They detailed several weaknesses in the guard rotations, as well as how to gain access to the Emperor's pagoda. The possibility of simply sneaking in and defeating the Emperor, instead of having to commit to a long and costly siege, certainly was attractive.

Xiaoshi had spoken to Kongming more after that. Kongming was the least flowery court official Xiaoshi had ever met, though admittedly there hadn't been many. The man was focused, driven, and in general not a bad person to be around. It had impressed him. Enough that Xiaoshi as the leader of the rebellion had asked Kongming to take command of the rest of the army once they had decided on the plan to assault the Emperor.

The rest of the army would be performing a feinting maneuver, which would try to draw out the Imperial Army . . . while Xiaoshi would be invading the tiger's den. Of course, the storyteller didn't know any of that—Kongming had kept things quiet enough that nothing had leaked.

Xiaoshi sighed as the tale came to a close.

"And in that sacred grove of peach blossoms, an oath was sworn!" the storyteller proclaimed to the tavern. "The oath that shall shake our world to its foundations!"

Xiaoshi took another swig of wine and closed his eyes.

It was time. In the end . . . it would all come down to him. Tianlan, lacking a body of her own, would never be able to do it. So he had to act. For both of them. For all of them.

→

It was surprisingly easy to enter the Imperial City. All Xiaoshi had to do was put on his rice hat and walk in the front gate with the rest of the line of people fleeing the fighting. He had learned early on that most people couldn't sense his Qi unless he was actively using it, and so the guards barely gave the "mortal" in their midst a second glance.

It helped that Tianlan was keeping a locus of her power near the army itself, so to other cultivators it felt as if he was with the army.

He walked past the muster fields, just inside the walls, and past the army that was preparing itself for war, the soldiers and cultivators grim faced as they prepared to sally forth . . . without their Emperor.

At least he knew that the Emperor would be exactly where he wanted him.

The man had been cooped up in his tower for over a year according to Kongming and cared little about what was going on outside, other than to demand that the General of the Azure Sky defeat the rebels.

Xiaoshi snuck into an alleyway, changing into the clothes that Kongming had given him. The clothes of a servant of the Imperial Palace, one of the low-ranking ones.

Nobody looked twice as he entered the palace below the floating pagoda and found an abandoned annex to wait.

He sat with Tianlan, meditating as he heard the horns sounded. The army of cultivators marched out of the capital, the great gate shutting behind them.

They simply sat together in her domain, staring at a sky full of stars. Xiaoshi's heart was surprisingly calm, considering what he was about to do.

"Are you ready to cast down the heavens?" he asked Tianlan. The woman smirked.

"The heavens? Nah. But that old fart?" She slammed her fist into her palm. "We'll beat the hell out of him. Don't you worry."

Xiaoshi laughed, his heart feeling lighter. Whatever else the Emperor was . . . in the end, he was just a man.

→

He leapt from the earth to the floating pagoda, alighting at a servants' entrance. Normally they would use the floating rocks to ascend and descend from the palace . . . but the Emperor had ordered them removed, such was his desire not to be disturbed.

Xiaoshi took a deep breath, then opened the servants' entrance door.

He walked into another world.

Instead of a pagoda with a hundred and eight floors as he had expected, he walked into the center of a storm.

It was the Emperor's Domain; there, his world was imposed over the world, and it consumed the entire inner palace.

Xiaoshi had to pull on his Qi to prevent himself from being instantly shredded to the bone in the maelstrom. His eyes narrowed through the battering winds as he beheld a star shining in the sky.

The Qi of the Emperor.

Xiaoshi floated off the ground and into the raging storm, heading for the shining blue orb in the center.

Surrounding the Emperor and being assimilated by his Qi were thousands of reagents. Perhaps hundreds of thousands of them. Spirit Beast Cores, medicines, and untold numbers of rare and valuable Spirit Plants. The entire bounty of the Azure Hills was being concentrated into one man.

As Xiaoshi flew closer, he even saw a Temple Dog pup, the little creature spasming fitfully on occasion as he was assimilated into the Emperor's body and soul.

The Emperor was cultivating. His Qi pulsed, the churning storm growing stronger, and there were twenty-seven constellations burning behind him.

Xiaoshi had never before seen the Emperor's face. None of the officials had, either. The man always addressed everybody from behind curtains. He had dark hair in a pristine topknot and a well-trimmed goatee. His skin was pale, like fine jade.

The only imperfection was a band of freckles across his nose and cheeks as well as the top of his chest.

The man paid Xiaoshi no mind as he continued to cycle his Qi.

Xiaoshi opened his mouth to call out to him, to challenge him—

"Do not interrupt me, boy," the Emperor stated simply, his voice calm and commanding. "Begone from my sight, repent for your sin of wasting my time, and kill yourself. Do this, and I shall not hunt your bloodline to extinction later. I would slay you this instant, but I do not wish for your unworthy blood to stain my soul."

Xiaoshi felt the surge of power as the man focused some of his intent. The weight was heavy, commanding. If Xiaoshi had been anybody else, the sheer pressure of the Emperor's words might have caused him to obey.

Instead, he gritted his teeth and pulled on *his* power.

A tiny patch of earth formed beneath his feet as Tianlan, deep in his soul, began to chant.

'And so the great Ancestor, Shennong, commanded his disciple in the ways of preparing the fields . . .'

The illusory realm, the Emperor's domain, an entire world imposed on reality, shuddered. And then it was invaded.

Amethyst eyes snapped open as the emperor stared down at Xiaoshi. His calm countenance was shattered in an instant; green and gold began to invade his realm, crawling up the world like vines strangling a tree.

[Till the Land]

The Emperor stared down at Xiaoshi and clicked his tongue. A bead of sweat forming on his brow was the only sign that this had unnerved him.

The entire sky had broken, forming a solid bedrock foundation. The storm was no longer all-encompassing. It was as it should be when the earth invaded, forming the counterpart to the realm of the sky.

A five-element formation sprang to life behind Xiaoshi, as Tianlan's voice continued to echo.

[Fell the Trees, Divert the Waters, Break the Rocks, Sow the Seeds, Reap the Harvest.]

Each word was a pulse, ravaging the world as energy crawled up Xiaoshi's arms and his legs, forming armor of solid Qi. His eyes sparked with a thousand colours.

The Emperor sat high in the air, in the heavens. Xiaoshi stared at the man from where his own feet were planted upon the ground.

"For your crimes against the people of the Azure Mountains, come and face *justice*, old man."

The Emperor's eyes were focused completely on Xiaoshi. The reagents, floating in the air, were sucked into a spatial ring.

"Crimes? Justice?" the man asked, then laughed. It was a short, sharp, angry thing. "I have committed no crimes, and my will is the justice of the heavens."

His eyes began to glow, burning purple stars, as a blade of starlight formed in his hand. His freckles connected with burning white light, forming a constellation on his skin.

"But I shall thank you. Your prattling is annoying, but you have delivered me a most welcome gift. *Yourselves.* You shall be of great use to my cultivation."

Xiaoshi clenched his fist. The domain around him shuddered under the action, like a great fist had grabbed it.

The sky exploded. The ground detonated.

The heavens met the earth.

→

For three days and three nights, the Emperor and Xiaoshi battled.

The Emperor's world shuddered and shook as bands of light the size of a city defended him. Starlight hot enough to put the sun to shame erupted, attempting to break Xiaoshi.

It was a crucible. In a single blow, the Emperor would have felled any other who challenged him.

Xiaoshi was less skilled. But the Emperor's domain, his very existence, was an offence to the world; Tianlan had commanded it. Cracks crawled through it, the world outside fighting this imposing force, eating at him and wicking away his Qi.

Eruptions of starfire were diverted like they were a backyard stream. Qi constructs were shattered like rocks. The Emperor's mighty weapons and armor, legendary ancient relics, were hewn away as by a man with an axe.

Each blow was assured, for the moment that led up to this had been planted long ago, and now the Emperor was being forced to reap his own harvest.

And finally, the Emperor was struck. Xiaoshi's fist ploughed into his ribs, tearing through every protection the Emperor could bring to bear.

Organs pulped. Bones shattered. The strike was so powerful the very earth reverberated with the hit.

And then . . . the Emperor fell.

His domain, which had fought against the world, dissipated.

In the end there was just a man, lying where the Emperor of the Azure had once stood.

He coughed wetly as he lay slumped against the wall of the giant pagoda.

"Why? Why would you do all this?" Xiaoshi asked the fallen man. He stared at the Emperor, not really expecting an answer.

The man laughed again, blood welling up from his lungs.

"Boy. You still know nothing. Why is this land covered in mist? Why does the world end at the edge of the Mist Wall?"

Both Xiaoshi and Tianlan paused at the question. Neither knew the answer.

"Let me show you, then, the truth of this place."

His Qi surged, and the man lunged.

Xiaoshi was slow to react—the strike hit him.

But instead of doing damage, it captured his vision. His world filled with stars and constellations, tearing his sight free from his body to speed across the land.

His gaze was forced into the Mist Wall, and then through it into the Great Beyond.

Demons. Legions upon legions of demons, marching towards a shining beacon of light in the distance. They slaughtered and rampaged, capered and danced as they destroyed and tortured everything they caught, consuming them whole.

A world of blood and fire, a world of unimaginable suffering.

The beasts in their legion sat just outside a wall of mist, prowling around the edges, and searching for a way inside.

It was a barrier, forged by one bloodline.

The barrier, however, slowly began to weaken, and monsters started to slip through the cracks.

"Xiaoshi! Xiaoshi! Are you okay?!" Tianlan shouted into his mind. He heaved breaths of air and rose from his stupor, rage once more taking him. Just what had the Emperor done? What had he shown him?!

He meant to demand answers . . . but instead received only a smile from his defeated foe.

It was a grin half mocking, and half the smile of a man who looked like a great weight had been lifted from his shoulders.

For the Emperor of the Azure was already dead.

"Xiaoshi? What happened?" Tianlan demanded again, as Xiaoshi began to pant harshly.

"I'm . . . I'm fine, Tianlan." What the hells had that been? Was it real? Was it one final act of petty revenge to leave him with this horror?

Xiaoshi didn't know.

→

He staggered down the flights of stairs in the pagoda, the Temple Dog pup cradled in his arms. He had released it from the ring, the storage ring somehow having survived the battle.

He was exhausted, utterly exhausted, and Tianlan wasn't much better. She was barely awake when they finally reached the bottom floor and stepped out into the predawn world.

He'd expected a long drop to the ground but was instead surprised to find that the great, floating pagoda was already on the large pedestal that had been beneath it. The foundation was full of cracks, but it was still standing, even after falling from the sky.

A great roar sounded out from the bottom of the pagoda's stairs. The majority of it was one of joy, but beneath the shouts of joy was an undercurrent of fear and sorrow.

Xiaoshi looked down at the crowd looking for his friends. Rumblin' Yao was the easiest to spot, covered in war paint. On one side of the plaza were the rebels. On the other, Imperial soldiers were throwing down their weapons and falling to their knees. All of them were beaten up and bloody from the battles they had fought outside the city.

"The Hero has defeated the Emperor of the Azure!" Kongming roared, his voice carrying above them all. The sound echoed all over the city.

Xiaoshi closed his eyes a moment before the sun broke the horizon.

It was finally over. He could finally go back home.

He smiled, feeling Tianlan's own joy, and once more opened his eyes. He started down the steps . . . then paused, as Kongming, at the head of the steps, fell to his knees.

"This Kongming pays his respects to the Emperor!" the man shouted.

Xiaoshi paused, utterly befuddled.

What the hells was Kongming doing? Nobody would actually—

"I pay my respects to the Emperor!" another man shouted, following suit.

And then another. And another.

"Cai Ruolan pays her respects to the Emperor."

"The Tie Clan pays their respects to the Emperor!"

A hundred thousand people. A hundred thousand voices. The Spirit Beast kings nodded in respect. Only Altan and the tribes kept their heads up, but he was smiling.

Tianlan was even more confused than he.

Him, Emperor? He was about to deny it. He would have to say no, wouldn't he?

But even as he opened his mouth to deny it, there was a flash of starlight, and a cold feeling—he remembered the demons from the vision.

He swallowed thickly.

Thus did the Emperor of the Azure die. Thus did the Emperor of the Azure ascend.

CHAPTER 38

THE BREAKING OF [天] PART 7

Xiaoshi's concentration was absolute as he did battle with his hated enemy. His strikes were perfect, slashing a thousand times in the blink of an eye. It was artistry, pure and simple, when he dismantled his foe and cut him down. But as always, there was a legion to take his foe's place.

He took a breath and surged ahead, prepared for the next bout.

"That's it for today, my Lord," Kongming said kindly as Xiaoshi sighed and set down his brush.

"I should have punched you in the mouth the second you opened it that day," Xiaoshi shot back.

'*And give him one from me too*,' Tianlan grumped, taking a moment from her sulking in her domain. His dear friend wasn't exactly enthusiastic about paperwork.

His prime minister laughed.

"And *that* is why you are the most suitable for the role, my Lord. The heavens lead, and the earth follows. This is the way of the world. Without a guiding star, how are we to prosper?" Kongming asked, his smile warm.

Xiaoshi just sighed. Why did Kongming have to be so damn earnest? The man left with a chuckle, heading for the scribes.

Xiaoshi sighed and rose, staring out the massive window out into the capital.

The weeks after the Emperor's death had been the most grueling in Xiaoshi's life. Fixing every problem, appointing advisors, helping out the injured, issuing pardons . . . It was all one big blur, even with Tianlan encouraging him all the way, despite her distaste for what was happening.

But even after that, his work wasn't done. He had been concerned by the Emperor's vision . . . but when he had gone and felt out the Mist Wall, it had been as strong as ever. The bastard, despite all that he had done, had reinforced it before he died.

Xiaoshi . . . didn't exactly know how to feel about that.

He saw the people of the city eagerly scraping the man's name off monuments and burning books that extolled his virtues. Xiaoshi hadn't ordered it . . . but the rage of those the Emperor had wronged demanded justice.

So he said nothing and merely watched.

Even the environment was changing. The area around the capital was getting colder. A lot colder, and more in line with the rest of the province. The strange, leafy plants were dying, and this high up in the mountains, he knew the land itself would soon become poor to farm.

There were already talks of changing the location of the capital city.

But *that* was an issue for later.

"Let's go home, Tianlan," he finally said, weeks after the grand battle. Things were calm enough now.

□

The dreams started happily. On one of the best days of Tianlan's life.

"Looks just like we left it," Tianlan whispered as she stared out at the little village.

In the distance she could see a figure in the watchtower scanning the horizon—probably Boyi—smell the cookfires, and hear Linlin's sweet voice carried by the gentle breeze. Xiaoshi's emotions swelled in time with her own. They had made it.

Home.

It had been a hectic few months to get back here, especially after Xiaoshi had become Emperor.

Tianlan knew Xiaoshi was annoyed with how often she prodded at him to at least send a message . . . but he wanted to deliver the news himself, instead of just sending a messenger to pick their friends up from their hidden village.

Really, *the Emperor*? She still couldn't tell why exactly he had agreed to the position. Neither of them wanted to be sitting on that stupid chair. She could feel that much. He hated most of the time his butt was parked in that chair, working through papers and studying every book Kongming had given him.

He said it was his *duty*. That he owed it to everybody and he needed to become their pillar, so nothing like this would ever happen again.

He was studying the old Emperor's notes, too. He had visited a bunch of places and used their Qi to reinforce the Mist Wall, to stop the demons.

Xiaoshi was trying to be something he wasn't, and she didn't know how to feel about that.

Their connection was . . . tense these days. Something told Tianlan to break it, but she easily pushed the thoughts aside. He was her Connected One. The first person to share everything with her and let her feel the world.

She would stay with him until the end, no matter how bad things got. That was what friends were for! Or so everybody she had heard talk about friends said.

She liked the sentiment.

Still, he was calming down now, as he almost hesitantly approached the village, turning back into his old self. He looked up at the guard tower again, where a man squinted down at him—and then that man's eyes opened wide with surprise.

"Hey! Hey! Xiaoshi is back!" Boyi shouted from his tower.

There was a great cheer from the village.

Everybody dropped what they were doing and surged forward, Linlin in the lead. Her eyes were wide and full of hope as she leapt into a tackle-hug.

Hands clapped his back.

There was no weariness. There was no decorum, like the other people in the capital.

They were simply home.

Tianlan's heart felt like it was going to burst.

She wanted to meet them. Meet them properly.

No, she *needed* to.

She knew she shouldn't—she knew that it was best for her to stay within her domain.

But the call couldn't be denied. Their war was over.

And maybe . . . maybe if she had a body, she could help Xiaoshi out better. In here, she couldn't really act.

So she pulled herself out of her domain.

The ground cracked and rumbled. Stone flowed like water, into the shape of a woman. It gained definition and colour.

And then, out of the dirt, came Tianlan.

She blinked at the silent crowd, a bit disoriented at, for the first time, being alone in her head.

"Hello, everybody!" she shouted eagerly, announcing herself. Her Qi filled the world . . . and suddenly they knew who she was.

The looks on their faces were priceless.

Almost as priceless as when, later that night, Xiaoshi finally told them what had happened.

All three of the Bo brothers fainted in sequence.

□

It was strange, having his thoughts to himself after what felt like an age . . . but he was glad that Tianlan was enjoying herself. They were still connected; he could still call on their combined Qi.

He was happy that she could live her life without being so tied to him. Seeing her smiles always brightened his day, as she found something new to taste-test or tried some new dance Ruolan had shown her.

Xiaoshi governed as best he could. He taught the people to honour the earth and receive its blessing. To love the ground they lived on.

He stayed for two years with Altan's tribe and did what the prior Emperor never could, convincing them to join his banner through bonds of brotherhood. He held great conclaves, to speak with the people and listen to their ills, with Tianlan often at his side. The Spirit Beasts had their territory protected. And all the while, he was supported by his prime minister and Tianlan.

At first people were a bit confused by her presence, but explaining her away as "a valuable companion who aided me against the Emperor" eased their worries.

When it came time to move the capital, Xiaoshi chose his old home of Pale Moon City. It had quite a few advantages and was already a bustling city from the trade in ore and mining. There was another reason too. Maybe it was a bit petty of him, but watching Wu's face as he had to kowtow before the new Emperor had been an utter delight.

Yet even as the realm prospered, he still felt a nagging worry in the back of his head that followed him back to his private quarters at night. That had him pulling open a secret compartment and taking out a map.

A map of the Azure Hills, with twenty-eight constellations drawn on it: a grand formation that had been in the process of being carved into the earth by the Emperor.

Carved into the earth and inlaid with Pale Moon Ore, it would be used to reinforce the Mist Wall.

He would not simply wait for things to get bad. Xiaoshi would stop them before they could happen.

He would *never* subject his people to the treatment the Emperor of the Azure had given them.

The Emperor of the Azure had laid the groundwork of the formation. Xiaoshi would seize it and use it for his own ends. Instead of taking . . . he would empower the land. He would empower the people so that even if he fell, they could continue to ward off the demons.

And thus he commissioned his largest projects yet.

A mountain that would be a place to train the future protectors of the Azure Mountains, just in case . . . and a grand formation to empower Tianlan.

He did not work alone. The Emperor's previous slaves aided him gladly. Lady Cao Li and the monkeys of the Crystal Mountain had been chained together. Both had been forced to toil endlessly, crafting formations and tearing the bounty of the earth from the ground to fuel the madman's lust for power and resources. With them, he turned the Emperor's formation into something that he could work with. They taught their saviour and Emperor gladly.

He commanded villages to be built in order to facilitate his grand design. Each one was given a title . . . and each chief took that title as their name.

He hoped his preparations would be enough, or better yet, unnecessary. That the last vision the Emperor had given him had been just out of spite.

But he knew in his bones this was coming.

□

She remembered the blessed life she lived.

Tianlan travelled the length and breadth of the Azure Hills. Sometimes with others, and sometimes alone. She met a hundred thousand people and a hundred thousand Spirit Beasts.

It was the happiest time of her life.

She helped farmers take in their harvest and went into the depths of the earth with miners, aiding them in dredging their ore and gems. She worked marble with masons and hauled wood for architects.

Each day she learned something new, she found something else to try.

They called her the Green Lady, Mother Earth. People recognised her by the mud on her shoes and the dirt smeared across her face, even when she wore the fine clothes Xiaoshi had gifted to her.

She loved the people who lived in the Azure Hills, and they loved her.

But she kept one thing secret. One thing sacred. No matter how much she wanted to connect them all to herself . . . that bond was for her and Xiaoshi alone. The man who had shown her all of these wonderful feelings in the first place.

Each and every time she returned to Xiaoshi, he listened to her tales with a smile. He built her a grand palace and entertained any request she had of him.

Any request, save spending more time together, like the old days.

Her Connected One was very, very busy keeping the Azure Hills together. But every time she asked if she could help him, she got the same response, followed by a loving smile.

"You should live life how you please, Tianlan. I'll be fine."

□

The world in the crystal accelerated into a blur as a rooster watched, reduced to flashes of scenes and emotions.

Playing with the Temple Dog pup that he named Dian.

Carving a mountain in two and using it as a place to unite them all. The Dueling Peaks.

Visiting the orphanages with Tianlan and drinking with her under the stars.

Hunting with Altan as they swung through the trees.

Composing absolutely horrible poems with Kongming. The man howled with laughter at Xiaoshi's every attempt . . . even if his own weren't any better.

Attending the Ascension Day festivals with Tianlan and Linlin undercover, only to be found by Ruolan, Kongming, and Altan. For the first time in a long while, they all felt like children again, eating greasy food and drinking cheap rice wine.

Ruolan and Linlin wearing nothing but smiles as they beckoned him closer.

Rumblin' Yao making new roads for his people. The massive Wrecker Ball teaching the Earth's Wrecker Stance to a blind boy, so that he could see the world through his feet.

Listening to a rather amusing tale from the Eighth Correct Place. He and Tianlan had dredged up the silver of the earth so that those villagers would know prosperity for their stubborn resilience. Xiaoshi would never abandon them or fail to reward a servant for their hard work.

The world sang the praises of the First Emperor. There obviously had been nobody before Xiaoshi.

And then, one day, there appeared a black, corrupted spot on the ground.

The demons were getting through the Mist Wall again.

CHAPTER 39

THE BREAKING OF [天] FINAL

He fought them, of course. When his back began to itch and his whole body ached, he knew that there were demons coming through the Mist Wall. It was a recent development that he could feel them at all. He never could before, when he'd been with Tianlan.

It took him entirely too long to realise that she had taken all the pain into herself before, and now separated, he was experiencing but a fraction of her pain.

He sallied forth wherever he could find them and destroyed them utterly. They were an itching, maddening nuisance, to the point that Xiaoshi thought he might go insane from it.

"How do you stand it?!" he demanded of Tianlan.

His dearest friend smiled. "It doesn't hurt that much. I can take it," she replied, pulling up her sleeve and exposing the black spots on her arms.

There were twice the number upon her than him, and he felt his heart sink. One of the people he had sworn to protect was suffering. One of *the* most important people to him.

"It's fine! We'll work together like the old days. I'll take this half of the province, you take that half, and we'll handle things!" she said with a smile.

Tianlan fighting and getting even more hurt felt wrong. It was a failure, on his part.

"You're already helping enough, Tianlan. I've got a plan. We just need to sit tight a little longer and I'll banish the demons for good," he said instead. He saw Tianlan perk up at his statement. "I don't really need to do this much paperwork anyway. I'll put it on Kongming and then have myself a little adventure, like you're so fond of. It's been a while since I had a break."

"Are . . . are you sure? I can definitely help," Tianlan said.

"It's fine. It's just a few demons, and I'm getting rusty!"

"If you're really sure," she whispered, but Xiaoshi was already leaving.

He had to last. He had to last, and all would be well.

□

The dream started to go from pleasant to bitter.

Tianlan spent many days meditating. Searching across her body, finding demons, and clearing up the infected spots.

They were hurting Xiaoshi, and that was something she couldn't abide.

Her awareness of her body had faded, but she could still do this much.

All she knew was that her Connected One was beside himself with worry. His pointed questions about how much the infected portions hurt, however, were brushed off.

She could stand a little pain. He already had enough on his plate, without a bit of soreness from her worrying him further.

She could endure wounds deeper than this. He had some kind of plan, he always did. Even if he was being cagey about it right now.

□

Upon the first solstice, the energy of the land surged as his people performed their acts to perfection.

The Mist Wall was reinforced. *It worked.*

"Xiaoshi, what the hells was that?!" Tianlan shouted, barging into the room. Her hair was frazzled, and she looked like she had just been woken up.

Tianlan waking up had been an unexpected but welcome side effect of everybody empowering the earth.

His dearest friend was feeling better than ever.

Once more, he was able to keep his promise of a better world. Once more, he held up the sky for everyone. Tianlan lived her days without fear and without pain.

His people invented wonders. Giant distillers, to wick impurities out of anything fed into them and refine it to perfection. Grand arrays, even for the meanest of homes, courtesy of Lady Cao and Mengde's formations. Vermin were driven out, and food was kept fresh even years afterwards.

The Dueling Peaks grew and grew as more formations and more arenas were added on.

The people were happy.

Though . . . it was not without its sorrows. Ten years after the formation was established, the first person he loved passed.

Linlin wasn't a cultivator. She could never become one. Her hair turned grey, and her face wrinkled. No amount of reagents could stave that off. No medicines would aid her.

At a mere one hundred and ten, eighty-five years after Xiaoshi became Emperor, Linlin died of old age.

He remembered the grand funeral. He remembered Tianlan's tears as she bowed her head. But beside those tears was a wonderful smile. One full of pride, when she congratulated Linlin for a long life.

But most of all, he remembered the hollow feeling in his chest at losing her.

But he hardened his heart and kept moving forward.

Or at least tried to. There were no more Dragon Veins to dredge. He and Tianlan would never get any stronger. They had completely plateaued.

□

Tianlan hugged a pillow tightly to her chest. She still remembered sweet lullabies and fingers through her hair.

The world around them prospered; their people made great monuments and amazing cities. They crafted wondrous devices and forged ahead with smiles on their faces.

It was Tianlan's honour and privilege to watch them grow. It was her greatest joy to be with them.

She watched the tournaments at the Dueling Peaks. She wandered the ravine with Altan and took part in their festivals. She bounded all over the province with Dian, the Temple Dog always in good spirits.

She loved her people. And in turn, they loved her.

And yet despite the fact that they were managing to hold the line—despite the fact that they never inflicted on their people what the Azure Emperor had—Tianlan and Xiaoshi did not speak as much as they used to.

Perhaps it was Linlin's death that made them drift apart just that bit more?

Tianlan hadn't really noticed it at first, but then she realised the dreams where they sat together had become increasingly rare.

The days where they talked started to become a memory; both of them were so consumed with their own lives, and every time Tianlan went to see if Xiaoshi was all right, they would just end up drinking heavily and reminiscing about the past.

She felt kind of hollow. Empty. Like something important was slipping away from her.

□

A decade passed.

Even with the reinforced Mist Wall, more and more demons were getting through, and both he and Tianlan had to spend increasing amounts of time fighting . . . and Xiaoshi was starting to feel the strain. He was getting slower, for some reason.

Now, even stronger demons were trying to slink into his home. These demons were quieter. More subtle . . .

They had attacked Kongming while his friend had been off inspecting a northern town. Xiaoshi had somebody do it often, after the Eighth Correct Place debacle. He was honoured and humbled that his people trusted his word so much that they would brave the constant floods. It was just bad luck that Kongming had gone himself.

He marched up to his bedridden prime minister.

"My Lord! You need not concern yourself with my well-being," Kongming started, only to cut off when Dian growled at him.

"He smells like a demon," his loyal canine companion declared. "His Qi is corrupted. Underneath, it smells of blood and oil."

Kongming smiled sickly. "The demons' poison is powerful. Try as they might, even our mightiest healers cannot take the rot from my blood."

Xiaoshi grimaced, while the Temple Dog paused, eyes narrow at the proclamation.

"Dian. Do not insult our friend again," Xiaoshi commanded, and the dog bowed his head. Xiaoshi sighed at the piteous look on Dian's face and scratched behind his ears before turning back to Kongming. "Do you need a leave of absence? I can appoint another prime minister. Anything you need and it's yours, Kongming."

His old friend smiled. "I ask only that I continue my duties until my death. I wish to see our Empire prosper, even to my last breath."

What could Xiaoshi do but agree? Tianlan and the best physicians worked on him, doing everything they could. From grand formations to the best resources, they poured everything they could into ridding Kongming of the poison.

But they never could completely eliminate the Demonic Qi from his body. It lingered on in him, in his blood . . . but at least they seemed to have stopped it from hurting him.

→

Slowly but surely, Xiaoshi's promise to his people started to fail. Empowering Tianlan and the Mist Wall wasn't happening fast enough. It wasn't good enough, and even with his best efforts demons were getting through. Once more, Xiaoshi had to make an army. He had to increase the taxes, even though he had sworn he wouldn't. He had to set his people to toil on projects.

No matter how he swore he would not be like the Emperor of the Azure, he found himself contemplating measures that were the same; the only difference was that there were no whips yet, with people *forced* to work on the necessary projects that would keep the demons out.

The realm began to suffer. The people whispered that it was the vengeance of the wicked. But they rarely learned of the extent of the damage.

Each time a demon entered, it was a statement that maybe Xiaoshi had been wrong to say that he was better than the man he had overthrown.

They were getting more devious, the demons, as they snuck in their forces. They tried to prey on the outermost villages, but Xiaoshi would not allow it. Whenever they broke through the Mist Wall, he was there to fight them.

Their Qi was getting less painful . . . but their tactics were more concerning.

The worst part was the whispers. The filthy things had started *talking* to him. Even as he dueled them, even as he broke them, they whispered to him.

They spoke lies, a thousand lies: that Tianlan was going to kill him, when this was all over. That he would die and fuel her power.

But he was a cultivator, so obviously that was foolish. He was stronger than the Emperor of the Azure. How would he die, of old age? Surely he would ascend and become immortal, wouldn't he?

He did his best to ignore them . . . but a little voice in the back of his head knew otherwise.

Xiaoshi knew they were telling the truth. Because when he looked into a mirror, he saw it. Whenever he moved, he was beginning to feel it, despite the Qi coursing through his veins, and Tianlan's gifts. *He was getting older.*

□

Tianlan was so happy that they were working together again. They had been so busy lately! She hadn't even seen Xiaoshi in four years! It might have been . . . well, it might not have been under ideal circumstances, but once more it was the two of them against the world. Fighting a just battle against wicked forces.

They were once again the protectors. And just like before, everybody was united. There were no real battle lines, as the enemy would try to infiltrate from all sides. Instead, they had rapid reaction forces, ready to take the fight to the enemy.

But Xiaoshi just seemed tired. She did her best to cheer him up. She talked of their old times together, and all the good times they had ahead after this was all over.

"Together until I die, huh?" he asked, as Tianlan slung an arm around his shoulder. There was an odd tone to his voice.

"Yup! I can't say I'm looking forward to eating your mouldering bones, though. You taste *horrible*," she teased, poking him in the side.

His smile froze, and their connection twanged unpleasantly, enough so that Tianlan could feel it.

"Xiaoshi? You okay?" she asked him worriedly.

He grimaced. "Nothing. That just wasn't very funny," he said after a moment.

"Then that's *your* fault, you're the one who said my sense of humor was great, and now you're changing your mind?!" she demanded.

His smile returned. But it was still dull.

□

Xiaoshi didn't know if he felt betrayed or not. He wondered if her words really *were* just a joke.

The demons seemed ever more gleeful, as they taunted him.

Something ugly welled up inside him, even as his bones started creaking more and more.

Xiaoshi had learned quite a bit from Cao Li and her monkey friends when the formation had been created. They had made sure to stress the risks of what they had made—how if somebody ever found a way to tap into the Grand Formation, it could be used for ill.

But they had trusted him. He was the Emperor who had freed them. Of course he would always have their best interests at heart.

Quietly, and with Kongming's help . . . he made some changes to the formation.

→

On the night of the solstice, it was just himself and Kongming. The man's wounds still stunk of Demonic Qi, but Xiaoshi's old friend doggedly soldiered on, assisting Xiaoshi in every way he was able. He had been instrumental in helping Xiaoshi change the formation, and he was the only one who understood. He was Xiaoshi's right hand, after all.

Xiaoshi had commanded Dian the Temple Dog to keep Tianlan company as she travelled across the countryside.

Mostly because he didn't know if the dog would consider his actions tonight just. And he couldn't bear to see the look in Dian's eyes when the ritual was completed.

"Are you sure?" Kongming asked him as Xiaoshi stood in the center of the province. In the center of the formation.

"Yes. Yes, I'm sure."

The formation was now one of consumption.

He could feel the Emperor of the Azure's smug grin from beyond the grave. He could taste the mocking laughter.

It would drain all of the power that his people were using . . . and funnel it wholly into himself. It wouldn't hurt them. He'd made sure of that. But it *would* take all their power for a moment. Millions of cultivators and Spirit Beasts would fuel his ascension. Just like the original Emperor had planned.

He needed strength to battle the nightmare to come. He needed strength to protect all of his people.

This path was a dead end. He couldn't afford to die of old age. He couldn't afford to remain this *weak*.

He could feel the ritual commence.

He took a breath as the power of an entire province began to surge, upon the night of death and renewal.

He was prepared.

He touched the frayed, golden threads that remained between him and Tianlan. He would sever them and start a new path. It would destroy the connection between their souls.

He raised a metaphorical axe to sever it—and paused.

Was . . . was he really just going to throw all of it away? Was he really going to abandon his bond with his dearest friend?

The characters around him spiraled and whirled.

He remembered Tianlan's smile.

He hadn't talked to her about this. He hadn't said goodbye, and now he was just deciding things on his own.

He was leaving her, just like Linlin had left him.

He paused as the power swelled.

How long had it been since they'd really, truly talked? How long had it been since he had stopped confiding in her? Thirty years? Forty?

Every time they'd met, she'd tried to support him. She had even offered to abandon her body for the duration of the war, so they could be as one once more, and he had refused her.

She had always been there for him. And now he was about to throw it all away without even a word.

He gently touched the golden threads again.

And let the power go. He felt his Qi drain away, entering the connection between himself and Tianlan.

No. He couldn't do it. He couldn't hurt her like that. He couldn't take advantage of his people like this either. He'd have to find another way—

"Xiaoshi!" Kongming's strangled voice called in warning, before he let out a racking cough. Blood splattered to the floor.

Xiaoshi turned, worry forming in his heart at the tone of his prime minister's voice.

That was all he received before a sword entered his back and punched out of his chest.

No. Not a sword. A bladed limb.

The demon attached to the other side of it, growing out of the puddle of vomit and blood that Kongming was hacking out, *grinned.*

But not at Xiaoshi. At the spiraling set of characters, which had just started to fade.

"It was most unpleasant, thy methods for attempting to remove me," the demon mused, sparing a glance over at Xiaoshi. The creature was oddly eloquent. More blood poured out of Kongming, the man shaking as he was rapidly exsanguinated, which formed the rest of the demon's body. "This Zhong Shen shall congratulate thy efforts. Thy pitiful attempts almost succeeded. We must further refine the Twilight Cuckoo's Triumph."

Demonic poison burned in Xiaoshi's veins. The monster tossed him negligently aside.

Then it stepped into the center of the province.

Into the center of the consumption formation.

It tapped the Dragon Veins with a single glowing finger, causing the blue characters to turn a sickly purple.

"Now, *dance for me*, my friends."

□

The dreams led to her nightmares and she remembered *the moment it all began to break.*

Tianlan hummed as she leapt over mountains, heading towards the Lake Districts. Dian bounded beside her, the big fluffy dog on the lookout for demons and ready to protect her . . . not that she really needed it. Still, it was nice to have another friend along.

They could drink together. She had bottles of wine, as well as fruit juice, on account of Ruolan's . . . condition.

Pregnant! Seriously, Ruolan had hidden it for months, the dummy! Holed up in her mansion and scared out of her wits at becoming a mother.

Tianlan would have little Ruolans and Xiaoshis to spoil soon, and she was very much looking forward to it.

She smiled as she bounded over yet another village, the people below fully immersed in their dance.

And then she paused, as she looked closer.

They seemed . . . kind of out of it. Their eyes had gone blank, glowing with crimson light. Their bodies started to twitch and writhe.

"Mistress. Something is wrong—" the Temple Dog began.

The sky turned red.

There was a ripping, sucking feeling in Tianlan's chest.

A sucking feeling that was pulling down her connection with Xiaoshi.

She fell to the ground, coughing and gagging. She reached up a hand and saw that blood was pouring out of her nose.

What—what is Xiaoshi doing?!

She scrambled and writhed, her legs spasming nervelessly even as Dian barked, terrified at what was happening to her.

All the while, people danced faster and faster and *faster*.

Tianlan started screaming, as her connection pulled and pulled and pulled—

□

The demon's body swelled and shuddered. It twisted and snapped, gorging itself on Tianlan's Qi and the souls of Xiaoshi's people. Everybody was connected through the formation.

Everybody was vulnerable.

And all Xiaoshi could do was watch, demonic poison continuing to paralyse his limbs. Watch, while the demons won.

They had tricked him. They had played him. And now they had beaten him.

No. He had beaten himself, hadn't he? His own hubris was his fall.

He could feel Tianlan's panic flood down their link, the sensation stronger than anything he had experienced.

She was dying, and it was all his fault.

Tears welled up in his eyes. The monster was laughing while it gorged itself on power. It was ignoring him.

Xiaoshi grunted, and with shaking limbs he tried to heave himself up, but instead he sprawled forward, his face slamming into the ground beside a part of the formation that he had been warned about.

The cascade inhibitor.

The part of the formation that would prevent the Elemental Conversion from running out of control.

"Never *touch this part while the formation is in operation,*" Cao Li had said, her voice firm. "*When we're channeling this much power, anything disrupting this part of the formation will have catastrophic consequences.*"

Xiaoshi summoned the last of his strength and pulled his fist up.

"*I'm sorry, Tianlan,*" he whispered.

The formation broke. The demon's laugh cut off in its throat as every control matrix in the formation abruptly stopped working.

The Qi in the formation tangled, twisted, and then—bereft of the guidance of the formation—*split.*

The demon's body swelled like a piece of fried dough, cracks forming all over its carapace, the light of more Qi than it could handle shining through the gaps.

"*Oh,*" the demon said, its voice faintly surprised.

And then the world broke, as all of the Qi from millions of people and Spirit Beasts, as well as the full might of an Earth Spirit, rebounded back into the earth.

□

Tianlan shuddered, each golden crack on her form pulsing as the world came to an end.

Wood to Fire. A forest turned into a raging inferno that changed night to day for the entire Empire.

A mother bear screamed, as she burned.

Fire to Earth. Hot springs and magma turned to stone. The earth bucked and heaved like a living thing.

Enormous rocks hammered into the earth. The people stared at the sky, their eyes blank. The formation broke them just as much as it was breaking the land.

Earth to Metal. Marble and granite changed to iron and tin, killing the earth and poisoning the water with heavy metals.

Rumblin' Yao stayed true to his oath to Xiaoshi, protecting all that he could within his shell, even as it killed him.

Metal to Water. The vast mines exploded, as Pale Moon Ore turned to ten times its volume in liquid.

Three quarters of the new capital was swept away, forming Pale Moon Lake. All that was left was the outermost section of the city, with the least of the administrative palaces.

Water to Wood, as the lakes and rivers were choked by an endless expanse of green.

The Lord of the Lake roared, roots and leaves consuming his flesh. The great lord dove to the bottom of the lake, burning his soul to prevent the water from going away completely.

His children howled with him, their horns sloughing from their skulls.

Then the energy discharge hit the center of the province.

The tops were knocked off a thousand mountains. Most of the debris hit the Mist Wall as they flew, vaporizing from the fury of fluctuating stars. But enough came back down to earth.

The demons outside it screeched when the cataclysm hit them, the burst of light and Qi shattering thousands of their portals and vaporizing millions of the beasts.

The survivors awoke to a dying world and with broken memories. Though they couldn't be called memories anymore, Demonic Qi poisoning and deluding. Their very souls had been wounded. Millions were dead or dying.

Yet none called it a cataclysm, because to their fractured souls and addled minds, *the world had always been this way.*

The Spirit Beasts screamed and raged as the rampaging Qi mutated their bodies. They went completely insane as their lords succumbed to the devastating Qi deviations.

A blind man had to drive what was once his best friend away from the corpse of his father, as the Roadspinner, now Wrecker Ball, screamed with rage and hate.

Men and women slaughtered each other in the aftermath. For food. For resources. For the dregs of Qi leaking out into the world.

Ruolan, a babe at her breast, picked up a sword used for opera, which she had sworn to never draw in anger . . . and called all who would be with her under her banner.

□

Xiaoshi awoke to a tongue licking at his face.

"Master. *Master*," Dian whimpered. His dear friend's teeth were cracked, and his eyes were mad and wild.

Xiaoshi groaned as he raised a hand. He'd meant to raise both of them, but he only had one arm.

And one leg.

But he was alive, at least for now. He groaned, letting the Temple Dog help him up. He was somewhere on the ruins of a mountaintop, having been flung from the old capital, the center of the province.

All that was left *there* was a hole in the ground.

The Mist Wall was visible in the sky now. Covering the sun and turning everything monochrome and grey.

He touched the part in his soul that was once connected to Tianlan yet felt only a ragged stump.

He touched the earth and was met only by silence.

He just wanted to curl up and die. But he was still alive. And if he was still alive . . . then he was alive for a reason.

Perhaps he had some role left to play.

His companion bore him onwards, and Xiaoshi took in the devastation he had wrought. That he had wrought by changing the formation and betraying his friend.

It was a sucking, hollow feeling.

Had it been pride that had blinded him? Had it been something else?

He didn't know. He couldn't know. All he had left was the crushing guilt.

He trudged forwards, his heart hollow, until he came to Pale Moon City—or what was left of it. A single outer borough was all that remained of the mining city.

He managed to form a semblance of order in Pale Moon. What was left of his Qi was used to cut through some of the people's madness, as they instinctively recognised their Emperor. He barely had any strength, but a snarling Temple Dog put to rest any thoughts of looting and arson for the populace.

He prepared them as best as he could, expecting demons to come winging out of the sky at any moment.

But none ever materialized.

For over a month, he waited. Nothing came.

□

The Mist Wall churned with lightning and power, slowly starting to fade away. He expected any weakness to immediately be capitalized on. He expected the legions of hell to push their way through the stellar barrier.

Yet not a single one came. Something else had drawn their attention. The Azure Mountains were not to be consumed by them.

So he made a record. A record of his memories.

He wanted . . . he wanted somebody to know, eventually. To know what happened here.

To know what had destroyed Tianlan. What had destroyed his people and left them like *this*.

With the last of his power, he placed a compulsion upon the earth.

Whoever was to be his successor would be guided to this crystal. Then they could learn all the secrets within and become the Master of the Azure Mountains. The Lord of all the people within.

A Lord better than both him . . . and the Azure Emperor.

"Go. Take this somewhere safe. If I do not return within the year . . . take care of yourself, my friend," he whispered to Dian.

His dear friend, his most loyal, was loath to leave him.

But his command rang in Dian's ears, and the Temple Dog obeyed.

It was the last Dian ever saw of his master.

The memories in the crystal ended there.

□

Xiaoshi watched as Dian went to do his bidding, the memory crystal clutched in his mouth. His heart was heavy.

For he knew that he would never see Dian again.

Xiaoshi's body was finally giving up. Finally dying. He wouldn't last the year.

He hoped Dian would forgive him and move on. He hoped the dog would find a better master.

Xiaoshi had one last task to perform. He started walking.

It took him nearly a month, in his condition. He had to dodge bandits and highwaymen looking for easy prey. But . . . he managed it. He managed to reach the location that would always hold a place in his heart.

He went to the place where he had buried his parents' funerary tablets, so long ago. His first farm. It was overgrown with weeds, and there wasn't a single trace left of it.

But it was his. His first place. His first heaven.

The place where he had met Tianlan.

Xiaoshi, on shaking limbs, lowered himself to the earth and pressed his forehead to the soil.

He closed his eyes and wept as his heart slowly stopped beating.

That was how Emperor Xiaoshi died. Not in a palace. Not with a grand funeral.

The worms claimed his flesh, and the earth his bones.

□

Tianlan awoke to agony. Her Qi, her lifeblood, was spilling out of her. Her body was just gone, a shattered pile of rubble.

She was broken and delirious. Fractured, and barely a person. She was nearly blind, deaf, and mute . . . but she could still feel. There was somebody approaching a Dragon Vein. One of her wounds, which was leaking Qi into the air.

"Help . . . me," she begged the approaching figure.

The figure that evolved into Ruolan.

Her eyes were cold and hard. Her face was full of wrinkles. There was blood splattered across her cheek.

Ruolan knelt down, fingers brushing against raw Qi as it dissipated into the air.

'*Ruolan. Ruolan, help me,*' she begged, reaching out tendrils of light to connect to her friend.

But Ruolan couldn't hear her.

The cultivator dug deep into the exposed Dragon Vein and ripped what little she could take out.

All across the province, it was the same story, as Tianlan died, over and over again.

Tianlan screamed and screamed, begging for help that never came.

It took over a decade, but her screams of anguish and pleas for aid petered out into bitterly spat curses.

She cursed them. She cursed their methods. She cursed their bloodlines. All the rats that gnawed on her bones for power to hurt their fellows were things that did not *deserve* her blessings.

She cursed them and cursed them and cursed them until the blackness slipped in at the edges, and what was the earth returned to it.

She never noticed that even broken, her words had some power.

□

Even in this mad world, there were some things that were respected. They remembered, even through their damaged and mutilated souls.

A dance on the solstice. A dance that was important. It protected them.

So every year, they performed it without fail. They performed it, standing on the corpse of a spirit who hated them and loved them at the same time.

The dance was a proclamation of love and respect. Love and respect, despite them ripping and tearing the dwindling resources and Qi out of Tianlan's flesh with abandon.

The world got brighter and brighter. The land got less dangerous as the Qi faded. Slowly, as the generations passed, the people healed.

Until all that remained was the Azure Hills.

□

Bi De's eyes were on the face of Xiaoshi: the last memory within the crystal. He gazed at the anguish within them. His mind was a whirl as he pondered the tragedy of Xiaoshi and Tianlan.

A perfect copy of the formation that had empowered the Earth Spirit bounced around in his head when the crystal imparted its memories.

It practically begged him to take up Xiaoshi's final wish, to ascend to the top of the Azure Mountains and command all its people.

To be the steward he couldn't be.

The crystal offered the location of stashes of reagents that none would have uncovered. It offered power, formations, and a hundred thousand long-dead cultivation styles.

A ghostly, spectral being slowly swam into view. Its eyes were closed, like it had been slumbering for a long while. It was weak, like the Temple Dog, yet growing in strength as it floated forward.

"You, who hast found the crystal. By the orders of mine Master, you are the successor. This one is sworn to your service." The ghostly apparition began to open its eyes, smiling warmly at Bi De. "It shall aid you in any way it can, for the ascendance of the—"

The spirit blinked. Consternation stretched across its features.

Then it blinked again, squinted, and struck the side of its head twice.

"*A chicken?*" the spirit asked, incredulously.

CHAPTER 40

NOT JUST ONE PILLAR HOLDS THE SKY

Bi De stared at the spirit.

The spirit stared at Bi De, its head tilted farther to the side.

Once upon a time, the spirit might have resembled a man. But, like the Temple Dog, time had done it no favours. Its face was smooth, like polished stone, and it didn't have any features except its glowing eyes. It was now just a being of blue light.

Its incredulity, however, was one that was profoundly common. It was quite amusing that even this ancient spirit had the same reaction as so many others. All who gazed upon Bi De had that moment, the moment of shock and confusion, and Bi De had to admit that he was slowly coming to enjoy their incredulous reactions. Which way would their faces twist? Would they hold up their hands to the heavens in consternation? Would they shout out "Impossible!"?

It almost made him want to start carrying a recording crystal around like Disciple Yun Ren just so that he might record an image of their reactions. Bi De dismissed that thought—actively recording an image seemed rather rude to him, so instead he contented himself with filing away the amusing faces people made. At least he'd be able to tell his fellow disciples of it; it was always amusing to compare the shocked reactions between them.

The amusing thought faded as Bi De's turmoil reasserted itself.

He gazed back at the spirit, willing it to speak its peace. It was twitching, its form fuzzing and destabilizing. Perhaps after so long a confinement it was as the Temple Dog had been. No being should be subjected to such a thankless task without acknowledgement.

Taking pity on it, he cleared his throat. "Greetings, Honoured Spirit. This one is Fa Bi De. I apologise for disturbing you. Might I aid you in some way?"

The spirit buzzed, and its entire form shuddered. "SpIRit bEASt?" it asked, its "voice" twisting and grating harshly before it focused sharply on him. There was a feeling of intent. Of Qi.

The endless expanse of the crystal trembled slightly, and Bi De felt something reach out and touch him. It was not hostile, but it pressed upon him, and after a moment Bi De allowed it past his defences. The touch filled him for a moment and it felt like his very soul was being weighed.

"Strong foundation, noble spirit. All requirements of the Lord are equaled," the spirit said in a bewildered voice, seeming to have forgotten that Bi De was there at all.

"Thank you for your kind words," Bi De replied, causing the spirit to jolt. It seemed almost panicked when it turned back to Bi De.

"Forgive this spirit, Young Lord! Your form was merely . . . *unexpected*! But truly, you do fit the qualities that were set by the Emperor!" the spirit declared, clearly shoving off its previous trepidation. Its voice lost its confusion, and took on a rapturous edge. "This one is Shenguashi, the polished benevolent stone of the Emperor, tasked with finding his successor! It may have been a . . . very, very long time, by this one's reckoning, but now this one may fulfill its duty! Rejoice, great and noble cock. For you have the qualities that befit an Emperor! You shall be heir to the legacy of our beloved saviour and bring peace to the realm. This spirit shall guide you upon this fated journey!"

The spirit approached Bi De eagerly, its eyes just *slightly* tinged with madness.

For one moment, Bi De was trapped in indecision. How did one respond to an ancient spirit's declaration of your destiny to become the next Emperor?

Bi De was all for confronting issues head-on. But *today*? After all that he had seen?

Sighing internally, Bi De tried for a diplomatic response. "I require some time to meditate upon what I have witnessed. It has been a day of revelations." He was quite exhausted, and that was the truth. He needed some time.

The spirit froze. It had grown animated during its rapturous speech, but at Bi De's words it deflated and fuzzed out for a moment.

"As the Young Lord wishes. Fret not, this one shall devise a plan for thy ascension in the meantime!" the spirit said, almost desperately. "Return to the crystal tomorrow, Young Lord, and I shall have everything prepared!"

Bi De nodded to it in acknowledgement.

Shenguashi seemed to take this as a sign of acceptance from Bi De. Bowing once to Bi De, he then flew away into the starscape of memories.

The rooster took one last look at the vast expanse of shining memories that had revealed so much to him, then carefully extracted himself from the crystal.

→

As he gradually grew more aware of his body, Bi De kept his eyes closed. Sensations returned to him bit by bit. He could feel the light of the moon, streaming in through the windows. The warmth of the blanket on his back, draped over his body. He extended his senses and reached out; he could feel the Qi of each and every member of Fa Ram.

He breathed in and out, slowly calming his racing heart. His world was not caught in the flames of war and suffering. The world he returned to was peaceful, and its denizens slept without fear.

Bi De let out a shaky breath and tried to separate his own emotions from the feelings projected into him by the crystal. He took another few calming breaths and let his energy cycle.

Then he opened his eyes.

The living room was illuminated by the moon; the hearth had burned down to embers. The bright moon spilled in through the window. It was the room where everyone gathered. At this time of night Bi De expected it to be empty—

Yet on the couch was Bi De's Great Master.

His Lord was still awake, reading a medical scroll that the Healing Sage had given to him and running his fingers through Brother Chun Ke's mane. Both Sister Ri Zu and Yin were asleep against the great boar's side.

Bi De felt a surge of affection for them. He had been considering going to the roof to contemplate . . . but seeing them here like this, being alone was the last thing he wanted.

An unnamed emotion welled up in Bi De as he stared at his Great Master . . . no, the man who might as well be his father.

He rose from his position and walked to the couch, hopping up beside his Great Master.

"Hey, buddy," his Great Master whispered, a gentle smile on his face. He put down the scroll he had been reading to turn and look at Bi De. Whatever he saw when he looked at Bi De made his face fall. "That bad?" he asked, reaching out and brushing his fingers against Bi De's wattles.

Bi De leaned into the touch and nodded. He stayed quiet, not quite trusting his voice just yet.

"Need some time?"

Bi De nodded again.

"Then take your time. I'll be here." His Master scooped Bi De up from beside him and settled the rooster into his lap. His fingers dug into the feathers of Bi De's back, massaging out a soothing rhythm.

The touch calmed his trembling Qi. Beside them, Chun Ke, Yin, and Ri Zu stirred but did not wake.

As the soft comfort of his Master's hand brought peace to Bi De, he closed his eyes again and focused upon the earth-shaking revelations he had been delivered.

The size of the mountain he was sitting upon had been unveiled to him. He knew his Master's strength, and envisioning anyone stronger than him had always been a difficult task. How could *anything* match the Master of Fa Ram?

Seeing the true scope of cultivators that even his Great Master had warned him of shook him.

The sheer power of Xiaoshi and all those who had lived before was utterly humbling. Ruolan, the opera singer, had been in the Earth Realm. There were farmers and miners at the end of Xiaoshi's reign who would be equal to Bi De in power.

It was one thing to hear it . . . and another to see and feel a man create a star and *throw it* at somebody. To *feel* the heat and the light and the Qi.

The world was vast, and never before had Bi De understood so keenly his place. He was not the strongest.

Bi De took another breath, calming his trembling Qi.

Xiaoshi. Tianlan, who was now connected to his Great Master. The Demon War . . . and the breaking of an entire province. His thoughts swirled from revelation to revelation before settling on Xiaoshi.

He could not truly judge the man. Once upon a time, Bi De himself had been tempted to consume a friend. To consume his own *kin* when accosted by Chow Ji. To be tempted was forgivable, but to go through with the act was not. That he had in the end stopped himself was commendable—how he had gotten there less so.

Bi De could see where the man had gone wrong. His self-imposed isolation. Xiaoshi had insisted on shouldering everything, doing everything himself. He'd shared nothing of his burdens, lied to even Tianlan, his closest companion. Bi De has seen how even in the little things, he had spurned the support of his friends. All out of a desire not to worry his friends, until it had all come apart in the end.

Xiaoshi was, in a way, a dark mirror of Bi De's own Master. What could have been. His Great Master too would not abide others harming his family. He could see the path of escalation that his Lord could have taken, while hating every moment of it.

For them, he would fight, and fight, and fight until he stood atop a pile of ashes and claimed the Azure Throne—all for their sakes.

The hand ghosted through his feathers.

No.

He would not allow that to happen. His Great Master would live a life he enjoyed, free of the bonds that path would place upon him. Bi De would do everything in his power to prevent that from happening.

All of them would.

Just the same, he was sure all of them would aid with the other part of the equation.

Tianlan. The Earth Spirit. The existence he had been giving his Qi to. The source of most of his Great Master's power.

At first, he had considered her more akin to a god than anything. Nameless and faceless. Eternal and all powerful.

Bi De, even knowing what he knew now, still found her worthy of the reverence he had given her. Everything he had seen of Tianlan had only deepened his admiration. She too had awakened in her own way just as he and the other disciples had, leaving behind the base nothingness to reach for something more. The Earth Spirit was kind and generous to all that she had met. A nurturing, friendly goddess who had supported her people without complaint. The other half of the pillar. The world upon which they all walked. Invincible, and eternal. Or so he had thought.

But now . . . now he knew just how vulnerable she really was. Her Dragon Veins were shattered. Her body had been broken . . . and for untold eons she had likely believed that her greatest friend had utterly betrayed her.

She had lived as a shattered, hurting husk. Until his Great Master had connected with her and started the cycle anew.

Bi De would not let her suffer. She would be healed. She would be made better, one way or another, for she did not deserve the fate that had been visited upon her. This, Bi De swore. He would do everything in his power to aid her.

And hopefully protect both her and his Great Master from the ones who had been at the core of it all.

The demons.

They had already shown themselves. If Bi De had to guess, *the Twilight Cuckoo's Triumph*, the ability that the demon in Kongming had used, was what had infected Zang Li. The beasts had survived, and with Tianlan growing in strength, they could possibly be attracted back into the province. They were *already* here in some numbers.

The histories said that the demons were defeated by the First Emperor. But some of them, the arch deceivers that they were, had passed on their blood and abilities to humans, forming Demonic Cultivators. It was why those cultivators were so hated; they used the blood and teachings of the archnemesis to empower themselves.

It was a threat that would need to be faced eventually, yet one Bi De did not know how to truly combat.

Bi De grimaced. He had longed for answers, and now that he had them, he was left with challenges so far above his reach he could not comprehend how he would face them. Perhaps those answers should have *stayed* buried.

They certainly complicated things.

He took another breath, drawing comfort from his Great Master's ministrations.

But there was no going back now that he had unearthed them. Now he knew what had happened to the formation, and he knew what had so damaged the land.

Those who did not learn from past mistakes repeated them.

And Bi De was no fool.

He may not have had any ideas on truly solving the issues yet. But he knew what he could do. What he had to do.

He would share everything he had learned with his fellow disciples and ask for their aid. Bi De vowed to never become that lone, crumbling pillar that Xiaoshi had become.

There may have been something appealing about being the sole pillar. About being the strongest, and the strongest alone.

To stand alone at the peak . . . *was to stand alone at the peak*. There were none to catch you if you fell.

Here, they would sharpen each other and figure out a course of action.

Together.

So he faded off to sleep as his Great Master stroked his feathers, taking comfort in the knowledge he was not alone.

While drifting off to sleep, there was one thing that nagged at his tired mind.

Though Bi De had *recovered* the crystal . . . he hadn't truly found it. An old crone had given him a map directly to its location.

He had not yet spoken to her. He had wanted to figure out what exactly was in the crystal first. But now that he knew, it was time to ask her a few questions.

CHAPTER 41

THE GREAT AND NOBLE EMPEROR

And that is all that has been revealed to me."

Big D fell silent as he finished his summary from his place at the chalkboard. We were all seated around a table before him, where he'd spent the last few hours recounting to us his tale. Our little group was made up of me, Meimei, Xiulan, Chunky, Peppa, Tigu, and Rizzo.

He'd talk to everybody else later, but for now, it was just us. He'd said he wanted us to help him figure out what to do.

We had gotten the CliffsNotes version, since it just wasn't feasible for every one of us to individually check the memories ourselves. Entering the crystal to view everything would have taken at least a couple of days.

Even with the short version, listening to Big D recounting the crystal's memories was like listening to a tale straight out of some tragic Shakespearean play.

The Tale of Xiaoshi and Tianlan: The Saga of the Azure Mountains.

In the quiet after Big D finished, I sipped at my tea and looked at the crystal, which floated off to the side. Everybody else was silent, clearly digesting the tale. I glanced at Meimei. My wife's eyes were narrowed into slits, and she was chewing on her thumbnail, deep in thought. My other disciples were similarly pensive. Xiulan in particular looked lost. She had gotten some pretty hard shocks—like finding out that the origin of her martial style was traditional opera of all things! Not to mention the surprise that the last Emperor and her direct ancestor had uh . . . had *relations.*

The whole thing . . . I won't say that I'd *expected* it, but I had been fairly certain *something* fucky had been going on ever since the whole formation had been revealed. Some part of me had suspected something simmering in the background, because of *course* my life couldn't just be simple.

To be honest, it was better than what I had been expecting. Tianlan wasn't some kind of strange parasite leeching off me until she became a demon god or some shit. There was no doomsday clock over our heads in regards to the formation.

It was a broken piece of land that needed fixing, and a pack of demons that might, or *might not*, be active.

Which I *won't* jinx by saying that it sounded manageable. The demons could obviously be a large threat . . . but it was one that I could tell *other* people about, like the cultivators in the rest of the Crimson Phoenix Empire, provided they believed me.

This had the trappings of some kind of "fated story" written all over it. But the point was, I had options other than "gather a ragtag band to save the world."

Hopefully, at any rate.

"Thank you for telling us all of this, Big D," I said, nodding to him. The rooster bowed in return. "But you're right. We'll have to come up with a plan, *together*, on what to do in this situation. Any ideas?"

"Yes!" Tigu shouted like she was in class, immediately raising an arm.

"What do you think, Tigu?" I asked.

"I'll set up a scouting rotation!" Tigu replied immediately. "We shall range far and wide to see if there is anything out of the ordinary! We can use recording crystals like the ones Disciple Yun Ren has to document anything we find!"

She was focused and *absolutely* serious right now. More like a hardened military woman than the happy girl I had gotten used to. She was a tiger that would devour anything that got in her way.

Pain and pride mixed in my chest. My little girl, ready to go off to war, for the sake of her friends and family.

"We'll train, get stronger, and protect our home if there are any demons. As for the crystal itself . . . I shall trust the First Disciple's judgement." She crossed her arms at the statement, looking away from Big D, who smiled at her.

"They shouldn't be able to get close to the house, at least." Meimei's voice was calm and matter of fact. "Even before I was a cultivator, I could smell there was something off about Zang Li. So if they try to hide, I can help sniff out any . . . *vermin*."

Her eyes went cold, two flinty amethyst chips that looked almost like they were shining with malevolent light. "And if push comes to shove . . . well. *Demons don't count as people.*"

Rizzo, sitting beside her, chuckled darkly. '*Yes, yes. What murder-poisons affect-hurt demons? A good-fine question, Master.*'

Both Tigu and Big D leaned slightly away from the two women as they muttered under their breath about ingredients they had to procure.

'*Chunky protect home. Help Big Little Sister,*' Chunky said quietly. '*Make sure no more hurt.*'

Peppa nodded from beside the boar. '*The poor dear. She seemed dreadfully injured.*'

"She's well enough to *headbutt* people," Tigu replied, dismissing the sentiment

'*Well, you* do *have a very headbuttable face,*' Rizzo ribbed.

"Haaa? Say it again, wormtail!" The cat-turned-girl glowered at the rat, who simply snickered.

Big D sighed as the two broke into an argument. Peppa watched on, amused, though Meimei had already pulled a piece of paper out and was scribbling furiously on it. I caught the words "blood necrosis" and "transmission vector" as my wife plotted horrible war crimes.

I, on the other hand, turned to the only person who hadn't spoken yet.

Xiulan was staring straight ahead, her face locked into a frown.

↔

While the others were focused on the demons, or protecting Fa Ram, all Cai Xiulan could think about was the crystal.

Or rather, the knowledge it contained.

Xiulan chewed her lip. It had been a shock to realise that her legendary Jade Grass Blades were opera props. And to learn of the . . . general disposition of her Honoured Ancestor. Her face flushed as she recalled Bi De's description of the woman: "The Healing Sage, as she is when drunk."

Which told her all she needed to know, really. Once she had a chance to look within the crystal . . . she would have to steel herself before witnessing that. Lewd and crass as the memories might be, it was still knowledge about their long-forgotten ancestors. The progenitor of their entire line. Most of the Azure Hills only had scraps of history preserved. Bits and pieces of knowledge about their founders, and even their styles could be said to be fragmentary.

The crystal was full of information that the Sects of the Azure Hills would quite literally kill for. It was a *true* connection to their ancestors. A chance to fix their corrupted and warped styles and regain what they had lost so long ago.

It represented both danger and opportunity in equal measure.

The first of the dangers was the Crimson Phoenix Empire. Knowledge that the Emperor they had sworn their oaths to was not the Emperor that they currently served? Well, that certainly wouldn't go down well.

They *couldn't* be the Empire of the Azure Hills. Such a challenge would be met with swift reprisal from the Crimson Phoenix Empire, and that was a fight that they *certainly* couldn't win.

Xiulan doubted anyone sane would consider rebelling against the Crimson Phoenix Empire. Time and the cataclysm Bi De had spoken of had eroded whatever loyalties might have existed. They were as much a part of the Empire as any other province.

There was only one person under the heavens who could get her to raise her swords in remaking an ancient empire . . . and he was the only man she knew who would likely utterly reject the possibility.

And thus, Xiulan pushed those thoughts aside and focused instead upon the potential opportunity.

For the crystal could make her plans to unite the hills a reality. Returning with this? It would cement her claims and help her forge the ties to bind them.

Although . . . even *thinking* about disseminating this knowledge to a select few was a rather novel thing. The old part of her, the part of her that hailed from the time before Fa Ram, urged her to simply hoard all the knowledge for herself. To keep it all and leave the others in the dust, for that was the way of a true cultivator. However, it was something she could use, so she had to think of how best to use it.

Knowledge of their ancestors. The truth that they had all been under one banner in the past, instead of disparate, feuding Sects. Those who joined with her would have all the power of their forebears granted to them . . . while those who refused would be left in the dust.

The outright domination of the other Sects using the ancient knowledge didn't sit entirely well with her. Her plan had been more in line with forging lasting, cooperative bonds with the Young Masters and Mistresses.

Those who would resent her controlling such a wealth of information were liable to try and steal it, or call their members to war to try to take it by force of arms.

It was a bludgeon that would ensure their loyalty. She didn't *want* to use it as such, though. She just . . . wanted peace, unity.

She could even just leave it here and set about her plan without it.

Xiulan sighed. Why couldn't things just be simple for once? She ceased her woolgathering and looked back up at the table. Tigu and Ri Zu were still bickering, while the others watched. But Xiulan could tell that Jin was patiently waiting for her to speak.

So she cleared her throat, catching their attention.

"Jin. Bi De. If you had brought this to my Sect, the Verdant Blade would have sworn their undying loyalty to you in a heartbeat. Whoever bears this crystal and the knowledge within . . . is, effectively, the Lord of every Sect within the Azure Hills."

The table went silent again.

"There are two real options in the use of this knowledge," Xiulan continued. "To hide it away from the Sects . . . or to use it as bait, to lure them in and control their movements. That is the value of the knowledge within this crystal to the Sects of the Azure Hills."

The table was quiet, everyone digesting her words.

Finally, Jin broke the silence.

"Or we could just give it to *all of them*."

Xiulan just stared at him. Just *give* people advanced cultivation advice. Just give them knowledge that they would gladly beggar themselves to possess. That they would sell their sons into slavery and gift their daughters to warm that person's bed in order to even get a glimpse at it.

And yet . . . as she thought about it, it *did* make a certain sort of sense to disseminate the knowledge to all.

Honour would demand that all who received the knowledge act with all due courtesy to the gifter. It had the potential to remove the thought of those attacking her and her Sect for the crystal, or even getting desperate enough to snoop around Master Jin's farm.

It was a novel solution. Something to think about, at least.

The mood was once more solemn and contemplative. Until she saw a mischievous look in Jin's eyes as he turned to the First Disciple.

"You know, there *was* one last thing that was bothering me," he began with the utmost solemnity in his voice. "Does this mean I have to call you my Lord now, seeing as you're apparently the Emperor's heir?"

The rooster physically recoiled, and Xiulan snorted at the question. "Heavens, Master, no, of course . . ." he began, denials springing to his beak.

And then he saw the grin and huffed at his Master's teasing words. Bi De coughed into his wing.

"Great Master, you are obviously more qualified than I," the rooster replied, his eyes narrowing. "Shall we proclaim you tomorrow, or today?"

"I didn't find the glowy crystal with the will of the Emperor in it, Bi De. *I'm* just a farmer."

Xiulan heard Chun Ke snort and she felt her own smile start to steal across her face—until the bow fired an arrow directly at her.

"Looks like you're the Empress then, Lanlan," Meiling said, looking up from her notebook and turning to her with a little smirk.

Xiulan froze at the statement.

'*Empress Xiulan, we are not worthy*,' Ri Zu squeaked, bowing low.

"Who wants to join my rebellion?" Tigu asked.

Well, technically, I do have a blood claim—er . . . well, no, no thank you, I most certainly do not wish to be proclaimed Empress. I have a hard enough time with my own Sect, thank you very much, she thought.

She cast about for anything that dismissed the claim . . . and then remembered the laws on inheritance.

"My Honoured Ancestor and the Emperor never formalized my family's status," she said, "While the children of concubines may inherit, it requires specific provisions. Therefore, by all laws, this Cai Xiulan is not eligible to inherit the throne."

The room lapsed into stunned silence at the solemn declaration, though there were a few chuckles after a moment. Jin sighed and shook his head.

"We'll talk again next week. I gotta run some ideas past the Lord Magistrate as well. Bi De, I trust you to tell everybody you think should know."

The rooster bowed. "Of course, Great Master."

"And . . . thank you, for trusting us all like this."

The rooster flushed, looking around the table. Xiulan smiled and nodded at him, gratified and humbled by the rooster's trust.

"Now . . . let's go get some lunch and some more tea." Jin's command took them all out of their seats, the tension dispelling.

A world-shaking revelation . . . and then lunch.

It was amusing how often that happened around here.

The others had already eaten, and though Wa Shi was obviously curious about what they had been talking about, the fish kept his peace, clearly trusting that he would be told when he needed to be. He was remarkably unbothered by such things if they did not involve his stomach.

They resorted to one of Jin's favourites. Xiulan still had no idea why they were called *sandwiches*. The name was foreign on her tongue, but the result was, as with most things Jin made, delicious.

It was two simple pieces of thick, crusty, toasted bread, served with pickled vegetables, smoked meat, and dried herbs from the garden. Jin always packed his high enough that it looked like he would have to unhinge his jaw to get it all into his mouth. Meiling's were significantly thinner, though she often added a few drops of honey and some cracked peppercorns.

Tigu made hers like Jin's . . . and then begged for bites of Meiling's, which her friend bore without complaint from years of her little brother doing the same.

Xiulan, on the other hand, guarded hers well from Tigu's questing fingers no matter how much she pouted. It had some of the smoked deer Gou Ren had made, along with some spicy oil, pickles, mushrooms, and cheese.

While Chun Ke, Pi Pa, and Ri Zu could eat their sandwiches just fine, the First Disciple had his deconstructed. He would peck each ingredient in turn, including the special ones that Wa Shi had helped him create.

The pepper worms weren't *terrible*, in all honesty, though her Petals would have coughed blood seeing her eat bugs.

They ate their fill, and in what felt like no time, they were finished. Tigu's begging eventually won . . . no, Xiulan took pity on the cat, and gave her a bite of her sandwich.

The little devil had gone "eh" and waved her hand dismissively at the taste.

Xiulan was in the middle of teaching her a lesson, her fingers digging into Tigu's scalp, when she heard Bi De's voice.

"I mean to travel to Verdant Hill myself. There is one I must speak to, and I shall only be a few hours."

Jin looked at the rooster as he balanced the plates and dishes he had collected to be cleaned.

"Need anything for the road?" Jin asked, but the rooster shook his head in denial.

"I do not need anything, Master. Thank you for the offer."

Bi De turned and began to walk for the front door of the house, only stopping so Chun Ke could nuzzle his feathers in goodbye.

Xiulan stood up and approached the rooster before he left. Taking a place at the door, her face solemn, her back straight just as she had seen done a hundred times.

"Cai Xiulan pays her respects to the Emperor," she intoned, affecting a perfect bow.

Bi De's eye twitched.

Almost as if they had choreographed it, though they had not, Tigu speedily took up a position opposite Xiulan to bow as well and said, "Rou Tigu pays her respects to the Emperor."

Xiulan shot a glare at the cat. Really, rebelling under Xiulan, yet declaring her loyalty to Bi De? The cat was courting death!

Well, it was probably because Tigu had seen the rooster's irritation. A figure flashed down from above the doorway to land lightly before the rooster and added her own bow.

'Hong Ri Zu pays her respects to the Emperor!'

The First Disciple's attention turned back to Xiulan.

And then she was out of the room, an explosion of feathers following behind all three of them as the First Disciple made his wrath known.

Xiulan ended up with her head shoved into a snowbank . . . but this time, the rooster had to work for it.

Progress.

CHAPTER 42

THE CRONE

Bi De alighted before a tiny coop that was nestled against the wall of Verdant Hill. It was an old, slightly rundown-looking affair, with a thin fence around it with a little yard for storing animals. There were several signs placed facing the fence that bordered the lot with another, similarly rundown-looking place. They loudly proclaimed that "Shu" fornicated with dogs and was ugly and bald.

The lot directly beside it mirrored this with its own signs, stating that the woman who lived next to him was a witch who conspired with demonic goats and similarly had carnal relations with every man and horse in Verdant Hill.

Bi De considered these for a moment before deciding it wasn't his problem. He was here for a different reason.

Before the front door lay a goat. The beast placidly chewed her cud, staring at the empty air.

Bi De coughed, trying to get her attention.

After several seconds, during which the goat did nothing, he tried again.

"Excuse me," he asked. There was another pause, but slowly, the goat turned a lazy eye to him and chewed a few more times.

"Is the Mistress of the house in?" he asked politely.

The goat considered him and cocked her head to the side at his voice. She swallowed the cud in her mouth, then lifted her hind leg lazily.

The goat's cloven hoof smashed against the door with a resounding *bang* that sent the whole shack rocking.

There was the sound of a head hitting something, a pot falling, and then a screech of outrage.

"Lan Fan, you dare?!"

A familiar old woman burst from the shack, brandishing a broom. One of her eyes was milky white the other was wide and wild, rolling around like it had a mind of its own. Her hair was disheveled and her robes unkempt. She looked like she had been jolted awake. A cat with only three legs followed after her, his eyes narrow with wroth.

The goat regurgitated her cud and started chewing it again, looking distinctly unimpressed by the pair of angry residents. As the woman shook her broom and took in a breath to begin an undoubtedly crass tirade, Bi De seized his chance.

"Grandmother. Do you have a moment?" he asked, his voice coming out of the crystal around his neck like it always did these days.

The woman glared at her goat before she turned a gimlet eye to the rooster on her fence. She huffed, then turned around, stomping back inside. The three-legged cat snorted and reentered the house after giving Bi De a once-over.

She had left the door open, however, so Bi De took that as an invitation to enter the small, cramped shack. It was as he remembered it. Carvings of animals hung everywhere, and knickknacks, stones, and other assorted objects were strewn all about, filling the space. There was a bed with an abundance of blankets on it, and the old three-legged cat had claimed it.

To his surprise, when he entered he saw that the old woman had actually started making tea, instead of just giving him hot water like last time.

"So? Was the map useful?" she demanded without looking back at him. "You certainly took your time with it, boy."

Bi De blinked at the sudden question. "Yes. It was indeed useful to me, Grandmother. It led to a discovery of great significance. For that I thank you."

The old woman grunted as she pulled out two tea mugs. She glanced at them both. One was in good condition, but the other had several chips out of its top.

She placed that one in front of Bi De and took the better one for herself.

"So, here to just thank me, or ask the question, eh? Everybody always has *questions*."

Bi De paused at the emphasis on "questions" but forged ahead anyway.

"You are correct, Grandmother. I do have a question, if I may ask it." The woman waved dismissively at him as she pulled the water from the fire and poured it into the cups. "Why did you give me *that* map, in particular?"

She paused and turned to him. The mismatched orbs, one blind, the other hale and piercing, stared straight through him as the room seemed to darken. Her eyes narrowed, and she took a moment to digest his question. Then she spoke.

"It seemed like a good idea at the time. Why, what did you find there, anyway?"

"You did not already know?" Bi De replied, taken aback by her curiosity.

The woman snorted. "What? Were you expecting me to have all the answers? Was I supposed to be some grand puppetmaster? Too bad! I have no clue what's going on either! Never do. Kahhahahahaha!" The woman descended into cackles, her eye rolling madly.

She laughed so hard she had to hold on to the table for support.

Several minutes later her laughter slowly subsided, and she sighed. Into the awkward silence, the rooster asked:

"But . . . then may I ask how you came across this map?"

"Come across it? *I made it*."

Bi De paused at the blunt answer. The old woman chuckled at the confusion on his face. "What do you know of divination, boy?"

"As in . . . foreseeing the future? My Great Master said that such a thing is normally unreliable. That trying to change fate could set it in stone."

"Huh. That lost boy always has surprises, that one," she said, her eyes growing faint and her tone wistful . . ." Though I suppose he's not *really* lost anymore, is he?" She refocused on Bi De. "But he's right. Divining the future is . . . *unreliable*. Trying to change it? Nigh impossible. Wasted years trying. Do you know how maddening it is? To see a cultivator follow your visions to the letter . . . and then have a mortal defy *them* completely by accident and stubbornness? Fate laughs at us; believe me, I know. Gives me a damn headache just *thinking* about it."

She glared at the wall of her house, in the direction of the other shack, before shaking her head.

"It's not all peering into the future trying to defy fate. Sometimes it is simply *seeing*. Past. Present. This little ability of mine was quite in demand, before I retired!"

Bi De heard a hiss. The old tomcat on the bed was positively glaring at the old woman.

The woman rolled her eye and broke into a massive grin that showed off her missing teeth. "Oh, this old lady used to be quite the jade beauty, yanno? Every man and woman under the heavens desired me, but it was a tiring life, a bit too full of excitement and *accidents* for my taste."

At that, she glanced at the cat on her bed, her eye flicking to the missing limb, and she scratched idly at her stomach. It was the same place Loud Boy had kept touching the brief time Bi De had known the boy. It was the spot over her dantian, the source of her cultivation. "So! I did what your Master did. Left it all behind! Everything! Found the weakest, most out-of-the-way province. Heh. Did you think he was the first to have that idea, eh?"

Her eyes sparked with mirth.

"It does seem to be a more common desire than one would think," Bi De mused, stroking his wattles. "Though, Grandmother, why choose this particular place?"

He glanced around at the . . . *used* building. It was a bit drafty, especially for her advanced age.

"Ha?! What's wrong with my house, you pile of feathers?"

Bi De froze at the aggression. "I am merely concerned for your well-being, Grandmother. It can't be very warm, and cutting the firewood . . ."

The old woman snorted. "I'm tough, and my skin's more leather than flesh. I'll be fine. Besides, I like it here! It's a fantastic place to live! Young men run away screaming, thinking I'll curse them, and instead of trying their hand with poisoned words, prominent ladies give me tea! And I think I'm close to finishing off that old bastard next door! *Kahahahahahahaha!*"

Her laughter trailed off, and she took a sip of tea.

"But it wasn't always so nice. I used to live down near the big city, and my life there was torment! Barely a week in this damn province, I started getting visions. It was annoying! So *annoying*, the flashes of memory, of some strange cataclysm long past. A spirit, bound to the land, moaning weakly about how it needed to find an heir."

The old woman took another drink.

"So I made a deal. It would shut up, and I'd send a worthy successor on their way."

"You promised to help it *so it would stop annoying you*?" Bi De asked incredulously.

"You got a better reason? The bastard sent me all over these damn hills, making that map and marking *that* location. Then I simply asked the fates where a good successor would show up . . . and moved here. At first, I was going to give it to the young Magistrate! He fit the bill! He would have been a grand Emperor! But . . . he might have gone mad from the stress. So I decided not to risk it . . . and he's too pretty to go out on an adventure. Have you *seen* his behind? Tight! *Tight like a tiger!* And he walks around town for us gals every day! Kahahahahahaha!"

Bi De stared, concerned, at the cackling woman.

"Then . . . then there was that boy. That lost, lost boy. He fits. He *fits*, you know?"

"Yes. I know."

"But I'm soft in my old age! I couldn't do it! A boy that lost needs to put down roots, not keep wandering. And besides . . . he brought me back my goat. *Always* reward a man who brings you your goat."

Bi De snorted at the simple answer.

"And then there was *you*. Well. It wanted an Emperor. And what is a rooster but the Lord of a farm?"

So was it mere chance? Or . . . was it truly fate? Bi De didn't know, and he doubted he would get a real answer out of the woman.

"I see. Thank you for your trust, Grandmother."

"Keh! Don't be so damn polite, you brat. *I did you a disservice.*"

"Be that as it may. A boon can wind up a disservice, and a disservice a boon, can it not?"

The old woman cackled once more. "Oh, you have *no idea*."

Bi De smiled at the old woman. He did have a long while before he would be returning home . . .

"I still do have some time, Grandmother. Would you like to hear of my journey and what was in the crystal? Or is it pointless to tell a tale to one who can see the past if she wishes?"

"Why do you think I made the tea? Come sit! I know some parts. But good stories are still enjoyable, even if you know what's going to happen. All that's left is to see if you're good at telling tales. My favourite talespinner is Tao the Traveller! And to think people think he's full of hot air! Kahahahaha!"

She grinned in challenge at him.

Bi De steeled himself. He would do his best to rise to the occasion.

"It started like another tale. One we both know very well . . ." he began.

→

And so Bi De told his tale to the old and eccentric woman. She listened intently, chuckling, heckling, or interjecting whenever she wished, the old tomcat lying on her lap. Lan Fan the goat had ventured inside as well, placidly chewing her cud as always.

"Huh," the old woman muttered when he was done. "Now that *is* a tale."

"Indeed. Though . . . I must admit that there are still many questions. The Mist Wall, for one. One would think there would be some memory of it . . . but the Healing Sage said that in all the texts she has read in the archives, none of the histories mention its existence."

The old woman scratched at her chin. "Well. It's not exactly a secret . . . but it's not advertised too much either. Once, the entire world was covered in those Mist Walls; there were some in every province, protections against the demons—but it makes for a poor story that we were cowering away like rats in the walls while the demons largely ruled the world outside. At least until we got our act together and fought 'em off. Pha!"

Bi De blinked at that revelation. He would certainly need to find a better history scroll soon, if that was the case. "I suppose. Thank you for the tea, Grandmother. I should go."

"Mm. And thank you for the tale and the company, young man. But don't come over too often. I hate guests. You . . ." She suddenly trailed off, her brow furrowing.

"Grandmother?" Bi De asked, concerned. Her face had lost all expression—she stared into space as if nothing else existed. Both the cat and the goat looked at her in alarm.

Then, all of a sudden, the crone took a deep breath. Her eye rolled wildly in its socket, and she started to breathe heavily. Sweat beaded on her forehead.

"Grandmother—" He started towards her, but her hand suddenly shot up and pointed at him.

And then Bi De *saw*. It was hazy, like a dream. The vision swirled and suddenly coalesced.

From the central plains and their fortress cities, warded against demons, did the Crimson Phoenix Empire march, fresh from their victory at what would be called Demon's Grave Ravine.

Something had happened to the demons. Some great devastation. And there would be no hesitating. They forged onwards, beating back the threat.

In their expansion, they found a hundred thousand hidden realms and powerful fortresses. Curtains of fire, citadels of gemstones, and shields of blinding light held the diaspora of humanity, tiny torches against the demons. Some they found broken and ruined, their protections failed and people eradicated.

Others, sensing the demon power waning, opened of their own accord, releasing their charges back into the world and adding their strength to the wings of the Phoenix.

Until one day, as they pressed ever northwards, they came across fading protections.

Cultivators of the ascendant Crimson Phoenix Empire were quick to notice and breach the massive "hidden realm." It was one of the largest they had ever found. They expected riches, resources, and people who would be willing to lend their might to the ever-growing crusade.

Instead, they found the Azure Mountains. A Qi desert. Sects, as weak as they had ever seen. Resources that even bare Initiates struggled to get use out of.

A broken, weak place without any redeeming qualities . . . save for that it was land, and it was present.

And so an envoy of the Emperor was dispatched.

"The Emperor demands your loyalty! Bend your knees, and you shall know prosperity!" the man called to the people, his Qi a shining beacon that even the entire population working together couldn't hope to match.

Emperor. Emperor. The word tickled in the back of the people's minds. They served an Emperor . . . didn't they? A great Emperor, who had protected them all.

The people of the Azure Mountains bent their knees without a single drop of blood being spilled.

And thus, the area was added to the Empire. Tianlan Shan, the Azure Mountains. Or rather, the officials fixed the characters for the province's name. The character for mountain and hill were corrected. Shan *was the spoken word for both, so perhaps the weaklings that had named their province had used the wrong character by mistake?*

They were now the Azure Hills, because there were no mountains here.

As abruptly as it began, it ended. Reality snapped back into place. The old woman's hand dropped, and an expression returned to her face. She panted heavily, her face locked in a frown.

Then she spat to the side.

Bi De, shaken by the sudden vision, steadied himself before speaking to the old seer. "Grandmother?"

". . . happens sometimes," she grunted, shaking her head. The cat on her lap nuzzled against her, while the goat sat back down and started chewing again, the action grinding and almost *violent*-looking. "Now . . . you were just leaving, yes?"

Bi De bowed his head. "Yes. I could ask the Healing Sage, if you require assistance . . . ?"

"It's fine, boy. Now out! Out! Shoo! Or I'll be having chicken soup for dinner!" the old woman scolded, making wild gestures with her hands, getting more energetic with each passing moment.

Bi De smiled and bowed to her. However, his departure was interrupted again, this time by a knock on the door.

The crone's entire body twitched, and a massive grin stole across her features.

"Oho? It's time," she muttered. She quickly stood and straightened out her dress, before she stomped over to the door and wrenched it open, gazing at a man on the other side. He was old and bald, with thin limbs and liver spots. The man had one hand behind his back, and his face was locked into a frown.

It was the same man that the crone had gotten Bi De to scare as payment for her map, all those months ago.

"Oh! If it isn't Bald Shu, darkening my doorstep!" she said with a sneer, surreptitiously reaching for a rather old and soft-looking root vegetable beside her door.

"Hag. Today was the final straw. I'm going to have to do something that I've been thinking of doing for a *long* while," the man announced, his voice surprisingly strong compared to his appearance.

The crone's lips twisted into a grin.

"Oh? And what *are* you here to do, Shu?" the old woman leered.

The man set his shoulders and drew himself up to his full height . . . which was the exact same size as the old woman in front of him.

"You wretched woman! You live on your own, with no sons or daughters to take care of you! No wonder you act this way! So! Take this as a declaration of my intent!"

The crone's smile had grown as she watched him shout. Until the man suddenly dropped to a knee, smoothly pulling a bouquet of snowblossom flowers hidden behind his back. The beautiful, icy blooms looked like snowflakes. "If no one will take care of this spirited woman, then I will!"

The woman's jaw dropped open. She stared, utterly dumbfounded at the kneeling man . . . but there was no disguising the flush that crept up her cheeks.

"You—you?!" she stammered as her hands rose, almost unbidden, to take the flowers.

For a brief moment, the crone seemed almost *young*.

"Hmph! I'll meet you tomorrow, woman! And make a respectable lady out of you yet!"

With that, the man stood and turned on his heel, beginning his march back towards his house.

The old woman staggered back into her house, her face aflame.

"Wha? How . . . he wasn't supposed to—" the woman mumbled, before her face went completely red. "You old bastard! *Me,* needing to be taken care of?! Needing to be respectable?! Tell that to yourself!" she shrieked.

The mushy tuber in her hand sailed out the open door towards the marching man—and missed completely. It looked like the old woman had tried to lead the shot . . . and the man hadn't gone in the direction she had predicted.

The man frowned at her. "You dare?" he asked, crouching down and collecting snow in his hands, while muttering something about her courting death.

The old woman cursed, then immediately stepped out into the snow to do the same.

Bi De watched, dumbfounded, as two elders began a childish scuffle.

For some reason, it looked like the old woman was purposefully stepping into some of the projectiles, yet judging by her cursing it was *completely* unintentional.

Bi De watched for a moment longer.

"They complement each other quite well, do they not?" he asked the old tomcat.

The cat had a smirk that looked entirely too familiar . . . before he was once again, just an old cat.

CHAPTER 43

REJECTION

Bi De hopped across the rooftops of Verdant Hill, heading towards the palace in the center. While he was quite satisfied with what he had learned . . . his smile was not from that. He snorted to himself at the shouts of outrage and cursing that still drifted up from the streets, as well as the shrieks of children.

Bi De had just been leaving, after watching the fight rage for a moment, when he'd witnessed a shift in the balance of power.

Grandmother, her good eye rolling, had offered a child who had shown up to watch the battle a goat ride if he intervened in her behalf against "the bald one."

The child had obliged.

The escalation had prompted Bald Shu to offer sweets in retaliation to a pair of brothers who had been passing by.

Now there was a miniature war in the streets, as snow flew every which way and dragged more and more people into the chaos.

Chuckling, Bi De reached his destination, landing on the Grand Coop of the Lord Magistrate. Before, this had been the biggest building he had ever known.

Now he knew how small it really was.

He had all the answers that he had sought, by coming to the crone. Yet instead of a puzzle completed . . . it only revealed a larger puzzle to solve later.

He had been given a map . . . and now through a series of events, a spirit thought he was to be the Master of the Azure Hills.

And yet the task was one that Bi De thought could not be completed. Apologise to Tianlan? He would convey the message to her as soon as he was able. Repair and protect her? To his dying breath.

Reform an empire?

He did have to admit that something deep within him found the idea appealing. To have an entire province as his flock. To rouse them in the morning and protect them from the foxes and the wolves. It was in his nature. He was a rooster, the greeter of the sun . . . and it was his duty to protect and lead.

He was interested, as well, in the lessons Shenguashi would see fit to impart on ruling and politics. The subject matter, whenever his Great Master discussed it with Disciple Xiulan, was most intriguing.

But . . . did he really want to *rule*?

No. No he did not.

But the spirit had been unstable. Extremely unstable. Politely refusing was likely to damage its essence, as its purpose for existing would remain unfulfilled. He needed a good reason for *why* he could not become some manner of Emperor.

With a sigh, he looked down at the giant coop again. The giant that was now small.

He mulled over what he was going to speak to it about.

□

Deep in the depths of a crystal, the spirit that was given the name Shenguashi took stock of itself.

A new Lord and Master. Its purpose would be fulfilled. A sense of *rightness* formed over the construct.

But . . . there were problems to be attended to as well.

The spirit knew it had been in stasis for a long, *long* time. Asleep, to prevent any degradation of itself . . . yet it appeared that those measures had not proved wholly effective. There was corruption in its bits of "self." Like some other being had been stored beside it. Entire swathes of time were missing.

Missing missing missing—was it missing anything important?! Would it fail in being a teacher? Would it fail in its duty—

The spirit shuddered when it felt something flicker within it, and the sudden tide of emotion stopped.

It was troubling, the missing time. It had no idea how many years had passed. But it was nothing to be truly *worried* about. Additionally, different parts of its matrix were still activating.

The time was irrelevant. The time that had passed outside was immaterial. All that mattered was the present, and that its maker's will be done in the present.

Even Shenguashi's new Lord and Master, the heir to a glorious, prosperous, and beautiful Empire was . . . well, a *chicken*.

It was not ideal. *Not ideal, not idealnotidelnotideal—*

But it had to teach anyway.

Teach! Make Emperor! Command of Creator! Purpose!

But it was fine. It was going to be fine. Nothing to worry about. The rooster was noble. A true Lord!

And Spirit Beasts could turn into humans, anyway. Many chose not to, preferring their own forms over being human. However, the noble rooster would surely see the wisdom in having a form better suited to ruling.

The spirit shuddered.

It shook itself . . . and then there was a feeling. Another consciousness suffused the crystal.

Its Lord, its Master had returned.

Its purpose was available.

The spirit's matrix shuddered.

"Young Master!" Shenguashi shouted eagerly as it manifested before Bi De. "Greetings, Young Master. This one has been preparing for your arrival! I trust you have given your purpose all due consideration!"

The spirit saw the resolution in the rooster's eyes. It was true! He had the bearing of an Emperor.

The rooster took a breath. "I must apologise, Spirit, but this one cannot become Emperor of the Azure Hills."

"Excellent, we can begin—" The words finished processing. The spirit shuddered.

That . . . wasn't right. It wasn't right it wasn't right it wasn't right—

Rejection. Rejection. Rejection. *It would not be able to complete its purpose.*

Why? Why the rejection?!

"Is this about your form? Worry not! You can turn into a human! Though you are indeed a magnificent specimen, it is no issue!" Shenguashi tried, its Qi bubbling erratically even as it babbled to stall for time to think.

The rooster shook his head. "It is not my form. There are several reasons. Firstly, I have meditated upon what I have seen in your creator's crystal. One reason for the fall of these hills was that there was a sole pillar holding it up. They were strong, but if that pillar falls, then so too does the rest. This Bi De would request that, instead of myself being the sole inheritor of your Master's will . . . that the august spirit before me teaches several people in the ways to make this land prosper. That way, if something unexpected happens, not all will be lost."

That . . . that was actually a good idea. The rooster had no heir yet, so teaching another would be a wise idea! Teaching many would be even better. Even now, the rooster proved his forethought! But refusing outright to be Emperor?

The spirit's matrix spasmed.

That was *not* ideal. But the rooster was offering to introduce Shenguashi to others!

That *was* ideal!

If the *rooster* refused to be Emperor . . . but still wished to learn. It matched all the criteria of Shenguashi's creator.

In time, the rooster would come around! It was fate! To follow the request of a future Emperor while trying to convince that same person to be an Emperor was a quest most ideal! Two tasks done at once!

The spirit would say two birds, one stone, but ah . . . that seemed . . . less than ideal.

"The second reason, however, is by far the more pressing issue, on why *none* can become Emperor of the Azure Hills. What do you know of the Crimson Phoenix Empire?" the rooster asked.

The name did not register for Shenguashi. "A rival state from the Great Beyond?"

The rooster grimaced, then breathed out silver light.

A map formed from nothingness. The Azure Mountains, as seen from above. Shenguashi grimaced, his creator's pain a phantom upon seeing the broken land. Pale Moon Lake. The Grass Sea. It was where the most people had lived—and consequently, the areas most devastated by the fall.

"This is the map I have of the Azure Hills."

"The Azure *Hills*?" Shenguashi asked.

"Yes. And this . . . this is a map of the Crimson Phoenix Empire."

The map, to Shenguashi's surprise, started *expanding*.

There were other lands beside the Azure Mountains. That much was known for certain. The Great Beyond was surely home to them.

But Shenguashi was unprepared for the extent of things, as borders formed and names swam into existence. The Howling Fang Mountains. Yellow Rock Plateau. Green Stone Forest. Raging Waterfall Gorge.

The spirit could only stare at these places . . . and yet the map *kept expanding*. Phoenix's Rest Plains. The Alabaster Karsts. The Goldgrass Steppes. Soaring Heaven Archipelago. Storm Breaker Coast. Forge Bellow Volcano. Seeping Water Swamp. The Amethyst Caverns. The Sapphire Strand—

It just kept growing, and *growing*, more and more and more names appearing. Rolling Dune Desert. Emerald Leaf Jungle. Poison Fog Valley.

The map expanded until it once more touched the ocean, forming a complete landmass.

It utterly *dwarfed* Shenguashi's known world. It expanded east, west, and south, to the extent that it could hold over *fifty* Azure Mountains within it.

The spirit's matrix buzzed.

"And this . . . this all is the Crimson Phoenix Empire?" Shenguashi whispered.

"Every province upon this map is a part of the Empire, *including* the Azure Hills. And it has been this way for thousands of years." The rooster before him let out a breath. "It is enormous, is it not?"

The world of Shenguashi's Master . . . was so very, *very* small.

Something in the spirit's body spasmed. It went through a hundred thousand scenarios, provided by its Lord. It went over rebelling against another unjust ruler. It spoke of uniting the hills.

But this? This big? This many enemies?! This many, which would each likely fight against the Azure Mountains' ascendancy?

All at once, everything stilled. The corroded parts of its matrix pulsed.

Oh. Of course there could be an Emperor of the Azure.

They just *also* had to be the Emperor of the Crimson Phoenix Empire.

The bubbling panic faded.

"Your servant sees, Bi De. That is indeed a problem. But this one has no objections to your current plan. I wish to meet those who would see this land prosper!"

The rooster blinked, clearly shocked, but a tentative smile overcame his face.

"I see. Thank you for being so understanding. I shall go and call my Master. He wishes to meet you as well and listen to some of this tale."

With that, the rooster disappeared from the crystal.

Shenguashi turned to the map.

Overthrow an Emperor, and install a new one.

That was how his Lord became Emperor.

The spirit would most certainly have to learn more, but it had waited for thousands of years. A few more wouldn't hurt!

Bi De reentered the crystal, along with another. Another, that made Shenguashi's essence thrum.

"May I introduce my Great Master. Rou Jin," the rooster announced. The man, who was filled with Golden Light. The light of Tianlan. The Master of the Earth.

The spirit stared in awe. Its ancient matrix activated, forcing out a question.

"Will you be the Emperor?"

The man stared directly at Shenguashi.

"Hell nah," he replied.

CHAPTER 44

CONTINUE

What changes with a massive revelation about the past? What changes once you see the entire sordid story, laid out with all its warts? When the damage that persisted to this day finally comes to light?

Not much.

Oh, the tale was interesting, all the sound and thunder. Drama and terrible cost. It would make a good opera. Any scholar or writer from the Before would have gone full Xianxia for something like the memory crystal if they'd known it held this kind of story.

And it had been amazing to see the past of the Azure Hills.

I guess I should have felt something more than sadness and sympathy for the dead. Something stronger, like Xiulan and Big D did, but I was too far removed from it. I had no real strong feelings about it, other than sorrow for Tianlan. If I were someone else, I might have tried to rush out to fulfill a dying man's wish, or tried waking up the sleeping Tianlan so I could fix everything *today*.

But I was a farmer, a husband, and a soon-to-be father.

I had chores to do.

I left Big D to show people the crystal and went about my day. The animals who were still *animals* needed to be taken care of. They needed to be fed and watered and let out from their barns into the winter wonderland that was my home.

I smiled as I watched our three balls of fluff—Afro, Pompom, and Fuzzy—bounce around the property, like snowballs themselves. Two cows and their calves followed them, breaking into a run and ploughing through the snow, jumping and kicking like overexcited puppies.

Modern wisdom said to keep them in the warm barn for the winter . . . but the animals were literally bred for the cold weather up here. The cows had grown in shaggy winter coats and the sheep were decidedly plump; they could take a little winter weather.

Besides, being cooped up was no way to live.

The sheep in particular were in a good mood today, and they looked truly magnificent. Their fleece had come in thick with strong, crimped locks, and I knew we would be getting some high-quality fiber come spring. At least I didn't have to find a seller for all this stuff. We'd be using it all up ourselves. Or rather, my wife would be using it all.

Seriously, if she were suddenly transported to the Before like I was taken here, she could make a living as a high-end tailor. Meimei didn't think there was anything really special about the fact that she could make clothes that wouldn't be out of place in a magazine. It was a minor point of pride, but, in her words:

"*Every* woman should be able to do this much."

Which, to be honest, I supposed was true from her point of view. *Every* lady from Hong Yaowu knew how to make and mend clothes. Most from Verdant Hill could too. It was just one of those things that people had to do. You could rarely afford to just go out and buy clothing, so you had to make it yourself.

And it wasn't purely a "girls" thing either. Gou and Yun knew how to sew patches, even if they preferred to get Meimei to do it because her stitches were cleaner.

I turned my attention to the cows next, as they started to root around in the snow too. I smiled at the beasts, who played with their calves. They had grown up fast, and the ladies were going to stop giving milk soon . . . but our experiments in sterilization and pasteurization had borne fruit. A quick shock with Meimei's Qi, and as long as it was kept cold . . . well, we hadn't found an expiration date yet.

I still had a small bottle from the day we'd first tried it, at the beginning of spring. It was starting to taste a bit herby, but it was still good to drink and cook with.

Even the stuff *without* Meimei's Qi pumped into it, just heated and primitively bottled, lasted for two weeks.

The materials science wasn't quite up to par to make cans just yet, but it would help out in preserving things in Hong Yaowu.

Still, at the rate we were going through the stuff I would probably need a couple more cows. My little family kept growing, and the farm needed to grow as well, if I wanted to keep up.

And if any of them became sentient . . . then, well . . .

Don't be a dick, try to help them with their problems, and treat them like oddly shaped humans. No murderous Spirit Beasts would be raised here, no sir! I had read too many stories about AI rebellions to say no if anybody asked me if they had a soul.

I would like to think that I was rather a dab hand at this whole process of accidental sapience.

Even if it never got any less stressful.

Though . . . it was kind of weird. In Xiaoshi's time, there was a distinction between Spirit Beasts who helped humans, and were kind of people, and Demon Beasts, who acted more like the Spirit Beasts I was more used to.

I wonder what had changed?

Had demons corrupted them somehow? Were the Spirit Beasts just different back then? Or had cultivators gotten a bit too greedy and now every Spirit Beast just attacked most people on sight out of some kind of self-preservation instinct?

I sighed and shook my head. I just didn't know enough. I looked back up and snorted at the sight that greeted me. Chunky had come to watch over the cows and sheep . . . and he had a new item, courtesy of Gou Ren, strapped to his back.

The mobile chicken coop's exterior was modeled after a traditional inn, and the tenants could *technically* fit Plato's definition of man if they were plucked. Diogenes was nuts, but he had a great sense of humor.

The chickens were clucking up a storm from their new mobile home. I had long since learned the different meanings behind their little noises. They were making the "happy/excited" clucks as they poked their heads out from the little doors and stood upon the rooftop. Some were on Chunky's mane, teasing out hairs to line their nests, and a particularly brave one perched on Chunky's left tusk, looking like a captain on the bow of a ship as the snow broke around the boar like waves.

Chunky trundled forward, *oinked* at the other animals, and turned his head to the forest. It was a good idea. I had a feeling that there were going to be some nasty winds soon. Not enough to force everybody back inside . . . but still unpleasant.

The animals fell in behind him quickly, and Chunky continued onwards. I smiled and waved to my Chunky boy, and he nodded back, his eyes crinkling.

As he walked past the house on his way to the bridge, I began to chuckle.

Ha, a wandering inn.

My mood improved, I went back into the barn, took off the nice coat Meimei had gotten me, and grabbed my handy shovel to muck the stalls. I have to admit, with the beautifully carved handle Tigu and Washy had given me it almost felt like a sin to actually *use* it instead of hanging it up like an art piece on the wall.

But they had made it for me to use, and use it I would. The shovel just felt *right* in my hand. Better than any other haft I had ever held.

The stalls didn't need much mucking, the feed levels were good, and there were no vermin that I could see. There was an owl in the rafters, but I left her to her sleep.

After that, I set down some fresh straw, cleaned off the shovel, and wandered back out into the cold. I pulled my red hat down a little; I hadn't gotten dirty, so I put the jacket back on.

I then started my rounds with the rest of the farm, checking over the fence myself and looking for anything amiss. I trusted Big D and everybody else to report anything . . . but it was just my way. To wander, think, and look at my home for myself. Miantiao and Yin were both in the greenhouse, the rabbit helping heat the room and tending the plants, while the snake just liked the warmth.

When I got to the drop hammer, it was pounding away at something—Gou Ren had begun working on another project with Bowu and Huo Ten.

The rest of the farm was quiet, and there was nobody else really out today. So I simply wandered and my mind wandered with me. My Qi, out of habit, started to saturate the ground.

I could feel it: the connection to Tianlan. With our intertwined pathways, it took a bit to distinguish between the Earth Spirit and myself.

At least I finally knew *why* I was so strong. It wasn't all my own power, after all. Though . . . I wondered why she hadn't really *told* me. Or interacted with me outside those strange, half-remembered dreams that were feeling less and less like dreams the more I thought about them.

Was it fear? Was it some sort of trauma, that she thought I would hurt her if I knew about her, like she thought Xiaoshi had hurt her? In the memory of the end, the man had tried to contact her, to no avail; he had known that she was still alive in some form.

Those were all questions for later. For now . . . she was asleep, and hopefully having good dreams.

I sighed again and my lips quirked into a smile. Turns out farming really *was* some crazy cultivation method. Who knew?

I let my Qi flow into the earth until I felt like I was empty.

Not for power. Not for her strength, even though I might need it in the coming years. But because it was the right thing to do.

And then I turned around and wandered back home.

→

What hit me every time I got back to the house after being out for a while was the smell.

I could never describe it right; it just smelled like home. The spices. The wood planks. The fire of the hearth. The *people*.

It never failed to put me at ease.

I checked in on Big D and Xiulan, their hands touching the crystal and their eyes closed. They weren't in any trouble, so I continued into the main room.

There, Meimei and the girls were working on cloth together, all gathered around the loom and taking turns as they performed the time-honoured tradition of shooting the shit, while Meimei taught everybody how to use the machine properly.

I guess the loom was kind of like the ancient version of a women's club. Xianghua, Peppa, Rizzo, and Tigu were all talking and giggling.

Judging by Tigu's personality, a person could be forgiven for thinking that she would rebel against learning to sew or do other "womanly things," but Tigu, being Tigu, defied expectations like a true cultivator, as the tomboy loved sitting beside Meimei and helping her weave.

I left them to it and instead wandered over to the table where Gou Ren, Yun Ren, Bowu, and Huo Ten were sitting looking over a piece of paper. Bowu and

Gou Ren had finished whatever they had been working on earlier when I was outside doing my rounds. They had what looked like a hand-pushed machine next to them, and one of them was *very* familiar.

"An inter-row tiller?" I asked, staring at it. It was right from my drawings, the machine that was used to agitate and aerate the soil in between rice rows.

Gou Ren perked up at the comment. "Yeah, Bowu managed to get the axle right, and Huo Ten got us the ore. It needs a few more tests . . . but I think we can work with this. It doesn't break down a quarter as much as the other one we made!"

I raised an eyebrow, impressed. They had seen a few shitty drawings, heard a few half-baked ideas . . . and then managed to form something coherent from it.

"This is *really* impressive, guys," I said, looking things over and giving Bowu's hair a ruffle. He beamed, and Gou Ren and Huo Ten exchanged high fives. Yun Ren just nodded and continued to look at the paper on the table, which was an aerial recording of Hong Yaowu that had been drawn on and annotated.

"Planning the fields for next year?" I asked, taking a closer look. Gou Ren *would* be teaching the people of Hong Yaowu my farming methods next year . . .

Yun Ren chuckled, looking up from the proposed alterations with a skeptical brow raised. Nezan the fox was looking on, his lips twisted with amusement. "He thinks himself an Emperor, with all these changes. Look at this, he wants to practically redesign the entire village!"

Gou Ren looked embarrassed. "Hey, it was just a couple of ideas . . ." he grumbled.

I looked closer. Yeah, it was drastic, but as far as I could see it was well-designed . . . just overly ambitious.

"I'll grab my own notes. Yun, could you make another one of these?" I asked him, and he gave me a mock salute.

We spent a good few hours poring over that map, planning fields and irrigation ditches. I had a few more pieces of equipment, like the seed drill, that Bowu was looking at with interest.

Eventually Chunky came in, and Washy appeared from where he had been napping under the ice.

Which led to another discussion, this one about diverting a river for the improvements to irrigation, which I was a bit leery of. I'd read too many tales of fucking up the area downstream, but it could have merit.

Eventually, though, things started disbanding as we all started to get ready for dinner.

I was just about to get Xiulan and Big D when they walked into the room. Xiulan was rubbing her forehead and seeming vaguely troubled.

"You okay, Lanlan?" I asked her.

The woman looked up at me, her mouth drawn into a line.

"The spirit asked me if *I* would become the Emperor," she said, sounding befuddled.

"Oh?" I asked.

"Naturally, I refused," she replied. "I do not know if I trust this spirit."

I snorted and shook my head.

That was how the day ended.

Earth-shaking revelations didn't have to change things right away . . . or at all, really.

Besides, the New Year was nearly upon us . . . as was the party in Verdant Hill.

CHAPTER 45

TRUST

Liu Xianghua allowed her eyes to rove around the little procession; she was part of a small caravan. They had set out from Fa Ram yesterday, to travel to Verdant Hill for the New Year festivities that would be taking place there. In doing so, they had stopped off at Hong Yaowu, since most of the village was also heading in the same direction. The cultivators of Fa Ram had aided the villagers in packing their goods, while Chun Ke and Master Jin had forged ahead to clear the road of snow. The mortals were chattering among themselves as they travelled along the cleared road, their mood light and festive.

Xianghua herself sat in a cart as it rumbled down the road, leaning against Gou Ren's arm. Her Gou was dozing lightly in his seat. Xianghua was quite excited. The New Year had once been the most consistent time she had to sneak off and spend time with Bowu . . . at least until the previous two years, when she had started being called to meetings by the Elders and her father.

Which meant sitting around and pouring the old bastards drinks while they talked in circles and reminisced. *Two damn years* she'd had to sit through that, and she was looking forward to the fact that this year was a return to form: she and her brother, observing festivities and eating entirely too many sweet pastries.

Though this year, she would have more than just herself and her brother.

"We're makin' good time, eh?" Gou Ren's mother Hu Li asked in that thick accent of hers from the other end of the cart. She was hanging onto the side like she were a much-younger woman, her eyes flitting around the road.

"Yeah. Our boys did good work," Ten Ren said with obvious pride, a soft smile on his monkeylike face. Both the foxlike woman and monkeylike man grinned at each other. One was vulpine and animated, the other amused with a hit of mischievousness. Their faces were weatherbeaten and starting to get wrinkles. They had blemishes and scars, the complete opposites of Xianghua's own parents . . . and yet to her they were superior in every way.

Xianghua smiled down at the dress she was wearing. A gift from Hu Li—one that the woman had inherited from her own mother. It fit surprisingly well, as did the rest of Xianghua's current attire.

"Feathers, or something more traditional?" Mother Hu Li had asked, as she held up baubles to be woven into Xianghua's hair. Wearing the trappings of

Mother Hu Li's tribe would have made the vein in her father's head bulge. In times past, she might have done it to spite him, but it was important to Hu Li, and it made her happy, so Xianghua had agreed.

"Feathers are the superior option," she had stated simply, and the wonderful woman beamed at her.

Ten Ren, while she had been trying on the dress, had taken his own sons and Bowu out hunting. The man was quieter than his talkative wife, content to simply sit and listen until the time came when he could crack a joke.

The boys had returned late that evening, each with a spectacular haul . . . including Bowu. Her little brother had trekked through the forest all day hunting with Father Ten Ren. Bowu had proudly shown off the rabbit he had taken: a single, lonely hare. But Ten Ren had nodded, praised the catch, and shown the boy how to butcher it. That was his way—quietly showing, and then letting one figure things out on their own.

When Bowu had accidentally punctured one of the organs, instead of striking the boy for his failure, Ten Ren laughed it off. He ruffled the bewildered Young Master's hair with pride and earned a grin in response that lit up like the sun.

Xianghua watched the two of them, having politely declined Ten Ren's offer to join Bowu's lesson. She'd had her own time one on one with Father Ten Ren, and her brother needed some of his own moments with just the two of them.

Speaking of her brother, at that moment he was jogging beside the caravan while talking to the Young Chief Xian. With easy strides belying muscles made for speed, volunteering to fetch and deliver items was his excuse to break into a sprint. Taking on every opportunity to move these days, it seemed her brother was making up for lost time.

It was . . . good.

Liu Xianghua was content. The warm, pleasant feeling in her chest had persisted for months and made the world just seem brighter. She did not need to concentrate to smile these days; she needed to concentrate to erase the ever-present slight upturn of her lips.

Everything was just . . . the best it had been in a long time. Her brother had been healed, even if he still was not a cultivator. She'd learned new things! Even if most of them were mortal in nature, sublime arts like Ha Qi were certainly great pearls. She'd gotten to spend time with Xiulan and Tigu. Both of them were always eager for a spar that didn't have the underlying *tension*; she was free from the worry of "What if somebody takes this too far?"

Her father would have hated every moment. Her mother too. She was "slacking." She was not maintaining her fighting spirit. And the biggest sin of all, *she was acting like a mortal.*

Her father would have slapped her until she couldn't stand up anymore.

And yet, even as she did all these things, these actions that would supposedly diminish her power and make her lesser . . . she grew.

She was not like Xiulan, a virulent weed that sprouted and grasped at the sun. Her growth was slower. But delicious, Qi-packed food, powerful sparring partners, and her own feelings of absolute peace had proved perfect for her cultivation.

Like a rising river, she had ascended to the Fifth Stage of the Initiate's Realm and was now brushing against the Profound. Her brother had guaranteed her a new, more powerful engine within the New Year, one that, in his words, would "utterly eclipse those other pieces of junk."

Xianghua let out a breath as she turned her eyes to the sky.

For all of this, the Sect would have lavished attention upon them and poured resources into their development.

Here . . . they were rewarded with *trust*.

Her own Sect was at times leery of her motivations, because of her repeated defiance of her father's will. Her father hadn't trusted her at all . . . though he *had* been right to suspect her.

But here? Bi De had shown her the crystal and the ancient arts of her ancestors within, expecting nothing in return.

The noble blood of a dragon, however weak and diluted, flowed within their veins. She had knowledge that would upend the entire Azure Hills . . . and it had been given to her freely.

She was still processing the information . . . but it was absolute proof, at least, that her ancestors had been noble; they had willingly fought against the monster that had been the Azure Emperor. Then they had housed thousands of refugees during the demonic incursion. Their legacy and domain . . . it was something *worth* preserving.

"Hey! Damp Pond!" Tigu's voice startled Xianghua out of her introspection. The caravan had rolled to a stop at a small clearing. "Help us cook lunch!"

Xianghua snorted at the demand.

"Very well! Thank me for my benevolence!" she called after Tigu, who responded with a rude gesture.

Xianghua shook her head and untangled herself from Gou. She would have her work cut out for her, whipping her Sect back into shape.

But for now? For the next week?

She turned and met Gou Ren's eyes. The man was smiling at her.

This week was a festival. Serious planning would begin after it.

□

"And . . . well, that's everything, Teacher," Jin said, sitting across from the Lord Magistrate.

The Lord Magistrate kept his face carefully neutral, but internally he was as calm as a sailor in a maelstrom, with about the same amount of swearing. He fought a twitch across his brow, staring ahead with serenity.

It had almost been a good day.

It had started well enough; the New Year's Festival was scheduled to start the following day. Everything was ready and today was supposed to be a time of relaxation, for the most part. He had completed all the planning over a year ago, and the people he had doing the festival setup had become exceedingly efficient at their jobs, needing little supervision.

Of course, he would have to be available for any last-minute additions, changes, or problems, but for the most part he had been looking forward to overseeing the last of the preparations and enjoying the crisp winter air as his plans came seamlessly to fruition.

Instead, like a storm in a cloudless sky, Rou Jin had shown up, asking for assistance with a *delicate* political matter.

His mood had soured, but he was still quite pleased that the young man had sought his counsel.

Indeed, it was only after his wife had said something that the Lord Magistrate really started to warm up to the idea.

"My darling, think of it this way," she had said, looking down at him reproachfully from where he was bound to the bed. "The de facto Master of the Azure Hills comes to you, and you alone, and says, 'Help me, teacher!'"

Indeed it *was* a very fine way of looking at things. He was held in such esteem that a powerful cultivator looked to the Lord Magistrate for approval!

It did also help that Jin was quite a quick learner, attentive, and held on to his every word.

So the Lord Magistrate had been mollified and—he'd thought—prepared for any "delicate diplomatic incident" that the young man could bring.

Naturally, the heavens had seen his hubris and decided to punish him for it.

As retribution, he'd gotten a rather fantastical story about a memory crystal, an ancient empire, the secrets of the past and what to do with them, and several of Jin's own ideas.

Why? Just . . . why?

Now all the Lord Magistrate could do was sit back in his chair.

His stomach began to churn unpleasantly . . . until he was drawn back out of his gloomy thoughts by the sight of Jin's expectant face waiting for his judgement. For the Lord Magistrate of the Verdant Hill to weigh in and provide a solution to the possible destruction of the Azure Hills.

He took a deep breath and forced down the feeling of utter despair and *really* thought about what was happening.

The formation that the demon had used was effectively destroyed, from what Jin had said. It had been thousands of years since then . . . and Jin had contingencies if there were demons involved—namely, contacting the Cloudy Sword Sect itself if things proved dire.

He also had an idea of what to do with the knowledge, an idea that would hopefully stop any and all cultivators from coming and bothering him by giving them bait *elsewhere.*

The Lord Magistrate felt his shoulders start to unclench.

Because . . . really, it actually seemed that things were already well in hand? The only reason why Jin was involving him was because the young man trusted his judgement . . . and knew that the Lord Magistrate would tell him if he found anything truly wrong with the ideas presented.

He thought about it further.

It was not the solution the Lord Magistrate would have chosen; he would have likely buried the damn thing and told not a soul. But giving the knowledge of Sect techniques away while keeping most of the past a secret—or at least Tianlan's status as an Earth Spirit, to keep people from bothering her—was viable, if they figured out how to copy the information out of the crystal.

Jin *did* have a plan. And though there was some risk . . . the outcome might be desirable.

Of course, when cultivators were involved, there was *always* the chance for things to go explosively wrong.

But for now . . .

"I believe your ideas are feasible," the Lord Magistrate finally said. "I commend your thinking on this matter, my student."

Jin let out a small breath, then smiled. "I thought it would be all right. I mean, the last thing I want is a war or something to break out. What kind of *idiot* would want to be Emperor of a field of ashes?"

The Lord Magistrate knew *several,* from his time in Pale Moon Lake City, though he couldn't help but smile at the younger man's grumbling.

"Indeed. At the moment, there is no time limit. A few trustworthy people know of this crystal. You hold all of the advantages, and can thus take your time deciding on a course of action. Careful planning and preparation is the key for any battle—on the field, or with words. I shall meditate further upon this myself. I'll need at least a week to consider the options we have before us, but there are no glaring issues that I can see with what we have discussed."

"Thank you for your insight, teacher," Jin said formally, clasping his hands together. Some more of the tension bled out of the room, the gesture signifying the end of the time where they were master and student. "Sorry to spring this on you so soon before the festival."

The Lord Magistrate waved it off. "I shall not hold it against you, Jin. Better to address problems rather than let them ferment into disaster."

"Well. Now that that's out of the way . . ." Jin bent, taking up a package from beside him.

"More syrup?" The Lord Magistrate eyed the jar Jin freed from the paper.

Jin shook his head.

"Spirits, this time. Mead, and a few of the other distillations. Also this . . ."

The Lord Magistrate smiled at the Seven Fragrance Jewel herbs.

"Thank you for your generosity, Jin. You do me much honour."

The young man scratched at his cheek.

"You've helped me out a lot. It's the least I could do—though there is one more thing!" the man said, reaching into his pack. "This is for your wife. Meimei said she used this to help with her damaged senses?" The Lord Magistrate froze at the lengths of soft, supple rope, crafted by a cultivator, along with the blindfold. He nearly choked, his eyes darting back up. Only to meet the pure, guileless smile of Rou Jin.

"Thank you. We both appreciate your continued concern for her health," he said, forcing a smile.

"I'll see you later, teacher. If you need anything, just give me a call!"

Not so long ago, those words would have sounded mocking.

Now the Lord Magistrate just nodded.

"Enjoy the festival, Rou Jin."

The young man stood and left the Lord Magistrate alone with his thoughts.

History from thousands of years ago, eh? He always did enjoy reading about the Scholar-Generals . . .

He had no use for the techniques, but perhaps they would permit him to see some of the legal documentation stored in the crystal.

CHAPTER 46

RING IN THE NEW YEAR PART 1: THE BOYS

The town of Verdant Hill was . . . quaint. That was all Bowu could really say about it. He had been to Grass Sea City during the New Year. The fireworks had blocked out the sky and the entire city glowed from the lanterns.

Yet even though it was quaint, it was still enjoyable.

"And that's where we beetle fight!" Xian whispered conspiratorially, pointing at a side alley that had a log post turned sideways at the end of it.

Bowu gave a single, serious nod at the alleyway.

"Don't worry. I won't tell Auntie," he whispered, and Xian's grin got wider as they set out into the town once more, Xian making good on his promise to show Bowu around. At that moment, everybody else was at the Zhuge Compound with Mister Zhuge and Big Sis Meihua.

Bowu's face flushed and he scratched his cheek.

The woman had heard that her father was teaching him how to blacksmith . . . and had grabbed Bowu and showered him with kisses.

And then she'd told his sister *to her face* that she was stealing him and Bowu was *her* little brother now.

Xianghua clearly hadn't known whether to be angry or impressed at the audacity of the mortal woman, but she had taken the declaration seriously and ended up in an hour-long argument with the woman about who was the superior sister between them.

Well, it had been an hour before Bowu decided to leave. They had gotten the tea out and were still arguing when he left with Xian—Tigu, Ri Zu, and Wa Shi had just sat down to watch.

And it wasn't like he minded hanging out with Xian. The fact that Auntie Meiling trusted him to make sure they stayed out of trouble was something he had never before experienced.

He had always been the one that had to be looked after, or had wound up pushed to the side. Or worse, pitied like he was incapable of completing any basic task.

But now *he* was the reliable big brother.

It was a nice feeling.

They wandered around town, Xian pulling him along at a pace that would have sent Bowu tumbling to the ground just a few months ago, yet now he kept up with indulgent ease.

Until a man stepped out into their path as they ducked down a side street to avoid the stalls being set up.

Xian slammed into his legs, and there was a *crack* and a splatter as the man dropped his wine bottle.

"Haaaa? Watch where yer goin, brat!" the drunk man snarled.

Bowu narrowed his eyes at the inebriated, belligerent man. *He* had stepped into *Xian's* path.

"Ah. I'm sorry, sir," Xian said, scratching at the back of his head. But the man just glared, his eyes hazy.

"Kids like yeh need a few smacks to straighten 'em out," the drunkard growled, and Bowu tensed. He might not have been a cultivator . . . but he had still been the Young Master of the Misty Lake Sect. He had been learning how to fight since he had learned how to walk.

One of the drunkard's friends made a sound of protest seeing his companion draw an arm back with an open hand. Little Xian looked shocked for a moment, before his own eyes narrowed, his body tensing for a dodge.

"Cease your wicked acts," a voice commanded, cutting through the sound of the alleyway. The offending fist was roughly grasped by somebody else.

The drunk whirled, coming face-to-face with two unnerving eyes and a beak.

Bowu at first thought some kind of Spirit Beast had wandered into town, but it turned out that the demonic head was simply a chicken mask. The person was wearing a wolf-fur vest and had a spear strapped across his back. The appearance rubbed at a memory—the attire was familiar for some reason. Beside him was a shaggy white puppy that was halfway to dog, its teeth bared and a low growl issuing from his throat.

The drunk paled and tried to pull his arm away, to no avail. The masked man didn't budge and Bowu realised this outlandishly dressed man—no teen, the proportions weren't right for him to be a man—was a cultivator.

A single push slammed the drunk into a wall hard enough to wind the sloshed bastard, and he slid gagging down the wall while the cultivator turned to face his equally soused companions. One of them stared incredulously at the bottle in his hand before pouring it on the ground with a newfound zeal for sober living.

"Begone," the boy commanded.

The drunk scrambled to his feet and disappeared along with his companions.

Once they were out of sight, the cultivator turned to the two boys and inclined his head slightly. "Are you both well?" he asked, his voice muffled by the mask.

Bowu glanced at Xian, who had a considering look on his face.

"We're fine! But . . . uh . . . are you the Torrent Rider?" Xian asked.

The cultivator's chest puffed up with pride, and Bowu realised exactly who this was. He had heard of the person in front of him before from Jin.

"Indeed, I am. I see my name has spread all the way to Verdant Hill!"

"Yeah! Big Sis told me about you. You're Bi De's student, aren'tcha?" Xian asked.

The boy wearing the chicken mask stepped backwards with shock. Reaching up and pulling the mask to the side, he revealed a young and boyish face, shock etched all over it.

"You know *Master*?!" he demanded, shocked.

"Yeah! He's here, I'll take you to him later. I'm showing Big Bro around town!"

"Ah . . . yes, please," the young man declared, bowing. "This one is Zhang Fei! It's a pleasure to meet both of you!"

The sudden switch from brash cultivator to polite young man got a snort out of Bowu.

"So . . . where are you from?" Bowu asked Fei. He remembered the story about torrent riding from Jin. It had sounded fun . . . and now, with his leg healed, he could actually try it.

Thus did they all venture into the town.

Fei turned out to be a pretty funny kid. He was a cultivator, true, but he was like Bro Gou Ren and his eyes started to sparkle when Xian started explaining the "awesome things" Bowu could make.

It was the start to a beautiful friendship. They met up with Bi De and the rest of the people at the Zhuge Compound and got to watch Fei show off his spear techniques. One thing led to another and Bowu ended up sparring with him for a bit.

The fight was close, but in this case experience trumped overpowering strength. Bowu managed to get him with a feint . . . yet instead of being upset that a mortal had managed to beat him, Fei had started earnestly asking Bowu for pointers.

It was weird . . . but it was nice. So they talked for a while, until the conversation drifted back to torrent riding. Unfortunately, it was the middle of winter, so Bowu wouldn't be able to try it for a while.

That was until Xian, grinning like Wa Shi with a new food to try, announced his idea.

Several hours later, all three of them and a fish were lined up in front of Jin. The man had his arms crossed over his chest, and his lips twitched as he struggled not to laugh.

The guard who was behind them was just as amused. The owner of the bathhouse? Not so much.

There was water *everywhere*.

↔

Zang Wei, known as "Loud Boy" to his friends, was deep in meditation. In his mind, he visualized a golden stove. The stove was broken, its shattered guts scattered and glinting in the blue light pouring endlessly from its jagged wounds. Zang went carefully, reuniting each piece with the whole, lessening the light's escape.

It was hard work, but it was going to be worth it. He could repair his cultivation. He *would* repair his cultivation.

He set one more piece of shattered stove, barely as big as a fingernail, into its place before letting out a breath and opening his eyes to a stone room.

He was getting close now. So *close*. He glanced around at the empty bottles, the Shrouded Mountain Sect's reparations going to good use.

Any day now . . .

His stomach rumbled, letting him know of the hours he'd already spent here today. This stone room had a surprising amount of Qi in it, which made it a prime spot to enact his repairs . . . but it was cold, damp, and out of the way.

He was just about to start for the door when it opened and a head peeked in. The woman on the other side had ragged but still lovingly repaired clothes. Her eyes widened on seeing Wei.

"Hey. You're up," Big Sis Minmin's deep voice carried easily over the din. A small smile tugged at the scar that continued onto her neck. She had incredibly curly hair and a glare that could scare the clouds off a mountain.

She was also the kindest and sweetest member of Rags's gang. She had a tray of food in her hands and was clearly just about to set it down for Wei.

"Yeah. I made good progress today. Thanks for bringing food for me, Big Sis." It still irked Wei that her voice was deeper than his, but he was still growing! It would deepen soon enough . . .

He hoped.

"I was just going to come out for today anyway."

Minmin nodded. "Everybody else is still eating . . . and the Boss is back. C'mon, there's room at the table."

Wei perked up at the mention of Rags, following the older woman back out and down the stone hallway of the Farrow Gang's honest-to-heaven *fortress*.

He had been absolutely gobsmacked when he had come out of the tunnel hidden in the side of a mountain. Rags had spoken so irreverently of their "hideout" that Zang Wei had expected a shack in a gloomy forest.

It looked almost like the design of the Dueling Peaks . . . but it had none of the interesting stuff in it. No moving doors or pulleys, and it had been long abandoned when Rags had first found it.

None of the interesting stuff, save for a series of pictograms carved into a wall that was the basis for Rags's fighting style.

Still, it was a nice place. Lots of rooms, and it was surprisingly clean. Though . . . that may have been due to Rags's other gang members.

Big Sis Minmin and Loud Boy pressed against the wall to avoid a group of rowdy youngsters before continuing into the hubbub of the main hall. Conversation and laughter enveloped them as they stepped out into the concourse.

Rags's gang was rather . . . different than Loud Boy had been expecting at first. It turned out all the people with him at the Dueling Peaks were the only ones who could actually fight.

People like Big Sis Minmin, Little Shou, Bro Kuang, and the Iron Head brothers.

The rest of the Farrow Gang? Kids, grannies, and grandpas.

The poor and the broken from Grass Sea City, led to a place of their own by a charismatic idiot.

Wei couldn't hate Rags for it. The fool couldn't read a single character before Wei had taught him how . . . But he was a friend and a good guy to his "gang."

And said friend was currently drinking his shitty, cheap booze as he lazed about at the head table, watching other people put up red decorations. Rags raised a hand in greeting . . . and Wei chucked him a piece of wood with several characters on it. Rags caught the missile, fumbling both the wood and his drink, not expecting it.

"Test time!" Wei stated cheerfully, sitting down beside his sworn brother. Minmin and the Iron Head brothers laughed as Rags let out a groan.

"You little shit! Seriously?!" he exclaimed. "It's the New Year, and I just got back from guarding another caravan!"

Wei ignored him and started into the food Minmin had gotten him, the woman letting out a throaty laugh that sounded *really* nice.

"Come on, what does it say?" Loud Boy demanded as Rags grumbled. Rags glared at the offending piece of wood, and then his face broke out into a massive smile.

"Ha, you little bastard. You thought you could get me with this! But—" Rags pulled out his own piece of wood.

On it were the exact same characters Wei had written. The calligraphy was terrible—but it said, proud as day, the same words Loud Boy had given Rags.

New Year's blessings upon my brother.

Wei flushed at the message. Rags had gone out of his way to learn how to write his gift to him.

"Raggedy bastard," Wei muttered, impressed.

"Loud-mouthed brat," Rags returned.

Both of them stared at each other . . . and then burst out laughing.

"Good to see you again," Wei said, reaching forward to clasp forearms with Rags.

"Same. It's not quite the same without my ears ringing from your voice!"

Wei shook his head. "How was guarding the caravan?"

"Ha! We ran into some bandits! But they took off as soon as they saw us. The legend of the Great Rags!"

Wei shook his head while Rags launched into another tale that was surely exaggerated.

But it still resonated with Wei. It lit a fire in his gut.

Wei had a bit more work to do on his core . . . and then he would be able to stand alongside his sworn brother once again.

"Also, we got another thing," Rags said, producing a letter. "Our sister sent us this!"

"Tigu sent us a letter?"

"Aye! Through the company! We have a little package as well! She sent us food and some of her Master's booze!"

"New Year's blessings, eh?" Wei asked.

Dong Chou, known as Rags, grinned and opened the letter, moving to hand it off to Wei, but Loud Boy shook his head.

"Come on. At least try first."

Rags paused and then sighed, giving Wei a halfhearted glare. He put the letter in front of him and with a halting voice, he began.

"*I, Rou Tigu, greet you, my sworn brothers! It has been a long time! All is well . . .*"

↔

"What did the Azure Jade Trading Company want, Father?" Tie Delun asked as he hammered another rivet into the plate. The forge was hot enough to melt steel, yet he worked close to the flame with his shirt off so that he could better get a grasp of the temperature.

"One of their outriders had a message for you, my son," his father replied. His bulk filled the doorway, though it had been built large enough that he wouldn't have to duck to enter.

"A message for me? From whom?" Tie Delun asked.

His father smiled beatifically. "He said it was from somebody named *Rou Tigu . . .*"

Tie Delun of the Hermetic Iron Sect was on his feet and had the letter out of his father's hand faster than he had ever moved before.

CHAPTER 47

RING IN THE NEW YEAR PART 2: HIGH ABOVE THE CLOUDS

High atop the lonely Cloudy Mountain, Senior Disciple Lu Ri stood at attention with the rest of the Senior Disciples. They were lined up in two rows, facing the peak of the mountain. Beside them, the rest of the Sect was assembled in blocks. The closest to the dais were the Core Disciples, followed by the Inner Disciples, and lastly the Outer Disciples.

It was the time of twilight at the peak of the Cloudy Mountain. The mountain was so tall that looking to the west allowed one to see the setting sun, while looking to the east one could see only darkness and stars, the sky split between the two.

They were all waiting to be addressed.

They did not have to wait long. It was customary for the ranking Elder of the Cloudy Sword Sect to appear in a burst of Qi. Today, Elder Ran simply walked. Traversing the rows of disciples standing at attention, he kept his gaze fixed, his back straight, and his arm aloft, holding a torch that burned with blue fire.

He reached the head of the rows of disciples, set the torch in its place just before the summit, and bowed.

All of the disciples bowed with him.

The torch represented the fallen Brothers and Sisters of the Sect, along with all of their ancestors. It was placed slightly higher than all of the disciples, but not directly upon the point where the mountain truly met the heavens. That place belonged only to the ascended. According to Lu Ri's research it was the first time this particular ceremony had been performed in eighty years. Normally, when they celebrated the New Year, nothing really changed. The disciples were occasionally allowed into Crimson Crucible City, but otherwise? Aside from a brief ceremony conducted by a Senior Disciple, it was just another day of cultivation.

Elder Ran turned his attention from the torch and to the disciples, and Lu Ri could feel his intent wash over them all. Some of the Outer Sect Disciples, who had been shivering and looking mildly ill from the height and the cold, abruptly stopped and stood taller.

Nodding, Elder Ran smoothed his well-trimmed beard.

This has been a trying year . . . for all of us," Elder Ran began, his eyes scouring the faces of the assembled disciples of the Cloudy Sword Sect. "I will speak the truth to all of you. There was a rot in our Sect, as you well know. A rot that attacked the core of our very ideals. It was a slow and insidious killer, one that even we Elders must admit blindness to."

Elder Ran kept his eyes on the disciples. None moved, staring straight ahead and hanging onto the Elder's words.

"But I can say now that this rot has been dealt a mortal blow. The crumbling of our Sect's foundations was caused by negligence and complacency, and it can only be fixed by diligence and duty." His voice became firmer. "And in this regard, I can only praise you all, disciples of the Cloudy Sword Sect. Those who have erred have been corrected. Those who knew not the proper path have been set upon it. You have taken the lessons of the Honoured Founders to heart, and in seeing your dedication, this old man can only feel pride."

Elder Ran lifted his hands in the formal gesture of respect: that of a court functionary, with his hands open, rather than the martial salute of a closed fist.

There was an undercurrent of shock as the Elder paid his respects to his juniors. "You have all risen to the tasks placed upon you. When our ancestors look down from the heavens, know that they smile upon us."

"Therefore, your diligence shall be rewarded. Disciples, this is my last command to you for the year: go and be merry. Any and all rowdiness will be forgiven tonight."

There was stunned silence after the Elder gave his order.

Then one of the Outer Disciples let out a tentative cheer.

Elder Ran chuckled and smoothed his beard.

→

Lu Ri was not one for parties. He much preferred silence and solitude, yet even he could not help but enjoy the atmosphere.

There had been a banquet waiting for them when they descended the mountain, with dumplings and fine wine. Other Sects would have certainly had more lavish-looking fare . . . but the Cloudy Sword Sect had unparalleled quality. Lu Ri knew because he had helped organise it. The Master Spiritual Chef Chao Chen had been contacted. Such chefs were exceedingly rare and generally only worked when they pleased, but the man had been intrigued by the chance to work with rare ingredients from the southlands. The Qi-laden foods were likely better than any the disciples had ever tasted, and the brewers that supplied the Emperor's household had parted with several barrels of the finest wine.

It was an indulgence . . . but in the grand scheme of things it was a small one. Lu Ri agreed that the Sect needed some kind of release after the pressure they had been placed under.

The Core Disciples, once surly at being forced from their compounds and their complete focus upon their own cultivation, had more considering airs about them as they gazed upon their juniors. Lu Ri knew that several Core Disciples had been surprised at the insight of their Juniors on the topic of cultivation. Others had led their Juniors out of the Sect and into battle against rampaging Spirit Beasts and cultivator bandits. Still others had ventured to tournaments, crushing all the opposition they encountered.

Such simple interactions had caused the Outer Disciples' abilities to grow in leaps and bounds, and the Sect was feeling more united than it had in years.

Lu Ri could not help but smile. He closed his eyes and listened to one of the Core Disciples playing her guzheng, her sublime skill echoing across the mountains along with her voice. Another Outer Disciple joined her. His skill was lesser, but his instrument and voice supported hers as they sang an old song about capturing the moon in their cup.

"A beautiful night, is it not, Senior Disciple Lu Ri?" Elder Ran's voice was quiet and unlike his normal tone when they talked business. Lu Ri opened his eyes in time to see the Elder take a seat, two companions sharing the evening air.

"It is indeed beautiful, Elder. The stars smile on us this night."

Elder Ran nodded at Lu Ri's words.

"Indeed. The solstice, the Phoenix of the Empire, and the New Year. All are tidings of hope and renewal, and this old man must confess he is feeling quite optimistic. We have you to thank for your efforts in finding Jin Rou . . . and waking us up from our daze."

Lu Ri simply bowed in respect. "Thank you for your kind words, Honoured Elder."

The Elder nodded and turned away from the mountain, towards the open air to where, far below them, Crimson Crucible City lay hidden beneath the clouds.

Elder Ran waved his hand like a child brushing away some sand. The clouds that shielded the Sect from view were wiped away in a single stroke. And not just the Qi-dense clouds below the Sect—*every cloud in the sky*, as far as the eye could see, simply moved out of the way, leaving the view unobstructed.

The city glittered below them, looking for all the world like a beautiful jewel.

"I remember loving the fireworks. I used to sneak off down the mountain to watch them during the New Year's celebrations. Will you have a drink with me and watch the show, Senior Disciple?"

"It would be my honour, Elder Ran," Lu Ri said, lifting the bottle of alcohol so he could pour his Elder a cup.

Elder Ran smiled, and with another wave of his hand the air in front of them distorted as he used the [Thousand Li View], bringing their vision right down into Crimson Crucible City.

The New Year festivities were in full swing. The city was painted red with all of the lanterns that had been erected, glowing crystals within them shining brightly. Enormous dragon puppets with floatstone in them soared through the air, their mouths letting out a volley of red and gold sparks. Drink flowed like water. Bao, potstickers, and noodles poured out of restaurants in a never-ending tide. The sweets that were made would form mountains. The city heaved with the force of its celebrations, loud, chaotic, and boisterous.

But as a massive gong rang, the pounding of the drums ceased. The people shouting and singing paused.

Each and every man and woman turned to the sky, ready for the fireworks show.

They did not have to wait long.

The first firework was launched out of a massive tube. It was the size of an ox, spewing green fire from its rear as it roared into the sky, climbing higher and higher and higher until it erupted in a detonation that, if it had been on the ground, could have leveled a city block. Green and blue sparks shattered the sky, not to be shown up by a secondary detonation of red with gold sparked around it.

The people of Crimson Crucible City packed as much gunpowder as they could into their fireworks, to send them as high as they could, trailing fire as they tried to reach the heavens.

None had ever succeeded, but every year a lucky few managed to pierce the clouds around the Sect.

Those lone few sparks were the only trace of festivities the disciples normally saw amid the shroud. But tonight . . . one could see over almost the entirety of Raging Waterfall Gorge.

Each little town and village was another spot of light. And above each one, there was another detonation.

The two of them watched for nearly an hour as the colours burst and thunder echoed.

Until finally the Elder turned back to Lu Ri.

"I must confess some curiosity with what you're working on, Senior Disciple. You've been quite busy, and this old man was wondering what has one of our rising stars so consumed."

Li Ri's eyes widened at the compliment. Him, a rising star of the Sect? The very thought was almost absurd! "This Disciple is in the preliminary testing phases of implementing a more cohesive system for mail," he replied.

Elder Ran looked at Lu Ri in surprise. "Oh? Elaborate, please, Disciple."

"Yes, Elder. In this Disciple's studies of the Founders' works, and that of the Scholar-Generals who created the Empire's bureaucracy, much emphasis was placed on the use of independent couriers. However, during this Disciple's time in the mortal world, he found the system exceedingly inefficient for moving large volumes of messages. Mortals complain often of delayed mail . . . if mail arrives at all. Yet this is not *solely* about the mail of mortals."

Elder Ran made no move to interrupt Lu Ri and simply gestured to continue.

"The Empire itself is almost like a creature. The people are its blood. The roads, its veins and arteries, its cities and farms are its organs . . . and the mail could be said to be nerves. What would happen to the Empire—to this civilization—if one were to effectively cultivate the speed at which information travels?"

Lu Ri held his breath, watching the Elder stroke his beard. Then Elder Ran smiled. "That is indeed interesting, Senior Disciple Lu Ri. That is the conclusion many have come to in their contemplations upon the world. That civilization itself is *alive* in some sense. Indeed, there are even some treatises by the Honoured Founders that discuss this very topic. I shall have them delivered to your room." Li Ri paused. He had come across the same conclusion as one of the Honoured Founders . . . *independently*? Pride swelled in his breast. "Continue this line of reasoning and your tests. I approve of them."

"It shall be so, Elder Ran," Lu Ri replied, looking over the city. Perhaps . . . perhaps the entire journey to find Jin Rou had been more fruitful than it had first appeared.

CHAPTER 48

RING IN THE NEW YEAR PART 3: THE OLD MEN

Hey, you drunken old bastard.

It's been a while, Gramps. I thought you were dead, old man, but it's good to hear from you again. Lots of things have changed since we last saw each other. I don't know if you heard about what happened, but, there was an incident with the Cloudy Sword Sect . . .

Fireworks sparked and banged. The smell of food filled the air. Laughter and shouts of joy were the overwhelming sounds as the soldiers of the army camp celebrated the New Year.

Two particularly enterprising, if foolish, men had even managed to fashion a dragon puppet so big it could be worn by Jade Armors. The mortal-controlled golems, thrice the height of a man, leapt and bounded. Technically, it was a breach of protocol.

Shen Yu simply smiled at the antics of the men.

"It's been a while since we've done something like this," Shen Yu mused to Xiao Ge. The men, who had both been disciples of the Cloudy Sword Sect, were sitting at a table together on top of a hill near the edge of the Imperial Army's encampment. Both were powerful cultivators who stood at the top of this world. They could have sat within General Tou Le's tent and been waited on by his staff, but that was contrary to what both men wished for.

"A very long time indeed. Why, I remember when that used to be *us*." Ge pointed down into the camp, one soldier rubbing another's back as he vomited.

Shen Yu laughed. "Ah, just like old times, eh?"

"Indeed, just like old times. You're nearly as spirited as you used to be," Brother Ge ribbed.

Shen Yu simply took a drink at the statement. His hand absently rubbed his storage ring, where the source of his improved mood sat.

You told me that when a man makes a choice, he has to follow that choice to the end. So I left the Sect. I could not bear to stay there any longer.

There were a couple of incidents on the way. I nearly got eaten by an Earth-Crushing Devil Serpent . . .

Shen Yu's smile widened and he turned his attention back to his brother.

"I am merely satisfied with the state of things," Shen Yu returned, raising his cup. Brother Ge had a knowing smile on his face.

Shen Yu hadn't exactly been secretive about how many times he had read Little Rou's letter, looking over the handwriting he had personally taught the boy. How much it had lifted his heart, seeing the irreverent little shit calling him an old bastard and mailing dung to him!

His temper had largely cooled after reading the letter. Little Rou had refused to be anybody's stepping-stone. And thus, he had set off from the place of his birth with determination in his heart.

He had abandoned the familiar and seized his destiny with his own two hands.

There was no possible way Shen Yu *couldn't* be happy with the kind of drive Little Rou had shown, willingly walking away from the Sect.

By Lu Ri's account he had even gotten stronger after leaving the Sect, just like Shen Yu had!

Well, Shen Yu was *technically* still on the register. Brother Ge and Brother Ran had left him on as a courtesy, even if they had parted ways amicably.

There was one problem, though.

Thank you for trying to look out for me. I appreciate it, even if how things ended weren't the greatest. Thank you for all the time and effort you spent teaching me . . . But I will not be pursuing cultivation any longer.

If that is a betrayal of the care you gave me, or the lessons, then I can only apologise. The years I was in your care were some of the best in my life.

So thank you, Grandfather, for your time and consideration. This Jin Rou has nothing but gratitude in his heart for what you did for a poor orphan.

That was the only part of the letter that had concerned Shen Yu . . . and he didn't fully understand it. The words were nearly incomprehensible. He could tell through the letter that Rou still had conviction. He still had drive and passion. He had not *broken*.

Perhaps Rou thought he was no longer worth Shen Yu's time? That had to be it. Little Rou was diligent, and maybe, like Brother Ge suggested, Shen Yu had laid it on a bit too thick with his talk of the boy being weak in their training. That had only been meant to inspire and motivate him, and it had . . . But after his crushing defeat had he come to finally *believe* that?

Yet when he pondered further, Shen Yu did not think so. He seemed . . . more sure of himself. His brushstrokes were too confident.

The other option . . . well, he had written that he had found a woman. Perhaps that was the issue? Love made men do foolish things. Shen Yu understood that all too well.

Everything . . . everything could still be fixed. Little Rou just needed some proper motivation. Shen Yu had once had dark thoughts of abandoning his path. Had he himself not lived like a mortal vagabond for a time? Yes, some proper motivation, and Little Rou would be back on his path!

Shen Yu, his grandfather, would be happy to give it!

When they had destroyed the demons and he had repaid the Emperor's favour, he would visit his grandson, recenter him, and all would be well.

And . . . this detour would be over *soon.*

Shen Yu and Brother Ge's attacks had been successful. They had found the demons' main nest. The last linchpin in their network.

It had been far larger than either of them had anticipated. Far, far larger, making Shen Yu glad he had decided to cut loose and had found it before it finished whatever plan the demons were using it for.

But it was so large that even Shen Yu and Xiao Ge could not approach lightly . . . Even they, cultivators in the Imperial Realm, would need support—if only a General that would hold shut the gates and prevent any of the beasts from escaping.

He hadn't exactly been expecting the extent of their reinforcements, however. The Emperor wasn't leaving much to chance with this one.

Shen Yu raised his eyes to the sky as a great prow broke through the light cloud cover and started to descend.

Shenfeng, the Divine Wind, an ancient flying ship the size of a small town, was a behemoth of heaven-steel, floatstone, and skywood. The pride of Soaring Heaven's Isle, and some would say the entire Crimson Phoenix Empire. It was the reason why the Soaring Heaven's Isle Sect, one of the few all-female Sects of the Empire, was mentioned in the same breath as the Cloudy Sword Sect.

On the deck of the great ship were Outer Sect members, the Midship girls, pulling on the rigging and adjusting the aim of the weapons. Its escorts flitted around the vessel, the ladies of the Four Winds soaring in the heavens on aetheric wings.

It always was an impressive sight. Just as impressive as yesterday when Brother Ge had put out a call for travelling members of the Cloudy Sword Sect.

They had received only five of them, but Shen Yu would give Brother Ge good odds of taking on the Divine Wind with them. Their intent was sharp and their minds focused. They had all been away from the Sect for years . . . but Shen Yu supposed that would have been a benefit.

And on the tallest mast stood Tianzhe Minyan, the Divine Falcon of the East Wind, Second Lady of the Soaring Heaven's Isle Sect. Her snow-white hair was immaculately tied into a braid and her skin was nearly the same pale colour. She was a woman carved from the finest jade. She still had her veil on, for men could be driven mad by her beauty, but Shen Yu knew her face *very* well.

As he knew the rest of her body. He locked eyes with the woman, whose eyes narrowed the moment she saw him.

Brother Ge rolled his eyes at the smile on Shen Yu's face.

"Brother, the last time we met she swore she was going to rend you limb from limb."

"She's sworn that the last three times, yet my limbs remain unrended. For such a cold-looking woman, she hides a great fire within. Is her passion not wonderful?" Shen Yu replied, waggling his eyebrows.

Brother Ge just laughed.

Just like old times, he thought.

Shen Yu contented himself with watching as the ship continued to descend, before looking out once more at the encampment that stretched for hundreds of li in every direction. Serried gleaming ranks of Jade Armors stood, Sect banners waved in the wind, and a million mortal soldiers rose and prepared to stop the lesser demons from escaping the wrath to come.

For now, they were enjoying themselves. But in two days they would be on the march, ready to finally end things.

Shen Yu closed his eyes. It had been far, *far* too long.

If I never see you again, then this is goodbye. If you're just being a lazy shit . . . then I'll see you at some point, old man.

I humbly pay my respects to my grandfather, though he is a bastard.

Rou.

Shen Yu took a sip from his wine as the soldiers roared and cheered the arrival of the ship, launching more fireworks into the air.

Minyan landed in front of himself and Brother Ge, her piercing eyes boring into him and her fingers tapping on the hilt of her blade.

He would finish everything up here . . . and then go and see his boy.

That was a promise.

□

The world seemed to shift when three figures appeared within a dark cave, their bodies shifting and flickering like living shadows.

The dark figures seemed to be assessing each other for a moment before, as one, they turned to a spot in the room that was just slightly darker than the others and sank to their knees.

"We pay our respects to the Demonic Master," they intoned as they clasped their fists in front of them.

"Greetings, my Disciples," an ancient voice replied. "How go thy endeavours?"

There was a brief silence before a male voice spoke. His voice was refined but sounded slightly strained.

"Shenhe of the Shrouded Mountain Sect is moving more swiftly than anticipated. We did not manage to shut down one of our operations in time, and she has found and destroyed every outpost we installed south of the Frost Spine. She has prisoners . . . but they are not of any real rank and will be largely useless to her. Of more concern is just how *tenacious* this assault is. Lu Ban, he . . ." The voice trailed off.

"Speak your mind, child."

The male shadow paused before his voice became rougher and less refined. More natural. "He fucked things up, Master. We've lost an *entire* technique branch."

There was a croaking chuckle from the shadow. "That he did, that he did! I never imagined that the Shrouded Mountain Sect would be so swift to move, nor Lu Ban found so easily! Such bad luck, eh? Ah, that child. If he weren't dead, I would be visiting a hundred thousand tortures upon him right now."

The words were casual and spoken like a grandfather talking of a rowdy boy despite their grim contents. "Well, there is nothing for it. Keep evacuating the cells. Destroy what you must. Shenhe may get a few more before it's done, but that is simply the price I shall have to pay. Though, do see if you can arrange something for this Shenhe, if you can?"

"Yes, Master. Your will be done."

"Excellent! Excellent! Now, my little butterfly?"

A female voice echoed next: "My apologies, Master. I haven't been able to get into the mountain again. Security is too tight."

"That was anticipated, my little butterfly. The other project?"

"Yes, Master. I made contact with him in the brothel . . . though it goes slowly. Zhang Zeng did not care overly for his son. It's difficult to stoke fatherly rage within him, but his pride is proving a more available target."

"Excellent. Excellent, my dear. With any luck, he'll cause a mess of things and all will be well."

Intent turned to the last shadow.

"Everything is proceeding apace, Master. No changes." The voice was cold, hard, and difficult to tell if it was male or female.

"Good, good. Well, this has been a *most* interesting year." The patch of darkness sighed and undulated for a moment before within it, an old man became visible. He was wizened and wrinkled, looking positively ancient. The old man flashed a toothless smile. "Let's see what fortune brings us in the next one, no?"

CHAPTER 49

RING IN THE NEW YEAR FINAL: AULD LANG SYNE

Tigu stood in front of a stall, tossing a ring up and down in her palm.

"One more try? Are you *sure* about this, girlie?" the stall owner asked, his smile vaguely slimy.

Tigu just smiled at him. The first two throws had been to test her theory. Now it was time for her victory.

Tigu loved festivals and parties.

The thumping music. The laughter and rowdiness. It just felt . . . right when everybody was having a good time, and most of all, they were *including her* in that good time. They didn't stare at her strangely. They didn't try to pull on her tail, or chase her around like she was some sort of curiosity.

She was just herself.

She flitted from place to place in the town of Verdant Hill, as her Master and Mistress had commanded all of the disciples to "have fun."

So Ri Zu had leapt into her hair, and she stole—*convinced* Shaggy Two, her disciple, to come with her while the Torrent Rider took off with Bi De, Misty Boy, and Little Xian. The dog was growing big, but he was still the cutest and fluffiest thing in the world. He had even remembered his training! This time, when she greeted her disciple, he properly guarded his belly.

While it was no Dueling Peaks, there certainly were plenty of things going on. Instead of what fun people could make for themselves, or Chun Ke giving everybody rides, there were stalls lining the streets, some with games and prizes. There she had found several children from Hong Yaowu, "chaperoned" by Ty An . . . who Tigu knew just liked having an excuse to play the games.

Some of them were quite challenging. Challenging to the point where Tigu guessed they would have been impossible for most people, but it was a surprisingly good test of accuracy and dexterity.

Until Tigu realised that if it was slightly challenging to *her*, it would be near completely impossible for any of the children who were visiting the stalls and trying to claim their prizes.

Ri Zu had been as incensed at their duplicity as Tigu had been.

Tigu, however, did what she did best. She had a righteous cause . . . and now she was going on a rampage. In her wake, there lay a dozen stunned stall owners, all in awe of her might. She'd conquered them with ease but had not slain them utterly. They could continue to exist and provide entertainment for others. This one, however, deserved only complete devastation. The only stall where the man was truly cheating.

Tigu's sharp eyes had caught him pulling on strings and jostling the rings loose.

He had even dared do it to *her* . . . and now, she had the counter to his devilish move.

"Win, Big Sis!" even the normally silent Little Liu begged. The girl Tigu had taught to carve was staring with as much emotion as she had ever seen on the child's face.

"Ha! Tigu is gonna win, easy," Ty An said with a sneer, looking to remain aloof . . . but that was ruined by the fact that she had several empty bags of sweets on her person and was eyeing the massive bag greedily.

Shaggy Two, by her feet, yipped.

The rest of the Verdant Hill children were staring at Tigu, half with worry, half with fervent hope.

Tigu let fly the ring in her hand. It had to be a gentle touch—any amount of force and the ring would bounce right off the slightly-too-big-for-it peg. But with the right amount of force . . . just so, it would stick the landing.

Then, as it settled, she stamped her foot at the exact same time the stall owner pulled on a string under the counter, a fail-safe he had devised that was connected to the pin—one that would knock the resting ring off, should it land correctly. The vibrations canceled each other out, and the ring settled in its place.

The man, looking panicked, pulled again. But he was just a man. He had no cultivation, and Tigu was in the Profound Realm.

Another tap of her foot, and the ring stayed up.

The man's jaw dropped.

There was silence for one beat, and then another. Finally, the children around Tigu burst into cheers.

The owner of the stall stared at the ring.

"And! We have a winner! An amazing throw!" the man said, trying to sound magnanimous or impressed, but she couldn't miss the clear dislike in his eyes.

Tigu held out her hand for the enormous sack of candies. The man huffed, looking annoyed . . . and after she had the candy in hand, Tigu tossed out some more money.

"Again," she demanded.

The stall owner froze, and swallowed.

Tigu scored two more victories, but on the third, the man seemed for just a moment like he wasn't going to give her her prize.

A slight bit of Tigu's intent hit him—his eyes bugged out, and cold sweat broke out all over his face. He was only too quick to hand her her prize before he started making excuses that he had to close early.

Tigu extracted two pieces as her prize . . . and then handed the sweets off to the rest of the swarming children.

Ri Zu chittered with amusement. A moment later, Tigu made to leave, only to get held up by Ty An . . . who flashed her a bottle of rice wine. Ty An's eyebrows waggled. "Me, you, Bowu, and the new guy. After the kids are in bed, yeah?" she whispered conspiratorially.

Tigu nodded and bumped Ty An's fist—then set off back into the town, wondering where she should go next.

Bi De was with Xian, Misty Boy, and the Torrent Rider. The Blade of Grass and Damp Pond were being boring, just sitting around in a tavern with Gou Ren. Chun Ke and Pi Pa were at one of the parks on the outskirts, where people rarely ventured, having a "date" to use her Master's words, and they weren't to be bothered. Wa Shi was with Yun Ren, recording images of the festivities and sampling the food. Finally, Master and Mistress were still with Meihua and Tingfeng, talking about children and other topics that Tigu thought were quite dull, making her rather glad she had been released.

She shook her head and turned her attention back to the town, wandering past several tables where people were playing games of chance.

'*Hey . . . can we sign up for that?*' Ri Zu asked.

Tigu glanced in the direction Ri Zu was pointing.

New Year Mahjong Tournament the letters boldly proclaimed. Personally, Tigu thought the game was rather boring if she wasn't teasing people until they got fed up and hit her. She had known how to play properly for months . . . but occasionally slapping down a completely nonsensical hand alongside a nonsense epithet for the play was absolutely hilarious. The reactions never got old.

But while *Ri Zu* couldn't openly participate, Tigu could.

'*If you don't want to—*'

"Sure. Let's see how far you get. But really, you need to master a human form of your own. It makes these things *so much* easier . . ."

→

Several hours later, the sun was mostly set and Tigu was sitting in the main square along with everybody else as it filled up. She was leaning up against her Mistress and scratching Shaggy Two's luxurious fur while her Mistress praised Ri Zu, who had a bronze coin in her hand. The rat was a bit pouty, but she wasn't really upset about third place. Ri Zu had ended up losing to two old men. One was lacking hair; the other, the victor, was missing an arm and an eye and carried with him a little doll of the Blade of Grass tied to his waist.

"A good-luck charm. Who can be luckier than the woman who killed that monster?" the old man had said, at Tigu's inquisitive look.

Indeed, his wounds had been caused by a sword, and not somebody particularly skilled with the weapon either. The cuts were ragged and had left thick scars.

Mistress had once mentioned treating refugees of a village assaulted by the bandit, and a good number of them had stayed in Verdant Hill.

Tigu idly wondered if she should give him one of Bi De's feathers, so he would have a charm from the *true* victor over the bandit, since the man had been a good and worthy opponent for her fellow disciple.

He had been kindly, genuinely impressed at the plays Tigu made for Ri Zu . . . and then had utterly crushed the rat with a happy smile on his face.

"A few more years and you'll have it," the man had praised her . . . before limping over to what looked like his grandson, who helped him walk off back into the town.

Now Tigu was simply relaxing. Most people were in the square, listening to a woman called Lady Wu, Mistress's teacher, play a traditional song on her guzheng for the crowd. She was the latest in a long line of people to enter the space cleared and start performing a song.

Eventually, the nice tune ended, and Tigu realised what her Mistress had been waiting for.

For the next to enter the center of town, after bowing to Lady Wu . . . was Tigu's Master.

Mistress smiled and waved as he gave them all an exaggerated wink. "I'd like to dedicate this first to my wife," her Master called out, and several people laughed and jeered, "and to Verdant Hill. The best town in the Azure Hills!"

That got more cheers, and more laughter, as her Master cleared his throat. Several people from the crowd that Tigu didn't know shouted her Master's name. He unlimbered his Ban Joh, then strummed a few chords.

Finally, he began to sing.

"Friendship lasts forever, as the earth and sky; How can I forget old times' friends?"

Tigu had heard the song in her Master's strange language. "Auld Lang Syne," he had called it, and he had spent a long time translating it, trying to find words that rhymed.

"We once all day wandered in the blue mountains of our hometown; we too, have been through hard times . . ."

Her Master's powerful voice carried through the town. The song was slightly melancholy—an ode to the end of the year and all the good memories that were accompanied by it.

"How can I forget old times' friends!" Tigu shouted out, accompanying her Master's voice.

Her Master glanced up with a smile.

"Let's raise a cup and heartily drink; friendship endures while the world lasts!"

"How can I forget old times' friends!" several more people shouted, as Master gestured to the crowd.

Ri Zu on one shoulder. Bi De on another. Xiulan, Xianghua, Gou, and Yun. Bowu, Xian, and little Liu. Pi Pa and Chun Ke. Wa Shi.

Friends. Tigu snuggled up closer to her Mistress as she rocked back and forth, whispering the lyrics Tigu had heard before under her breath.

It wasn't traditional in the slightest. But nobody in the town cared. After all, it was an interesting tune on an interesting instrument . . . and they could all sing along.

"How could I forget old times' friends?" the town roared, as her Master's instrument twanged out the last few notes . . . and then he started into another song, this one far more upbeat.

□

And thus, another year ended.

One that had been full of hardship and strife.

But on that night, there was no dwelling on the battles and conflict of the world in Verdant Hill.

The Lord Magistrate's stomach was not bothering him at all, so his wife invited him to dance, her steps so full of vigor—before, all she could do was stand and rock back and forth.

A heavily pregnant woman was invited to dance to the upbeat, rolling tune by the most beautiful girl most had ever laid eyes on. Both of their smiles were radiant as they spun together, their feet pounding to the music.

Beside them, a man who looked like a monkey and a tall woman with feathers in her hair, wearing a dress from the tribes of the north, dazzled all with their movements, so in sync were they.

Those who were not distracted by them were instead cheering on a rabbit who bounded through the air, somehow looking graceful.

The people of a gambling den roared with laughter each time they got fleeced by a literal monkey, too amused and too drunk to care how much money they were losing.

High above, a young man rose on a dragon's back as they watched the town below glowing.

Two pigs leaned against each other, sharing a meal.

An ox, near the shadow of a building, watched a puppet show. The Demon Slaying Orchid kicked around Sun Ken. None could hear the plough laughing at the treatment of its former wielder.

An orange-haired girl ran her hands along the top of an old, three-legged tomcat's head, and then stood, leaving when another girl and two boys called her over.

A rooster shook his head in amusement with a rat on his back, and left four teens to get into mischief with a bottle of drink they *probably* shouldn't have had . . . and then laid eyes on something most amusing.

A stall that was selling dolls. One of which had bright orange hair, made out of yarn.

The owner of the establishment looked incredibly weirded out as the rooster approached. But the animal had exact change.

The next day, on the first day of the new year, a rooster awoke the land with his melodious cry.

And if that hadn't woken the town up, the shout of outrage as the girl found the doll of herself tucked in beside her certainly did.

And thus began the second day of the festival.

CHAPTER 50

ROLL AWAY THE WINTER

The world was getting warmer.

Just slightly, but it was there. Oh, the snow kept falling and would cover the ground for months yet, but the depths of winter were behind us now and spring was creeping closer. On the calendar of the Before, it would have been around February.

I took a deep breath in through my nose as I stood atop the hat of the General That Commands the Winter, looking out into the horizon, over the hills and far away. It was a great view from here, higher than pretty much all the hills around.

Originally, I had come up to do some maintenance, but the good General was holding up remarkably well this winter. His ash eyes hadn't faded at all this year, and his buttons were vibrant as ever. It barely took effort to clear the snow off of him.

The worst part of him was his nose, which had been replaced for the third time yet was once again almost a nub. The animals had gotten to it. The native birds, mostly. Big D and the others had offered to stop them, but honestly, that was what it was there for. If I had wanted the nose to last, I wouldn't have used something edible. Besides, it was fun to look out the window and see the fluffy birds and enormous woodpeckers come and take some food. It was a midafternoon pastime to sit and keep track of which creatures visited the General. The snowman was practically a giant bird feeder, with many roosting in his big hat.

Which . . . honestly said a lot about how successful we were. *I could afford to have a bird feeder.* I could spend some of our hard-earned food on animals . . . and it didn't matter.

I would have enough food for tomorrow. Hells, I could buy enough food for us to eat for the next *forty years* if I felt like it. Nobody who lived here would ever know the pain of hunger—and if it came down to it, nobody in the entire commandery of Verdant Hill would need to fear a spoiled harvest. Between my and the Lord Magistrate's preparations, famine would be one disaster we could weather.

Saving the world always seemed a bit too abstract and unreachable to me. Feeding a neighbor in need?

That I could do. One step in making this place just a little bit safer.

That was what mattered.

I took another breath, just drinking in the sight of the land, but was distracted a moment later when a tune drifted up to my ears.

"*Dada da da da da da dah, la da dah da di dah* . . ." I heard Tigu hum to herself as she worked on another ice sculpture. Yin was beside her and staring with concentration at a rough chunk of ice that could have been the beginnings of a snake. The melody was exactly that of "Auld Lang Syne." It had been a traditional New Year's song where I was from, which I had decided to belt out during the festivities. It had, back in the Before, been seen as overly sappy. You still sang it anyway, as it was a tradition, but there had always been a number of smirks when people sang the song ironically.

I hadn't exactly been expecting people to find the song so touching and poignant, which was dumb, because the song *was* meant to be exactly that.

Pops and Uncle Bao had looked like they were holding back tears by the time I was done. After I had stopped playing, I got practically swarmed by people complimenting it.

I'd made sure to tell them I wasn't the original author of the song. It would have felt scummy, taking credit for something like that.

After that, the rest of the night had gone well, and I'd ended up dancing a bit with everybody. I had intended to stay sober in solidarity with my wife, but Meimei had just rolled her eyes and shoved some booze into my hand. The festivities were just as good as last year, and I had gone to bed in a great mood . . . only to be awoken by Tigu ranting about the doll of herself that she had found in her bed, decrying its quality and the missing details.

Her complaining stopped after Meimei had taken one look at it and promptly decided it was cute.

And it *was* cute. It had big eyes and orange yarn hair. It was very, very cute. My girl's first official piece of merch . . . that she would be getting royalties for.

Tigu had been reduced to grumbles, to Xiulan's amusement . . . which was also cut short when Meimei had found the vendor and bought a Demon Slaying Orchid doll.

"I've finally succeeded at bringing you into my bed," Meimei had said with the biggest shit-eating grin I'd ever seen on her.

We had both dolls on our dresser, and the one of Xianghua, too. I had gotten one to tease her as well, though she seemed more flattered than flustered.

I shook my head and looked down at the sculptures Tigu was making. She had seemed pensive after Meimei's declaration that the dolls were cute . . . so today everything she was making was effectively chibified. Small, squat, and cute. The most prominent was a very happy-looking boar with a bunch of birds perched on him.

For the rest of the gang, it was pretty much a day off from work. Almost everybody was at the kung fu poles; Xiulan and Xianghua had decided that they were great for agility training for hockey, so they were skating around the poles like dervishes along with Peppa, who was, as always, deceptively agile.

Meimei was off to the side sitting on our chair and all bundled up, watching with a smile. She had slowly been scaling back the amount of physical activity she was doing.

I knew she wasn't fragile or anything, though none of what I considered normal for a pregnancy was happening, and I had lived through a couple of expecting aunts and some female friends. There were no mood swings, no cravings, no swollen legs . . . the only thing that really said she was pregnant was the fact that she needed to go to the bathroom a bit more.

That, and the fact that she looked like she had a beach ball stuffed under her shirt. Her stomach was getting big. Really big. Not that there were any other signs that her body had changed. No stretch marks, no varicose veins or flabby skin. Boy, women went through hell when they had kids . . . but I guess cultivation had its perks. I wouldn't have minded the stretch marks either way, but Meimei seemed pretty pleased with things, so I was happy too.

That, and there had been some growth in . . . *other* areas. Neither Yun Ren nor Gou Ren could ever tease her about having a flat chest now, something my wife was immensely pleased with, though she'd had to alter all her clothes a bit.

I was aware birth was dangerous in this time period. Knowing she didn't have to fear infection and had the ability to heal basically any tear, and the fact that Pops and a midwife would be here, well . . . it did wonders to calm some of my nerves.

I worried less about my own child's birth than I had earlier in the year with the cows. Which was probably good, because Meimei would have cuffed me if I pestered her as much as I did them. I was also avoiding thinking about afterwards too much. One step at a time.

Meimei caught my gaze and smiled, waving up at me. I gave her a thumbs-up and hopped down from the General.

It had been a nice, relaxing day so far . . . and it was only going to get better. I landed in front of the greenhouse in a single jump, feeling like I had merely stepped from a ledge rather than several stories in the air. I smiled at the glittering edifice of glass and iron and opened the first set of doors, coming into the first part of the greenhouse. It always kind of felt like an airlock or something sci-fi. And to basically everybody living on this world, *it kind of was.*

Outside was a winter wonderland, but the moment one walked through the door they entered an otherworldly place. Inside the building was the warmth of high summer, where fresh fruits and vegetables dangled on the vine.

The tomatoes were wet with dew. The sunflowers Yin had planted stood strong and tall. The potatoes, carrots, and cabbage were as verdant as Xiulan's swords.

And today, they had hit *optimal ripeness*. I could just tell. And after months of preserves and pickles, we would be eating well tonight. Out of everything from the Before, having the convenience of fresh fruits and vegetables on hand all the time was one of the things I had missed the most.

And now, here they were.

Not even in my second year yet.

Maybe I was a Xianxia protagonist after all.

The speed of my cultivation was top-notch.

CHAPTER 51

THE FOX AND THE PLOUGH

Su Nezan, the Spirit Fox—or rather a fragment of Su Nezan—looked on as his nephew clashed with Cai Xiulan. He was curled up on a rock at the moment, watching the friendly bout; Yun Ren kicked up snow with every movement, trying to shroud his blows. In contrast, Xiulan moved without disturbing the snow, her light steps letting her sway like a blade of grass dancing in the wind. Summer's Sky was keeping its help limited today, to better build the boy's foundation. Nezan smiled at the look of concentration on Yun Ren's face and studied him for a moment. The blood of the foxes was still weak in his veins . . . but it was changing him. His teeth were sharper. His eyes, when angered, turned to slits. And his face was slightly softer and more androgynous.

He could be mistaken for any one of their clan, him and his mother. Indeed, Nezan's female form was the spitting image of Nezin Hu Li . . . if two decades younger. Truly, they carried similar blood.

The woman had been most amused by a fox calling her niece when they'd met just before the New Year's festival. As had her husband, who started calling the monkey, Huo Ten, Uncle, much to the confusion and bashfulness of the poor creature.

Neither of them *really* believed that they had Spirit Beast blood in them.

Nezan was pulled out of his introspection when Xiulan suddenly darted forward and tapped Yun Ren's arm. The boy winced and shook it out, but nodded at the rebuke and resettled into his stance, ready to receive his senior's instruction once more.

The beautiful woman was certainly a better teacher than Nezan ever was, and he could see the effects their spars had on his nephew's form. He was a man of action, Yun Ren. He learned only by *doing*. She was by far his nephew's superior, but under her instruction Yun Ren's movement was becoming more refined.

The fox smiled as he watched them duel for a moment longer, before directing his attention elsewhere. This morning, Jin had declared it was "free time," and so everybody was doing as they wished. A good portion had chosen to train today.

Farther away from the spar, Gou Ren settled into a stance beside Tigu. The pair began to move through the motions of a martial form together. They were quite synchronized, and the form was full of power strikes that suited the larger man more than Tigu.

Nezan turned to look in the distance at a sudden peal of laughter. On the river, Rou Jin skated with Liu Xianghua. The man was doubled over and howling with laughter at something the woman had said. As for her part, Xianghua looked confused but tentatively smiled. The fox wondered just what the girl had said to set off the boy. He'd have to find out later.

His gaze drifted farther out, to the fence in the distance, where Bi De the rooster hopped and kicked along it. Little Ri Zu was behind him, her silver needle flashing, and the rabbit Yin hopped after them both, her body wreathed in a corona of light.

The sound of a hammer starting to pound drew his attention next as the forge house began to belch smoke, and then a rumble in the ground alerted him to Chun Ke. The boar was twice the size of a horse today, and he carried with him in his sleigh Little Meiling, while Wa Shi the dragon pranced beside them. They were heading off into the forest on a leisurely stroll.

It was peaceful, almost idyllic.

Zang Wen, his dearest friend, would have *loved* it. When she had finally cut ties with the Shrouded Mountain Sect all those years ago, and when she was finally healed enough from her less-than-friendly departure, she had delighted in her freedom, charging around with the foxes of their little village. Such a passionate soul she was, rebounding after years of her Sect trying to turn her into another weapon against the foxes. She was their light, their heart and soul. She had barely gotten to experience the world and the joys it could bring.

And then she had died defending what had once been her sworn enemies.

Nezan idly wondered how many of the village had survived the centuries he had been sleeping for.

His eyes roved over those present as they strove to improve, as they traded pointers, and as they worked with each other.

Yes, Wen would have loved it here. And probably loved teasing the lady of the house as well. She had a fox's humour and disposition at times.

From what he had seen, Little Meiling, while she gleefully poked at Xiulan, was rather weak to any return fire.

The fox shook his head as he turned his eyes back to the training. The training . . . like they were preparing for a war. He had heard the whispered conversations, about the crystal and how they were growing stronger to aid Jin and protect the Azure Hills.

Nezan's amusement died slightly as his thoughts turned from the lovely sights to the crystal.

The crystal had been . . . *interesting*. He'd been surprised, and maybe a little disappointed, at how easily they had let him in on the secret. Nezan hadn't even had to work his wiles on anybody! It would have been quite the challenge, too. He looked too much like the Xong brothers' mother in his human form for them to take the bait. Indeed, Little Gou's expression had been just as horrified as Yun Ren's was whenever he appeared in his female form and started flirting with somebody. Cai Xiulan would have tossed him on his ass with a polite smile—she was a true Young Mistress, the kind who tended to be horribly repressed, just like Wen had been.

Xianghua would have just started stabbing. The woman was just the right amount of unhinged, and absolutely loyal to her chosen man. Tigu would have begun sculpting him, completely missing any subtext, and Meiling would have aggressively stared . . . but likely told him nothing. Really, that little girl was a dirty old man in a woman's body! He approved! He had already tried to tempt Jin, as a joke, and the man had dismissed him completely. It hurt his pride as a fox, it did! Instead, he had been *invited* to learn about the crystal. He was quite touched that his nephew had vouched for him, and was also satisfied at how his nephew's companions accepted Yun Ren's judgement.

It was almost disappointing.

Though, naturally, he had assumed there wouldn't be much to it.

A crystal from the Azure Hills. It wasn't like there could be anything truly interesting on it, he had thought.

The spirit pestering the chicken if he wanted to be Emperor, then looking spectacularly annoyed after it said the words, was amusing. He'd thought it would set the tone for the entire crystal.

He was wrong. Very, *very* wrong.

Although the majority of the information would likely be of great value to any historian, Nezan cared little about the past of the province. He had known that the Misty Fang was once a bastion against demonic incursion. And it wasn't like the Crimson Phoenix Empire didn't base most of their legitimacy on the fact that the First Emperor and the Scholar-Generals had been the ones to largely end the demons as an existential threat.

To the world outside the Azure Hills, the knowledge contained . . . wasn't exactly something that wars would be fought over, especially since the children weren't foolish enough to try to secede from the Empire.

Nezan approved. They were cute and a bit naïve . . . but they weren't *stupid.*

If that was all, that would be the end of it. A point of interest and that was it.

Or that was all it would be, had he not seen the strength Xiaoshi had been capable of. The strength the Path of Shennong could muster.

Nezan was no stranger to battles. He had fought a war with his dear Zang Wen, the Summer Sky Thunder, against the Shrouded Mountain Sect.

Xiaoshi's might have made his dear's pale in comparison.

He had known that Jin was strong. The man could surely match Nezan with the power he had displayed during the Dueling Peaks Tournament.

Nezan still didn't have a grasp on the full extent of Jin's power; only that it was vast enough that even if he had battled Nezan's dear friend at the peak of her power . . . Nezan had a feeling she would most certainly lose. Even the Elders of the Shrouded Mountain Sect, if they were alone, could conceivably fall to Jin.

But Xiaoshi? Xiaoshi from the crystal? His power was on yet another level. That was the kind of man who could, with a single swing of his fists, clear out the entire mountain of those bastard squatters. The scum that had assaulted the Misty Fang, who had slain so many of his kin.

They would finally be destroyed. It would be the work of years, but the plan formed in his mind.

All it required was a few pushes, and then he could bring war here . . . after he integrated himself more. He knew much . . . and if he said so himself, he was quite the entertainer. Little Meiling already liked him, and he had spent a long, *long* time playing caretaker to his kin's children. He dared to say that he was quite good at it.

Uncle Nezan, the kindly fox whose tricks and pranks everyone loved, could make this place his home. He could stock the pantry. Entertain with his guzheng. Be the rascal deadbeat, the one who got chased around to the amusement of the children, while he looked after them and took them on adventures.

Part of the family.

And all the while, he could weave a spell around the Shrouded Mountain Sect. It did not have to be illusions; the fox bloodline was powerful . . . but words and warm flesh were just as devastating as the beguiling powers of Da Ji.

And what would Jin do, when the Shrouded Mountain Sect showed up on his doorstep?

Why, Jin might smite them just as Xiaoshi had smote his foes. He might march on the mountain and tear out Nezan's sworn enemies, root and all. He had the backing of the Cloudy Sword Sect. Those of the Shrouded Mountain would be utterly destroyed. And Yun Ren's uncle had asked nicely for a boon, after he had aided him throughout the battles, and who could call the other foxes to war to help defend Jin's home?

Well, the Misty Fang would be theirs again.

His form was made of pure Qi, but he could feel the swirling eddies of his power. He couldn't stop the sick, twisted smile that crawled across his face—

"Hey, Nezan! Ya listening?" The words shattered Nezan's concentration, and he glanced up at the face of Yun Ren.

Nezan shook his head and plastered a genuine smile on his face. "My apologies, nephew! I was just . . . engrossed in my own thoughts."

Yun Ren nodded as he took a seat beside Nezan. "Well, like I was sayin', I'm goin' back to Pale Moon Lake City soon, and since I'm heading there anyway, I was wondering if you wanted me to stop by your place first? Or if there was anywhere else you wanted me to go?"

The boy's smile was bright. He was obviously thinking of his Biyu back in the city. "I've already got a few places for Summer's Sky to see," he continued. "There's a village called Cha Meng just a bit off the path that's supposed to have really, *really* good tea. Elder Hong said the palace in Pale Moon Lake City used to order their tea exclusively, so I was gonna swing around and get some!"

Summer's Sky rattled in its sheath, obviously happy to go on the adventure.

Nezan grimaced.

"I am fine, nephew, there is no place I need to be first. Go to your darling! I want to see this Biyu in person!" Nezan said, forcing his voice to come out chipper even as his hatred for the mountain rolled in his guts.

Yun Ren sighed. "Could you tone it down a little for her? Please?"

Nezan laughed, his mood lightening some. "Of course I will . . ." Yun Ren perked up. "*Not!*"

Yun Ren's face fell. "Bastard," he grumbled.

"Indeed I am! I do not believe my parents were wed in the human sense—now, though, you have done well with your blade practice. I do believe it's time to work on your illusions!" Nezan commanded, as he hopped up onto Yun Ren's shoulder.

The boy groaned, but started walking to do as Nezan asked. He did have a bit of a skip in his step, however.

"That excited to be out exploring again?"

"Yeah. I asked Summer's Sky to tell me about all the old wielders, Wen especially. I've asked it for every place Summer's Sky remembers her saying she wanted to visit. I've got a list, and all I need is a map. You said she wanted to explore, right? Well . . . I just thought . . . I could visit everywhere she wanted, ya know? For Summer's Sky, and, well, you wanted to go with her, right?"

The words were a blow to Nezan's gut. The smile, it struck the fragment of a greater whole to his core.

Yun Ren had never met Wen. And yet he wished to honour her. To follow *her* dream. His dearest Wen's. He wanted to give Summer's Sky tea, and he wanted to go to places *Nezan* wanted.

And there Nezan was, plotting how to drag his earnest little nephew and all his friends into a war simply for the fox's own vengeance.

And if that war happened, Yun Ren would fight. He would fight, for his family and for his friends, without hesitation and without question. He would fight, and die for them, like Wen had fought and died for Nezan's family.

For a battle and a slight that Yun Ren had nothing to do with. The Misty Fang had been in the Shrouded Mountain Sect's hands since Nezan's childhood, so, so long ago. His war was *thousands* of years old.

Where had he gotten the guts to drag people who had shown him nothing but kindness and hospitality to war with him? To plot and scheme and *use* the bloodline of his Honoured Aunt?

Nezan's Qi construct shuddered. He looked back at the others. The smiles on their faces. Those faces were replaced with faces he knew intimately. His family, crowding around Wen, laughing with her.

Blood leaking out of mouths, guts steaming on the ground, screams as lightning burned them to ashes—

No. No. What was he doing? What was he *thinking*?

He was a fox. A wicked, devious creature, filled with the blood of Da Ji. The bane of gods and kings.

We are not the slaves of our blood was the first Teaching of their Honoured Aunt.

Nezan's dark plans were bottled up, then carefully pushed aside.

No. To bring war here . . . he could not, *would* not do such a thing. It was a betrayal of the highest order, and he would not feed into that part of Da Ji's legend. Nezan had his honour—and if he carried out that plan he would never be able to look Honoured Aunt Su Nezin and his Dear in the eyes, if he ever met them in the afterlife.

Nezan took a deep breath as Yun Ren entered the clearing where he practiced his illusions. The rocks were a riot of colours and fractal patterns—beautiful, if vertigo-inducing.

Nezan shook off the lingering feelings and focused. Besides, there was a chance that the Shrouded Mountain Sect would screw up on their own. There was already animosity there.

So instead . . . he would take precautions. Keep an eye on things. Just because *he* wouldn't start anything didn't mean the Shrouded Mountain Sect wouldn't.

He . . . he had some contacts still. Some kin who would be able to keep an eye on things for him and make sure that the Shrouded Mountain Sect stayed on their side of the line . . . and make sure that these wonderful, if a bit naïve, children could have just a bit more peace.

His lips curled into a smile. He dearly hoped Jing Ai was still alive . . . if only to see her face when Jin refused her advances.

It was cute how much the man only had eyes for his wife.

Nezan nodded, watching Yun Ren work for a moment . . . before he flexed his own Qi. One of the rocks changed, colours spreading like ink—like Nezan had learned from Yun Ren.

His nephew turned and stared at the image. He bit his lip, struggling not to laugh.

It was the image of a rather tall man screaming in pain, with Summer's Sky stuck in his ass.

"Damn it! One time! You stick somebody in the ass one time . . ." Yun Ren complained, Summer's Sky rattling with amusement.

↔

The blade known as Summer's Sky was content. Eighth Wielder's progress was acceptable, and his growth interesting to observe.

More importantly, the tea here smelled excellent. The cultivator known as Meiling was adept at brewing many, *many* kinds of tea, as was her creator, Hong Xian.

It was interesting. It was pleasant. Summer's Sky approved of both of them.

Summer's Sky was beside Friend Nezan as the Eighth worked. The Fox had been lost in his thoughts quite often recently, and Summer's Sky had noticed the look on his face that said he had been thinking something that the Seventh wouldn't have approved of.

Luckily, there hadn't needed to be any intervention. Friend Nezan had calmed himself.

The Seventh always said that Friend Nezan stopped himself before he did any truly foolish things.

Summer's Sky did not wish to contradict the Seventh, but Summer's Sky had counted four hundred and forty-five instances in which the Seventh was incorrect. Friend Nezan *often* did things that Summer's Sky considered stupid, like eating that *clearly* bad piece of meat one thousand one hundred and thirteen years ago. Or when he'd insisted the price would go up on those teapots, and they would be rich when they resold them. Or the time with the swing, the ropes, and the bottle of perfume.

On second examination, that hadn't been stupid. Merely baffling.

Summer's Sky's wielder sent a burst of intent down their link. The emotion contained was curiosity.

"Hey, Summer's Sky?" the Eighth Wielder asked as he crafted another illusion and placed it onto the rocks.

Summer's Sky directed its full attention to its wielder. '*You have a question, Eighth Wielder?*' Summer's Sky responded.

"Yeah . . . I was wondering . . . . Well . . . I saw the sword in that crystal thing, and it looked like Sun Ken's sword. That guy was talking about artificial spirits and it got me wondering . . . everybody always said Crimson Tooth, or I guess Sun Ne now, had a demon in it . . ."

'*Eighth Wielder is correct and incorrect. The plough contains a blade spirit. Not a demonic spirit,*' Summer's Sky stated.

The Eighth Wielder paused. "What?"

'*The plough contains a blade spirit. It is weak and degraded, but active,*' Summer's Sky confirmed.

The Eighth paused and turned to look fully at Summer's Sky.

"How long have you known *that*?"

'*Three months, twelve days,*' Summer's Sky replied, omitting the smaller denominations of time. Most wielders didn't care and considered the exact time irrelevant.

"Huh," the Eighth muttered. "Well, do you guys, like, talk at all?"

Summer's Sky sent a burst of neutrality down the link. '*Blades do not speak to each other unless they are locked in combat.*'

The Eighth Wielder considered the statement.

"Why not?" he asked back.

Summer's Sky paused at the rebuttal. Why . . . not?

"Ha! He has you there, darling!" Nezan said, amused.

Indeed, why not? Summer's Sky pondered the statement. The first and foremost was that the blades needed to be touching for the spirits to truly interact; while their wielders fought, so too did the Spirits, ripping and tearing at each other as they clashed in mirror to their wielders. They tried to disrupt Qi flow in the other blade, and in extreme cases one could even kill their opposite.

Summer's Sky had only truly interacted with foes. Spirit Weapons, even in the Howling Fang Mountains, were rather rare. They were given to their wielders and they bonded with them, or they remained sleeping in storage. Peaceful interaction simply wasn't an option. Merely possessing a blade with a spirit was an advantage: they were far more resilient to techniques that disrupted Qi flow, and they could remain sharp and durable when a more mundane weapon would fail. They had their own Qi flow and could better modulate the energy within their "bodies," smoothing out eddies of Qi, and they also attempted to disrupt Qi flow in each other, which just happened to be used to its greatest effectiveness in combat.

'*Interest. Approval. Summer's Sky requests to speak with the other Spirit Weapon.*'

With a shrug, the Eighth picked up Summer's Sky and headed out of the forest, towards the other spirit weapon wielder.

Summer's Sky left the Eighth to convince the ox, whose attention was purely on the other weapon. A plough. Summer's Sky was mildly impressed that the spirit had survived the transition. It was remarkably hardy to have continued to exist, with its form bent and twisted from a sword to an implement meant to cut earth.

The ox nodded tentatively at the Eighth's request; Summer's Sky was placed against the plough.

For the first time in its life, when Summer's Sky touched another blade, there was no raging torrent of Qi or even an attack that met it.

Curious, Summer's Sky pressed forward and manifested into the world of the other. Summer's Sky's form was that of the Seventh Wielder; Wen had spoken with Summer's Sky the most and, in honour of their relationship, the blade's spirit adopted her form. Long, braided, golden hair ran down Summer's Sky's back. Blue eyes examined the world. A white robe and red sash clothed it.

To Summer's Sky's surprise, the world wasn't a forge like most of its opponents' worlds had been. It wasn't a hellish world of blood and slaughter, a raging river, or Summer's Sky's own domain of blinding light . . . It was a warm, inviting plain, surrounded by mountains. The sky was filled in by golden cracks.

Summer's Sky took a closer look at the mountains. Most of them had deep cuts in them. The blade looked at its feet, where there were hundreds, no, *thousands* of perfectly straight furrows in the ground, leading off into the distance.

Summer's Sky approved. The cuts were very nice.

Looking up, Summer's Sky began its search for the other. *Sun Ne*, the one called Jin had said. It didn't need to look far.

Before it stood a wild-looking child of indeterminate gender. Their hair was brown, messy dreadlocks. Their skin was tanned and their clothes were a bright, eye-searing yellow, decorated with smiling suns.

Sun Ne's concentration was absolute as it dragged its hand along the ground and produced a perfectly straight cut, striving for perfection.

"Cut cut cutcutcut! Cut cut cutcutcut!" the child muttered, a look of absolute peace on its face.

Summer's Sky waited until the cut was complete and the child sat back to examine their handiwork.

"Greetings," Summer's Sky intoned.

The wild child's head snapped up. Its jaw dropped and it stared, dumbfounded for a moment, at Summer's Sky.

They stood together. The child looking on in shock, and Summer's Sky standing calmly before it.

"Greetings," Summer's Sky's monotone voice tried again.

The child kept staring, looking scared and confused.

"Greetings. This one is Summer's Sky. It wishes for peaceful dialogue. Do you accept?"

The child stared blankly, then shuffled its feet in uncertainty. Abruptly, an ox appeared out of the ether, standing beside the sword spirit. Internal manifestation of the wielder? Interest. Approval.

The child took strength from the appearance of its wielder, took a breath, and looked directly at Summer's Sky.

"Do you . . . like cutting things?" Sun Ne asked.

"Yes," Summer's Sky answered honestly.

The child's eyes brightened.

CHAPTER 52

GROWTH UNDER THE SNOW

Cai Xiulan stood, panting, in the middle of a forest clearing. Her breath came out in steaming gouts; her brow was slick with sweat; and she had several new bruises. Her swords hovered in the air behind her, two glowing blades of jade that looked to be inlaid with gold. Those were the only two at the moment, and they wavered slightly.

Her opponent was in no better shape. Tigu was crouched low, her legs trembling. She had a couple of drops of blood on her face, where Xiulan's swords had managed to find purchase in flesh harder than steel. The small cuts were already gone, however, healed by Tigu's Qi.

Her sharp eyes roved over Xiulan's form before she sighed, her intense look of concentration fading.

"Draw?" Tigu offered.

"Draw," Xiulan confirmed. They could have probably done one last attack . . . but then both of them would have become too exhausted to walk home. Besides, this was less a bout to find a victor and more the fact that both of them had wanted to practise new techniques.

In that case, the battle was a victory for both of them, considering how much Xiulan's lower back stung. Tigu had become much faster over the past months.

Xiulan raised her hands in a martial salute, and her opponent did the same. Respect was clear from both sides of the battle.

"Good fight!" Tigu said, a bright smile on her face.

"Good fight," Xiulan returned, a soft smile of her own on her face. They were certainly stronger ever since they had come back from the Dueling Peaks. Her experiences had refined her abilities.

Tigu had always been good at fighting, her natural aggression and eye for openings making her a deadly threat, but now she had caution, movement techniques, and a pair of high-quality bracers that let her spare her arms whenever she blocked blades, an extra layer of protection.

Both of them rose from their bows, and Tigu started stretching. She did look a bit out of place in her more standard attire. Having one's arms, legs, stomach, and most of their chest exposed in the middle of winter looked a bit cold; cultivators in the Initiate's Realm could still be affected by mundane weather, but now?

Xiulan could have stripped naked in the middle of the province's harshest blizzard and been fine. Both of their bodies were far, *far* more durable than they had been last year.

Tigu finished her stretch, her arms rising above her head as she flexed every muscle, her abs, biceps, and shoulders on full display. They complemented her appearance, accentuating her wild face. In the summer, with her tan, she looked downright exotic in a sea of pale and milky-white skin tones.

"So, what did you see that you think I should improve on?" Tigu asked as they began to walk back to the house.

"Your movement technique needs to come out faster. You still have slightly too much buildup, so it makes it obvious when you're trying to use it. Have you had any luck with 'kicking the air so hard it becomes solid' like Jin suggested?" Xiulan asked.

"I'm still too inexperienced! It's starting to feel a bit more solid, but . . ."

Discussing their bouts was not a recent thing between them, but ever since Jin had started training more, the talks had become more in-depth. Jin had an interesting perspective on training. They had even recorded a few of their fights in his crystal, and then he had played it back for them as they sat inside by the fire.

Xiulan could remember every second of the fight, but seeing it from a different angle had been most enlightening. Jin had said it was fairly standard practice where he was from to record fights, and then have a panel of one's Seniors and instructors go back over it.

While most Sects recorded their enemies, to find weaknesses, few ever really did it for themselves.

He also did it for them when they were playing Ha Qi, to find minute flaws in their skating form. Truly, the quality of training at the Cloudy Sword Sect was something else. No wonder they were so mighty.

They completed Tigu's assessment before pivoting to Xiulan.

"Your control over your blades is well-executed, even when you have so many active at a time," Tigu mused on Xiulan's swords. "What are you up to now? Forty-eight?"

"Yes, forty-eight Blades of Grass," Xiulan confirmed. It had been both shocking and humbling to realise that even after her cultivation had been burned, she had taken the Sect's techniques even further than her Honoured Father was capable of.

As far as she knew, nobody in her Sect had gone past forty in centuries . . . since the time of the founding and Honoured Ancestor Ruolan's Fans of Grass.

Xiulan had many misgivings about her Honoured Ancestor's . . . *colourful* personality, but the woman's brilliance could not be denied. Her every action humbled Xiulan . . . but she could not copy the woman's style fully.

Xiulan's own technique was a cross between the more martial form and the original opera performance. Distinct from both, and slowly, *slowly* turning into something of her own.

"But it's incomplete," Tigu said after a moment. "There's still something missing. The number is large . . . but that's all. From thirty-two to forty-eight does not feel like the jump in power that it should be."

"I agree. It's running up against a block . . . and I think I may know the answer I need to break through it. It will have to wait until the spring . . . but the grass will grow again," Xiulan said to her sparring partner.

Tigu grinned at Xiulan's conviction.

"I'll hold you to that—" she began as she stepped out of the tree line and back onto the fields of Fa Ram.

And then both of them were promptly hit by a veritable tidal wave of snow. It slammed into them and had enough Qi in it to bowl both cultivators over. Qi that they recognised, of course.

For a moment, the snow Xiulan was under felt like she was buried under a mountain. Then, as her Qi touched it . . . it just became snow again.

She pushed herself off her back to a seated position, her head covered in white powder. Tigu sat up beside her, looking a bit dizzy.

Then, in front of Xiulan, a rooster's head popped out of the snow.

Bi De shook his head to clear it.

"An excellent blow, Master," the rooster called out, sounding slightly dazed.

"Hahahahahaha! See? I've got a few tricks of my own—ah." Jin's laughter boomed, and then cut out abruptly as he realised he had caught both of them in the crossfire. "Sorry, Lanlan. Sorry, Tigu."

"No harm done," Xiulan replied as Jin walked up to them. He held out his hand and Xiulan took it, allowing herself to be pulled to her feet. "Has your time today been fruitful?" Xiulan asked. Tigu was already out of the snow and brushing herself off. Bi De had emerged from the snow as well, combing his ruffled feathers.

"Yeah, it's actually going surprisingly well!" Jin said, and hefted his weapon, leaning it on his shoulder.

Xiulan raised an eyebrow at it.

"It's perfect, huh?" Jin asked, his voice full of mirth.

Xiulan stared at the shovel and its beautifully carved hilt, courtesy of Wa Shi and Tigu.

"It has a truly exemplary pedigree," Xiulan responded, considering the "weapon."

Jin started laughing.

"It's a legendary weapon, passed down through the ages . . ." Jin began, listing the qualities that made the shovel a perfect weapon. His arm slung around her shoulder as he started to wax poetic about the benefits of a shovel over a sword.

Xiulan just shook her head with amusement at his antics.

But it *did* seem like the shovel suited him.

→

Xiulan's day progressed from there. Training, cooking lunch, playing Ha Qi with Xianghua, and now bathing. Each day, even when Xiulan tried her hardest, seemed like barely any work at all.

Though they were going to have to renovate the bathhouse soon—it was getting *incredibly* crowded. Jin had already increased the size of the tub once, but it simply wasn't enough to accommodate four women and a pig when they all decided to bathe together.

At that moment, Yin was floating in the center of the tub, heating the water with the power of the sun mid-nap. Tigu was using a single finger to rub soap into Ri Zu's fur. Xianghua was listening intently to Pi Pa as they discussed calligraphy. Those two were out of the tub and on the bench against the wall where one could sit if they just wanted a steam bath. The pig was stepping on Xianghua's back, kneading knots out of the cultivator.

Xiulan had Meiling nearly in her lap as she washed the other woman's hair. Meiling hummed in approval when Xiulan's fingers dug in deep, like Meiling did for her. Her legs were nearly entwined with Tigu's, and if she raised her knee, she would touch the dozing Yin.

While it was small and cramped, it was kind of nice.

The boys certainly didn't seem to mind, though the boys also splashed each other with water, beat each other with birch branches and towels, and then jumped in the frozen river while whooping like wild men.

Or after they finished their baths, they would stand in the living room wearing nothing but towels and start *flexing* while grunting manly encouragements to each other.

Which always distracted Meiling, Xianghua, and Tigu, teach for different reasons. Xiulan herself had to admit she had . . . *observed* a few times.

They had all cultivated their bodies well.

And while Xiulan and the girls didn't flex at each other, jumping into the cold river was bracing. There was a certain sort of thrill in doing it . . . and knowing that the men in the house were all gentlemen who ignored them.

It was still a novelty that she was comfortable enough that she could let her guard down.

She finished washing Meiling's hair and pulled her back so the woman rested against Xiulan's chest. The swell of her belly stuck up through the water.

Meiling sighed, content.

"Your chest makes a very nice pillow."

Xiulan rolled her eyes. "You're very lucky you're pregnant, otherwise I would be trying to drown you right now."

Meiling chuckled, yet neither of them made any move. Xiulan had, after all, used Meiling as a pillow enough times . . . after particularly bad nightmares.

Her mood soured at the thought before she pushed it away.

Indeed, everybody had fallen asleep at least once on Meiling's lap to a hummed tune and gentle fingers weaving through their hair. Meiling was skilled from years of taking care of her little brother, and Xianghua swore that it was a manner of sleeping potion she used. Even Yun Ren had claimed that Meiling's thighs were the only part that were never considered bony.

There was even a ranking of "best place on a person to use as a pillow." According to Tigu, Ri Zu, and Meiling, the best place to sleep on Xiulan was her chest . . . which was certainly embarrassing.

Gou Ren had commented on the restful properties of Xianghua's behind, which of course the woman was proud of, and everybody—when she wasn't listening—agreed that Pi Pa's bulk made a good place to lay one's head. Jin also ranked highly, his arm a firm pillow that Xiulan hadn't yet tried—though the undisputed "best pillow" was, as always, Chun Ke.

Xiulan sighed in contentment, simply lying in the warm water.

Xianghua and Pi Pa then entered the tub and water spilled out.

Xiulan was shoved against Pi Pa and Tigu. She had a brief underwater scuffle with the cat and Xianghua, who each claimed their portion of leg space.

That lasted until Pi Pa managed to time a stomp so it hit all three of their feet at once.

Peace resettled in the tub, for the time being.

→

That night, Xiulan found herself on the roof.

It was her usual spot when she was feeling off center . . . and tonight her body had urged her up. She'd had a dream. Not a nightmare, it wasn't that harsh, but she'd had a dream about the Valley and Sun Ken, which had occurred just a little over a year ago.

It was still tender and raw, to see the people out celebrating the death of Sun Ken. Not in the celebrations themselves—no, they could taunt the man all they liked; he was a bastard who deserved the mocking—but in the fact that she was the one who was featured so prominently.

She still couldn't watch the plays for long. They always made her feel melancholy and left a sour taste in her mouth at the undeserved praise.

The pain, after everything, was still there. The deaths of the soldiers still occasionally weighed on her at night, just as they had when she'd first come back to Fa Ram.

But there were no more nightmares anymore. The promise she had made—that nothing like that bastard would ever happen again—and the people in her life dulled the ache.

A year. It had been a year since she had come to Fa Ram. She didn't know whether time had flown by, or it felt like they had all been friends for years.

They had fought for each other. Bled for each other.

Xiulan took a deep breath and let her spirit begin to wander. Through the connections in the earth. The connections to Tianlan.

The first lesson from Jin came to mind, back when she had thought him an unfathomably ancient Master.

Everything is connected.

He was more right than he had realised, back then. It really *was* all connected.

Xiulan let out a breath as she felt a warm presence approach.

She turned her head to see Jin, a smile on his face and a cup of tea in his hand. Xiulan patted the roof beside her. Jin sat and handed her her cup of tea.

"Thank you, *Master* Jin," she teased.

Jin rolled his eyes.

"Of course, *Senior Sister*."

She bumped him with her shoulder.

He bumped her back.

Together, they watched the moon rise.

CHAPTER 53

THE LAST SIGH OF SNOW

Deep, deep below there was another world. It was a place apart. Solid and ancient, yet ephemeral and young, Here the sky was black as pitch, and had been for months. It was lit only with shining stars, and traced with golden cracks running through the endless void.

The earth was coated in alabaster-white snow, broken by the jutting obsidian rocks that reached for the sky.

It was silent here—a silence so profound that to break it would be sacrilege.

In this quiet world there was a hill where white, black, and gold met. A little house stood on the hill. A small, homey building, sturdy and well-maintained surrounded by masses of snow. Light spilled out of a window as round as the green door next to it. A thin trail of smoke rose into the air from its red brick chimney above a tiled roof. There was a pile of wood stacked against the side of the building, though the pile had obviously shrunk through use.

The house would have looked lonely, but it had a companion: a crooked and clumsily made snowman stood tall and strong beside it. His hat was perched at a rakish angle and his grin was jaunty and bright.

It had stood vigil beside the house, keeping it company during the long night.

□

"This is it," Loud Boy said quietly. He stood in a grotto in the southwest of the Azure Hills, where the water, undeterred by the freezing temperature, still flowed. The air was still cold, but waterfalls sprayed and sparkled, and the barest hints of vegetation flourished. The scent of the sea whispered past him.

It was a beautiful oasis, and yet somehow forlorn. The place . . . where he had first become a cultivator. Where the little orphan had taken his first steps on the path to greatness.

He remembered the rage and the ambition that had fueled him back then. The fury. One boy, one orphan, against the unfair world that had ripped everything from him.

Now he wasn't quite so alone.

His companion stared around, wide-eyed wonder in his expression. "I'm not one to talk, but how the hells did you *find* this place?" Rags asked.

"Got a little lucky," Loud Boy replied. "I tripped and bashed my head into the entrance. Turns out my head was stronger."

Rags snorted in amusement, turning back towards the stone wall that they had entered through. The pair lapsed into silence. Arrayed around Loud Boy were all the reagents he needed. The spiritual pills received from Cai Xiulan. The repayment from the Shrouded Mountain Sect.

His dantian was mostly sealed. All it needed was the last push.

One last push, and then he would be a cultivator again.

"We'll throw a big party after you succeed!" Rags declared. "So quit stallin' and get to fixin', yeah?"

Loud Boy—Zang Wei—smiled at his friend and sworn brother. Rags's confidence in him . . . well, it did make him feel good.

"Yeah. Don't worry, we won't stick around for long," Zang Wei replied, rolling his eyes. He let out a breath as he walked to the middle of the grotto in the center of the formation.

Then he sat down and began to meditate.

He followed the steps in the scroll he had been gifted. The reagents lifted into the air, spiraling around him. His stomach heated up, his Qi nearly boiling—no, more like a blacksmith's forge heating up, melting metal, and fusing it together.

It swirled and swirled. Raging like a storm—until he was suddenly inside one.

The tempest was a familiar place. He had been here before, when he had first met his benefactor. When he had first learned of cultivation.

From the clouds descended a dragon's head. It was huge. Gargantuan. Every description that Zang Wei had given did not do the enormous creature justice, so large was he. His scales were bright blue, and his body shone with the light of constellations. His yellow eyes sparked with the unfathomable fury of a storm.

To Zang Wei, it was confirmation. He had succeeded in repairing his dantian.

He was a cultivator once more.

Once, twice, thrice the dragon coiled around the sky, before his eyes speared Zang Wei.

The boy kowtowed before the enormous creature.

"Great Dragon. I have, as you told me, gone out into the world and seen it with my own two eyes. I have endured many hardships . . . and now, I return."

The tempest quieted.

'*The last time we spoke, I asked you a question, boy. Do you have an answer for me?*'

The great dragon's voice boomed like thunder, splitting the sky.

'*What is the nature of this world?*'

When this question had first been asked so long ago, Zang Wei had no answer. So he had been bid to go out into the world and return once he had that answer.

His initial travels had been . . . harsh. The world had been unkind. And in those early days, he'd thought that the nature of this world was *suffering*. The world was an unfair, miserable place.

But then he'd met his friends. Friends who had raised him up. Friends who had joined their hands with his. Friends who had supported him, even at his lowest. Even when his dantian was broken, his cultivation shattered, he was not abandoned.

The smiles of Cai Xiulan, of Rags . . . of Tigu . . . flashed in his mind.

And he came to the true answer.

Loud Boy smiled up at the tempest.

"The nature of the world . . . is that it is," Zang Wei declared. "It is suffering and sorrow. It is joy and companionship. It exists. And it is what we make of it."

The storm dragon stared down at Loud Boy.

'*Your dantian was shattered; your cultivation was ruined . . . and you come back more optimistic than you left?*' the dragon asked him.

"Yes."

There was a rumble like a peal of thunder—and the great storm began to laugh.

"I don't mind that answer, boy," the dragon rumbled in his ear.

And then Loud Boy opened his eyes. Qi swirled around his body, a dragon tail coiling around his arm, and ethereal horns on his brow.

Behind him, Rags let out a whoop of joy.

□

The house on the hill only had one room. While there was a table and a set of chairs, most of the little house was taken up by a plush bed. The interior was warm, with only the glowing coals in the fireplace providing a dim illumination.

In the plush bed, a single figure lay sleeping. A little girl, whose body was covered in golden cracks. Despite her thinness, her cheeks were plump and flushed with colour. She looked fairly healthy, instead of the gaunt and skeletal appearance she had once worn.

She was cocooned within her blankets, with only her head and her messy hair peeking out. Her eyes were closed tight, yet they darted around underneath their lids, clearly in the throes of a dream.

Or a nightmare. One of many, that had troubled her sleep.

She shook slightly, twisting under the covers. Her lips drew back into a pained grimace. Tears welled in closed eyes, leaking out and dripping down her cheeks.

A choked sob came from her throat. Even as the wounds of her body healed, the wounds of her mind still ravaged her.

She dreamed of sundering and breaking. But most of all . . . she dreamed of demons.

□

It was tiresome. It was all so tiresome, Elder Zang of the Shrouded Mountain Sect thought, as he stood and let the inquisitors perform their rituals.

Really? As if he, an Elder of the Shrouded Mountain Sect, would fall prey to a demon's tricks. His son might have been a waste of resources, but he was beyond such things.

Still, it was required by the ancient protocols. Tradition that required him to suffer this indignity. Checking in with his Juniors, instead of being able to come and go as he pleased.

It made his blood boil.

"All procedures are complete. Elder Zang, please continue at your leisure," the inquisitor said, bowing his head.

Of course everything had come up negative, but he could still feel the slight intent in their gazes. He said nothing as he moved past them, through the gilded halls of the Sect, and to his personal pavilion, taking up several li near the top of the mountain.

Because it was *his* blood that had fallen prey to the demon . . . or whatever had taken the sprog.

Zang still had his own doubts. Doubts that this "Master" who had killed his son truly had ties to the Cloudy Sword Sect.

He sighed. His good mood after visiting one of the courtesans had all but evaporated. The woman was skilled in her arts, and in conversation. Her fingers were soothing. A welcome balm to his soul.

"My Lord, why would they ever doubt you? It must be foul play; others must have conspired against you," the woman had asked, appalled, as she'd served him more wine.

Zang frowned at the woman's words.

She was right, Zang did suspect foul play . . . but there was something about this that didn't sit right with him. It made him restless.

He opened a drawer in his quarters and pulled out a scroll, unfurling it.

He had a feeling in his gut that somebody *had* conspired against him . . . and continued to do so.

Somebody he would be looking into with great interest.

His eyes fell upon the map of the Azure Hills.

□

The little girl trembled in her bed, shaking under the weight of demonic intent, crushed under their grasping hands.

But she was not alone in her little house. Or at least, never alone for very long. The door opened to a massive, imposing figure. It was a hulking creature bigger than the house the little girl lived in, so large it would not fit through the door.

Yet somehow, the creature did fit. Between one step and the next, the behemoth was a behemoth no longer. The beast was rather small now, about to a man's knee, not including the load of firewood stacked upon its back.

The little boar pulled shut the door behind him and deposited the wood next to the fireplace. A soft whimper drew his attention to the shattered girl in the bed. The boar took notice of his charge and grunted. After his trotters were dutifully wiped of snow and water, he leapt onto the little one's bed, shrinking down to an even smaller size. His little nose pressed against the child consolingly as she moaned, her teeth clenched tight, the sobs racking her body.

The little boar shuddered with her in sympathy. He pressed himself against her and, as Chun Ke had always done . . . took some of the darkness away.

The little one's sobs calmed. The leaking tears slowed while the boar lay with her, his solid presence calming her. Soothing the old pain and banishing the bad memories.

As she eased into a more restful sleep the boar carefully got up. He wiped away her tears, then smoothed down her hair and made sure to properly tuck the little one back in.

Once he was satisfied, he turned his attention to the rest of the house.

□

In Pale Moon Lake City, a young woman stretched her arms above her head, done with her task. Her voice escaped with a little squeak as her shoulders popped and muscles relaxed after hours of sitting hunched over a desk.

Biyu the crystal carver smiled down at her desk. It was littered with piles of old scrolls that she had used for references. A series of blueprints and plans—which when stacked together would form a pile several inches thick—shared the space with the clutter of references and writing tools.

They were her blueprints—original, not copied. Blueprints that would, hopefully, be used to carve the first storage ring produced in the Azure Hills in, well . . . *forever*. They didn't actually have a record of when the last one had been produced.

Biyu's gaze drifted from her desk to the workshop walls. Glowing crystals provided light, illuminating the hundreds of specialized chisels and knives crafted by master artisans; a special set of chisels had even been imported from Howling Fang Mountain just for this project, costing the kind of fortune that Biyu had no reference for.

It was just so fantastic. So amazing! It was all Biyu could do to leave them on the shelf, instead of taking them down and just admiring every single one of them . . . again. The last time she had done that her Master had walked in and burst out laughing over the fact that she was rubbing her cheek along the wood.

Biyu had merely been trying to . . . *acclimate* herself to the tools! Everybody knew that your tools needed close contact and proper maintenance! She had seen her father and the other sailors he worked with hugging the masts of their ships or whispering sweet nothings to their fishing nets. It was natural!

She shook her head and sighed.

A storage crystal. A *real* storage crystal. She closed her eyes for a moment and the memory of a smile crossed her thoughts, of a hand that held hers, supple and strong. Biyu grinned. Whenever she thought about the crystal, she couldn't help remembering Yun Ren. Biyu could hear his excited voice talking about his art. She loved his passion, a mirror of her own with crystals. She wanted to share in his joy again: to see all of his recorded images, and to listen to his stories. To be the one who made the crystal that helped him accomplish his dreams.

She glanced at the veritable stack of flat crystals, incremental improvements to the image-recording lens, as the Masters were now calling them.

It was their best seller. Both because of the price . . . and because they took barely any Qi at all to operate. One could use reeds with a higher concentration of energy to be the catalyst . . . or even a normal person with a bit of control over a mortal's limited Qi.

The nobles were going absolutely crazy for them. All for "broken" defunct crystals she had turned into treasures.

Biyu sighed, rubbing at her eyes. Maybe she should ask her Master for some time off. Yun Ren did say she could visit whenever she wanted, and she wanted to show him the improvements—

One of the crystals on the wall slowly started to increase in luminescence. It was one that let her know that a guard was requesting her attention. There were no sudden sounds or doors slamming open here, for fear that someone could miss a cut on the immensely valuable crystals.

Only the subtle glow, which would disrupt nothing and startle nobody.

She stood and walked over to tap the crystal twice, knowing that the request would be transmitted to the crystal's twin outside.

She had to only wait a moment before the door opened, revealing Chua, her guard for today.

"Ma'am, you have a visitor," he said quietly.

Biyu tilted her head, confused at who would be visiting her . . . until she saw the figure that walked in behind Chua.

Yun Ren's smile warmed her heart. She dashed from her position, and he laughed the moment her arms wrapped around his neck.

"Yun! How is everything?! Oh, I made you a new crystal!" She started babbling immediately, which was a bit embarrassing, but Yun Ren seemed to enjoy it as he hugged her back.

They both pulled back so they could look at each other, Yun Ren's normal little smirk replaced with a genuine smile.

"I'm doin' good, Biyu. And I hear you're doin' well too, right? Had a chat with your Master, for a little, since you were busy."

"Oh yes, it's amazing. I get to work with so many new tools, it's great!"

Yun's laugh was punctuated by a second deeper chuckle that caused Biyu to jump.

"An enthusiastic little gem, aren't you?" a smooth voice asked, as something materialized on Yun's shoulder. Biyu froze at the sight. The white fur. The red markings. The yellow eyes.

"Ohheavensitssocute~!"

The fox's eyes widened, and then the absolutely adorable creature began to *preen.*

It was the start of a very nice week.

Biyu learned how to skate. Yun Ren learned how to wind-surf on the ice of the lake. She ended up carving part of a crystal with Yun's sword, the weapon commenting that "Little Brother Sun Ne would find its report acceptable."

Nezan loved Biyu's collection of bows. The fox said they made him feel absolutely *fabulous.*

□

With careful and well-practised movements, making barely a sound, the now-larger boar grabbed the fire prod in his teeth and stoked the flames. He placed another log on the fire. He trundled around the house, clearing away what looked like patches of tar, the substance accumulating in the corners of the room.

He cleaned it from the house and gathered it in a reed sack, which had been woven when the house was first made. Done with his cleaning, he took the sack far, far away, to the top of a mountain in the distance.

There, he lifted the bag to the heavens.

The golden cracks in the sky responded. They pulsed, and from high above, Qi collected like drops of dew. A dizzying array of energies flowed down. Chun Ke sensed a silver droplet of moonlight. Grass, growing strong and nourishing everything around it. A fierce and mighty intent, the blades of a protector. An herbal scent, tangy and medicinal. Misty illusions and sturdy, rocklike endurance that others could depend on. A captured instant of a storm's wrath, hidden within a lazy, babbling creek. A void, wrapped in warmth and duty. The burning gold of the sun. The earth and glass of a spirit starting on a path of renewal.

Medicine, and a will to help, contrasted by the dim light of the stars.

And finally . . . gold. The cracks themselves pulsed as golden liquid seeped out of them, racing to the location of the other drops.

The gold of a man who loved the little patch of land he could call his own.

The drops of Qi swirled together, growing heavy upon the golden scar like rain upon a leaf . . . and waiting for one last piece.

The boar's Qi, life and growth, flowed up to join the Qi above. The prismatic orb shuddered and swirled, mixing every colour, every scent, and every taste from the gathered Qi into one single, shining drop.

It was suspended in the air for just a moment before it dropped.

It fell, landing on the reed bag full of tar. When it met the tar within, it acted more like honey than water: enveloping the impurities within and burning them away until there was nothing left.

The boar, satisfied, his task complete, closed his eyes.

□

"It's time!" Bi De's Great Master declared. He stood at the head of the disciples, his arms crossed and his gaze resolute.

Each and every one of them was in the ceremonial garb of this most glorious of times. Their heads were covered by their red hats, their bodies by the red-and-black-checkered robes called Flan Nel.

The snow was melting ever so slightly; the air had the promise of spring . . . and that could mean only one thing.

The pots were prepared; the firepits were dug.

And the trees were tapped.

Sap flowed like water and was boiled away as they toiled and toiled, crafting the sweet elixir known as maple syrup.

□

The boar was not the only one who visited. In the depths of the dream world, there were others.

A man, two halves fused with golden cracks, hummed songs, told fantastical stories about little men that stole from dragons, and argued with the other half of himself. Both of them seemed to enjoy the arguments; there was no real animosity between them. After all . . . they were nearly the same man.

A woman with freckles that formed like constellations on her face visited too. She patched up blankets and told stories of her childhood, as gentle fingers ran through the little one's hair. In her stomach, a spark grew, getting larger and larger every day.

Sometimes, the little girl's power, unconsciously, reached out towards that light. To cradle it. To let her power flow into that little spark and inhabit it . . . but always, some sense of her awareness, even while sleeping, stopped short of taking such a step.

A woman with long hair and a pretty voice was the quietest; she simply sat, silent. A constant warm presence. Adding nothing to the dream but the peace she carried within her.

A cat who was a girl occasionally visited. She carved into the wooden beams of the house and added more decorations to the carvings she had already created.

A rooster stared at the sky with a gimlet eye, waiting for the dawn.

Days passed, that were not days, but an endless night.

For all the sky was eternal, the little girl within the house changed.

The tremors and tears came less and less. Not every day was a nightmare; some of her dreams had her smiling. Sometimes she felt at peace.

She stirred slightly as the sky, once pitch-black, grew brighter and brighter.

As the snow grew soft and slushy and began to melt.

And as Tianlan, deep in slumber, began to stir.

□

"Jin?" Meimei whispered.

"Yes, love?" I returned.

"This week," she stated simply, her hand against her stomach.

CHAPTER 54

WATER

The last week of Meiling's pregnancy certainly changed things for her.

She was currently bundled up in a blanket, seated on a pillow near the fire. Chun Ke was acting as a backrest, which was common enough, but the coiled dragon surrounding them was new. Her fingers were scratching through the dragon's mane as she sat, still a bit amused. Wa Shi's favourite bag of mixed nuts and dried berries was beside her; he kept trying to get her to eat . . . and the things he brought her were devoid of any bite marks. She was flattered, truly, to be held in such esteem.

She hadn't really been allowed to do anything without somebody bouncing up to help her. She'd been forced to come up with some tasks for others just to cut down on the hovering.

Tigu, Bi De, and Xianghua were all out aggressively patrolling the perimeter, warding off *what* dangers she couldn't fathom. Gou Ren had been sent off when she'd claimed she had a craving for stew and requested he hunt something for her. She appreciated it, she truly did, that Gou cared so much about her . . . but he was a ball of nervous energy and did not help her peace of mind at all.

They were all acting rather silly, in Meiling's opinion.

She supposed everything like this crammed into the last week was better than suffering through it for months. It was novel and kind of cute—she could stand being pampered for a week. She at least had some peace and quiet right now, though.

At least Jin wasn't hovering. Her husband, aside from looking slightly constipated these past few days, was a veritable bastion of calm control and competence. He took charge with easy grace and still wasn't babying her, for which she was grateful. He was actually out now, picking up her father, and had said he would go to Verdant Hill to see if Meihua wanted to visit.

Three people, aside from her backrest and the dragon—whom she couldn't have deterred with chores and phantom threats so easily—were still in the room. Pi Pa was writing down a checklist of everything they needed, and Ri Zu was rereading everything she could get her paws on about the birthing process.

There was probably a bit of karma here, considering how much her student was poking and prodding at her every hour to check her over. Meihua had been right: it was annoying as hell, but Meiling managed to keep her temper in check. The rat meant the best, and she would accept it for what it was.

The last person in the room was the most tense. Meiling turned to her main "guardian." Xiulan was standing in the corner of the room, her muscles stretched as tight as a bowstring. Her swords floated behind her, ready to slice any would-be intruders.

Meiling sighed. Xiulan had been getting steadily out of sorts as the day progressed. Her brow was furrowed, and she kept shooting glances at Meiling. She had even gone back to her overly formal speech, treating whatever Meiling said like it was an order from an Empress.

Meiling had worked entirely too hard on smashing through that shell, and having her retreat back into it was frustrating.

"Xiulan, what's the matter?" she finally asked. Her friend was startled out of her silent reverie at the sudden question.

"I am well, Senior Sister—" she started, but Meiling was entirely out of patience.

Meiling reached back over the boar and onto the couch, where she grabbed a pillow and then hurled it. Her weapon sailed through the air at her target before Xiulan's hand snapped out and caught it. Both Ri Zu and Pi Pa turned to look at the commotion.

"Xiulan," she stated simply and with mild reproach.

Xiulan blushed.

"It is an unfounded worry," the other woman deflected.

Meiling's eyebrow arched higher. Xiulan's resolve wavered and then collapsed. Her friend sighed and ran her hand through her hair, then stood and started walking forwards. She stepped over the coils of the dragon and knelt down beside Meiling.

Xiulan carefully took Meiling's hand in her own, her fingers on Meiling's pulse.

She chewed her lip for a moment before looking directly into Meiling's eyes.

"There have been no signs of this . . . but . . . oftentimes, as a woman's cultivation rises in rank, pregnancy and birth can become more traumatic," Xiulan finally said. "The child can destabilize a woman's foundation and occasionally even provoke tribulation. My own mother had this to a minor effect and was rendered unable to use her combat arts for a full three months due to her unstable Qi. There are also tales of a child completely consuming their mother's cultivation . . ." Xiulan trailed off before sighing again. "I don't want to see you hurt, Meiling." The earnest words struck Meiling's heart.

"Xiulan . . ." she started to say, then trailed off. It was something Meiling and Jin had heard about, but they'd assumed that the signs for something like that would start early. It was still a worry, but even if it damaged her cultivation it didn't really matter all *that* much to Meiling. If it wouldn't kill her, and if that was the price she had to pay for her child . . . then Meiling would endure it.

"I have already shared my worries with Ri Zu, and she thinks there is nothing to indicate such a thing happening to you . . . but still. You already know that I tend to worry a bit too much, Senior Sister."

Xiulan's lips quirked into a smile. Meiling couldn't help but smile back.

"Well . . . I think my guardian should be slightly closer at hand, don't you?" Meiling decided, pulling Xiulan's arm. There was no resistance as Xiulan sat down beside her.

The day became slightly less tense . . . until Xiulan reached out to take a nut. Wa Shi's head snapped up and the dragon growled at her.

Xiulan glared back and picked out the nut anyway. She bit down and chewed aggressively on it.

The only reason there wasn't a fight was because Meiling was there.

It was funny until Ri Zu decided to do another checkup, "just in case." Meiling poked Xiulan in the side the entire time for making Ri Zu worry even more.

→

Morning turned to evening as people came and went, until there was a bit of a commotion outside the main house.

Meiling was curious, but the door soon opened to reveal Yun Ren with a bright smile on his face. She had actually been expecting him sooner.

"Haven't popped yet?" he asked cheekily as he leaned down to embrace her. Meiling rolled her eyes. At least she could count on Yun Ren to not be a worrywart.

"Not yet. A few more days. How was Biyu?" she asked back, and Yun Ren scratched his cheek.

"She's doing good. Gonna visit in the spring, she said, so . . . there's that to look forward to. How much do I have to bribe you to *not* tell her every embarrassing story you know about me?"

Meiling simply *stared* at him. She was actually disappointed he had asked. Of course it would be too expensive for him to afford . . . but she wasn't *heartless*. The *really* bad stuff could wait until after they were married.

Yun Ren sighed. "Hey, worth a shot, right? But I gotta get back out and help Jin carry everything in."

"Everything in?" Meiling asked, raising an eyebrow.

"Well, *yeah*. Everybody gave something to Jin when he grabbed your pops. Jin's got enough food to feed an army, and Auntie Li said more people are going to be coming over—"

"Meimei! My darling, how are you?!" Before Meiling could start to parse that they were going to have *more* guests than she'd thought, Yun Ren was unceremoniously pushed out of the way by Meihua, her friend marching in with her own son tied to her back. Little Jinhai's dark eyes were looking around curiously at the menagerie of people and animals. "Oh, you're positively glowing! All right, I've got some things I've learned which were absolutely invaluable—"

Meiling smiled as Meihua started talking her ear off.

She had been there for Meihua . . . and now Meihua was here for her. Like it always was.

Hu Li came in next, then her father, and finally Jin, carrying enough food that the mound went over his head.

Her heart started beating faster in her chest—the nerves had finally hit.

→

Many a scholar or poet likened the birthing room to a woman's battlefield. Where life and death hung in the balance between screams of agony and gushing lifeblood.

Meiling found the comparison rather apt; like a battle, the unexpected was what turned victory into defeat nine times out of ten. And the unexpected could be mitigated, or dealt with, by proper planning and a good doctor. Meiling rather liked to think of herself as an expert on the circumstances of birth. She had helped her father and the village midwives deliver enough children until she had learned enough to have been the one in charge.

She had certain expectations for how this was supposed to go and had been mentally preparing herself. She was rather small, so quite a bit of tearing was to be expected at the minimum.

She had also expected to be a bit more . . . alone for some reason; she was giving birth in a far-off house, after all. She'd expected Jin, her father, the Xong brothers, and maybe a midwife for aid, and she'd thought that that would be enough.

Reality, however, was nothing like her expectations. Hong Meiling, daughter of Hong Xian and Liling of Pale Moon Lake City, may have thought of herself as a simple farmer's wife, but the world did not agree.

She was, after all, the lady of the household, and she had a number of people, including a crowd of powerful cultivators, who very much wanted her alive and well—and for her birth to go as smoothly as possible.

Even as her mind went down every possible way it could go wrong, the more rational part of her supplied the solution: normally starting and ending with the fact that any damage she could possibly take could be healed away. Ripping and tearing? Gone in an instant. Bleeding out? A dose of sparkling herb essence and it would taper to a stop. If need be, they could even do the horrifically risky procedure that involved cutting open the mother's stomach . . . and she would probably live.

The baby, too, would probably be safe. They had run every test they could think of and then some.

Now she sat with what was effectively a war council. It was actually a little funny, if she thought about it, though in the "this is funny because I'm trying not to freak out" kind of way. With two days to go, it was the last chance to prepare.

Her father sat at the head of the table, the position given to him by Jin. Ri Zu had taken a seat beside him. Pi Pa was to his left, duty rosters arranged in front of her. Then the rest of the large table was filled out with everybody else at the farm along with Hu Li, who'd accompanied Meihua when she had come with her father.

Her father finished flipping through the pages before him, then cleared his throat.

"I have completed my examination and I concur with my daughter and apprentice Ri Zu: there are no complications that I can currently detect. The babe is positioned well, and when the labour signs start in full, things will proceed normally," her father said, his voice matter of fact. "As you can see here, things . . . are just about as perfect as I can imagine."

He gestured beside him to a nearby slate. A slate with a hazy image on it. It had been Jin's idea. Ri Zu's Qi could take what amounted to impressions—impressions that Yun Ren filled his Qi with and then projected as an illusion onto a page.

It resulted in the rough outline of a baby. *Her* baby. She could see the pudgy arms and head, along with the line that was the umbilical cord.

Such examinations were normally uncomfortable at best and inexact at worst. At least she wasn't a cow, where the procedure involved sticking a hand up to the elbow in the poor creature's ass, but there was enough poking and prodding in a sensitive area.

But it . . . wasn't *this.*

It was a sight that struck her to her core. Her mouth was dry just looking at the image of *her* child.

A warm hand settled on her shoulder, and she looked up to see Jin smiling at her. While Meiling was starting to get nervous, Jin had come to a place of complete and utter calm. Zen, he called it. He was in, if not a good mood, at least at peace that he had done everything he could for her and it was out of his hands for now. She took comfort in his steadiness. He would move heaven and earth if she needed him to . . . but right now, all they could do was wait.

Meiling managed to drag her eyes away from the grainy image, rendered in shades of green, and refocused as Pi Pa's voice called out.

'*The schedule is as follows. Miss Yin, Young Sir Wa Shi, you're in charge of heating the water and the cloth,*' the pig commanded, and the rabbit and the fish nodded. '*Young Sir Bowu and Young Miss Xianghua have volunteered to aid you. Young Miss Tigu has requested to be on guard duty along with the First Disciple. My Dear is on standby, should we, for any reason, need anything from Verdant Hill or Hong Yaowu.*'

Her voice called out the roles one after another.

'*Young Miss Ri Zu, Miss Hu Li, Miss Meihua, and Young Miss Xiulan will be assisting the doctor in his duties. If the Mistress's prediction holds true . . . in two days, the Young Master will be welcomed into this world.*'

Young Master. It was tradition to hope for a male child . . . Meiling's heart pumped so hard that she could feel it in her temples. She felt ill, and there was pressure in her stomach—

Oh.

She abruptly stood, to the shock of the table, and walked out of the room, heading outside into the chilly air. She stepped off the veranda onto the snow, not even feeling the cold slush.

"Mei? Mei, are you all right?" Jin asked as he rushed after her.

Meiling took a few deep breaths.

"I didn't want to get the floor dirty," she said after a moment. Honestly, it was a completely absurd thought, but it was one she had just acted on—since she knew what was happening.

"Don't want to get the floor dirty . . . ?" Jin asked, a confused lilt in his voice.

She felt something break inside her and warmth flooded her gut. Fluid dripped into the snow.

Jin's eyes bugged out.

It appeared, even with the fact that she was *so sure* . . . the child within her was just ever so slightly impatient.

Took after her, if she was honest.

CHAPTER 55

THE BATTLE

A wise turtle once spoke to a red panda of the illusion of control, using the metaphor of a peach pit. Both, honestly, had fair points. The red panda had declared that he could direct where the tree grew, that he could control it through sunlight and water.

The turtle replied that he could, but no matter what he did, he could not force the peach tree to be anything but a peach tree.

The answer, I had always thought, lay somewhere in between, even if actually *living* that advice was the hard part. To account for the things you could control, and accept and respect the things you couldn't.

Some things just *were*. And right now I, realistically . . . couldn't do anything to change what was about to happen.

So I took a breath, and let it all go.

□

I stared at my wife, frozen for a moment. My heart was still beating a thousand miles a minute in my chest, yet a strange sort of calm came over me. Meiling stood there nervously staring back, standing in a small puddle of liquid. She had walked out of our home because she didn't want to make a mess. Her water had broken.

Father. I'm going to be a father very, very soon.

I took a breath.

She looked a little unsteady. Her eyes were wide, fear welling up in her features . . . until her eyes met mine.

I smiled at her as I walked forward, holding out my arms. Meimei wobbled towards me and we hugged, standing together in shin-deep slush.

Her tense shoulders relaxed.

"You're right, it would have gotten the floors dirty. The whole thing will. So obviously, you'd best stay outside. Lemme know when you're done and we'll let you back in," I said, my voice full of sarcasm.

Meimei choked out a laugh.

"Sorry. Didn't know what else to do . . . and cleaning the floors kind of sucks," she muttered.

I snorted. She was right. Even with cultivation, cleaning the floors was annoying. What I wouldn't give for a vacuum cleaner that wasn't named Washy or Peppa.

"Tell you what. You don't have to do any cleaning at all for a while after this. We got a deal?" I asked her.

"Deal," she agreed. I pulled back from her and the odd expression on her face was gone.

"C'mon, let's get your cute butt back inside." I nudged, and she giggled.

"I have a cute butt, huh?" she asked, like she didn't know how much I liked her butt.

I just stared at her and slung one arm around her shoulder, leading her back to the house.

Back to Pops and Rizzo, who had swung into motion the moment they'd realised what was going on.

I stayed with her, leaning against my side, as we walked to the room that had been set up specifically for this day. She seemed a bit shell-shocked but was coming down from the panic, breathing deep.

"Just like all those other times . . . but my turn," she muttered under her breath.

She was awaited by Pops and Rizzo, Meihua, Hu Li, and Xiulan. With one last touch . . . I let her go.

I had accounted for and controlled everything I could; now it was time for me to sit back and let the experts and nature do their thing. Now all I had left to do was wait.

Wait, as my wife entered her own battlefield.

↔

"I raise this cup to you—heroes and martyrs all! We shall drive back the darkness and remove this filth from the land!" Brother Ge's voice rang out, reaching every soldier in the encirclement. He did not have to raise his voice, for it sounded to cultivators and mortals alike that he was right beside them, speaking personally to each and every man. To them, it felt like his eyes were upon them and them alone. It felt like one of the Elders of the Cloudy Sword Sect was judging them worthy.

Shen Yu stood slightly behind his sworn brother. He did so out of respect for the Cloudy Sword Sect and these pitiful men who would soon have the wrath of hell coming down upon their heads as mere mortals.

The mortals stood in their gleaming ranks, their eyes blazing with determination.

They were all ready for what was to come, even if they were woefully equipped to face it.

In that, Shen Yu could agree with the ideals of his old Sect. There was some value here. These mortals . . . he could respect their bravery, if nothing else. Without the might of cultivation they yet stood, ready to fight.

"Now, drink with me! For our ancestors! For our descendants! For the Empire!"

Three sips from the vessels that each man held. Three sips of a mix of alcohol and a potion that would render them more resistant against the demons' corruptive Qi.

"For our ancestors! For our descendants! For the Empire!" the men roared as one, a thunderous rumble that matched Ge's own voice.

Ge always had been good at these speeches—better than Shen Yu, at least. There was a certain amount of nobility about the man . . . always had been, even centuries ago, when he was still wet behind the ears as they stormed their first demonic Sect.

It had been a long, *long* time since those days. Although the scale had certainly increased. This was one of the largest operations Shen Yu had ever taken part in. For hundreds of li, the fortifications stretched: ditches, ramparts, and killing fields, all surrounding what looked like a red crack that was floating in midair. Normally, it would be near invisible—but now it was engorged, pulsing like an infected wound.

Some demons would spill out when the cultivators pierced the wound. They always did.

When the army ripped open the world and pressed into the demons' home . . . the rest of the beasts would pour out in a flood. Lesser creatures, coming by the thousands, while the cultivators were busy within.

And these men would be the only thing there to blunt the charge into the heartlands.

They would die by the thousands . . . but they would do their jobs well.

The speech ended, Shen Yu took a breath, and General Tou Le sent the men to their positions.

It was time.

The ambient Qi in the air rose as the formation finished charging.

A lance of light speared through the air and rammed into the red, pulsating gash in the world.

The world broke open like a rotten and infected boil. Black liquid gushed out as a portal formed in the air, leading to a twisting, corrupted realm where no light shone other than the dull red of some baleful star. The ground was black and twisted, and the world itself seemed to rebel against the demonic presence.

For a brief instant, one could see the ravening demonic hordes as they surged forwards.

Then the ballista on the *Divine Wind* fired, the massive ship shuddering. Explosions that could consume entire villages ripped holes in demonic ranks and broke open the bridgehead.

"Brave sons of the Phoenix! Advance!" General Tou Le roared.

↔

Meiling had been expecting a lot of things when it came to this point. She knew she was small and slim, so birth was likely to be hard on her, no matter Hu Li's jokes that Meiling had "birthing hips." It was nothing like she had expected. Oh, it hurt a bit . . . but that was it. It was mostly pressure.

Her mind was clear as she took deep breaths. Her father, Ri Zu, Meihua, Xiulan, and Hu Li were with her. Everybody else was just outside. The door was open, so they could poke their heads in if they wanted to.

Meiling wished that Jin were right beside her . . . but it was bad luck to have the father too close by during the birth.

It was kind of embarrassing to have her legs hiked up and people who weren't her husband between them poking around . . . but it was necessary.

Ri Zu was as calm and professional as Meiling's father as they did their work.

"You're dilating well, if a bit quickly," Xian stated. "Contractions are normal."

"Look at this, Meimei. You called me a resilient weed . . . but you're doing better than I did," Meihua joked as she dabbed a cloth along Meiling's sweaty forehead.

Meiling smiled at the jab.

"It's damn unfair is what this is!" Hu Li grumbled, and leveled a glare at her sons through the walls. "Couldn't those two have been more considerate?!"

Hu Li's labours had lasted a full day each for her sons.

Gou and Yun had last seen Meiling when she'd entered the room, her brothers in all but blood each wrapping her in a hug as tight as they could muster.

Yun Ren had tried to look aloof, but his eyes had given him away, as had the slight tremor in his hand.

Gou Ren hadn't even tried to hide his own anxiety. It was easy to forget that he had just turned eighteen some days past . . . or at least it was until his hardened, refined features melted into that of the boy she had patched up on far, *far* too many occasions.

It had made Meiling misty-eyed that both of them were so concerned for her. They might have had their little fights, but when everything was on the line . . . the Xong brothers would have come with her to hell.

Bitching and moaning all the way, but they would be there.

Meiling felt her body tense slightly, and she let the contraction happen. She got the feeling that she could stop them, or at least control them better . . . but she just let them flow naturally.

One slightly more painful one hit, and her hand clenched. Xiulan, her silent sentinel, made no noise as Meiling's fingers tightened on her own. She just kept up the circles she was rubbing on Meiling's back.

She was there and just staying out of everybody else's way, a silent pillar of support.

And so things continued for two hours more. It was a bit boring, if Meiling was honest. She lay back, took breaths, and waited.

Part of her was waiting for the complications or for something bad to happen.

But nothing came.

'*Dilation is complete. Everything looks good. Master . . . you can start to push.*'

Meiling took another breath. This was it. A son or a daughter. The worry of every woman was the sex of their firstborn. A son was lucky . . . a daughter always led to tension, pressure, to secure the family line.

All sorts of nastiness could arise from that . . . but Meiling knew it wouldn't apply in her case. Jin didn't care. He had told her he was fine if *all* his children were daughters.

She turned to look at the open door and caught her husband's eyes as he looked in.

He smiled at her and nodded.

You got this, he mouthed, absolute confidence in his eyes.

↔

A battle with so many cultivators was necessarily chaotic. Even this twisted realm heaved under the force of their Qi.

Swords flashed. Thunder rumbled. Techniques and the roars of warriors matched the howls of the demons in their intensity. The *Divine Wind* fired as fast as it could reload. The fairies of the Soaring Heaven's Isle turned into fierce falcons, their Mistress, Minyan, the foremost among them. Everything that flew was an offence to them, and the demons died in droves under cutting winds and freezing shards of ice.

Minyan's eyes flashed, and a section of ground ten li across was simply pulped from air pressure alone.

The battle was *home* to Shen Yu. The struggle. The will to survive. His sword split a Demonic Warform in two, the building-sized creature falling in half . . . as did twelve of its brothers. Brother Ge kept pace, the two of them watching each other's backs. The sky turned black and descended upon the demons as Ge cut loose. The Raging Cloudy Sword Formation surrounded and enveloped everything in its path. The weak simply perished, the clouds filled with such powerful sword intent that their enemies turned to dust, cut into a hundred thousand pieces.

The strong fared little better when Ge used the *true* might of the formation. He was one with the thunderous storm. Present within every inch of space. He was simply *there*, his sword descending like an executioner's judgement, within the whole length and breadth of the black cloud.

And yet though he was there, at the same time, he was not. Each and every attack launched at him passed through the cloud without ever even coming close to touching him.

Nothing could even make a sound before he ended them, dead the instant they touched the billowing darkness.

The shock of their brutal assault had shattered the leading edges of the demonic horde, but it was only the beginning. Their true prize lay farther in, at the center of the hidden realm, where the most powerful demon would reside.

The lesser beasts started to panic as the advance ripped through them like a scythe through a rice stalk. Little portals started to open up, and they sought to flee into the real world . . . only to run into the defensive emplacements.

The cultivators let them go, their efforts focused on getting to the center.

Their eyes were peeled for tricks and traps. Shen Yu noted the demons' own emplacements, half built, even as he destroyed them.

Then . . . the world rumbled.

A hill in the distance shuddered . . . and started to grow. Baleful eyes opened, and a sword that could split mountains in two stabbed into the ground as the monster started to rise.

Shen Yu slowed in his advance; the air grew so thick it was like breathing in sludge.

A Hellforged Demonic Titan.

"It appears that heaven has intervened on our behalf," Brother Ge stated from beside Shen Yu.

Indeed. The horrific beast, the same one that even the Founders of the Cloudy Sword Sect found difficult to contend with, was only half-finished. Its armor was missing in places, and one of its eyes flickered and spluttered.

Shen Yu was reluctantly forced to admit that the Emperor had been right to call him. This . . . this was worrying. It was the largest buildup of demons in thousands of years . . . and they had caught the bastards with their metaphorical pants down.

If it had been a few years later, the enormous construct of blood and hate would have been complete. Shen Yu frowned, ascending into the sky. His frown deepened as he saw the construction pits.

As would have its brothers.

The ballista from the ship hammered into the massive monster, and it staggered . . . but remained standing.

It roared. A physical thing that sent some of the lesser cultivators flying.

Then there was a surge of Qi. A black form landed on the Titan's shoulder. It was almost human-looking and carried an enormous axe.

Another landed on its head—this one covered in slavering maws, each dripping lava.

A third rose into the sky on ebony wings, like a twisted butterfly.

Not one, but *three* Demonic Generals.

"How polite. One for each of us," She Yu mused. Brother Ge appeared beside him a second later, stepping out of his black clouds.

"Indeed. I shall be magnanimous, and kill them swiftly," the man said.

Minyan just scoffed, her eyes boring into their adversaries. A lesser creature would have died from the hatred that radiated from her body . . . and several nearby demons did, their hearts literally freezing in terror. Spines of ice erupted from their chests and they slumped to the ground.

Shen Yu's sword shuddered as his Qi ran through it.

[Unconquered Blade of the Soul]

↔

"Push! Push, that's it!"

There were no dramatic last-minute reveals or enemies.

"I can see the head! Good job, Meimei, you're doing great!" Meihua encouraged her. I clenched my fist as Meiling groaned, just the slightest hint of pain in her voice.

There were no massive blasts of Qi or strange formations.

'*Everything looks good!*' Rizzo squeaked.

Preparation and planning carried the day.

"Seriously? It doesn't hurt?" Hu Li demanded, staring at Meiling with no small amount of envy.

I simply sat and waited, with Big D on my shoulder and Tigu in my lap.

It was all I had to do, because it was out of my hands . . . and in theirs. And no amount of being able to punch good would change that.

"The head is almost out!"

↔

Outside the great rift was a battle that would be immortalized for generations. Tiny holes ripped in reality as demons poured out of them, trying to escape the wrath of the cultivators—and met a wall of stalwart spirit and Imperial steel.

Halberds rose and fell with desperation-fueled strength, some shattering on black carapace; bows and crossbows fired so many arrows it might as well have been rain. Jade Armors waded into the worst of it, the golems never resting. Their pilots roared oaths and battle songs, chanting the names of the Jade Armors' previous pilots to lend them strength.

Choking fog and impossible biology rose to meet them. Poisoned blades and maddened fury met grim resolve. The demons funneled into choke points and scrabbled at defensive emplacements.

It was a battle that looked like it was the end of days. Human blood and corrupted ichor coated the ground, mixing and turning into rivers. Cultivator officers and defensive formations slowed the superhuman beasts just enough for mere men to land fatal blows.

It was merely the dregs of the other battle raging within the rift.

The air shuddered as the elements came to life, ravening lightning and blazing fire combating blasts of black-tinged light. Heroes who had lived for hundreds of

CLASH!!
CLASH

years and thought themselves to be the pinnacle of might fought and died much the same as the mortals outside.

A bald cultivator wearing the robes of a penitent fought with suicidal bravery against the war construct, further ripping open the holes that had been made by the great ship that was still bombarding it.

A formation of Raging Clouds created a safe zone, an impenetrable bastion that was both attack and defence, as the disciples of the Cloudy Sword Sect funneled the majority of the demons into their blades.

The blackened sky had been painted with swathes of beautiful blue as the power of Soaring Heaven's Isle cut through the darkness and imposed its will upon the world. A falcon battled a twisted butterfly that spewed poison and beams of light.

Farther away, a silent cloud compressed into a single point, all of its power brought to bear on a monster spewing flames so hot the stone around it evaporated; a hellscape of lava and toxic fumes surrounded the combatants.

The last was a duel of blazing light and twisting shadow. New valleys were carved into the earth, and the world itself cried out in pain under the power of two Sovereigns of cultivation.

The unconquerable sword met an axe made of darkness and chitin with city-shattering force.

↔

There was a scream of pain, and then a groan of effort.

There was a gasp, and then a moment of silence.

And then . . . there was a great breath taken and the wails of a baby.

Everything in that moment froze. I stopped being able to hear properly. I stopped being able to really think.

Xiulan came out of the room with a beaming smile on her face and said something that I didn't parse. The only thing I could hear was the crying of a baby.

I rose to my feet, my limbs slightly unsteady, and took a step toward the room.

Xiulan's smile just got wider as I staggered up to and past her.

The room had a peculiar smell to it. Blood and bodily fluids.

But I ignored that. My senses condensed to a single point, to a single person.

I looked at Meiling. She was exhausted, and sweat dotted her face and ran down her cheeks. Her hair was stuck to her face. She was disheveled and exhausted.

She had a baby against her bare chest and tears in her eyes. She turned to look at me and she smiled.

My wife was the most beautiful I had ever seen her.

↔

The roars of victory resounded as mortals cheered. The great rift in the world wobbled and started to destabilize.

Shen Yu limped out of the rift with Brother Ge and Minyan. Minyan's arm was a corrupted, ruined mess, hidden in her sleeve; Brother Ge was breathing harshly through burned lungs, his body a patchwork of burn scars.

Shen Yu touched the wound in his side while he stared at all the mud and blood.

Another battle. Another victory—but not one that had been assured. This was the most brutal demon assault in at least a thousand years.

He was tired. So tired . . . but also satisfied.

A victory for the ages.

He sighed and nodded to General Tou Le—the man was on a horse, for his legs were missing at the knees.

Shen Yu's duty was finally done.

He looked at the mortals, some of whom were sobbing. Others were cheering, heroes who had defended their home and family.

For the first time in a long time, he felt a kinship with those little men who could not touch the heavens.

Defend home and family.

How mortal a drive . . . yet how human it was too.

↔

She held the swaddled babe out to me, a little tuft of brown hair on the top of their head. Our child wailed, and I took them gently into my arms.

Amethyst eyes opened as the crying calmed for a moment.

I held my child . . . and all was right with the world.

CHAPTER 56

HARD-WON VICTORY

Meiling was utterly exhausted. She could barely keep her eyes open. She was still drenched in sweat and felt a bit sick after what she had been through, even though it had been, in all honesty, a simple birth. It had been fast, and easy to the point of being textbook—which she was grateful for. She could barely imagine going through what Hu Li had experienced. Twenty-four hours instead of six. Now *that* was hell . . . and she knew some women even had to labour for a day and a half.

She wasn't done quite yet, either. She was glad Jin had taken their child . . . because she still had business to attend to. The unpleasant spasms in her core continued as the afterbirth progressed, her father and Ri Zu remaining between her legs to remove the umbilical cord and placenta. It was worth it to see the look on Jin's face as he looked at their child, their son, with joy.

Despite her exhaustion, she couldn't help but smile as she saw the look of absolute wonder as he held their son for the first time.

A son. They truly were lucky.

Her dear husband was completely and utterly entranced. The child's cries quieted while Jin rocked him back and forth gently.

"Good job, Meimei. Good job," Meihua whispered in Meiling's ear as she dabbed down Meiling's forehead with a damp cloth. Hu Li simply nodded to her, the older woman patting Meiling's thigh.

"See? *Toldja* you got them birthin' hips," Hu Li teased. Meiling snorted . . . but was too tired to retaliate. Xiulan ran her fingers through Meiling's hair, getting some of the tangles out before leaving to go and talk with the others still outside the room. The spell finally seemed to break on Jin, as he properly held their son to his chest. His eyes then turned once more to her.

Meihua and Hu Li glanced at each other, before both women stood and gave them some space.

Jin walked towards Meiling and knelt down beside her.

"Hey, beautiful," he whispered, one hand coming to rest on her cheek. She leaned into the touch. Beautiful? She probably looked disgusting.

Meiling huffed and held out her arms. Jin smiled and returned their son to her so that the baby could rest his bare cheek against Meiling's chest. She stared at the wrinkled, absolutely adorable face and paused. It was a little strange, because she thought most fresh babies were ugly. He was wrinkly and just a little bit like a dried prune, like all fresh babes were, but he was *hers*, so he was handsome in spite of his pruny shape!

Abruptly, tears sprang to her eyes. The pain. The effort, and the hardship, had all been worth it.

They both stared for a moment at the life they had made together.

"He's got your hair," she mused as she looked at the tuft of downy brown.

"And your eyes," Jin said fondly, before he blinked. "A boy, then?" He sounded surprised, and Meiling arched an eyebrow.

"Xiulan *did* say as such when she went to get you."

"I kind of . . . *wasn't paying attention*," Jin admitted. "And it doesn't really matter, right? Son or daughter . . . both are good, eh?" Jin continued, his voice thick with emotion.

"I suppose it doesn't, does it?" Meiling replied with a smile. They leaned closer into each other . . . and moment by moment, the exhaustion faded. It felt like their hearts were beating in sync.

The moment lasted until her father gently cleared his throat.

Both of them started and glanced up. Her father's eyes were wet with tears and his forehead damp. His grin was the brightest Meiling had seen in years, full of fondness. Ri Zu was upon his shoulder, her ears folded back and the tiny cloth she was drying her eyes with in her hands.

"I'm sorry to interrupt . . . but I think we have others who wish to see," her father said with gentle amusement.

She turned her eyes to the doorway, where a truly impressive pileup was staring in, yet not daring to come closer. She supposed it was time for her son to meet his siblings and aunts and uncles . . .

Meiling nodded, not really trusting herself to speak, and beckoned them closer.

It was like a dam broke. Tigu was the first to scramble forward, followed by Yun and Gou, and then the rest of their disciples. Bi De was the most hesitant of them, and seemed troubled, yet started forwards as well, hopping up onto Jin's shoulder so he could take a better look.

"You good, Meimei?" Gou asked as he dropped to his own knees, looking at her with concern. Tigu nodded rapidly from beside him.

"It sounded like you were engaged in a fierce battle, Mistress!" Tigu stated, her yellow eyes searching and nose likely smelling the scent of blood. Meiling cupped her cheek with her free hand.

"I'm fine," Meiling managed to croak. "Just tired. You're right though, Tigu. It *was* a fierce battle."

"But you came out victorious!" Tigu declared, mollified, but she abruptly looked pensive as her gaze turned to the bundle in Meiling's arms. "And this is the Young Master," she muttered. There was a complicated expression on her face.

Then Tigu sucked in a breath and stood. She clasped her hands together in a formal salute and bowed. "Rou Tigu pays her respects to the Young Master!" Meiling saw the rest of the animals start in shock, before they too began to stand up straighter. Meiling frowned at the sudden oath, of all things. It was flattering, but not quite what she'd had in mind. "She swears to serve him faithfully—"

Jin's hand landed on Tigu's head in a short chop, cutting her off.

"*Little Brother.* Not Young Master. *We're family,*" Jin said to her. "That means Big Brothers and Big Sisters need to guide him well . . . not *serve* him, okay?"

Tigu looked up at him with her big yellow eyes. There was something oddly vulnerable in her expression.

". . . okay," Tigu murmured meekly, in a manner that seemed almost surprised.

"Now . . . say hi to your little brother properly, okay?"

Tigu stumbled forward on shaky legs and knelt down so that she could see the baby again. He was asleep, Meiling's son. Already dozing in spite of the commotion.

Tigu peered at him curiously before seeming to decide something. She huffed. "Very well! He shall grow to be a fine man! With Rou Tigu as his sister, how can he be anything but?" she declared, hands on her hips. Mieling glanced at Jin, and her husband shook his head in amusement.

Tigu was soon nosed out of the way by a massive boar.

Chun Ke was rarely pushy, but at that moment his tail was wagging, his nose was twitching, and his trotters were tapping on the ground excitedly.

His nose pressed gently against the child, and then Chun Ke *oinked* happily. Pi Pa stood beside him, offering a little bow.

The next most eager was Xianghua, to Meiling's surprise.

"Ah! He's just as ugly as Bowu was!" Xianghua stated, nodding her head. "How wonderful!"

Meihua looked scandalized at the statement, but Meiling took the compliment for what it was—Hu Li just burst out laughing. A moment later, Yun Ren came back downstairs with the recording crystal.

Some were less interested than the others. Bi De bowed politely, but he seemed to keep his distance, lost in his own thoughts. Yin and Miantiao were merely curious. Wa Shi squinted at the baby before shrugging, not exactly knowing what he should do.

Huo Ten ran a gentle finger across the baby's face, before smiling. '*This Huo Ten has taken care of many young ones. If you need aid, I can carry him on my back for a while.*'

Meiling smiled and nodded . . . but she was fast fading.

In the end, she could barely keep awake as Jin and Xiulan helped her to the bath and bathed her. She was glad for the help, since after a little bit her child awoke and started trying to feed for the first time. She was rather occupied as they helped her get all the sweat and afterbirth off her.

There would be more congratulations and praise for her tomorrow, when the rest of the village arrived, but there wouldn't be any party for the newborn until he was at least a hundred days old. That would wait for the end of his first hundred days. Only then would a child receive their name. Meiling had no doubts that her son would thrive.

She drifted off, dreaming of names.

CHAPTER 57

STIRRINGS

All right, there we go. All clean again, my little man," I said as I finished tying the new, fresh piece of cloth around my son's waist. His eyes were still closed, and there was no real response other than a little croon, but that was perfectly fine by me.

Scooping my son up into my arms, I headed back to the couch where Meimei was sitting.

She smiled at me as I held our son in the crook of my arm. He was tiny enough that I could practically hold him in one hand. Across from us, Meihua was seated with Jinhai on her lap and Tingfeng beside her. The two of them had been giving us advice as we relaxed in a relative lull period . . . which would last until our son had to relieve himself again.

Tingfeng seemed a bit amused. I was, after all, hitting the cultural "woman's work" barrier, but quite frankly I didn't really care. "You know, I don't believe I've changed our son," he said.

"What, never changed a diaper before?" I asked.

"No, our maid takes care of such things," he stated. Right . . . they were pretty wealthy, the Zhuge Clan. "Your disciples were quite eager to be of aid, Brother Jin. Why not oblige them?"

I pondered the question for a moment. He was actually kind of right. If I asked, any number of people would drop what they were doing. But . . .

I shrugged. "I think a man should know how to do at least some of everything." That and it wouldn't feel right to dump everything onto them. I had helped bring this life into the world, and damn it, I was going to help with everything. Even the worst jobs.

Even if Meimei had outright refused a fifty-fifty split of the chores around child rearing. Some cultural stuff dies hard, though it was kind of funny that we had a little argument about me doing *too much* as a father, instead of too little.

"Your 'Before people' were very strange," she had informed me the previous night, then demanded I go to sleep and leave our son to her. I'd only pouted a little and spied a lot. Mei was beautiful in the moonlight and so was my son.

Meihua leaned over, taking a better look at the sleepy, freckled face as our son fell asleep against Meimei's chest.

"Awww, I can't wait until he starts smiling. That's the best part, you know?" Meihua said. "The smiles. And the giggles."

We were still a ways away from that, but it was something to look forward to.

The first week after the birth passed in a bit of a blur, I'll be honest. The early days of being a parent were rather unfair for us, compared to other people. For one thing, we were cultivators. Waking up every two hours? It was a cakewalk for both of us, and we could probably keep that up for months. Enhanced senses meant we could nearly instantly pinpoint if our son was hungry, was just fussy, or needed to be changed.

I could never call it easy, really, but it cut out a lot of the unknowns, just being what we were. And that gave us time to enjoy ourselves.

I woke up every morning to my son sleeping on Meimei's chest, Meimei awake before me with a radiant smile on her face. It was nice. She looked healthy, instead of having bags under her eyes like you would expect on a new mom.

It was utterly fantastic, although it was accompanied by a feeling I couldn't describe. A paternal instinct? I don't know, but whatever it was, I liked it. The feeling was mixed with gratitude that I could be with Meimei every step of the way.

The other thing that made it pretty easy was my job.

Unlike a lot of people, I could *afford* to be present. I had no hour long commute to the city and back to work, leaving me exhausted at the end of the day, with Meimei alone in the house to tackle everything on her own. That would have absolutely sucked. My job was right here at home, and I was kind of on vacation already. In the last days of winter there was nothing really to do. The ground was half frozen or a mud pit or, like the General That Commands the Winter, just plain frozen—the towering snowman was still holding strong.

There was food and clothes and safety. I had created all of that. I'd made a place for my family, which was a hell of an ego boost and made me feel like the king of the world.

Honestly? We were overprepared compared to most parents with their first child. I had already done some of this stuff in the Before. Never with a baby as . . . *fresh* as this, but I knew how to change diapers and clean bare asses. Hells, I had done a stint in a wastewater plant what felt like an eternity ago, so the smell didn't even bother me.

Meimei, though? Compared to her, she made my experience look like I was an amateur. At ten years older than her younger brother, she had been his mom, so this wasn't her first rodeo . . . to say nothing of taking care of other people's children—and ours wasn't sick or vomiting everywhere.

Together, we could have handled everything. Together, we were more than enough.

But it wasn't just the two of us.

As the saying went: it takes a village to raise a child . . . and our friends and family were all in.

Like *really* all in.

Meihua had offered to feed our son for the night if we needed to get some sleep. Which was a little strange to my modern sensibilities . . . but was apparently something of a common practice.

In this level of development? It paid to have a good friend who had given birth around the same time, to the point where some women apparently tried to plan their conception around other women . . . just so that they could have some uninterrupted sleep.

It also kind of made sense that Gou Ren, Yun Ren, Meiling, and Meihua were so close when Hu Li mentioned that she had taken care of all of them at least once.

On top of the two extra mothers, ready and willing to help, we had a horde of aunties and uncles waiting in the wings in case one of us looked like we were flagging.

From the constant patrols, to the barrage of people asking if we wanted them to change diapers—Tigu for one had practiced how to tie diapers until she could probably do it in her sleep. Hell, she had made it a contest . . . and then Xianghua had won. There was never a moment where we didn't have an offer of help. It wasn't just family either—a stream of well-wishers from Hong Yaowu had kept coming to congratulate us, bringing gifts and advice.

It was . . . well, *humbling* to know that so many people were willing to do so much to help us.

Although not everyone had quite the same reaction. Bi De had been sitting on the little rocking crib I had made, keeping watch over my son every night. Some of the apprehension I noticed after his birth seemed to have faded from the rooster . . . but it was still something to talk about.

I took a breath and let it out as I listened with half an ear to Meimei and Meihua's conversation. I glanced out the window, at the last days that we would have snow, and let a smile cross my face.

Another year had come and gone . . . and despite the pain and terror I'd experienced when I'd first arrived on this world . . . I was . . . grateful.

I could safely say . . . I was enjoying my life.

Running away from the chance at unlimited power was probably the best decision I had ever made.

□

Deep, deep under the ground, in a place that was yet wasn't, the blackened sky turned pink, with the soothing tones of the rising dawn.

The snow, save for the snowman, had all melted, exposing brown, flattened grass. The black, jagged rocks had lost some of their foreboding look in the new dawn light, reflecting the changing sky.

And within a little house on a hill, a little girl stirred. She tossed once, then turned, and then groaned, as awareness started to return to her.

First to come, as always, was the pain. It was *always* the first thing she felt upon awareness. The old friend that had been with her for thousands of years.

But it felt . . . weaker. The ripping pain, like searing knives, was a duller ache instead of a sharp slice. She could almost ignore it. It was an ever-present constant in the back of her mind, rather than an impossible-to-ignore weight.

Her consciousness drifted in the stillness, for it was not yet entirely time for her to fully awake.

She took a deep breath in, expecting the acrid tang of impurities that she expelled from herself while she was sleeping. But her nose found only the scent of a merry fire.

Something told her that that wasn't right. Perhaps something had gone wrong, and she hadn't managed to expel the impurities within her. Her senses started to cast about. Like a man in the dark, stumbling forward.

Smell, touch—

And the taste of Qi on the wind.

Over a dozen different flavours. Over a dozen different little roads off into the distance. Meandering paths, rather than a massive, ripped-open road.

Warmth. Affection.

Not pain and terror.

Her featherlight touches continued down golden links, until she felt something new.

A tiny little spark of gold.

A tiny spark of gold that was her Connected Ones.

Tianlan's arms wrapped around something small and in need of protection.

A little orb of golden light.

It was precious. It was beautiful, even with her half-consciousness.

She held it closer to her chest, in a protective embrace.

It was something she had longed to do—she had never gotten to hold her two best friends' child.

It was one of her most painful regrets. Even if they had betrayed her in the end.

As her consciousness began to fade again, however, she did have a thought. If it was a regret in the past . . . well . . . Ruolan's descendant was here . . .

↔

"Jinx," I immediately called before Xiulan could say anything, recovering as she was from her own sneeze.

"Ji—" She cut herself off and pouted as I rubbed my nose. Her sneeze was just about the only thing that wasn't dainty about Xiulan. It was as loud as mine—either one of us could cause the glass in the greenhouse to rattle.

Xiulan kept grumbling as we tended to the stocks of Spiritual Herbs and checked on the beehive. While I spent most of my time with Mei, I did still do a few chores. The bees seemed to be doing well! After I had put them in the greenhouse I'd had second thoughts, realising that it could have had adverse consequences, but I'd managed to luck out. I could have accidentally killed the whole hive, which would have been bad.

Still, if they could be moved in and out with no consequences, that was pretty great!

I hummed as we worked, infusing my herbs. Xiulan's much-nicer voice flowed with mine, making a surprisingly good harmony.

We were expanding the plots, so we could keep producing medicine and also have them for seasoning. We had also managed to grow a cutting of the Ten Poison Resistance Herb, one of Xiulan's wedding gifts, and I couldn't wait to get more of them. Like the Lowly Spiritual Herbs, they tasted pretty good. Sweet and sour, they would make a fine addition to my slowly growing collection of tasty seasonings.

It didn't take too long with somebody helping me work. The pots were all finished fairly fast, the sprigs of herb growing big and strong.

I was on complete autopilot as I came to my last bucket. It looked like it had already been harvested, but that was wrong. It contained the weird root that I had found almost two years ago now.

Honestly? I gave the thing Qi mostly out of habit, and a little bit out of curiosity. I still hadn't found out what it was—

I paused, my hands on the soil. Squinting, I moved my finger through the dirt until it bumped up against a slight deformation.

A small growth from the root, starting to poke out from the soil.

Huh.

"Took you a bit, eh? Well . . . you go at your own pace, little buddy," I murmured.

CHAPTER 58

THE STORM

In the north, winter never truly went without a fight. Even with spring nearly upon them, there was always one last storm, the vengeance of winter. When the sky turned black and screamed down from the Sea of Snow, roaring defiantly one last time at the warm wind of spring.

And this one . . . it was a bad one. A Devil Storm. Once every ten years or so, the north would send down a storm of such magnitude. A storm that seemed actively malevolent, with billowing, pitch-black clouds. Old wounds would ache; docile animals would rear and panic. Men and women would have their faces turn grim.

With it came snow, ice, and freezing rain. The gale-force winds battered the tile rooftops and slung freezing-cold waves of slush that could get big enough to bury and drown a man. Thunder howled and lightning crackled.

It was a terrible thing, the Devil Storm.

□

"Shore up what you can, but do not dally! Buildings may be rebuilt; your lives are a more precious thing!" the Lord Magistrate of Verdant Hill's voice rose above the intensifying winds as he walked through the town. The people didn't stop to gawk at him, merely jumping immediately to carry out his commands. It required much practice to project one's voice so, and he most certainly was not a natural. He had practised relentlessly to achieve the desired effect . . . and drank plenty of honeyed water afterwards.

His throat would need it. And he would need a place by the fire. He grimaced and pulled his coat tighter around his body as another blast of wind seared through the streets—the Devil Storm blowing in an unseasonable cold. The lower hem of his robe was wet and partially frozen with slush already, and he was most grateful for his fine boots, lest his feet be frozen too.

His eyes darted around the town and the scene of organised chaos within it. The plans put in place were being followed to the letter, the guards racing around and helping the people of Verdant Hill board up windows, batten down doors, and secure what they could.

It was not what he wanted to be doing today, but whenever the coterie of grandmothers showed up, with the mad woman at their head and a goat at her side, the Lord Magistrate had learned it paid to listen.

And it doubly paid to listen when they spoke of a Devil Storm. He had not known that old lady to be wrong. She could feel it in her bones, she said, and so the Lord Magistrate listened.

The orders were received without complaint, plans swinging into action with the ease of long drills, but there was always *some* amount of chaos. That was just what happened.

He marched quickly through the town. The guards had already been out and about earlier, knocking on doors and informing the people of the Lord Magistrate's will. Those in the poorer districts were welcomed within the palace's main hall, just in case their houses could not stand up to the battering. The palace was warm, and its thick walls and roof were proof against any storm the north could throw at them.

Still, one last check before he went in himself. He noticed a man struggling with a board, attempting to nail it to his window and keep it shut.

The Lord Magistrate looked around for a guard, but he was alone for once, so he grimaced and marched over to the struggling man, the only one on the street at the moment.

He grabbed the other end of the board for the man, stabilizing it so he could finish driving the nails in.

"Thanks, Broth—" the man started to say, turning to smile at the man who had helped him, before realising who it was. Awe entered his eyes, and suddenly the Master of Verdant Hill felt a bit less cold. "Lord Magistrate?!"

"Was that the last thing you needed to do?" he asked the man.

"Yes, Lord Magistrate! I took my wife and child to the palace first!" the man replied.

The Lord Magistrate nodded.

"Good man. See to your fellow people of Verdant Hill, but do not tax yourself unduly."

"Yes, Lord Magistrate! Right away, Lord Magistrate!"

He nodded and let the man go so he could continue his final checks. A few more hammered-in nails, a few conversations with the more well-off clans—whose courtyards and homes were similarly sporting extra guests—and a visit to a lone mother who needed some assistance getting her bundled-up gaggle of children to the palace were his last tasks.

He ordered the captain of the guard to close everything up . . . and then he could *finally* get warm.

The sky was completely black as the Lord Magistrate entered the halls of the palace, pulling off his hat and almost groaning with pleasure at the feeling of warmth and safety.

He hadn't liked the look of the clouds rolling in . . . though he knew he would be safe in the heart of the seat of his power, comfortable.

His eyes roved over the main hall. It was full, but it wasn't *packed*. The blazing hearthfires overpowered the cold, and he could hear the tones of an expertly played guzheng drifting through the air.

The mood was downright optimistic, with the children even looking outright excited, as bedrolls were laid down.

The Lord Magistrate smiled at their antics when he handed his coat and boots off to a servant and received fire-warmed and blessedly dry clothes. The servant bowed, with a murmured "Lord Magistrate."

He took a cup of tea from the local tea shop owner, brewed to perfection. He received a report of the capacity of the palace, and the amount the firewood and food would cost, which was honestly a pittance compared to the looks of utter admiration from him sheltering his charges within his own home.

He walked through them, muttering the appropriate words to those who wished to speak with him. He was . . . not really paying too much attention, but the comforting words were what the people needed to hear.

Soon enough, he arrived at the guzheng player, his lovely wife. Lady Wu smiled at the Lord Magistrate, surrounded as she was by her audience.

He smiled back, her dexterous fingers played a song of spring, drowning out the howling wind.

Once the storm blew over, his outriders would be dispatched. They would set off, braving the elements, seeking the villages, and reporting back to him damage that needed to be repaired.

But for now . . . there was nothing more he could do but sit and wait. He hoped Jin wouldn't be upset that his congratulations were delayed . . . but he had a feeling his student would be understanding.

□

Despite the Devil Storm's presence, its fury seemed . . . *blunted*. It was a small thing. The wind still rattled doors as children huddled in blanket fortresses. Its cold fingers still ghosted under doorways and probed at the fires, as if they were lives to snuff out.

But its full might was restrained; the tides of slush shuddered but did not fly like the ocean waves; the bitter-cold freezing rain fell and melted before it could ice homes over. The gale winds raged yet only shook loose a few roof tiles and rattled the doors, rather than blowing entire houses down.

For there was a guardian in the land.

His name and title were grand. A defender of unparalleled ferocity.

Intent had made him. First, it had been a joke, and yet . . . he was so much more than his initial conception. For in that joke was a core of belief . . . and a spark of power from a little dreamer.

His eyes were black as pitch and utterly unflinching as he stared down the full might of the north wind. His hat, the symbol of his station, was tall and grand. He even had a loyal subordinate close by, lending him just a bit of his strength.

The General That Commands the Winter faced the storm . . . and smiled.

□

In the Eighth Correct Place, the ground heaved and rumbled as rain, snow, and ice poured down the Gutter in the middle of it. It was full to the top, and some water spilled over its sides . . . But the great work held.

The people, taking refuge in a forest that had once been overrun by wolves, watched in awe at the sheer amount of ice and water thundering down the Gutter—so much so that even the Torrent Rider dared not test his luck in the merciless surge.

Instead, he raced from village to village, the mask of his Master tight upon his face. He herded the sheep to sheltered areas; he plucked those foolish enough to wander close to the Gutter from its killing stream; he carried the elderly from their homes to safety, a smaller, more mundane hero.

Yet a hero nonetheless.

He worked and toiled without cease, as clouds turned day to night, spitting and howling.

But the houses stood firm and strong. They stood triumphantly. They were, after all, in the Correct Place.

□

The good General faced the howling gale; he faced the lashing rain. He stayed standing when by all rights he should have fallen over.

But even the mighty General could not face this onslaught alone, reaching so far as he was. His subordinate fell first.

The Warden That Sends Forth the Flying Ice and Snow toppled slowly, power spent. His icy heart turned to slush, yet he had done his duty well. His smile faded for the first time all winter as he collapsed, fallen in the line of duty.

And then the General stood alone. For not one day, but three, did the Devil Storm batter and smash at him. His smile faded. His body was ground down.

But he stood. He stood until he was a featureless white pillar, with a hat that miraculously did not blow off.

He shuddered and shook, he trembled and cracked . . . but he did not fall.

He remained standing as the sun rose high in the sky, pure, and beautiful, and warm.

The General That Commands the Winter stood . . . and didn't fade.

His body might have broken, but his crystal heart remained.

CHAPTER 59

THE SNOW GLOBE

Well, that was a lot better than we were expecting, wasn't it?" Bi De's Great Master asked as his feet pounded across the now bare stone of the road. His hands flashed out and he scooped up branches of fallen trees, either tossing them off the path or, in the case of an entire tree, kicking it up to carry it upon his shoulder without breaking his stride.

Bi De hopped beside him, copying his movements and using precise gusts of wind to fling off the leaves and smaller debris that had accumulated. Gou Ren, Yin, Bei Be, Wa Shi, and Tigu raced along with them, cleaning up the debris they missed. A wave of water followed in their wake, blasting away any dirt that had been swept onto the road. Chun Ke brought up the rear, pulling the cart with Uncle Xian, Liu Bowu, little Xian, and Ty An. Zhuge Tingfeng had already been returned to his home.

"Indeed, Master. It was good to see that everyone escaped undue harm. The Healing Sage and Uncle Xian were both concerned about the storm, but it appears the howls of the wind were worse than the damage inflicted."

Fa Ram had escaped nearly unscathed, save for some downed branches. Indeed, Bi De had found the storm . . . pleasant, even. While the storm raged, they'd remained untouched. They had spent the entire second day in the greenhouse. It was far enough away from any trees, so the chance of the winds being strong enough to break the reinforced, Qi-forged glass was slim.

They had all gathered to watch the raging rains and sleet as they lashed against the windows, the warmth around them feeling like it was the height of summer. They played board games, and his Great Master, for the first time, managed to defeat Chun Ke at go.

Which was a great victory—the Master had defeated one beyond him. The boar had always been surprisingly good at the game, despite his difficulties and injury.

They also watched the flights of bees, as they too felt the coming spring and were starting to truly awaken.

The Great Master, upon hearing how destructive these Devil Storms normally were, had raised the question of seeing if anyone needed aid, and the Healing Sage had bid the Great Master to check on Hong Yaowu and Verdant Hill. Loath though the Master was to leave his child . . . he had, in the end, followed his instinct to help and set off with the cart and supplies, ready to give his aid.

He had delivered Hong Xian to his people . . . but they too had escaped nearly completely unscathed. A few roof tiles were missing, but that was about it.

The only true casualty was the final collapse of the village's snow golem, who had been looking haggard anyway. His body was now a tiny slush pile.

The great golem's corpse was surrounded by inconsolable children, and Hong Xian the Younger was holding a funeral service . . . complete with a funerary tablet.

The children seemed to think that the Warden That Sends Forth the Flying Ice and Snow had something to do with the lack of damage, so there were already plans to build another next year. They had even managed to find the golem's hat from where it had blown off into the trees.

Bi De's Master had picked up a few other helpers along the way, and thus departed to Verdant Hill. The road here had been in much worse condition. It was covered in hip-high slush and hundreds of fallen branches, but they were cultivators—they simply waded through each and every impediment, sweeping the path clear with ease.

Verdant Hill was a bit worse off, but again, to Hong Xian's befuddlement . . . it wasn't as bad as storms had been in the past. It certainly *looked* bad, and there was trash everywhere . . . but the people of Verdant Hill were already cleaning it up. Compared to the devastation Bi De had seen at the Dueling Peaks, it was nothing.

Indeed, the Lord Magistrate had been in the finest spirits Bi De had ever witnessed in him, a bright smile on his face. He was mildly injured, several rope abrasions on his body, but that was to be expected. He was aiding the men of Verdant Hill, along with Archivist Bao, in setting up a crane, the rope and pulleys letting them lift up the numerous roof tiles they needed to replace.

From preliminary reports delivered by minor transmission stones, the outriders were reporting similar circumstances in the closest villages.

"It's all due to the Warden's help!" Little Xian had decided. The Lord Magistrate looked utterly baffled, until it was explained exactly who the Warden *was*.

"Yes, the snow golems," the Lord Magistrate said, his earlier cheer back. "My messenger mentioned the one at Hong Yaowu, and the men built their own small one. Next year I hear that there's going to be some kind of competition between the outriders and the guards, something about our men refusing to be beaten by the villages."

The man chuckled and then stood tall, forming the gesture of respect.

"Thank you all for coming," the Lord Magistrate continued. "Your willingness to lend our Verdant Hill aid is appreciated and speaks to your virtuous souls. If you wish to give us any help, I am not a man to refuse your benevolence—but we do have things well in hand. I would like to have a drink with you, however, my student. I hear things have gone well?"

And thus, after a day of putting roof tiles back on buildings and sweeping streets, as well as lunch with the Lord Magistrate . . . they were on their way back home.

Past the fields, bare dirt now visible. Past the earth and rock, now exposed once more. And past the first little shoots of plant life. Active as soon as the sun hit them, they raced to be the first to bloom.

It was close. It was so close now Bi De could taste it, as the beating heart within the earth thumped louder and louder.

↔

After a long day of cleanup duty, we finally made it home. It had been difficult leaving the farm, but in the end I wanted to be a man my son could look up to. So I'd gone to see if my neighbors needed any help.

Seeing the hell that weather could wreak up close was always something.

I knew how bad storms could get, and this had been quite the nasty one . . . but it hadn't turned out too badly. And it was always great to see the community banding together. I had been a part of enough cleanup operations after flooding and ice rain, so it was old hat to me.

A few roof tiles? Nothing. Cleaning up the roads would take longer, but it was doable.

So instead of funerals and sorrow, we got the good feeling of a job well done. Sure, there was damage, but like the road, it was more an exercise in community bonding than anything strenuous.

We came back through the gate of my farm in high spirits, ready to relay the good news to those who had stayed home . . . and I instantly noticed something. The yard was completely clear, the wood of fallen branches stacked up.

And I knew the culprit.

The good thing about super medicine is that your darling wife heals fast, without any scarring or stretching.

The bad thing about super medicine is that Meimei was, upon being given her clean bill of health, trying to do strenuous activity. The polar dip she had taken during the storm was fine, but she should still be resting!

I wanted to pamper her, damn it! But Meimei was bringing down planters and sorting out some of the soil I had made for her, Xiulan and Rizzo her assistants. Her eyes were gleaming as she prepared everything for spring, our son tied to her back so she could carry him around wherever she went.

But I wasn't one to be outdone by my wife.

I sent out my dutiful disciples and we started on our last preparations.

The tools were inspected and sharpened. The fields were staked out. Commissions for my drop hammer were given to Bowu, who grinned like a loon when I entrusted him with the task; Ty An, who was visiting Tigu, rolled her eyes and rolled her sleeves up and immediately started pumping the fires of the forge.

We were a well-oiled machine now. All the kinks of last year had been mostly smoothed out, and once more we would be expanding. Expanding with new fruits and vegetables, new experiments, and new . . . things.

Like a drill we moved forward bit by bit, each and every year.

One of the last things was to finally put the General to rest as well. Part of me wanted to see just how long he would take to melt . . . but in the end, I decided to give him a send-off like last year.

Namely by shoveling him into the river. He was basically pure ice from the storm, but it didn't really impede me any . . . at least until I got to the middle of him.

'*Again, it is some form of ice crystal, but I have no idea what kind. Ice crystals are hexagonal in shape; this one is a sphere,*' the monkey stated.

Huo Ten scratched his chin as he held the perfect sphere in his palms. Last year it had looked just like another piece of ice, a diamond-shaped fragment. Now it was a perfectly smooth sphere, dark like the frozen pond water. The globe was flecked through with gently drifting motes of white—like stars or gentle snowfall. '*If I had not seen it before, I would even say that this was already cut. Of course, some crystals grow 'perfect,' but it is very rare . . . In short? This Huo Ten had no idea what this is! It is interesting, though . . .*'

The monkey handed it back to me, and I stared, completely nonplussed, at the sphere. I shook it.

The little motes within went wild, like they were caught in a storm.

My giant snowman formed a snow globe in the middle of his body.

I licked my lips, staring at it for a moment longer.

"You know what? Not the weirdest thing I've seen," I decided, even as I wondered if little Xian's theory about the snowmen protecting them had some merit. It wasn't *actually* commanding the winter, was it? "Thank you for your service, General. You sleep tight now, okay? We'll see you next year."

I stared at the globe for a moment longer before taking it back to the cold storage. The area had already been packed with river ice, so our fridge would last until next year . . . and we had added another room to it. A room with a door, beyond which Tigu's sculpture collection lay.

We now had the full set. A naked ice sculpture of literally everybody who lived on the farm.

It was amazing what Tigu could get people to do by just asking them nicely . . . with no hint of any bad intent.

And honestly, they were getting a lot better.

I shook my head as I started out of the cold storage.

Last year, I had my wedding. This year . . . ?

Well. I was excited to find out.

CHAPTER 60

THE YOUNG ROOSTER

As the days slowly got warmer and warmer, we became more and more active, though I was in a slightly melancholy mood. This time last year I was rushing towards a wedding; this year, I was moseying on forwards and taking things a day at a time. I felt the land beneath me stirring more and more, like a kid tossing and turning in bed.

The end of winter was within the week now. I could feel it in my bones. Soon it would be spring, and . . . Tianlan would be awake. I don't know if I was looking forwards to that conversation, but it was something that needed to happen.

She couldn't be too bad, not with all the help she had given us. It still weighed on my mind, though, and often woke me up early.

Still, my nerves would wind down quite quickly at the beautiful sight that greeted me every time I opened my eyes: my wife on her side, dozing, and our son in between us.

It truly was the greatest. I smiled at the freckles dusting both of their noses and resisted the urge to plant a kiss on Meimei's nose.

It was fantastic, let me tell you, to have Meimei all healed up already. She was similarly ecstatic . . . and as long as we kept it short and sweet, well, we managed to catch up on some time we had, er, missed.

We had to be careful, though. Meimei didn't want to get pregnant again quite so soon. Maybe in a year or two? We'd have to talk about it.

But until then, fun was back on the menu for both of us. Three cheers for over a dozen willing and able babysitters.

I just lay there for a moment, basking in the warm bed . . . until a rooster started to crow, Big D's voice echoing across the hills.

I stared at my son, amused as his eyes snapped open.

There was one thing that was funny in the mornings.

As the rooster crowed, a tiny voice rose up with it. Not one of pain, or hunger, but just a little squeal as my son decided the best thing to imitate in the morning was a rooster.

I snorted while I stared at the baby beside me, trying his best to pop a cock-a-doodle-do. Meimei, her eyes open, heaved a similar sigh, fond exasperation on her face.

"Of all things . . ." she muttered, planting a kiss on his forehead. "At least he has strong lungs."

"Little De here does have quite the pipes, doesn't he?" I joked.

Little De. *Xiao De.* A pun in another language, because *Xiao Didi* meant "little brother"—what Tigu had taken to calling our son.

I paused. Well, it was kinda awkward to just refer to my son as "the baby" all the time. Milk names, or "name before your official name," were sometimes given to children to drive away evil spirits.

My grin spread across my face. If he ever figured it out some time in the future, my son would be *so* pissed at me. Or he would never learn and figure his nickname just came from his "strong uncle". . . and really, it did.

"*I know that smile,* husband," my wife deadpanned. "What exactly does that name mean?"

I told her. Most wives, I think, would be offended that you wanted to make your kid's nickname an inside, kind of rude, joke.

Meimei's cheeks puffed out, and then she started cackling.

"Oh? *Little De*, you yell so much!" my wife scolded him affectionately. The baby giggled.

And that was how my son got his nickname. It brought a smile to my face every time I said it.

↔

Bi De held out his wing, a feather tracing the character for "strength" before amethyst eyes. Amethyst eyes that held a spark of interest and intelligence within them as they followed the red feather.

The eyes were watching, *trying* to understand. Not quite able to articulate anything yet, but there was no mistaking what it was.

Bi De smiled all the same.

"He likes you," Bi De's Great Master said, smiling at them both. "I think it's the colours that draw his eye. You are a handsome devil."

Bi De shook his head with amusement. Indeed, his plumage was something he took great pride in. Feathers the colour of fire, with a jade-green tail, and wings with sapphire blue decorating the top of them. They shone in the light and were coveted by all who laid eyes upon them.

"Little De has a good eye, then," Bi De declared pompously. His Great Master's smile widened, and Bi De felt himself flush. For his Great Master to give his own son a protective name after Bi De, it was most flattering. It showed in how much regard his Lord held his First Disciple, that Bi De's name would be the bane of evil spirits for his own son—even if none would dare to inch close to the babe in Fa Ram.

Bi De . . . found himself caring for the babe more than he'd thought he would . . . and not just because his milk name had been given in Bi De's honour.

His Great Master had made it very plain to the disciples that nothing related to the child was their *duty* . . . only their responsibility if they accepted. If they did not wish to change the soiled cloth, then they did not have to. Bi De had learned just in case, but so far he had not had to perform that task.

"He sure does. He's got his momma's peepers," his Great Master declared, looking fondly at the child, before turning to Bi De. "And you're calmer around him now. You were a bit on edge for a couple of days there." His voice was conversational, though also concerned.

Bi De nodded. Of course his Lord had noticed his apprehension . . . but that was now dust in the wind. Bi De's concerns had been laid to rest. The spark in the amethyst eyes.

"I was worried that he might be like the ones that I have sired, dull and without presence, but . . . I suppose humans do not work like that in the first place," Bi De said. "But it was obviously folly."

His Great Master paused, the man's smile falling.

"Oh . . ." he suddenly whispered, looking stricken. "*Bi De . . .*" He trailed off, compassion and pain clear in his voice. Bi De hopped from beside the babe to his Master, to look him in the eye and reassure him.

"I believe I have come to a sort of peace with it, Master. Or if not peace, understanding." He hadn't mated with the hens in a while. Ever since he'd gotten back home, really. "It was base instinct that drove me, like Tigu's dislike of Ri Zu. Thoughts of what was 'right' that I had not questioned. A man sires many children, and takes the worthy to continue his name. I did as my instincts commanded . . . and, well, nothing happened."

His Great Master grimaced, and his hand came up to rest on Bi De's head. He was silent for a moment as his fingers worked.

"No father should have to go through that."

Bi De leaned into the touch. "I have meditated long upon this. This Bi De supposes he is an anomaly. In my journeys, I have not met another chicken with a spark. Nor another fox like Basi Bu Shi, nor multiple wolves, nor rabbits . . . Only Pi Pa and Chun Ke are the exceptions, but they are like yin and yang, so make some sort of sense. We were either born with exceptional talent . . . or there is some other factor at play. Spirit Beasts, like the Blaze Bears, all seem to have some innate sense of self, while we . . . we all are different. And so there are two choices: seek to better understand it, or wait for the heavens to smile upon you." His Master chewed his lip, eyes focused completely on Bi De. The rooster did not like his Master feeling such obvious distress over Bi De's revelations.

"I have decided to forgo that, for the moment. If I am to be a father, I must be as skilled as yourself . . . and to accomplish that, I must do a lot of study. Perhaps it shall be attained through the use of some sort of transformation. Perhaps I shall never sire children, and like the Gramps of your tale, take in an heir. But that is for the future . . ."

His Master nodded, still looking concerned.

"Then . . . what do you want to do in the future? I know that you said that you wanted to protect Fa Ram, but . . ."

Bi De considered the words.

The journey he had gone on, venturing all around the Azure Hills, had been satisfying. Going forth into the unknown, learning, and meeting the others who lived there. Witnessing their customs and seeing their special dances had been enjoyable.

And then coming home and telling the others all about the places he had been was satisfying in its own way as well.

"I want to better understand myself," Bi De replied. "There are two parts: one that yearns to go out into the world, to explore, and learn more about it, and the other that wishes to stay here and defend, to protect and watch over this wonderful place and see it grow. If I can, I should like to do both. A wanderer, and a protector. After all, I must live up to the sign you made, no?"

His Master's mood lightened, and he snorted. "Yeah. The whole world will know to respect the rooster." They lapsed into silence for a moment. "That was a bit heavier than I thought it would be," his Master admitted. "But thanks for telling me. We'll figure things out . . . together, if you'll have us."

Bi De bowed his head, once more humbled by his Master's support. His Lord glanced to where Little De had become distracted by motes of light, then held out his arm.

Bi De hopped onto his Master's shoulder as the man set out into the yard. The yard where the grass was going green and the first flowers were racing to open.

Out into the beautiful sun, just like old times.

CHAPTER 61

THE EMPRESS OF THE GREEN PAVILION

At the Beginning of the Time of the White Death

Vajra sat upon the wall of the barrier, her wings buzzing occasionally and her abdomen working as the pleasing vibrations of the Emperor's hum resonated through the Green Pavilion. Beside him, Beautiful Bi De and Stalwart Chun Ke worked, their magnificent forms acting in tandem to attend to the pots of soil and raise the Green Pavilion, Palace of Eternal Warmth, to new heights.

Vajra was rather glad she had observed the ancient rites of the White Death—preserving her best soldiers and allowing the rest to perish at the end of their short lives.

There simply were not enough plants and nectar within the Pavilion for a full muster and growth of the hive—enough was here for a bumper of brood at the start of the Season of Plenty, but it would be impossible to support her hive at full mobilization.

Still, it was through no fault of the Emperor's. The realm was new and had to be made from scratch, and thus Vajra would be patient.

In time, the Coldguard would have much to do . . . but for now there really was nothing. They did not need to vibrate their bodies to keep the hive at an acceptable temperature as living heaters, so instead Vajra commanded them to frolic and dance—and hopefully draw the Emperor's eye.

For she had been right in her earlier devotion: this man was truly the Son of the Heavens and the Earth.

"Let me tell you the story of how I died," the Emperor said as he gazed at the Empress. His words were as heavy as the mountains.

The Emperor had conquered death—and not just conquered death; he had the knowledge of vast hidden realms to prove it.

Truly, she had the luck of the heavens to land in the service of such a powerful Emperor! Oh, when the time of the White Death ended, Vajra would send out a thousand heralds to proclaim his dominion over this land, conquer every hive, and slay every Flying Demon that dared show its face!

Vajra could not wait.

Unfortunately, she did not draw the Emperor's eye that day, for after he completed his row, the Master of this Land stood. "Right. I'll go check on the table.

Miantiao said it was pretty much done," he called out. Beautiful Bi De and Stalwart Chun Ke stood with him as he exited the Pavilion.

Vajra stopped dancing and buzzed as he exited the hidden realm.

But though he left, that did not mean this palace was empty. She gazed around at the others within the Green Pavilion. Her eyes landed first on the White Blazing Star, the white rabbit that dozed in the barrier room, heating it. Vajra had thought little of the servant at first, but now? After truly experiencing the heat? Oh, if only Vajra had command of such a fearsome beast during the war—her tactic of cooking the Flying Demons within their carapaces would have been trivial. With her immaculate command and the brute strength of the White Blazing Star, victory would never have been in doubt.

Vajra felt the sorrow and longing well up within her for the Empire that had been lost to the Flying Demons, and her wings buzzed without conscious command. Then she forced the feeling away. There was no medicine for regret. And really, would she have known such wonders if she had won? No. The defeat had merely paved the way for her to ascend to new heights.

The other one in the room—the Empress—was a dominating, tyrannical presence.

She sat upon a chair, reading a scroll, with a contented smile on her face. Vajra studied the woman closely, looking for any weakness in her most formidable rival. Indeed, she was most powerful, and if Vajra wished to be the Emperor's Empress, then there would be political maneuvering involved. The woman was, after all, some sort of . . . healer. Vajra knew that was important, but such things were supposed to be content working from the shadows. And she had heard the woman complain about politics. Well, Vajra, a good vassal, would take such annoyances off her hands—

Thistleflower eyes rose up and landed on Vajra's form. It took all of Vajra's concentration not to freeze and let the woman know she had been observing her. The Empress's eyes were as her soldier's stingers: sharp and piercing. They tore into Vajra's armor and laid her bare as the woman's nose wiggled like that of a Blaze Bear smelling honey.

Vajra acted like one of her Coldguard and began cleaning her antennae.

The woman's nose worked again before she shrugged and turned back to her scroll. "Not enough Qi, I don't think . . ." she muttered.

Vajra felt her body shudder. That gaze had certainly been . . . *something*.

Perhaps . . . *Empress* was slightly too ambitious a goal for now, even with the Emperor's favour for her hive's honey. Vajra the Boozemaster was a powerful title . . . but evidently not powerful enough to challenge the current Empress. Nay, hubris would not be her downfall.

Instead, she would curry favour.

She took off from her position and landed before the Empress on one of the pots of dirt nearby. Then she launched into her most elaborate and intricate dance, in hopes of appealing to the woman.

The Empress glanced at her and took in another breath.

"Strange little thing," she muttered, but allowed Vajra to dance for her.

"She's cute! Look at her work that hairy butt!" the Emperor's voice boomed. Vajra flinched at the statement. She had been so intent on her dance that she hadn't taken notice of him reentering. But he had a large smile across his face as his wonderful, *wonderful* finger reached down to stroke her hair.

Vajra nearly fainted from pleasure.

She was still recovering when the Emperor placed down a glittering pane of barrier, supported by tree-branch struts.

"A table made of glass now too?" the Empress sighed, her eyes roving over the glittering, shimmering piece.

"It fits the room. Got that feng shui," the Emperor said with a nod.

"It does look nice—" the Empress started to say, then paused before turning her piercing gaze on the Emperor. "Since when do *you* care about feng shui? I've done my best, but our house is a mess, going by traditional—"

Vajra, however, merely listened with half an ear to the argument. The Emperor was clearly teasing the Empress, baiting her to get more and more annoyed at him—till eventually, she realised what he was doing and stuck her tongue out at him while he laughed.

Vajra's eyes were fixed upon the glittering pane.

Upon the glittering *stage*.

A command was sent out. Her troops answered.

And a great dance upon the glimmering barrier began.

"See? Vajra likes it. If bees like something, it's totally good feng shui," the Emperor reasoned.

The Empress opened her mouth, closed it, opened it once again, and then closed it and sighed.

She instead sat back and watched the performance.

→

And thus, the season of the White Death continued.

That season, Vajra played host to the Emperor himself more than she had in the entire Time of Plenty. The buzzing of her soldiers, he had said, soothed him. She had danced for him over a hundred times, to his pleasure and enjoyment—even sharing the stage twice with Beautiful Bi De as the Emperor played the sounds of the heavens from his Ban Joh.

She'd also shared the stage with one of her rivals, though the Blade of Grass, as she was called, was far too fat to stand upon the glittering dais. Naturally, Vajra outperformed her . . . though the woman's bigger body commanded vast attention.

The Emperor continued to treat her and all her drones kindly, running his enormous fingers over their fuzzy abdomens without harming them at all and eliciting vapours on all her Coldguard. He chuckled with his wonderful rumble as they all swooned and passed out in his firm grasp.

Really, the worst part of this place was losing access to his grand steam room . . .

But this view was good too.

Vajra and her hive were glued to the barrier wall, their eyes peering out into the gloom.

Her Emperor was most merciful, allowing her to witness him as he braved the White Death without a care and plunged into water Vajra knew would slay a drone instantly with its icy coldness. With him went his beautiful, mighty cock, plumage stunning even through the frosted barrier.

The others weren't bad either. The wet, *glistening* muscle—!

Several of her Coldguard fell off the barrier, buzzing with happiness.

Vajra's abdomen wiggled in contentment.

→

It was time.

Even through the shimmering barrier, Vajra could feel the change that was taking place outside the Heavenly Green Pavilion. It was the sun. The way its position changed, becoming more and more intense, which meant the Pavilion required less of the White Blazing Star's warmth.

Her hive was full of activity. The first spring brood sat in their legion as the Coldguard tended to them, feeding only the choicest pieces of jelly and pollen from the most Qi-rich plants. Already, the larvae were nearly twice the size of what they should be, her enlarged cells using the bounty of the Emperor's gift to her.

"Yeah, I think they're all in here. Leave the door open just in case, though," the Emperor's voice came through. "Gotta find a better way to do this next year. Don't want to stress them out too much."

Their fortress was lifted in mighty hands; they could hear the *thud* of feet and feel the bite of the outside wind as the Emperor returned them to their previous location, placing the fortress upon the elevated stilts.

Vajra could taste the first flowers on the breeze.

It was time.

Vajra gazed imperiously at her ranks of Coldguard. Normally they would be ragged and half-dead at this point. But instead, they stood, still tall and proud.

'*It is time. Awaken the dreamers*,' she commanded.

The cells of her finest warriors were gathered from where they had been placed to rest. They were heaved out with all their gilding and glory.

Ritualized dances directed Qi and energy. Reed banners were waved, heralding the return of the deathless.

'*Bane of the Black Lances, She Who Purged the Reeds—Arise.*'

A pulse of an Empress's will. The cells, made of the finest wax . . . flexed. Drops of preserving honey trickled out, but far, *far* less than there should have been.

One leg burst out of the side of the cell. Then another, like it was merely another molt.

With one strike of her wings, the rest of the wax shredded.

And a behemoth rose. Her carapace was iridescent blue. Her stripes the deepest black.

The connection rammed into Vajra like the booming laugh of the Emperor. And suddenly, she was *more.*

They both were.

The Bane of the Black Lances rose, born again just like the Emperor had been. One by one, her Immortals rose, their droning, powerful buzz filling the air.

Oh, how thankful Vajra was to the demons that cast her so low.

Vajra's wings started to buzz with laughter as more and more of the cells of the deathless burst, revealing soldiers who had become the equal of any demon.

Vajra the Boozemaster, servant of the Emperor, would amass for her liege a mighty tribute.

Wings opened and began to buzz.

All lands were his; all glory to Fa Ram!

↔

"Man, the bees sure are getting busy already. I love how industrious they always are . . ."

CHAPTER 62

THE NAME

It was another good day on Fa Ram. Bi De had just completed his patrol around the perimeter of his home. He'd had a wonderful time examining the buds that had started to grow upon the trees, observing the awakening animals he had come across, and feeling the warming breeze rustling through his feathers.

Upon his return, he found his Master waiting for him with fresh tea; his Great Master smiled upon him as Bi De spoke of the changing world.

"It is in the subtle differences that this one finds the most profound. The size of the buds growing upon the branches. The fungus slowly fruiting with vigor in the rotten logs. The world truly is just . . . alive."

His Great Master grinned at the statement. "It really is, isn't it? I can't wait until the flowers really start to open up and we can start to sow again," his Master mused, sipping his tea. Bi De could not wait to begin the work of the spring and summer. To once more grow with the plants of spring. "So, did you see anything else interesting while you were out?"

Bi De took a sip of his tea before responding. "I saw Man Gi, off in the distance," Bi De replied after a moment, remembering the flash of red fur, the same colour as the vest he wore.

"Oh? You saw Man Gi again?" his Great Master asked, and the rooster nodded.

"He seemed in fine health, but fled when he noticed my gaze."

Man Gi. The only other fox to receive a name of power from his Great Master. The disheveled and tattered-looking animal was either the smartest, or the luckiest, creature without a spark Bi De had met. The beast had somehow managed to survive both his and Tigu's purges before they had learned that some predators were necessary for the function of the cycle of life. Indeed, the hawks and the mink were repopulating now, but they knew their places.

"He's a wily old man, that Man Gi," his Master said, chortling.

Bi De almost hoped that the fox did gain a spark, if only so that he could have a conversation with the beast. He wished to understand the brethren of his once-sworn nemesis. To have tea, and truly understand what drove their kind. Tigu was a predator, yet she could control herself. Nezan was too far removed, even though he too was a fox. Bi De wondered, if offered food to satiate the hunger in his belly, could Basi Bu Shi also have been a disciple? Would Bi De have been able to train alongside a fox?

Bi De didn't regret his actions. He merely imagined what could have been.

"Indeed. He is a credit to his line. Perhaps I should ask Nezan to speak with him?" Bi De returned.

Both of them chuckled at that, his Master shaking his head.

Another bout of laughter followed, and they turned their heads to the couch where the Healing Sage, Yao Meihua, and Disciple Xiulan were sitting.

Xiulan had Little De cradled in one arm. With the other, she held her braid and was ghosting the soft locks over Little De's face, causing the babe to giggle along with his mother, who was looking on.

The Blade of Grass stared at the babe in fascination, her crystal-blue eyes sparkling with warmth and tenderness even as the babe slobbered into her hair.

"Little one, little one, look here~" Meihua tried, her own braid tickling. But she was completely ignored—Xiao De kept his eyes fixed upon the brown locks of Xiulan, even making a sound of displeasure when Xiulan pulled her own hair away.

"See? Look at him, he already knows well the touch of his aunt!" The look Xiulan gave Meihua was positively smug, and the other woman pouted, their duel over who would be the "best aunt" a constant petty rivalry.

The Healing Sage laughed and brought her own green hair to tickle, only to be met with another grunt of disapproval.

Xiulan's expression went from smug to panicked.

"Oh? Xiao De, you spurn your own mother for your pretty aunt? You *dare*, O son of mine?" the woman said reproachfully in a mocking yet gentle tone.

The couch full of women further devolved into giggles as the two males watched on for a moment longer. His Master smiled softly, while Bi De took a sip of his tea. He wondered how his own glorious feathers would hold up against Xiulan. She had been remarkably inventive in caring for Little De, despite never caring for a child before. Using her Qi abilities to make the glass baubles float above the child in a circle was inspired.

He wondered idly if he could conjure moonlight for the babe? It would be something to try later.

Soon, though, the pair finished their tea and the Great Master stood. He checked the position of the sun and considered it, before turning to where Xiulan was being accosted by her companions.

He took pity on his disciple.

"Meimei, you still want to go for that walk?" he asked, and the Healing Sage perked up, ceasing her prodding of the Blade of Grass.

"Yeah! I want to check on the mushroom farm!" she called back.

Soon enough, the Master and Mistress of Fa Ram were ready, walking out the door arm in arm with their babe tied to Meiling's back. A more private walk, just for the three of them, it had been decided—a fortuitous choice that everyone was happy to oblige, for there was another grave matter to be discussed by the household.

"Is it time?" Bi De asked Tigu when she walked out from the shadows.

The girl nodded.

"Then let us assemble."

→

There was tension in the air in the Great Manor House of Fa Ram. All could feel it as Bi De entered the room where everyone save the Master, Mistress, and their son had gathered.

He nodded to each grim face, striding to his place at the head of the table.

Indeed, the tension was higher than it had been during the height of when Tigu and Ri Zu's animosity for each other was at its worst. The room was full: all of the disciples were present, as were Meihua and Hu Li. They all eyed each other warily; victory here meant a victory everlasting.

"We shall commence the meeting," Bi De declared. "Speak your piece, my friends, and keep your calm—I know this issue is a matter of great contention."

Bi De referred, of course, to the true name of Little De; The Great Master had asked for suggestions, valuing their input as always. That had begun a secret war among all those present, each vying for their selection. A conflict that the First Disciple hoped to end.

"You're just saying that because no matter what, you've already won, Big De," Tigu grumbled, before she sucked in a breath and stood. She strode over to the nearby slate board and picked up a piece of chalk. With powerful, slashing strokes, a character was written.

"Behold, a worthy name!" Tigu shouted. "Kai! Victory! Our little brother needs a powerful name, and this name is best!"

She remained at the head of the room, her glare focusing upon any who would dare challenge her suggestion.

The first to strike back was, surprisingly, Ri Zu.

'*Why something so forceful?!*' Ri Zu demanded. '*Why not something softer and kinder? He comes from a family of healers! And thus, Lee would be a fine name!*'

"Because this name has impact!" Tigu shot back.

"There are a *lot* of Lees," Meihua murmured.

"Lee is the worst name!" Xianghua spoke up, sounding irritated. "This Young Mistress knows of fourteen among the servants of our Sect. Small Lee, Skinny Lee, Bony Lee, Lanky Lee . . ." Her eyes narrowed as she rattled off the names.

Bowu snorted from beside her. "Big Sis banned them from serving her, since she can't tell them apart."

Ri Zu wilted at the defeat, pouting.

'*Jiangen,*' Pi Pa stated after a moment. '*A strong root. It would fit, would it not?*'

"I don't hate it!" Tigu declared, and another name was added to the list.

"Shandan," came from Meihua, and Xiulan nodded from beside her.

Chun Ke, with an enigmatic smile, grunted, '*Zhuye; Red Leaf.*'

'*Like a maple leaf?*' Ri Zu asked, her gaze considering.

"Jin, like his pops?" Hu Li tried.

"Like in our village?" Xian asked. "It's tradition in Hong Yaowu to name sons after their fathers but . . ."

"Oi, dun look at me. Ten Ren named our boys!" she replied, her accent slipping out. "And unless you want something strange from my family like Baatar, or Kotan . . . Those'll get people looking at you funny for bein' a tribal, no reason to put a kid through that shit . . ." the woman muttered, looking away.

"Xiaoshan?" Xiulan suggested. "It's a bit close to . . . *his* name, though."

Xiaoshi. The first emperor. Would it be something that their Master considered?

Or perhaps something like Tianshan . . . but "heavenly mountain" was hopelessly arrogant.

'*Wan,*' Wa Shi offered, and some conversation paused. Wan. It wasn't a bad name, really, except for one thing.

"Wan. *Rou* Wan? *Meatball?!*" Tigu demanded. "You dare call my little brother *meatball*, you gluttonous bastard?!"

'*Look at him! He's all round and meaty looking*!' the fish fired back. '*Besides, meatballs are powerful!*'

The room descended into chaos; an argument began that lasted until the Great Master returned home.

CHAPTER 63

KING OF THE WORLD

The Imperial Capital of the Crimson Phoenix Empire was situated upon five hills named after the five representations of the body of Fenghuang, the phoenix: Virtue, Duty, Propriety, Credibility, and Mercy.

The pillars of the Phoenix were pillars of the Empire.

Upon these five hills stood the pinnacle of what the Crimson Phoenix Empire had to offer. Thousands of pagodas housing the noble clans. Hundreds of stadiums, to test the limits of cultivators and mortal warriors alike. The capital heaved with trade and industry, smoke and flame belching from its famous forges. Sights from the thousands of li that the Empire encompassed were on display. From the trees and the fruits of the south, to the pelts of the north, to the gems of the east, and much more. In the very air above the city, captured islands from the Soaring Heavens Archipelago floated, laden with more buildings and industry. It was a place of incomparable wonder.

The Imperial Palace itself formed the heart of the teeming metropolis, a city within the city, forbidden to the unworthy. An immortal flame burned at the pinnacle of its largest pagoda: the Fenghuang's fire itself, lit with seven colours, captured within a bowl that bore the symbol of the taijitu.

It was said that those born within the light of the fire rarely knew sickness or ill health; the fire drove away all that would harm the trueborn sons and daughters of the Phoenix Rest Plain. Even the lowest street rat of the wondrous city would raise his nose in arrogant superiority to the nobles of the far-flung frontiers. For they lived in the nest of the Crimson Phoenix.

And now, the city of millions swelled to encompass a triumphant army.

A million soldiers marched into the capital, invited by the Emperor so that he could personally gaze upon the valiant defenders, his victorious soldiers.

The news of the victory over the demonic hordes had spread like wildfire, and millions more from the surrounding areas had made a mad dash to witness the parade.

High above the city was the imposing form of *Shenfeng*, the *Divine Wind*. The flying ship was bedecked in colour, flanked by smaller vessels. Petals of spring flowers, white chrysanthemums, fall leaves, and flakes of snow rained from its decks into the city as the beautiful fairy sisters flitted around them.

While the symbol of Soaring Heavens Isle was foremost among the banners, the Sect had deigned to allow others the honour of the great ship bearing their banners aloft.

The parade marched through the grand thoroughfares of the capital. First came the Emperor's own Household Guards, clad one and all in heavenly steel—his favour was clear, as the qilin riders marched behind an enormous Temple Dog. Lord Chen Huo, the Eternal Guard of the Heavenly Flame, had come down from his post to welcome the returning champions.

Then came the cultivators. The Immortal Heroes, led by Xiao Ge, the Black Clouds of the Silent Sky. He was wounded, yet bore his scars with dignity. The mighty immortal's grave injuries lent truth to the titanic struggle with the demons. What trailed behind the few experts of the Cloudy Sword Sect were banners upon banners that represented the many ranks who formed the grand army.

Finally, came the soldiers. Rank upon gleaming rank, bearing banners of fire. The mortals, who had held the line against lesser demons.

The cheers and chants reached a fever pitch as they finished rounding the fourth hill and started towards the fifth, where the gates of the Imperial Palace lay.

Up five thousand steps they marched, never once faltering or wavering, until they came to a courtyard—so vast that all the men of the Army that Guards the Gates could fit in with room to spare.

The cultivators and men stood proudly before a pavilion. An open-air building on a dais, shrouded in a curtain and fire.

As one, mortal and cultivator alike dropped to their knees.

"We pay our respects to the Emperor!" the soldiers thundered in a single voice, a boom that reached out beyond the city walls.

Although it was lit from behind by seven-coloured fire, none could truly see the Emperor's face hidden behind a curtain. Yet they didn't have to. There could be no mistaking the sheer majesty of the man shrouded in fire.

"*Rise*," the Emperor commanded, and his Qi flared like the morning sun. It burned out like a wildfire, saturating the courtyard and racing to all corners of the city, a presence of heat and light that did not burn. It was a heavy weight, one of a firm and guiding hand.

The Emperor of the Crimson Phoenix Empire stared upon them—a man who was closer to a god.

The mortal soldiers wept as his presence filled them.

"Heroes of our Empire. It does please us to see your return . . ."

□

". . . and we do thusly recognise your meritorious deeds."

It was the one thousand, one hundred, and third time His Imperial Majesty, the Third Emperor of the Crimson Phoenix Empire, had said that phrase today, though the majority of those had been to especially proficient mortals. The less able were seen to by the scribes.

He was seated upon his dais, behind a wall of blazing fire. Fei Xinxhao of the Mount Huandi Sect was prostrated before him, the man receiving his reward.

The mortals had, according to ancient custom, received their rewards first, so that the cultivators could be given the full concentration of the immortal Emperor.

Stipends for the fallen were distributed in perpetuity to any spouses or children; a mere hundred or two years of money going to the families was considered generous to the mortals, but it was a drop in the treasury.

If only *all* of his subjects were so easily pleased.

"We reward you with this Thousand Poison Antidote, as well as the ability to take but one text from the Phoenix Library. Do not squander this chance."

"This Fei Xinxhao thanks the Emperor for his benevolence." The cultivator bowed low and retreated from the Emperor's presence, the smile on his face radiant. A legion of scribes next to the throne dutifully recorded every word.

The man retreated, keeping his eyes low in the presence of the most powerful man in the Empire. His Qi was a pressure upon everyone here, reminding them of their place.

"That is the last of the meritorious upon the rolls; speak now, if one feels as if any contribution was overlooked."

He stared in particular at Xiao Ge, for his reward had not really been a reward at all. The man had asked for the Cloudy Sword Sect disciples to be called upon more, not less, in contrast to what he had asked in the past centuries.

It was a sudden change in priorities that the Emperor had to investigate. There were whispers, of course. Upheaval within the Sect.

None spoke up while he was examining the acting master of the Cloudy Sword Sect. The Emperor frowned, the action invisible behind the curtain of flames.

"*Then go. Bring glory to our Empire,*" he commanded.

"We pay our respects to the Emperor!" the voices once more chorused, and the cultivators filed out of the room.

"*Was there anything else?*" he asked his chief scribe, the man's forehead pressed to the floor.

"No, my Emperor."

"*We will retire, then. Continue your work.*"

"Yes, my Emperor."

His Imperial Majesty, Emperor of the Crimson Phoenix Empire, stood from his throne and exited through a doorway hidden behind it.

Once he was safely in the passage beyond, the most powerful man in the Empire removed the bracer that was on his arm and heaved a breath. The effort to maintain it all wore on him. He stared at the bracer, a symbol of power, and a quiet reminder of his own limitations.

With it and the formations of the city, he could achieve a power that most cultivators could never hope for.

But the upper ends of his strength were a lie; a bottleneck had halted his advancement long ago.

The Emperor's Qi was augmented by the works of his ancestors, a polite fiction to those without true strength that the Emperor's power was absolute. Few could see the truth. Of those that were confirmed to know were Xiao Ge and Tianzhe Minyan. Others, the Emperor was not sure.

The Second Emperor might have been able to battle the likes of Xiao Ge on an equal footing—but he, the Third Emperor, would be defeated utterly outside the seat of his power.

So instead of the force of arms, he wielded a different weapon, the weakness of all humans: greed, love, and the thirst for power. He played the Sects off each other, lest they get ideas. Seating arrangements were weapons. Grand speeches were his sword, and yet still his power over the Sects had declined over the years.

The Empire was growing too big and unwieldy. As the proverb went: the heavens are high, and the Emperor is far away.

It had been even harder with the slow retreat of the Cloudy Sword Sect, the Empire's finest supporters. It had surprised him when the wind changed and the Cloudy Sword Sect had attended him. Xiao Ge had arrived, penitent about his absence, content to play his part like the old days. The Cloudy Sword Sect could still be counted on to honour their old oaths—a righteous bludgeon against the unvirtuous.

The Emperor's stride took him past the Inner Palace and towards the deepest location of his home.

He touched his ring to the door, and suddenly he was elsewhere.

A hidden realm, made by his ancestors: a vibrant garden, full of soothing Qi. He let the feeling of dew from the waterfall land on his skin, and he smelled the sweet scent of the flowers.

He let out a breath and continued deeper into the garden, where there was a place for entertaining guests. Normally, there would be one of his trusted concubines from the Imperial Harem. But today, it was a different sort of distraction.

"Took you long enough, Fengyan," a rather grumpy voice echoed from where the man was seated at a chair. Shen Yu yawned indolently from his seat.

His wounds were bandaged and covered with paste. The Imperial physicians had examined him and managed to repair the worst of it. Now, all he needed was rest and time.

Fengyan sighed at the slovenly nature of his friend.

→

Fengyan, the Third Emperor, examined the recording of the battle before him. It had been taken by Shen Yu for his personal viewing. The Emperor's face was marred with a frown at the war constructs and the blasts of light that struck it. He raised an eyebrow at the appearance of a penitent and his charge against the Hellforged Demonic Titan.

"So . . . the diviners were right. There is a challenge every age, and we must rise to meet it," he muttered after he deactivated the recording crystal.

"Tch. There's always a challenge. You don't need diviners to tell you that," Shen Yu replied.

"Indeed there is—but they got the general location right, and even the size of the threat."

"First time since—" Shen Yu cut off the thought and sighed. "Whatever. I'll allow you to praise them this once, Fengyan."

To most, such disrespect to the Emperor was equal to treason, but there was a time where Fengyan had called this man Senior Brother. That was centuries ago, now. Shen Yu was one of the few men—and sometimes Fengyan would say the *only* man—who could get away with it. And even he had his limits.

But their time as brothers was long, long ago. Before the forty-eighth prince had been deemed the only one worthy enough to succeed the Crimson Phoenix Throne. The rest of the Imperial line had either sworn binding oaths to him . . . or been culled, before his Lord father, the Second Emperor, had disappeared forever.

Fengyan respected his father . . . but the duty the man had left him with was not an easy one.

"No more calling them the bastards of three fathers, or saying that when this turned out to be so much less than they predicted you would castrate all of them?" Fengyan asked, using the crass tones he had learned while travelling the inner city in his youth.

"No. They were right to ask you to 'call on your strongest champion.' Even if it was at an immensely inopportune time." Shen Yu had been very upset when he had found out why Fengyan had called upon this favour. His frown exaggerated the wrinkles on his face.

"I am still getting used to you being . . . *old*," Fengyan said after a moment, watching the lines as they shifted on his face.

Shen Yu shrugged. "I feel old more and more. My experiences have weathered me. It's not right to look like a young whippersnapper when I feel like this. Besides, the ladies don't seem to mind! Like a fine wine, I am! Better with the wrinkles! Unlike you, babyface! You still look like the last fifty Young Masters I had to crush!"

"Like fine wine? You look like the ass of a Crag Turtle."

Shen Yu barked a laugh as he raised a bottle to his lips and drained the crystal vessel. The vintage was over a thousand years old, made by one of the rare few cultivators who completely indulged in a beneficial passion. It was easily worth ten frontier cities.

It was also the eighth one that Shen Yu had finished since he had arrived. He sighed as the taste hit and slumped into the seat.

"It was a near thing. If they had completed their constructs it would not have been as much a victory as we hoped. At least one of us would have fallen . . . if not all of us."

It was rare to hear his ever-confident friend speak like that.

"Then we are blessed by the heavens," the Emperor said before rising. Shen Yu nodded before picking up another bottle. He got halfway through draining it before the Emperor snatched it out of his hand and downed the rest himself.

Shen Yu's eyes widened before he began to howl with laughter.

"You little brat! Years ago, I would have tanned your hide for that!"

"Attempt it at your peril, Shen Yu. The wards in here are quite powerful."

"Feh. You've gotten too cheeky, you bastard. And it's been too long." Both men smiled at one another, before the Emperor raised his hands in the gesture of respect. When he spoke next, he spoke as the Emperor and not as Shen Yu's old friend.

"You have come when you were called, our loyal subject. We hold your oath to us fulfilled."

Shen Yu stood from his chair and bowed back. "This Shen Yu pays his respects to His Imperial Majesty."

There was a pulse of Qi, as the contract completed. A pressure on both of their souls released, just slightly.

"So. What happened in the Cloudy Sword Sect?" the Emperor asked, though he knew he probably wouldn't get a straight answer, if he got one at all. Xiao Ge was Shen Yu's sworn brother, and Shen Yu would never say anything to harm him.

Shen Yu knew that he had to make the attempt, and he knew the man didn't begrudge him it.

"Some manner of incident. It's been resolved, and I dare say your job will be easier because of it."

Which was as good as he was going to get . . . and it was *some* peace on his mind.

"What do you plan to do now, Shen Yu?" Fengyan then asked as he conjured a chair so he could sit at the table beside his friend. More bottles of wine appeared at the snap of his fingers. He poured them both a cup.

Shen Yu seemed to consider something before he sat back down.

"I'm going to see my grandson."

The Emperor of the entire continent nearly spat out the wine he had drank. Instead, he composed himself and simply raised an eyebrow.

"I thought you said you were never to sire another child," he delicately prompted.

Shen Yu's last son had been . . . an experience. Nearly a million subjects dead, five cities sacked, three Sects destroyed, four more crippled, and enough cultivation resources wasted that it had set the Empire back centuries.

Shen Bu had been quite a thorn, until the mad dog had been put down by his own father.

It had been a messy affair that had left Shen Yu in the Empire's debt. Shen Yu had sought to redeem his son's sin with three tasks repaid.

One task remained.

"Adopted. From the streets of Crimson Crucible City."

"I guess there is a story there?" the Emperor asked, his eyebrows raised. Shen Yu lit up like he hadn't seen in centuries.

"You should have *seen* the way he shoveled," one of the most powerful cultivators in the Empire declared loudly.

Fengyan allowed himself to rest for a while as he listened to an old friend speak fondly of his found family. Shen Yu allowed himself to be animated and open. Like the old friends they were, even when they both knew in their hearts that they might have to kill each other one day.

They could never be like how they used to be. Not entirely. But at least for the moment, Fengyan was Fengyan.

He did not have to plot a course that would see thousands dead in the *best* circumstances. He did not have to execute loyal subjects so that he could retain a less loyal but more useful one.

He could simply have a nice drink and listen to the tale of a street boy shoveling shit.

It was quite amusing.

→

Eventually, however, Shen Yu had to leave.

And the Emperor had to once more don his mantle.

He met with his legions of ministers and scribes and decided the affairs of state. It had been a lot worse before he had expanded the bureaucracy and created the Archive Reform. The Empire had simply been too big, so he had needed more people to run it.

But that project was finally bearing fruit. He had his scribes, and he had less minutiae that he needed to observe.

"*Leave the Empire more powerful than you inherited it,*" had been his father's last command.

He didn't quite know if he was succeeding.

But by his oath, and the Mandate of Heaven, he was the Emperor.

The Phoenix's flame would be everlasting—no matter what he needed to do to keep it burning.

CHAPTER 64

SPRING

The first thing Tianlan became aware of was noise.

It took her a moment to place the sound, so deep was her slumber. But it came to her, for it was unmistakable.

A rooster's crow, heralding the sun as it broke the horizon in her domain, signaling the start of spring.

It was not how she normally awoke. She remembered, ages ago, waking to the acrid tang of impurities that were deposited in her "home." It was always a slow, gradual thing, however. This was a jolt to her senses, but not in an unpleasant way. The call was . . . *invigorating*.

The second thing she became aware of was a feeling. *Warmth*. She felt *warm*, comfortable, and safe; she was curled up in a nest of blankets, with the dying embers of a lovingly tended fire in the hearth.

There was no pain. None of the hundred thousand fractured voices screamed in her mind. Her blood did not steadily leak from cracks in her body.

Not wanting to open an eye just yet, she examined her body. Her tongue poked around in her mouth and found all of her teeth, the ones that had been missing regrown. Her fingers ghosted over her limbs; the hard, golden-metal replacements for her missing body parts were soft and felt like skin. She tapped at her eye, but that was still a flat pane, the orb still gone. She was still damaged; but she was more whole now than she had been when she'd fallen asleep.

When she had first become herself once more, a year ago, she had been running mostly on excitement and wonder at simply being conscious again. That was what had fueled her interactions. But now? Now, she couldn't feel the weariness deep in her soul. The grasping hand that tried to lull her back to sleep. Tianlan felt *rested.*

Her one working eye opened. Sunlight streamed in through the window, warm and comforting as she glanced around the room. It was clean and fresh smelling, like somebody had come in to air it out—and as she saw the pressed snowflower on the table beside her bed, she realised somebody *had.*

Multiple people. She could, at the edge of her memory, remember stories. Hands, stroking her hair. A warm nose that tucked her in tighter. The scent of grass, the comforting smell of medicinal herbs, and even the feeling of moonlight shining on her, standing vigil.

The feelings that chased the darkness away in her slumber. The feelings that had cut through the nightmares and made her nights restful.

Tears welled up in her good eye as she slowly sat up, casting her senses out. Seeking those who had granted her the gift of peace.

The easiest to find was her Connected One. Her awareness followed their connection, until she could see him, standing in the real world.

Jin.

His back muscles stretched, and sweat dampened his brow as his hoe bit into the earth. His Qi poured out of his body with each motion, unconcerned with perfection or extracting every drop of value. Instead, it was focused on mending and protecting the vast and resilient earth he walked on. He gave his all to her, just as he always had. His Golden Qi, full of his desire to help and a love for his craft, flowed into her. It enhanced her, repairing her shattered body and broken Dragon Veins.

But his was not the only Qi, unlike how it had been in the beginning.

Upon his shoulder was a rooster, eyes sharp and ever vigilant. His Qi radiated off his body, following his Master's into the soil. The light of the moon was less tender than that of the solid power of gold, but it was a dutiful warden. It was fast, fierce, and vigilant, rooting out any impurity that might dare to hide in her Qi.

His flock trailed behind her Connected One, and the rooster guided them with expert clucks. He sent them forth to sup upon the worms and insects within the soil, occasionally hopping off his Lord's shoulder to partake himself. When he returned to his Master's shoulder, he would let loose another call. Proclaiming to all the world that it was spring, exulting in the time of new growth with all his heart.

When Bi De called, others would call with him. She felt a tug of amusement from another one of her connections, this one as developed as that of Jin's. She followed it, away from Jin, and was met with her Connected One's other half.

Meiling let out a "hey-oh!" as the rooster's cry filled the hills. She was arranging and rearranging her garden layout, looking it over with a critical eye before shaking her head and adjusting the placement of a pot. Her Qi was quiet. Understated, compared with Jin's. But it worked with the Golden Qi seamlessly, fortifying and enhancing the golden patches.

With her was little Ri Zu. She dutifully attended to her Mistress, the two of them working together to take what they needed out of storage. Ri Zu squeaked and chittered while the two women casually quizzed each other on anatomy. Her Qi found the little, hard-to-reach places of impurity, guiding the moon and the Golden Qi to make sure nothing was missed.

A cry came from another little spark nearby. A nameless babe, propped up on blankets within his mother's reach, watching the world with a simple, sublime joy. Tianlan felt her connection to him. A tiny thread linked them, marking him as one of hers. He was too young to draw upon his Qi, but the little bits that were there flowed between them like one being.

From there, the house caught Tianlan's attention, for there was darkness there, though its ravenous hunger was controlled and quiet. What the moonlight could not purge, and what medicine could not cure, the void destroyed utterly. Sometimes it even tore out the pieces that were too far gone to mend, so that resources could go elsewhere. But even though it caused Tianlan some pain, she knew it was not unkind. The destruction it provided was necessary.

It was strange to think of the Void as cheerful or kind, but it was. Pi Pa gossiped away with . . . one Tianlan wasn't familiar with. The beautiful woman was working with the pig, her own son tied against her back and a bright smile on her face.

She watched the two of them take their tea and biscuits out to the fields, passing by Meiling and Ri Zu, heading for the outer fields.

There they chanced upon a contest. The descendant of Ruolan, Tigu, and a woman with a passing resemblance to the Lord of the Lake were dueling. They sowed the new fields by jumping in the air and throwing the seeds, coating them in Qi so that they would not break. The seeds landed in perfectly straight, perfectly cut furrows—and when no victor could be decided, they simply started on the next one, their trick shots becoming more and more elaborate.

Tianlan's heart ached as she stared at Cai Xiulan. The woman with the golden crack in her chest, a reminder of what she had been willing to sacrifice to protect those she loved. Yet she had once again reached the same level she had been at before she'd burned, her Qi a vibrant light to Tianlan's senses.

Tigu was Tigu; there was nothing else to be said, and Tianlan was looking forward to teasing the both of them. The Girl Who Was a Cat was happy, so happy, as she jeered and japed with the other warriors and listened intently to the final woman who began a lecture on "how to be a good sister."

Naturally, according to Xianghua, she was the best sister in the world, and Tigu could merely hope to be a distant second. The woman was not one of Tianlan's . . . not yet, at any rate. Her misty Qi flowed into the ground without a thought—especially when Tigu launched herself at the woman, shouting that she was courting death.

A great dragon watched on, laughing at the ensuing duel in between sips of tea he'd received from the pig. His storm of Qi rained upon the freshly sown fields, watering them. The draconic deluge was awash with fortifying might, the vitality of the dragon's power, given freely, saturating everything he gazed upon. It provided for the new seedlings a measure of his own power—if only because a bit of Qi now meant that they would be more delicious later. Tianlan smiled as she sensed the dragon's gluttonous smacking of his lips as he dreamed of spring's bounty, and all the wonderful food they all would share.

But there were some missing. She cast her senses around the farm, looking for the others, but they were not there.

With a frown, Tianlan followed the connection farther. She paused when she realised how much her domain had expanded. Previously it had been confined to a thin line along the road. Now the core of it was a bubble that saturated a massive area, encompassing Hong Yaowu completely and reaching halfway to Verdant Hill. Tianlan grimaced at the feeling of the ancient ritual point. It was amazing that people still lived here—but it had been . . . *his* decision to found this place.

She didn't know if she liked it.

She dismissed the thought when she came into Chun Ke's presence.

His dependable Qi was a beacon of warmth and safety. He felt her senses upon him somehow, and smiled at his Big Little Sister. For a brief moment, his eyes unfocused, and he was there beside her, a kindly snout sniffing. She smiled at the examination and patted the curious nose. Content that she was all right, he once more departed.

He was with solid Gou Ren, as he instructed the people of the village in how to sow the fields in the way of her Connected One. He was a foundation, strong and pure, with the slowly growing demeanor of a leader in his own right. When he spoke, the people listened, redoing their fields . . . though not without some help.

Bei Be, Sun Ne, and Yun Ren helped craft the new fields, the plough exalting in the perfect cuts. Yun Ren seemed spectacularly amused as he used a sword for his part, a piece of an old fox howling with laughter lazing nearby with snacks. The artifact blade radiated curiosity, finding its circumstances interesting.

Yin, the bright sun, pulled a new seed drill *entirely* too fast along one of these new fields. Atop it sat two of the newer additions to the farm. Bowu cackled with maddened laughter as his new creation performed to his exacting standards, while Huo Ten the monkey whooped and hooted beside him.

Finally, there was Miantiao. Tianlan could still feel the well of grief within him, hidden behind his eyes. But today he had a smile on his face as he watched the young ones play. She sent reassurance down their small connection and allowed him the moment of peace.

Tianlan travelled to the extent of her reach: past the first ritual point, then past another. She seemed to extend across a good portion of the north. She was still a fraction of the size she had once been . . . but she was there. She was stable.

She almost couldn't believe it, as she brushed her senses along the connections. It wasn't like the grand ritual. It wasn't a funnel of Qi, directed by one person's intent. It was a myriad of different flavours and emotions. It was like her connection with him. But somehow more intense. More familial. It was almost overwhelming, to be truly connected to so many others. It was what she'd wanted so long ago.

→

For a while, she just basked in the feelings that the spring and her people brought her. The joy of a day of honest work. Gou Ren blushed and grumbled when he saw that Jin had done most of his fields for him while he was helping the village. The man was grateful, but he had wanted to do it himself.

They had a grand feast, using up the last of their leftover preserves. Pickles and salted fish, fresh fruit from the greenhouse, fiddleheads, and morels. It was an eclectic mix, yet none complained. Jin started strumming on his instrument, and Ruolan's descendant picked up the tune.

Xiulan was getting a lot better at dancing, as she swung each member of the farm into a merry jig; Meiling, for the first time in months, got to try the mead. Her cackles echoed over the farm, as did her off-key voice.

It was wonderful. It was utterly wonderful. Tianlan's heart pounded in her chest as she simply watched—watched until they all went to sleep, ready to rise bright and early for more work tomorrow.

Tianlan sighed when she left them, returning to her body. She hummed with contentment, the nightmares seemed so far away today. Finally, she arose from her bed, humming one of the tunes Jin had played—and realised that her humming was accompanied by a familiar sound.

The tones of a Ban Joh drifted in through her window.

Her Connected One was *here*.

For a brief moment, Tianlan hesitated. Memories of . . . her past welled up within her. *Pain.*

Then she shoved the memories of *the traitor* away. This one . . . this one wasn't like him *at all*. He wasn't a bastard who would betray her and rip her apart.

She looked down at the rags she was wearing and took a breath. There was a brief moment of concentration, and then her clothing changed.

Instead of fine silk or rags, she was now clad in the garb of a farmer. A modest dress and a practical top—the only decoration that of a maple leaf and a wheat stalk. She stood and walked to the burnished bronze disk that served as a mirror, really looking at herself. No more bashed-in teeth. No more brutal scars. Even the gold cracks had smoothed out. She wasn't some emaciated wretch anymore.

She was Tianlan.

She opened her door and stepped out into the night. Out under the field of stars, unmarred by golden cracks, each and every one shining brilliantly and illuminating her realm. There was a patch of packed snow right beside her house—coal eyes and a smile of all things atop it—but the rest of her realm was covered in grass.

She swallowed thickly as she looked forward and saw him. Her Connected One was sitting on a rock, not too far from her house.

His fingers lazily strummed. Once, twice, he hit bum notes, sending it twanging. But he recovered and kept on playing.

He played until the song was finished. The last notes faded into the air.

Jin turned to her. His face was still split in two, welded together by a band of gold, but the fused line was smaller than she remembered. She barely felt any of the turmoil within that had once dominated him. Only a feeling of peace.

Less two souls mashed together, and more one person.

Tianlan froze, with his gaze upon her. She knew that she had . . . not exactly been completely truthful with him. Fear had kept her from interacting outside their dreams.

What would he do? How would he react? She knew he had wanted to run away from cultivation—and here she was, making him everything he didn't want to be.

But instead of the expected recriminations, he smiled at her.

"Good morning, sleepyhead," he said, his voice warm.

A smile crawled across Tianlan's face as she felt the wellspring of calm and honest joy at seeing her awake—at seeing the little broken wreck of a creature she was.

"Good morning," Tianlan whispered back.

He nodded and patted the rock beside him. Hesitantly, Tianlan took first one step, then another. And then suddenly, she was seated beside him.

For the moment, there was silence.

"Nice to *really* meet you," Jin eventually said, looking at her with amusement. Tianlan flushed and kicked her feet, looking away.

"I'm sorry. For not really trying to talk to you." He needed an explanation she didn't have the words for, but she didn't need to find them—the connection between them was open. Her fear, anxiety, and now hope suffused their bond.

Jin didn't get angry. He simply nodded. She supposed it was easy to understand, when you could feel exactly what the other person was feeling.

A hand landed on her head as he ruffled her hair. "You've been helping us out a lot, huh? I would have said thank you sooner."

"But you do," she corrected him.

"Hm?" He turned, confusion on his face.

"You do say thanks. All of you. What was it you taught to the others? 'We give to the Land, and the Land gives back.' You healed me. It should be me, you know? Saying thanks." Tianlan turned to look at him.

He mulled over her words, then sighed and shook his head, a fond smile on his face. "Ooh, well. We'll call it just aboot even, then, eh?"

Tianlan giggled at the strange, thick accent he put on. "Call it even," Tianlan agreed.

"Buuuuttt. I'm not the only person you need to say hi to, yeah?" he whispered to her, and pointed down, off the rock.

Tianlan blinked, then turned to where his finger was pointing. Pointing at the tables being set up, where Chun Ke was trundling happily, and Xiulan was furiously chopping imagined foods . . .

And where Meiling was standing, her hands on her hips, radiating displeasure, her narrowed eyes upon Tianlan. The gold glow of her freckles seemed just slightly sinister.

"She ain't too happy you tried to go to sleep in a hole in the ground. Call her Big Sis. It normally stops her from being so angry."

Jin's hand landed on Tianlan's back, and before she could gather her courage, she was launched into Meiling's arms.

"Hello, little one," Meiling said, her smile absolutely terrifying. "I trust that you'll not be foolish next winter?"

Tianlan took her Connected One's advice as she stared into two baleful purple stars. "Yes, Big Sister. I'm sorry." Tianlan sniffed, instantly surrendering.

Meiling's eyes softened, and Tianlan was scooped up into a hug—warm, and safe.

There was a seat for her, there at the large table. She was near Tigu, arguing with Ri Zu about the name of a child, and beside Jin and Meiling, sandwiched between them.

Slowly, hesitantly, she started to smile.

Her people. They were all here . . . and all connected.

→

Tianlan's feet pounded to the beat, and Xiulan's did the same across from her. The Dance of the Elements had more happy memories for her than bitter ones.

Xiulan had gotten better. She was no Ruolan and never would be—but her passion was just as beautiful as Ruolan's utter mastery.

But the drums eventually had to end. They clapped their hands together and bowed, then were immediately swamped by the others, laughing and trying the moves for themselves.

Tianlan's heart was full to bursting. Her head felt like it was swimming. But . . . there were two missing from the scrum of people.

The first one. The one who had started her healing.

Jin.

He was seated off a bit to the side now, simply watching with a smile on his face. He did that sometimes. He separated himself and just enjoyed other people having fun. She could feel the pride within him—he had enabled this. They were happy because of his hard work. Bi De was upon his shoulder, the rooster made of moonlight standing tall and proud, as he too observed the gathering.

Her own feet took her in that direction, none of the others noticing she was going.

"Having a good time?" Jin asked.

Tianlan plopped down beside him on the rock. "No thanks to *you*! I thought Meimei was going to turn me over her knee!"

He barked out a laugh and stared down at the others. "Well, I'm glad you're in high spirits at least." He paused for a few seconds, seemingly considering something. "Can we talk for a minute?"

With a bit of privacy went unsaid. Bi De bowed his head and took off from Jin's shoulder. After a moment, Tianlan obliged him. With a wave of her hand, the distance increased, until they were on top of a hill a thousand li away.

They drifted into companionable silence, for a moment . . . before Jin sighed.

"Tianlan?"

"Yes?"

"Could you tell me what happened?"

Tianlan paused at the question. In another time, she might have deflected. But tonight . . . tonight, she couldn't. She could hear the duet of Meiling and Xiulan belting out the song about the donkey, their voices echoing off the hills.

She took a deep breath—and then startled a little, as Chun Ke was suddenly there, having sensed her distress.

She buried her fingers into the mane of the ever-reliable boar . . . and nodded. She owed him that much.

She owed all of them that much.

→

Slowly, haltingly, she began her tale. Of how she first came to be. Of . . . *Xiaoshi*. Of the Azure Mountains before the fall of the Mist Wall.

The story was painful. It hurt, dredging up the things she had tried so hard to forget. But for him? For her Connected One . . . she could bear it.

He listened to her attentively, one arm around her shoulder.

It was almost fond, the beginning parts. The middle parts too, as she told him of playing with Ruolan, Rumblin' Yao, and the Crystal Masters. Of how they had made one people from the disparate clans.

Which made the fall all the more painful.

"It wasn't the breaking that hurt the most," she whispered, her voice wavering. "Not really. If they were all fine, maybe I could have . . . maybe I could have been fine with it. But it wasn't that. The worst part . . . . the worst part was that they *turned on each other for it*."

"They killed each other," she continued. "Our friends, *they killed each other*. Spirit Beasts and humans alike were butchered like animals. The bonds we forged—people who had sworn to die for each other . . . to the *cultivators*, it meant *nothing*. I cried and begged! I shouted until I had nothing left to give!" In that moment, her voice was the raging of the rapids, and the all-encompassing fury of a mountain ripping free from its foundations. "They tore out my blood and broke open my bones to get at the marrow! They ripped up any part of me that was still intact for their *worthless pills*. And as my Qi faded, they dug deeper and deeper, so that they could feast on the dregs! *And then they used me to kill my own people.*"

She could still feel it. Their acrid Qi, riddled with impurities. The world suddenly seemed *so small*, as the tears dripped from her eye. Jin was barely up to her knee—Tianlan had become less a girl and more an amorphous mass of dirt and plant life. The rage and hatred and grief pounded in her ears and made her vision fade.

But Jin was still there. Chun Ke was there. Jin did not move from the suddenly towering mountain that had once been Tianlan. He simply pressed his hand against her, his Qi warm, gold, and soothing. Chun Ke whimpered with sorrow, his eyes watering as he looked upon her.

Slowly, she shrank. Her body once more became flesh and blood, until she was small enough for her Connected One to hold. His arms wrapped around her like the walls of a fortress, proof against the horrors outside.

She could feel the pounding of his heart. The compassion. The shared grief, as he felt her pain.

He held her as she took deep breaths.

→

Silence once more took hold of the realm. She had climbed out of his lap, but they were still together, watching the stars.

All that was left was the beating of two hearts. Until Jin spoke again.

"Thank you for telling me, Tianlan."

"You already knew parts of the story," she whispered. He hadn't been surprised. She could feel that much from him. He had *known*. She expected him to deflect, or say he had learned from some inconsequential place.

"Bi De found a memory crystal by a man named Xiaoshi. It was recorded in his dying moments."

For a brief moment, the rage came back.

"Oh? And what did *he* have to say?" *The traitorous bastard.*

"That he fucked up massively, that he was to blame for everything, and that whoever found the crystal needed to search for any way to revive you, just so that he could apologise," Jin said, his voice calm and even.

Tianlan stared.

She opened her mouth, and closed it again.

"What?" she asked, a sudden numbness flooding her chest.

That . . . that wasn't what had happened—he had betrayed her, broken her out of his own selfish will . . . yet she could feel that everything Jin said was the truth.

"Bi De," Jin called, and a rooster of moonlight appeared, carrying with him a crystal. He placed it in Jin's hand, gave a curt bow to the both of them, and left.

"You don't have to look at this tonight," Jin said. "It's a bit heavy, for just waking up. But . . . I think you should see this. Or at least the end. I mean, I kind of think he was an idiot . . . although . . . I think it might help if you hear him out."

Tianlan stared at the crystal.

Part of her just wanted to smash it. To ignore it and sever the tie completely.

But one small part of her . . . it hoped. It hoped that her oldest friend had not betrayed her.

Tianlan reached out, and after a moment of hesitation, she touched the crystal.

□

Demons. A battle in a sanctum. The moment when Xiaoshi nearly betrayed her . . . and then pulled back at the last second.

A demon, maiming the souls of everyone she had ever cared about.

"I'm sorry, Tianlan," Xiaoshi gasped, and broke the formation. His heart burned with the desire to save her.

Tears poured from an Earth Spirit's eyes.

It rained for the next week.

□

But like all things, both the rain and the grief did not last forever.

Tianlan Shan, the Spirit of the Azure Hills, was drawn from her fugue by the feelings of joy and determination that touched her soul.

It was time for the spring planting to begin.

Her Jin, her Connected One, rested his shovel on his shoulder as he looked out over the fields, even though they were wet, and the rain was cold. She could feel his joy. She could feel the deep, enduring love he had for his home, his Qi mingling with hers.

And it was not just from Jin. It was from all of them. She could feel Meiling and Bi De and Tigu and Xiulan and Chun Ke—each and every one of them felt the same way. And it was not just love for the land. She felt it in their Qi, as they offered it to her freely.

They loved *her*, too.

The past was a bitter thing, full of regrets, misunderstandings, and pain. Yet it was the present that comforted her. It was the present that washed those feelings away.

One last tear fell for an old friend.

↔

My eyes widened as the rain stopped, and the clouds broke. A glimmer of golden sunlight speared down. My home was beautiful even when it was raining. But under the new light? It took my breath away.

I felt a gentle tap on my soul.

'*Hey*,' Tianlan whispered, doing the mental equivalent of holding my hand.

"Hey yourself," I replied. "Are you all right?"

'*I don't know*,' she answered honestly. '*But . . . I think I will be.*'

I used my Qi to do the mental equivalent of ruffling Tianlan's hair, and she leaned into the touch.

"Then let's get to work! This delicious rice isn't going to plant itself!" I declared.

A great cheer erupted behind me, with one voice the loudest of them all. Another little cry joined the rooster's call, my son adding his own voice to the chorus.

"You tell 'em, Big D," I said, smiling as Tianlan giggled along.

The warm wind of spring ghosted over the hills.

EPILOGUE

MARCHING ON THE HILLS

Shen Yu stood on the bow of the great ship, the *Shenfeng*, as it cut through the sky. The wind was in his hair and blowing through his beard. The birds and beasts of the sky without Qi approached the construct curiously; those with any sense fled from the overwhelming power the artifice produced. Behind him, the deck was a hive of activity. The fairies of Soaring Heaven's Isle maintained their ship while Brother Ge traded pointers with the new recruits of the Cloudy Sword Sect.

Shen Yu ignored all of it. His gaze was fixed on the steadily approaching Cloudy Mountain.

It had been . . . three hundred years since he had been back upon the mountain, striding through the halls of the Sect. As he looked at the distant peak, shrouded by clouds, he felt conflicted. The Cloudy Sword Sect was where he'd begun. It was his nest, before he could spread his wings and fly. It was his rock, for though he might have left the Cloudy Sword Sect—their rules and regulations too rigid for his taste—he still held to the ideals of the Honoured Founders, if not the letter of their law. He lit a candle every year for his fallen brothers; he drank in remembrance to the Masters who had seen his talent.

He had trusted the Sect utterly.

More than any cultivator *should* trust something besides themself, if he was truthful with himself. He had thought nothing of leaving something precious in their care, for his old Sect was righteous and took their oaths seriously.

Of course Little Rou would be safe there. Put in the same nest that had nurtured Shen Yu, he too would spread his wings and fly in time, while Shen Yu took care of an obligation that could not be ignored.

He had been with little Rou for ten years; for most cultivators it would be the blink of an eye, but to him, it had been enough. He couldn't help but care for the boy. Rou was more a proper descendant than his last spawn. He'd known hardship from a young age and was unspoiled. He knew how to work hard, he knew how to *suffer* to achieve his goals. He was upright and righteous without letting it get in the way of what needed to be done. He reminded Shen Yu so much of himself that it hurt.

Rou was everything Bu hadn't been. Or he was what Bu *could* have been . . . if Shen Yu hadn't had a hand in ruining the boy. He had doted on him too much.

Helped too much. And in the end, it had all been for nothing. His little Bu, his son, had become a *monster*.

Jin Rou. With him, Shen Yu finally had a chance to fix the mistakes of the past. He had a chance to wipe the stain of dishonour, to leave a legacy.

Then, through negligence and rot, the Cloudy Sword Sect had *broken* that precious boy.

Worse than that, they had nearly *killed* him.

The little shit who replaced wine with horse piss, just like Shen Yu had done to Brother Ge and his old sectmates. The boy, who had taken in all of Shen Yu's teachings and was on the cusp of becoming his own man.

To have such potential, such drive smothered in the nest was always a tragedy.

To have it happen to Little Rou made his blood boil and his organs clench. It made him want to vomit blood and erase the mountain that he stared at. It was a hard thing to love something so greatly.

Only the strong bond between himself and Brother Ge stayed his hand. His brother had accepted responsibility for the mistake immediately, and the thought of fighting him to the death was unacceptable. He didn't know if his spirit could ever recover from such a battle. But even that wouldn't have been enough if Rou had died.

The little worm who had harmed him, however? That creature's life was forfeit. Or better yet, Rou could decide what to do with him. Yes, yes, that seemed like the best option. What sort of grandfather would he be, to take away his grandson's vengeance?

Shen Yu took a deep breath as his hands clenched and he tried to calm himself, banishing the anger and betrayal.

Someone had obviously sensed his distress, however, and a second later, a hand trailed along Shen Yu's shoulders as Minyan floated behind him. The Second Lady of the Soaring Heaven's Isle Sect was once more clad in pristine robes and her veil. Such a shame—her beauty was always a sight to behold. Icy-blue eyes regarded him. Minyan was recovering well from the battle, but one arm was still covered in seals and bandages.

Her presence dispelled his mood fully as her Qi brushed along his.

It was the other reason, besides his still-healing body, that he was upon the great ship. One simply did not spurn the company of Tianzhe Minyan, be they man or woman. She was still, as ever, a tiger. She had clawed him quite thoroughly, but Shen Yu was quite adept at making this particular tigress purr.

"'*Sunlight shines on the Raging Gorge, in a prismatic haze. From afar, like a veil, do the waterfalls hang.*'" Minyan's musical voice recited the ancient poem.

"'Water cascading three thousand feet from the sky. Is the Celestial River falling from heaven on high?'" Shen Yu completed it, and Minyan smiled beneath her veil. He had spent ages memorizing all the poems in his youth just to impress her, but in the end, despite their dalliances, they'd always ended up going their separate ways.

"The aging of your body has done wonders for your voice," she sniped.

"Indeed. The timbre has improved, while your singing voice is as sweet as ever," he said before waggling his eyebrows at her.

"Hmph. You're a bastard, Shen Yu," Minyan huffed, before turning her eyes to the land below them. "It has been nigh on four hundred years since the *Shenfeng* saw these skies," she mused, "and nearly the same length of time since I have set foot within the Cloudy Sword Sect."

"Indeed, it has been a while since our Sect has been able to offer you hospitality, Divine Falcon of the East." Brother Ge's voice came in next as he approached them both at the bow of the ship. "In return for the generosity you have shown us, we shall hold nothing back."

"See that you don't, Black Cloud," Minyan said before turning slightly to look upon the eight men and six women wearing the robes of Cloudy Sword Sect Initiates, being transported to the mountain instead of having to walk. "Though I must confess you recruited far more than I thought you would."

Brother Ge looked back at the new recruits, mostly soldiers taken from the survivors of the mortal army who had shown aptitude, or from the Imperial City itself.

They had been receiving Ge's personal instruction, and Shen Yu had even seen some of the Soaring Heaven's Isle girls listening in on Brother Ge's lectures. His brother had spent many an hour lecturing Shen Yu when they had first become friends; Shen Yu could recite what they were learning from the other man by heart.

"They all have potential. I would be remiss not to recognise them," Ge stated simply.

Minyan turned her eyes to one of the female disciples in particular, her intent focusing on the meditating student. Then she clicked her tongue in annoyance when she beheld the potential within.

"Take care, lest I poach that one from you."

"You are welcome, as always, to try. Mastering temptation is a vital art," Xiao Ge responded.

The two elders snorted at each other. They were, in the end, rivals. As all cultivators were.

As all cultivators *had* to be.

→

"We greet the returning Heroes, and our Honoured Guests!" the ranks of the Cloudy Sword Sect Disciples boomed as one. Shen Yu paid them barely any attention as he entered his old Sect. He remembered having to gather like this. He also remembered *hating* it. It was tedious and boring, time better spent studying than greeting people who barely cared about them.

Yet he couldn't help but stand slightly straighter as he sensed their Qi and intent. Their Qi felt solid and immutable as law; yet like the clouds above, it was ready to unfurl and cover the land in shadow.

Thus he was welcomed back into his old Sect.

Stepping foot onto the ancient grounds of the Cloudy Sword Sect was like stepping into the past.

The massive gates, decorated with the images of the first wars, where men fought demons. The stone buildings and the green roof tiles.

It was a stark kind of beauty, one he appreciated. There was an almost otherworldly quality, for no mortal could have ever built this. This was a place disconnected from the dirt and grime of the mortal world below. It was truly the abode of cultivators, intended solely for cultivation.

He paid little mind to Brother Ge and Minyan's verbal sparring as she fished for information about some manner of disturbance in the Sect. There would undoubtedly be a few pretty fairies doing the same this night—and many young men suddenly accosted by their greatest weakness. He doubted it would lead to any real conflict; they were too polite for that.

The feast later was delicious. Shen Yu listened as the young ones told tales of their ferocious battles against the demons. It was amusing, their antics, the fairies and the Cloudy Sword both trying to impress each other.

The ceremony for the fallen was a more bitter affair. Shen Yu partook, his body and mouth flowing through the actions and words that had been repeated far, *far* too many times. He lowered his head for those so beneath him, like Master Zhao Da—who had eclipsed Shen Yu utterly back then—had bowed his head.

He paid his respects to his old Sect.

And then . . . and then he wandered.

He appreciated the fact that no one followed him.

He travelled first to the balcony where he had spent many a night, staring up at the stars. One of the support beams had been repaired recently, but on the bottom of the cliff side, where none could see, he could still spot the place where he had carved his name.

He walked through the gardens where the Lowly Spiritual Herbs—or as they were more commonly known, Seven Fragrance Jewel herbs—were grown. He had been amused to know that such precious plants were given such a humble name by the Cloudy Sword Sect.

He went to the Outer Sect dormitories, which were clean and regimented. He remembered the food being the best he had ever tasted, way back then. He had spent many a night in those dorms, studying and reading the works of the Founders and trying to improve himself.

He meandered to the sparring ring, where he had gained his first true friend in this world when Ge had offered his hand after knocking Shen Yu down.

Next was the library. To a certain spot where he'd told Rou he could study freely, and even hide his notes. To his surprise, when he looked he found there were notes. His heart seized as he recognised Rou's hand—detailing a technique that would surpass what the Cloudy Sword Sect had for growing Spiritual Herbs.

Shen Yu couldn't help the grin that stole across his face at that, nor the pride in his chest. He carefully took the notes, in case Rou wanted them later.

His steps were lighter after the library, and he continued his journey. He found his steps bringing him to the secluded place in the back of the Sect, where he and Ge had taken to drinking, and then roped Ran into joining their conspiracy when he had found them.

He went up a level, to the Inner Sect, and to the dedicated medical facilities. There he and Ge had spent many a night recovering, after fierce battles with the Demonic Sects.

He also saw the pavilion, where he had been recognised by Master Cao Ci. The old Master had praised his efforts and allowed him to go higher than he had ever imagined.

It became a blur, after that, as he roamed. The tournament grounds, with its cheering crowds. The Wall of Martyrs and the names. The garden, and its sweet fragrance, where Ran, Ge, and himself had sworn brotherhood to each other.

A hundred thousand good memories. Memories of an urchin rising up to challenge the heavens.

All of them, now tinged with a slight bitterness that Rou had not gotten to see the true beauty of the Cloudy Sword Sect.

Shen Yu stopped before the enormous gate: the exit to the Sect, and the gateway to Crimson Crucible City.

There was a certain finality to this last place. The doors where he himself had exited and gone forth into the world.

Shen Yu simply stood there, his breathing calm and steady, and wondered what his life would have been like if instead of his open hand, Ge had offered his fist.

It did not paint a picture Shen Yu liked.

He grimaced. Hopefully, *hopefully*, things were still salvageable with Rou. Hopefully, he still had his legacy.

He felt the presence of Brother Ge approach. The man projected his movements, and Shen Yu knew that if he wished to be unbothered for a while longer, Ge would leave.

Instead, Shen Yu allowed him to approach.

"Shall I take you to the culprit so that you may render your judgement?" Ge asked quietly.

"His fate is for Rou to decide. No, take me to your man, the one who found him. I shall reward him for his efforts," Shen Yu said. If only because he wouldn't be able to stop himself from killing the rat who had dared to derail a better life for Rou.

Brother Ge nodded. "Very well. Our Lu Ri is a good egg. You shall not find him wanting."

↔

Lu Ri, Disciple of the Cloudy Sword Sect, sat at a table under the moonlight and once more thanked his kindly Senior Sister for putting him through hell by training him to resist intent. Senior Sister Yeo Na had even returned to the mountain, with Elder Ge's retinue, so he could serve her some tea and get her an appropriate gift.

Because he was sitting across the table from an intent that was every bit the equal to—no, it was *stronger* than Elder Ge's aura.

Lu Ri kept his composure as *Shen Yu* stared at him.

Shen Yu, the Unconquered Blade.

One of the strongest experts in the Empire. His name was little known among the mortals, for he cared little for their adulations and time had turned the tales of his climb to the heavens into myth and legend. The mortals knew him only as some wandering, legendary hero who appeared and changed the tide of history with every breath and swing of his sword. Demonic Sects shattered. Rebellions crushed. Legendary treasures unearthed, and terrible Spirit Beasts felled.

To those who reached for the heavens of the younger generation, it was often a shock to learn that Shen Yu, the man whom they'd grown up reading stories about, was real, so astounding were his deeds.

And *that* was who Jin Rou's benefactor was. No wonder Elder Ge had spat blood. They had harmed the tiger's cub and were armed with nothing but their fists and a prayer against the beast's fury.

Lu Ri waited as calmly as he could as Sword Intent surrounded him, ready to end his life.

Keeping his focus, Lu Ri reached out, picked up his tea, and sipped it.

Shen Yu, his eyes burning, suddenly softened at the action, and the man burst out laughing.

"You're right, Brother Ge! This one is good! You have my praise, Senior Disciple Lu Ri. Your composure impresses this old man!"

Lu Ri, his heart pounding, bowed his head at the praise. "Thank you for your kind words, Honoured Expert. How may this Lu Ri aid you?"

"You're the one who found my boy, correct? Tell me how you did it," Shen Yu demanded.

"It is a long and at times tedious story. Would you like the abbreviated version?"

Shen Yu seemed amused. "Tell your tale in full, Disciple. Leave *nothing* out."

And thus, Lu Ri told his story: of trekking for six months through a Qi-starved desert, and the actions that he'd undertaken in order to find Jin Rou.

The expert listened to Lu Ri intently. He told his tale to the impassive man, though at times the man's eyes twinkled with amusement, which was a good sign.

Until finally he asked a question. "Did you feel his cultivation?"

"His cultivation was not something this disciple could comprehend. It was powerful, but subtle," Lu Ri responded immediately. "If this one had more time to study it, perhaps, but . . ."

That, at least, drew a pleased smile—the man suddenly seemed utterly relaxed.

"I see," Shen Yu stated, "And then?"

"Then, I left and did not push, as instructed. This pleased Jin Rou, so he offered me a way to contact him and said he would offer me his hospitality should I need it."

Shen Yu mulled over Lu Ri's words . . . and then nodded again.

"You have done well, Disciple Lu Ri." He glanced at Elder Ge, who had been smoking his pipe. The Elder nodded. "Now I shall allow you to guide me to my grandson personally."

Lu Ri paused at the declaration.

Well . . . it appeared that he would be heading back to the Azure Hills quicker than he'd anticipated.

ABOUT THE AUTHOR

Casualfarmer started writing after listening to his parents' stories on their long drives to visit relatives. He had been saving money from his food-service-industry job to go to college for teaching when the COVID-19 pandemic hit. *Beware of Chicken* is Casualfarmer's first original story. He lives in Ontario, Canada.

BEST. CHICKEN. EVER.

You thought Beware of Chicken was good reading it with your eyeballs?

Give those eyeballs a good rest. Close them, and imagine the audiobook... an aural experience brought to life by the smooth stylings of award-winning narrator Travis Baldree. Baaaaaaa-caw.

Available on Audible right now!